Skye O'Malley

BY BERTRICE SMALL

Adora

Unconquered

Beloved

The Spitfire

A Moment in Time

To Love Again

Love, Remember Me

The Love Slave

Hellion

Betrayed

The Innocent

A Memory of Love

The Duchess

THE O'MALLEY SAGA

Skye O'Malley

All the Sweet Tomorrows

A Love for All Time

This Heart of Mine

Lost Love Found

Wild Jasmine

Skye O'Malley

Bertrice Small

BALLANTINE BOOKS / NEW YORK

Skye O'Malley is a work of fiction. Names, characters, places, and incidents are the products of the author's imagination or are used fictitiously. Any resemblance to actual events, locales, or persons, living or dead, is entirely coincidental.

2007 Ballantine Books Trade Paperback Edition

Published in the United States by Ballantine Books,
an imprint of The Random House Publishing Group,
a division of Random House, Inc., New York.

BALLANTINE and colophon are registered trademarks of Random House, Inc.

Originally published in trade paperback in the United States by
Ballantine Books, an imprint of The Random House Publishing Group,
a division of Random House, Inc., in 1980.

ISBN 978-0-345-29256-8

www.ballantinebooks.com

Book design by Susan Turner

146119709

To Pamela Strickler and Jan DeVries with love
because they deserve it, and because they understand
my people almost as well as I do.

PROLOGUE

"WHAT THE HELL DO YOU MEAN SHE CAN HAVE NO MORE CHILDREN?" demanded Dubhdara O'Malley of his brother. The O'Malley, chief of Clan O'Malley, was a big man: six-foot-four, arms and legs like thick tree limbs, ruddy, sunburnt skin, snapping blue eyes, and a mop of dark hair that was just getting a sprinkling of silver. "You priests are always prating that the purpose of marriage is to procreate. Well, I've done what the Church wanted, I've gotten children on her, and not one of them a living son! Now you tell me I must *stop?* But I don't suppose you'll be granting me an annulment so I can wed with some fresh and healthy blood? Faugh! You make me sick!"

Father Seamus O'Malley, looking almost his brother's twin though not quite as dark of skin, viewed Dubhdara with genuine sympathy and understanding. He knew how he felt, but there was just no help for it. His sister-in-law couldn't take another pregnancy. The midwife had been quite certain about that. Another child would take Lady O'Malley's life. That would be outright murder.

The priest drew a deep breath. "You've been married ten years, brother, and in that time Peigi's been pregnant ten times. She's miscarried three. This birth nearly killed her."

The O'Malley whirled, bitterness flooding his rugged face. "Aye," he said. "She's miscarried thrice—and all boys too! The only one of my sons she managed to birth lived barely long enough for you to baptize, God assoil his wee soul. And what am I left with? Girls! Six girls! Five of whom are as plain of face as their mother. Faugh! Damn! I thought surely *this* time . . ."

He paced the room angrily, caring nothing that his harsh words were overheard by the woman who lay, half dead and weeping with bitter disappointment, in the next room. She had prayed so hard for a son. She had made a novena every month of her confinement. She had fasted and sacrificed, giving to those less fortunate than herself. And what was the result of her piety? Another girl, and the knowledge that she would now never be able to bear her husband a son.

Unknowing and uncaring, Dubhdara O'Malley raged on and on. "Why could she not give me sons, Seamus? Why? I've gotten a brace of healthy lads on lasses about the countryside, but my own wife can give me nothing but girls! I wish to God she had died and the female brat with her!"

"God forgive you, Dubhdara!" exclaimed Seamus O'Malley, shocked to his soul.

O'Malley shrugged. "At least I might start anew, but wait and see, Seamus! You wait! She'll outlive me yet! No! I'll not stop trying. I must have a legitimate son! I must!"

"You get Peigi with child again, Dubh, and she dies, I'll have the Church on you! It'd be deliberate murder, for I've warned you what will happen if she conceives again. The midwife said she almost bled to death. The wee lass she's borne is healthy and strong though, thanks be to God."

O'Malley made a derisive noise.

"What will we baptize her, Dubh?" encouraged the priest.

O'Malley thought a minute. "Call her Skye after the place from which her mother came. Her oldest sister, Moire, can stand her godmother."

"She needs a godfather too, brother."

"You be her godfather, Seamus. Six daughters is too many to provide dowries for, so I intend Skye O'Malley for the Church. The Church'll take a smaller portion, and 'tis fitting that the future nun's godfather be a priest."

Seamus O'Malley nodded, satisfied. It was high time his brother singled out a daughter for the Church. But then the priest looked closely at his new niece for the first time, and was quickly certain that this was not the daughter Dubh would send to a convent. His five older nieces were, as their father had said, plain as pikestaffs. With their ordinary brown hair, their pale gray eyes, they were like little sparrows.

This child, however, was a bird of paradise. Her skin was gardenia-fair, her eyes a wonderful blue, like the waters off Kerry, and she already had a thick headful of black curls like her father's. "No," said Seamus O'Malley softly to himself, "you are definitely not convent material, Skye O'Malley!"

He smiled down at the babe. If she fulfilled her promise, her beauty could be bartered for a powerful match. The Church would be delighted to accept a less spectacular O'Malley, one whose dowry could be enriched by sister Skye's good fortune.

On the following day, Skye O'Malley was baptized in the family chapel. Her mother, still weak from childbirth, was not present, but her father and five older sisters were. Moire, aged ten, and the eldest, became Skye's godmother. Looking on admiringly were Peigi, nine, Bride, seven, Eibhlin, four, and Sine, eighteen months.

When Seamus O'Malley poured the holy water on the child's head, Skye did not cry out as custom decreed, thus allowing the Devil to depart her. Instead, to everyone's shock, she made a sound very much like a giggle, and for the first time Dubhdara O'Malley looked at his new daughter with interest.

"So," he chuckled, his blue eyes narrowing with speculation, "it's not afraid of water, is it? Well, she's a true O'Malley at any rate. Maybe I'll not be giving you to the Church after all, Skye O'Malley. What do you think, brother Seamus?"

The priest smiled back. "I think not, brother. Perhaps one of the others will be better suited, and even has a true vocation. Time will tell, Dubh. Time will tell."

The O'Malley took his new daughter from his brother and cradled her in the crook of his big arm. With his startlingly bright blue eyes, shoulder-length black hair, and bushy black beard, he very much resembled a pirate. Indeed, his sea-roving activities bordered on piracy. However, his fierce appearance did not frighten his new daughter at all. She gurgled contentedly before closing her eyes and falling asleep.

As the O'Malley left the chapel with his brother, his five older daughters trailing in their wake, he did not relinquish his hold on the infant. The bond between Skye and her father had been formed. And when Peigi O'Malley's milk refused to come in, he chose the wet nurse himself—a healthy, pretty farmgirl whose bastard had been strangled by its umbilical cord.

Six months later Dubhdara O'Malley departed on a seagoing expedition which would keep him away from Ireland for several months. To his priestly brother's outrage, he took baby Skye and her wet nurse, Megi, with him. "You're a disgrace to the family, Dubhdara O'Malley! What the devil will people say about Megi? And if that's not bad enough, you're endangering the child! I'll not have Skye harmed," roared the doting uncle.

The O'Malley laughed. "Stow your gab, Seamus! I'm not endangering Skye. She's already gone sailing with me for a day or so. She likes being on my ship. As to Megi, I would be endangering Skye if I did not take her along. Megi's milk is better for Skye than a goat's, which is the only alternative."

"And I suppose you'll deny you've been fucking with Megi."

"No, I'll not deny it. You know I like all the comforts."

The priest threw up his hands in despair. There was nothing he could do with his brother. Dubh was the most carnal man he knew. Well, one good thing would come of it. At least poor Peigi would be safe from her husband's lust for the time being.

In the summer of 1541 the O'Malley of Innisfana sailed out of his stronghold on Innisfana Island, into the western seas. It was the first of Skye's many voyages. She took her first tottering steps on the heaving deck of her father's ship. Her small baby teeth cut marks into the ship's wheel. While her wet nurse, Megi, cowered in her bunk, fighting seasickness and praying she wouldn't drown, Skye O'Malley clapped her fat baby hands and laughed at the storms.

The baby became a toddler, and the toddler a little girl. Dubhdara O'Malley was the lord of the seas around Ireland. He had many ships and several hundred men who answered only to him. Skye soon became his acknowledged heir and a favorite among the rough sailors. She was spoiled and cosseted by them all. She barely knew her mother and sisters, and had no time or patience for them and their silly lives.

In the spring of 1551 Skye's mother died. Soon, her uncle Seamus urged that Skye stay home and learn some woman's ways, to sustain her in marriage. As the priest pointed out to his brother, Skye's husband was more likely to appreciate a wife who could run his home than one who could navigate a ship through the fog. Reluctantly, O'Malley sent Skye home to Innisfana to learn how to be a lady.

Angry at being taken from her beloved sea, Skye set about making her older, married sisters' lives miserable. She quickly learned, however, that Dubhdara O'Malley's mind was made up. She must learn womanly arts. So, as her father wished, Skye set about making a good job of it. When her next older sister, Sine, was married a few months later, Skye had become accomplished in the household arts and was scheduled to be wed next.

But though Skye had learned the womanly arts, she had not become a biddable female. Not Skye O'Malley!

PART I
IRELAND

Chapter 1

It was a perfect early summer day in the year 1555. Innisfana Island, its great green cliffs tumbling into the deep and sparkling blue sea, shone clear at the mouth of O'Malley Bay. English weather, the Irish inhabitants of the region called it, and it was nearly the only English thing they approved of. There was a slight breeze, and in the skies above the island the gulls and terns soared and swooped, their eerie *skrees* the only counterpoint to the breaking surf.

Standing tall against the horizon was O'Malley Castle, a typical tower house of dark gray stone. Rising several stories high, it commanded a view of the sea from all its windows. It had a wide moat, and beyond that moat was—of all things—a rose garden, planted by the late Lady O'Malley. After her death, now four years past, the new Lady O'Malley kept the garden up. Now in full bloom, it was a riot of yellows, pinks, reds, and whites, a perfect background for the wedding of the youngest daughter.

Inside the tower house, in the main hall, the five older daughters of the O'Malley family sat happily gossiping with their pretty stepmother while they sewed and embroidered the bride's trousseau. It had been a long time since they had all been together.

Now, each had her own home, and they all met only on special occasions.

They were as similar now as they had been as children. Medium-tall, they all ran to partridge plump. It was the kind of comfortable figure that kept a man warm on a cold night. Each was fair-skinned with soft peach-colored cheeks, serious gray eyes, and long, straight, light-brown hair. None was beautiful, but none was ugly, either.

The eldest, Moire, was twenty-five, and had been married for twelve years. She was mother to nine living children, seven sons. Moire stood high in her father's favor. Peigi, at twenty-three, had been married ten years and was mother to nine sons. Peigi stood even higher in her father's favor. Bride, twenty-one, had been married eight years, and had only four children, two of whom were boys. Dubhdara tolerated Bride, and constantly exhorted her to greater productivity. "You're more like your mother than the others," he would say ominously.

Eibhlin, eighteen, was the only one with a religious calling. She had been such a quiet little thing that they hadn't even suspected her piety until the boy to whom she was to be wed succumbed to an attack of measles the year Eibhlin was twelve. As O'Malley considered a possible replacement bridegroom for his fourth daughter, Eibhlin begged to be allowed to enter a convent. She genuinely desired that life. Because her uncle Seamus, now bishop of Murrisk, was present for the talk, Dubhdara O'Malley was forced to give his consent. Eibhlin entered her convent at thirteen, and had just recently taken final vows.

Sine O'Malley Butler was sixteen, wed three years, and the mother of one boy. She was eight months pregnant but she would not have missed Skye's wedding.

The married sisters were dressed in simply cut, full-skirted silk dresses with bell sleeves and low, scooped necklines. Moire was in a deep, rich blue, Peigi in scarlet, Bride in violet, and Sine in golden yellow. The lacy frill of their chemises peeked elegantly up through the low bodices.

Eibhlin struck the only somber note. Her all-covering black linen gown was relieved only by a severe white starched rectangular bib, in which was centered an ebony, silver-banded crucifix. About her waist the nun wore a twisted silk rope, also black, which hung in two plaits to the hem of her gown. One plait, knotted into three knots, symbolized the Trinity. The other, knotted in the same manner, symbolized the estates of poverty, chastity, and obedience.

By way of vivid contrast, her sisters wore chains of wrought gold or silver about their waists, and each woman had attached to her chain a rosary, a needlecase, a mirror, or simply a set of household keys.

Because this was an informal home gathering, the married sisters wore their hair loose, parted in the center. Sine and Peigi had added pretty arched linen caps. And of course Eibhlin, whose hair had been cut when she took her vows, wore starched and pleated white wings over her white wimple.

Presiding over this gathering was Dubhdara O'Malley's second wife. Anne was the same age as her stepdaughter, Eibhlin, and as pregnant with her fourth child as was her stepdaughter, Sine. Anne was a pretty woman, with chestnut-brown curls, merry brown eyes, and a sweet, sensible nature. Anne's silk gown was of a deep wine shade, and fashioned identically to her stepdaughters' gowns. But over her ruffled bodice Anne wore a double strand of creamy baroque pearls. None of the O'Malley daughters had resented their father's marriage to Anne and everyone liked her enormously. One could not help liking Anne.

For nine years after Skye's birth Dubhdara O'Malley had obeyed his priest brother's edict, and stayed out of his wife's bed. He really did not wish to kill Peigi. Free of yearly pregnancies, Peigi regained her strength and even began to bloom. Then, one night, Dubhdara O'Malley had arrived home from a long voyage. It was late. He had no current mistress, and there wasn't a servant girl in sight. He had gotten drunk and sought his wife's bed. Nine months later, Peigi O'Malley died giving birth to the long-awaited son, born September 29th and baptized Michael. The little boy was now almost six.

Within an almost indecently short time O'Malley had taken his second wife, a girl of thirteen. Nine months from their wedding day Anne had birthed Brian; a year later, Shane; and in another year, Shamus. Unlike her meek predecessor, Anne O'Malley possessed good health and high spirits. This child she carried was to be the last, she told her husband firmly. It would also, she assured him, be a boy. Five sons should give him the immortality he craved.

O'Malley had laughed and slapped her playfully on the backside. His daughters took this to mean that he was either in his dotage or growing mellow with age. Had their own mother ever made such a statement she would have been beaten black and blue. But then, Anne O'Malley was the mother of sons.

Moire looked up from her embroidery to gaze with pleasure

about the hall. It had never looked so nice in their mother's time for she, poor soul, had spent much of her life in her own rooms.

The stone floors were always well swept now, the rushes changed weekly. The oak trestles were polished to a mellow golden hue, reflecting the great silver candlesticks with their pure beeswax tapers. The big brass andirons were filled with enormous oak logs, ready to be lit when the evening arrived. Behind the high board, prominently displayed, hung a large new tapestry depicting Saint Brendan the Monk on a sky-blue background, guiding his ship across the western seas. Anne had designed it, and had been working on it almost every evening of her married life. It had been a labor of love, for the second Lady O'Malley adored not only her bluff, big husband, but their sons and their home as well.

Moire's eyes lit upon several big colorful porcelain bowls filled with roses. Their pungent, spicy scent gave the room a wonderful exotic smell. Moire wrinkled her nose with pleasure and said to Anne, "The bowls are new?"

"Aye," came the reply. "Your father brought them back from his last voyage. He is so good to me, Moire."

"And why not?" demanded Moire. "You are good to him, Anne."

"Where is Skye?" interrupted Peigi.

"Out riding with young Dom. I am surprised at your father in pursuing this betrothal. They do not suit at all."

"They were promised in the cradle," explained Moire. "It wasn't easy for Da to find husbands for us all, for we've none of us large dowries. Skye's marrying the heir to the Ballyhennessey O'Flahertys is the best match of us all."

Anne shook her head. "I fear this match. Your sister is a very independent girl."

"And it's all Da's fault for he has spoiled her terribly," said Peigi. "She should have been married off two years ago at thirteen, like the rest of us. But no, Skye did not want it. He lets *her* have her way all the time!"

"That's not so, Peigi," Eibhlin chided her sister. "Anne is correct when she says that Skye and Dom do not suit. Skye is not like us in temperament. We favor our mother while she favors Da. Dom is simply neither strong enough nor sensitive enough to be Skye's husband."

"Hoity-toity, sister," said Peigi sourly. "It amazes me how much the wee nun knows about human nature."

"Indeed and I do," replied Eibhlin calmly, "for whom do you

think the poor women of my district pour out their unhappiness to, Peigi? Certainly not the priest! He tells them it is their Christian duty to be abused by their menfolk! And then he adds to their guilt by giving them a penance."

The sisters look shocked, and Anne broke the tension by laughing, "You're more a rebel than a holy woman, stepdaughter."

Eibhlin sighed. "You speak the truth, Anne, and it troubles me greatly. But though I try I cannot seem to change."

Anne O'Malley leaned over and fondly patted her stepdaughter on the hand. "Being a woman is never, ever easy," she said wisely, "no matter what role we choose to play in life."

The two young women smiled fondly at each other with complete understanding. Then everyone looked startled as they heard shouting in the entry hall below them. As the noise came toward them up the steps the O'Malley sisters glanced knowingly at each other. They recognized the voices of Dom O'Flaherty and their sister, Skye.

As the two burst into the main hall, Anne O'Malley was again struck by the beauty of the two young people. She had never seen two more physically perfect people, and perhaps this was why her husband insisted on the match. Anne shivered with apprehension.

Dom O'Flaherty threw his riding gloves on a table. At eighteen he was of medium height, slender, with beautifully shaped arms, hands, and legs. Having inherited his French grandmother's coloring, he had glorious, close-cropped, curly golden hair, and sky-blue eyes. He affected a tailored short beard that hugged the perfectly sculpted sides of his face and ended in a softly rounded point. Because he was angry, however, his fair skin was now an unattractive, mottled red. His handsome face with its long, straight nose and narrow lips was contorted with rage.

"It's indecent!" he shouted at Skye. "It's indecent and immodest for a maiden to ride astride a beast! My God, Skye! That horse of yours! When we're married I will see that you're more suitably mounted upon a palfrey. What ever possessed your father to let you ride that big, black brute, I'll never know!"

"You lost, Dom," came the infuriatingly cool reply. "You lost the race to me, and as you always did when we were children, you try to retaliate by clouding the issue. Well, let me tell you what you can do with your bloody palfrey!"

"Skye!" Anne O'Malley's voice was sharp with warning.

The girl looked to her stepmother, then laughed. "Oh, all right, Annie," she acquiesced prettily, "I will try to behave myself. *But,*

Dom O'Flaherty . . . hear me well. Finn is my horse. I have raised him from a colt, and I love him. If we're to be happily married, you must accept that, for I have no intention of exchanging him for a rocking horse just to soothe your male pride."

And while her bridegroom fumed, Skye signaled to a servant to bring some wine. As if in afterthought, she ordered some for Dom as well. Flinging himself into a chair, he glowered at her, but all the while his eyes roamed her body and he thought how beautiful she was in her dark-green silk riding habit. The skirt was divided, and the neckline open, plunging into the valley of her young breasts. Tiny beads of moisture had gathered on her chest and the sight excited him. He realized that he longed to possess this lovely young woman.

At fifteen Skye O'Malley was well on the way to fulfilling the promise of unequaled beauty that she had shown at birth. She stood every bit as tall as her betrothed. Like him, she was beautifully proportioned, with a slim waist that moved into softly rounded hips. Her breasts were small but full. She had a heart-shaped face. Her eyes were still the color of the seas off the Kerry coast, sometimes pure blue, sometimes dark, sometimes azure with a faint hint of green. They were fringed in thick ebony lashes that brushed tender pink cheeks. Her nose was slim, turning up just slightly at the tip. And if you looked carefully you could see a few soft, golden freckles across the bridge of her nose. The red mouth was surprisingly seductive with a full lower lip, and when she laughed she revealed small, perfect white teeth. Her skin was the color of cream and seemed even fairer by the contrasting mass of blue-black hair that tumbled about her shoulders.

She excited Dom very much, although he, it seemed, did not interest her. She far preferred galloping that great black stallion of hers at breakneck speed about the countryside, or sailing off with her father on some piratical adventure. The realization was quite a shock to his pride.

Dom O'Flaherty was not used to indifference from the fair sex. Women ordinarily made fools of themselves over him, and he was very proud of his sexual prowess.

Dom tried to console himself with the thought that once he bedded her she would soon be tamed. Hot-tempered virgins usually turned out to be passionate lovers. He licked his thin lips in anticipation, and quaffed his goblet of wine. He was not aware that his betrothed was eying him with disgust. Dom O'Flaherty would run to fat in his middle years, Skye decided.

Again from the entry below came the noises of arrival. Anne O'Malley rose to her feet with a smile. "Your father is back," she said, "and it sounds like he brings guests."

Two large wolfhounds, several setters, and a large terrier all bounded into the hall. One of the wolfhounds trotted up to Anne and dropped two small velvet bags at her feet. Bending, Lady O'Malley picked up the bags and, loosening the strings, poured the contents of one bag into her cupped hand. She stared at the sapphire-and-diamond necklace that nestled in her palm. "Holy Mary!" she gasped.

Dubhdara O'Malley chuckled with pleasure from the doorway. "Then you like it, lovey? There's earbobs, and a ring to match in the other."

"Like it? Oh, Dubh, it's the most beautiful thing I've ever owned! Where . . . ?"

"Portuguese galleon got itself blown off course and then wrecked aways up the coast. We were just in time to save the captain from the scavengers. He was most grateful."

Anne said no more, but she read between the lines. It was obvious that her husband and his crew had battled coastal wreckers for possession of the damaged galleon. The O'Malleys had been pirates for centuries. It was their way of life. Undoubtedly the captain of the unfortunate ship and the survivors among his crew were now housed in the dungeons below, where they would spend the next several months awaiting ransom. Anne shuddered and reminded herself that such thoughts were not her concern.

"And where's my wee lass?" demanded the O'Malley.

"Here, Da." Skye rose from her chair and came forward.

Seeing her garb, he frowned with disapproval. "Still riding astride, poppet?"

"Don't scold me, Da," she wheedled him prettily. "It was you who taught me, and I simply can't gallop Finn sitting sideways. It's most unnatural."

The O'Malley cocked an eyebrow. "Must you gallop him? Wouldn't a nice trot do you? You must think of the babes you're going to bear Dom now, poppet."

She ignored his last remark. "Have you ever tried to trot with one leg slung over a pommel, Da? The last time I tried it I ended up with bruises all over my—"

"Skye! We've guests!"

For the first time her attention was drawn to the man by his side.

"My Lord," she heard her father say, "this is my youngest daughter, Skye, who will shortly be the bride of young O'Flaherty. Skye, this is Niall, Lord Burke, the MacWilliam's heir."

"*Niall an iarain,* Niall of the Iron," she said softly. This was a famous man, the secret dream lover of half the maidens in Ireland.

"I see my reputation precedes me, my lady Skye."

"It is an open secret that you are Captain Revenge, and that you conduct those daring raids against the English who live in the Dublin Pale. Of course, no one would dare accuse you of this."

"Yet you, my lady, do not fear me," he murmured, holding her fast with his gaze until she blushed.

The voice was deep and sure, but as smooth as fine velvet. She shivered. She raised her eyes to his. They were a silvery gray, and she imagined that in anger they would be colder than the far northern sea, but in the heat of passion they would be fiery warm like rich wine. Guilty color flooded her cheeks at these immodest thoughts. The gray eyes twinkled infuriatingly, as if reading her mind.

He towered over her by a good eight inches. His smoothly shaven face had been tanned by the outdoors. The short-cropped hair was as midnight dark as her own.

Raising her hand, he kissed it. It was all she could do not to snatch it away, for his lips burned her flesh like a brand. Sweet Mary, she thought, he's so much more sophisticated than Dom, yet he's only ten years older than I am.

"My lord, welcome to Innisfana," she murmured politely. Dear God! Was that husky, breathless voice hers? And why was Anne staring at her so strangely?

Her father's voice brought her back to reality. "These are for your dowry, poppet," he said, handing her a marvelous collection of rubies set in gold. They were a necklace, earrings, bracelets, a ring, and a hair ornament. Everyone exclaimed, and Dom O'Flaherty congratulated himself as though he had been personally responsible for choosing his bride.

Skye clutched the jewelry to her. Thanking her father, she left the hall. *Damn!* thought Anne O'Malley. She has been attracted to Lord Burke. And why not? Now why couldn't Dubh have betrothed her to a strong, fierce man like Lord Burke instead of that vain boy, O'Flaherty?

Skye walked up the stairs to her chamber with what she hoped was great dignity. She was quite surprised that she could move at all, for her legs were shaking terribly. She was very confused, and not just a little frightened by her reaction to Lord Burke. She hoped she hadn't behaved like a green maid, but never had she had this kind of a reaction to a man.

She had never seen Niall Burke before, though his romantic and military escapades were legend. As she had dared to say aloud minutes before, he was known to some as the famous Captain Revenge, who caused havoc for the English and their Irish allies whenever he felt that their policies were not serving Ireland.

Captain Revenge exacted a high penalty from English overlords who dealt unfairly with their native Irish underlings. Once, in an escapade later to have all of Ireland laughing up its sleeve, Captain Revenge had made love to the daughter of an important English nobleman who had estates in Ireland. Having learned the layout of her father's castle from the love-besotted girl, Captain Revenge ransacked the castle's treasure room and used the nobleman's store to pay the taxes of several impoverished Irish families. The English accepted the money and rendered receipts. When the deception was uncovered, it was too late for anything to be done, and the English fumed with impotent rage. Certainly they suspected the connection between Captain Revenge and Niall, Lord Burke. But what could anyone do? London's policy was that the overload of Mid-Connaught was not to be antagonized. He was, after all, an ally—an ally to the English being anybody not openly waging war against England. And too, they asked themselves, what possible real damage could one high-spirited young man do?

He was indeed a fascinating man, thought Skye, and when their eyes met there had been a moment of deep recognition.

Safe in her room, she watched as Molly, her maid, prepared her bath. Molly thought the lady Skye bathed too much, but Molly had to admit that her mistress smelled better than anyone she knew. She took the riding clothes from the girl and, brushing them, put them in the wardrobe. Skye divested herself of her undergarments, pinned her long hair up, and climbed into the tub.

The warm water felt good. Slowly Skye rubbed the cake of scented soap between her hands, then washed her face. Niall Burke. Niall Burke. Her mind repeated his name like a litany. He was so tall. He had made her feel petite, which she most certainly was not. He had been dressed in the English fashion, with elegant particolored hose and matching green pantaloons to the knee. She imagined the rippling muscles beneath the green velvet doublet. She suddenly wondered what it would feel like to be crushed against that broad chest, and to her shame the little nipples on her small breasts hardened, thrusting above the water.

What on earth was the matter with her? She had never had thoughts like these before. She knew so little about what went on between men and women, and Dom had certainly never inspired her. In fact, for all his good looks, Dom repelled her.

Molly took the soap from Skye, finished washing her, and dried her off with a linen towel. She had barely finished wrapping the girl in a silken chamber robe when a knock sounded on the door. Molly opened it, bobbed a flirtatious curtsey, and admitted Dom O'Flaherty.

He sauntered in with a lascivious look to his bride-to-be, whose young body was well outlined by the robe. "I have to leave you for a few days, Skye. Sir Murrough has sent word that I am needed. I will be back in time for our wedding."

Skye's heart soared. He would be gone, and Lord Burke would be here! "Go with God, Dom," she said sweetly.

For a moment there was an awkward silence, then Dom reached out and pulled his betrothed into his arms. "No kiss, lovey? You would send me on my way without the least sign of affection?"

"We're not wed yet, Dom. I don't have to kiss you."

"Don't have to?" he exploded. "Christ, Skye, don't be such a little prude! You'll have to do more than kiss me in a few days' time!" Damn, but she was a sweet armful, all perfumed and warm from the bath. He could feel his desire growing. He sought for her mouth, but she squirmed away.

"No!"

His blue eyes narrowed in anger, but then he laughed. "All right, lovey. But in a short time I'll have you begging for my kisses." He mocked her a bow, then turned and left the room. She shuddered.

"Oh!" squealed Molly. "He's a lusty one to be sure, mistress! You'll have good bedsport with him, and that's lucky in a husband!"

"Be quiet, you little fool!" snapped Skye. "Instead of drooling over my betrothed, fetch my new burgundy velvet gown. I intend on wearing it tonight with the rubies Da gave me."

Molly scurried to obey. Skye O'Malley was a better mistress than most, rarely cruel, but not above administering a slap now and then. The maid laced her mistress into a little beribboned busk that pushed her pretty breasts up so that they seemed almost to spill from her pale-pink underblouse. The nearly transparent sleeves were striped in gold. Carefully Skye drew her stockings up her shapely legs. They were pink silk, embroidered with a flowering vine of gold thread, and had been made in Paris. Several petticoats followed, and then the dress. A beautiful creation of the finest, softest velvet, it was a shimmering, jewel red, with a full, flowing skirt. Slashed sleeves revealed the pink-and-gold-striped sleeves of the underblouse.

Skye now sat, careful not to wrinkle her skirts, before her precious mirror while Molly brushed her dark hair until it shone with bluish lights. She was not allowed to bind it up until after her marriage. This had been a source of great frustration to Skye, especially at sea, but her father had been very firm about it. She might braid it, but the braids must hang long.

"No O'Malley maiden puts her hair up until she weds," he stated, and there was no point in arguing.

Looking at herself in the mirror, however, she had to admit that her long, wavy hair was beautiful. Especially now, as Molly placed a little gold lace cap with a tiny veil on her head. Skye clasped the ruby necklace about her throat and studied the effect. The great stones glittered almost savagely against the creamy softness of her bare chest, and when she caught her breath she noted with surprise that her breasts swelled provocatively beneath the glittering rubies. The jeweled hair ornament was to be put aside until she wore her hair up, but she slipped on the earrings, bracelet, and ring. Sliding her feet into red velvet shoes, she stood.

"Lor', mistress," breathed Molly reverently. "I never seen you look so beautiful! What a pity Master Dom's not here now to see you. You could drive a man to madness!"

Skye laughed, pleased. "Do you really think so, Molly?" Secretly she was wondering whether Lord Burke could be driven to madness. Her insides fluttered with fearful, delicious anticipation. She almost flew out the door, bumping into her pretty stepmother as she did so.

"Gracious, Skye," laughed Anne O'Malley. "If you would impress the hall, then you must not rush so. Make a grand entrance . . . slowly gliding . . . thusly, my love." She demonstrated prettily.

"Your pardon, Anne. I did not hurt you, did I?"

"No, love, but stop so I may look at you. Dear heaven, how lovely you are, and not yet grown. If young Dom could but see you now . . ."

Skye made a face. "I don't want to marry him, Anne!" The words tumbled out all by themselves.

Anne O'Malley was suddenly serious and fully sympathetic. "I know, love. I know, and I do understand."

"Please, Anne, *please* speak to Da. He adores you, and he'll listen to you. He'd do anything for you!"

"Oh, Skye, I'll try. You know I will. But it will do no good. Your father is a man of his word, and he has given his word on this marriage. You're the last of his girls, and he wants you well settled. Young O'Flaherty is a very good match for an O'Malley of Innisfana."

"I hate him!" came the whispered reply. "He's always undressing me with his eyes."

"Perhaps it will be different when you're wed," soothed Anne, though in her heart she knew it wouldn't. "Maidens are often fearful of the unknown. But really, there is no cause for alarm, my love. Tomorrow I will come and explain it all to you, Skye."

"Speak to Da, Anne! Please, promise me you will!"

"I will, Skye. I promise I will."

The two women moved down the steps to the main hall of the castle, and all the while Anne was aware that Niall Burke's eyes were fastened to her beautiful stepdaughter. At the bottom of the steps he was there, tucking Skye's small hand in his arm, wordlessly sweeping her away while Anne watched helplessly. No one else saw the dangerous, hopeless attraction between the two. She *must* speak to Dubhdara!

The floor beneath Skye's feet seemed to have disappeared. She was floating. Shyly she glanced down at the hand covering hers. It was big, and square, and brown. It was magically warm, and she could feel the strength hidden deep within it. Her heart was pounding. Why did he affect her this way?

They walked over to the great fireplace, which was flanked by enormous stone lions. It was red with the oak logs that now burned merrily with an occasional crackle and snap. They stopped and observed the leaping flames for a moment. They did not look at each other, but merely stood side by side.

Finally he spoke. "Why do you tremble when I touch you?"

"I am not used to the attentions of men," she answered him breathlessly.

Turning her so that she faced him, he looked down at her. "I do not understand that, Skye O'Malley, for you are outrageously fair. Has no man, even your betrothed, whispered sweet words of love into your little shell ear?"

"No." Her cheeks were softly pink now, and her voice was so low that he had to bend to hear her.

Niall Burke was enchanted. He felt something strange sweeping over him, possessing him, rushing him onward to something his inner voice warned against. "Look at me, sweetheart," he commanded her. "I promise not to bite you, though God knows you're a tempting morsel."

Shyly she raised her blue eyes to his silvery gray ones, and for a moment Skye felt as if she were drowning. She realized he felt it too! Neither could tear their gaze away. They were suspended in time, their souls flowing back and forth between their bodies, twining into one perfect being.

A great guffaw of laughter from the other side of the hall broke the spell. With shock, Niall swore, "Christ! What is it you do to me, little witch?" He was astounded by himself. "Turn your eyes from me, Skye darling, before I shame us both." He signaled a servant bearing a tray of wine goblets and, snatching two, gave one to Skye. He gulped down the other, welcoming the burning sensation that spread through his stomach. It gave him something to concentrate on, to prevent himself from carrying this girl away from the hall forever.

When dinner was announced, Lord Burke, as the highest-ranking guest, was seated next to the bride-to-be. He was artful enough to hide his troubled emotions, but the meal tasted like sawdust to him. He was a man of the world, experienced beyond most, but the girl had affected him as no other female had ever done. He admitted to himself that he desperately wanted to bed the wench, but there was a great deal more to it than that, something he had never felt before. It had all come on him so quickly that he couldn't understand it.

Niall Burke was the only son of Rory Burke, the MacWilliam of Middle Connaught. The MacWilliam had almost despaired of ever having an heir. All three of his wives had died in childbirth. The last of them, Maerid O'Brien, had given him his only child. From the moment of his birth Niall had been a strong and healthy lad, but the MacWilliam anxiously protected him.

His wet nurse ate at the MacWilliam's table so that the lord of Mid-Connaught could oversee her diet. The baby's nursery was kept well warmed in the winter and dry in the damp weather. No child had ever been so well taken care of. Even his sleep was overseen by a night nurse who sat first by his cradle, and later by his bedside, monitoring his every breath.

Despite it all, the boy flourished. Convinced that he had a lively heir, the MacWilliam finally eased his stranglehold. Intelligent, Niall was educated first by the priests and then sent to England for polish at Cambridge. In sports there was no one to touch him, and because he could not be bested in any field, he was called Ironman.

He could run faster than any man in Ireland, was unbeaten in wrestling from the time he was twelve, was both an excellent swordsman and an excellent falconer. He swam as though born to water, rode like a centaur, and could follow a stag's trail better than most hounds.

Niall proved a lusty animal between the ages of fourteen and sixteen. There wasn't a serving wench in his father's castle, or a girl in the surrounding countryside, who was safe from his attentions. Gradually, however, he calmed down and became more discerning.

Rory Burke adored his only son. And in the number of Niall's bastards scattered about the countryside, the father saw a resurgence of his branch of the Burke family.

Rory now wanted his heir safely wed to a suitable young woman. Niall, however, had preferred to remain free.

But today had changed that. He had fallen instantly in love with Skye O'Malley. Never having been denied anything in his entire life, Niall fully expected to have her.

On Niall's right sat Eibhlin O'Malley, and throughout dinner he devoted himself to the nun, much to Eibhlin's secret amusement. Like her perceptive stepmother, she had seen the sudden, powerful attraction between Skye and Lord Burke. She pitied them both.

After dinner, O'Malley suggested that Skye show the O'Malley rose garden to Lord Burke. It wasn't an unusual request, for Dubhdara was proud of his youngest daughter's beauty, wit, and manners. He enjoyed impressing his guests with her. Anne could only hope to God that Lord Burke remembered Skye was to be wed in a few days.

Niall and Skye walked slowly from the hall, down the steps to the entry, and across the lowered drawbridge. Neither spoke. The mauve and golden twilight of the early Irish summer gave more than enough light. The air was cool, with an occasional slight breeze that carried to them the sensuous fragrance of the roses.

"My mother planned this garden for years," murmured Skye. "She loved roses. It was the one thing Da indulged her in. He had bushes brought in from all over the world. It's a beautiful garden, isn't it?"

"It is most charming," replied Lord Burke gravely.

"Thank you."

They walked a bit farther, in silence once more. As they came to the end of the roses, Skye turned to go back to the castle, but Lord Burke touched her shoulder and she stopped, her face upturned. His strong arms wrapped about her. A flame of fierce joy shot through her. She had known this would happen! She had wanted it to happen! His dark head dipped, and Skye O'Malley's lips parted slightly like an opening rosebud as she received her very first kiss.

To her great surprise his lips were soft. She hadn't expected that in a man. Then he was drawing her even closer, and the mouth on hers became demanding. Instinctively she answered that demand, freeing her arms and sliding them around his neck so that their bodies touched. For a brief moment she was floating. Then suddenly, abruptly, he released her mouth. His eyes were dark with passion. Looking down on her, he muttered huskily, "I knew it! I knew it would be this way with you!"

For the briefest moment reason returned, and she began to tremble. Concern filled his eyes and, catching her face between his thumb and forefinger, he whispered, "No, sweetheart! Don't regret, or be afraid of me. God, not that! I could not bear it!"

"I . . . I don't understand," she whispered. "I don't understand what is happening to me."

"To us, sweetheart! It's happening to me too, Skye! I barely know you, but I'm in love with you. I have never been in love before, Skye, but I know that I am in love with you."

"No!" Tears rolled down her cheeks. "You must not say these things to me, my lord. In a few days' time I am to wed with Dom O'Flaherty."

"But you don't love him, Skye!"

"My lord Burke! You know the way of these things. I have been betrothed since the cradle."

"I will speak to your father at once, sweetheart. You must not marry young O'Flaherty!"

She looked at him wonderingly. "Are you not contracted, my lord?"

"She died before we could be wed. I did not even know her. Come, sweetheart, I would kiss you again." His mouth swooped down, and Skye gave a small cry of joy as she yielded herself wholly to him.

It was utter madness, yet he loved her! This great and famous man loved her! And dear God! she loved him. She, the level-headed Skye, had fallen in love at first sight. She could feel his powerful body restraining itself in its desire, and she loved him the more, for if he tried to take her now she would give herself gladly, and he must surely know it.

Reluctantly he loosed her, his eyes warm and caressing. "Skye, sweet Skye! How you intoxicate me, my love! Come, sweetheart.

Let us return before I lose my head." He took her hand and led her slowly back to the castle.

Anne O'Malley watched them enter the hall, and silently she despaired. Skye's cheeks were flushed, her lips softly bruised with recent kisses, her eyes dreamy with anticipation. Anne rose from her chair. She had to talk with her husband! Suddenly a pain tore through her belly, her waters broke, soaking her stockings, shoes, and her petticoats. "The baby!" she cried, doubling over clutching her swollen middle. Instantly she was surrounded by the women. Dubhdara O'Malley shouldered his way through the crowd and, picking up his wife, carried her out of the hall and upstairs to their bedchamber.

No one could believe that a woman who had borne three children so easily would have such a difficult labor with the fourth, but Anne O'Malley struggled for two days. Eibhlin, trained in midwifery, worked hard. But the child was large, and turned the wrong way.

Four times the young nun turned the baby to the correct position, and four times the infant reversed itself. Finally, in desperation, Eibhlin turned the baby a fifth time and, finding its small shoulder, gently grasped it and drew the child slowly down the birth canal. After that, Anne was able to finish the job. As Anne had predicted, it was a son. The boy weighed over ten pounds. He would be named Conn.

Dubhdara O'Malley came to his young wife's bedside. They had bathed her and put her between clean, lavender-scented sheets. She had been given a nourishing drink of beef broth mixed with red wine and herbs, which would stop the bleeding and help her sleep. She was exhausted.

The room emptied. O'Malley bent and kissed his wife's cheek. He looked somewhat older, for he had suffered untold agonies at the possibility of losing this loving woman.

"No more, Annie! I am happy to settle for five sons, and the bonniest wife in Ireland! I don't want to lose you, love."

She smiled weakly and patted his hand. Then suddenly she remembered her promise. "Skye . . ." she began weakly.

For a moment he looked puzzled, then his brow cleared. "Skye? Ah, yes! The wedding is scheduled for tomorrow. You'd not have it called off, eh love? Well, don't worry, Annie. Skye will be wed tomorrow, never fear. You just rest and get strong, and if you're awake before tomorrow evening I'll send the bride and groom in to visit you."

She tried to speak, tried to tell him that he must call it off, that the wedding of Skye and Dom would be a terrible mistake. But the herbs and exhaustion had taken effect. Anne struggled to speak, but could not. Her eyes slowly closed and she couldn't open them again. Anne O'Malley had fallen into a deep, drug-induced sleep.

Chapter 2

Dubhdara O'Malley stood looking down at his sleeping daughter. It shocked even him to realize how beautiful Skye really was, and he wished he had the name and the fortune to assure her a nobler husband than young O'Flaherty.

He bore no love for the English, but he knew that their royal court was at this moment the center of the earth, and he thought how Skye would shine there.

Still, he hadn't done badly by her. Her husband would be the next chief of the Ballyhennessey O'Flahertys, and Skye would be mother to the chief after Dom. He had her safely settled. He'd miss her, though. Well, he chuckled to himself, why not admit he had a special place in his heart for the lass? She was pure O'Malley. Himself in female form, and like none of his other children.

For a few minutes more he watched her in silent wonder, and then he gently shook her by the shoulder. "Wake up, Skye! Wake up, lassie."

She resisted, having no desire to be yanked from the dream in which she and Niall were kissing. He persisted, however, and finally she opened her eyes a bit. "Da? What's the matter?"

"Annie's been delivered of a fine, healthy son, poppet. But she's fair worn with the effort. Still, she doesn't want your marriage postponed. The wedding feast will go on as scheduled, but you and Dom are to be married in an hour in the family chapel. Get up, Skye lass! This is your wedding day!"

She was instantly awake. "No, Da! No! Anne promised—"

"It's all right, love," he interrupted. "It's all right with Anne. She's sorry to miss the festivities, but she knows that, with a castle full of guests, we couldn't postpone it."

Skye sat up, her long dark hair tumbling about her white shoulders. Her eyes were enormous and deep blue in her heart-shaped face. He shifted his eyes uncomfortably from the perfection of her small breasts, visible through the thin lawn of her shift. "Da! Listen to me, please! I do not want to marry Dom O'Flaherty! Oh, why won't you listen to me?!"

Dubhdara O'Malley sat down on the edge of his favorite child's bed. "Now, poppet, we've been over this before. Of course you're going to marry Dom. He's a fine young man, and it's a good match for you. These bridal nerves are natural, but you must not give way."

Why didn't he understand? "No, please, Da! No! I hate Dom! I cannot . . . I will not marry him!" There was an hysterical edge to her voice.

"Skye!" His voice had become stern. "Enough, now! I have postponed this wedding for two years in hopes you would outgrow your willfulness, but no more, poppet! You've no reason to cry off, no religious calling, only silly maiden fears that will have vanished by this time tomorrow." He stood up. "Make yourself beautiful for Dom, poppet." And he left her.

Skye began to weep, a combination of frustration, anger, and fear. Great, gulping sobs of anguish poured hot and salty from her eyes until they were almost swollen shut. Molly, finding her young mistress in this shocking state, turned about and sought the lady Eibhlin. The young nun came instantly and, taking her younger sister into her loving arms, tried to soothe her. When the sobs had finally abated, Eibhlin laid her sister back on her pillows and mixed some herbs in a goblet of wine that she made Skye drink. The medication would soothe her. Eibhlin had seen cases of bridal nerves before.

Next the nun took soft pads of linen soaked in rose water, and lay them on Skye's closed eyes.

"It will take the swelling down," she told Molly. "We'll let her rest for half an hour, then dress her for the wedding."

Very soon thereafter, Skye O'Malley stood beside Dom O'Flaherty in the castle's candlelit chapel and was wed. All the guests agreed that there had never been a more beautiful bride. Her gown was of creamy white satin with a deep, square neck edged in a wide ruffle of silver lace. The low neckline gave the groom a fine view of her breasts, and Dom O'Flaherty licked his lips in anticipation at the sight of small, pink nipples.

As the elderly priest intoned the ancient Latin words of the ceremony over them, the bridegroom thought lasciviously of how he would pillow his head tonight on those soft breasts. When she raised her hand to receive the marriage ring, Dom noted the richness of her gown for the first time. The sleeves were slashed, the inserts filled with silver lace. This lace also edged the wrists. Her beautiful black hair was unbound, in recognition of her innocence, and topped by a simple wreath of sweetly scented white flowers.

She was whiter than her gown, and had Dom bothered to look closer, he would have seen the helpless, trapped look in her eyes. The drug given her by her sister forced her to comply with the farce. Her responses were so low that they could barely be heard, and she moved like a puppet. Her family assumed it was bridal nerves.

They were pronounced man and wife. They turned to face their families and, at that moment, the chapel doors were flung open, revealing Niall Burke, his face anguished, his eyes stark with a pain that only she could understand. Skye simply wanted to die.

"Kiss the bride! Kiss the bride!" came the ribald shouts.

Dom O'Flaherty turned Skye so that she faced him. "Now," he said triumphantly, "you belong to me!" His mouth found hers. He forced his tongue between her soft lips and into her mouth. Around them came the crude cries of encouragement. The tongue was soft, and demanding. Seeking to escape this horror, Skye fainted.

"Ho!" shouted Dubhdara O'Malley, well pleased. "Here's fine proof of my lass's innocence! Her first kiss and she swoons! Loosen her laces, lad. You're no stranger to women's clothes, or so I'm told."

While the laughter that greeted O'Malley's sally echoed around the chapel, Dom O'Flaherty picked up his bride and carried her from the room. Helplessly Niall Burke watched as the unconscious Skye was borne back to her room. He wanted to hit the smug young man who cradled Skye in his arms with such obvious pride of ownership.

For the first time in his life, the heir to one of the most powerful families in Ireland had been thwarted. For the last three days Niall had tried unsuccessfully to see the O'Malley, but Dubhdara had been unavailable to his guests because of his young wife's lying in. Under the circumstances, Niall hadn't expected them to marry Skye off so quickly. He had thought he had time to speak with the O'Malley. Though the situation would have been embarrassing, there would have been no real disgrace in O'Malley exchanging the heir to Ballyhennessey for the heir to the MacWilliam of Mayo.

Niall pushed, along with the family, into the bedchamber. Dom laid his burden upon the bed. With nimble fingers the bridegroom loosened the girl's laces. Momentarily forgetful of his audience, Dom caressed the soft, creamy swell of Skye's breast. The hunger in his pale-blue eyes was unmistakable, and Niall felt a murderous rage well up in him.

"Now, now, my son, we'll have none of that until tonight,"

chuckled O'Malley. "Your bride's got to be able to stand for all the toasts that'll be drunk at the feast, and she'll be in no condition if you have her now."

O'Flaherty flushed amid the leers and snickers. Then Eibhlin pushed through the crowd to Skye's side and, kneeling, began to rub the girl's wrists. "Molly—the wine, please. And a burnt feather. Da, it would help if all these people left. You too, brother Dom. If Skye is to be up to enjoy her own wedding feast, she must rest now."

The room slowly emptied, and Eibhlin and Molly raised Skye up. First the feather was burnt and waved beneath her nose, then the drugged wine was forced between her lips. Skye coughed, choked, and opened her eyes. "You fainted," said the nun drily.

"He . . . he put his tongue in my mouth, Eibhlin," said Skye, visibly shocked. "He . . . he said that I belong to him."

"You do."

"*No! Never* to Dom O'Flaherty! *Never* to any man!"

Eibhlin turned. "You may leave us," she told the reluctant Molly. Then Eibhlin said quietly, "It's Niall Burke, isn't it, Skye? Dear Lord, he didn't take your virginity?"

Miserably, Skye shook her head. "He wanted to wed with me, Eibhlin. He was to speak with Da."

"But he didn't, or if he did Da said no. You're married to Dom O'Flaherty, Skye. You must face it. It is your duty to be a good wife to him. He loves you and he is your lord in the eyes of the Church."

"I cannot, Eibhlin! I simply cannot! I hate Dom, and I can't bear his touch."

"Some women are like that, Skye. Perhaps you are one."

"No! When Niall Burke kissed me it was perfect! I wanted him! The way a woman wants a man . . . in marriage. But I don't feel that way about Dom."

"Go to sleep, little one," said the nun soothingly. "In a few hours' time you must hostess your wedding feast."

Sighing, Skye lay back. The herbs were doing their work, and suddenly she fell asleep, her face still wet with tears. Eibhlin shook her head. What on earth possessed Da to insist on this marriage, knowing Skye was so against it? He had always indulged his youngest daughter, adoring her lavish beauty, delighting in her love of the sea. He had never before forced her into something.

Eibhlin speculated. Perhaps their father wanted the last of Peigi O'Malley's daughters out of his house so that he could be free to enjoy his second wife, and his five sons. At any rate, though she would never admit it to Skye, the nun shared her sister's dislike of O'Flaherty. He was stubborn, far too vain, and for all his fine education, woefully ignorant. Eibhlin sighed. There was simply no help for it. It was a man's world, and a decent woman was either a wife or a nun. Perhaps, she thought wistfully, it would be different someday. Eibhlin went back to the chapel to pray for her sister. There was nothing else she could do.

When Skye awoke several hours later, the terrible reality of her situation swept over her once more. Her knowledge of men was limited, but she instinctively understood that her husband was the sort of man who preyed on the weak and helpless. Dom liked winning. She must not let him know how upset she was.

Slowly she rose from the bed, feeling just slightly dizzy, and bathed her face in rose water. Still unlaced, she breathed deeply, clearing her head. She whirled at the sound of the door behind her, furious that her privacy was to be so quickly disturbed. "How dare you enter my chamber!"

He smiled lazily. "You forget, Skye pet, that I have the right to enter your chamber whenever I choose to do so. I am your husband."

She shivered. "I forget nothing, Dom," she bravely answered. He moved toward her, and her courage cracked. "Don't come near me!" She backed away from him, but he kept on until she felt the edge of the bed against the backs of her legs. The look in his eyes terrified her, and she had to force herself to stand straight, to look directly at him. She could hear the sound of her own heart drumming in her ears.

"Your maiden shyness pleases me—to a point, Skye." His hand caressed her cheek, slid down her neck to her shoulder, then gripped the soft flesh. "I am your husband and I will brook no disobedience from you. Your father has spoiled you badly, but I will not. I will school you as I do the bitches in my kennel, and you will do your duty by me. When you err, I shall punish you. Do you understand me, Skye?"

"Yes, Dom." Her eyes were lowered in apparent compliance, but really to hide her smoldering hatred.

"Good," he said, his voice softening a little. "Now come here to me, pet." He took her chin between his fingers and forced her head up. His wet mouth ground on hers, and his tongue forced itself between her clenched teeth. She shivered with revulsion. The wet lips were on her throat. He pushed her onto the bed and, atop her, pulled down her gown, exposing the small, perfect breasts. His mouth opened to capture a little pink nipple, and she screamed.

He stopped, raised his eyes, and looked down on her. "Please Dom, we must face our guests." Groaning with frustration, he stood up slowly and, giving her a venomous look, stumbled from the room.

Outside in the hallway he stopped a moment to catch his breath, to massage the ache in his groin. She was right, damn her! He didn't dare take her until tonight, but he needed to cool the fire in his loins! At that moment his wife's buxom maid came around the corner.

Dom O'Flaherty's blue eyes narrowed speculatively, and a quick winning smile lit his features. Molly stopped, eyed him, and instantly ascertained his need. Wordlessly she took his hand and led him around the corner into a darkened alcove. She loosened his codpiece, and gasped with delight. "Oh, my Lord! You'll more than do!" her arms slid up around his neck and she whispered excitedly, "Give us a kiss, love." He bent to find her mouth, all the while fumbling to raise her petticoats. He backed her up against the stone castle wall, and Molly wrapped her legs about his waist. Clasping the plump cheeks of her buttocks in his hands, Dom O'Flaherty buried himself deep in the servant girl's willing warmth. He worked himself back and forth, not caring that he was banging her head against the wall. She moaned, half with pleasure and half with pain. He obtained his release quickly. Molly was set back down on her feet and, straightening his garments, O'Flaherty left her without so much as a word or a glance. Molly slipped to the floor, whimpering.

Skye, who seldom prayed outside church, was thanking every saint in the calendar for her temporary reprieve. Tonight there would be no reprieve. She would be forced to submit to whatever it was men did with women. She had some vague ideas, but her sisters had never discussed sex, and Anne had not gotten around to enlightening her. She was going to be at Dom's mercy.

She took her brush and removed the tangles from her hair. Then, smoothing the wrinkles from her wedding gown, Skye opened the door and left her room. Dom appeared from the darkness and, arm in arm, they descended into the hall below to greet their guests.

The festivities had begun without them, and a cry went up as they entered. Dubhdara O'Malley, already half drunk, lurched forward and escorted his daughter and her new husband to the high board. Skye was horrified to find herself with her husband on her right and Lord Burke on her left.

"Good evening, Mistress O'Flaherty. My best wishes on your future happiness," he said formally.

"Thank you, my lord," she answered. She dared not look at him lest she begin to weep again, but her hand shook as she reached for her goblet. Noting this, his heart contracted painfully.

The O'Malley of Innisfana had spared no expense. Huge bowls of raw oysters, platters of prawns and shrimp boiled in white wine and herbs, were set on all the tables. Whole sea trout broiled and stuffed, first with salmon then with smaller fresh-water trout, and finally with small shellfish, were placed at intervals on the tables. The bridegroom stuffed himself with raw oysters, loudly reminding everyone of their aphrodisiac quality.

The next course consisted of whole swans, capons in a lemon-ginger sauce, larded ducks, plump golden broiled pigeons, whole baby lambs, sides of half-cooked beef dripping their fat and bloody juices, potted rabbits, small pasties of minced meats, bowls of new lettuces and small green onions in vinegar; silver trenchers of bread and crocks of sweet butter. No one went thirsty, for silver pitchers of wine, both red and white, and earthenware pitchers of ale were placed on all the tables and kept filled.

The last course consisted of shaped jellies in all colors, custards, fruit pies, wheels of sharp cheeses, sweet cherries from France, and oranges from Spain. The chef, hired for the occasion, had done himself splendid credit with a magnificent marzipan confection. Its top decoration depicted a married couple, the bridegroom's cod-piece conspicuously large, the bride with a coy smile upon her face, her eyes fixed on the bulge.

Toast after toast was drunk. Some were ribald, some thoughtful. Finally Dom O'Flaherty turned to his bride. "Go prepare yourself for me, pet. I am well fed by your father's gracious bounty. Now I would feast on your sweet flesh."

Her cheeks reddened and she shivered. "I must bathe," she answered. "There was no time this morning."

"How long?"

"An hour."

"Half, Skye. I will be denied no longer."

She stood, and immediately a shout went up. Gathering her skirts up, Skye fled the hall followed by her sisters and, behind them, a group of laughing young men. If they caught the bride or any of her maids, they would be allowed a kiss as forfeit. With incredible swiftness the O'Malley sisters gained Skye's chamber—where the young couple would spend their wedding night—and slammed the door, successfully shutting out the young men.

Before the fireplace a small steaming tub of water stood ready.

Skye looked gratefully to her servant. "Bless you, Molly, you anticipated me."

"Knew you didn't have time before," replied the maid, helping Skye undress. The sisters busied themselves putting Skye's beautiful gown away and straightening the chamber. Sine took the warming pan and ran it smoothly beneath the bedcovers. "Nothing cools a man's ardor like cold sheets," she observed.

Skye kept her mind on her bath. If she allowed herself to think of what was coming she would go to pieces. She glanced about her bedchamber. Aside from the flowering branches placed there in keeping with the old pagan fertility ritual, it seemed the same. The large black oak bedstead, hung with azure blue velvet, had been freshly made with fine linen sheets redolent of lavender. The tall matching armoire was now empty, of course, her clothing having been packed for transport to her new home. She washed quickly, stepping out of her tub into a warmed towel. Her lovely body was rosy from the heat of the water. Molly quickly dried her and lavishly applied scented powder with a lamb's wool puff. The sisters sneezed as the excess filled the air.

"Open the window a bit," commanded Moire. "And fetch the silk robe, Molly."

Skye flushed. "Oh, no, Moire! Not *that,* for pity's sake."

"Skye!" Moire's voice was sharp. "It's an O'Malley family custom, and we have all followed it. Lord, sister, you're the fairest of us all. There's nothing for you to be ashamed of, lass."

"But for all those leering men to see me naked!"

"We O'Malleys are proud to show we come to our husbands unblemished. You will follow the custom as we all have." The silk robe was loosely wrapped around the bride, and then Moire said, "Peigi, unbolt the door. I hear the men coming."

Peigi had no sooner stepped back from the door when it burst open and the laughing guests poured into the little room. Dom O'Flaherty had already been partially disrobed by his friends. Dubhdara O'Malley stepped up to his youngest daughter. He was very drunk, but he could yet play his part.

He held his hand up for silence, and the room quieted. "This is the last of me daughters to be wed. As with all my girls, I am proud to show that she comes unblemished, and free of pock marks, to her bridegroom." He nodded to Moire and Peigi, who drew the simple robe from Skye and let it slip to the floor. The girl was now completely naked. As she turned, the sisters held up Skye's long dark tresses to show the assembled guests that nothing was hidden beneath her hair. In the candlelight, her beautiful body glowed like mother-of-pearl.

An audible sigh rippled through the room as the men and women admired and envied the young virgin's perfection. The bridegroom was visibly affected. Skye was exquisite, with her small, pink-tipped breasts, her slim, long legs ending in slender, high-arched feet.

Suddenly the guests were thrown into shock as Niall Burke pushed forward, boldly allowed his silver eyes to slide over the bride, and announced, "O'Malley! As your overlord I claim the *droit du seigneur* of this woman."

The master of Innisfana swallowed hard. "A poor jest, my lord," he replied, now very sober. He was hoping to God that Burke was only drunk, but he knew Burke wasn't. "My daughter's no peasant wench," he stated firmly.

Lord Burke drew himself up to his full imposing height. His proud glance swept the room. "I am your overlord, Dubhdara O'Malley. You swore obedience to me on my tenth birthday. It was by my most generous hand that you received this barony of Innisfana. Our laws demand that you comply with my request."

"No!" shouted Dom. "She's mine! Mine! And I am not your vassal."

Lord Burke looked scornfully at the younger man. "I will remind you, O'Flaherty, that your family owes obedience to my father—whose deputy I am. I claim the *droit du seigneur* of your bride. Will either of you gentlemen endanger your families and insult me over a girl's maidenhead? Besides, O'Flaherty, when I am finished schooling her she'll be much more to your taste. You are not, I understand, very good with virgins."

There was a sharp intake of breath around the room. Dubhdara O'Malley shifted uncomfortably. Then suddenly it came to him that the final decision rested with his new son-in-law. "I yield to you, my lord," he said quickly, nearly sighing with relief.

The complete silence in the hot little room was finally broken by Dom's voice. "I'll pay a penalty, my lord," said Dom. "You have but to name it."

Niall Burke eyed Dom arrogantly, then drawled, "Your life, or the wench's maidenhead."

A gasp went up. This was high drama, the sort of thing that would be spoken of for years to come in both the halls and hovels of Ireland. Why was Lord Burke so intent on having the bride? To be sure, she was a lovely creature, but it was very rare for an overlord to claim the *droit du seigneur* of a vassal's bride.

Dom O'Flaherty whitened, then reddened, with fear and helpless rage. His eyes swept over Skye, then back to Lord Burke. He pictured them locked in an embrace. Damn the bastard! thought Dom. He's got me trapped! At last he said savagely, "I yield. And damn you to hell, my lord Burke!" Turning, he stamped from the chamber, followed quickly by the O'Malley and the rest of the guests.

Niall Burke walked slowly to the door of the room and, shutting it, slammed the bolt home. Turning back, he looked at Skye. Throughout the whole exchange, she had remained as silent and still as a hiding rabbit. "I do mean to take you," he said quietly.

Her eyes were enormous, blue-green against her white face. "I know," she answered softly. "You'll have to tell me what to do. No one has ever told me what is required, and I am very ignorant. Anne didn't have time to explain," she finished helplessly.

A warm smile lit his features, and he was suddenly her Niall again. "I think, sweetheart," he said in a kindly voice, "that the first thing would be to get you into bed. You look chilled." With a sweeping movement he pulled the covers back and, scooping her up, gently tucked her beneath the down coverlet.

"Kiss me, Niall." It was a simple request, and it was also the first time she had called him by his name.

"I have every intention of doing just that, Skye. Give me but a moment to divest myself of my clothes."

"Please, now!"

Had she been anyone else he would have made a ribald jest. She was so intense. So urgent. Instead he bent, kissed the lips she offered. It was a sweet kiss, and they were both loath to stop, but finally she drew away. "I had to be sure it would be as lovely with you this time as it was the last. When Dom kissed me today I wanted to die because he revolted me so."

"And is it still as lovely, my darling?" His silvery eyes caressed her warmly.

"Yes, Niall. It is still lovely."

Thoughtfully, without haste, he removed his clothes and approached the bed. "Have you ever seen a man naked before, Skye?" The firelight from the small corner fireplace flickered across his bare body.

"Only the top part. The sailors often strip their shirts off when it gets too hot. I've seen bare feet, and part of the leg too." Her eyes slowly traveled the length of him, lingering a moment on his sex, then blushingly moving upward.

He grinned mischievously at her. "I trust I meet with your complete approval, sweetheart," he teased, climbing into bed with her.

Her heart-shaped face was very serious. "I don't understand how it works."

"Let me worry about that," he answered. Taking her into his arms, he rolled her beneath him. "Ah, Skye! Sweet Skye! I have dared much for you, my darling." His mouth found hers again, but this time it was different. His lips teased, playing lightly across her mouth, her fluttering eyelids, her forehead, cheeks, chin, and lastly the tip of her nose.

The shock of his sweet assault left her slightly breathless, and she was certainly not ready for the warm hand that gently cupped her breast. "Oh!" Then, "Oh, Niall, I am sorry I am so small," she apologized shyly, unable to meet his warm gaze.

"You are perfection, Skye. See how sweetly your breast nestles into my hand? It is like a little white dove." He bent his dark head and kissed the pink peak, pleased that it hardened almost immediately beneath his lips.

Gently he pressed her back among the pillows, lightly straddling her. His warm mouth now pressed kisses all across her trembling breasts, taking pleasure in her rapid rise to passion. Her beautiful hair billowed shining and dark across the white linen pillows. Head thrown back to reveal the slender column of her throat, she tempted the warm lips to leave a string of burning kisses down the quivering flesh.

His big hands slipped over her torso, enjoying the silken skin. Suddenly Skye was afire, and she moaned helplessly, frightened. Her body felt liquid. She was languid, yet filled with a great strength at the same time. His voice murmured soft and reassuring words of love.

Still she gasped softly, surprised as his fingers gently explored her, probing tenderly, forcing the tension from her body. Then she became aware of a new touch, that of his manhood, hard against her soft leg. Gently his knee nudged her thighs apart. The pulsing root of him touched the tip of her womanhood, and in a sweet haze of fear and desire she heard him say, "It will hurt you just once, Skye. After that there will never be pain again, my love."

"Yes! Yes! Oh, please, yes!" she panted, not even knowing what it was that she sought, but desperately wanting it. A deep, burning pain quickly receded, leaving her filled with a wonderful, throbbing warmth. His silvery eyes met her blue ones, and passion mirrored passion as he loved her. For a moment they hung suspended in time and then she cried out her pleasure as his hardness broke, filling her with his creamy juices.

After a few breathless minutes he rolled away and cradled her in his arms. He stroked her hair, marveling at its soft density. When he spoke again his velvety voice held the faintest hint of a tremor. "Thank you, Skye, my little love. Thank you for the most precious gift a man can receive from a maiden."

She moved so that she could see his face, her new womanhood making her brave. "I have waited all my life for you, Niall Burke. Do not leave me now, for I should sooner be your leman than Dom O'Flaherty's wife. I would go where you go."

He sighed. "I cannot let you go now, Skye. We will get your marriage annulled based on your adultery with me. I have no intention of returning you to O'Flaherty. We will leave for my father's castle in the morning. Your husband is a vain peacock. A fat financial settlement and a new and noble bride should soothe his swollen pride."

"You will not leave me?" Her eyes were shining with happiness. "Oh, Niall! I love you! I love you so much!"

"God, sweetheart, I adore you!" He kissed her hard. "I love you too, my darling. I love you!"

Their bodies melted together once more. Skye was completely overwhelmed by these new and delicious stormy sensations sweeping over her. Her body responded to his every touch, eagerly seeking each new thrill.

He lay on his back and, lifting her, lay her atop him. Her blushes delighted him. Shyly she hid her face in his shoulder. He chuckled. "Nay, sweetheart, now you must love me."

"But Niall, I don't know how," she protested.

"Touch me, Skye. It's the best start."

She sat up, her legs on either side of his torso. She couldn't quite meet his gaze yet. Shyly she touched his chest with a trembling hand. The dark mat of hair was soft, his skin smooth and warm. Her hand moved to his shoulder, then down his well-muscled sword arm. In a sudden bold move she leaned forward and brushed his cheek with her breast. Niall softly caught his breath and waited for her next move. Slowly she rubbed his face and then a hard little nipple was against his lips. It was now Skye's turn to gasp as she found the taut little peak in the warmness of his mouth. His tongue teased it, sending darts of fire through her. She wriggled, eyes half closed.

His arms came up around her, and she once more found herself on her back. He caught her hand and drew it down to his manhood. Unbidden she caressed him with devastating effect. He groaned into the dark and tangled night of her hair. The clean, heathery smell of her soap, the warm woman scent of her body maddened him. Again he slid his great sword into her sweet sheath.

Sighing, she took as much of him to herself as she could. Her arms held him as tightly as his held her.

"Put your legs about me, my darling. I cannot have enough of you." His voice was strange, fierce and husky. Obeying, she cried out softly as she felt him drive deeper into her soft body. The world about her exploded into a whirlpool of pleasure upon pleasure. It could get no better, and yet it did—with each smooth thrust.

"Niall! Oh, Niall, I die!" she finally sobbed, seemingly unable to bear any more. He was experienced enough to control their spiraling rise, but he could not stop loving her. "Just a little more, Skye. Ah, God! You're so sweet! I don't want to stop!" he muttered thickly. "No! No! Don't stop! Please, no!" she whispered back frantically. She did not want to leave this marvelous world. Deeper! Deeper! Faster! Faster! They were lost in each other. As they climaxed together she gave a long wail, half in joy, half in sorrow.

Gathering her to him, he crooned low, "Ah, Skye! Sweet Skye! You are perfection, my little love. Pure perfection! I love you so, sweetheart."

Her blue-green eyes were heavy with exhaustion, but they shone with love. "Give me a son, Niall!" she whispered fiercely.

Tenderly he stroked her cheek. "In time, my darling. In time. Now sleep, Skye, my love. In the morning we will face the world with the shocking news that we would be together. We will need to be well rested to meet the uproar that's sure to follow."

"You meant it when you said you wouldn't leave me?" Her voice trembled.

"Aye, sweetheart! Only the devil himself can separate us now, Skye."

"I'd go with you into Hell itself, Niall," she answered passionately.

At last, enclosed in each other's arms, they fell asleep, trusting the power of their love.

Chapter 3

IN THE GRAY HALF-LIGHT BEFORE DAWN NIALL BURKE AND SKYE lay sleeping. Heart hammering, the little pot boy crawled through the unshuttered window and for a brief moment stared quite openmouthed at the two people lying on the bed. Both were naked. The man was on his stomach, face down, his arm flung across the woman. She was curled on her side. The pot boy, who was rarely freed from his kitchen, thought the two were the most beautiful sight he had ever seen. He felt saddened at what he must do. The woman stirred in her sleep and, guiltily recalling his duty, the boy tiptoed across the room. Softly sliding the bolt back, he opened the door.

Dubhdara O'Malley and three of his men-at-arms came silently into the room. O'Malley nodded to his retainers. Niall Burke was swiftly pulled off the bed, a cloth stuffed into his mouth. Then he was half-dragged, half-carried out of the room, the door shut softly but firmly behind him. Fiercely Niall struggled against his captors, who hustled him down into the main hall of the castle. He was not afraid, for he knew that if it had been his life they sought he would already be dead.

"You'll not yell, my lord?" O'Malley asked him when they entered a room down the hall.

Niall shook his head. His arms were freed and the gag was pulled from his mouth. He took up the goblet of ale placed at his hand. Drinking it, he began to dress in his clothes, which the little pot boy had thoughtfully brought along. Niall Burke was furious, but arguing with the O'Malley stark naked put him at a disadvantage. His antagonist spoke first.

"You will be on your way immediately, my lord. Young O'Flaherty has spent an unhappy night, drinking and abusing Skye's maid. The sight of you now could drive him to rashness. I should not like to answer to the MacWilliam if his heir were harmed."

Niall yanked on his boots. "I want Skye's marriage annulled, O'Malley! For three days I tried to get to you, to ask you to call off this marriage. I love Skye, and she loves me. I want her to wife. I'll see that O'Flaherty is pacified with a new bride and a large bribe. Why do you think I did what I did last night? To *amuse* myself, man? I love your daughter, O'Malley, and I hope my action will force O'Flaherty to give her up."

Dubhdara O'Malley looked amazed. "Laddie, laddie! If I have nothing else in this world I have my good name and my good word. The word of Dubhdara O'Malley has never been questioned because it is as good as gold. I have never broken my word! I will not do so now. Skye was betrothed to Dom as a child. Even if I had postponed the marriage, your father would not permit you to marry an O'Malley of Innisfana. For you, it will be an O'Neill, an O'Donnell, or an O'Brien—daughters of the high aristocracy. Not my little lass."

Niall's silver eyes flashed. "She is fit to be a queen, O'Malley!"

"Ah, laddie, you'll get no argument from me on that account! But my daughter is Dom O'Flaherty's wife till death parts them. You've exercised the *droit du seigneur* on the bride. There is nothing else here for you. Go home. Leave me to mend the broken fences, and my child's broken heart."

"I will not leave without Skye, O'Malley! She comes with me!"

The master of the castle barely nodded to his men. Niall Burke was tapped lightly on his head, rendering him unconscious. "Carry him to the boat, and tell Captain MacGuire to take him home. MacGuire's to put this letter directly into the MacWilliam's hand, and await a reply," O'Malley said tersely.

O'Malley sat watching a moment as his most honored guest was slung over the shoulder of one of his men and removed from the hall. Then, without a backward glance, O'Malley returned to his daughter's bedchamber. He shook her awake gently. "Skye, lass! Wake up now."

Slowly her blue eyes opened, then widened in surprise. "Da?" Her gaze quickly swept the room, and her voice became a frightened whisper. "Niall?"

"Gone, Skye. Niall Burke has gone home."

"No! He promised we would never be parted! He promised!"

"Men frequently make promises in the heat of passion that they have no intention of keeping," said the O'Malley brutally. "Get up and get dressed, daughter. You'll go with Eibhlin to her convent on Innishturk until Dom's temper cools, and we're sure you don't carry Burke's bastard. I'll send someone to help you dress."

"You're lying to me, Da! What have you done with Niall?"

"I'm not lying, Skye. Burke has gone home."

"Where's Molly?"

"She's sick this morning," O'Malley said as he left the room.

Skye sat numbed. He had *promised* they would not be parted! He had meant it! She knew he had meant it! Where was he? Had they killed him? Oh, God, no! She began to tremble. No. Of course they hadn't killed him. Her father would not kill his overlord's heir.

Perhaps, said an evil voice in her head, perhaps he is telling you the truth. After all, your experience with men is not great. Perhaps the great lord's heir has amused himself with you, and has now gone back to his own. Her heart began to hammer fiercely, and for a moment she thought she would faint. Then, from deep inside, Skye called on the reservoir of strength she had built up over the years. If she listened to doubt she would go mad. She must trust to her intuition. Skye O'Malley would not give in to panic.

Climbing from the bed, she walked naked across the chamber and drew her clothing from a leather-bound trunk. She began to dress, first pulling on her underclothes, then a skirtlike object. This garment was a design of Skye's own fashioning. O'Malley had objected to his daughter wearing men's clothing, but Skye had felt hampered aboard ship by long skirts. So she had made her skirts into wide pants that came below the knee. Beneath, she wore hose and knee-length leather boots. She had cut her chemises off at the waist, hemmed them, and worn them beneath her silk shirts.

Washed and dressed, her long black hair braided and affixed atop her head, she gathered up a dark plaid cloak and left the room. She found a man-at-arms waiting, and directed him to fetch the small trunk in her room and see it safely stowed in the waiting boat.

Regally, she descended the stairs. Below, in the castle's main hall, her father, her sister Eibhlin, and Dom awaited her. Dom looked terrible. His eyes were badly bloodshot and puffy, and his face was marked with several scratches and bruises. She steeled herself for the confrontation. "Good morning, Dom." He eyed her angrily, nodded, but said nothing. She shrugged, then turned to her father. "I am ready to go, Da, but before I do I want to know the truth. Niall would not have left me unless forced."

Dom O'Flaherty's light-blue eyes widened, then narrowed. He turned to his father-in-law. "What the hell treachery is this, O'Malley? It's bad enough that Burke demanded the *droit du seigneur* of my bride before the entire district. Now it appears she was in collusion with him!" He whirled on Skye. "You little bitch! How long has it been going on? How long have you been whoring with Burke? I ought to beat you black and blue!"

Skye eyed her husband coldly. Her voice was calm and level. "I met Niall but a few days ago, Dom. Yes, we are in love. I do not understand how it happened, but it did. I do not particularly like you, Dom, but I would not have hurt or embarrassed you deliberately. Niall Burke wants to marry me. Give me an annulment. You don't love me. Niall will arrange for you to have a new and noble bride, and a fat financial settlement to soothe your wounded pride."

Dom looked as if she had lost her mind. "Have you given me a half-wit to wife, O'Malley?" He turned on Skye. "Listen, you little fool! The MacWilliam isn't about to let his heir marry with the likes of you. Niall Burke is a rake. He wanted only to fuck with you, which I've no doubt he did quite well if his reputation is warranted. It's over! Now you'll go with Eibhlin to Innishturk until I'm sure Burke's seed did not take root. When you come home to me, Skye, you'll be a proper wife—like me or no—and you'll go no more awhoring. Get out of my sight now, woman!"

"Da!"

"Obey your husband, Skye. He is your master now."

"Never!"

Dom O'Flaherty leaped the distance between them and, grasping Skye by the arm, slapped her brutally several times. Shocked, for her father had never hit her, she could only try and protect herself from his blows. "Whore! I warned you what would happen if you disobeyed me!" He shook her hard. Furious and fearful both, Skye pulled away angrily.

"Whoreson!" she hissed. "Hit me again and I'll stick a knife into your black heart!"

"Enough!" roared O'Malley, stepping between the two. "Enough, Dom!" His voice was sharp. "Eibhlin, take your sister to the boat, and *go.*"

Skye's eyes were almost black in anger. "I'll not forgive you for this, Da," she said quietly. Shooting him a look of pure hatred, she left the hall with her sister.

Outside, the day was chill and gray. The wind whipped the women's cloaks about them as they hurried across the drawbridge and through the rose garden. For a moment Skye stopped. Her eyes softened and swam with tears. Plucking a red rose, she inhaled its fragrance, sighed, and continued on her way, carefully picking her way down the path that led from the cliff top to the damp beach below. A sailboat and two of her father's men waited on the beach. She could see her trunk already in the boat. One of the men helped Eibhlin into the little craft. Skye brushed aid aside, clambering up into the craft and seating herself in the stern. She took a firm grip on the tiller. While one sailor pushed the boat from the damp sand, the other hoisted the sail.

The sailor Connor grinned, nodded, and sat back when Skye took the tiller. They'd be at Innishturk Island in a jig time, for no one could sail a boat like Mistress Skye. The other sailor, newer to O'Malley's service, sat silently.

Skye tacked the boat smartly across the castle's sheltered cove and nosed it into the open sea. The day was turning fair, and there was a good breeze. The small boat skimmed across the deep blue waves. Innishturk, but a few nautical miles away, was easily visible. Skye carefully set her course to bring the craft in on the piece of coast closest to Eibhlin's convent.

Eibhlin wanted desperately to talk to her, but Skye suddenly looked older, and very forbidding. The young nun was suddenly sad. What could she possibly say to cheer her sister? What did you say to a woman forcibly married to one man when she deeply loved another? Once again, Eibhlin felt the frustration of being a woman in a man's world. Again she asked herself why it was so.

Then Eibhlin saw a terrible bruise beginning to form on Skye's left cheekbone. Silently the nun dipped her handkerchief in the icy cold sea and, squeezing it out, wordlessly handed it to her sister. A brief smile was her thanks, as Skye took the wet cloth and held it to her injured face.

Innishturk came closer, then closer, and soon the little boat was scudding up onto the beach. Eibhlin was lifted out. In her element now, she commanded, "Bring Mistress Skye's trunk, Connor. Padraic, you stay with the boat."

"Yes, Sister." "Aye, Sister."

Skye swung herself over the side of the boat and dropped lightly to the sand. She knew the way quite well, for she had often come with her father to see Eibhlin. Silently she trudged up the path from the beach. At the cliff top she undid a small wicket gate, and held it open for her sister and the panting Connor. The gate swung shut, and they were on the convent grounds.

Ahead of them stood St. Bride's of the Cliffs, built over one hundred years before. The convent was built around a quadrangle, the four towers of its corners rising stark against the sky. The dark gray stones of the main building were weathered by the wind and the sea. There were several outbuildings for the convent livestock, a bakehouse and a washhouse. At the convent portal—a double oaken door bounded in brass—they stopped.

"Connor will have to wait here," said Eibhlin. "I'll send someone to bring your trunk."

"I'll wait with him," said Skye quietly. "If I am to be cloistered for a month I'd just as soon postpone my captivity."

Eibhlin did not argue. She pulled on the bell. When it was answered by the portress, she entered hurriedly.

Alone with Skye, Connor observed, "Strange place for a honeymoon if you ask me."

"I didn't!" snapped Skye, "but it's as good a place as any when you're wed to the wrong man. Repeat that, you old gossip, and I'm sure to be beaten for it."

"The O'Malley never laid a hand on you in your life, lass!"

"No, he didn't, but the little bastard he's married me to did. The bruise on my cheek is a mark of his affection."

Connor saw nothing wrong with a man occasionally giving his woman a clout to keep her in line, but he was truly shocked that a bridegroom would beat his bride of one day. Mistress Skye was not just any lass. She was special. Besides, he was related to her maid, Molly, who'd barely survived her night with O'Flaherty. Better to warn the young mistress.

"I'd best say this straight out, lass, so's you'll be on your guard. O'Flaherty took Molly to his bed last night. Fair killed her too. Made her do all kinds of things no decent man would ask of a woman. Then he beat her half to death and kicked her out. When you've got to go back to him, be careful."

Skye's face betrayed no emotion. "Will Molly be all right?"

"Her bruises will heal."

"Tell her if she chooses not to serve me anymore I'll understand. If that is her decision she may remain at the castle to serve my stepmother. Tell the lady Anne that I will need a stout serving woman of middle years and plain countenance. If I am forced to return to him, I would not expose another young girl to O'Flaherty."

The convent portal creaked open again and Eibhlin came forward, escorted by two stout nuns. Skye bid Connor farewell, then followed her sister through the door. Her trunk would be brought in by the other nuns.

The two sisters walked silently through the long hallway until they came to a heavy oak door. Eibhlin rapped on the door. A voice bid them enter, and they obeyed.

Seated in a chair was one of the most beautiful women Skye had ever seen. Her oval face was serene beneath the white wimple, with its starched and pleated white wings. Her black habit was relieved of its severity by a stiff white rectangle of a bib upon which rested an ebony crucifix banded in silver, a silver lily on its face. Kneeling, Eibhlin caught the aristocratic hand and kissed the silver-and-onyx ring of office.

"Rise, my daughter," came a cool, cultivated voice.

"Reverend Mother, may I present my sister, Skye. Skye, this is the Reverend Mother Ethna."

"Thank you, Sister Eibhlin. You may return to your duties now. Mistress Monahan from our village went into labor this morning, and you have our permission to attend her."

Eibhlin bowed herself out, and the Reverend Mother Ethna waved Skye to a chair. "Welcome to St. Bride's of the Cliffs, Lady O'Flaherty. Your father has already apprised us of the reason for your visit. We will endeavor to make you as comfortable as possible."

"Thank you," Skye said tonelessly.

Quiet brown eyes surveyed Skye, and the nun appeared to be debating with herself. Then she said, "I was Ethna O'Neill before I took the veil. It was my niece to whom Lord Burke was betrothed. She never knew him, but I did. He has a most winning way about him." A small smile played about the corners of her mouth.

"We met but a short time ago," said Skye, softening somewhat. "I don't know what happened to us, but we are in love. Da simply would not listen. Niall wants to have my marriage annulled so we may wed."

The nun shook her head. "Perhaps he can arrange it, or at least get the proceedings started while you're here."

"You're the first person who's not told me that the MacWilliam won't let his heir marry with an O'Malley of Innisfana."

The Reverend Mother laughed. "Ah, these men and their pride! Take heart, my daughter. The MacWilliam is a stern man, but he loves his son. But tell me, child, have you no feeling for your young husband?"

"I do not love Dom, nor did I ever wish to wed with him. I begged my father not to force me to it, even before I met Niall Burke. In fact, I did not wish to wed at all until I met Niall. I do not believe a woman should have to spend her life with someone she dislikes."

"So," chuckled the nun, "you're a revolutionary like your sister, Lady O'Flaherty."

"No. And please, I beg of you, Reverend Mother, do not call

me Lady O'Flaherty. I shall never acknowledge Dom's name as mine. I am Skye O'Malley!"

"Very well, Skye O'Malley, we shall try to make your stay with us as pleasant as possible." The nun picked up a bell and rang it sharply. It was instantly answered by a little novice. "Sister Feldelm, this is Skye O'Malley, Sister Eibhlin's sister. She is sheltering with us for several weeks. The West Tower guest suite has been prepared for her. Will you please escort her there?"

"Yes, Reverend Mother," said the novice, bobbing a curtsey. "If you'll come along with me, Mistress O'Malley."

"You are free to go wherever you chose on the grounds, Skye, and the chapel and public rooms of the convent are open to you. You need not keep to your rooms."

"Thank you." Skye turned to follow Sister Feldelm.

"My daughter, I shall pass on to you any information I receive."

Skye flashed her a small smile, then followed the novice out.

How sad, thought the Reverend Mother. Another young woman pushed into an unhappy marriage. She wondered what the MacWilliam would do. She knew what he would not do. He would not let Niall have Skye, for he sought a better match for his heir. Damn him and the others like him for the fools they were! Hadn't they yet learned that overbred wenches invariably proved to be bad breeders? A good sturdy lass of less elegant lineage made a better wife.

The Reverend Mother Ethna realized that beneath the gallant defiance, Skye O'Malley was a frightened and desperate girl. If the child was to be disappointed, best she learn it now so she might face her grief with the nuns. In the time she was with them, they could, with the grace of God, help her make peace with herself.

Alone in her apartment Skye inspected her surroundings. There were two rooms, a good-sized dayroom, and a small bedroom. Both had fireplaces. The bedroom fireplace was set into the corner. The room held only a big oak bed with claret velvet hangings. There was no room for any other furniture. The size of the bed amused and puzzled Skye until it dawned on her that the convent probably relied on the generosity of its friends to furnish its rooms. Giggling to herself, she wondered what the nuns thought of the great bed. It faced the one small window in the bedroom, and looked out over the sea.

The dayroom was a bright, pleasant room with windows on two sides. They faced north, giving a far view of her home on Innisfana Island, and west across the open sea into the setting sun. On the east wall of the room was a large stone fireplace flanked by two great carved winged angels. To the north of the fireplace was the stout oak door that served as an entry.

On the opposite side of the fireplace a small floor-to-ceiling bookcase had been built into the wall, matching a larger one that shared the south wall with the paneled bedroom door. Before the lead paned western windows was a polished oak refectory table with armchairs at the head and foot. To one side of the fireplace was a settle and on the other a comfortable chair. There was a large carved chest, and in the space between the windows stood a little prie-dieu with an embroidered cushion. Skye's trunk had been placed in the bedroom, beneath the window.

The convent's benefactors had been more than generous. Heavy claret-red velvet draperies hung from all the windows, and a large Turkey carpet in reds and blues was spread across the floor, matching a smaller one in the bedroom. Skye later learned that the O'Neills had furnished the West Tower's guest quarters when their own Ethna became the head of St. Bride's of the Cliffs.

Skye's days quickly took on a comfortable pattern. She rose early, and attended mass in the convent's chapel. She was not particularly religious, but she prayed now that Niall would soon come for her. Afterward she obtained her own breakfast from the kitchen and went off by herself to walk across the convent grounds. A small sailboat belonging to the order was placed at her disposal, and Skye spent many hours sailing and fishing to pass the time. The convent soon enjoyed a number of fresh seafood dinners courtesy of their young guest.

The main meal of the day was served at two in the afternoon, and Skye ate it alone in her dayroom. The evening meal was served after vespers, and sometimes Eibhlin joined her young sister. Otherwise Skye was again alone.

The convent had a surprisingly fine library, and the bookshelves in Skye's dayroom were also well filled. On very wet days, she read. Skye O'Malley was a well-educated woman for her day. She could speak her native Gaelic as well as English, French, and Latin. She could write, and though she might not sew as fine a seam as her sisters did, her needlework was passable and she could knit.

She knew how to run a household, understanding provisioning, salting, conserving, preserving, soap-making, and perfume-making. She knew the rudiments of brewing and household medicine. She had been taught to keep accounts, for O'Malley firmly believed that the only way to avoid being cheated by one's own steward was to do one's own household accounts. And as if that were not enough, Skye was one of the finest navigators her father had ever sailed with. The O'Malley often joked that he thought his daughter could smell out her ship's destination.

Though she saw the nuns as she moved through the uneventful pattern of her days, Skye actually spent most of her time alone. The order of St. Bride's was not a cloistered one, nor was it a begging order. The nuns were workers, devoted first to their God and second to the poor. Some of the nuns were teachers and others gave medical aid to the surrounding area. The rest farmed for the convent, cooked, knitted, sewed, and did the farm and household chores.

Skye adapted instantly, and entered into the spirit of the convent, doing her share of fishing, snaring rabbits, and one day even bringing down a young buck. The venison was a rare treat for the nuns.

Skye needed that constant physical activity. Had she not worked so hard she might never have slept. Why had Niall not communicated with her? Surely he understood the anguish she was feeling. He could not, she was sure, have made love to her with such exquisite delicacy while intending to leave her forever.

It might have eased her mind to know that Niall Burke suffered no less than she did. He had clawed his way up through the swirling darkness to discover himself trussed like a damned Christmas goose on a cockle of a boat that was bouncing all over the ocean. The bearded captain of the little boat gave him a wicked but sympathetic grin.

"So, you're awake, me lord."

"Where the hell am I?" snarled Niall. "Unloose me at once!"

The captain looked unhappy. "Ah, now, your worship, I can't do that. If I were to unloose you, and you became violent, which I can see you're sure to do, I'd be in terrible trouble. Take Lord Burke home to the MacWilliam was what the O'Malley told me to do, and that's just what I'll do."

"At least sit me up, man, and give me a dram. I'm cramped, my head feels like the little people are mining gold inside it, and I'm not sure I won't be seasick."

Captain MacGuire chuckled. "All right, lad. You don't ask a great deal of a man, and I'm no fool to make you any more uncomfortable than you already are." Bending, he hauled Niall into a sitting position, his back against the mast, and held a flask to his lips.

Niall gratefully swallowed several gulps of the smoky, peat-scented whiskey. It hit the pit of his stomach like a burning rock, but almost immediately it began to spread its warmth through his cramped, wet body. "So the O'Malley sent me home?" he said thoughtfully.

"Aye, me lord, and you've slept as peaceful as a babe most of the way. We're just about there."

Niall craned his neck and looked to the coast, but he was not a sailor and the distant landscape looked all the same to him. "How long?" he demanded.

"A bit," came the infuriatingly vague answer. "See that little point over there? Once we're around it you're home. That's where we'll land, and then I'll walk you from there. I've a message to deliver to the MacWilliam."

"Walk!" Niall exploded. "We'll take the first available horses we can find. The MacWilliam's stronghold is a good stretch of the legs from the sea, man. Do you ride?"

"About as good as you sail, laddie."

"Then God help you, MacGuire! You'll soon be as uncomfortable as I am now!"

When they finally reached shore the captain untied his passenger and helped him from the boat. Niall Burke rubbed his wrists where the ropes had chafed him. He was anxious to be home so he might speak with his father. He clambered up the hillside from the beach.

Without even looking to see if MacGuire was with him, Niall strode quickly away, following a faint path. After about a half-hour they came in view of a thatched roofed farmhouse. Next to the farmhouse bloomed a kitchen garden of herbs, carrots, and other root vegetables, cress, and a few bright flowers. The nearby fields, well kept, were already colored with barley and rye. And in a pasture just beyond the garden a dozen sleek horses grazed peacefully. There was no sign of life, though MacGuire could have sworn he had seen smoke coming from the chimney. "Ho! The house! 'Tis Niall Burke, and a friend."

After a long moment the farmhouse door swung open, and a big man stepped out. He called back out into the house, "It's all right, Maeve. It's his lordship." The man came forward, a grin on his face, and clasped Niall's hand in his own large bearlike paw. "Welcome, my lord! How may we serve you?"

"I need two horses, Brian. This evil-looking fellow is Captain

MacGuire, one of the O'Malley's men. He'll return the horses to you later."

"At once, my lord. If you're not in too great a hurry, the wife is just taking bread from the oven."

Niall Burke's silvery eyes crinkled in appreciation. "Ah," he breathed. "Maeve's bread with her own honey! Come on, MacGuire! I've a treat for you, despite the fact that you've treated me badly." The captain in his wake, he burst through the door and swept up a sparrow of a woman into his embrace. He held her high above him, lowering her to smack kisses on both of her flushed cheeks while she laughed and scolded him to put her down. "I've come for your virtue—and your fine bread, Maeve love!" he teased, returning her to her feet.

She gave him a friendly whack, and said, "None of your naughtiness now, Master Niall. 'Tis long past time you grew up. Come along with you, and your friend too. Sit down. The bread's just from the oven."

They obeyed her and sat. Niall, turning to MacGuire, explained, "Maeve was my nurse until I was seven. Then she deserted me to wed with Brian. As a boy, I used to come here often, for she bakes the best bread in the district. And for some reason her bees make the best honey you've ever tasted."

"It's the salt air," said Maeve. "It gives the honey a wee bit of a nip."

MacGuire shortly found that Lord Burke was no liar, and he said to Maeve, "If you had a daughter who could bake half as well as you do, mistress, I'd wed with her in a thrice."

Maeve flushed with pleasure. "If you return this way, Captain, stop for a meal with us."

"Thank you, mistress, and I will!"

"The horses are ready, my lord," called Brian from the doorway.

Niall Burke stood up, licking a drop of honey from his finger like a small boy. "Let's go, MacGuire. I'm anxious to be home!"

The captain was surprised to see two fine, well-bred mounts waiting. They mounted and, with a wave to Brian, rode off.

"Your peasants must be prosperous to have any horses at all, let alone such fine ones," observed MacGuire as they cantered along.

"These are our horses," answered Burke. "We keep good horses with several specially chosen families for just such purposes as these. That way, we're never stranded." He then spurred his horse to a gallop. "Come on, man," he called to the captain, who was bouncing up and down on his mount, looking decidedly uncomfortable. "I'm for home!"

Niall Burke was to regret his haste. No sooner had he entered into the MacWilliam's presence than the O'Malley's letter was handed over to the great lord. MacGuire was sent off to be served refreshment, and Niall stood impatiently while the MacWilliam, his strong features darkening, skimmed over the parchment. Finally the MacWilliam snorted and, looking angrily at his son, roared, "Well, you arrogant puppy, I hope you have a helluva good explanation for your conduct! Dubhdara O'Malley's ships are vital to the defense of this area, as is the goodwill of the Ballyhennessey O'Flahertys!"

Niall, of course, had not read the letter. Caught off guard, he blurted like a schoolboy. "I love her, Father! I love Skye O'Malley! I tried to speak with O'Malley, and get him to call off the wedding. But his wife went into labor before I could talk to him. She had a hard birth. He was unavailable all that time, and they wed the girl ahead of schedule, practically in secret."

"O'Malley wouldn't have called off the match, you young fool! It was made years ago. He was bound to it! And a damn good match it was for his youngest lass. How dared you interfere?"

"I love her, and she loves me. She detests the O'Flaherty bastard they've wed her to! She always hated him, even before we met."

"And you felt that gave you the right to claim the *droit du seigneur* of the bride? Jesus, man! If you were anyone else I'd kill you! You're lucky O'Malley has a sense of humor. The girl's been sent to her sister's convent to be sure your night results in nothing worse than embarrassment."

"I love her!" shouted Niall. "I want her marriage annulled so I may wed her. There must be a bishop in this family."

"Over my dead body!" roared the MacWilliam. "O'Malley's ships are valuable to me. His wench is not. I'll have no pirate wench mothering my grandchildren! I've arranged for you to wed with Darragh O'Neill, the younger sister to your late betrothed. She is thirteen, and ripe for marriage. You'll be joined in three weeks' time."

"No!"

"Yes! Listen, you young idiot, take O'Malley's girl as a mistress if you wish, but you cannot wed her. She already has a husband. And from what I hear of him, once he takes her to bed, you'll become just a pretty memory to her."

"Go to Hell!" Niall Burke stormed out of his father's study and got gloriously drunk. The following day, his head feeling twice its normal size, he was summoned back to his father.

"This," said the MacWilliam, "was brought for you this morning. I have taken the liberty of reading it, and can only say that O'Malley's daughter is wiser than you are. She obviously has more sense than you do. Here."

Niall snatched the parchment and read it with shock.

My lord Burke:

I have retired with my sister to her convent of St. Bride's on Innishturk Island, where I shall pray to Our Lady that the shameful night we spent together bears no unhallowed fruit. What we did was wrong, and I can only hope and pray that my husband will forgive me. I beg that you forget me, and for the good of your soul enter into Christian marriage with a good woman at the earliest possible moment. May God go with you always.

Skye, Lady O'Flaherty

He wanted desperately to deny what he read. And, after all, he had never seen her writing. Was it a forgery? The hand, however, was sweetly rounded and feminine, and he recognized the imprint on the wax seal as the one she wore on a ring. Perhaps they had forced her to write this message. But he knew how stubborn Skye was. They could have burned her feet with hot irons and she'd not have written it, had she not wished to do so. Damn her! Damn her! Was that all he meant to her? A shameful night? Damn her for the fickle bitch she was! Anguished beyond anything he had ever known, Niall blinked back his tears and said hoarsely, "I'll marry Darragh O'Neill." Then he dropped the letter and strode from the room without a backward glance.

The MacWilliam waited a moment to be sure his son had gone, then said, "You can come out now, Captain MacGuire. Go back and tell the O'Malley that his strategy worked. My son will be wed in three weeks' time, and will give him no further trouble."

MacGuire bowed, nodded wordlessly, and departed.

Alone, the MacWilliam felt a twinge of conscience. He loved his son deeply, and hated denying him anything. Still, when given the choice between an O'Neill and an O'Malley for his daughter-in-law, there was only one choice the MacWilliam could make. Yes, Niall would settle down quite nicely with Darragh O'Neill. By this time next year he would have a grandson.

Chapter 4

An especially nice thing came of Skye's stay at St. Bride's. Walking on the beach one day, she came across an injured young wolfhound, not quite full grown. The poor creature was half starved, its ribs plainly visible. Its fur was so filthy and matted with salt that it was difficult to tell the dog's true color. Its leg had been caught in a rock crevice. Hearing the weak bark, Skye ran to the dog, who looked up at her hopefully and thumped his long tail in a friendly fashion.

"Ah, poor beastie," murmured Skye sympathetically, and set about freeing the dog. Carefully she removed the small rocks about the animal's leg. And then, as gently as she could, she drew the leg from its prison. The dog winced, but did not growl. Skye patted him. "There, love, come along now and let's find some food for you." The dog fought his way to his feet and limped, stumbling a little, after her.

The nuns were as sympathetic as Skye had been, and allowed the dog into the convent. His origin and owner remained a mystery. The island peasants would not dare claim the royal canine. Peasants kept only working dogs, such as terriers, mastiffs, and mongrels. The Irish wolfhound, that great killer of wolves and other predators, belonged to the ruling class, as did Irish setters.

Skye named the dog Inis, after the favorite hound of Partholan, an early settler in Ireland. Inis attached himself to her with a singular devotion. He walked out with her in the mornings, sailed with her in the convent's little boat, and slept with her at night, spreading his great lanky frame across the foot of her bed. Within a few weeks he had regained his normal adult weight, one hundred sixty pounds, and stood thirty-eight inches high. Bathed, his fur became a shining silvery gray that reminded Skye of Niall's eyes. Inis's ears and the feathers on his legs were black. The hound was Skye's slave, his soulful eyes lighting up with pleasure each time he looked at her.

Skye needed the dog's love, for Niall Burke appeared to have forgotten her entirely. And then there came the day when her show of blood arrived right on schedule. She wept into Inis's soft neck, her heartbreak complete.

The Reverend Mother Ethna sent a message to the young

O'Flaherty informing him that his wife was not pregnant and a week later Dom arrived to claim his wife. The Reverend Mother personally showed him into Skye's apartment. "I would have come sooner," he said, smiling smugly, "but I was obliged to attend Niall Burke's wedding to Darragh O'Neill."

Skye fainted. When she came to she was lying on the settle. She heard Dom speaking solicitously to the nun. "I did not realize the news of Lord Burke's marriage would so unsettle my lady."

"Did you not, my lord?" said Ethna O'Neill coolly.

O'Flaherty smiled and, ignoring the nun's sarcasm, continued. "I realize it is unusual for a gentleman to spend the night in your convent, but I really do not think my wife should be moved until the shock wears off."

The Reverend Mother Ethna had decided she did not like Dom O'Flaherty, but she did agree with him that Skye should not be moved right now. She was forced to assure him that, though it was unusual, it was not forbidden him to spend the night under St. Bride's roof. He was welcome. Dom thanked her politely, then asked if she would take his wife's hound, see that it was fed, and have it put in the stables with his men and horses. Inis, who had taken an instant dislike to Dom, was removed under protest.

They were alone. Dom O'Flaherty walked to the settle and said coldly, "I know you've recovered your swoon, Skye. Now get up and greet your lord and master properly."

Slowly, she rose and placed a quick kiss on his mouth. He chuckled and with lightning swiftness pulled her close. She tensed and he laughed. "Ah, yes. You don't like me, do you, wife? How unfortunate for you for you'll soon be spreading yourself wide for my pleasure, and my pleasure alone. And when I'm deep inside you I'll wipe all thought of Niall Burke from your mind!" His mouth ground down on hers, and she beat her clenched fists against his chest. Then suddenly she was rescued by a knock on the door. Dom smothered a curse and called out sharply, "Come in!"

Two nuns, each laden down with a tray of steaming food, hurried in, their eyes lowered. Placing their trays on the great refectory table, they hurried out as quickly.

Skye pulled from her husband's grasp. "How thoughtful!" she exclaimed brightly. "We have been sent supper."

"I've no appetite for food yet," he said in a surly tone.

She raised the cover of a dish. "Look! Boiled shrimp! And here's a lovely capon, and a small joint of mutton! If we don't eat it now, it will get cold."

"Let it!" He came swiftly up behind her and loosened her laces, sliding his hands around to cup her breasts. "This is what I'm hungry for, Skye," he said, squeezing her flesh. "The food will wait. Your laces are loosened. Go into the bedroom, finish undressing, and wait for me in the bed."

She closed her eyes to squeeze back tears. "Oh, Dom!" she pleaded. "Not here! I'll do whatever you want me to, but not here in this holy house. Not here!"

"I hadn't considered it that way," he said thoughtfully, "but the idea of fucking you in a convent appeals to me. Shall we pretend you're a young nun about to be ravaged by a Viking chief?" She blanched at his sacrilege, and he snarled, "Quickly, Skye! I'm hot for you—having been denied my marital rights for over a month!" He punctuated his words with a light slap to her cheek.

She wanted to fight him, but she had been so badly broken by the news of Niall's marriage that she couldn't find the spirit. She fled into the bedroom and, with shaking fingers, pulled her clothes off and climbed into the big bed. A moment later, Dom entered the room, drinking from a goblet of wine. Placing the goblet on the nightstand, he undressed swiftly, letting his clothes fall where they dropped. When he turned to enter the bed she bit back a cry of terror. Niall had been a big man, but Skye's husband was unnaturally large, enormous. Seeing her fear, he chuckled. "The wenches in Paris call me Le Taureau! Do you know what that means?"

Terrified, she nodded. "The bull." Her voice was a whisper.

"Aye, the *bull!*" he said proudly. "And I am, wife! Now spread yourself wide. I've got something for you!" He tore back the covers she clutched to her breasts. The sight of her naked body inflamed his lust, and he flung himself on her.

Skye managed to gasp, "But Dom! I am not ready!"

He raised himself above her, and gazed down at her. "You're not ready?" His look was incredulous. Had he not been so astounded he might have hit her. "You do not have to be ready, Skye. I am!"

And she felt herself being ripped asunder by his monster sex. Before she could cry out, his hand clapped over her mouth. He pushed himself into her, muttering all the while, "You're tight as a drum, woman! Burke's cock must be no bigger than a worm, to have left you so tight!" He grunted his pleasure while, beneath him, her eyes reflected pain and fright. She tried to lie still, hoping to ease the pain, but she couldn't. She writhed in an effort to escape him, and mistaking her actions for growing passion, he laughed. "I knew it! Beneath all the ladylike manners you've the makings of a good whore! I'm a lucky man!" And he drove deeper and harder into her. "Don't fear, lovey," he panted, "I'll teach you many a good trick to please us both!" Then, with a growl of pleasure, he collapsed.

For a moment they lay sandwiched together, then O'Flaherty got up and, returning to the dayroom, poured himself more wine. Skye felt tears gushing down her cheeks, but she made no sound for fear of angering him. She heard him lifting the covers of the dishes, sampling the food. He didn't think to offer her any.

Coming back into the small bedroom, clutching a chicken leg, Dom sat on the side of the bed. He patted her backside. Skye feigned sleep, hoping he would leave her in peace. She heard the sound of his slow, methodical munching, and then the leg bone hit the floor. "Spread yourself!"

Resistance was useless. She was his wife, his chattel. She obeyed and was once again subjected to pain and degradation. When he was through this time he rolled off her and fell asleep on his back, snoring contentedly. Skye waited until she was sure he slept soundly, then crept from the bed. She could barely walk, but she would have crawled on her hands and knees to get out of that room.

Gaining the dayroom she shakily poured herself some wine, spilling half on the table. Adding some more wood to the fire, she collapsed into the large chair.

Niall! His gentle hands, his loving mouth! He had sought to please her while teaching her to please him. Damn him! Damn him! She had been betrayed. They had all been right. The great lord's heir had only been amusing himself with her, and his lust for her innocence was no less foul than Dom's lust to subdue her. A hand dropped on her shoulder, and she started, looking up with dread.

"I woke, and you were gone," he said plaintively. "You're weeping! Still sad I'm not Niall, eh?" She wiped at the tears guiltily, quickly shaking her head, and his tone softened a bit. "I probably hurt you," he said matter-of-factly. "Well, don't worry, Skye. It'll get easier with use, and you'll soon stretch to take my bulk. Come on, lovey. Let's fuck a bit more, for if you can't sleep then I've not used you enough. Besides," he chuckled lasciviously, "you're a far sweeter piece than I thought you would be."

All the rest of the night, while she endured her husband's embraces, she hated Niall Burke with a growing fury, and considered how she would revenge herself on him one day. Oh, yes, he would pay for her broken dreams.

And a similar scene was being enacted miles away, at the stronghold of the MacWilliam.

Darragh O'Neill Burke had been destined for the Church since her birth. Her eldest sister had been betrothed and eventually wed to an O'Connell. Her middle sister had been betrothed to Niall Burke. But Ceit had died suddenly last winter, and Darragh, who had been in her beloved St. Mary's convent since the age of five, was brought home to take her middle sister's place in the marriage bed.

It was a particularly tragic choice, for Darragh O'Neill had a true religious vocation. When it was decided that she would replace her sister, Darragh was two days from taking her final vows. Her father and his troupe of men had arrived with much noise and shouting, just in time to prevent Darragh's blond hair from being shorn. O'Neill had waived the return of Darragh's dowry from the religious order, knowing that this would make Darragh's mother superior more easily amenable to his change of plan. He lost nothing by it, as the money had been paid in full eight years prior, just as Ceit's dowry had been paid to the MacWilliams at the time of her betrothal.

The mother superior explained the change to the horrified young nun, saying smoothly that God and Our Lady had quite obviously made other plans for Darragh. Darragh must accept God's will with good grace. She would leave the convent immediately and wed Lord Burke. Weeping bitterly, the girl obeyed.

Thus Niall Burke was greeted on his wedding day by a pale girl whose red-rimmed eyes gave evidence of much weeping. As he had not been fully informed of her religious commitment, he was annoyed that she should face the marriage with so little enthusiasm.

Later that evening, when the bride and groom went to bed, Darragh fainted at the sight of her naked husband. Niall gently elicited an explanation from Darragh. Touched, he gently stroked the pale blond hair. "I think that, under the circumstances, there's no need for us to hurry the physical side of our marriage," he said quietly. "Let us take time to know one another better."

The truth of the matter was that Niall had no taste for raping unwilling virgins. And he cursed both their fathers for their blind stupidity. The girl had a deep religious commitment, and he questioned whether she would ever get over that. He laughed bitterly.

They had torn him from the woman he loved, who would gladly have given him sons, because his father didn't think her highborn enough! And in her place they had given him a dedicated nun! It was too funny, and he would have laughed again had he not become aware that his new wife still seemed troubled.

"What will people say if the sheets have no bloody stain tomorrow?"

He chuckled. "Ah, Darragh Burke, 'tis truly innocent you are. Many a lass has played at carnal games before marriage, yet flown the bloody sheet the morning after her wedding. Move over, lass, and I'll show you."

Wide-eyed, she watched with amazement as he took the fruit knife from the bowl by the bed and pricked the inside of his thigh. A small trickle of blood flowed forth, staining the sheets. Darragh's virtue was thus proved while her husband's honor was saved and his prowess attested to.

It had been now two weeks since their wedding night. Darragh reasoned that her virginity had been saved forever, and as she had long ago dedicated that precious gift to God, she had no intention of giving it to Niall. She would keep his house, but that was all. Niall's kindness on their wedding night seemed a weakness she could continue to exploit.

Once again, as he had every night since their wedding, Niall gently tried to make love to his wife. Darragh's inexperience prevented her knowing how patient her husband really was. She was determined that he would not succeed, but he was equally determined he would. If he must be married to this girl then she would mother his children. Now Darragh informed him that she would be his bride in name only. Her virginity belonged to God.

"You cannot force me as you did poor Skye O'Malley, my lord. I can but imagine the poor woman's shame!" she finished righteously.

At the mention of Skye's name Niall's head whirled, and he stared with revulsion at the cold, pious, feelingless creature they had wedded him to. A tiny, fair-skinned, flat-chested girl with watery blue eyes, white-blond hair, and a prim mouth was his wife. The comparison between her and Skye with her gardenia skin, flowing blue-black hair, and blue-green eyes was ludicrous! Skye, with her sweetly rounded small breasts, rosebud mouth, and innocently eager passion. Skye! Dom O'Flaherty's willing wife . . . who had given Niall a night of bliss only to destroy his happiness almost immediately with a cold letter. He groaned. Skye would soon give Dom sons! And so, he decided with growing anger, would Darragh O'Neill Burke give her husband sons.

Seeing the grim purpose in his silvery eyes, Darragh fell to her knees clutching her rosary beads, her lips moving silently in prayer. Niall angrily snatched away the beads and, pulling Darragh to her feet, ripped the white linen nightgown from her. Catching her in his arms, he kissed her deeply, forcing the narrow lips open. She fought him, clawing at him with surprisingly sharp nails, squirming wildly. Darragh truly believed that God would strike her husband with a bolt of lightning for his impudence, and she prayed it would kill him. As they fell back onto the bed and she felt his great manhood penetrate her maidenhead, Darragh called on every saint in the calendar to avenge her. But soon she was moaning at him to continue, her skinny legs wrapping around him, her lean hips finding the rhythm and moving with it.

Afterward he felt disgusted with himself, and with her as well. He had never in his life forced a woman, but she had driven him to it with her denial of him, and the mention of his beloved, treacherous Skye.

Women! They were all alike. They said one thing, meant another. Beside him, his wife sniveled and complained, "You hurt me! You hurt me!"

"It always hurts the first time, Darragh. It'll get better now."

"You're never going to do *that* to me again. Never!"

"There'll be no immaculate conceptions in this family, *wife,* and besides, you enjoyed it. I know when a woman likes it, my dear. And like it or not, it's your duty to give me sons. You might even admit to liking it eventually. There's nothing wrong with a woman taking pleasure with her husband."

"Never!" she spat at him as he pulled her back into his arms. His big hand stroked her tense body soothingly. "I'll endure it, for it is obviously God's will, but I'll hate it every time you stick that awful thing inside me."

"Have it your own way, my dear," he said. "Just remember that I was no more anxious for this marriage than you were. I would just as soon you stayed in your convent." And he thrust into her again, making her cry out. "Give me a couple of sons, Darragh, and I'll leave you in peace forever."

And down the coast, across the water on Innishturk Island, Dom O'Flaherty bent over his beautiful wife, pumping smoothly. Skye was too sensuous a woman to deny her body its release. She let herself begin to fall away into a lovely world of sweet sensations, and then she heard her husband moan. He collapsed atop her. She had not reached her own heaven, but he didn't care. Niall had cared. She turned her head away from Dom, a tear sliding unchecked down her cheek. Damn Niall. Would he never stop haunting her?

Chapter 5

THE MACWILLIAM HAD COMMANDED THAT HIS VASSALS KEEP the twelve days of Christmas with him. They came from all over Mid-Connaught, including Dom O'Flaherty and his bride of several months.

The hospitality was lavish, for unlike his less powerful neighbors, the MacWilliam's tower house had sprouted three additional interconnected towers over the years. Consequently he now owned a fine stone castle, built along Norman lines around a gardened and cobbled quadrangle. His guests were housed quite comfortably. Although Skye's father's tower house was most comfortable and very well furnished, the MacWilliam's large castle was lavish by comparison.

There were four O'Flahertys partaking of their overlord's generosity. Dom's father, Gilladubh, and his younger sister, Claire, had come with Dom and Skye. Skye frankly hoped that they could find a husband for Claire O'Flaherty, though neither Claire's father nor her brother seemed to realize that, at fourteen, Claire was practically an old maid.

The girl was pretty enough, with thick, flaxen braids, Dom's pale-blue eyes, and a pink-cheeked complexion. But there was something sly about her, something Skye did not like. On the one or two occasions Skye had attempted to correct the girl for minor faults, Claire had complained to both her father and her brother, and Skye had been told to leave her be. Behind the doting men's backs, Claire had smiled smugly at her sister-in-law. But Skye had had some measure of revenge when she caught Claire helping herself to Skye's jewelry. Boxing the girl's ears soundly—which gave Skye great pleasure—she warned her that if she stole again she would have Claire's head shaved.

"And if you complain to either Dom or your father, *dear* sister," Skye's voice dripped sweetness, "you'll be bald for a year."

Claire O'Flaherty needed no further warning. The fierce look in Skye's eye convinced her that her brother's wife was not the soft fool she had originally thought she was. From that moment on the two women maintained a wary truce. Now Skye was determined to marry the girl off as quickly as possible, to get her out of her house.

Skye had known that Niall would be at the Christmas gathering. She soon learned that he was to be their host, as his father was suffering with gout. If Niall expected to find her heartbroken, she would soon disabuse him of that notion. In the six months since Dom had taken her from St. Bride's she had made a kind of peace with herself. She did not love her husband nor did she ever believe she would, but she played the obedient wife.

Her mother-in-law was long dead, and the running of the O'Flaherty household was left entirely in her hands. Claire seemed not to care, or even have the necessary knowledge. Skye did her job well, which pleased her father-in-law. Gilladubh O'Flaherty was an older version of Dom, a pompous lecher with a penchant for fine wines and good whiskey. Skye soon learned to avoid his quick hands, once going so far as to brandish a candlestick at him and threaten to expose his outrageous behavior.

Sitting on the MacWilliam's fine guest bed in her petticoats and beribboned busk, she brushed her hair with angry, vicious strokes. Tonight Skye O'Malley would be as beautiful as she could make herself, and she would hold her head up before the arrogant Burkes and O'Neills. It was her good fortune to own a more magnificent wardrobe than most women did, for her father had always delighted in showing off her beauty.

Mag, her tiring woman, brought her gown and laid it carefully across the foot of the bed. She held a small round mirror for her mistress, and Skye skillfully outlined her eyes with kohl and put just the tiniest bit of red to her cheeks, giving her fair skin a faint, healthy blush. Her shining dark hair was smoothly parted in the center, carefully tucked into dainty gold wire cauls, then pinned on either side of her head. Lastly Skye applied to the deep valley between her breasts, to her wrists, to the base of her throat, and to the back and sides of her neck, a rare perfume made especially for her of musk and attar of roses. Let him smell the scent of roses on her! Let him remember, and know she cared not!

Skye stood up, and Mag hurried to help her mistress into her gown. The tiring woman quickly laced the dress and then stood back to survey her lady. A toothless smile split her weathered face.

"Aye, you'll break his fickle heart, my lady! One look at you in this gown, and he'll wish he'd stood up to that old devil, his father!"

"Is Lady Burke so displeasing to the eye then, Mag?" asked Skye with feigned disinterest.

Mag cackled with laughter, and hugged herself. "Nay, lady, she's pretty enough. It's just that you're so wickedly fair."

Skye smiled a little cat's smile. "Get my jewel case, you old crone!" she ordered affectionately and, when the woman hurried to obey, snatched up the mirror. Holding it away from herself, she studied her reflection. The gown of deep-blue velvet *was* beautiful, and its low, square neckline revealed her snow-white breasts. The bodice flowed into a full skirt, parting in the center to reveal a Persian blue underskirt of heavy satin, embroidered in gold and silver thread. Her shoes matched her gown, but her stockings were pure silk, and matched the underskirt right down to the embroidery. Skye twirled slightly, and was pleased to see that the stockings would show to great advantage during the dancing.

Mag held open the jewel case and Skye lifted out a sapphire necklace, the large square stones interspersed with round gold medallions, twelve in all, each representing a sign of the zodiac. At the bottom of the necklace a large pink pearl teardrop hung provocatively between her breasts. There were sapphires in her ears and she wore three rings, a sapphire, an emerald, and a large baroque pearl.

Dom strode into the room and asked jealously, "Are you dressing to please Niall Burke, Skye?"

"Rather to please you, my lord," she said smoothly, "but if my gown displeases you I will change to whatever gives you pleasure."

He eyed her carefully. He knew there wouldn't be a woman at tonight's banquet to compare with her. She would be the fairest creature in the hall. And she belonged to him! He would be the envy of every man there. Roughly he pulled her into his arms and buried his face in the warm scented cleft between her breasts.

"Don't!" Her voice was sharp. Familiarity had removed her fear of him, and now only a veiled contempt remained. "Don't, Dom. You'll put me in disarray." He stepped away from her. "How handsome you look," she quickly noted. "Your sky-blue velvet goes quite well with my deep blue."

"Day and midnight," he said, offering her his arm.

She laughed. "Careful, my lord, you verge on the poetical. Your fine Paris education may not have gone for nought after all."

The banquet hall of the MacWilliam's castle was a great room with heavy beamed ceilings and four fireplaces. They blazed now with giant-sized logs. Tall narrow windows gave views of the snow-covered countryside, the plainness of the hills and fields broken at intervals by large stands of black, bare trees. To the west the hills were stained orange-red with the sunset. The room was crowded with elegantly dressed guests. Servants scurried to and fro with trays of wine, amid a low steady hum of voices.

As they entered the hall the majordomo announced them and Skye felt the eyes of the entire room on them. The story of her wedding night was yet spoken of throughout the district, and now the nobility of Mid-Connaught watched to see the first meeting of the O'Flahertys and the Burkes since that fateful day of last May. The gossips had to admit that Skye and Dom were an outrageously handsome couple.

Skye and Dom moved with a stately slow pace as they proceeded down the length of the hall to greet their host and hostess, Niall and Darragh. Skye kept her head high, her face expressionless, her glance at a point just above the top of Niall's head. For a brief instant she gave in to her curiosity and glanced at his face. His silver-gray eyes were ice, and sent a wave of bitter coldness sweeping over her to penetrate the very core of her heart.

She was puzzled. She had expected a smug smile, certainly not this disdain. She was discomfited by his attitude, but a quick glimpse of the tiny woman at his side restored her confidence. She felt joy surge through her with the knowledge that Darragh Burke was, for all her noble breeding, no beauty.

They had reached the dais now, and Skye looked past Niall and his wife to where the MacWilliam sat, his painful leg cushioned upon a stool. She flashed Niall's father a brilliant smile, her even little teeth almost blinding in their whiteness. The old man let his glance sweep over her, and it gave her great pleasure to see the regret in his eyes. Now they both knew that he had made a mistake. She swept him a graceful curtsey. "My lord."

It amused him to realize how quickly she had read his thoughts. He enjoyed a worthy adversary, and she would make one. If he had been twenty years younger he would have made an attempt to bed her himself. "My friend, Gilly O'Flaherty, tells me you're a good wife to his boy," growled the MacWilliam.

"I am," she answered him coolly.

"I thought you were happiest being a pirate wench."

"I am that too, when I can, my lord."

"And are you good at that too, Lady O'Flaherty?"

"I'm good at whatever I set my mind to, my lord."

He chuckled. "Welcome to you, and to your husband," and then his eyes crinkled wickedly. "Undoubtedly you both remember my son. Niall."

She felt Dom stiffen beside her, and she squeezed his hand reassuringly. They would not even acknowledge the insult. Dom's good manners asserted themselves with the knowledge his wife stood by him. The two men bowed curtly to each other.

Then Niall's eyes raked her cruelly. "I see you're already with child, Lady O'Flaherty," he said loudly.

"Aye, my lord. Wed *seven* months, and *six* months gone with child. The women of my family are known to be prolific breeders." She spoke as loudly as he had. Then she turned and insolently eyed Darragh Burke. "I see your own bride of half a year is not yet as fortunate as I. Are you, my dear?"

Darragh flushed. Her "nay" was audible to all. Skye smiled sweetly, curtseyed again and, taking her husband's arm, turned away. Behind her she heard the MacWilliam chuckle.

Skye allowed Dom to seat her by the fire. She stared into the leaping flames as he went in search of some mulled wine. She was almost shaking with suppressed fury. How could Niall behave in such a fashion?! He had shamed her before the entire county on her wedding night, left her after making extravagant promises he never intended keeping, and now he pretended that he had been the injured party! The bastard! A goblet was shoved into her hand and she gulped a mouthful of wine to calm herself.

"You were magnificent!" she heard her husband say. "By God, you showed Niall Burke, and in front of all Connaught too! Not that I think it would be easy to get that skinny, overbred O'Neill wench pregnant. I don't even envy him the task," he laughed.

"Shut up, you overblown fool!" she hissed at him through gritted teeth. God, why were all men such idiots? "I don't give a tinker's damn for Niall Burke, but I'd not insult the MacWilliam's hospitality, so try not to be too obvious in your glee, *husband*."

Dom looked at her strangely, but before he could say another word Anne O'Malley came to greet them. She sent Dom off to join his friends, then settled herself comfortably and looked at her stepdaughter. "Was it wise to insult Niall Burke and his wife?" she asked.

"Was it wise for him to insult me?" Skye snapped.

"You still love him."

"I hate him! For pity's sake, Anne, speak of something else. The babe has a tendency to make me weepy, and I'd rather not be misunderstood."

"Of course," said Anne O'Malley sagely. "It would hardly do for Niall Burke to think you weep for him."

"I never realized before what a bitch you can be, *stepmother,*" said Skye evenly.

Anne laughed. "Oh, the babe does make you testy, doesn't it?"

"He," said Skye. "Dom and his father are convinced it's a lad, and they will accept nothing less."

"Oh, I see. And how goes it with you otherwise?"

"Quite well, actually, Anne. Da did me a great service in wedding me to Dom. Not only have I gained a lecher for a husband, I also have one for a father-in-law. My husband's sister is a common bitch not averse to stealing my possessions when she can, and whining to her father and brother when she's caught. It's a charming new family I have. I am most grateful to Da.

"My new home is in a shocking state of disrepair, and despite the fine dowry Da gave me, I am told that no money can be found to put it to rights. Half the household items I brought to O'Flaherty House, the silver bowls and candlesticks in particular, are mysteriously missing. In short, I am the mistress of a dung heap peopled by a vain and randy old cock, a vain and randy young cock, and a flighty hen."

Anne was shocked. "Do you want to come home until the child is born, Skye?" Sweet Mary! She couldn't let Skye have her baby in that place!

"God, yes! I do want to come home, but they'll not let me for the next O'Flaherty must be born in his own home, Anne. I would appreciate it, however, if you could arrange for Eibhlin to come to me immediately after Candlemass. Though the child isn't due until early spring, a late-winter storm at the wrong time could delay her, and I would be frightened if she were unable to reach me in time. Besides," Skye smiled wryly, "I need the company. Claire is none, and neither she, nor Mag, nor our old cook knows about birthing a child."

Anne was now very upset. "What of the other women in your household? The maids? The laundresses? Is there no midwife in your village?"

"The few women we can get to work for us come from our nearby village each day and return to their homes at night. They love their children, and no family would allow their daughters in my house because of Dom and his father. They will work O'Flaherty lands, and pay O'Flaherty taxes, and fight for the O'Flahertys, but too many of their girls have been abused by the O'Flaherty men for them to allow their daughters in our house. Even so, Dom and Gilly have had their share of the poor creatures. They go out on horseback and hunt them down while the girls are working in the fields! The O'Flahertys' reputation is so bad that even Claire has no tiring woman of her own."

"I knew it was all wrong from the beginning," said Anne. "I knew it!"

"Then why didn't you speak to Da as you *promised* me, Anne? You encouraged him to wed me off the very morning of Conn's birth!"

"No, no, Skye! That's not so at all! I tried to tell your father right after Conn was born, but they'd given me herbs in wine to make me sleep, and your father misunderstood me. When I finally awoke two days later, you were wed, and had already been sent to St. Bride's."

"Then you did not betray me to get me out of the house?"

"You foolish goose! Whatever made you think such a thing? Once you were firmly wed there was nothing I could do. I only wish your father had waited. Even though he was firmly set on the match, perhaps I could have prevented the afterward."

"No," said Skye softly. "At least with Niall Burke I learned that love can be sweet—not true, but sweet. Had it not been for him, I might have gone my whole life believing all men were animals."

"Some men are more vigorous in bed than others, Skye."

"Dom is a pig," was the flat reply.

"Why do you hate Niall if you're grateful to him?"

Skye's eyes blazed blue fire, and her voice was rock hard. "Because he betrayed me! Because he swore he loved me! Because he promised to have my marriage annulled, to wed with me. Instead he crept from my side before the dawn without even so much as a good-bye kiss and rode merrily home to wed his high O'Neill! I will *never* forgive him for that, Anne! *Never!*"

In the silence that followed, Anne O'Malley struggled terribly with her conscience. She knew the full truth. Finally she decided that silence was the best policy. To tell Skye the truth now would do nothing more than hurt and anger her further. Nothing could be changed now. Skye was wed, and pregnant with her husband's child. Niall Burke was wed. If either of them learned now of the deception that had been practiced on them it would only cause greater unhappiness. Who knew what those two strong-willed, passionate people would do if they ever learned the truth?

Anne was saved from further talk by the announcement that dinner was served. Once in the banquet hall they separated, for in deference to the O'Malley's value to the MacWilliam, O'Malley and his wife were seated higher up on the board than Skye and Dom, who were seated much below the salt. Dom, however, cared not one whit, for thanks to his wife's beauty and wit, he was very much the center of a gay group of young people, some of whom were well-endowed wenches with bold eyes. He anticipated a pleasant Twelve Days of Christmas.

And Skye sparkled, determined to show Niall how indifferent she was. It seemed to those who sat in the more favored places at the table that those below the salt were having a far better time than those above it. There was simply no denying that young Lady O'Flaherty was a delightful and charming beauty.

Skye ate carefully, taking of the first course only a thin slice of fresh salmon, and of the second only the wing of a lemoned capon. She ate two small pieces of newly baked brown bread, liberally spreading the butter across it with her thumb. Around her, the other guests gorged themselves on dish after dish, but Skye was revolted by the overrich menu. When the sweet was served she enjoyed a small tart of dried peaches, licking the clotted cream from about her mouth like a child. Watching her from the high board, Niall longed to kiss that mouth as much as he longed to strangle her for her perfidy.

As the meal drew to a close, more of those seated above the salt began drifting farther down the table to cluster about Skye. Occasionally great bursts of laughter issued forth from the group. When the dancing began Skye refused all but the least strenuous dances, but even so she never lacked for partners. She moved proudly, and with much grace, her gown showing to great advantage. Her blue eyes sparkled, and her smile flashed again and again.

At the high board Niall Burke sprawled in his chair, glowering, his big hand clutching his jewel-studded goblet so hard it was a wonder the stem was not bent. His silver-gray eyes, pantherlike, half closed, followed her wherever she went. Occasionally he took great gulps of the dark red wine, emptying and refilling his cup several times. She was beautiful, damn her, and even in her present state outrageously desirable.

"Young Lady O'Flaherty is most popular," ventured Darragh.

"Aye," he growled, suddenly standing up and striding away

from his wife to join the dancers. The young man partnering Skye suddenly felt a hard hand on his shoulder. Looking up to see his scowling, black-browed host, the young man quickly stepped aside. Niall clamped an arm about her waist and took one of her hands in his. Her smile faltered, but she never missed a step.

"Should you be dancing?"

"I am expecting a child, my lord. I am not mortally ill with a wasting sickness."

"You've changed, Skye."

"Nay, my lord. I have simply learned not to put my faith in pillow talk."

They separated, and she wove in and out of the figure, meeting him again on the other side.

"I find it hard," he said, "to understand the workings of a fickle woman's mind. You behave as though I rejected you instead of the other way around."

"You betrayed me. You left me without even a good-bye, and hurried home to wed and bed your 'dead' fiancée! I had no chance to reject you, but I do now!"

"I was not betrothed to Darragh O'Neill until after your marriage, Skye. It was her dead sister, Ceit, who was to be my wife."

Again they were separated by the figure. When they met again, he said, "I would never have wed Darragh had it not been for your letter."

Skye stopped dead. "What letter?" she demanded of him.

One look at her face told Niall Burke that something was very wrong, but they were in a roomful of people, some of whom were eying them with speculative curiosity. "But of course you're exhausted, in your condition, Lady O'Flaherty. Allow me to escort you to a seat, and get you some chilled wine," he said loudly, leading her from the floor. He found her a seat within a windowed alcove. Though they were plainly visible to the entire room, they had the privacy to talk without being overheard. Niall snatched two goblets of wine from a passing valet, and handed her one.

Understanding the need for deception, she leaned back with half-closed eyes feigning exhaustion. Her heart was hammering, not from weariness but from the sudden realization that they had probably been tricked. "What letter?" she asked again.

"I did not leave you willingly, Skye. Your father sent a little lad up the vine outside your window, and the boy opened your bedchamber door to the O'Malley and his men. I was gagged, and taken from the room. I explained our plight to your father, but he would not listen. Rather he had me knocked unconscious, and taken home by one Captain MacGuire. The next day I was given a letter in which you repudiated our relationship. For God's sake, Skye, the handwriting was feminine, and I recognized the seal as the one on your own ring."

"We all have these rings, Niall. All my sisters, even Eibhlin."

"I did not know," he sighed deeply. "It would seem, my love, that those two old spiders, our fathers, have gotten their way by foul means. Damn them both!"

"Do you love her, Niall?"

"No. She was to be a nun, and in her heart she still is. She spends more time on her knees than in our bed."

"I'm glad!" she said fiercely, and he understood.

"The child—?"

"Is Dom's. There is no doubt, Niall. I swear it! Do you think I would be here if it were not?"

"Have you learned to love him then?"

"I will never love him, but I am his wife as you are Darragh's husband," she said quietly. "And now, my lord, bid me good night, for we are fast becoming the center of curiosity in the hall and I see Dom coming."

"I will find another opportunity to speak with you," he said. He did not leave her side, but stood waiting until Dom joined them. "Your wife is fatigued from the dancing, O'Flaherty. You must take good care of her since she carries your heir. You're very fortunate in that respect."

Dom, taken off guard, was speechless. Niall bent over Skye's hand, briefly but tenderly kissing it. "Good night, Lady O'Flaherty." Then he was gone across the floor to rejoin the dancers.

"Will you escort me to our room, Dom? I am very tired." She fought to keep her voice flat. Dom must not know! Not even suspect!

"Of course, my love," he answered, his voice sweet. Helping her up, he walked her slowly from the hall. When they had gained their room she asked him to call her maid. "Nay, love, I'll maid you myself, Skye." His voice had become soft and caressing. It was a dangerous sign. "There wasn't a woman tonight who could compare with you," he murmured. "Every man envied me my beautiful wife. Every one of them imagined what it would be like to stick himself in you, but I'm the only one who can do that, Skye, *aren't* I?" He had her bodice unlaced now, and drew it off. His fingers swiftly drew her gown and her petticoats down and off. Then her chemise, and finally she stood naked and shivering in her embroidered stockings with their gold ribbon and silk rosette garters. Slowly he let his eyes wander over the new fullness of her breasts, and the sweet swelling of her belly. His hand caressed the living roundness, and Skye, barely breathing, prayed he would be satisfied by this show of ownership.

"Kneel on the edge of the bed, Skye."

She shivered. "Dom, please! It's not good for the child."

"Kneel, you little bitch! Or do you want me to believe what my eyes told me when I looked across the hall tonight to see the fine Lord Burke bending solicitously over my wife, ogling her tits? And you! You encouraged him!"

"No! I didn't!" Every muscle in her body tensed. Then, sighing, she knelt on the edge of the bed, her knees drawn up beneath her. Her hands were clenched into tight balls. There was no fighting him. Resistance brought further punishment.

He looked down at her, so meek, so obedient. He was angry with her, and tempted to sodomize her, for he knew how she hated that particular degradation. But he feared for the child. It was *his son,* and it bound her irrevocably to him. Without the child she might run to Niall Burke and become his leman, making the O'Flahertys the laughingstock of all Connaught.

He did no more than loosen his codpiece and his organ, swollen already, burst forth. He saw her shiver again, and the feeling of power her fear gave him aroused him further. He easily found his way inside her, sliding his hands beneath her breasts to play with the very sensitive nipples while he moved himself with long smooth strokes. "Your hound does it this way to the bitches in my kennel. I've watched him many a time," he murmured, biting the back of her neck. She said nothing. To her relief he was finished quickly. "I'm going back to the hall now," he said. "Get some rest, Skye." Fastening his clothes, he was gone.

For a few moments she lay quietly, her face wet with silent tears. Then she stood and, removing her stockings, wrapped herself in a soft woolen robe before lying down again. If she could have boiled her body she would have done so, but even that would not rid her of the memory of his touch, the smell of his lust on her skin.

She could not stop the tears from flowing. It had all been too much. Learning that her father and the MacWilliam had conspired to keep Niall from her had come close to breaking her heart all over again. It had been easier when she could simply hate Niall. Exhausted, she slept.

The sudden sound of the door latch rasping woke her and she tensed. Dom was back, and probably drunk. She lay quietly, hoping he would believe she was sleeping.

"Skye," came the soft whisper.

"Niall!" She sat up. "Are you mad? In God's name go quickly before Dom returns! Please, my lord!"

He shut the door quietly and drew the bolt closed. "Dom is lying in the hall in a drunken stupor with his friends. My page is watching. Should Dom awaken the lad will warn us long before he can get here." Dearest Heaven, she was beautiful, her black cloud of hair swirling about her shoulders, her eyes enormous and dark with concern. Niall sat on the edge of the bed and drew her into his arms. "You've been weeping." It was a statement.

"It was easier when I thought you'd betrayed me," she said softly, believing he would understand.

"For me also, my darling." He reached out and caressed her dark hair.

"Your wife—?" She had to ask.

"Is keeping one of her interminable vigils in the chapel. She does it to avoid me, but I care not. Bedding her is like bedding a dead thing."

"Oh, Niall . . ." Her voice broke, and she buried her face in his shoulder.

"Skye! Ah, love, don't weep! Damn, Skye, you'll break my heart!" His mouth gently found hers. Sighing deeply, she slid her arms about his neck, and gave herself over into his keeping. His hand found the swell of her breast, and it seemed so natural, so right. She pulled her lips away from him long enough to whisper, "Yes, Niall! Oh, please love me!" Then her mouth fused fiercely to his again, and she was lost in a burst of searing passion that swept over her body instantly, nearly rendering her unconscious.

His hand gently caressed the ripening mound. "I wish to Heaven he were mine," he muttered huskily. "God! You're so beautiful with the babe growing in you, like one of the old Celtic fertility goddesses."

"I prayed so hard," she whispered. "When I was at St. Bride's I prayed you'd gotten me with child. How I wept when I found it wasn't so. Eibhlin says they feared for my sanity. Then Dom came . . ." her voice trailed off.

"I'll kill him," Niall said quietly.

"And what of your poor wife? Would you kill her also? What harm has that unfortunate creature done to either of us? You say she was to be a nun, and from what you tell me she had a true vocation. Has she not been harmed as deeply as we?" Skye drew a deep breath and pulled away from him, her blue eyes intent. "Niall! Oh, Niall, my love! We are inescapably wed to other people. There is no hope for us. I love you, Niall, but when I return to Ballyhennessey I want never to set eyes on you again. I cannot see you and keep my love for you from the world. Dom is already suspicious. I want no trouble between the two of you, for he is foolish and apt to be treacherous. I am not so innocent as to beg that you forget me. We will not forget, either of us, but we must part."

He pulled her back into his arms. "I cannot bear to lose you again," he said brokenly.

"Oh, my love, you never really had me," she answered sadly.

For a few minutes longer they clung to each other, unwilling for the bittersweet interlude to end. Then, kissing her tenderly, he laid her back against the pillows. "I'll find other times during this visit when we can talk," he said. "Promise me one thing, though. Promise me you'll ask my help should you *ever* need it. I will not rest easy if you do not give me your word, Skye, and swear to it. I'll not have O'Flaherty mistreating you."

"I do not fear Dom. As long as I play the beautiful and docile wife for him in public, his vanity is fed enough." She would not tell him the truth, tell him of her husband's degrading ways in their bed, for it would only infuriate Niall and there was nothing he could do about it. "Sit with me but a moment longer," she begged. Smiling, he took her hand. She closed her eyes. Soon she was asleep. Gently drawing the featherbedding over her, he unbolted the door and slipped from the room.

Making his way back to the banquet hall, Niall dismissed his page for the night. Then, turning to seek his own quarters, he almost collided with a young squire. "Your pardon, my lord, but the MacWilliam would see you." Niall nodded and immediately sought the old man's rooms.

He found his father sitting up in bed, a nightcap upon his leonine head. His gouty foot was freshly bound, and he held a goblet in his hand. Niall bent and sniffed the cup. "I thought malmsey was bad for your foot," he noted.

"That quack of a doctor tells me everything is bad for my foot. I suppose if I could still fuck he'd tell me that was bad for my foot also," was the flinty retort. The MacWilliam paused. "I would say that the beauteous young Lady O'Flaherty is bad for more than your foot, Niall, my son."

The two men eyed each other, and the MacWilliam sighed. "I was wrong to force you into marriage with the O'Neill lass. I can see O'Malley's girl would have made you a better wife. Christ! Wed seven months, and already with child! And she carries the babe well. What a breeder! She'll give O'Flaherty a houseful of sons, and still have a waist a man could span with his two hands. And what a beauty . . . that hair, and those Kerry-blue eyes, and those marvelous tits! Damme, I wish I weren't so old!"

Niall laughed, but his father now continued in a more serious tone. "Keep away from her, Niall. O'Flaherty won't wear the horns of a cuckold gracefully. He'd kill you if he catches you with his wife. I know you were with her in her bedchamber tonight while her husband lay drunk in the hall. Be careful, lad! You're my only son, my heir, and I love you. Until you get a legitimate son, we're not safe."

"Rest easy, Father. Skye and I but talked. If we had done it in public the gossips would have had a field day."

"You *talked?!* God's nightshirt! If I were twenty years younger and alone with that beauty, it would not have been talking I'd have been doing!"

Again Niall laughed. "Come, Father, she's six months gone with child."

"There are ways, boy."

"I know, and perhaps if the child were mine—but it's not. Besides," and here Niall eyed his father firmly, "finding out the trick that you and O'Malley played to separate us has made Skye very vulnerable. I would not hurt her further. I love her."

"If she lost the babe then she'd be free of O'Flaherty," said the old man slyly. "His wife, yes, but free to come to you . . . and she would. I'd recognize any bastards she gave you as my heirs, for I strongly doubt the O'Neill girl will ever conceive."

"Don't tempt me, Father. If you think Skye worthy to bear our heirs, then surely she is worthy of our name as well. You see her as nothing but a brood mare who will secure our immortality, but I love Skye. I have never wanted any woman but her for my wife." He took a deep, ragged breath. "But O'Flaherty is strong and healthy. He will probably live forever. She and I have no hope."

"His death could be arranged . . . but you're too noble for your own good, Niall! Love has made you a weakling. If you don't mean to claim the woman for your own, then keep away from her else her husband kills you in a fit of jealous rage," growled the old man.

"Or I kill him," mused Lord Burke quietly.

Chapter 6

Skye's son, Ewan, was born in early spring. Eibhlin helped deliver her new nephew, having come to the O'Flahertys' immediately after Twelfth Night. Eibhlin was shocked by the poverty of the O'Flahertys' tower house. Anne had, of course, repeated Skye's descriptions of her home, but the nun had assumed that Skye's bitter disappointment over her marriage caused her to exaggerate. Now she saw that everything Anne had reported was dismayingly true.

The masonry of the tower house was in poor repair and there were drafts everywhere. The floors were covered by nothing except dirty, much-used rushes. The few wall hangings were threadbare and virtually useless for warmth, let alone comfort. The furniture was sparse as well. Eibhlin was puzzled. She knew that her father and stepmother had sent a number of fine pieces along to Skye, but when she questioned her younger sister all she got was a mumbled answer about Gilly and Dom and their endless debts.

Having her sister with her made it a happy winter for Skye. Ewan's birth was a relaxed and easy one, and Eibhlin left four weeks afterward. She returned within several months to aid her sister once again, for Skye's second son, Murrough, was separated from his brother by but ten months.

Murrough made his entry into the world during a brutal mid-winter storm. Fortunately this birth was also an easy one, for Eibhlin had other factors beside the baby to contend with. The strong winds had blown so hard that the floors of O'Flaherty House were covered with half an inch of snow in some places. It had blown through cracked walls and the sheepskin-covered windows. The fires had gone out several times, and Eibhlin had been hard-pressed to keep her sister and the newborn boy warm and dry. Eibhlin was angry. She was ashamed that her sister should live this way. Skye's dowry gone to pay gaming debts, or for wine, or to buy gifts for the women Dom and his father amused themselves with. Eibhlin made herself a vow: Skye would have no more babes, especially so quickly, until Dom grew up and took his responsibilities seriously.

"Ten months between babes is too soon," she scolded. "Now you must rest at least a year or two before conceiving again."

"Tell Dom," said Skye weakly. "He'll be on me within the

month. Despite his whores, he harbors a constant lust for me. Besides, I thought I could not conceive as long as I nursed Ewan."

"An old wives' tale that has done more harm than you can imagine," replied Eibhlin. "*And* I shall talk to Dom myself. Then I'll give you the recipe for a potion that will prevent conception."

"Eibhlin!" Skye was both amused and shocked. "And you a nun! How on earth do you know such things?"

"I have as much knowledge as a doctor," replied Eibhlin. "More perhaps, since I have also learned midwifery and herbal medicine from the old ones. Doctors scorn these things, but they are wrong to do so. I can tell you several ways to prevent conception."

"But does not the Church forbid such wicked practices, my sister?"

The nun answered forcefully, "The Church has not seen innocent babes dying of starvation because there are too many mouths in the family to feed. They have not seen little children and their sickly mothers freezing to death, blue with the cold, because there are not enough blankets or clothes in the hovels they call houses—not even food or wood for warmth! What do the well-fed priests and bishops, snug in their stone houses on this snowy night, know of these poor souls and their endless torments?

"I help where I can, Skye. For those innocent and superstitious poor I offer a 'tonic' to help them regain their strength after the ordeal of several births. They know not what I give them. If they did, they would not take it because they truly believe the Church's threat of eternal damnation. You, sister, are not so foolish."

"No, Eibhlin, I am not. And I want no more of Dom's children. I will not be made old before my time, nor shall I nurse this child knowing what I do now. One of Dom's women gave birth but a month ago. She has breasts like udders, and it will amuse me to have her nurse both Dom's son and his bastard. She can live in the nursery with both boys and have Ewan's wet nurse for company."

"You've grown hard, Skye."

"If I were not, Eibhlin, I should not be able to survive in this house. You have been here enough to know what the O'Flahertys are like."

The nun nodded. "Have you had any luck in finding a husband for Claire?"

"None, and I'm not likely to unless I can convince Da to dower her. Gilly and Dom have gambled away the dowry left to Claire by her mother. There's nothing left. And if I didn't know better, I would swear she was a half-wit, for she cares not. The few young men who have come calling have been met with indifference. One is too fat, another too lean. This one is a buffoon, but that one lacks a sense of humor. One is too ardent in his wooing, and another has no blood in his veins. I don't understand her at all! She has no religious vocation, no passion for anyone so far as I can see. Nor does she seem to desire to control her own life, as I did. She cares for nothing."

"Perhaps she is merely content to stay with her father and brother. Some women are like that."

Skye looked candidly at her sister. "Do you really think Claire O'Flaherty is like that, Eibhlin?"

"No," came the quick reply. "She's a sly and secretive girl for all she looks like an angle. There is something . . ." and here Eibhlin hesitated, loath to criticize yet genuinely concerned. "There is something unwholesome about Claire," she finally finished.

Skye agreed. But there seemed nothing she could do with Claire unless she could find a husband for her. What bothered Skye most was that Claire always appeared to be laughing at her, hugging some secret to herself that she would not share with anyone else, least of all Skye.

Eibhlin soon left to return to St. Bride's, but she talked to Dom first. He said later, "Since your sister tells me your health will suffer if I get another son on you, you can hardly complain if I seek diversion elsewhere."

"Have I ever complained before?" she asked him, amused, hiding her delight in the knowledge that she would be spared.

"Nay, you're a good lass, and you've given me two fine boys."

Skye smiled sweetly, and bit her tongue to keep from laughing. Dom saw her only as a credit to himself. She had become, he thought, exactly what he'd always wished her to be—a gracious chatelaine and a good breeder. He was willing to be generous now, to leave her alone for the time being.

Her life now took on a sameness, giving her the peace she craved. She worked to run the estate so that it supported them all and still paid the MacWilliam his annual tribute as their overlord. Neither Dom nor his father cared what she did as long as they had the time and the wherewithal to pursue their own pleasures.

She drove her peasants hard, though she was fair. Used to the laxity of the O'Flahertys, they had gotten out of hand. At first they resented her, but when winter came and the peasants found themselves warm, dry, and well fed for the first time in years, they blessed their lady. She had managed the miracle of preparing them for winter.

Then Ewan was past two, and Murrough sixteen months, and one day Skye realized that in all those sixteen months Dom still hadn't come near her. Silently she blessed the woman or women who were keeping her husband amused. And it came to her that it had been many months since she had heard any gossip linking Dom with any particular woman. It was a disquieting thought.

It was June again, and Skye was eighteen. The weather was unusually sunny and warm for Ireland. Her healthy, fully healed young body was beginning to crave loving once again, even Dom's. Though they had been invited twice more to spend Twelfth Night with the MacWilliam, she had kept to Ballyhennessey, using her pregnancy as an excuse not to travel, and playing ill the second time.

She dared not see Niall again, although both her mind and her body craved him with a desperation that almost tore her apart. With the knowledge imparted to her by Eibhlin, she might easily have become his mistress, with no one the wiser. The temptation had been fierce, but she held herself in too high a regard to be anything less than his cherished wife.

Dom and his father had attended the Twelfth Night revelries. Skye had insisted that they go to the MacWilliam's castle, leaving her behind with her babes. Though she had impressed upon the two men the importance of every opportunity in finding Claire a husband, they had returned both times to say that no suitable husband could be found. Skye could not understand it. Thanks to Dubhdara O'Malley, Claire now had a respectable dowry that neither her father nor her brother could steal. Either the girl was being too fussy, or else there was someone in Claire's life whom she knew was not suitable, but foolishly sought after anyway. Skye was determined to find out what was going on, for Claire O'Flaherty was seventeen now and Skye did not want to have her with them the rest of their days.

Skye picked her time carefully, choosing an evening, after the meal, when both Gilly and Dom had disappeared. She had seen Claire head for her own rooms at the very top of the tower house. Skye had never been there before. She had never been asked, and there had never before been a reason to violate Claire's privacy.

When the house had quieted, she slowly climbed the stairs to her sister-in-law's apartment. Entering the dayroom, Skye was shocked to find many of her long-missing dowry items. The windows were hung with the French velvets she had planned to use in her own chambers. The small polished oak sideboard Dubhdara and Anne had had made particularly for her stood against one wall. On it was her small silver tray with her hand-blown Venetian goblets and decanters! "God's nightshirt!" she swore under her breath. "I'll skin the sly bitch!" Dear God! There were her silver bowls and candlesticks! Stunned, then furious, Skye was about to storm off to seek out her husband and demand an explanation when she heard laughter and the murmur of voices—one very definitely masculine—from the bedchamber above.

So, she thought, Mistress Claire does have a lover! Well, whoever he is he'll soon find he has himself a new wife, unless, God forbid, he already has one. Serf or lord, she'll wed him! Silently Skye crept up the stairs, reaching the little landing, then neared the bedchamber's half-open door. The closer she got the more vividly she heard the sounds of vigorous lovemaking. Reaching the door, she peeked into the room.

What she saw confirmed her suspicions. Claire and a man, both naked, were intertwined. Color flooded Skye's face at the sight of Claire's long, white legs wrapped tightly about her lover. He brutally rammed himself into the writhing, straining woman. Claire began to moan.

"Harder, Dom! Harder! Yes, yes, brother darling! It's so good! So good!"

Skye felt the first wave of nausea sweep over her as she clung to the door. Dom! Claire's lover was Dom! Her own brother! Slowly Skye slipped to the floor, still clutching the door, faint with the sight.

"Whore!" Dom growled. "What a little whore you are, sweet sister mine. Shall I fuck you until you can't stand up? I've done it before, haven't I? Tonight, however, it pleases me to fuck you till you beg me for mercy, and then you'll pleasure me in a hundred other ways I can invent!"

"Yes, yes . . ." breathed Claire. "Whatever you want, my darling! I'll do whatever you want! Oh, Dom, don't I always?"

Still on her knees, Skye was frozen with both horror and terror.

"On your hands and knees, bitch!"

Claire scrambled to obey, and was quickly and cruelly sodomized by her brother. Skye felt the bitter taste of bile rise in her constricted throat as Claire panted, "Hurt me, Dom! Yes! Hurt me!"

Still Dom did not spend. Now he lay his sister on her back and, straddling her, put himself into her open, eager mouth. Skye closed her eyes to blot out the sight, but she could not close her ears to the throaty, gobbling noises made by Claire, or the groans of pleasure made by Dom. Unable to contain herself, Skye sobbed aloud.

Claire shrieked, "Oh, my God! There's someone here! Someone has seen us!"

Dom leapt from the bed and, yanking the door fully open, caught sight of his half-fainting wife. "Well, well," he murmured nastily, "what have we here? It's my sweet wife."

Claire's eyes narrowed. "Bitch! How dare you spy on me!" she shrieked.

"I wasn't s-spying." Skye's voice was shaking. "I came to t-talk to you about getting m-married."

Dom began to laugh uproariously, but a look from his sister quieted him. "Married?! Why on earth would I want to marry, you ninny?" rasped Claire. "The only man I've ever loved is Dom, and I don't ever intend leaving him. *He's mine!* The only reason he married you was for the money, and to get heirs. He's got both now, and we don't need you at all, except to run the estate for us. So get out of here, and don't ever come back again snooping and spying!"

Skye turned to flee but Dom's big hand grasped her shoulder. His other hand slid around to squeeze her breast and as the nipple hardened he laughed softly. "It's been a long time, Skye."

She tried to pull away. Claire snarled from the bed, "Leave her be, brother! You don't need her as long as you have me!"

"Be quiet, bitch! She has pleasured me too, and now I think I would have you both at the same time."

"No!" wailed Skye, struggling to reach the door, but his arms closed about her and Claire, a sudden vicious look in her pale-blue eyes, reached out and ripped Skye's gown from her. As her sister-in-law's body became more visible, Claire's gaze softened, becoming almost dreamy, and she reached out again, this time to caress Skye's body. Skye shrank from her touch, sick with revulsion. Claire laughed nastily. "Let me have her first, brother. Let me prepare her for you, please! You can watch while I love her. Remember how you loved watching me and the little maid I once had?"

"No, Dom! Oh, God, no!"

Dom smiled sweetly at his sister, his eyes bright with memory. Then he nodded. "I'll watch, but when I'm ready, Claire, you must give over. Promise me now? No teasing like you did with little Sorcha."

"Yes, darling," Claire purred, and then with Dom's aid they tied the struggling Skye's arms to the bedposts.

Claire straddled her victim and, holding Skye's head between her hands, she kissed her slowly, and wetly. Skye seemed faint and, laughing, Claire began leisurely to explore the shrinking flesh. The degradation she was inflicting added to her enjoyment. Taking Skye's nipples between her thumb and forefinger, she rolled them gently before bending and sucking on them. Bound though she was, Skye fought to escape, but her helplessness only stimulated her antagonist.

Slowly Claire slid her lush body down Skye's until their breasts and bellies met. Then she rotated her pelvis and mons veneris against Skye's, murmuring vilely, "Don't tell me that, with all the sisters you have, you've not done a bit of girl-fucking in your time. And remember—while we pleasure each other, Dom is watching us and readying himself for both of us, big bull that he is. Don't fight me, sister, for now that you know about Dom and me there's no reason we cannot share him and enjoy each other all the time."

Skye turned her head away, ashamed of what was happening to her and confused by the stirrings of desire she was beginning to feel. Claire thrust and moaned against Skye's helpless body with increasing fervor until suddenly Dom pulled her away and, mounting his wife, thrust into her.

Skye screamed, which only seemed to madden him. Claire was now kneeling within Skye's view, slack-mouthed with lust as she watched her brother use his wife. When Dom had sated himself with Skye he rolled off her and loosened her bonds. He pushed her away, pulled his sister over, and mounted her next. Skye curled into a tight, protective ball, and sobbed. She had never felt so fouled in her entire life. She knew that if anyone so much as touched her again, she would kill.

Strengthened by this realization, she marshaled her courage and crawled off the bed. Stumbling across the room, she reached the door. Dom and his sister had finished by this time and Claire saw her. She cried out, "She's escaping, Dom! Get her back! I want her again!"

Dom lurched off the bed and lunged for his wife. Skye had now wrenched the door open. As he reached out for her, Skye sidestepped him. Dom stumbled through the door, lost his balance, and fell screaming headlong down the flight of stone steps leading to his sister's day chamber.

There was a stunned silence. He lay still, twisted grotesquely.

Claire leaped from the bed and stood gazing down into the room below. Then she turned on Skye and howled, "You've killed him! You've killed Dom!"

Holy Mother forgive me, thought Skye, but I hope so! Then as relief brought strength sweeping over her, she turned on Claire and furiously slapped her, leaving the imprint of her hand on the girl's face. "Shut up, you vicious little bitch! Shut up!"

"We must get help," whimpered Claire.

"Not yet."

"You *do* want him dead," came the horrified accusation.

"I'll not deny it," said Skye flatly, and Claire shrank away from her. "But before we can get help we must all dress. How will it look to the servants to find the three of us mother naked? I'll not put that scandal on my sons. Get dressed! Then go and fetch me some clothes from my room. Quickly!"

The procedure seemed to take forever, but at last both women were dressed. Struggling together, they forced Dom into his clothes. To Skye's sorrow, he was still breathing.

"Now," said Skye, "rouse the house."

"What will I tell them?" quavered Claire.

"That Dom has had an accident. I will handle the rest. Go, now!"

Claire fled, shrieking loudly enough to rouse the entire household, and quickly the room was filled with babbling servants. Skye calmly directed the removal of her injured husband to his own rooms. The family's surgeon was sent for and arrived as the dawn was breaking.

Dom lived, but it would have been better if he had died. His spine was broken in two places. He was paralyzed from the waist down. He would not walk, or function as a man, ever again.

Skye thanked the surgeon, paid his fee, and sent him away. Then she took on the O'Flahertys. Gilly blustered at her. "Claire says you're responsible for my son's condition."

"Your son is responsible for his own condition," replied Skye coldly. "Last night after the meal was finished and I had seen to my household duties, I went to your daughter's rooms to speak to her about arranging a marriage. I found her and your precious son fucking merrily! And it was not the first time they had engaged in this . . . *incest!* When I tried to flee from them they ripped my clothes from me, and used me vilely! Both of them! I tried to escape again and Dom lunged at me. When I stepped aside he fell through the open door and down the stairs. I'm only sorry he didn't break his damned neck! It would have saved me the trouble of caring for him. If you still believe that I have wronged your son, Gilly, then we will take our case and place it before the MacWilliam."

"Yes!" sobbed Claire. "For once in your life, Father, take the initiative! Dom will spend the rest of his life half a man because of her! She deserves to be punished!"

Skye drew herself up proudly and looked down upon the vengeful Claire. "Yes, Claire," she purred. "Take your case to the MacWilliam. Do! And then be prepared either to prove your virginity before the midwives' panel or name your lover! Who will you say it is, Claire? One of the serfs? I think not. You're far too proud a bitch to admit to fucking with a serf. Who then? There is no one else! No one ever comes to visit you. No one! Perhaps you could claim the Devil for your lover. In a sense, you'd be speaking the truth."

Skye's father-in-law looked suddenly old, and defeated. Claire wept helplessly. Skye's next words held a finality. "I am going home to Innisfana," she announced. "And I am taking my sons with me. I will not be back. Since Claire loves her brother so deeply she will remain here to care for him for the rest of his life. I will see that Da withdraws her dowry. She has no chance of a decent marriage without it, and I would not, knowing what I do now, see her wed with some poor unsuspecting lad. She will be fed and clothed at my expense, or she may go with what she has. The choice is hers.

"Frang the bailiff will run the estate for me, and answer to me alone. This is, after all, to be Ewan's inheritance someday and I want it turned over to him in good condition.

"Gilly, you will be taken care of, but my father's lawyers will shortly have a paper for you to sign that will prevent you from gambling away any part of the estate. Mark me well, Gilly. I will not pay for your wines, your women, or your gambling debts!"

"Father! Are you going to let her do this to us!?"

Gilly stared straight ahead and Skye smiled triumphantly. "Yes, Claire, he is! He knows the alternative. I will bring *my* case before the MacWilliam—*and* before the Church! If I do I will accuse you not only of incest with your brother, but of witchcraft as well! You deserve to burn for what you've been doing!"

"I love him!" Claire screamed.

"You were his *sister!*"

"I loved him," Claire repeated, "From the time we first bedded when I was but a maid of eleven. I was the only woman who ever really satisfied Dom."

Skye looked pityingly at Claire. "In the years that Dom has left we will see how much you really love him."

In the morning Skye bid her husband an unemotional farewell. "I hope you enjoyed what you and your sister did the other night, for the memory of it will have to last you a lifetime!"

"Bitch!" he snarled at her. "What kind of a woman are you to leave me?"

"A better woman than you ever knew or appreciated, Dom. Your conduct with your sister has wiped free any obligation on my part toward you. Farewell."

He struggled to rise. "Bitch! Come back! I command you, Skye! Come back!"

She never turned back. His voice, alternating between curses, threats, and pleas, followed her until the sound became quite unintelligible and finally faded altogether.

Skye rode away from the O'Flaherty house, Ewan before her on her saddle. Behind her were the carts carrying her younger son, the two nurses, and her household goods.

But when Skye reached Innisfana several days later there was no peaceful haven there. Dubhdara O'Malley lay dying, having been badly injured by a falling mast in a storm as he was bringing his ship home. A stubborn man, he had refused to die until he reached his home, and until he had seen his youngest daughter. The messenger he sent to Skye had found her as she took ship for Innisfana Island.

She was barely in time to bid her father a final farewell. Tearful, she kissed his cold and sweating brow. "I'm back for good, Da."

He nodded. Explanations were unimportant now. "Your brothers are too young for the ships yet," he gasped weakly. "You've got to take charge for me."

It never crossed her mind that he was thrusting a huge responsibility upon her. She answered simply, "I will."

"You're the best of them, lassie. Even the boys."

"Oh, Da," she whispered. "Oh, Da, I do love you!"

"Skye, lass, this time follow your heart," were Dubhdara O'Malley's last words to his favorite child. He died a few minutes later, holding her hand.

Her beautiful blue eyes overflowing, she looked wordlessly to her uncle Seamus. "I heard him," he said, "and I'll uphold your rights, Skye. You're the new O'Malley, and may God be with you for you'll be needing all the help you can get."

Skye looked to her stepmother. "I heard him, and I trust you," said Anne. "You'll do right by us all. Besides, it's your full brother Michael who is the next male in line, not my lads."

"In this family," answered Skye, "it's not necessarily the eldest, but the most competent. At least two of your boys show more promise than Michael. He's most like my mother, lord help him. He's more likely to follow Our Lord Christ than the sea. Am I not right, Uncle?"

Seamus O'Malley nodded. "He'd asked me to talk with Dubh. He wants to enter St. Padraic's and become a priest."

Skye turned to Anne. "You see. It rests with Brian and Shane now."

As quickly as the family of the O'Malley chief could be assembled, they determined the length of the wake and the date of the funeral. With Seamus O'Malley and Anne to back her, Skye was reluctantly recognized as the new O'Malley by her brothers-in-law and her very shocked sisters. Her clansmen and vassals came quickly, almost joyfully, to pay their homage to Skye, the new O'Malley.

The next step was a journey to the MacWilliam's stronghold to pledge him her fealty. Only Anne, Eibhlin, and her uncle knew the truth behind her leaving her husband. All three were horrified, but swore to keep the secret. Seamus O'Malley added to his niece's mystique by claiming that she had returned home because of a dream in which her father called her from over the waves. The men who had sailed with her father and with her when she was a child circulated once again the old tales of her bravery and skill. The MacWilliam would have been hard pressed indeed to deny Skye her inheritance.

She rode into his stronghold with all her captains escorting her. Niall Burke watched her arrival from one of the towers of the castle, and wondered what would happen between them now. She rode astride, as she had in the old days, and upon the black stallion, Finn. She was dressed in Lincoln green hose, over which she wore high brown cordoba leather boots, and a mid-thigh-length doeskin jerkin with silver buttons. Beneath the jerkin was a cream-colored silk shirt with small pearl buttons. Her glorious blue-black hair was parted in the center and twisted into a smooth coil at the nape of her neck. Her gardenia skin was a little flushed. Upon her left hand he could see a blue flash, and knew she wore the great sapphire ring that had been her father's seal of office.

He descended from the tower, and strode swiftly to his own quarters. To his surprise Darragh was waiting for him. The three years of their marriage had been a bad joke, and he rarely saw her, let alone cohabited with her. It was obvious that she would never conceive him a child. She had never come to him willingly, and each time he had taken her it had been a battle in which she yielded to the flesh and then did penance for her weakness. She had had coarse brown robes made up for herself, robes that resembled those worn by her old religious order. She rarely bathed, believing it a concession to the flesh. For over a year now she had spent her days and nights in constant prayer. He no longer went near her. Her personal habits disgusted him, and attempting to claim his rights seemed now like raping a nun, a thing for which Niall Burke had no taste.

He greeted her courteously, and she replied, "Lady O'Flaherty is here to see your father, Niall. Why has she come?"

"Her father has died, Darragh, and it was his deathbed wish that she take over his duties until her brothers are grown. She is now the O'Malley, and she has come to pledge her fealty to her overlord."

"And what of her husband? I have been given to understand that she tried to murder him and then left him, taking his sons with her. He lies paralyzed for life with only his loyal sister to care for him."

"Where did you obtain this information, Darragh?" He kept his voice quiet and level.

"I have a letter from the unfortunate Lady Claire O'Flaherty begging me to intercede with the MacWilliam on her poor brother's behalf."

"I do not believe the tale, Darragh. I have never known Skye to be anything but generous and thoughtful."

"Those are not the qualities that made the O'Malley leave her in charge of his small empire," noted Darragh shrewdly. It was an unusually sensible observation for Darragh.

"Skye would never harm anyone. I refuse to believe it!"

"Of course you do not believe it. You lust after her, but for the sake of your immortal soul you must not yield to her wiles, Niall!"

He laughed bitterly. "Whose wiles would you have me yield to then, *wife?* Yours? Let me tell you something about Skye O'Malley, my dear. The last time I saw her she told me she never wanted to set eyes on me again because, through an awful quirk of fate, we were wed to other people. I then said I would kill her husband. She chided me, asking what I would do with my own wife, kill her also? She said you had been as wronged as the rest of us were, and we must all make the best of our situations. She would tempt neither herself nor me by seeing me again."

"Ah! The most wicked ones are always the most clever, Niall! She has skillfully misled you into believing her virtuous. Beware of her! Beware!" And with a strange look in her weak blue eyes, Darragh turned and left him.

Niall went about the business of changing his clothes. His father had told him he wanted him there when the O'Malley swore her fealty, for she must swear it not only to the MacWilliam, but also to his heir. He debated whether to be elegant or simple, finally settling on black velvet because it was both.

Entering the main hall of the castle, he was surprised to find that Skye had not changed from her riding clothes. Her captains at her back, she knelt. Placing her hands in the old and gnarled ones of the MacWilliam, and then into Niall's warm firm grasp, she twice swore her loyalty to the Burkes, then rose gracefully to accept their kiss of peace. Lord Burke noted the pride and love flowing from the eyes of the rough-looking O'Malley captains. That they adored her was obvious, and he was reassured to know that she would sail with such devoted men.

Then suddenly, to everyone's shock and embarrassment, Darragh appeared in their midst, her nun's robes swirling about her, and cried out, "My lord the MacWilliam, on behalf of the O'Flahertys of Ballyhennessey I cry for judgment against this evil woman! Oh, wicked whore of Babylon, your days of evil are numbered! The Lord God will strike thee down with fire and the sword!"

Skye looked swiftly to Niall, her eyes filled with pity.

"Clear the hall, dammit!" shouted the MacWilliam, red-faced and very angry. When all but the four of them had gone, the old man turned on Darragh. "I hope, madam, that you have a bloody fine explanation for this intrusion, and for your unwanted charges!"

"No longer 'madam,' sir, but Sister Mary Penitent. That was to have been my name before you stole me from my convent, and forced me into carnal bondage with your son. It will soon be my name again, for I will no longer remain here, but return to St. Mary's. Before I go, however, I will right a great wrong done by this wicked woman. First, she deliberately crippled her husband. Then she willfully deserted him, stealing both his sons and his money. She must be punished! God demands it!"

"What the hell nonsense is this?" roared the MacWilliam.

"She claims to have a letter from Claire O'Flaherty," said Niall quietly to his father.

"The lying, deceitful bitch!" said Skye furiously, and the MacWilliam and his son grinned at each other.

"All right, O'Malley, what's your explanation?" demanded the old man.

Skye glanced scornfully at Darragh. "Is she strong enough to hear the truth of this? It's not very pretty."

"Speak, O'Malley," commanded the MacWilliam.

"Claire O'Flaherty lies, my lord. I caught her and her brother, my husband, in incest." Skye outlined the story, concluding, "When I dodged him, he fell down a flight of stairs."

Darragh Burke, who had turned white at the mention of the word "incest," gave a moan of horror and fell to the floor in a faint. The MacWilliam and his son glanced briefly at her, then returned their attentions to Skye.

"The surgeon said Dom will never walk again. Under the circumstances, I feel no obligation to him. The estate was in a ruinous condition when I married Dom. Your annual tributes had not been paid in three years, but it is all paid up now, thanks to me. The O'Flaherty lands are again prosperous because of my skillful management. This, despite Dom's having gambled and whored away my dowry. Claire O'Flaherty owes me for every mouthful of food she consumes, every drop she drinks, the very clothes on her back. She might have been safely wed, but for her own crimes. It was her choice to remain at Ballyhennessey and commit incest with her brother rather than wed her own man. When Dom was injured I told her she could stay and nurse him or go, as she pleased." Skye looked hard at the MacWilliam. "If you feel her charges have merit, my lord, I will abide by your decision."

The old man reached out and gently stroked Skye's beautiful hair. "There is no merit in her charges, O'Malley," he said gruffly. "If she will not accept my decision in this matter, then I shall turn her over to the Church. They will deal with the wench far more harshly than you or I would." He smiled at Skye. "Now, lass, will you accept my hospitality for a few days' time? You've come through a hard time and you've great responsibility ahead of you."

She smiled back at him, and he thought again how extraordinarily beautiful she was. For the briefest moment he regretted his age and his infirmities. He envied his son this beautiful woman who would undoubtedly become his mistress.

"I will accept your kindness, my lord, but only for a day. You're right in that I am now laden with responsibilities. My father's entire fleet stands awaiting my orders, and they must remain idle until I have studied his books. My eldest brother prefers the Church to the sea, and though I will train him in my father's ways, for boys are known to be fickle creatures with changeable minds, I doubt that Michael will change. Therefore it will be my half-brother, Brian, who's most likely to become the next O'Malley. He is but six now. It will be at least ten years before he can take over his duties. Then, too, there are my own two sons to raise."

"Stop, lassie!" said the MacWilliam. "You're exhausting me. It's too much for a woman to take on, and I wonder at your father, God assoil him."

Skye looked at the old man proudly. "My father knew I would not fail him. He might have chosen any of my sister's husbands, or even my uncle Seamus, but he chose *me. I am the O'Malley!*" Then her look softened, and her eyes, which had been a deep purple-blue, lightened to a clear blue-green. "Tonight, however, I shall be just Skye O'Malley, and your most grateful guest." She turned without another word and walked from the room.

The MacWilliam bellowed for a servant, who quickly removed the still unconscious Darragh. "If you mean to have the O'Malley lass," he said to Niall, "you had best tame her quickly, my son. This is no milk-and-water wench, but a full-blown woman. Once she gets the bit of power into her teeth, you'll not easily get a bridle on her. I'll see if I can start annulment proceedings on your marriage, for the O'Neill girl belongs back in her convent. As to O'Flaherty, the health of a cripple is precarious at best. I trust you're not too noble to object if we assist him now to a better life . . . discreetly, of course."

Niall shook his head without hesitation. "May I speak to Skye of marriage?"

The old man grinned wickedly. "If 'twill aid you in your wooing, yes, and I imagine you'll need all the help you can get. She's a strong-minded woman."

Niall grinned back as he strode from the hall and headed for Skye's chambers. His heart was singing. She was his! They would finally be together, and they would make marvelous love, and she would bear him strong sons and beautiful daughters, and they would be happy. He burst into her room, startling Mag, and a half-clothed Skye.

"My father's starting the annulment proceedings, my love. We can soon be wed!"

He reached out for her, but she eluded him. "Mag! Get out! I'll call you." Then, "Don't touch me, Niall! I cannot bear to be touched. I told you what they did to me. I never want to be touched again! I am happy you're to be free of Darragh O'Neill; but find yourself another wife, my lord. My husband lives, and even if he did not, I would not remarry. I will never again put myself at a man's mercy." She shuddered deeply.

He was stunned. This was not the girl he had known. "Skye, my love," he began gently, "I know they have hurt you; but *I* never hurt you. Remember how it was with us? It was sweetness beyond measure. Come, love," and he held out his hand to her, "come let me love you, and wipe away the unhappy memories."

"Niall!" Her eyes filled with tears. "Please understand. I cannot even bear for Mag to touch me. My own good Mag. I bore Dom's brutal lovemaking for three years. Even then I remembered how it had been with us, and I prayed that someday we could be together. There was no obscenity that Dom forced upon me that spoiled you for me, not ever. Not until the night he and his vile sister . . ." She could not go on.

He finished it quietly for her. "Until the night they both raped you."

"Aye," she said, and was silent once more.

"I *do* understand," he said as his deep voice, soothing and tenderly warm, sought to reassure and comfort her. "The wounds are still too new and I, in my happiness, have foolishly assumed you would share my joy at the prospect of our being together again. Forgive me, my love. You have suffered two wicked shocks, and now you're burdened with an awesome responsibility. You'll need time to adjust, and you shall have it, sweetheart!"

Her lashes were silken smudges against her pale skin. A great wave of pity washed over him as two crystalline tears slipped from beneath her closed eyelids and down her cheeks. He wanted to reach out, enfold her in his arms, comfort her, wipe away completely all the terrible hurt. But he stood with clenched fists and fought to maintain a rigid control on himself lest he frighten her, and risk losing her forever.

Finally she spoke. "I love you, Niall. I have never loved anyone else."

"I know, Skye," he answered quietly, "and that is why I will wait."

"What?!" Her wet jewel eyes flew open.

"Yes, my precious love. Wait. In time the terror will fade, and when it does I will be here, Skye. Be it a month from now, or a year. Or ten years."

"You need an heir, Niall. Your father wants one so very much."

"You'll give me one someday, my love."

"You're mad." But a small smile played at the corners of her mouth.

"Not mad, my darling, simply in love with a wild and sweet vixen who will eventually come home to me again."

Suddenly she held out her hand to him. He grasped it, and felt her tremble, but she did not pull away. "Give me time, Niall. I will come back to you! I know now that I will! Just give me time."

A wonderful warm smile lit his face, turning his mouth up at the edges, crinkling his silvery eyes at the corners. "Madam, I offer you whatever time you need, for I have surely never known anything better worth waiting for than you." He bowed low over her slim hand, his cool lips gently brushing her skin, sending a small shiver—was it revulsion, or was it desire?—rippling through her. Then, straightening, he turned and left her chambers.

Skye stood frozen, barely breathing. He loved her! Despite it all, he still loved her! He was willing to wait! And now, as she felt the blood begin to course through her veins, warming her as she had not been warmed since that terrible night, she knew it would be all right. The horrible memories were fresh, but she would heal eventually. And when she did, Niall would be waiting!

On the following day the O'Malley thanked her overlord for his hospitality and, after a short ride to the coast, sailed home to Innisfana Island. Within the month word came to the MacWilliam that the transition from the old to the new O'Malley had been made smoothly, and that the fleet was sailing once again.

So Niall Burke waited. The healing process had begun for Skye, and when it was complete they would be together forever. He would not go to her before then. There was plenty of time.

Chapter 7

A YEAR PASSED, AND DOM DIED. HIS DEATH, THOUGH SUDDEN, was not unexpected. With the loss of his legs he had lost the will to live. Claire O'Flaherty disappeared shortly after the visit of an English cousin, and only Gilly remained at Ballyhennessey, a sad shadow of his former self, content to spend his days and nights in a drunken haze. The estate was well managed by Frang, the bailiff.

The small, prosperous trading empire of the O'Malleys grew

more prosperous through Skye's skillful handling, and the MacWilliam was forced to admit that Dubhdara O'Malley had known exactly what he was doing when he had placed his daughter in charge. How she would behave in wartime was another matter, and he had yet to call upon her for that.

At nine, Michael O'Malley was more a priest than child, his calling so obvious that Skye finally sent him to school at the monastery of St. Brendan's, preparatory to his entering the priesthood at sixteen. He would not take his final vows until he was twenty, by which time his two oldest half-brothers would have wed and probably produced heirs.

Brian and Shane, at seven and a half and six and a half, had begun the process of learning about the sea, about ships, and about their late father's half-legal, half-illegal methods of doing business. Brian was assigned to a ship named *Western Wind,* and Shane went aboard the *North Star.* Neither ship would ever be out when the other was also out, and occasionally the boys were at home at the same time, which gave Skye a chance to see her half-brothers working together, and to evaluate them as they grew. Each was a true O'Malley, taking to the sea as to an old and respected friend. Skye wished her father could have seen them, for he would have been proud.

With the aid of Bishop O'Malley, and the donation of a fine manor to the Church, Niall Burke was finally given an annulment from his wife Darragh O'Neill, and she happily returned to her convent, where she quickly took final vows. On his son's behalf, the MacWilliam sent to Seamus O'Malley and formally requested his niece's hand in marriage. With her permission, the negotiations would begin at once.

"I don't know now," said Skye mischievously.

"Christ's bones!" roared the bishop, for a moment so like his late brother that his niece burst into laughter. Looking very aggrieved, the bishop demanded, "What do you mean, you don't know now? From the moment Niall Burke looked at you nothing would do but that you have him! Now you can, and you don't know if you will? God Almighty, woman! Make up your mind!" His plump face was red, and his blue eyes almost black with anger.

Skye's laughter died in her throat. Kneeling, she leaned her silky head against the prelate's knee. "It isn't because I don't love Niall, Uncle. I do. He is the only man for me, and he always will be. But I am no longer a girl whose only interest is her man and their babes. Perhaps I never really was."

"Beware, lassie," warned Seamus O'Malley. "This is the MacWilliam and his heir that we deal with. They are your overlords."

"Let them beware also!" shot back Skye. *"I am the O'Malley!"*

Seamus O'Malley mastered his temper. "What is it you want, Niece? Specifically."

"My marriage must not affect my status as the O'Malley, and neither must my husband or my father-in-law interfere with that. The responsibility for the clan remains mine until I see fit to pass it on to one of my brothers. Da wanted it that way. I will not have the Burkes dabbling greedy fingers into the O'Malley coffers!

"I will come to them with a dowry worthy of a princess, but that is all they will receive. I want no interference by the Burkes into O'Malley affairs."

The bishop nodded. "'Tis shrewd you are, Niece, but I don't know if we can get the MacWilliam to swallow such a big pill. He's a sly old man."

"Come, Uncle, you're a brilliant negotiator. Did you not arrange with your 'friends' in Rome for Niall's annulment? We both know the reason the MacWilliam seeks me for his son is not my bonnie blue eyes or my pretty tits. He looks to our ships, but they are not mine to give. They belong to my half-brothers, and I will not cheat my father's sons out of their inheritance even to gain my own happiness. I offer that wicked old man a bigger dowry than any of his 'better-bred' wenches, and I also offer him something even better than money, for I am a proven breeder of sons! Tempt him with that! For all his cleverness he has but one heir. I will give him half a dozen more."

The bishop laughed. "You're a very naughty wench, Niece. Your attitude toward the holy sacrament of matrimony is really quite shocking. I am tempted to pile you with penances."

"I will accept them gladly, Uncle, if Niall Burke truly loves me." She became deadly serious now. "This is what I must know. The last time he accepted his father's will too easily, and did not fight for me. Now he must battle the MacWilliam to prove his love."

"And if the MacWilliam refuses your terms?"

"He won't. But if he did then Niall would wed with me anyway if he really loves me."

"Very well, Skye. 'Twill be your way."

"Thank you, Uncle," she replied meekly with downcast eyes, and he chuckled and fondly whacked her backside.

The MacWilliam angrily roared his outrage, but Seamus

O'Malley stood firm. Even after Skye wed with Lord Burke she was to remain the O'Malley, and she was to retain complete control of O'Malley affairs.

"The O'Briens have a fine lass ripe for marriage," said the MacWilliam slyly.

"The devil take her," shouted Niall, and the bishop masked his smile. "'Tis Skye I want, and Skye I'll have even if I must slit your scrawny throat!"

The MacWilliam looked at his son with an injured air. "If you're that hot for her then you might as well have her. I hope you'll quickly breed me several grandsons before much more time has passed. I am not growing any younger."

Seamus O'Malley returned to his niece, happy to tell her that her terms had been accepted, and that Niall Burke had been willing to fight for her. The O'Malleys were in a state of great excitement because one of their own was to wed with Niall Burke. Yet Skye remained calm throughout.

"You must be made of ice," remarked her sister Peigi. "He's what you've always wanted. And God knows his reputation with women would set an ordinary woman to fainting. You've already had a taste of his lovemaking, so surely you must be excited to finally be marrying him."

"I am, but we're not wed yet, Peigi. I am fearful of rejoicing too soon lest I awaken to find it all nought but a dream. If I remain quiet and unobtrusive I will not attract the undue attention of those spirits who might envy me my good fortune."

"God ha' mercy, little sister, what unchristian nonsense is this? Thank the Lord you do not run our business so foolishly."

Skye shook her head, but said nothing further. She knew that even here in the heart of devout Christian Ireland, food and drink were placed upon the doorsteps nightly in offering to the little people. She knew that certain maidens of unblemished virtue were marked as sacred, and the keeping of their virginity placed in the care of an ancient Celtic demon who materialized to destroy the violator if the girl's innocence was threatened. She and the men of her fleet made verbal obeisance to Mannanan MacLir, the ancient Irish sea god, before each voyage.

It had been almost eighteen months since she had seen Niall, and she was somewhat frightened, for in all that time she had been free of men's demands. Her aversion to being touched had eased somewhat, and Mag could again bathe and dress her.

As if sensing her fears from afar, Niall Burke came unannounced to Innisfana Island. He found her in her mother's rose garden clipping some late blooms. For a few minutes he stood in the shadow of a tree and watched her. He realized he had never seen her in a moment of leisure. She was dressed in the Irish fashion, wearing a bright red skirt of soft, lightweight wool. She had tucked it up, and he saw that she was bare-legged and barefoot. Her blouse was of fine linen, as white as many washings could make it. The sleeves were short, and it was deep-necked, revealing her breasts when she bent to inhale the sweet fragrances of the flowers. Her blue-black hair was loose and billowed softly about her shoulders in the light breeze. She carried a wide, nearly flat straw basket, half-filled with roses. Her giant hound, Inis, walked slowly by her side.

She was lovelier than he had remembered, and his heart beat a little quicker when he realized that this beautiful woman had consented to be his wife. The young innocent of fifteen was long gone. He barely remembered her now, as this lovely creature of nineteen quickened his blood. He let his eyes feast on her, enjoying the soft pink in her cheeks, the way her lashes made a dark smudge against her skin. Her slim figure moved with such grace. It gave him pleasure just to watch her.

After a little longer, he stepped from behind the tree and the big hound stiffened, his hackles rising. Inis growled low in warning.

"I am glad to see you so well guarded, Skye."

"Put your hand out, Niall, so Inis may get your scent." She patted the dog. "Friend, Inis. Niall is a friend."

Lord Burke suffered himself to be thoroughly sniffed. He patted the animal, speaking reassuringly to him, receiving first a long searching look from the liquid amber eyes, and then finally a wet, cold nose pushed into his palm.

"He likes you!"

"And if he hadn't?"

"You might have had difficulty claiming your rights once we're wed, my lord," she said mischievously.

She sobered suddenly, and he did too. Then he held out his arms to her and, without a moment's hesitation, she walked into them. His arms closed securely about her, and she stood quietly listening to the rapid beat of his heart just beneath her cheek.

"I love you, lass," he said quietly.

"And I love you, my lord Burke. I would seal that love with a kiss," she said softly, raising her head. His mouth gently found hers. At the first touch of his lips she panicked, but his big hand caressed her hair and he murmured against her mouth, "No, love, it's Niall, and I love you." With a sigh she gave herself up to him, and when he released her at last, her eyes were shining with joy.

"Is it all right now, sweetheart?" he asked, already knowing the answer.

"Yes, my lord. For a moment . . . but it quickly passed."

"I will always be gentle with you, Skye."

"I know." She smiled happily. "How long were you watching me?"

"A few minutes. You're a charming sight barefoot, and clipping roses."

"But hardly dignified," she blushed. "As the O'Malley, I should have sailed out to meet you, my betrothed husband."

"Leave the O'Malley at sea, my love. I prefer shoeless lasses, especially the one now in my arms. Besides, you did not know I was coming. And but a day behind me is himself, anxious that your uncle perform the betrothal ceremony here in two days' time, and that we sign the contracts. Would that please you, pet?"

"Oh, Niall! Yes! Yes! Yes!"

"And then," he continued, "we can be wed in three weeks' time after the banns are all read."

"Yes!" Then her face fell. "No. It cannot be in three weeks' time. Damn! I must go to Algiers, and we sail in a week."

"To Algiers? Why?"

"It has been suggested that we set up a trading post in Algiers, and I cannot give my approval unless I have investigated the situation myself. I must not waste O'Malley gold, or O'Malley resources."

"Why must you leave next week? Can't you go another time?" She could hear the irritation in his voice.

"Oh, Niall, I am sorry. In order to gain a trading license in Algiers we must have permission from the Dey, who represents the Sublime Porte in Constantinople. Without the Dey's approval we cannot trade safely in the Mediterranean."

"Why not simply bribe him?"

Skye laughed. "We are going to, but the Turks do things differently than we do. We are rather straightforward, whereas they demand grace and elegance, even in their business dealings. When the Dey learned that the head of the O'Malley company was a woman he demanded to meet me. My representatives dared not refuse him. So I must go or else risk insulting the Dey. To insult the Dey is to insult the Sultan. In that case we would not get the trading permit. Worse, our ships would be marked as fair game by the Barbary pirates who sail out of Algiers under the Dey's supervision. We would be ruined. I have to go. The appointment is set."

"How long?"

"At least three months."

"Three months? Dammit, Skye, it's too long to be separated from you!"

Her eyes lit up. "Come with me, Niall! Sail with me to Algiers! I know we must allow our families the privilege of marrying us off with pomp and fuss. But once we're betrothed and pledged to wed, no one will think to mind if you accompany me. We can have our church wedding when we get home. Come with me, my love! Oh, please come with me!"

It was a wild, impractical idea, and he almost said no. Then he thought of the long days and longer nights ahead. Niall Burke took a deep breath and said, "Yes, Skye, my love. I'll sail with you, though I must be mad to do so."

With a cry of joy she flung herself into his arms.

Several days later, in the same chapel that had seen Skye's baptism and ill-fated marriage to Dom O'Flaherty, her betrothal to Niall Burke was celebrated. She regretted the absence of her father at the moment of her greatest happiness, but the MacWilliam's open joy eased her sorrow.

The ceremony was barely over when Skye left her husband-to-be and their guests in the care of her sisters, so that she could oversee the preparation of her ships. They would sail in a fleet of nine ships. Skye's flagship was the *Faoileag* (the Seagull). With her would be her father's ship the *Righ A'Mhara* (King of the Sea); Anne's ship the *Ban-righ A'Ceo* (Queen of the Mist), which had been a wedding gift from her late husband; and the six ships belonging to Skye and her sisters. These were known as the six Daughters for each was named a "Daughter of . . ." They were *Inghean A-Sian* (Daughter of the Storm), *Inghean A'Ceo* (Daughter of the Mist), *Inghean A'Mhara* (Daughter of the Sea), *Inghean A'Ear* (Daughter of the East), *Inghean A'Iar* (Daughter of the West), and the *Inghean A'Ay* (Daughter of the Island).

Each ship was carefully prepared and provisioned, and the crews were handpicked by Skye. She wished to make a good impression on the Dey. Permission to trade with Algiers meant untold wealth.

Thus it was that, one week from the day of his betrothal, Niall Burke found himself standing on the quarterdeck of a ship as it sailed south out of O'Malley Bay into the rolling blue Atlantic

Ocean. He was not a sailor by nature, and had no special feeling for the sea. Nevertheless the weather was tolerable and he quickly found his sea legs. What he could not find as easily was an end to his amazement—for Skye O'Malley in command on the sea was completely different from the woman he knew and loved.

She was amazingly competent, highly knowledgeable in areas of which he had little or no understanding. The men about her did her bidding unquestioningly, and listened to her with open respect. Had she not been his sweet Skye in the privacy of her cabin, Niall would have been genuinely frightened of the Amazon who commanded this small fleet. Fortunately, Niall Burke had a sense of humor, and he quickly realized he was going to need it.

Though he shared the captain's quarters with her, he slept alone in a single bunk in a small side cabin with the wolfhound Inis as his companion. The great dog had attached himself to Niall with a singular devotion that delighted Skye, for Inis had hated Dom. Lord Burke amused himself by training the dog. It was intelligent, but lacked manners. Niall also spent a good deal of time in the company of the same Captain MacGuire who had returned him to the MacWilliam several years back.

It was MacGuire who began to teach Niall the rudiments of seamanship, for as he succinctly put it, "The O'Malleys are all half fish, and if you're to wed one, you'd best understand why they love the sea even if you don't." Niall Burke listened, learned, and began to have great admiration for those who made the sea their life.

He spent the evenings with Skye, though she would not share her bed with him. "I am not a passenger on this voyage," she told him. "If I were needed in the night, and we . . ." Her blue eyes twinkled, and he laughed in spite of his disappointment. To reward his patience she flung herself into his arms and kissed him ardently, her soft breasts pressing provocatively against his pounding heart, her little tongue darting teasingly about his mouth. Niall pushed her back, and kicking her legs from beneath her, they fell to the big captain's bed. Skye felt her shirt buttons opening as if by magic, and his mouth burned into the soft flesh of her breasts, nuzzling against a suddenly hard nipple, sucking until the throb between her legs was almost unbearable.

Then he lifted his head, and his silvery eyes stared down at her with tolerant amusement. "You're captain of this ship, Skye, but I will, if you don't mind, be captain in our bedchamber. If you tease me like that again, I'll have you on your back before you can say 'Sail ho!' Do you understand me, sweetheart?"

"Aye, Captain," she answered, and he was flattered to see the admiration in her eyes.

The weather remained miraculously fair as the *Seagull* and her sister ships sailed farther south, avoiding the treacherous Bay of Biscay entirely by the simple maneuver of keeping far enough out to sea. They now sailed shoreward, rounding Cape St. Vincent, ploughing across the Gulf of Cádiz, and through the Straits of Gibraltar into the Mediterranean.

They were but a few days out of Algiers when a freak storm struck the O'Malley fleet, scattering it haphazardly. The wind and waves were tremendous. The heavy rains soaked into the decks and through into the below-decks area. Just when they thought themselves safe, the storm having died, the boom of a cannon brought them face to face with Barbary pirates.

The pendant sent them by the Dey to insure their safe journey had been ripped away in the storm, and they were under attack by two ships. There was no choice but to fight. Skye's men were delighted. Laughingly they broke out the weapons and turned with relish to meet the enemy. The grappling hooks flew, and the *Seagull* found herself pinioned against a pirate ship. Below decks, her gun crews worked frantically to sink the fast-closing second ship while above deck, Skye, sword in hand, led her men in defense of her ship.

Horrified, admiring her courage but scared to death for her, Lord Burke grabbed his own sword, but MacGuire held him back. "She's doing fine, laddie. Stay with me. You go to her now, and she'll be more concerned for your safety than for her ship's. She doesn't need you. If she does we'll go, but for now we'll just defend this area from the mangy infidels." And clay pipe still clenched between his teeth, he leaped forward to engage a burly, bearded, turbaned ruffian who was attempting to gain the quarterdeck. Knowing MacGuire was right, Niall joined in the fight to keep the quarterdeck free.

The *Seagull's* gun crew succeeded in sinking the second enemy ship, and a great shout of triumph went up from the O'Malley men. With renewed vigor they began to force the invaders from their decks and off their ship. The grappling hooks were disengaged and, slowly, a border of water began to appear between the two ships. The pirates fled back to their own vessel.

What happened next was never quite clear in the minds of the sailors who lived through it. A freak wave—a remnant of the recent storm—hit the ship sharply, broadside, and Niall Burke found himself pitched overboard into the sea. He heard Skye scream his name, and then Inis hit the water near him and swam to his side. He could see a boat being quickly lowered, and he knew it would be only a matter of minutes before he and the dog were safely back aboard the *Seagull.*

On the ship above, Skye raved in a manner previously unknown to her crew. "Jesu! Jesu! You idiots, hurry! Lower the boat before he drowns! If either he or the dog is drowned I'll keelhaul the lot of you all the way back to Ireland!"

The boat hit the water and was swiftly rowed toward Lord Burke and Inis, both of whom were treading water. Skye leaned from the quarterdeck, frantically directing the rescue. In the foaming sea Niall's dark head bobbed next to Inis' silvery black one. Intent on the rescue, they all forgot about the pirates. The pirate captain and his crew had been staring, amazed, and now the captain nodded to one of his seaman.

The pirate was swung swiftly across the gap between the two ships. Grasping Skye firmly about the waist, the man lifted her from the deck of the *Seagull,* and the two of them swung back to the pirate ship.

She turned on him with a shriek of fury, nails clawing, but her captor laughed, his teeth white against his tanned face and black beard. As she struggled with the man, she heard her own crew shouting, but the pirates were now breaking out muskets and shooting down into the water in an attempt to hinder the rescue of Lord Burke. The rescue boat finally reached Niall, and he and the dog were hauled into it.

"Thank God," sobbed Skye. She heard Niall call her name and, taking her captor unawares for a moment, she fought free and shrieked, "Niall! Niall!"

He stood up in the boat and shouted desperately, "We're coming, beloved! We're coming to get you!"

There was a sharp crack of a musket, and a bright blossom of scarlet burst from Lord Burke's chest. Skye stared in horror, then screamed endlessly as she watched him fall into the little boat. "I've killed him! Oh, sweet Christ! I've killed him!" And with a moan of anguish she slid down into the darkness that rose to free her of her pain.

PART II

ALGIERS

Chapter 8

THE GARDEN OF KHALID EL BEY HAD BEEN DESIGNED TO BE A haven of perfect peace. Rectangular in shape, it lay directly behind the Bey's villa, a two-story marble building high atop the city of Algiers. The view from both garden and villa was magnificent, allowing a panoramic vista of the city below with its recently built Turkish fort—called the Casbah—and the blue Mediterranean lapping at its feet.

There were orange and lemon trees in the garden as well as tall, full pines, and roses of every imaginable color. A T-shaped pool, its longer bar interspersed with spraying fountains, ran the length of the garden. The paths held carefully raked light gravel, and small white marble benches were placed at intervals along them. There were three distinct sounds in the garden of Khalid el Bey. The tinkling of fountains, bird songs, and the murmur of the breeze in the pines. Occasionally, the buzzing of a bee intruded itself.

The only human inhabitant of the garden at this moment was a beautiful young woman who lay dozing on a portable chaise longue. She wore a simple pale-blue caftan, and her slim feet were shod in gold leather sandals. Her skin was very fair with the faintest blush of pink on her cheeks, her eyelids softly shadowed in blue kohl. Her thick blue-black hair lay curling in gentle disarray about her shoulders.

Khalid el Bey, who had come into the garden from the villa, stood silently watching the woman. He was a tall man in early middle years, his dark hair just beginning to silver slightly at the sides. His skin bore a faint golden tint, which set off his short, black beard. His amber-gold eyes were fringed in long, thick, dark lashes, unusual in a man but most attractive. Khalid el Bey was neither fat nor thin, but possessed a firm, well-muscled body which he exercised regularly. His face was oval, the eyes set well apart, the nose long and aristocratic, the lips thin but still sensuous.

Now, as he stood gazing quietly down on the lovely woman in his garden, he knew that his instincts had been correct. She was indeed a great beauty—though when she had been brought to him two months before, one would not have known it. She had been thin then, her hair matted and lank. And she had been suffering from shock. Still, he had seen a valuable jewel beneath the filth, and despite Yasmin's objections had bought her for his House of Felicity.

She had healed slowly. He himself had spooned nourishing chicken broth between her cracked lips during that first week. His gentleness had communicated itself to her, and it was to him that she first spoke.

"Who are you?"

"My name is Khalid el Bey."

"Where am I?"

"You are at my house in the city of Algiers."

She became silent again. After a moment she ventured, "How came I here?"

"You were brought to me by Capitan Rais el Abdul. Tell me now, my beauty, what is *your* name?"

"My name is Skye," she answered him.

"And where do *you* come from?" he probed.

Her enormous sapphire-blue eyes seemed bewildered, then filled with tears. "I don't know," she sobbed, "I don't know where I come from. Surely this Capitan Rais el Abdul must know."

Khalid el Bey shook his head. "No. You were transferred to his ship from another. The first vessel was just going out on a voyage and hailed the Capitan, who was homeward bound." Then seeing the fear in her eyes he spoke soothingly. "Do not be frightened, beautiful Skye, I am sure your memory will return soon. We know you are European, for we are speaking French, though your accent is not that of a native Frenchwoman. Rest now. We will talk again."

But her memory still had not returned. His Moorish physician had examined her throughly. Her age was between eighteen and twenty. She was not a virgin. In fact, she had borne more than one child. She was free of disease, and had all her teeth. Because the physician could find no evidence of a head injury, he concluded that the memory loss was due to some terrible emotional shock, and that her mind refused to remember.

Her beautiful blue eyes, which changed from sapphire to blue-green as her moods changed, opened now and looked at him.

"My lord Khalid."

He smiled. "How are you feeling, my beautiful one?" Sitting down beside her, he caressed her dark hair.

"I am ever so much better, my lord."

"We must talk now, Skye."

"Of what, my lord?"

"You know that my name is Khalid el Bey. But I have another name, Skye. I am called the Whoremaster of Algiers. I own many houses filled with beautiful women whose very reason for existence is to please the men who come to visit them. I own the women—as I own you."

"You do?!" She was incredulous. "You own me?"

"Yes, Capitan Rais el Abdul bought you from the first Capitan, and then he sold you to me."

"Why did you buy me?"

He smiled. Her memory loss had affected so many areas, including her knowledge of worldly things. "I bought you, Skye, because I intend to train you to be the finest courtesan Algiers has ever known. Then I will place you in my best house, which is called Felicity."

"What must I do, my lord?"

"Do you remember nothing of lovemaking?" She shook her head. He sighed. "I will have to have Yasmin instruct you in certain matters. Then I will personally instruct you. We will begin tomorrow, for the doctor has assured me that you are well enough."

"Yasmin does not like me, my lord Khalid."

"Yasmin is a slave, like you, Skye. She will do as she is told. If she should distress you in any way you will tell me."

"Yes, my lord Khalid. And thank you," she said softly. "I will endeavor to learn well so you will be pleased."

He mused later on her answer. If, as he suspected, she was a highborn European, then she was also a Christian. Yet the loss of memory had left her free of both her religion and its ethics. If he could introduce her to the physical delights of lovemaking and make it pleasant for her, he could make her the most famous courtesan since Aspasia. It was a magnificent challenge, and one he was looking forward to with great enthusiasm.

That evening when Khalid el Bey had finished his meal, he dismissed his slaves and, giving orders to his majordomo regarding his bed partner of the evening, welcomed the woman who oversaw his most famous brothel. When Yasmin sat opposite him he marveled at her beauty. He knew she was close to forty. Still, she was a Circassian, and they were famed as the most beautiful slaves in the world. He had purchased her over twenty years before from a breeding farm. She had been the first of his special women. Thanks to her, he had been able to place his business above his competitors.

Brothels in Algiers, for the most part, had been confined to the waterfront and served sailors of all nations. The wealthy residents of the city had private harems, and needed no such services. But the flesh peddlers of the city had overlooked one important market. Algiers, being the chief city on the north African coast, entertained many wealthy visitors. These had no women available to them. Khalid el Bey was the first to meet that need, and he became famous doing so.

The women in his House of Felicity were the most beautiful, the most skilled, and the most entertaining in all of Algiers. There were no two alike, for Khalid el Bey especially prided himself on offering variety. Though others had tried to imitate him, they had all failed miserably, leaving him with the undisputed title of "the Whoremaster." Not only did he own the House of Felicity, he now also possessed full or part interest in almost every house of prostitution in the city.

He was admired and respected by the other businessmen for, though very shrewd, he was scrupulously honest. Still, few men really knew the man, and his origins were a mystery. Though many thought him a Moor, he was actually Spanish. He had been born Diego Indio Goya del Fuentes near the city of Granada, the second son of an old and noble family. He was well educated for his time, and might have gone on to marry and lead the circumspect life of a sixteenth-century Spanish nobleman. Then fate, in the guise of a beautiful Moorish girl named Noor, had intervened in the young man's life. They had been desperately in love, but Noor had been as firm in her faith, Islam, as any devout Christian was in his.

Diego Goya del Fuentes had long been betrothed. Now his sisters took malicious delight in teasing his fiancée about Noor. The fiancée, a prim, religious girl, felt it her moral duty to inform the Inquisition of the existence of the Moorish maiden. On the day that Noor was burned at the stake as a heretic, Diego stood helpless on the edge of the city square, his hooded face wet with tears, watching as the gentlest, kindest person he had ever known was burned to death. She was tortured cruelly, yet as the flames licked her graceful body, her sweet voice lifted in a song of praise to her god, Allah. That day, Diego Goya del Fuentes disappeared from Spain forever.

He wandered for several years through Europe and the Middle East, finally settling in the city of Algiers. He changed his name to Khalid, the title "el Bey" being his by virtue of a journey to the holy cities of Mecca and Medina. He converted to Islam in honor of Noor's memory, though he felt no strong religious leaning.

His feelings for women were ambiguous. On one hand, he remembered his lost love and her gentle sweet ways. On the other, he recalled his sisters' malice, and the cruelty and ignorance of his fiancée. Perhaps this explained why, though he enslaved women into the profession of prostitution, he was a kind and good master.

Skye had touched him as no woman had since Noor. Her helplessness appealed to him, and this was why he now carefully instructed Yasmin about her care. But Yasmin argued, "Why do you fuss so over this one girl, my lord? She is like a thousand others." The Circassian's voice was spiteful, and Khalid el Bey hid a smile. Yasmin had been in love with him for years but he felt no more for her than he had for the others. No woman had claimed his heart since Noor.

"Skye is like a child now," he explained patiently. "Although she recalls some things, her loss of memory has wiped out all carnal knowledge. She knows nothing and has no prejudices. If we handle her carefully, we may mold her as we desire." He cleverly emphasized the *we,* and Yasmin leaned forward eagerly.

"This would really please you, my lord?"

"Yes, Yasmin, it would. Skye is not simply a pretty face or body. I sense a good mind behind those lovely blue eyes, and that is what her specialty shall be. Like the courtesans of ancient Athens, Skye shall entertain the gentlemen with a skilled body and with her intelligence as well. She will not be used for those of our clientele whose tastes run to the bizarre, but rather for elegant men, men of culture—such as the Ottoman commandant of the Casbah. Or perhaps the sea captains who come to us from the Italian states, France, or England. Together, Yasmin, you and I will make Skye an intriguing, exciting, much-sought-after woman."

"I will do my part, my lord Khalid. I will teach her all I know. Even certain things I have kept from the others. Skye shall be unique, and she shall be perfection."

He smiled his wonderful smile at her. "You have always exceeded my faith in you, since the very beginning, Yasmin. Thank you." He twice clapped his hands sharply, then sent the answering slave for coffee. Turning back to the woman, he asked, "The women now in the House of Felicity are satisfactory?"

"Except two. The English girl, Sweet Rose, has fallen in love with one of her gentlemen, and consequently is balking at her job. With your permission I can correct that, for the gentleman involved wants to buy her and add her to his harem."

"Sell, but accept only the highest price for her. After all, we're losing a good investment. What of the other girl?"

"The gypsy Rhia is not adjusting, my lord. I think I must recommend severe punishment in her case."

"Why?"

"I sent her along with two other girls to a party of half a dozen young Turkish officers. They had requested they be allowed to play the rape game. We assigned them to the Suite of Clouds. It was arranged that, as the girls sat at their leisure, the Turks would break in and ravish them. It is a harmless game, and the officers involved are regular customers of ours, all highly recommended. While the other two girls fell in with the spirit of the game, shrieking and protesting prettily before yielding, Rhia screamed in earnest and fought wildly, severely scratching two of our guests about the face. Naturally they subdued her, and I am pleased to say that all six of them enjoyed her despite her protests. But the other girls, of course, felt slighted. They were angry that she should draw all the attention to herself in such a fashion. The officers complained, too, that afterward she wept as one demented. I finally had to remove her from their presence, and send in another girl."

"Has she ever before partaken of this sort of fantasy, Yasmin?"

"No. She was, of course, half wild when she came to us. But she's been treated well and has done very well with the gentlemen individually. I believed her ready for this sort of thing."

"What is her specialty?"

"Oral gratification, my lord, and I understand she is quite good at it."

Khalid el Bey thought a moment. "She was probably raped sometime in her life. The fantasy in which you placed her brought back the memory and hence her terror. Do not put her in such a situation again. Let her do what she is good at."

"You are too soft, my lord. Rhia offended our guests. When they ask, what shall I tell them has been done?"

"Do not wait for them to ask. Send a message to the two who were scratched that the matter has been taken care of, and offer them each an evening of pleasure at our expense."

"It shall be as my lord has said," answered Yasmin.

Khalid el Bey rose from the cushions and helped the Circassian to rise. "You must return now, I know," he said quietly, gently dismissing her. "You will come tomorrow and begin your instruction of Skye."

"As my lord commands," she said, bowing out of the room.

He almost sighed his relief. She was beautiful and loyal, but of late she had become clinging and presumptuous of their long association. He wasn't quite sure what he would do about her. To free her would only give her ideas above her situation, for she was a slave, born of slave parents. He smiled, thinking back to those many years ago when he had gone to a Circassian breeding farm with an Egyptian friend. His friend was a slave merchant in Alexandria, a connoisseur of beautiful young men and women, who preferred buying directly from the breeder so he might have the best selection.

The owners of the farm had paraded before their valued customer and his guest a variety of exquisite virgins and youths. Yasmin had been among them, and Khalid's friend remarked on her, saying that they had shown her to him in his two previous visits.

"Alas," sighed their host, "she is lovelier than an April morning, but I cannot seem to sell her. I have just about decided to breed her with our best stud."

"What are her bloodlines?" asked Khalid's friend.

"Pythias out of Iris," came the reply.

"Whew!" exclaimed the Alexandrian admiringly.

Khalid el Bey had no idea what they were talking about, but there was something touching about the little slave girl. "What is her age?" he asked.

"Fifteen," came the reply.

"A bit old. Is she a virgin?"

"Sir!" The farm owner was indignant.

Khalid el Bey laughed. "I will take her, my friend. I simply wish to know what it is I am buying."

An outrageous price was named which Khalid el Bey scoffed at, reminding the slave breeder of the girl's age and the possibility of her being barren if he bred her rather than sold her. They haggled back and forth until finally a price was agreed upon that suited Khalid el Bey but, according to the merchant, impoverished him. The money was exchanged, and Khalid el Bey found himself the owner of a beautiful Circassian slave girl with long blond hair and Nile green eyes.

When they returned to Alexandria he set about introducing her to the joys of physical love. She had been taught its many arts but had never used them. She knew the human body and its sensitive areas well. Her skillful fingers could bring an impotent man to a firm and long-lasting erection. She could sing while accompanying herself on the lute. She danced well. And after several weeks in Khalid el Bey's bed, she found that she performed very well there too.

Then one night Khalid el Bey had several guests in for the evening, and when the meal was done she danced for the company. Afterward he sent her to her room, telling her that perhaps one or two of his guests might visit her and if they did she was to please them for that would please him. In fact four of Khalid el Bey's guests came to her spacious quarters that night, and with each she was soft and charming and skilled. They left singing her praises, and Khalid el Bey rewarded his slave girl with a strand of coral beads. The next night and the night after and almost every other night after that, Yasmin pleasured her master's friends. Then another girl, Alyia, joined their household. Where Yasmin was fair, Alyia had skin like a dusky rose, thick and waving hair the color of a raven's wing, enormous brown eyes, and a pouting red mouth. To Yasmin's fury, Alyia shared their master's bed for several weeks. But then she too joined the Circassian in entertaining Khalid el Bey's friends.

Several months later, Khalid el Bey left his two women in the hands of his friend, the slave merchant. He made a quick trip, and returned several weeks later with two more girls. He moved them all to the city of Algiers.

They were installed in a small, beautifully appointed house, and every night Khalid el Bey's women entertained a variety of guests ranging from wealthy visitors to Turkish officers of the Imperial Ottoman Army who were stationed in Algiers. Within a year Khalid el Bey owned twenty beautiful women and a larger house. At the end of two years he owned fifty beautiful women who lived in two houses, and he had begun the construction of his present villa.

When the third year drew to a close the villa was finished, and Khalid el Bey was the undisputed Whoremaster of Algiers. Two things were constant. Yasmin remained the head of Khalid el Bey's women, gradually becoming less of a courtesan and more of an administrator and manager. And, there was not a girl who entered Khalid el Bey's service who was not first tried by him. It gave each of them a close touch with their master, for during the time they served him personally he loved and cherished them. He had never used force to bend a women to his will. Consequently his women all adored him.

With Skye he saw his greatest challenge. With the proper training she could become the finest whore he'd ever owned. Unlike the others, who all cherished the secret dream of being bought and married by one of their customers, Skye would have no such hopes as she had no knowledge of marriage. And if, as he hoped, she proved totally uninhibited, she could be taught some more exotic forms of lovemaking that would command a very high price.

The more he thought of her the more curious he became. Many times he had observed her secretly in the bath and in her bedchamber. Her figure was as lovely as her coloring, but it was her skin that intrigued him. It was flawless. Utterly flawless. Smooth, beautiful skin the color of rich cream, or was it old ivory silk? He longed to touch it with his sensitive fingers, his lips. Would it be soft? Yes, undoubtedly it would be soft. Would it be soft and warm beneath his mouth, or would it be cool and smooth? He shivered in anticipation. Although he enjoyed his women, it had been a long time since he had actually looked forward to one, and it would be several weeks until he could even consider sampling Skye's charms. He sighed, and went to his bedchamber. Perhaps the little houri who was to be his partner tonight could ease some of his longings.

At midmorning on the following day Yasmin began Skye's lessons in love. She looked with dislike on the young woman she intuitively knew to be the most serious rival she had ever had for Khalid's affections. Still, she reasoned, the sooner Skye was taught what she needed to know, the sooner she'd be out of Khalid's villa. And Skye must be taught well, for then Khalid would be pleased.

"Disrobe for me," commanded Yasmin, and when Skye quickly complied, her caftan dropping to the floor, Yasmin scolded, "No! No! You show all the sensuousness of a donkey! Let me show you." And her fingers undid the frog closings on her pink caftan as gracefully as if she'd been playing a musical instrument. Turning, she gently shrugged the garment from her shoulders, exposing her smooth fair skin. Slowly, slowly, she allowed the garment to slide downward, revealing the line of her back, her plump round buttocks, her legs. Then she turned to face Skye. Her breasts were big, but firm. Sliding to her knees, her head bent to touch the floor and she murmured huskily, "As my lord commands."

Then suddenly Yasmin stood up briskly and said matter-of-factly, "That is how to disrobe properly. You try it."

Quietly Skye picked up her robe and dressed. Then, imitating exactly and with equal skill Yasmin's movements, she removed the caftan again. Sinking to the floor at last, her dark head bowed, her soft voice clear and sweet, she said, "Is that what you want?"

"Yes," came the terse reply. "It is fortunate you learn quickly.

"We will now discuss perfumes. Sit down. No, don't bother dressing. I must show you the proper places to anoint yourself. A woman's body is a work of art, but in order to remain a masterpiece you must work at it constantly." She reached into the basket by her side and then handed Skye some green leaves. "Mint. Chew them. Your breath should always be fragrant and your teeth clean. All of our women are perfection. That is what makes them famous, and justly so. We are not common street trulls to be had for a few sequins." Yasmin carefully laid out several bottles on the carpet. "Musk, ambergris, attar of roses. All of our perfumes have one of these as a base." She uncorked them and held each out so Skye might smell. "Which do you prefer?"

"The roses."

"Good! I would have chosen that one for you myself. Though my lord Khalid tells me that you are not a virgin, there is an air of innocence about you that we will concentrate upon. It appeals to many men. I will use the attar of roses to demonstrate." She stood up and, taking the stopper between her thumb and forefinger, stroked it generously between the deep valley of her breasts. Carefully lifting each of the heavy globes, she perfumed beneath them. Next the stopper touched the base of her throat, the back of her neck, the soft spots behind her ears. Then came her wrists, beneath her arms, and in the blue-veined hollows of her inner arm. Yasmin dipped the stopper again and touched it to her navel, the backs of her legs, her ankles, the arches of her feet, and her Venus mound. "You must go lightly here," she explained, "for men sometimes enjoy the sweet taste of a woman, and that should not be overwhelmed by another scent."

Skye appeared puzzled, and Yasmin gazed at her enviously. "You really don't remember, do you?" she said. "Allah, how I envy you! It will be like the first time again for you, but without the pain of virginity." Then catching herself, she handed Skye the attar of roses and said brusquely, "Let me see you do it now."

Carefully Skye imitated her teacher, and when she had finished she looked expectantly toward Yasmin.

"You have forgotten one area," said Yasmin, taking the bottle stopper from her student. Cupping one of Skye's breasts, she dotted the scent beneath it.

"Don't!"

To the older woman's surprise, Skye's face was drained of color, her body stiff. Her eyes held horror. Yasmin was genuinely frightened. "What is it, Skye?! Are you all right?"

Slowly the fear drained from the younger woman's eyes, and she said, bewildered, "I don't believe I like being touched by another woman."

"What do you remember, Skye?"

"Nothing. I remember nothing, but when you touched me . . ." She shivered with genuine revulsion.

Yasmin was concerned. What if Skye didn't like being touched by men either? She could hardly be a successful whore then, and Khalid el Bey's investment would be lost. Normally Yasmin would not have introduced the subject of male anatomy until a later lesson, but she felt she must know before she went any further. If the girl was emotionally unstable she should be disposed of now. Yasmin clapped her hands and said to the answering slave girl, "Fetch my new eunuch, Ali."

Then, turning to Skye, she said, "There are two ways to geld a male. If it is done when they are young, all is removed. But the mortality rate is high. The other way is to remove the male's seed sac, but leave the rod. We buy only that kind of eunuch, for they are better-natured. They are also invaluable in teaching our girls the things they must learn about a man's body. Ah, Ali, come in! Come in! Skye, this is Ali. Is he not beautiful?"

The young man flushed. Skye let her eyes slide over him. He was indeed good-looking, tall, with softly golden skin, dark curly hair, and liquid brown eyes. "He is gorgeous, Yasmin. You are indeed fortunate."

Yasmin smiled smugly, then said sharply to the man, "Ali, disrobe!" She looked quickly to see the effect this would have on Skye. Would she faint? Was she fearful? The eunuch undid his long robe and, removing it, laid it carefully on a chair. Then he stood straight, awaiting further instruction. Yasmin glanced toward Skye. "What do you think of him?"

The younger woman looked puzzled. "As I have said, Yasmin, he is gorgeous."

"His nakedness does not offend you, or frighten you?"

"No, should it?"

"No, but some women are fearful nonetheless. Now, Skye, I want you to go to Ali, put your arms about him, and press your body to his."

Skye did as Yasmin commanded, sliding her arms around the eunuch's neck, rubbing instinctively in a very provocative way against the young man's soft body. He shuddered, nuzzled her ear, squeezed one of her buttocks, then cupped a breast in his hand. Her eyes grew dark with desire, and she swayed slightly.

"Mistress!" Ali's voice was pleading, and Yasmin laughed. She had learned what she needed to know. Skye might dislike a woman's touch but she enjoyed a man's. The lessons could continue. Without giving Ali another thought, she dismissed him. He fled, gathering his robe.

"What a funny creature," Skye observed. "Didn't he like me?"

Yasmin laughed again. "He liked you very much, and had you been alone he might have made love to you. I will allow him to do so when you have more knowledge. We use these young eunuchs for that purpose, as we can hardly practice technique on our gentlemen." She looked candidly at Skye. "You're a good student, but that is all we will do today. I will come tomorrow at the same time."

After Yasmin had dressed and gone, Skye sat quietly for a few minutes. Then her hands crept upward to cup her own breasts. Gently she caressed her body and was amazed to see her nipples harden. She thought about what it would be like to have a man stroke her, and felt a tingling between her legs. It was all so pleasurable. What other lovely things had her cursed memory wiped away? Sighing, she stretched naked on the cushions and fell asleep.

That evening Khalid el Bey sent for Skye. She was fresh from the baths and had just finished perfuming herself. Sliding a lightweight wisteria-colored silk caftan over her body, she ran barefoot through the short, carpeted hallway that separated her room from his apartments.

"How lovely you are!" he said as she entered the room. He noted the sheen of her skin and the way her midnight-colored hair curled in damp tendrils about her face. "Yasmin tells me your lessons went well. She feels you have a talent and will progress quickly. She is pleased with you, and therefore I am pleased."

Her face became radiant."I want to please you, my lord Khalid! Without you I should be nothing."

His big hand cupped her chin, and his dark eyes looked into her blue ones."I do not think so, my little lost bird. I do not think so."Then smiling, he asked gently,"What have you learned?"

"Just perfuming, and the proper way to disrobe before a gentleman."

"Disrobe for me," he commanded, sitting cross-legged amid the colorful cushions."Pretend I am to be your gentleman."

She stood very still before him. Her fingers hardly seemed to touch the tiny pearl buttons of her robe before it opened. He had not but the barest glimpse of her breasts when she twirled gracefully. The silken robe slid with agonizing slowness down the long line of her back and over the perfect twin moons of her buttocks. She turned to face him, her eyes modestly lowered. Sinking to the floor, she said softly but clearly,"As my lord commands."

For a moment he stared at the gleaming dark head that touched his slipper. He was amazed not only by her easy skill, but by his own reaction to it. Beneath his brocaded robe he was swollen and aching, and he couldn't quite believe it. He had always maintained a perfect control over his body.

She raised her head, and their eyes met. "Do I please you, my lord?" she asked innocently.

"Very much," he murmured huskily. Don't! Don't! his saner self warned him, but he heard himself saying, "Sit next to me, Skye." And when she nestled in the curve of his arm he bent over her and touched her lips. They parted easily beneath his, and he drew her scented breath into his own mouth. His tongue sought for hers, found it and they caressed one another with burning softness until he became aware of her hands seeking his, and placing them on her naked body.

"Touch me, my lord Khalid!" she whispered urgently. "*Please, please* touch me!"

Fighting to control himself, he allowed his hands to slide over her body. He had never felt such a desire in himself for any woman. Her skin was softer than anything he had ever known, and when she moaned with undisguised pleasure he trembled. He slipped his own robe off. You must not! She is unschooled! You will ruin everything! warned his saner self, but his lips slid down the pure pillar of her throat, and his hungry mouth captured a taut nipple, sucking passionately on it until, with an angry half-cry of desperation, he yielded to his own desires.

Swinging himself over her burning body, he impatiently parted her thighs and thrust himself into the welcoming warmth of her. She sighed and with a deeply rooted feminine instinct, she wrapped herself about him and moved her lush body to match his frantic rhythm. Her slender fingers slid down his long, smooth back, kneading his muscled buttocks until he whimpered with pleasure. Within her own body she felt a tingling tenseness that built with unbelievable intensity until, cresting, it burst over her like a giant wave lifting her high and then dashing her down into a swirling darkness.

"Skye! Skye! Ah, my beautiful beloved," he murmured against her ear. He caressed her gently.

"I did not remember until now how beautiful making love could be," she whispered.

"Do you remember anything else?" he questioned hastily.

"No. Only that I have done before what we just did, and that it was good."

"I should not have taken you," he said. "What if I had frightened you?"

"You did not frighten me, my lord Khalid, but perhaps I displeased you with my lack of skill."

He laughed weakly. "No, Skye, you did not displease me. It is true you lack the skill of a trained courtesan, but this same lack of skills has given me a very pleasurable time."

"Must I continue my lessons with Yasmin, my lord?"

"Yes. Your innocence has charm, my beloved, but there is no harm in your learning our ways. You will learn to pleasure your gentlemen in a variety of ways. It is your duty as a woman to be knowledgeable in the arts of love, and as Yasmin teaches you, you will show me."

She lay on her back breathing quietly and evenly. He lay on his side so he might gaze down at her. His fingers traced a delicate pattern down her breasts and torso. Shivering, she raised her blue eyes to him. Bending down, he kissed her mouth with great tenderness, then her eyelids. "Go to sleep, Skye, and sleep in the knowledge that I will watch over you."

Her eyes closed. He again wondered who she was and where she had come from. A noblewoman without a doubt, but from where? Her coloring ruled out the far north, and he did not believe her to be either Spanish or French. When she had first regained consciousness he had spoken to her in French and she had answered him, but he knew her accent was not native to France.

Could she be English, or one of the Celtic races? Unless she regained her memory, they were unlikely ever to know.

Khalid el Bey was not sure he wanted to know. Somehow this beautiful creature had insinuated herself into his heart. It had been a long, long time since he had felt more than just sexual satisfaction with a woman, but with Skye he suddenly felt something he had long believed himself immune to. That feeling was a longing for a real home, and it took a wife and children to make such a home.

He smiled at his fantasies. Surely he was getting old, for the first sign of age in a man like him was the longing for rest. He gazed again at the woman by his side. Was it possible? Did he really love her? What if he married her, and she later regained her memory? But that was unlikely. She would not regain her memory, or so his physician said, unless faced with the very thing that had shocked her in the first place.

Still, he would not move swiftly. He would allow Skye to continue her lessons. It could do no harm. And later he would make a decision about their future. He closed his eyes, sighed, and fell asleep.

Chapter 9

Yasmin was shocked. "You took an unskilled woman to your bed? What on earth possessed you, my lord Khalid?"

He turned on her. "You presume on our long association, Yasmin. Skye belongs to me, and I will do with her as I choose. I do not need your approval."

"I only meant—"

"You are an insolent slave," he said cuttingly. "I have rarely found it necessary to use the whip, but you tempt me now, Yasmin. You tempt me greatly."

She had gone very white. Flinging herself to the floor, she implored his forgiveness. "Get up," came the cold reply. "You will continue Skye's lessons, Yasmin, and if I should ever hear of your mistreating her in any way, I will sell you. Go now!"

The Circassian scrambled to her feet and fled the room. Her heart was thundering. In all their years together he had never spoken to her that way. Yasmin was deeply frightened. Was he in love? Allah forbid! The worm of jealousy gnawed at her heart, and Yasmin began to hate the woman called Skye with an impotent fury.

She dared not act openly against her yet, but once Khalid sent Skye into the House of Felicity, she would be at Yasmin's mercy. Yasmin thought with pleasure of a Syrian merchant who visited them twice yearly, and whose delight was in watching two women perform before he took them both. Knowing Skye's revulsion at another woman's touch, Yasmin intended to punish her by forcing her to participate in such a show. For now, however, Yasmin would bide her time.

She smiled at Skye as she entered her room and bid her good day. "Today," she said, "we will review yesterday's lessons, and go on to the study of anatomy, both male and female."

Skye nodded. Annoyed by her poise, Yasmin sought to shock her. "Tomorrow I will bring a girl from the House of Felicity with me, and she and Ali will begin to demonstrate to you the various positions of love." She stared hard at the younger woman.

"That should be very interesting," replied Skye with infuriating calm. "I would learn quickly and well so I may please my lord Khalid."

Yasmin had to bite her lip to keep from shrieking. Skye's lack of emotion was totally unnerving. Would she be one of those cold creatures who felt nothing at the height of passion? If that was the case then she would have to be taught to simulate emotion, for nothing frustrated or angered a man more than an unresponsive female. Yasmin realized that it might be harder to train Skye than she had previously thought. But train her she would, and when she was through Skye would be the most magnificent creature ever to grace the House of Felicity. Then Khalid would realize Yasmin's great value to him, and finally make her his first wife. She had waited so long for an opportunity like this, doing his bidding unquestioningly all these years, seeing to his interests.

Catching herself, she ceased daydreaming, called for her eunuch, Ali, and threw off her silken robe. "A thorough knowledge of both the male and female body is essential, Skye," said the naked Yasmin. "With small-breasted women such as yourself, the breasts are usually very sensitive, and most women are highly sensitive on the little button that lies hidden beneath the Venus mound. Demonstrate, Ali!"

Yasmin lay among the pillows, the young eunuch propped on his side next to her. Fascinated, Skye watched as he caressed the soft globes of Yasmin's breasts, using both his hands and his mouth. He worked slowly and as Yasmin's breasts became harder and firmer, a small moan escaped her. Ali shot Skye a small triumphant smile, which his partner missed. One hand moved lower to Yasmin's Venus mound. A finger probed delicately, rubbing gently, and another soft cry escaped the writhing woman.

Ali bent his head to touch with his tongue where his finger had lately been. The woman beneath him cried aloud her passion, and suddenly Skye closed her eyes and shuddered. In her mind's eye she saw a blond man and a blond woman intertwined together on a bed. It was evil! Her mind strained to remember, but she could not quite do so, and then a shriek of pleasure from Yasmin brought her back to the scene before her.

The older woman lay panting, her lush body covered with a fine sheen of perspiration. The eunuch lay on his back, his eyes closed. Gradually Yasmin regained her composure. Finally she spoke. "You have now seen one way in which a woman's body can give pleasure and be pleasured, though of course it is more important that you give pleasure. I will demonstrate that shortly, but first I want Ali to caress you as he has just caressed me. It is necessary that I see how you react in such a situation. Exchange places with me."

For the second time Skye felt uncomfortable. When Khalid el Bey had made love to her the other night it had been right, but she didn't want the sly Ali with his obviously knowing hands and mouth touching her, and with sudden defiance she said so. Startled at first, Yasmin was speechless, but she quickly regained her voice.

"I did not ask you whether you wished to do this thing. I have commanded you to obey me. How dare you even contemplate disobeying me? Our lord Khalid has put you in my charge, and if you disobey me I shall have you beaten."

"You do not dare to mark me," shot back Skye. "You are a slave as I am, and my lord Khalid would punish you greatly should you destroy my value!"

Yasmin smiled nastily. "It will not destroy your beauty should I have Ali beat the soles of your feet. The bastinado is an extremely painful but effective punishment for fractious slaves."

Skye paled, but said evenly, "I will not allow that creature of yours to touch me, and if you hurt me I shall tell my lord Khalid of your cruelty."

"What cruelty do you speak of, my lovely Skye?" Khalid el Bey stood in the door a moment before entering it. With inborn instinct Skye flung herself into his arms. "I won't do it, my lord! Please don't make me! Please!" His eyes softened, his arms tightened protectively about her, and he dropped a kiss on the top of her dark head.

Yasmin made an exasperated noise. "You tell me to train her in the arts of love, and when she will not obey me you condone it!"

"I will not allow Ali to touch me in *that* way!"

"I cannot gauge your sensuality if I cannot see it!"

Khalid el Bey hid a smile and said to Skye, "Will you allow me to caress you so Yasmin may learn what she needs to know?"

"Yes." It was said softly. Without another word he slid her caftan from her body and drew her down amid the cushions. His hands were incredibly gentle as they cupped and caressed her sweetly rounded little breasts, and she sighed with delight as he teasingly skimmed the soft, smooth skin with his skilled fingers. A warm hand fondled her belly and slid downward to touch that most sensitive of spots. She cried out her pleasure, and his mouth quickly covered hers in a burning kiss. As the pleasure faded slowly away, she opened her eyes to find him staring down at her, a strangely tender expression lighting his amber eyes. Then he turned his head, and she was struck by the hawklike beauty of his profile.

"Do you know now what you must, Yasmin?"

The older woman was very still, her green eyes huge and almost black in her pale face.

"She responds well to a man's touch, does she not, Yasmin?"

"To your touch, my lord Khalid," came the reply.

"From this moment on, Yasmin, you will not force Skye to anything she chooses not to do. You will teach her all you know, and she will practice her skills on me alone. Only I will correct or chastise her. Do you understand?"

"Yes, my lord." The woman shot Skye a look of pure hatred.

"Then that will be all for today." Yasmin and Ali were dismissed. Khalid stood up and, holding out his hand to Skye, said, "Dress yourself, my sweet. In the garden there is a rose called 'Love's Delight' that has just come into bloom today. I would show it to you."

They were alone. Skye drew on her caftan slowly. She slipped on her sandals. His deep voice cut the silence surrounding them. "What was it about your lessons today that disturbed you, my Skye?"

"When I saw Ali making love to Yasmin," she said, "I became uncomfortable, my lord. It was as if I had seen . . . something like that before, and it was evil. Yet I could not *really* remember. It frightened me. The eunuch, despite his state, was so sure of his power over Yasmin. He smiled at me in such an arrogant way, and I knew then that I could not bear it if he touched me. Have I displeased you, my lord Khalid?"

He put an arm about her. "No, Skye, you have not displeased me. Whatever you may have been in your former life, you were certainly not a wanton, and that pleases me. I think, perhaps, that I shall have to change my plans for you. Come now, and see the roses."

"You will not send me away?" Her voice was frightened.

"No," he held her by the shoulders and looked down into her upturned face. "I shall not send you away, my little lost love." And again she was puzzled by the tender look in his eyes.

Alone in the night, Khalid el Bey paced the rooftop terrace of his house. The sky above was black silk, relieved only by the crystal blue stars. The air was still, yet it was perfumed by the sweet scent of night-blooming nicotiana. It had become obvious to him that he couldn't make Skye a courtesan. Though her memory was buried, a strong moral sense remained. He would send a note to Yasmin tomorrow morning, stopping Skye's lessons. Whatever he felt she needed to learn he would teach her himself.

He had to admit to himself now that he was in love with Skye. Her revulsion toward Ali today was only a part of it. The truth was that Khalid el Bey did not want her in the House of Felicity pleasuring a different lover every night. He wanted her in his own house, loving him, and bearing his children. Yes, he loved her enough to honor her by making her his wife. He felt like a boy again, and for the first time since his love for Noor, he felt hope. Perhaps, he thought wryly, there was a god in the heavens, after all. At peace with himself, he descended the steps to his own quarters.

To his surprise, Skye was asleep on the cushions by his couch. For a brief moment he watched her, then he bent and dropped a kiss on her cheek. She stirred, opened her magnificent sapphire eyes, and sat up.

"I am afraid," she said in a rush, "I have angered you. And if you send me away—" she stopped, trying to gather her thoughts. "You are all I have, my lord Khalid. I remember nothing before you, and if you send me away I shall die!"

Tenderly he gathered her into his arms. "I have spent many hours alone with the night, my sweet Skye, and I have realized something. I have decided that there is only one fate for you." She trembled against him, and he stroked her reassuringly. "Your fate is to be my wife, beloved. I will love you, care for you, and protect you, my Skye. I have never before wanted a wife, and it has been many years since I really loved a woman. It has been my custom to make love, but not give my heart. Do you understand the difference?"

"Yes," she whispered. "You enjoyed their bodies, but not necessarily the women themselves."

He smiled in the semidarkness of the room. "You are wise, my Skye. Now, love, tell me if you are still afraid."

"No."

"And are you pleased with my plans for your future? Will you be happy to be my wife?"

"Yes."

"Sweet Skye, I . . . I love you, and I want you to be happy. If the thought of marriage to me displeases you, you must tell me so, for I would not have you be unhappy."

"You do me great honor," she said softly, "but I am not certain I love you, my lord. Surely you deserve a wife who loves you."

"The love will come, sweetness. I want you safe."

She raised her face to him. "Then gladly shall I be your wife, my lord!" Her blue eyes were shining with trust and even, he thought, a little happiness. "I promise to make you happy," she told him shyly.

"You already make me happy," he told her, and then his mouth sought hers, tasting and giving the sweet sensual delights she seemed to crave from him. His hands caressed the small globes of her breasts, and then his tongue was torturing the pink nipples to a peak of excitement, circling round and round the sweetly sensitive flesh until her breathing became ragged. He lowered her to the cushions and his hands gently spread her thighs. Tenderly he entered her, taking her there on the floor, delighting in her sigh of pleasure as his pulsing shaft thrust deep.

Her soft hands began stroking his back, sliding slowly down its length to cup and fondle his round buttocks. "Khalid! Oh, my Khalid!" she whispered with a hot little breath against his ear. He shivered. "Love me, my lord! Oh, love me well, my lord!" She exhorted him and, catching his rhythm, she moved with him until both of them were lost in the wildly spinning vortex of their shared passion.

So great was the desire they aroused in each other that Skye fainted and Khalid, to his amazement, came close to losing consciousness himself. As his seed thundered into her hidden valley he shook fiercely with the intensity of his passion. Drained, he rolled from her and gathered her into his arms, raining kisses on her beautiful face. "Oh God, I adore you! I adore you!" he murmured over and over again, and as she slowly climbed from the darkness she heard someone's voice worshiping her. "Niall," she murmured softly. "Niall!"

Khalid stiffened. "Skye, sweetness," he said gently, "Skye, open your eyes." And when she obeyed he said, "Who is Niall, my beloved?"

Immediately her eyes became clouded and confused. "Niall?" she asked, puzzled. "I know no Niall."

He sighed. Whoever Niall was, Khalid envied him very much. Skye must have loved Niall. Still—it was he, Khalid, who now possessed her, and he would not lose her, as this Niall had done. "Sleep, my love," he said cradling her against his chest. And slowly her breathing became even and regular.

He lay awake most of the night struggling with himself. Was it possible that she was regaining her memory, or was the outcry just a fluke, never to be repeated? The doctor had said that Skye would not find herself again unless faced with the identical situation that had caused her trauma, and the chances of that happening were so remote as to be impossible. There was no danger of her recovering. He *would* marry her! Was he not entitled to some happiness? He wanted her, and he wanted the children of her loins.

He rose with the first light, and left her sleeping. In his dayroom his body servant lay sleeping before the door. Gently, Khalid nudged him with a slippered foot. When the slave's eyes flew open, Khalid said, "Fetch my secretary immediately. I will be in the library." Stumbling to his feet, the slave hurried off. Drawing his white robe about him, Khalid el Bey went to his library to await the secretary. He arrived a few minutes later, rubbing the sleep from his eyes.

"I am sorry to bring you from your bed so early, Jean, but there are some urgent matters." The secretary nodded, sat, and took up his pen. A French captive, Jean gave thanks for his monastery education because it made him useful as a secretary. Otherwise, he would now be in the mines like so many others.

Khalid el Bey spoke. "Draw up manumission papers for the slave girl known as Skye. I want her legally free. Then draw up a marriage contract between the freedwoman known as Skye, and myself. Her bride's price shall be this house, the estate, and twenty-five thousand gold dinars. Consult the mullah for the exact wording.

"Then," he continued, "send for the astrologer, Osman. I wish a consultation today. Wait! Before anything you must send a message to the Lady Yasmin telling her that all lessons are postponed until further notice. Say nothing else. That should get you started. I will return later."

As Khalid el Bey left, Jean heard him order a waiting slave, "See that Jean is sent breakfast immediately," and the little Frenchman marveled that his master was so thoughtful. This was not the first time, either. The bey's good manners had won his secretary's loyalty from the very first.

Jean wondered what was in his master's mind. He could have any woman without marriage. Why marriage? And Yasmin would be very angry. But Jean's Gallic logic was on the side of his lord's decision. It was time he settled down and had children. And besides, the lady Skye was the fairest woman Jean had seen in years.

Khalid el Bey returned to his bedchamber. Skye was gone, and he knew she had returned to her own chambers. Following her there, he heard giggles coming from the bathing room and found Skye and the pretty twin Ethiopian slave girls all splashing about the scented pool. He watched for a moment, struck by the vivid contrast of their wet bodies—ivory and ebony, sleek and shining.

Skye saw him first and, swimming over to the shallow end of the pool, came partway up the steps and held out her hand in invitation. She was like a goddess standing there in her nude young beauty, and he could feel his desire rising. He held his arms out and the two slave girls scrambled from the pool to remove his robe. Nude, his desire became visible to all. Skye's blue eyes twinkled and, throwing him a saucy look, she dove back into the pool, giving him a delicious view of her sleek flanks. "Leave us!" he growled to the two girls, and dove after Skye.

He was amazed to find what a strong swimmer she was. She laughed mischievously at him and dove beneath the water to emerge in midpool. His own laughter sounded now. "Where in the name of the seven djins did you learn to swim like that, you vixen?"

Her blue-green eyes widened innocently, and she shrugged. "Alas, my lord Khalid. I know not. Are you not afraid to take such a wife to your bosom? Who knows what else I may know?"

He swam over to her and, gently, with a restrained passion that she instantly sensed, he took her face between his thumb and forefinger. His golden amber eyes regarded her gravely. "I am not afraid to take such a wife to my bosom, Skye. Whatever surprises are in store for us will only serve to make our life more piquant. I love you, my little lost one. I love you!"

Slim white arms slid up around him. Her small round breasts pressed against the dark furred mat of his chest as she offered him her lips. "Khalid, be sure, I would not hurt so good a man. You are all I know, and I should be lost without you, but is that enough for you? I can offer only myself, and I do not even know very much about who I am."

"What is between us is good, Skye. Your lovely body responds well to mine. We like each other, and more couples than not have started life together with less. Do not fear, my love. You do not cheat me. It is a good bargain we make between us. Your concern for me does you credit. But now, my beautiful one," he swept her up in his arms, "I want to make love to you again."

She wiggled, wet and protesting, against him. "It is morning!"

"A most delightful time," he agreed, laying her on the sun-warmed tiles that surrounded the pool. He straddled her.

"Someone will see us, Khalid," she protested.

"No one would dare to disturb us," he growled. His staff was hard and seeking against her thighs. "I want you, Skye. I want your tempting little body. I want you hot and sweet and yielding beneath me," he whispered against her ear. She shivered deliciously as his tongue explored her ear, and shivered again as he moved downward along the scented length of her neck, biting gently at her silken shoulder. Skye soon forgot the bright sunshine. Khalid's hands were on her hips, stroking and stroking the fires of her passions. He suckled at her breasts, drawing a cry of pleasure. "Open your legs for me, now, my love," he murmured. "That's it, my darling, take me into your fiery sweetness. Ahh . . . Skye, your little honey-oven is made for me! Hold me tightly, my love! Ahhh!"

His words aroused her greatly. His hands never stopped loving her body, and when his great rod entered into her she felt filled to overflowing with him. His body movement was strong and rhythmic, each stroke bringing her nearer and nearer to sweet oblivion. She climbed higher and higher. Then she was caught in a jeweled whirlpool, and she heard a long soft woman's cry mingled with a great masculine sob.

Her next conscious thought was that the sun was hot on her face, and she heard water lapping against the tiled sides of the pool. She opened her eyes, and looked about. He lay on his back, eyes closed, but his voice brought a furious blush to her cheeks. "You were made to pleasure a man," he said, "and I am grateful that that man is me. After we have breakfast, I shall see Osman the astrologer, and he will tell me what day this week is most favorable for our marriage. I am having Jean draw up papers freeing you, Skye."

She pressed herself into the curve of his arm. "Oh, my Khalid, you are so kind to me! I swear I shall make you a good wife!"

He smiled and caressed her. "I know you will, my love," he answered her.

They breakfasted on yogurt, green figs, and boiling-hot Turkish coffee. Afterward Skye returned to her own apartments, and Khalid el Bey welcomed Osman, who greeted him by saying, "So, my old friend! You have finally fallen in love again."

Khalid laughed. "I have no secrets from you, do I, Osman?"

"The stars tell me all, my lord. And they tell me some things about your love that you might be interested in knowing. She comes from a green and misty land to the north, a land peopled by strong spirits and great psychic forces. She was born beneath the sign of the ram which, like all fire signs, is a strong and passionate one."

Khalid el Bey leaned forward eagerly. "How can you know all this, Osman?"

"Because, my lord, such a woman has recently appeared in your own chart."

"I want to marry her."

"I cannot stop you, my lord."

"You do not sound enthusiastic, Osman. What is it you are not telling me?"

"She will not remain with you, Khalid. It is not her fate. Her fate is back among her own people, and so it is written in the stars. There are many men in her life, but she will always steer her own course, rule her own destiny. One man in particular stands out in her life. Their paths have crossed before and will most assuredly cross again. It is with this man that she shares her soul, my friend, not with you. Can you not just enjoy her while she is with you? Why must it be marriage?"

He was shaken. The astrologer had always been accurate. "Will it make any difference if I marry her?"

"No, my lord, it will not."

"Then I shall marry her. For I love her above all women, and would place her above all women."

"And when she leaves you, will you let her go?"

"She will not leave me, Osman. She will not leave me because of the children she will give me. She is not a woman who would abandon her babes. She will give me children, won't she?"

"I cannot be sure, my lord. She will be mother to several children, but without a comparison of her exact birthday and yours, I cannot tell you for certain."

"She will bear me sons!" he said positively, and Osman smiled faintly.

Still, he was concerned for his friend. The woman brought a confusion into Khalid el Bey's chart. There was a dark area now that Osman could not fathom, and it worried him. Still, if his friend insisted on marrying her, then at least he would pick the best day. He scanned his charts carefully, made swift new calculations, and finally pronounced, "Saturday, at moonrise, you will take her as your wife."

"Thank you, my friend. You will come, of course, and celebrate with us."

"Yes, I shall come. Is it to be a large celebration, Khalid?"

"No, Osman. Just a half-dozen or so are to be invited—my banker, the head of the merchant's guild, the mullah, the Turkish commandant, and my secretary, Jean."

"What of Yasmin?"

"I think not."

"Yasmin loves you, Khalid."

"Yasmin thinks she loves me, Osman, and therefore she will accept my plans because of her belief in me. Besides, she will have no further contact with Skye. I cannot allow my wife to associate with a whore."

Osman had to laugh. "There, my friend Khalid, speaks both the Spaniard *and* the Moslem in you." He stood up. "Until Saturday, my lord Bey, and I wish you luck with Yasmin."

Khalid el Bey sat pondering for a few moments after Osman had left. The astrologer was right. Yasmin would have to be dealt with, and the sooner the better. Rising, he called for his horse and, in the silent midafternoon heat, he rode down to the heart of the city, to the House of Felicity.

The building in which this famous brothel was housed was built around a planted courtyard that had a spraying fountain at its center. The side of the house facing the streets was white and devoid of windows or any decoration save the double-doored entry of blackened oak with polished brass studs. Guarding the doors were two huge black giants in scarlet satin pantaloons with cloth-of-gold sashes, turbans, and ridiculously turned-up shoes. Their large bare chests and muscular arms were oiled so that they gleamed in either sun or torchlight. They smiled broadly with flashing white teeth as their master rode past them into the courtyard.

Khalid el Bey dismounted, tossing the reins to a pretty young girl of ten who smiled at him in an adult and provocative fashion.

Both her feet and her budding breasts were bare, and she wore only white gauze pantaloons that revealed her round little buttocks. A clever innovation, he thought, for many of his Berber clients liked prepubescent girls best of all.

For a minute he stood and looked about the courtyard with a proprietary air. Everything was in perfect order. He was pleased. The brick walks were well swept, the shrubs well trimmed, the flower beds colorful and fragrant.

"My lord Khalid, you honor us!" Yasmin swept down the steps to greet him, her black-and-gold silk caftan billowing. An odor of musk was strong about her, and he could see her vermilion-tinted nipples through the sheer silk. Her golden hair was plaited with black pearls, and behind one ear was a creamy gardenia. It continually amazed him that she always knew of the arrival of an important guest, and was instantly there to greet him.

"My dear Yasmin, you are as lovely as ever." He chuckled inwardly as she bridled with pleasure. "Come. I wish to talk with you." He led the way to her apartments, waiting patiently as she served him coffee and small honeyed almond cakes.

At length she asked, "How is Skye?"

"That is what I have come to discuss with you," he answered. "I have decided she is quite unsuited for this sort of life."

"Praise Allah! You have come to your senses!"

He smiled faintly. "You do not like Skye, do you?"

"No!"

"Then you shall not be burdened with her any longer, Yasmin."

"You have sold her?"

"No. I am taking her to wife. The chief mullah of Algiers will join us on Saturday evening at moonrise."

Yasmin's face crumbled. Then, recovering herself as quickly as she could, she laughed weakly. "You jest, my lord. Gracious—how you startled me! Ha! Ha!"

"I do not jest," he said quietly. "Skye is to be my wife."

"She is a *slave!*"

"No, she is not. I have freed her. She was never meant to be a slave, Yasmin."

"And I was?"

"You were born a slave of slave parents, of slave ancestors. It is your fate."

"I love you! Does she love you? How can she? She barely knows you. But I know you, Khalid, and I know what pleases you. Let me!" and she fell groveling at his feet.

He looked down at her with genuine pity. Poor Yasmin with all her clever Mideastern sexual arts for pleasing a man. Yes, he had enjoyed them once, but they had also bored him to death. The Mideastern mode of loving was debasing to the woman. She was taught to please her master, who lay there, a nonparticipant except for the automatic ejaculation of his seed. It was up to the woman to please. The responsibility for his pleasure rested with her, and if she failed . . . the bastinado awaited.

How much better, he thought, the European way, where the man was in charge, his masculinity ruling and subduing his woman, her climax the most marvelous act of submission. It delighted the senses and soothed the male pride.

"I love Skye," he said, "the decision was mine. And you, my most beautiful and valued slave, have no right to question me."

"What will happen to me?" she whimpered.

"Nothing. You will continue your duties as before." After a pause he asked, "Would you like your freedom, Yasmin? Then I should pay you for the duties you now perform for me."

Yasmin was horrified. Her very slavery bound her to Khalid el Bey. Without it he could cast her off at any time, and now he probably would.

"Oh, no! No! No, my lord! I do not want my freedom."

"Very well then, my dear, it shall be as you decree. Now, get up, Yasmin, and see me out." He rose. Taking her arm, he raised her up. "You *really* are invaluable to me, my dear," he said in a kindly fashion, and though she knew it to be a tossed bone, she was somewhat soothed.

"When may I come and wish the lady Skye happiness?"

"I would prefer you didn't, Yasmin. Like any sensible man, I would prefer to keep my wife away from my business. And you, my dear, are a part of that business."

"I understand, my lord Khalid," she said smoothly, and thought bitterly to herself: Yes, I understand completely. You do not want your precious wife associating with a whore! And I am a whore!

They walked out into the sunlit courtyard, and the little girl brought Khalid's horse to him. The Whoremaster of Algiers chucked the child underneath the chin, then slipped her a silver piece. "A nice touch, Yasmin," he complimented her. Then, mounting the prancing animal, Khalid el Bey rode away.

Chapter 10

In the next few days the preparations for Khalid el Bey's wedding were made. The few invitations were issued, the feast and entertainment were planned, and the bridal chamber was decorated. Since Skye's memory loss prevented her from having any religious preference, and since she had been a practicing Moslem since coming under Khalid el Bey's protection, the chief mullah of Algiers found no impediment to the marriage.

On the afternoon of the nuptials six virgins from the House of Felicity arrived at Khalid el Bey's estate and were housed in the women's quarters. Unlike the Turks, who separated the sexes at a wedding, the inhabitants of Algiers were less formal. Although it was not necessary for the bride to be in attendance at the religious ceremony, which would be performed at the neighborhood mosque, she and other women were invited to the feast. For what was a celebration without soft and fragrant feminity?

The little French secretary, Jean, had been given his freedom in honor of his master's wedding. Jean had, however, elected to remain in Khalid's employ rather than return to his native land. He and the other guests were to be gifted with feminine companionship for the evening. Khalid and Skye looked over the girls and decided the pairing. "I think," he said, "the pretty plump little Provençale with the black-cherry eyes will do quite nicely for the mullah. He is yet a young man, but inclined to be overserious and weighed down by the importance of his position."

"Has he no wife to ease his travail?"

"No, Skye, he has not, although I know he is not a celibate."

"Then the choice is an excellent one, my lord, for should she insinuate herself into his affections she will make him supremely happy. I see beneath the youth and sensuality a proper housewife and mother."

Khalid chuckled. "Bravo, my Skye! I see that also, and should God will that it be so, think how grateful the mullah will be to me when his first son is born! Now . . . for the head of the merchant's guild, and for my banker, the delicious blondes. Each of these gentlemen is well into middle life. Each has a carping wife and a houseful of greedy, brawling children and relatives. What is needed here is simple, and quite physical. Maidens whose light-colored eyes fill with admiration easily, with big, soft breasts, and feather heads, who have only one desire, to please the master."

Skye examined the two girls. They were fluffy creatures who would amply fill the bill. "What of Osman and Jean?" she asked.

"The petite creature with the soft hazel eyes and thick, chestnut-colored hair comes from his own Brittany. They will be quite a surprise for each other."

"Oh, Khalid, how kind of you. The girl looks frightened, but Jean will reassure her nicely, and I will be delighted to have a friend in the house."

"Yes, she will be a friend for you. I hadn't thought of that."

"Let me guess the others, Khalid! The sweet-faced, grave-looking girl is for Osman!"

"Yes," his eyes were amused.

"Then that leaves that rather fierce-looking creature for the Turkish commandant. God, Khalid! She looks like she could devour a man. Is that a wise choice?"

"My love, there are many things you don't remember about human nature. The commandant of the Casbah fortress is a regular patron of the House of Felicity. His taste in women is, ah, somewhat sophisticated. Easy conquest bores him. He enjoys a woman who fights him. The girl I have chosen for him is half-Moorish, half-Berber. She is a wild little savage, and should delight him greatly. Now, my love, see that these maidens are bathed and clothed in time for the feast. The next time I see you, my sweet Skye, you will be my wife." His golden amber eyes warmed her. His mouth brushed hers tenderly, and quickly he turned and was gone.

She sighed. He was so good to her. And she still worried that she should not be marrying him. Something deep inside her nagged at her, yet try as she might, she could not understand what it was. Sometimes in her dreams there was a man, always the same man, but she could never see him clearly, she could only sense him crying out to her. It made no sense.

Sighing, she clapped her hands and the slaves came running. She gave orders for the six girls to be bathed and perfumed. Then she set about choosing their garments from the vast wardrobe in the harem quarters.

For the mullah's golden-skinned dark-haired Provençale it would be apricot silk pantaloons, a gold-embroidered sash, and a bolero fringed in little gold beads. Because of the heat and the lateness of the feast, she could forego the gauze blouses. The choice for the two blondes was simple: baby pink for both. For the Breton girl with her chestnut hair and hazel eyes, apple green was perfect. For the girl chosen for Osman, a sky blue would set off her dark-blond hair. Lastly, she chose flame-colored silks for the Turk's maiden. Handing the clothing to the servants, she gave orders for their distribution and returned to her own quarters to bathe and change into her own wedding garments.

At moonrise exactly, the chief mullah of Algiers performed the simple ceremony uniting Khalid el Bey in marriage with Skye, who became known from that moment as Skye muna el Khalid—Skye, the desired of Khalid. Then the groom and his guests returned to his house through the winding lantern-lit streets of the upper city, led by dancing, cavorting musicians whose reedy pipes and thumping drums pierced the dark velvet of the night.

The groom wore white silk pantaloons with silver-and-deep-blue-embroidered bands that stopped at the knee. His feet were shod in silver-colored leather boots. His shirt was also of white silk, open at the neck, with full sleeves and tight cuffs, over which he wore a white vest embroidered in silver and blue. It was all topped by a long white satin cape lined in dark blue. His dark head was bare, his short black beard had been well barbered.

Behind the closed shutters along his route, maidens and matrons alike peeped out and sighed with longing. The legendary Whoremaster of Algiers was a fairy-tale prince.

Behind Khalid el Bey walked the Turkish commandant of the Casbah fortress, Capitan Jamil. As tall as the bey, he was heavier set, and to the spying female eyes that watched, as sinisterly handsome as the bey was kindly. His face was long, as was his nose. His eyes were black and unfathomable, his mouth thin and cruel below a slim mustache. He was known to be cruel, even brutal, in his handling of fractious prisoners. Now, however, he strode along with his host and the other guests, chatting amiably.

"I understand your bride is a captive."

"Was," came the reply, "I bought her. Now she is legally free. And my wife."

"I had heard you were training her for the House of Felicity. She must be quite good at whatever she does if you have decided to marry her."

Khalid el Bey laughed lightly but he burned inwardly. "Skye has no memory of her past," he said. "At first I thought that to train a woman such as she might prove amusing. But she is actually far too innocent for such a life. I had been considering marrying and siring sons for some time now. But what respectable father would allow his daughter to wed the great Whoremaster? Skye is obviously of the upper class, wherever she comes from, and she is beautiful. Is that not an ideal choice for my purposes?"

"I am eager to meet your bride, Khalid."

They had reached the house now, and entered through the wide doors into the square hall where the bey's majordomo awaited. "Felicitations, my lord! Long life and many sons!" he cried, ushering them through into the banquet hall. Waiting slaves took the men's cloaks, and brought silver-chased basins of rose water and soft linen towels so they might bathe their hands and faces. Refreshed, they sat down upon the large plump cushions strewn about the table.

"Gentlemen," said Khalid el Bey, sitting at the head of the table, "it gives me great pleasure that you are here to share this moment with me. I would share my happiness with you, and so I present, to each of you, for your many nights of pleasure, a virgin who has been trained in my own House of Felicity." He clapped his hands and the six girls, all dressed in their butterfly colors, entered and moved swiftly to the gentlemen for whom they were intended.

"By Allah!" swore Capitan Jamil, "you do things with style, Khalid! Even in Constantinople I never saw such a display of elegant manners. I shall write the Sultan tomorrow telling him."

"Many thanks," said Khalid carelessly. He was more pleased by the reactions of his other guests. The head of the merchant's guild and the banker were pleasantly overcome by the two little blondes. And Jean was rendered momentarily speechless by the pretty girl who shyly greeted him not only in his own tongue, but in the dialect peculiar to Brittany alone. The chief mullah actually had a smile on his face—the first time Khalid had ever seen that phenomenon! And Osman was obviously quite taken by his maiden.

Capitan Jamil paused in his careful inspection of his "gift" to inquire, "And your bride, Khalid? Where is she?"

As if in answer, the banquet-hall doors opened and four black slaves in red silk breechcloths entered bearing a litter. They carefully set it down and the majordomo handed out the veiled occupant and led her forward to sit by the bey.

Her fine silk pantaloons were the soft lavender of early wisteria, cut low. A wide band of deep violet flowers on a gold background rose to just below her navel. She wore gold slippers embroidered with pearl violets. Her sleeveless bodice was violet velvet trimmed in gold braid with floral embroidery done in gold and seed pearls. She wore thin gold bracelets. A single long rope of pearls dangled from her neck, and great matching pearl tears bobbed in her ears. Her midnight-black hair was loose, and sprinkled with gold dust. A small mauve veil obscured her face below those marvelous eyes shadowed in blue kohl.

"Gentlemen, my wife, the lady Skye muna el Khalid," said Khalid el Bey as he reached up and undid her veil.

They were momentarily stunned into silence. Everything about her—her flawless skin, her dark blue eyes, the full red lips, the delicate, slightly upturned nose—everything was exquisite. Finally the banker found his voice.

"Khalid, my friend, I have four wives. If you put all of their beauty together, it would not equal half of your wife's loveliness. You are a most damnably fortunate man!"

Khalid el Bey laughed happily. "Thank you, Memhet! Your praise is received with joy."

Now the servants began bringing in steaming dishes; the gold goblets were filled with icy juices; musicians played discreetly from behind a carved screen. A whole baby lamb had been roasted, and was served now on a mixture of saffroned rice with onions, green peppers, and tomatoes. There were bowls of yogurt; purple, green, and black olives; and shelled pistachio nuts. The slaves passed hot loaves of bread, and placed upon each guest's plate a small whole roasted pigeon in a nest of watercress. As the fermented fruit juices began to relax the guests they became a bit noisier and freer, the men feeding choice morsels from their lips to the lips of their giggling companions.

The mullah sat on Khalid's right, Skye on her husband's left. Next to her sat Capitan Jamil, who had been unable to take his eyes off the bride. "What a pity," he murmured softly so that only she might hear him, "that Khalid decided to keep you for himself, my lovely. He could have made a fortune selling your charms. I would have paid a king's ransom to possess you first. Still, it is good to know the great Whoremaster of Algiers has a weakness."

A hot flush stole up her neck and cheeks but she said nothing. He laughed low. "You are the most beautiful woman I have ever seen, bride of Khalid el Bey. Your skin glows like mother-of-pearl. I shall dream for many nights of your long legs and perfect little breasts, which are like tender fruits. How I hunger to taste of those sweet young fruits." He leaned close to her as he reached for a handful of olives and his upper arm deliberately rubbed against her.

"How dare you accost me in such a manner!" she hissed angrily. "Have you no respect for my husband, who is your host? Or are Turks totally without honor?"

He drew his breath in sharply. "Someday, my beauty, I shall have you completely at my mercy. And when I do you will pay dearly for that insult."

To his annoyance, Skye did not appear frightened. She merely signaled the servants to clear the table and serve the next course. The coffeemaker, kneeling at his little table, began to grind the beans and boil the water. The slaves placed upon the board colored crystal bowls filled with figs, raisins, oranges, green grapes, candied dates, and rose petals. Silver plates of small honeyed cakes, with matching tiny bowls of sugared almonds, were put before each guest. Goblets were refilled with sweet liquid fruit sherbet chilled by snow brought from the nearby Atlas Mountains. The bey leaned over to kiss his wife. "You have planned everything perfectly, my Skye. It is as if you had been born to the duties of the chatelaine."

"Perhaps I was," she answered him softly.

The entertainment began. There were wrestlers, then jugglers, then an Egyptian fakir who made things appear and disappear. Lastly came the dancers. There were at least half a dozen of them to begin with, but in time only one very voluptuous creature remained, her sinuous body writhing passionately and more suggestively with each movement. Skye became aware of the silence that had overtaken her guests. Their chatter was gone, and the only sound in the room was the music—the insistent whine of the pipes, the heavy beat of the drums, the brass tals upon the dancer's fingers teasing their challenge to the musicians. Skye glanced about her and saw that some of the wedding guests had gone into the garden. Still others had begun to make love right there on the cushions. Blushing, she turned to her husband. With twinkling eyes, he stood and drew her up beside him.

"I believe," he said, "the time is ripe for us to make our escape. Come, my love!"

"Where are we to go, Khalid?"

"To a secret little villa that I own along the seacoast. We shall spend our honeymoon there, free of friends and business." He hurried her out into the cool night, stopping only to retrieve his cloak and to place one of mauve silk, lined in rabbit fur, about her. Before the house stood a great white stallion. Khalid el Bey leapt onto its back and, reaching down, lifted his bride and placed her before him on the saddle.

They rode down into the city and then to the sea, where they followed the beach for several miles. The moon dappled the water. Looking up into the velvety heavens, Skye caught her breath. The stars seemed so big, so near, and she was tempted to reach out and grasp a handful. Nestling in Khalid's arms, her head against his heart, she felt its sure and steady beat. As they rode she became aware of a familiarity about the roar of the sea and the salty smell of the cool damp air. For some reason these sensations soothed her, though she had no idea why they did. Khalid was silent, and she dared not speak lest she break the spell.

Finally he turned the white stallion from the beach, and she could see the black outline of a building on one of the hills overlooking the sea. As they came closer, Skye saw that it was a large round kiosk. There was a pleasant air about it. Large brass lanterns with hand-blown Venetian globes, their beeswax candles twinking a welcome, hung on either side of the silk-draped entrance.

Khalid el Bey drew rein on his horse, gently deposited his wife on the lawn, and dismounted. "Welcome, my beloved! Welcome to the 'Pearl Kiosk.' There are three rooms within—our bedchamber, a bath, and a dayroom. It belongs to you now, Skye, for it is my wedding gift to you."

She was astounded. His bride's price to her had been overgenerous, and now he gifted her with even more. She felt quite humble in the light of such great love. Skye suddenly felt her heart contract painfully. Looking up at him, she said, "Khalid, I do care for you, you know. Were you a poor man I should still feel this way, for it is your love for me that warms my heart and soothes my spirit, not the gifts you give me, though I am grateful for them."

"It is for just that reason that I enjoy giving you things," he answered her. "You are not a greedy little creature. Come now, sweetness, let us go in, for the night grows cool. Are you not the least bit curious to see your new gift?"

The doorway of the Pearl Kiosk was hung with multicolored diaphanous silks and in the entry hall was a long, narrow reflecting pool. Looking up, Skye caught her breath, for in the roof above the pool was a glass ceiling that matched the pool in size and shape. Therefore, the still surface of the pool now appeared to be filled with twinkling stars. The foyer was lit by gold and crystal lamps similar to those on the front of the building.

They first moved through a doorway on their left, where Skye found a beautiful dayroom with a fireplace that blazed merrily, taking the dampness from the air. The floor was lush with thick rugs. Colored glass lamps hung on thin chains from the gilded and beamed ceiling. Overstuffed furniture and pillows were covered in the finest silks and velvets, the colors like jewels—ruby, sapphire, emerald, amethyst, and topaz. The windows that faced the landside were small hand-blown rounds of pale-amber glass. There were low tables of inlaid mosaic tile and great brass bowls filled with red and yellow tulips. One small wall had a built-in bookcase filled with leatherbound volumes, the sight of which brought a glad cry to her lips.

"So," chuckled Khalid el Bey, "my good secretary, Jean, was not wrong. You *can* read. In what languages, my beloved?"

She looked a trifle shamefaced. "Jean seemed so horrified that I could read that I did not wish you to know. I wandered into your library one day and, seeing the books, I picked one up and opened it. It was French. I find that I am also able to read Spanish, Italian, Latin, and the language Jean calls English." She hung her head and said hesitantly, "I appear to possess another rather unfeminine trait. It seems I also write."

Khalid el Bey burst into laughter. "Marvelous, my Skye! Simply marvelous! It seems that you are a very intelligent woman, and while most men might be shocked to find themselves with such a wife, I am not. The ways of Allah are indeed mysterious. I originally intended to make you my most famous whore, but now I find you are educated, so, beloved, I shall instead make you my partner! When we return to the city I shall teach you myself, and Jean will aid me. Should anything ever happen to me, no one will ever be able to cheat you." He swept her into his arms and kissed her soundly. "What a delight you are, Skye!" he chuckled, and she felt warm and safe and very much loved. His amber-gold eyes twinkled. "We have yet to see our nuptial chamber," he murmured, carrying her from the richly appointed dayroom across the foyer. He pushed open the carved and gilded double doors.

The room into which they now entered had walls painted to resemble an oasis, with graceful palms, the mysterious desert dunes beyond, and above, on the ceiling, the wonderful black velvet North African sky had been recreated, complete with twinkling stars done in gold luminescent paint. Skye would discover that in the sunlight the false night sky was actually bright blue and that the stars were not visible at all. To continue the illusion, the rugs were of thick gold and cream wool, large potted green palms were placed strategically around the room, and the bed was partially draped to resemble a tent canopy. The room was very softly lit by tall lamps that resembled lotus flowers and burned scented oils.

Without a word he slid the sleeveless violet bodice from her. Then his hands pushed the pantaloons over her hips and, when she had stepped from them and pushed the little mass of silk away with her foot, he slid to his knees. She stood still while his elegant hands fondled her breasts. Then, moving to grasp her by the waist, he covered her torso in hot kisses. She caught at his head and pressed it against her wildly fluttering belly. The time for words was long past. For a moment he simply knelt there enjoying the silken feel of her wonderful skin, then swiftly standing he stripped off his own clothes and they walked to the bed.

It was the beginning of an incredible week. Skye had never been loved so tenderly, so passionately, so expertly, so completely. There was not a part of her he did not explore and worship, and he encouraged her to do the same with his body. Gradually she lost her shyness, became bold and caressed him in subtle ways that left him moaning. They made love in the early hours of the dawn, in the heat of the afternoon, in the dark of night. They swam naked in the foaming azure sea. They hunted antelope from horseback with their hunting cats, beautifully trained panthers, loping by their sides. Another discovery had been made by then—Skye could ride astride quite expertly. Once again he gifted her, this time with an exquisite golden Arab mare.

In the time they spent at the Pearl Kiosk they were provided for and waited on by an army of invisible servants who saw to every need. Delicious meals magically appeared, as did fresh clothes. When they desired to hunt, their horses and cats awaited them at the Kiosk front. Hot, scented baths were ready upon their return. Everything was done to make this time together perfect.

On the night before their return she lay half awake, exhausted by their lovemaking, content to listen to Khalid's even breathing. Suddenly she was aware that she had never been so happy. He surrounded her with love, security, everything she could want. Why was it, then, that she could still not give him her heart?

They rode back into the city of Algiers on the following morning. They were dressed identically in white. The sleek black panthers were by their sides, leashed, but nonetheless causing a stir as they moved through the crowded streets of the lower city. That same day, when they had resettled themselves, Khalid el Bey took his wife into the library where Jean sat working.

"Ho, Jean! I bring you a pupil."

The little Frenchman looked up with a smile. "Welcome home, my lord Khalid! Welcome home, my lady Skye! Who is to be my pupil, and in what?"

"I want you to teach the lady Skye the intricacies of my business. Should something ever happen to me she would be helpless without a thorough knowledge of it. Since she can already read, write, and speak in four languages it should not prove difficult as long as she can grasp simple mathematics."

"What are mathematics?" asked Skye.

"Here, mistress," Jean wrote a simple sum on a parchment. "If you take one hundred dinars and add to them another fifty dinars you have—"

"One hundred and fifty dinars," replied Skye, "and by the same token if you have one hundred and fifty dinars and take or subtract from them seventy-five dinars you will have remaining seventy-five."

The two men looked at each other in complete surprise, and Skye said, "Is that not correct, Khalid? Have I made an error?"

"No, my Skye, you have not made an error. You are quick and quite correct, is she not, Jean?"

"Indeed, my lord. Indeed!"

The bey laughed. "I think I leave you in good hands, my love. Do not be too hard on my good Jean, for he is invaluable to me." Khalid walked from the room, laughing softly to himself.

Skye seated herself demurely at the library table and looked expectantly at Jean, who was suddenly a little fearful that he had that rarest of creatures on his hands—an intelligent woman. Drawing a deep breath, he plunged into the business at hand.

For the next few weeks Skye spent most of her days with Khalid and Jean, closeted in the library, and she suddenly understood the true nature of her husband's business. She was shocked for a while. Then, realizing that Khalid had not invented prostitution, she accepted it.

She quickly understood that each house Khalid owned had to be treated as a separate entity. Those located on the waterfront, serving sailors of all nations, were provisioned far differently from the House of Felicity. The waterfront brothels served only beer, but in the House of Felicity and its two sister houses, the menu was quite varied. Even the women varied with the different establishments. On the waterfront, pretty but sturdy peasant girls were the choice, girls who might easily service two dozen men a day without ill effect.

Young women bought for Khalid's more elegant brothels were all beauties carefully schooled in proper Arabic and French so they might converse well. They were also taught good manners, hygiene, and elegant ways of dressing. Their sexual skills were excellent. The men who bought their company bought it for an entire evening.

All of Khalid el Bey's waterfront brothels worked their women five days a week and allowed them rest for two days. This necessitated keeping records on who was working and who was not. Each of these women received a hundredth portion of the fee collected for her services each night, and at the end of five years was given her freedom and the monies accrued. Most married and settled down. Some, however, took to the streets and were quickly lost. Others hired themselves out to lesser brothels and quickly found themselves overworked and disease-ridden. Most brothel keepers were not as careful with their women as Khalid el Bey, who kept two Moorish doctors on his staff and had his women checked weekly for the pox.

All of this meant voluminous records, and Skye found herself becoming very interested in her husband's business dealings. His brothels involved not only the care and well-being of people and property but the provisioning of those people and the upkeep of the property.

Problems were tripled in the more elegant brothels, for the women there had to be exquisitely clothed and jeweled. They needed oil baths and wore only the finest perfumes. But despite his vast outlay, Khalid el Bey was a rich man. Profits far exceeded expenses. And these profits had to be invested.

This was the thing that interested Skye the most, the investment of her husband's funds. Some of the money was placed with a goldsmith, Judah ben Simon. Some of it had been put into portable wealth such as loose gem stones. The rest was invested with the adventure ships belonging to an Englishman called Robert Small. It was shortly after their return from the Pearl Kiosk that Skye met this bluff sea captain.

One night as she and Khalid sat listening to love songs sung by a sweet-voiced slave girl, an uproar ensued from the courtyard of the house. Her husband leaped to his feet laughing and Skye could hear a booming voice saying, "Now, laddie, your master may be a-laying with one of his fancy pieces, but believe me, he'll stop to see me. Out of my way! Damme, Khalid, you old Moor. Where are you?" The door to the chamber flew open and a tiny-legged man strode into the room.

He was a most fantastic sight. His colorful clothes included puffed and slashed red velvet breeches, black silk stockings, a red velvet doublet embroidered in gold and silver thread, a long cape, and a flat hat with an egret plume. On a tall man the clothing might not have been so fantastic, but Robert Small stood only five feet tall. Powerfully built, he had sandy-brown hair and his eyes were a snapping blue. His round, weathered face was mischievous and kindly while also being the homeliest Skye had ever seen. The little man was as freckled as a thrush's egg. "Ha! There you be, Khalid, and as usual you've got some rare beauty by your side."

"Robbie, you're a wicked old man, and so I've no compunction in springing this surprise on you. The 'rare beauty' is my wife!"

"God assoil my soul, Khalid el Bey! True?" The bey nodded, and the Englishman bowed low to Skye. "My humblest apologies, madam. I hope you'll not think ill of me." Then, realizing he'd spoken English, he said, "Khalid, I know not what language your lady speaks. You'll tell her for me?"

"There is no need, sir," said Skye sweetly. "I fully comprehend you, and am not in the least offended. It's quite natural you should think me a whore, considering the nature of my husband's business. Now, however, you will excuse me, for I imagine you've much to talk about with my lord." She rose gracefully and, smiling mischievously, left the room.

The little Englishman chuckled. "How," he asked, "did a renegade Spaniard-turned-Arab end up with an Irish wife?"

"Irish? Skye is *Irish?*"

"God almighty, man! Didn't she tell you?"

"She doesn't know, my old friend. Several months ago I bought myself a rather bedraggled and frightened waif from a corsair captain. He had gotten her from an outbound captain who claimed to have captured her in a skirmish. He knew nothing of her history. When Skye regained her full senses she had no memory excepting her name."

"And so you married her! Lord, man, you're a romantic at heart."

"Wrong!" Khalid el Bey poured the Englishman a tiny cup of sweet Turkish coffee. "I had intended to make her the finest and most expensive whore the world had ever seen."

Robert Small sucked his breath in sharply. "Did you indeed, laddie? And pray tell what stopped you?"

"I fell in love with her, my friend. Not with just her face and luscious body, but with the woman I began to see emerging. She is without guile, and generous as well. She is also the least greedy female I have ever known, and when she looks at me with those marvelous blue eyes of hers I am lost, Robbie! Very soon, the thought of anyone other than myself touching her enraged me. I found that I wanted children and a loving wife, like a normal man."

"God help you, then, my friend, for you have a weakness now, and your enemies will use it against you. As long as the great Whoremaster of Algiers showed no vulnerability he was inviolable."

"Don't fret, Robbie, I have no enemies. Even my women respect me."

"Don't be a fool, Khalid!" It was said sharply. "All wealthy and powerful men have enemies. Look closely to yourself and to that beauty you've married."

For a few minutes the two men sat silently sipping their coffee, then Robert Small spoke. "I've made you richer again, Khalid. The ships we sent to the New World have returned laden with precious metals, jewels, and furs. The ones that traveled south returned with spices, slaves, and gemstones. I have, as usual, saved the cream of the female slaves for you to see."

Khalid el Bey was all business now. "Did we lose any ships or men?"

"No ships, but three men were lost on the *Swan,* off the Horn. It was a particularly bad storm, the captain tells me, but he didn't lose one slave."

"Good! And you, Robbie, how was your voyage?"

The captain chuckled and stretched his short frame out on the pillows, his hands behind his head. "Ah, Khalid, I wish you'd been with me. How often you've warned me of men's greed, and the vulnerability that greed brings in. And you were right! I found us a mine manager in the Spanish Americas who is a younger son with no hope other than to end his days a rum-soaked wreck. His oldest brother, their father's heir, married the girl he loved, and then arranged for him to be sent from Spain. He burns for vengeance, and so he has agreed to help us obtain six shiploads of gold for a percentage and passage back to Europe. It was a cheap price to pay, Khalid. We filled three ships this trip, and I've already sent three other ships."

"And how did this young don cover the theft? And how can we be sure he'll not betray us?"

"The first theft was covered by causing a mine to cave in. It'll take months to clear it out, by which time we'll have returned for the second load from the other mine. It will not matter if the

Spaniards learn then that they have been robbed, for we'll all be long gone by that time. The young don has a half-Spanish, half-Indian mistress he intends to marry and take to Paris with him. He can live quite well on what we pay him.

"The mines he oversees give up the purest gold I've ever seen, Khalid! The other ships in our fleet have carried back the finest furs imaginable, along with basketsful of turquoise, coral, jade, amethyst, emeralds, and topaz. I have, as usual, saved a choice selection of furs and gems for you, along with some excellent Indian pearls and spices from the Southern fleet. Everything else has been disposed of through our regular channels, and your monies are already with your banker."

"You are generous, Robbie, and quite thorough, as always. Perhaps you will allow me to do a little something for you now. Your ship was sighted by friends of mine this morning, and I knew you would be with me by evening. Go to the House of Felicity, and you will find a surprise waiting for you."

The Englishman grinned delightedly. "Ah, Khalid, you didn't have to go to any trouble."

The Whoremaster of Algiers grinned back, "She's quite to your liking, Robbie. Go along now so I may rejoin my own lady."

The captain scrambled to his feet. "If my surprise is that good I'll not be seeing you for several days, Khalid," and he was quickly gone.

Khalid el Bey stretched his long body in a catlike movement and called, "Skye!" She appeared immediately from behind a wall hanging, and sat down next to him. "You heard," said her husband.

"Yes, my lord. If this story is true then you are indeed fortunate to have such a partner."

"You can trust Robert Small with your life, my Skye. He is the most honest man I know. He has never cheated me. It is simply not in his nature."

"What awaits him at the House of Felicity? Have you found him some petite creature to soothe and comfort him?"

Khalid laughed. "No! Though Robbie is a bit of a man, he likes big, tall women. The maiden awaiting him stands six feet and has breasts like summer melons. I've been given to understand that Robbie's rod is as big as any man's, so they will both enjoy themselves."

They laughed together, imagining the little man and his Amazon mistress locked in sweet combat. Then as easily as they had begun to laugh they stopped, and she was in his arms again. He kissed her until she ached for him. His hands slid beneath her sheer pale-blue silk caftan, his long fingers teasing her nipples until she whimpered.

"Look at me, Skye," he commanded softly, and she struggled to raise her heavy-lidded eyes to him. "You are my wife, beloved, and I love you."

Now, for the first time, she looked deep into his warm amber eyes and realized that she felt deeply toward Khalid. With this startling realization, the heartache that had assailed her continually ever since she'd awakened to her new life in Algiers seemed to dissolve, leaving her feeling as light as a feather. She loved! This was what love was, and she could remember it! Her eyes filled with happy tears and she said wonderingly, "Oh, Khalid! I love you, too! I do! I know that now!" And pulling his dark head down to hers, she kissed him deeply. He, feeling her certain, unwavering love, found his passion bursting into an unquenchable flame.

Beneath his eager touch the silk of her robe tore away and his hands and mouth began their worshipful adoration of her. He loosened her lovely dark hair and spread it over the apricot velvet pillows. Then his long fingers gently traced her high cheekbones, moving down the fine line of her jaw to capture her small chin.

"Tell me again, Skye," he said softly.

Her sapphire eyes caught his amber-gold ones and held them unwaveringly. "I love you, my lord Khalid," she said firmly. "I love you!" Then she kissed him again, her little tongue teasing his mouth. He could feel her small round breasts rubbing against his chest and, unable to refuse the invitation, he lowered his head and nibbled on the hard, quivering nipples. His tongue pushed into her little navel and she eagerly thrust her torso toward him. He moved lower yet, his mouth seeking that most secret core. Tasting her seashell-like fragrance, his tongue darted like wildfire over the moist dark pink flesh. She whimpered, half in agony, half in ecstasy, her fingers catching at the dark hair of his head as he relentlessly pushed her beyond endurance. Amazingly, she did not shatter into a thousand pieces. She soared higher than she had ever done before. Then with great tenderness he kissed the soft inside of her thighs, pulled himself up over her, and gently took her.

Skye was frantic with unfulfilled passion. She had never known such love as this. Or had she? Her mind whirled in confusion, but Khalid's warm body soon overcame that. What difference did it make if she had loved before? Khalid was her husband. He loved her, and she loved him. Why should she torture herself with vague, flickering memories? All that mattered was now.

"Skye! Skye! Come with me, my darling! Now! Now!"

She met his ardor with her own, soaring as he did. Afterward, as she lay sated, she said quietly, "I want a child, Khalid."

He smiled in the darkness. This was further proof of her love. "I shall endeavor, my love, to give you everything you want—especially children."

Suddenly she laughed happily and, propping herself up on an elbow, looked down into his golden eyes. "I love you, and am loved in return," she said. "Whatever has been before in my life can matter little in the light of this love. If it were important, then surely I should have remembered it all by now. I know who I am. I am Skye, the beloved wife of Khalid el Bey, the great Whoremaster of Algiers."

Chapter 11

Niall Burke lay weakly back upon the scented linen pillows and, focusing his silvery eyes clearly for the first time in weeks, gazed out at the distant blue mountains. The landscape outside his window was a riot of lush vegetation. Pink and red hibiscus, cloyingly sweet gardenias, spicy roses, and crisp lavender were all growing in a wild mass that spread upward from the gardens to the flowering vines that clung to the villa wall. It was all so vibrant.

Now, totally immersed in the sights and smells, the shrieking of the darting parrots, Niall knew he would live. And fervently he wished he were dead.

The carved oak door of his room opened then, admitting a young girl whose big eyes lit up at the sight of him.

"Ah, Señor Niall. At last you are fully awake. I am Constanza Maria Alcudia Cuidadela. My papa is the governor of this island, and you are in his house." She put a tray on the nearby table.

Feeling like a fool, Niall was forced to ask, "What island is this?"

The girl blushed in pretty pink confusion. "Oh, señor, forgive me! You are on the island of Mallorca."

"How did I come to be here?"

"You were brought to us from the fleet in which you traveled by a Captain MacGuire. He explained you are a great lord."

Niall forced back a small smile. "Is MacGuire still here, Señorita Constanza?"

"Si, Señor Niall. Although the rest of your fleet sailed weeks ago, he refused to leave you. He said his mistress would not forgive him if he did. Would you like to see him?"

Niall nodded and the girl pulled the embroidered bellpull by his bed. "Fetch the Irish captain at once, Ana," she instructed the answering servant, then moved to straighten Niall's pillows. She wore a rose fragrance, which caused a sharp pain to tear through Niall. Constanza poured something from the frosty majollica pitcher into a silver goblet.

"It is the juice of the oranges from our garden," she said. "Drink it. It will give you strength." She gracefully handed the goblet to him, then sat and drew a small embroidery frame from a hidden pocket in her gown and began to stitch.

He drank, and was pleasantly surprised by the cool, tart sweetness that slid down his parched throat. He studied the seated girl over the goblet. She was, he decided, about fifteen, and very lovely. She was quite petite, with a tiny waist and generous breasts. Her skin was a pale golden shade, her hair a darker gold, and her eyes were the color of purple pansies.

He let his eyes wander about the room. It was spacious and pleasant, with white walls and a red tile floor. On one wall was a large dark wood armoire with intricately carved doors, and a long walnut table stood before the French doors opposite his silk-draped bed. There were two chairs by the table and an embroidered chaise longue by the bed.

"Is the juice good, Señor Niall? May I pour you more?"

"Thank you," he answered politely. Dammit to hell, where was MacGuire? As if in answer to his silent summons, the door flew open to admit the captain and Inis. With a joyous bark, the dog leaped onto the bed and lay down beside Niall, his tail thumping happily.

"So, lad, you've decided to remain among the living! Praise be to God!"

"Skye? Where is she?"

MacGuire looked most uncomfortable. Sighing, he admitted, "We don't know where the O'Malley is, my lord. When the infidels shot you down our first concern was to get you safely aboard. We knew they couldn't outrun us. But no sooner had we gotten you back to the ship than a damned rain squall hit, and we lost the bastards in a fog bank. We were nearer Mallorca, and so we brought you here. The rest went on to Algiers, but alas, sir, no trace has been found yet of the O'Malley."

For a moment, all was silence. Then Niall said, fiercely and simply, "I'll find her! I'll find her!" And he swung his legs over the edge of the bed trying to rise. Inis whined.

Constanza Alcudia Cuidadela rose swiftly and sped to his side. "No, No! Señor Niall. You will reopen your wound. It is still not totally healed." She slipped an arm about his back and gently forced him back to the bed. "Fetch my papa immediately," she hissed angrily at the stricken captain. "Ana, help me get the señor back into bed." She fussed about him like a little mother hen, puffing the pillows and smoothing the coverlet, and despite his anxiety he was amused by this little creature whose concern for him was so touching. "For shame, señor!" she scolded. "Ana and I have worked so hard to make you well! Why do you allow your captain to agitate you? If you cannot remain calm then I will not let him in to see you again."

He realized then that, although he was speaking Spanish with her, he had spoken Gaelic with MacGuire. She hadn't understood. He felt suddenly weak, but wanted her to understand. "My betrothed wife was kidnapped when I was injured," he said. "MacGuire tells me she has not yet been found." It was several moments before she spoke.

"You love her very much, Señor Niall?"

"Yes, Señorita Constanza," he replied gently. "I love her very much."

"Then I shall make a novena to the Holy Virgin that she is found soon," the girl said gravely, and Niall thought again how sweet the child was.

MacGuire quickly returned bringing an older gentleman with him. The man was of medium height with a short, dark, tailored beard, dark hair, and the coldest black eyes Niall had ever seen. He was dressed richly but soberly, his short velvet cape edged in a wide band of deep brown fur.

"Lord Burke," the voice was as cold as the eyes. "I am the Conde Francisco Cuidadela, and I am happy to see you conscious at last. Captain MacGuire tells me, however, that you are agitated about your betrothed. It is best that you hear the truth now."

"Papa!" the girl's voice was pleading. "Señor Niall is not yet strong enough."

"Silence, Constanza! How dare you presume to advise me? You

will come to me after vespers for punishment, and then you are to spend the night in the chapel meditating on filial respect and obedience."

The girl hung her head, beaten. "Yes, Papa," she whispered.

"Your betrothed wife is lost to you forever, Lord Burke, and the sooner you are able to accept this the better off you will be. Should she be found you could not possibly want her back. If she is alive, she has by now been defiled by the infidel, and no decent Catholic could live with that."

"No!"

"Be reasonable, Lord Burke. Captain MacGuire tells me the lady was a widow. Without the protection of virginity—for purity brings a very high price among the infidels—she was probably raped by at least the captain and officers of the ship that kidnapped her. If she survived that and was beautiful, then rest assured that she was sold into slavery. If she is still alive, she now graces some pasha's bed. It is not possible that you could want a woman like that back, even if she could be found. Under these circumstances, the holy Church would not hold you to your betrothal. The lady is as lost to you as if she were dead, and in all likelihood she *is* dead."

"Get out!"

The Conde bowed from the waist. "Your grief is understandable, Lord Burke. I shall leave you to it. You will soon see the wisdom of my words. Come, Constanza!" And he swept from the room, his daughter meekly behind him.

Niall Burke watched the door close behind the Conde and his daughter. For a moment the silence hung heavy in the room, then he said grimly, "All right MacGuire, talk! I'm no child to be wheedled, and if I've lived this long, you can bloody well be sure I'm going to survive. *Where* is the O'Malley fleet, and what's this nonsense about Skye being *lost* forever, and how the *hell* long have I been here anyway? Speak up, man, or I'll tear the tongue from your head!"

"You've been ill six weeks, my lord."

"Jesu!" swore Niall.

"The fleet went directly to Algiers and we were able to obtain an immediate audience with the Dey. He was most sympathetic and sent to every slave merchant in the city, offering a king's ransom for the O'Malley's return, or at least information leading to her return. It was like hollering down a rabbit hole, my lord—not even an echo. The Dey came to the same conclusion the Conde has. She never reached Algiers alive. What other answer is there?" Here his voice broke, and he wiped his eyes with the back of his hand.

In truth, MacGuire was more distressed by something he dared not tell the seriously ill Lord Burke. It seemed that there was one other possibility about the O'Malley's fate. The Dey had told him that Skye might have reached Algiers alive and then been sold privately. Private sale of captives was strictly illegal because it cheated several people, including the Dey himself, of their shares in the purchase price. But private sales were managed, especially sales of beautiful women. MacGuire reasoned that, if this had happened to Skye, then the Dey would not be able to trace her.

"I don't want to believe it, my lord, but if Mistress Skye is alive then where is she?"

Niall Burke was stunned. Skye dead? No! Not Skye. Not his vibrant Skye with her Kerry-blue eyes and her proud spirit. No! His shoulders began to shake as the dry sobs took hold and racked him mercilessly. Stumbling from the bed, he lurched across the room, through the French doors and out onto the terrace. All around him everything throbbed with life and *they* said his Skye was dead! Clutching the cool marble balustrade, he howled his frustration and anger at the unfairness of it all, howled and shouted until his voice was so hoarse that he made no sounds at all.

He felt an arm about him, heard a soft voice making soothing sounds he could not comprehend, allowed himself to be led back inside where he barely reached the bed before he collapsed, unconscious. Constanza Cuidadela shook her head as she drew the covers over him. She felt his forehead.

"The fever is back, Captain MacGuire. You must sit with him tonight for my father will not excuse me from my punishment. I will tell you what to do."

MacGuire nodded. "He's not an easy man, your father."

The girl did not reply. She went quietly about her business, caring for the unconscious Niall. Smoothing the pillows first, she next tucked the sheets about her patient and, finally, placed the frosted pitcher on the bedside table.

"You can do very little, Captain, except to keep him as quiet and as comfortable as possible. Ana will bring a basin of scented water shortly, and she'll come again during the night." The vespers bells began to toll, and Constanza said, "I must go. When the fever breaks, change his nightshirt and the sheets. Ana will help." And then she was gone.

MacGuire tended Niall throughout the night. Strangely, Niall was not restless, but lay ominously quiet as the burning fever consumed his big body. Diligently the O'Malley captain cared for his charge, bathing his forehead regularly with the cool, scented water, gently forcing the sweet juice down his throat. During the night, the servant woman, Ana, appeared regularly, bringing fresh water and juice for the sick man. Once she brought a tray for MacGuire with a small cold chicken, bread, fruit, and a carafe of sweet golden wine.

As she silently placed his tray on the long walnut table, MacGuire asked, "How is the lass?"

Ana's black eyes blazed. "She prays in the chapel for your master, señor," she said tersely. Then she left.

MacGuire ate hungrily, drank half the carafe, and returned to Niall's bedside. Toward dawn he dozed in his chair only to be startled awake by a great cry of anguish. Lord Burke sat straight up in the bed, his eyes tightly shut, the tears pouring down his face. He sobbed bitterly, "Skye! Skye! Don't leave me, beloved! Come back! Come back!"

MacGuire was immobilized for a moment by the terrible anguish. Then he reached out and shook the weeping man gently. "My lord! My lord! It's only a bad dream."

Gradually Niall quieted, and finally he lay back. His forehead was cool to the touch. Relieved, MacGuire struggled to change his sleeping friend's damp nightshirt.

After the first mass of the new day, Constanza appeared to check on her patient. Ana was with her. Constanza praised the worn captain. "You have done well, Captain MacGuire. Go and rest. I will tend to Señor Niall now."

"But you had no rest either, lass," protested MacGuire. "You must sleep. He's out of danger now. A servant can keep watch." He put a fatherly arm about her to lead her toward the door, and was shocked when she winced. A thin red line began to show through the sleeve of her gown, and the captain's eyes widened.

"Aye!" snapped Ana. "The Conde beat my sweet Constanza last night."

"Ana!" The girl was flushed with shame. "He is my father, and it is a father's duty to chastise an erring child. I challenged his authority. I was wrong."

"She is a saint, my *niña*. The Conde enjoys hurting her!"

"Ana! Please! If you are overheard he will send you away, and you are all I have."

The serving woman compressed her lips tightly, sighed, and nodded. MacGuire spoke again. "Has the Conde gone to his duties as the island's governor?" The women nodded. "Then, Señorita Constanza, I shall strike a bargain with you. I shall keep watch over Lord Burke until the afternoon siesta while you sleep upon the chaise longue. When afternoon comes, I shall go to my own rooms."

Ana smiled broadly. The captain was *muy simpatico* to her Constanza. Therefore, to Ana, he was a good man, a man to be trusted. A few minutes later she left the young girl sleeping comfortably, MacGuire guarding both Constanza and Niall.

In the late afternoon when the long mauve shadows were beginning to form and the midday heat to abate, Niall Burke opened his silvery eyes again. He instantly remembered where he was and the circumstances that had brought him here. A great burst of sadness washed through him, and he sighed deeply.

"How do you feel, Señor Niall?"

He looked to the slim girl. "Like the very devil, *niña,* but I seem to be alive, so I'd best get on with this business of living."

"Was she very beautiful, your betrothed?" The directness of the question was like salt in an open wound, and he winced. Drawing a deep breath, he replied, "She was the loveliest creature imaginable, *niña.* Her hair was like a black storm cloud. Her skin was like a gardenia flower in texture and color, and her eyes were the wonderful deep blue of the seas off Ireland. She was kind yet proud. And not only was she my dearest love, she was also my best friend, and I shall miss her for all the days of my life."

Constanza's eyes were bright with tears. "I can only hope," she said softly, "that someday a man will love me like that."

"I can see no reason why one wouldn't, *niña.* I cannot understand why you are not already married. How old are you?"

"Fifteen, Señor Niall."

"And have not half the eligible young dons on this island already sued your father for your hand? Or are they all blind?"

She smiled shyly, then blushed. "There will be no offer for me, Señor Niall," she said sadly. "My father long ago destroyed any chances of marrying I might have had. Last night when he told you about your betrothed you undoubtedly thought him harsh, but your plight brought back to him something he would much rather forget.

"Almost sixteen years ago the Moorish pirates raided this island, and when they left they took my mother as one of their captives. My father had been deeply in love with her, and he was frantic. He was able to ransom her six weeks later.

"I was born six months later. Though she swore before the priest and on every saint in the calendar, even on the Holy Mother's name, that the pirates had not touched her, my father could not bring himself to really believe her. Not ever. As she grew bigger with her pregnancy, he grew more distant toward her. She adored him, and it broke her heart. She lived just long enough to give me life, and then she died like a snuffed-out candle.

"The irony is that I look like her. Every day of my life I have been a living reproach to my father. In turn, he has held me responsible for my mother's death and he has cast enough doubt on my paternity that no decent family on Mallorca would allow their son to offer for me.

"I am his child, though. That is certain. Ana was my mother's servant before she was my nurse. She came with my mother from Castile when Mother was married to Father. She was with her the entire time Mother was kidnapped, and she swears to me that my mother knew no man but my father."

Suddenly Constanza stopped. She blushed beet-red. Realizing the cause of her embarrassment, Niall Burke said quietly, "Don't regret your words, *niña.* I have always been the kind of man to whom women talk. I understand now your father's words. He is a harsh man, but he meant to tell me the truth."

The girl knelt by his bedside, her lovely oval face turned up to him. "I am so sorry, Señor Niall. I know how sad the loss of your betrothed wife is to you, but God has willed that you live. We will both pray for your Skye's immortal soul, but you must also promise me that you will now get well."

Niall Burke was touched by her honest concern. He put his big hand over her small one. "Very well, Constanzita, I promise, but you must promise to help me. Will you?"

The hand beneath his trembled slightly, and she flushed a most becoming pink as her dark-gold lashes brushed her cheeks. "If you wish it," she said low.

"I wish it," he answered, releasing her hand.

In the next few weeks he grew stronger. The fever finally left his body, and his appetite increased. Eventually he was able to leave his bed and walk about his room. Then came the day that he ventured into the gardens. That afternoon was the happiest time he could remember in many weeks. He and Constanza, chaperoned by Ana, sat on the grass and picnicked on small meat pastries, juicy green grapes, and a delicate rosé wine. Niall told them stories of his boyhood in Ireland, and for the first time he heard Constanza laugh, a sweet trill of genuine mirth, as he told them a particularly amusing story about his youthful hijinks. He began to sleep again at night, and the nightmares of seeing Skye struggling in the grasp of the Barbary pirates began to fade away.

The O'Malley's fleet put into Mallorca's capital city of Palma again. They had spent several months in Algiers seeking their mistress, but in the end they had had to leave without even any information. The Dey, however, had given the O'Malley family rich concessions in hopes of placating them. It seemed there was no hope of finding the O'Malley alive. The Irish ships would sail home shortly under the leadership of Captain MacGuire. Niall, however, was still not considered strong enough for the voyage.

Niall entrusted Inis to MacGuire and gave the captain a lengthy letter to his father, pouring out his grief and closing with the admonition, "Make no contracts for me. I will, in time, do my duty by the family." Then, with a strange sense of loss, Niall Burke bid the O'Malley fleet farewell, watching from the terrace of the Conde's garden as the ships sailed out to sea.

Niall saw little of his host and was glad, for the cold Spanish don was not a man whose company Niall enjoyed.

One day Constanza suggested that he might feel up to riding, and he delightedly agreed. That afternoon he found himself upon a spirited roan red Arabian stallion, cantering through a field of colorful windflowers and anemones. Constanza rode with him, mounted on an elegant little white Arabian mare. She was a fine horsewoman with a good sure seat and gentle but firm hands.

In the heat of the afternoon they stopped in a meadow above the sea to rest their horses and eat the light luncheon Ana had packed. Constanza lay a little white cloth over the grass and set out their luncheon of crusty bread, soft ripe cheese, peaches, pears, and white wine. Niall unsaddled the horses so that they could rest. A tall, leafy tree shaded them all, and the air was heavy with the scent of wild thyme.

They ate in silence. After the meal Constanza spoke, "Soon you will leave us. Where will you go? Back to your Ireland?"

A small shadow flitted across his face. "Not right away, *niña*. I shall travel for a bit before I go back. But go back I must, for I am my father's only heir. My first marriage was annulled. My second never made."

"You will find happiness, Señor Niall. I pray every night to the Blessed Mother for you."

He cupped her face with a warm hand. "What a sweet creature you are, my Constanzita."

She blushed and pressed her cheek against his hand. Suddenly he wanted to kiss her, and he did. Pulling the girl into his arms, he bent his head down—found her mouth. She was trembling wildly, but she did not struggle. Emboldened, he gently parted her lips and plunged into the sweet cavern, seeking, finding, stroking the girl's satiny tongue with his own. One arm held her fast as a hand sought her full, young breasts.

Constanza tore her head away, gasping for air. Frantically she sought his hands. But it wasn't Niall she feared, it was herself. Niall Burke was a gentleman, and one word from her would halt him, yet she could not bring herself to say the word. No man had ever before kissed or touched her as he was doing. Her heart was pounding and she feared it might burst. Yet she did not stop him. His mouth was again on hers, tenderly searing her soul with a passion she had never even suspected she could feel. His fingers were undoing the laces of her bodice, gently pulling down her chemise.

Niall was amazed by the girl's easy acquiescence. He was positive she was innocent, yet she seemed to welcome his advances. He felt a momentary guilt but pushed it away. Skye was dead, he was alive, and Constanza Cuidadela was fresh and sweet. His eyes feasted on her young breasts, beautiful golden orbs, their proud dark-coral nipples tight like unopened rosebuds. Almost reverently, he caressed and kissed them, delighting in her soft cry.

Constanza felt an unfamiliar tightness building within her. It frightened her a little. She did not want him to stop, but suddenly he did.

"You are a virgin, aren't you, *niña?*" Her blush gave him his answer. "I will not dishonor you, Constanza," he told her gravely. "It would not be right if I spoiled you for your future husband, especially after your kindness to me. I had no right to do what I have just done. For that I ask your forgiveness and your understanding."

Constanza sat very still, making no attempt to cover herself. In the meadow the roan stallion screamed defiantly and brutally mounted the white mare, biting her silken neck and thrusting his great organ into her. Constanza rose and deftly shed the rest of her clothes. They lay in a colorful heap about her trim ankles. She looked at Niall proudly.

"I want you to do to me what your stallion does to my mare," she said softly.

Niall Burke felt the aching hardness in his groin. It would take a saint to refuse such an invitation, and he was no saint. Still, he was no rake, either. Then the idea was born in him. Why not? he thought. I will have to sooner or later. And so he said, "Will you be my wife, Constanzita?"

"Yes," she answered. He stood up, towering over her, and slowly pulled off his own clothes. She watched him, curious. Having no brothers, she had no certain knowledge of male anatomy. Before her amazed eyes his masculinity rose proudly like a battle flag. He took her hand, saying tenderly, "Touch it, *niña.* I promise it won't bite you . . . though it will love you well."

Her small hand closed about him, gently, virginally curious. He held his breath, afraid of frightening her. Her warm little hand cradled him, fondling him with innocent expertise, and he could not restrain an intense groan. Startled, she let go.

"I have hurt you!"

"Nay, lovey, you pleasure me beyond all," and he drew her into his arms and kissed her again. Her round breasts, hard now with her mounting passion, rubbed against his dark furred chest until the little nipples were raw with desire. Her torso pressed tightly against him like burning silk, trembling weakly as her legs began to give way. But her voice was low and strong.

"Take me, my Niall. Take me like the stallion took my mare!"

He lowered her to the ground, then knelt beside her. Her violet eyes were wide with wonder as he bent his head to catch a little nipple in his mouth. Slowly he sucked on it, watching with narrowed silver eyes as her breath came in short little gasps and her hips began to twitch. A caressing hand moved down her fevered body, and she jumped as he touched that most secret of places. His finger pushed through the soft defensive folds, rubbing insistently, and Constanza thought she was going to faint.

Her heart was leaping about wildly, and she was being buffeted by a great storm of new feelings, the like of which she'd never known. Her belly ached, and between her legs where his hand teased she ached in a different way. When he gently put his long finger into her she was relieved, but when he withdrew, the ache was worse and she whimpered.

"All right, lovey," he said softly, "I will make it better now," and he mounted her, parting her trembling thighs, and slowly entered her. She opened herself to him like a flower. Her eyes never left his face even when he reached her tight little virgin shield and pierced it, swiftly, so as to give her less hurt.

Constanza felt the slow, burning pain spread quickly up her, and she cried out. His lips covered her protest, his tongue probing her mouth, matching the rhythm of his throbbing spear. Something wonderful was happening to her, and she eagerly thrust her hips upward to meet his fierce downward thrusts. The pain was gone, and she was soaring like a bird in flight. Her little hands grasped his tight buttocks to bring him closer, and at the moment of her climax she tore her head away from him, shrieking her joy. Then she fainted.

Niall Burke lay panting in astounded exhaustion. Never had he experienced such passion in a virgin, and she had certainly been a virgin, as the blood on her thighs attested. Now she lay drained and unconscious. He studied her for a moment, this girl who would be his wife. She was certainly lovely, and although he wasn't entirely sure he liked her excessive passion she would certainly be a better bedsport than poor Darragh had been. The MacWilliam might be angered momentarily by a surprise bride, but if Niall was lucky he would bring her home to Ireland with a babe in her belly or at her breast. In that case, all would be forgiven.

She was barely breathing, and he pulled her into his arms to warm her, to awaken her. Her eyelids fluttered as she began her slow return to consciousness. He held her close, murmuring soft little words of endearment, and as her eyes opened to focus on his face, she blushed furiously.

"Oh, Niall, what must you think of me? But, oh, it was wonderful!"

He laughed. "What I think, *niña,* is that I am a very lucky man. You were quite magnificent. How do you feel, lovey?"

"I flew, Niall! I really flew! I feel so happy now, and I want to do it again!"

He chuckled. "We shall fly together again, lovey, but I think perhaps it would be best now if we returned to Palma. I must ask your father's permission to marry you." He stood up and began to pull his clothes on, but it was not easy to concentrate when Constanza lay naked at his feet on her bed of meadow flowers and soft green grass. He finally managed to return some measure of order to his garb and, holding out his hand, he said, "Come, madam, and I will maid you."

She stood, and he was again enchanted by the perfection of her slim body. Slowly she pulled on her undergarments, then the dress skirt, and lastly the dress top which he laced for her, first cupping the sweet round breasts and fondling them. Leaning back against him, she murmured contently.

He spanked her bottom fondly. "Pack the luncheon basket, *niña,* while I catch the horses and saddle them up."

They returned to Palma in the late afternoon. One look at Constanza's face brought a cry of joy from Ana. As Niall dismounted his horse the older woman grasped his hands and kissed them. "Gracias, Señor Niall! My Constanza will make you a good wife, I swear it!"

"Then you think the Conde will give his consent, Ana?"

A crafty look came into the woman's eyes. "He will at first refuse you, for he has never forgiven my *niña*'s birth. If, however, you tell him that you have dishonored his daughter then he will quickly consent, for he fears scandal more than anything else."

"In that case, Ana, I shall speak to him at once," smiled Niall.

"He is in his library now, my lord."

Niall bent down and brushed Constanza's lips. "For luck, Constanzita," he said, and was gone.

"Aiiieee, my *niña!* You have at last found a man, and what a man! He will keep your belly filled for years to come. It is what I have prayed for, *niña*. Someone to take you from the Conde, and his bitterness. Now you will have a good life, a normal life." She hugged the girl hard. Then, catching herself, she gasped, "In my happiness I have forgotten you, my Constanza. You are all right? He was gentle?"

"He was gentle, nurse, but I am sore and could use a bath."

"At once, *niña!* At once!"

And while Constanza bathed herself in a warm, scented tub, Niall Burke sprawled his long frame in a rather uncomfortable chair in the Conde's library. In his big hand he twirled the stem of a small wine glass. The Conde stared coldly at his guest.

"You are vastly improved in health, Lord Burke." It was more a statement than a question. "I expect you will soon leave us."

Niall nodded. "Soon, my lord, and when I go there is something I would take with me from Mallorca."

"A souvenir of sorts, Lord Burke?"

Niall could not resist a chuckle. "Of sorts," he said. "I wish to marry Constanza. I am formally applying to you for her hand."

The Conde's facial expression never wavered. "It is impossible, Lord Burke."

"She is previously contracted?"

"No."

"She is ill with some fatal sickness?"

"No."

"Then why do you refuse me? I am the only son and heir of a wealthy and noble man. In my country, my lineage is equal to your own. You would have grandchildren. And, as my wife, your daughter would lack for nothing."

"I do not have to explain myself to you, Lord Burke. I am Constanza's father, and I have refused your suit. My word is all that counts."

Niall drew a deep breath. "Is the reason for your refusal the fact that you doubt your daughter's paternity?"

Francisco Cuidadela grew white. "You are impertinent, Lord Burke. Leave me! I do not choose to discuss it."

Niall's silvery eyes narrowed. "Let me tell you how I spent my afternoon, Conde. I spent it enjoying your daughter's favors. She gave herself to me quite willingly, and I am pleased to say that she was a virgin. At this very moment my seed could be rooting in her fertile womb. You deliberately destroyed her chances of marriage here on Mallorca. Now not even a convent will have her. How will you face your friends when she grows big with my child? You are the last of your line, Conde, and your late wife's family is also long gone. There is no place you can send Constanza to hide her shame. Already I hear the laughter of your friends. And if King Philip should hear of this scandal you might find yourself rapidly replaced as governor here.

"On the other hand, if you accept my suit you will be envied your cleverness for catching such a fine prize as myself. But, of course, the decision is yours."

Francisco Cuidadela had gone from white to red and back to white again as Niall talked. Now the Conde made a strangled sound.

"Does that mean you accept, my lord?" asked Niall politely.

The older man nodded weakly, and Niall smiled, satisfied. "Tomorrow," he said, "we shall see the bishop and arrange for the first of the banns to be posted. Have your secretary bring me a copy of the marriage contract in the morning. I trust that Constanza's dowry will be quite ample, as she is your only child. Not that I care," he said, "but my father will expect it."

The Conde sent him a black look. Chuckling softly, Niall left the library. It was done. Once again he was betrothed, and he hoped that, this time, the union would produce children.

Constanza was not Skye, nor would she ever take Skye's place in his heart. He laughed ruefully. He had never loved anyone but

Skye. Why had fate been so cruel as to separate them just when they were so near to marriage? "Skye," he whispered her name softly. "Skye O'Malley, my love." He tasted the words on his tongue. No, she couldn't be dead! Would not her spirit have come to him, and wouldn't he have felt it if she were? Must he accept that she was dead when he truly could not believe it was so?

No, he would never love Constanza as he had loved Skye, but Constanza was sweet and good and deserved his full attention. She would have it too, he vowed; but when he closed his eyes to conjure up her oval face with its violet eyes and halo of golden curls he instead saw a cloud of black hair framing a heart-shaped face with laughing blue eyes and a soft red mouth.

"Dammit, Skye O'Malley," he swore. "I cannot help it that I am alive, and you are . . . are . . . Leave me in peace, my darling, to find some kind of happiness!"

He found Constanza and announced, "Your father has consented to our marriage, lovey. Tomorrow we shall have the bishop read the first banns at mass, and the contracts shall be signed."

"I cannot believe it," she breathed, her eyes shining. "How did you convince him?"

"I told him how we spent the afternoon," said Niall drily.

Constanza swayed. "Oh! He will beat me!"

Seeing her white face left no doubt in his mind that she did not exaggerate. "Has he beaten you before, lovey?"

"Of course. He is my papa. He is never an easy man, Niall, but knowing that I gave myself to you willingly will infuriate him. I am truly afraid."

"Don't be frightened, Constanzita. I will not allow anyone, even your father, to harm you."

With a contented sigh she nestled into his arms, and he felt better than he had in a long time. She loved him, she needed him, and it would be good between them.

The marriage contracts were signed the following morning and the first banns were read at the Palma cathedral's noon mass. By nightfall felicitations were pouring into the governor's villa from all the best families on the island. The Conde was particularly pleased when one of his friends who had spent time in London and Dublin congratulated him on obtaining such a fine catch for Constanza.

"Lord Burke's father is quite wealthy, my dear Francisco, and dotes on his only son as you have doted on Constanza. What a fine match! But then, you were always a shrewd devil, eh?" The two men chuckled conspiratorially, and the Conde began to feel that perhaps he had the upper hand after all. This tempered his unfriendly feelings toward Niall.

The banns were read twice again within the month and then on a bright winter's morning several days after the Twelfth Night feast had ended, Constanza Maria Theresa Floreal Alcudia Cuidadela was joined in holy matrimony to Lord Niall Sean Burke. The bishop of Mallorca performed the ceremony.

The sun streamed through the stained-glass windows of the cathedral, making beautiful wavy patterns on the pale-gray stone floors. The bride was preceded by six little girls in pale-pink silk dresses over miniature farthingales with short puffed sleeves, wreaths of rosebuds in their unbound hair. The children carried gilt baskets of flower petals which they strewed about lavishly.

Constanza clung to her father's arm, a vision so exquisitely ethereal that an audible sigh rose collectively from the guests. Her gown was a heavy white silk brocade overskirt on a cloth-of-silver underskirt. The upper sleeves of the gown were large puffs of white brocade, slashed to show the silver interior. The sleeves were edged in lace just below the elbow. The lower sleeves were thin white silk that clung tightly to the arm and ended in cuffs of lace. The white brocade bodice was tight, and began just above the swell of the bride's ample bosom. Modesty was preserved by a transparent silk chiffon insert that had a dainty, virginal, round lace collar.

Constanza's golden hair was unbound and topped by a wreath of white rosebuds attached by small pearl pins to a sheer cloud of lace that floated about her. In one hand she carried a bouquet of gardenias and about her slender neck was a single strand of pearls.

The groom, awaiting her at the altar, was equally elegant. His silk hose were red-and-gold-striped, his upper legs covered by puffed and slashed breeches of claret-red velvet. His short, high-collared doublet was of matching silk and open at the front to show an embroidered white silk undershirt ruffled at the wrists. Covering his doublet was an embroidered overjerkin of claret-red velvet, studded with freshwater pearls and gold beads. His rakish velvet cap was tilted to show its heavily jeweled underside, and a pink plume drooped from it. His shoes, tanned from the hide of an unborn calf, were gilded a pale gold.

Sword and dagger were *de rigueur,* and both of Niall's blades were of the finest Toledo steel. The hilts, however, were gold, and heavily jeweled in diamonds and rubies. Encircling his neck and spilling down onto his chest was a heavy gold chain with a large gold, diamond, and ruby medallion depicting a raised winged griffon.

The women eyed his broad chest and well-turned legs and sighed behind their fans. How on earth, they wondered, did that meek little milksop catch such a man? It was said that the couple would remain on Mallorca for several months before journeying to London and the court of the young new English queen, Elizabeth. Perhaps in that time they might have the opportunity to offer their charms to the handsome Lord Burke? They would show him what an error it was to wed in haste.

The ceremony ended, and with the bishop's permission Niall tenderly brushed the lips of his bride. Her shining eyes and sweet blush told him how happy she was. Smiling, he tucked her small hand in his arm and swept her down the aisle of the cathedral, back across the square, and into the governor's villa. Soon they were greeting their guests.

The Conde had spared no expense in the preparation of his only child's bridal feast. The tables groaned with sides of beef, whole young roasted lambs and kids, larded ducks, whole swans in aspic, lemoned and gingered capons. There were pigeon and lark pies with their flaky crusts steaming, and huge bowls of paella, red lobster bits and green olives showing brilliantly against the saffroned yellow rice. There were platters of boiled shrimp in white wine and herbs, a tub of raw oysters, platters of new green scallions, and tiny red love apples. Great loaves of white bread, both lean and long and fat and round, had been placed at intervals down the board. One whole table had been set aside for sweets. There were plates of molded jellies in red, green, and gold, dishes of sugared almonds, cakes, marzipan fruit tarts, and silver bowls of black raisins, purple figs, green and white grapes, and Seville oranges. Deep-red and golden wines and heady beer flowed from the villa fountains.

The musicians played lively tunes as they moved among the guests. At the head table Niall and Constanza sat in the place of honor receiving congratulations. Neither missed the admiring looks cast the groom's way by many of the ladies, and the bride's purple-pansy eyes darkened jealously.

"You look like an outraged kitten," he observed in an amused tone.

"I was thinking," she replied, "that the marquesa, for all her low décolletage and painted face, is at least ten years your senior."

Niall gave a whoop of laughter and kissed her soundly. "Oh, *niña,* what a sharp little tongue you have." Then his eyes caressed her, and he said, "Soon I shall teach you to use that naughty tongue in a sweeter pursuit," and Constanza felt a strong warmth sweep over her. Since that afternoon in the meadow he had not known her intimately. His behavior had been that of any proper gentleman with his betrothed. It had made her a little afraid, especially after her monthly show of blood had arrived on time. Perhaps he regretted his proposal but was too well mannered to withdraw it? Now, however, his eyes told her that she had been foolish to be afraid. As the relief flooded through her she felt quite giddy.

The afternoon lengthened and became evening. Finally Ana was at her elbow, whispering, and Constanza rose discreetly and left the courtyard. "Come in an hour, my lord," said the servant woman softly, and Niall acknowledged the message with a faint nod. Shortly afterward the Conde slipped into the seat nearest him.

"I did not mention it before, but Constanza's maternal grandmother was English. Part of her dowry was a house on the Strand in London. It is not large, nor elegant, but it has been kept in good repair. It came to me through Constanza's mother, and I have made it a part of your wife's dowry. My London agent has already informed the tenants that they must leave. The house will be staffed and ready for you when you reach London."

"My thanks, Don Francisco. The Burkes have long considered the value of a London house, and the Strand is an excellent location." He glanced about the festive courtyard. "My gratitude also for this day. It has made Constanza so happy."

"She is my daughter, Don Niall. Oh, I know that old gypsy witch, Ana, has convinced Constanza that I doubt her paternity and believe she killed her mother, but it is not so. Constanza was born with a heart-shaped mole on her right buttock. I have the identical mole, as do my brother, Jamie, our father, and our late grandfather. So did my two sisters. Any doubts I might have entertained were eradicated the moment I first saw my daughter.

"As to Constanza's mother, Maria Theresa was as frail as she was proud. The agony of being held all those weeks in the licentious clutches of the Moors shamed her as greatly as it shamed me. She died because she could not bear to be whispered about for the rest of her life. How could a simple peasant like Ana understand something like that?"

He sighed. "Be good to my Constanza, Don Niall. She is so much like her mother. When you take her away, it will be like losing Maria Theresa again." He then rose quickly, and joined a group of his friends on the other side of the courtyard.

Niall was astounded by these revelations, and the brief glimpse he had just had into the Conde's soul. No wonder he had been so generous with Constanza's dowry. It included an estate in Spain, the villa here on Mallorca, an enormous settlement in gold with the promise of more to come when the Conde died, and now a London house. He smiled to himself. The MacWilliam would be quite pleased, for Niall was certainly bringing home an heiress.

A servant refilled his goblet, and he watched the gypsy dancers with a growing feeling of peace. Quaffing down the cup, he rose and went to his room where he found his manservant waiting with a steaming tub. Silently, he bathed, sniffing appreciatively at the sandalwood soap. Standing up, he sluiced water down his body, and was carefully dried.

"Where is my lady?"

"She awaits my lord in the bedchamber next to his own."

"Tell Ana I am coming. Tell her to leave my wife. You are dismissed for the night."

"*Sí,* my lord."

Niall examined his naked body in the pier glass and was pleased by what he saw. His illness and idleness hadn't put any flab on him. He turned, picked up a small object from out of a drawer, and entered the scented candlelit chamber where Constanza lay beneath the coverlet of their bed. Her eyes widened at the sight of him.

"I sleep this way," he said by way of explanation.

"So do I, but Ana made me put on a nightdress. She said it was expected tonight."

"Shall we shock Mallorcan society, *niña?*" he asked mischievously. "Stand up quickly," he commanded, and when she obeyed he tore the dainty lawn gown from her body and tossed the pieces across the room. "And now, to assure my honor and proclaim your purity to all . . ." He held his hand over the bed and tightly closed his fist. Blood splattered the sheets in the center. Constanza shrieked, and Niall laughed. "Perfect, my love! Now the wedding guests will believe your maidenhead successfully breached." He wiped his hand clean of blood and tossed the linen towel in the fire. "It was a piglet's bladder filled with chicken blood," he explained. "Your Ana gave it to me this morning."

"Oh," she answered wide-eyed. "I never thought . . ." her voice trailed off.

He laughed. "Neither did I, but your Ana, bless her, did. I am glad she's coming with us. Now, you tempting little piece, come here to me! This last month I've gone half mad remembering our afternoon in the meadow."

"Oh, I have too!" she confessed. He picked her up and put her gently on the bed. Then he joined her. "Is that very shocking, Niall?"

"Hell, no, lovey! I'd rather you were eager for me than cold and retiring." He pulled her into his arms almost roughly and her belly fluttered in anticipation. How many times had she dreamed of that afternoon, seeing the red stallion thrusting his big penis into the quivering little white mare, and then seeing Niall looming above her, lowering his body onto hers, thrusting his own great penis into her. There had been days when she had writhed on her bed with the memory half a dozen times.

Now as he buried his face in her warm breasts, she sighed. Her golden orbs grew hard as his mouth drank first from one and then from the other. His tongue circled the nipples again and again until she begged him to take her. He laughed. Niall had recognized the wanton in her, and now he was curious to see how far he might drive her.

His warm tongue licked her soft, fragrant skin, moving downward from her navel, stopping, then moving up each leg from the knee, stopping again. She thrashed wildly, her blond hair tangling. Fascinated, Niall let his lips and eyes wander to the soft defenses of her womanhood. With gentle fingers he parted the plump folds to stare in fascination as her tender little button grew stiff and throbbing. His mouth fastened about it, and tasted its sweetness.

"Ohhh, dear God, don't stop! Please don't stop!"

Twice she climaxed under the ministrations of his demanding mouth. At last, unable to bear much more himself, he drove his root into her warm and fertile body. She cried out her pleasure, wrapping her legs tightly around him, moving fiercely with his rhythm, clawing at his back in her passion as he emptied himself into her.

Rolling off her, he saw that she was in a semiconscious state. He gathered her into his arms gently so that her return would be a warm and safe one. He was delighted with this marvelous, passionate creature to whom he was wed. It was almost too good to be true, and yet it was true. He had found the perfect mate, the woman from whose loins the next generation of Burkes would spring. Constanza stirred faintly in his arms. "Good-bye, Skye, my dear true love," Niall whispered softly, and turned to face his new young wife.

Chapter 12

The wife of Khalid el Bey was the most famous woman in the city of Algiers. Three nights each week she presided, unveiled, over her husband's banquet table. The all-male guests were shocked at first, but they quickly recovered, for the lady Skye was charming, witty, and gently spoken. It was said that she knew as much about running her husband's businesses as he did, but no man gave that rumor serious consideration, for it was too absurd. Allah had fashioned women for man's pleasure, and for birth, but nothing else.

All envied Khalid el Bey his beautiful wife, but none envied him more than Jamil, the captain of the Casbah fort. The Turkish soldier had quite a respectable harem, for he was known to be sexually insatiable. Favors from Captain Jamil were easily bought simply by presenting him with a beautiful, skilled slave. Still, Jamil lusted after Skye, desperate to possess her. She had intrigued him greatly by refusing his overtures. He bribed the women of Skye's household to smuggle in gifts of jewels, flowers, and comfits. All were returned, their wrapping not even opened. Furious, he managed to separate her from her guests on two occasions, only to be rebuffed, even insulted. Never in his life had Jamil been refused so strongly, and the insult rankled. He was determined to possess Skye.

Tonight he lay sprawled on a couch in the House of Felicity, watching with Yasmin through a two-way mirror. On the other side of the mirror was one of the city's most respected merchants, who lay naked and tied while two lovely young girls serviced him. One crouched over his head, her plump little pussy rubbing against his open mouth, while the other sucked frantically on the merchant's small, flaccid manhood. Finally, as their simultaneous efforts resulted in success, the girl at the lower end mounted the man and rode him to glory.

Jamil laughed heartily. "Poor darlings, he's not worth their effort. Send them both to me later and I'll reward them with a real workout."

"I thought you intended spending the night with me," she pouted. "I do not give my favors to just anyone."

"Would you deny me an appetizer before a gourmet meal?" he flattered her.

Yasmin almost purred. She enjoyed Jamil. He was the best lover she'd ever had—next to Khalid. Khalid, damn him, had ceased his visits since falling in love with Skye. A look of anger flashed across her beautiful face. Jamil caught it instantly.

"What is it, my pet?" he queried. "You have been increasingly irritable of late. Tell Jamil, and he will make it better."

She hesitated before admitting, "It is my lord Khalid. He is so changed. I do not know him anymore, and it is all the fault of his wife."

"She is quite beautiful," he said wickedly. "But of course, I do not know her."

"I wish to Allah she were dead! Then my lord Khalid would come to me again."

"Perhaps," he mused, "it could be arranged, my dear." He continued smoothly despite her startled look. "Of course, I should expect certain remunerations from you for my help. But what difference should the death of one woman make to anyone? Especially a woman with no memory, no powerful connections."

Yasmin was fascinated in spite of herself. "But, how?" she asked.

"If I wanted someone dead I should chose the time and place carefully, and then I should wield the blade myself. The fewer people involved the better, would you not say? Who would suspect you if we were seen to enter your chambers together on the night in question?"

"When, Jamil? When?"

He smiled. "Tomorrow night, my dear Yasmin. The sooner the better. I shall send a message to Khalid el Bey asking that he meet me at the Casbah fort. Afterward I shall simply deny that I sent any message. You and I shall be seen entering your rooms. I shall stay the night. You will slip out and walk to Khalid el Bey's house. Enter through the garden. The lady Skye should be alone, possibly even sleeping. Strike quickly, check to be sure you have succeeded, then leave."

"Why are you so willing to help me?" she asked, suddenly suspicious.

"We are friends, Yasmin. Khalid's woman means nothing to me, but you do. If my plan seems harsh, my dear, you need not act on it. The choice is yours."

"No! You are, as always, Jamil, direct and to the point. I will do it!"

The captain smiled toothily as Yasmin rose. She said, "I will send the two girls you desire to the baths and then to you. From this night on, anything you want in the House of Felicity is yours."

Jamil could not believe either his luck or Yasmin's gullibility. He would have to work quickly now. The slave-spy he had placed in Khalid el Bey's house would have to be informed and instructed in two tasks. The first would be to give the bey a sleeping draught in his wine so that he would retire early. Then the slave would tell Skye that a man claiming to know something of her past was at the front gate asking to see her. This would keep Skye out of the house while Yasmin entered the darkened sleeping chamber. She would kill the bey believing it was Skye.

He chuckled wickedly, well pleased with himself. His spy would be a tongueless mute soon after the murder and could not implicate him. In fact, he would see the hapless creature sold off. As for Yasmin . . . well, the penalty for murder was rather severe. A killer was tortured first and then thrown from the city walls onto the iron spikes that studded the walls. Sometimes a prisoner could linger for several days. Strangely, the women were the longest-lived. It would be interesting to see how long Yasmin would last.

Naturally, Jamil would offer his strong arm and protection to the grieving widow. The grieving rich and beautiful young widow, he amended his thoughts. An idea struck him. Perhaps he would marry Skye. He need not remain the Sultan's captain-governor of the Casbah fort forever. He could as easily retire here in Algiers as anywhere else. Besides, Skye would need someone to run Khalid el Bey's various business interests. Jamil had never had a wife, but with the bey's wealth in his pocket he could afford four wives as well as a fine harem. With unlimited money a man might have anything he desired. Jamil sighed, musing on the pleasure and wealth Khalid el Bey's death would bring him. To be sure, he would be losing a good and interesting friend, but that could not be helped.

His thoughts were interrupted by the entry of the two girls who had earlier entertained the merchant. Giggling nervously, for they knew his reputation, they knelt submissively at his feet.

"How may we serve you, lord?" they chorused.

He viewed them through cruelly narrowed eyes. "Let us begin with the same exercise you performed earlier on your merchant client," he said. "We will progress slowly and inventively from there."

And across the city, Skye lay awake hugging her happy secret to herself. There was no doubt now. She was with child, and oh! how happy Khalid would be when she told him! They had entertained earlier, and then he had gone off on his customary nighttime rounds of his houses. When he came back she would surprise him with the news. Smiling, she imagined the look on his face. She folded her hands protectively across her belly. It was much too early to feel any life, but she tried to imagine what the son of Khalid el Bey would look like.

Hearing his step, she rose and ran to greet him. His strong arms wrapped about her, and he kissed her very thoroughly. His mouth inflamed her, and when his hands slipped beneath her gauze gown to caress her trembling body she almost forgot what she had waited to tell him.

"Khalid! Stop! I have news."

"Yes, my love," he murmured, pulling her robe open to nuzzle at her pretty breasts. His mouth closed over a pointed nipple; he sucked hard on it, and she almost fainted. It was no use. She wanted him as much as he wanted her. Her news would wait. She swayed against him and he picked her up and carried her to the bed. Somewhere along the way their garments were shed.

He put her down on the middle of the mattress, positioning her body carefully. Then he straddled her just as deliberately, his hairy, well-muscled legs lying outside her smooth ones. Sitting back on his haunches, his heels against his tight buttocks, he reached out his hands to play with her. One moved forward to pinch gently at her sensitive little nipples, the other moved behind him to tickle the soft throbbing flesh of her sweet cleft.

Skye's eyes narrowed like a cat's and she murmured her pleasure. "So, my lord husband, you would tease me. Two can play at the same game." And she cupped the sac of his manhood in her right hand, rolling his balls with a provocative rhythm while her left hand stroked his rod with equal expertise. She elicited a groan of delight from him.

For several minutes they continued to caress each other until both had reached a peak of excitement that offered only one satisfaction. Skye enjoyed pleasuring Khalid as much as he enjoyed pleasuring her. As always, she felt a thrill of excitement as she watched him grow big and hard for her.

The bey watched his wife's growing passion with delight. She was so beautifully natural, so unlike all the skilled whores he owned. To have such a wife was a blessing for which he was deeply grateful. He swung off her body now and said, "Let me play the great desert stallion tonight, my Skye. Roll over, and be my little wild mare."

She knelt, her head resting on her arms, her white bottom facing him, ready. Kneeling, he gently inserted himself into her. Then one hand moved to squeeze and fondle her hanging breasts while, with the other, he did something he'd never done with her before. As she approached her climax, he pushed a finger into her anal orifice and sent her into such a frenzied climax that for one brief and terrifying moment he thought he'd done her some awful damage. Then, realizing that she had only fainted, he took his own release. It was a greater climax than usual because of his relief.

Afterward she lay relaxed in his arms and sighed with pleasure. "I was worrying," she said, "that our lovemaking would not be as much fun now, but I see that it can continue to be just as delicious."

"Why should anything be different, my love?"

"Because, my lord and husband, you are to be a father next spring. Is that not wonderful?"

The bedchamber was plunged into deep silence. Slowly then, awareness began to grow, and his face took on a brilliant glow. He caught her to him.

"You're sure?" he cried, tearfully, hugging her to him fiercely.

"Yes! Yes!" she gasped, laughing and crying at the same time.

"Oh my Skye! No one has ever given me a greater gift than you have given me in yourself. And now you will give me a child, too. It is too much, my love. Far too much. Thank you, thank you!" And he wept, still holding tightly to her.

Skye cradled Khalid to her breasts crooning to him. This wonderful man who had rescued her from God only knew what horrors, who loved her, had made her his wife and given her a wonderful life was thanking *her!* She wept with him and her heart swelled with joy.

"I love you! Khalid! Whoever I might have been I cannot remember, but I rejoice in the woman I am now for I am your woman. It is I who should thank you."

Silence again descended upon the room as the two lovers joined once more, tenderly, and Khalid bent to kiss Skye's faintly rounded belly. Then they slept, entwined together on the bed, until long after dawn.

It was Skye who rose first to greet the new day. Looking down upon the sleeping Khalid, she let the great love she felt for him sweep over her, leaving her teary. She noted every inch of him. The light sprinkling of silver gray that had begun to touch his dark, wavy hair. The faint scar on his left shoulder left by a wild Bedouin girl's dagger. The almost boyish look he had when he was asleep. Her blue-green eyes traveled the length of him. Then, shivering, she began to feel as if she were committing his face and body to memory. Shrugging the feeling away, she went to her bath.

Skye would always remember that the day progressed with an easy familiarity that offered no hint of the things to come. She worked with Master Jean on the books of the trading vessels, amazed that Captain Small had done so well. He was due again in Algiers any day now. They had recently received word of his arrival in London, where he had disposed of the last of the Spanish gold. She was looking forward to seeing Captain Small again, knowing how delighted he would be at her happy news.

After the midafternoon prayers, Jean's Marie brought them a light repast and the news that the bey had gone on his daily inspection rounds early as he wished to spend the entire evening with his wife. Skye blushed happily, then said, "My good Jean, you and your Marie have been true friends to my lord Khalid and me. I shall therefore share with you a secret known only to my husband. I am to have a child in the spring."

Marie cried, "Oh, madam! So am I! Is it not wonderful!?"

Delighted, the two women sat together and chatted happily while Jean chuckled with amusement. Following his ex-master's lead, he had, soon after acquiring Marie, legally freed her and then married her. He had learned that she came from a seacoast village located in Southern Brittany near Poitou. It was only rarely that Barbary pirates attacked the region, but on one of those infrequent raids, the fourteen-year-old Marie, a postulant at a local convent, was carried off. The pirate captain had stripped her habit off himself, but when he saw how attractive and how young she was, he locked her in a small cabin with several straw pallets, a bucket, and a tiny barred porthole. Two other pretty young girls quickly joined her, one her own cousin, Celestine.

The three naked girls clung to each other, terrified, through a long night. On the deck above their little prison, the anguished screams, pleadings, and sobbings continued throughout the night as the village women who were unfortunate enough to be married and older, or virgin but not pretty enough, were repeatedly raped and sodomized. At least two girls committed suicide by leaping overboard. Several died of abuse including a ten-year-old girl whose mother was strangled when she tried to knife one of the men attacking her daughter. Finally, toward dawn, the weeping survivors were all herded into an open pen on deck where they stayed for the remainder of the voyage—burned by the sun during the day, cold and wet in the night, and easily accessible to any sailor seeking sport.

In their tiny cabin Marie and her two companions were little better off. The heat during the day made the room an unbearable oven and the damp night air chilled them to the bone. This, coupled with the stink of the one bucket they had for relieving themselves, left them weak and listless. The bucket was emptied every other day. Food was shoved through the grate in the door twice daily. They often had a steaming bowl of a surprisingly tasty concoction of peppercorn- and herb-flavored gravy with tomatoes, onions, eggplant, and a tough, stringy meat that Marie suspected was goat. They had no utensils, but ate with their fingers and the small piece of bread allotted each. A pitcher of water went with the meal, and they quickly learned to conserve it.

When their ship reached Algiers the girls crowded together by the tiny porthole watching as their female relatives and friends were taken off the ship. Then from the bowels of the ship, the village men were brought up, filthy, their newly grown beards matted and lice-ridden. They too were quickly driven off the ship. As the three wondered what was to become of them the cabin door opened and the captain entered carrying something over his arm. Carelessly he flung them each a garment.

"Put 'em on," he commanded in rough-accented French, and when they obeyed he handed them each a heavy veil. "Pin it to your hoods and follow me," he said. "Open your yaps once, and I'll turn the lot of you over to my crew. They'd like that."

Frightened, they scurried after him up to the deck and down the gangway. On the dock was a large, closed litter.

"Get in," snarled their captor, and they quickly obeyed. "You're going to the baths to be cleaned and prettied up," he explained. "Do whatever they tell you to do. You'll be sold at auction tonight. Be thankful Allah gave you beauty with your purity or you could have ended up like the others in your village." He yanked the curtains shut and the litter began to move.

Celestine looked to her cousin Marie. "Shall we kill ourselves?" she whispered fearfully.

"*Non, non, chérie,*" scolded Marie. "We will pretend to meekly accept our fates, and perhaps later we can escape."

"But if we are sold we shall be separated," wailed Renée. She had been the village innkeeper's only child, and was terribly spoiled, having been raised knowing that her dowry was the largest of any girl's for fifty miles around. "How could you, a nun, suggest we yield to the infidel?"

"I am not a nun, Renée. I was a postulant for one short month. I do know, however, that God has forbidden us to suicide. Whatever I must endure in His name I shall. We are not in Tour de la Mer any longer, and it is unlikely we'll ever see it again."

At the baths the girls were scrubbed, massaged, bathed, denuded of body hair, creamed, and perfumed. Their long beautiful hair was washed, dried, and brushed until it shone. Marie's rich chestnut curls were appreciated, but the blond locks of Renée and Celestine made them far more valuable. They were garbed in transparent silks and fed a light meal of capon breast and sweet fruit sherbet.

Promptly at moonrise the auction began. As they watched, Marie felt a soft languor steal over her, and realized they had been drugged to insure their cooperation. Helplessly she watched as Renée was sold to a fat black Sudanese merchant whose delight as he bore her off was evident. Renée opened her mouth to scream, but no sound came forth. Only her terrified blue eyes told of her fear.

Girl after girl was sold, and then it was Marie's turn. Khalid el Bey quickly bought her, and because he looked kind she begged him to buy Celestine too. The bey was agreeable, but the eunuch who ran the harem of the captain-governor had marked Celestine for his master. Khalid el Bey was forced by etiquette to withdraw from the bidding for Celestine.

Marie was placed in the House of Felicity and trained as a courtesan. But when the time came for her to make her debut Khalid el Bey chose her to be a gift to Jean.

Celestine was not as fortunate. Her initial resistance to Jamil assured her immediate success with him. But the naive young girl fell in love with the cruel captain-governor, which made his interest wane. When he instructed his eunuch to sell the French girl off, Celestine committed suicide by leaping from the roof of one of the Casbah towers.

Marie had been devastated by her cousin's tragic death. It seemed especially sad in light of her own good fortune. Jean's strong love had supported Marie through the worst of it. But the captain-governor had made a bitter enemy in the young Breton girl. Marie did not know how, but she was determined to have her revenge.

Thoughts of vendetta, however, were far from Marie's mind on this day. She was delighted to know that her mistress was also pregnant. "I can deliver both our babies," she told Skye proudly. "My mother was the finest midwife in three villages, and I helped her many times."

"The doctor tells me," said Skye, "that I have borne more than one child, but of course I do not remember," she sighed. "I wonder about those children. Are they alive? Are they boys or girls? How old are they?"

"Madam must not fret," chided Marie.

Skye smiled sadly at the girl who, though several years younger than she, still attempted to mother her. "I cannot help but wonder if my children miss and mourn their mother," she said. Tears filled Marie's hazel eyes and Skye felt guilty and hugged the girl. "Now I've made you sad, and I did not mean to do so. I have heard that pregnant women are subject to emotional vagaries. Is it not true? I grow morbid, and you weep." She made a face at herself, and Marie laughed through her tears.

Skye smiled back, then asked, "Master Jean, are we through for the day? If so, Marie and I shall spend the rest of the afternoon luxuriating in the bath."

The bey's secretary nodded. As Khalid el Bey was a good, kind, and gentle man, so was his wife a great lady, and Jean was grateful that she extended her friendship to his wife. "Go along, my lady. You have gotten so far ahead of me with the accounts that it will take me at least two days to catch up." He smiled with contentment as the two women left him. Life was good here in the bey's household.

In the early evening before the meal was served, Captain Robert Small arrived at the bey's home, laden with gifts for Skye, shouting lusty greetings. Khalid delighted in the bluff seaman's thoughtfulness, but Skye was truly touched by the care that had so obviously gone into Small's choice of gifts. There were several bolts of fine China silk, rare spices, and a long strand of pearls from the East Indies. From the New World Captain Small had brought an intricately carved box of solid gold, lined in white velvet, containing the most magnificent necklace, bracelet, and earrings of Colombian emeralds that Khalid el Bey had ever seen. The emeralds, set in gold, glittered with a blue fire found in only the finest stones. "They reminded me of your eyes," muttered the captain, flushing with the words.

"Why, Robbie," smiled Skye, "how observant you are, and how

very, very generous." She bent and kissed his ruddy cheek. "My thanks."

"You'll eat with us," said Khalid. It was not a question. Skye left to inform the cook.

The seaman settled himself on a comfortable divan. "I need not ask, Khalid, for I see the married life suits you well."

"Very well, Robbie. Do you think fatherhood will suit me also?"

"She isn't!" A look of sheer delight crossed the Englishman's face as the bey nodded. "She is! By God, Khalid, you dog! My next trip back I'll have a fine gift for your son!"

"Or my daughter."

"Nay, man, a brace of lads first, then a lass to spoil is always best. Do it that way."

Khalid laughed heartily. "The deed is already done, my friend. We must take what Allah offers, and be grateful."

The dinner arrived quickly, and Robert Small lowered himself to the table amid the pillows. Skye sat at one end directing the servants. There was a whole leg of baby lamb rubbed with garlic and stuck with sprigs of rosemary set upon a nest of greens and surrounded by tiny roasted white onions. A white bowl held small green artichokes in olive oil and red wine vinegar. Another bowl was filled with fluffy white rice mixed with sesame seeds, sliced black olives, green peppers, and sautéed onions. There were flat dishes of boiled eggs, purple and brown olives, strips of red pimiento, and tender green scallions. A basket of round, flat loaves of warm bread and a silver dish of sweet butter completed the main course of this simple family meal. Discreetly attentive slaves kept the three crystal goblets filled with subtly spiced fresh pomegranate juice.

The main course finished, the slaves removed the plates and brought in silver bowls of warm, scented water and tiny linen towels. Desert consisted of a huge platter of fresh fruits, golden brown dates, round Seville oranges, great black figs, bunches of purple and green grapes, sweet red cherries, and both green and golden pears. A filigreed basket was passed, containing tiny pastry horns filled with a mixture of chopped almonds and honey. Skye brewed the dark rich Turkish coffee.

Afterward, hot steaming towels were offered to cleanse sticky fingers, and water pipes were brought to the gentlemen. Two pretty young girls played and sang softly in the background while the men smoked and talked. Skye noticed that Khalid seemed sleepier than usual, and she teased him. "It is I who should be tired now, my lord, not you."

Stifling a yawn, he chuckled. "Impending fatherhood is exhausting, my love. I cannot keep my eyes open. I am going to retire now before I fall asleep here. Robbie, stay. Skye has many questions to ask you, I know, and I have not given her a chance." He rose. Skye rose and stood within the curve of his arm.

"You do not mind if I remain for a bit?"

"No, my Skye. Fill your lovely head with all the things you need to know." He kissed her tenderly. "Allah, how fair you are! The white silk caftan and gold embroidery sets off Robbie's emeralds very well. The blue flame in their centers does indeed match your beautiful eyes." He kissed her again. "Don't wake me when you come to bed, my love. I'll sleep through the night."

She kissed him back. "Sleep well, my darling. I love you!"

He smiled happily at her, touching her cheek in a tender and familiar gesture. Bidding Robert Small a good night, Khalid left the room.

"You've been good for him," remarked the Englishman.

"He is good for me," she answered.

"You've had no return of memory, lass? Not even a glimpse?"

"No, Robbie, nothing. Sometimes a sound or sight has a familiar ring to it, but it is never anything I can put my finger on. And now I don't really care. I am happy as Khalid el Bey's wife. I love him dearly."

They sat talking for some time. At the back of the garden the little wicket gate creaked open to admit a dark, hooded figure. Slowly, carefully, Yasmin made her way across the garden, keeping well into the shadows. She saw two figures talking in the salon. One was garbed in white. It had to be Khalid. He had worn white that afternoon, while making his rounds. She heard a hearty laugh, and recognized it as Captain Small's. The captain and Khalid were talking and would probably visit for some time.

Yasmin wondered if she should wait until Khalid had gone to bed. The idea of disposing of Skye under Khalid's very nose was tempting. Yasmin wanted her master back, but she hadn't forgiven him for marrying Skye.

She crept on past the salon, keeping far enough away to avoid the lights. She heard the low murmur of voices, but could make out nothing of the conversation. No matter, she thought. Slipping into the villa through a long French window, she made her way up the darkened back staircase of the house to the main bedchamber. The door was open and she stood still for a moment, letting her eyes adjust to the dark room.

Yasmin knew the room well. Looking toward the bed, she observed the sheet-swathed figure. She hesitated no longer than a second. Moving purposely across the room, she plunged her dagger again and again into the sleeping figure who groaned once, then lay still. Unbridled joy surged through Yasmin. Dead! Dead! Her rival! Her enemy! Skye was dead! She wanted to scream her happiness.

Then behind her someone did scream, a long piercing wail of terror. Whirling, Yasmin faced a slave woman who was clutching at a crystal carafe of water. The carafe slid from the woman's hands. Yasmin stood stock still watching the crystal shatter on the tiles, the water mixing with it, spewing a rainbow of shattered droplets across the floor and rugs. Yasmin could not move. She stood frozen as the woman's screams echoed throughout the house.

At the sound of running feet, Yasmin shook herself back into action. Moving to the door, she shoved the slave woman aside and tried to flee, but the servant clung to her arm screaming, "Murder! Murder! She has killed the master!"

Allah! What was the woman screaming about? Yasmin wondered. Khalid was downstairs. She had killed Skye. Yasmin yanked her arm free and turned to run. Bumping into another body, she tried to push by, but her shocked eyes locked onto Skye's.

"Allah! No!" Yasmin gasped.

"She killed the master!" wailed the slave woman again.

"Yasmin! What has happened?" asked Skye fearfully.

Yasmin turned from Skye and stumbled back across the room to the figure on the bed. With icy fingers she pulled the sheet back. Seeing the cold, stiffening form of Khalid el Bey, Yasmin moaned with a pain so great she couldn't truly feel it all. Her fingers tightened again about the dagger. She whispered her anguish. "Forgive me, Skye!" and swiftly drove the dagger between her own breasts. Yasmin crumpled to the floor.

Skye knelt on one side of the woman, while Captain Small knelt on the other. Yasmin's ragged breathing was the only sound.

"Why?" whispered Skye. "*Why,* Yasmin? You loved him!"

The dying woman's eyes were glazing already. "Forgive me."

Skye swallowed the bitter hatred rising in her throat. This woman had just stolen her very life from her, and now begged forgiveness. She wanted to shout, no!, but then she heard Robert Small say quietly, "Come lass." Knowing what he wanted, she said softly, "I forgive you, Yasmin."

Yasmin sighed. Gathering the last of her strength, she said, "I thought it was you. Jamil p-planned it, but it was all for him, wasn't it? Jamil wants you. Beware of him." Then, as if a candle had been blown out, the life fled from her eyes and Yasmin was gone.

Skye stood. The room was bright now, lit by the lamps held by all the household slaves who stood clustered in tight little groups, some of the women beginning to sob. Skye stared at them, fighting to retain her control. She must not go to pieces now, as she had obviously done when she lost her memory. She owed Khalid that much, for he must be revenged. The Turkish captain-governor could not kill her husband and escape judgment. Who had heard Yasmin's confession? Only she and Captain Small had been close enough to hear the painfully whispered words. The next nearest people had been Jean and Marie. The slaves had all been afraid of coming too close.

Stepping over Yasmin's body, Skye moved to the bed and sat next to the still form of her husband. There was virtually no blood to be seen. By some twist of fate the dagger had pierced only vital organs, but no arteries. "I would be with my lord," she said quietly, and she heard the shuffle of feet and then the closing door.

Alone, she wept her terrible grief in silent pain, rocking back and forth, holding herself, as if that would prevent her from shattering. Her head ached and waves of pain and nausea began to rack her.

Suddenly she heard Robert Small commanding, "Voice it, lass! Voice your pain or else it will kill both you and his babe. Is that what you want? If so, take Yasmin's escape, for it's quicker."

She saw the Englishman standing by the door. He had never left her. Now, crossing the room in three strides, he grasped her by the shoulders and shook her. "Damn it, lass! Cry! Scream! Curse the heavens, but in God's name get it out!"

She sobbed softly once, then stopped. He hit her hard several times, and suddenly her resistance broke. Opening her mouth, Skye wailed her grief with such loud and terrible cries that they echoed throughout the house. The slave women, grieving softly until then, joined in their mistress's tragic lamentation and soon the whole house rang with grief. Shortly the sounds echoed through the entire neighborhood. People began to gather, and it was not long before everyone knew that Khalid el Bey had been murdered by his jealous slave woman, Yasmin.

Slowly Skye's grief eased. Looking a final time on her beloved husband, she bent and kissed his cold lips. Then, supported by

Robert Small, she left the room and walked downstairs to the bey's library. "Get Jean and Marie for me, Robbie. I must be revenged, and I will need help."

When the four of them were gathered together in private, Skye quietly repeated Yasmin's dying words to Jean and Marie. The Frenchman was shocked, but his wife sniffed, "I would put nothing past that evil Turk. Look how he killed my little *cousine,* Celestine. He has no real heart, that one!" She began to weep. "He claimed to be the master's best friend, and yet he killed him without a second thought because he wished to possess Madam!" Jean comforted his wife as best he could.

"We will both be revenged, Marie," said Skye, "but before we can be, we must lull Jamil into a sense of security. He must not even suspect that we know he is responsible for my lord's murder. Let him feel safe—and then we will strike!"

"You cannot revenge yourself on the Sultan's governor and remain safely in Algiers," said Robert Small firmly. "The dey would be forced to punish you in the Sultan's name."

"I cannot remain here under any circumstances, Robbie. The memories I have of Khalid and our life together would break my heart. And though I am capable of running the House of Felicity, who would do business with a woman? Sell everything here in Algiers, but do it secretly. Have the money transported to our London goldsmith."

"The house also?" asked Jean.

"The house, the seaside kiosk, sell all."

"What of the slaves?"

"Prepare papers of manumission for them all. I shall give each of them the price he or she is worth in order that they may all get started in another life. Those who wish to come with me may do so, but no one is to be told until we are ready to leave. I hope, Jean, that you and Marie will come with me. But if you choose to return to Brittany I will understand."

"There is nothing for us in Brittany, my lady. Our families are gone. Marie's entire village is gone. We would rather stay with you, for we love you as we loved the bey."

"Thank you," said Skye. "I would have been lost without you both."

There was a scratching at the door, and when Skye called out, "Enter," a slave came in to announce that the captain-governor was on his way up the driveway.

"Hold him off for a few minutes," she told Jean. He left the room immediately. "Robbie, you go too. I shall go upstairs through the secret passage here in the library. Marie, quickly!"

Skye drew two leather-bound volumes from a shelf and, reaching into that empty space, pulled at a hidden lever. The bookcase swung open to reveal an interior staircase. "Shut it behind us, Robbie," she said, handing him the books. Then the two women were gone. They hurried up the stairs, which opened out into Skye's old room.

"I cannot ever go back in *there,*" she told Marie, referring to the bedchamber she had shared with Khalid. She quickly stripped off her white silk caftan. "Get me the azure gauze chamber robe, Marie." Marie fetched the gown, smiled with appreciation of Skye's strategy.

"The captain-governor will be so blinded by lust," she remarked as Skye dressed, "that he will believe whatever you tell him, madam."

Skye nodded. "I must not rouse his suspicions," she said, "and I need time. Send my women to me, Marie. The captain-governor will expect to find the grieving widow surrounded by her weeping handmaidens, and I must not disappoint him." A look of physical pain crossed her face, and suddenly she began to weep uncontrollably, her sobs interspersed with bursts of hysterical laughter. "Oh, God, Marie! It is too macabre! How Khalid would appreciate the role I play."

Marie looked stricken, and the tears spilled from her eyes as she fled the room to do her mistress's bidding. Skye flung herself on the divan, weeping soundlessly now. *Khalid, oh, Khalid,* she thought desperately. Please God, please! Let me wake and find him sleeping safely next to me! But she knew in her heart that her prayers were useless. He was dead, and lost to her. She heard the door open softly, and then her women were clustering about her like bright little butterflies, sobbing and clucking with sympathy. Skye didn't even look up. She wept harder and soon she heard Marie's cry of protest.

"My lord Jamil! You cannot enter my lady's chamber! Her grief is too terrible to behold!"

"I was Khalid el Bey's best friend," boomed the captain-governor's deep voice.

Allah curse him! thought Skye fiercely.

"It is my duty to comfort his widow. Step aside! Khalid would have done the same for me."

Allah strike him down this instant, for I do not think I can face him without betraying my feelings, Skye silently shrieked. But she breathed deeply and calmed herself. Khalid *would* be avenged.

The door opened again, and she knew Jamil had entered. There was a flutter and she realized that her maidens had gone, leaving her alone with him. She sobbed piteously.

"Skye, my dear, I am so sorry."

She sobbed louder, fighting not to wince when she felt his arms about her. One hand imperiously forced her head up, and he stared into her eyes. He was somewhat taken aback by the depth of her grief, but he spoke nonetheless.

"Don't fear, beautiful Skye. I will take care of you as did Khalid." Allah, the emeralds she was wearing were worth a king's ransom!

"I am s-so alone now, Jamil."

"I will take care of you," he repeated, his eyes straying to her breasts. They seemed fuller than he had noticed before. Damn! He wished he could take her now, but it would hardly do to fuck the widow when her husband's corpse lay still warm in the next room. There would be plenty of time for that later on. If he acted too soon he chanced losing the juicy plum of her wealth.

She pressed against him, weeping afresh, soaking his silken shirt, half swooning into his arms. By the teats of Fatima she was a rare beauty! He could hear the ragged sound of his own breathing as his hot eyes devoured her lush body. He didn't want to release her, but he could hardly go on holding a half-conscious woman. Standing up, he carried her back to the sleeping couch and gently deposited her there.

Look your fill, you murdering bastard, she thought as she watched him through slitted eyes. *Dream your lust-filled dreams for dreams are all you'll ever have of me.*

Finally Jamil sighed reluctantly, and left the room. She lay quietly until Marie joined her, saying drily, "The household has been threatened with severe punishment unless you are properly cared for, madam."

Skye sat up. "The presumption of the man! He says he will care for me as did my lord Khalid! When he touched me it was all I could do not to vomit! Oh, Marie! Where is the justice in this world? Why should a man as kind and good as my lord Khalid die, and one as evil as Jamil live?"

The Frenchwoman's eyes again filled with tears. "*Hélas,* madam! Would I could answer you, but I cannot."

Faithful Marie remained by Skye's side all night. Neither really slept. Arrangements for the bey's funeral were completed in the morning, for the day was Thursday and unless he was buried by the sabbath sundown there could be no funeral until Saturday. The body was first washed, then wrapped in a seamless white shroud. The shroud had been dipped in Mecca's sacred Zamzam well when Khalid el Bey made his pilgrimage to the holy city.

Led by the captain-governor and the bey's beautiful tragic widow who was garbed entirely in white, a thin mourning band around her head, the funeral procession made its way from the villa through the city to the cemetery, following a careful ritual of lamentations by the women and readings from the Koran by the men.

The bey's tomb, a small, domed white marble building, overlooked the harbor. Carefully the body was laid to rest on its side, facing the holy city, and final prayers for his safe arrival in Paradise were said by the young mullah who had married them. Skye had allowed Yasmin to be buried honorably, and her shrouded body was placed at her master's feet in hopes that she would serve him better in Paradise. In her grief, Skye attempted to remain in the tomb with her husband and had to be carried out.

With sundown, Skye was safe from Jamil for twenty-four hours, and in those twenty-four hours Jean worked feverishly with Robert Small and Simon ben Judah to put the bey's affairs in order. The goldsmith, whose own sabbath followed the Moslem one, knew of several prospective buyers for the bey's business. They could not be approached, however, until Sunday, the first day of the week.

On Saturday morning a slave was dispatched to the Casbah fort, bearing a message for the captain-governor. Jamil read the neatly written words twice, as if seeking a hidden meaning.

"My lord Jamil. I am deeply appreciative of your kindness to me. For the next thirty days I shall be secluded in deepest mourning, and will receive no visitors. I know you will honor my grief." It was signed, "the lady Skye, widow to Khalid el Bey."

Jamil gritted his teeth with annoyed frustration. He was aware that he could hardly propose marriage to a newly widowed woman, but he had hoped to sweep her off her feet, thus preventing any other suitors from courting her. Then a thought struck him, and he smiled. The thirty days could easily work to his advantage. Skye was young and used to regular lovemaking. After a month of abstinence, she should succumb quickly. He smilingly dictated a proper reply to her letter.

"Lady Skye. Your period of mourning will be honored, though reluctantly. I shall call upon you thirty-one days from this date." It was signed: "Jamil, Captain-Governor of the Casbah Fortress."

Skye read the message and chuckled with delight. She could sense the pent-up frustration, and was pleased to hurt him even in this small way. Within a month Khalid el Bey's affairs in Algiers would be settled, and she would have made good her escape.

And as if Khalid's spirit watched over her, the days sped smoothly by and everything proceeded toward the sale of the bey's interests. Simon ben Judah explained smoothly to prospective buyers that there were those less reputable than they who might wish to cheat a young widow, so it was best that negotiations remain strictly secret. Since none of those involved wished others to know of the bidding, the secret was kept. When a bargain was finally struck, Skye found herself twice as rich as Khalid el Bey had left her. The monies, all in gold coin, were transferred to London. Both the villa and the seaside kiosk were sold to Osman the astrologer.

Osman was one of the few people she saw during her mourning. He had come one afternoon to tell her that he wanted the house and kiosk for himself and his beautiful slave woman, the same girl Khalid el Bey had given him. She sold to him readily, happy that someone she knew and liked would live in happiness in the places where she had been so happy. She and Osman sat in the villa garden and she served him Turkish coffee and small honey cakes.

"You are with child," he said quietly.

"Yes," she answered, not in the least surprised. "I had told Khalid the night before he. . . . He was very happy."

"You made him very happy, Skye. You were his joy. I warned him, however, that your fate was not with him. It is back among your own people, and you will soon begin that journey back."

"Oh, Osman! Did I cause Khalid's death?"

"No, my dear, you did not, and you must never blame yourself. Khalid el Bey played out his fate as it had been planned since the beginning of time. Now you must play out yours."

"Who am I, Osman?"

"I do not know, Skye, but I will tell you what I do know, what I told your husband before he married you. You were born under the sign of the ram. Your homeland is a green and misty place peopled by strong spirits and psychic forces. You will always control your own destiny, Skye, and you will eventually be reunited with your true mate."

"Khalid el Bey was my true mate!" she snapped angrily.

"No, Skye, he was not. He loved you deeply, never doubt it. And I know that you loved him, but there is another man, a stronger force in your life. He was with you before, and will return to you in time. Follow your instincts, my dear. They will never fail you."

"And my child?"

"Will be born safely, Skye, and live to a ripe old age, as will you."

"Thank you, Osman. I will always have my memories of Khalid el Bey, but to have his child is a far dearer thing. Thank you for the reassurance."

The astrologer stood up. "I will go now, my dear, and I shall bid you a final farewell now. Since I was away from the city when Khalid died, it is understandable that I pay my condolences now. If, however, the man who watches this villa so carefully for the captain-governor should see me here again it will certainly seem curious, and it will arouse suspicions, so I will not return."

"Jamil has set men to watch my house?" she exclaimed. "How dare he! The arrogance of the man!"

Osman laughed. "My dear, he fancies himself in Khalid el Bey's place and wishes to discourage any other suitors."

"I would sooner wed a snake."

"That will not be necessary," replied the astrologer drily. "You will easily escape him. He suspects nothing. When do you leave?"

"In two nights. It will be the dark of the moon."

"Good, but be careful. What of your slaves?"

"I have freed them, and will give them money to start a new life. Jean and Marie will come with me."

"Tell the others that I will employ any who choose to stay. Ask those who prefer to go to remain here until I come to take possession of the house in six days. If they go about their business as usual, the captain-governor's spies will suspect nothing. That will give you a four-day start. It should be enough to get you out into the western sea, and pursuit is virtually impossible then."

"Oh, Osman, how can I thank you?"

He smiled at her. "By playing out your part as Allah has foretold it, my dear."

She walked with him back into the house, bidding him a final farewell in the atrium. Taking his hand, she pressed it to her lips and forehead. "Saalam, Osman, my friend."

"Saalam, Skye, my daughter. Allah go with you."

During the next few days Skye's emotions fluctuated wildly.

She was frightened by the unknown awaiting her in the foreign-sounding town of London. She was elated by the fact she was outwitting Jamil, though frustrated that she could not inflict a terrible injury on him in retaliation for Khalid's murder. She was happy and relieved that Jean, Marie, and Captain Small would be with her, but sad to leave such good friends as Osman.

Then the night of her departure arrived, and she stood with Marie making a final inventory of the few things she would take with her. Most of her clothing would, of course, remain. This wardrobe was hardly suitable to a life in England. She would, however, take some caftans with her to be worn in the privacy of her bedchamber. The flowing loose robes would be comfortable as her pregnancy went on. The loose gemstones Khalid had kept, as well as her marvelous jewelry, were all sewn into the garments for safe transportation. She would take her wonderful gold brushes and combs, her crystal perfume bottles filled with rare and costly essences, and other things of a sentimental and personal nature. They were all packed carefully in carved cedarwood chests and passed quietly from servant to servant and finally to the silent English seaman who waited in the dark outside the villa's garden gate. Unaware of the little wicket gate, Jamil had no one watching it.

Skye climbed to the roof of the house and gazed for one final time over the city of Algiers. Below her, the night lights twinkled, and she heard, faintly, the murmur of life as it brawled and sobbed and laughed. Above her, the velvet heavens gleamed black, and she stared deeply into them as if trying to pierce through the darkness.

"Oh, Khalid!" she sighed, then jumped, startled by the sound of her own voice. She had not cried since the day they had buried him, but now she wept without restraint. She stood in the center of the roof terrace, her face upturned to the skies, letting her grief pour over her. And when she had finished she said softly, "I shall never grieve so deeply for you again, Khalid, my love. I have my memories, and I have our child, whom I regret will never know you. Now, Khalid, I must leave our home, and I hope you will wish me Godspeed. I wish you the same." She stood quietly, and a great peace flooded through her and she knew that he approved of what she was doing. "Thank you, my love," she said. Glancing around the terrace a final time, she descended to the ground floor of the house where the servants all waited to bid her good-bye.

She spoke quietly to each in turn, and they thanked her for their freedom and the money she had given them. For now, they had all decided to remain in Osman's employ. Her farewells over, she joined Jean and Marie and walked through the gardens and then through the little back gate.

By prearrangement, a closed litter awaited them. Entering it, they sat wordless, each wrapped in his own thoughts. The bearers made their way down into the city and to the docks. Captain Small awaited them, and no sooner were they aboard his vessel, the *Mermaid,* than the gangway and anchor were raised. While the first mate saw the ship underway, Robert Small escorted his passengers to their quarters.

Skye could not remember her arrival in Algiers, but she would always remember her departure. On a hill overlooking the harbor she could pick out the spot where her husband's tomb stood. Looming above the city she saw the sinister towers of the Casbah. Marie smiled grimly.

"We are well revenged, madam. This morning I sent the captain-governor a plate of sweetmeats in your name. I made them myself. One of the ingredients was an herb that will render the evil Jamil impotent for all time. He will never hurt another woman with his lust again."

"Marie! It is perfect! Imagine his shock, and then his shame! Oh, how I wish I might be there to see his agony!"

The two women stood watching in silence as the lights of the city disappeared in the distance. Then Marie put an arm about Skye and led her to her cabin where, for the first time in weeks, she slept soundly. With the tension gone from her life Skye suddenly began to behave like the pregnant woman she was. She developed peculiarities of appetite and was frequently sleepy. She became queasy and then seasick when the ship hit rough weather off the Bay of Biscay.

Marie and Jean sat with Captain Small one evening discussing Skye's welfare. They all agreed that London was not the place for a delicate expectant mother.

"It is your country," said Marie to the little Englishman. "Where would be a good place for Madam to have her *accouchement?*"

"There are many pleasant places near London," replied Captain Small, "but I would prefer she was someplace far from the city. It's not just the child we must worry about. The lady Skye has had the severe shock of her husband's murder. She ought to be in a quiet place. I have set course for my own home port, the town of Bideford in Devon. I own a fine big house several miles outside the town. My sister, Cecily, lives there. She will welcome you all, and adore taking care of the lady Skye. After the babe is born your mistress may continue on to London. But perhaps by then she will not wish to go."

Thus it was that the *Mermaid* rounded Hartland Point on a fine October morning to sail into Barnstable Bay and then a little way up the River Torridge to Bideford. As Skye stood at the ship's rail, watching the undulating woodland scenery that sloped down to the riverbank, she saw with sure instinct that this was a safe haven. Robert Small had been right. It was here that she would have her baby in safety. Whatever else came afterward, she would find the courage to face it.

As Osman had said, Skye was following her destiny.

PART III

ENGLAND

Chapter 13

The little town of Bideford, small though it was, was one of the most prosperous seaports in England. Under the personal protection of the great de Grenville family, Bideford was just entering the period of its greatest prosperity when Skye arrived there.

Set on the side of a long hill backed by a vast woodland, it sloped downward to the river Torridge. Bideford, surrounded by rolling hills, woodlands, fertile meadows, and orchards full of ripening apples, was a most charming, colorful English town.

Although it was a seaport town, it was not situated directly on Barnstable Bay. In order to reach Bideford, one had to cross the estuary, avoiding the dangerous bar that stretched across its mouth. The estuary was situated almost midway between Hartland Point and the Rock of Death. Facing the bar estuary, some twenty miles away, was Lundy Island. Its rocky, cloud-capped hills made Lundy Island a favorite haunt of Devon pirates and smugglers and their counterparts from all over the world.

Safely across the bar and into the estuary, which flowed upland, was the village of Appledore. At Appledore, the estuary forked, becoming the Taw River to the left and the Torridge River to the right. Now the countryside became lush with rich meadowland and fruit orchards. A few miles up from Appledore the river reached fertile, green Bideford. It was here, in the Bideford hills, that Robert Small had his house, Wren Court.

Captain Small had made arrangements to be met at the dock when he and Skye and the French couple disembarked, and the four rode through the town and up the hills on two chestnut and two gray mounts. The little party made a delightful picture riding against the trees, trotting up the bright green hills.

As they approached Wren Court, Skye cried, "Oh, Robbie! Why have you never told me what a beautiful estate you owned?" She reined in her chestnut mare at the crest of a hill, and sat gazing rapturously at the red brick manse. Jean and Marie pulled up beside her, and Robbie was forced to stop with them.

He blushed. "It's been in the family—the land at least—since the time of Henry V. Wren Court itself was built during the reign of Henry VII. That's why the house is shaped like an 'H'."

Skye turned her brilliant blue eyes on him laughingly. "You're far too modest, Robbie. I wasn't expecting anything so lovely."

"The family is landed gentry, Skye. There's always one or more of us standing for Parliament. Unfortunately, I never married and got myself an heir, and my sister Cecily was widowed before she could have children. I suppose I'll leave Wren Court to a family of distant cousins." He sighed, then shook his reins and the gray gelding bolted for home, the other three mounts racing close behind.

The house was exquisite, a small and perfect jewel of mellowed red brick, covered in places with shining dark ivy and surrounded by green lawn. The crossbar of the "H" was two stories high, the sides were each three stories high. Skye would later find that this two-story section contained a long and light entry foyer on the ground floor. This foyer had two sweeping staircases on either side, both of which led to the second-floor open picture gallery. As the entire second floor was open, the first and second stories together made a huge two-tiered room. The wings of the main floor, to either side of the entry, were the kitchens and dining rooms. The second floor, beyond the gallery, was given over to the library and salons and the entire third floor to bedrooms.

As they rode up the gravel drive, Skye was further enchanted by the streams of sunlight catching the many leaded windows, and the profusion of late roses perfuming the air. Above the circled doorway was the family's red-and-gold coat of arms. As they reached the house, four grooms came running to take the horses, and Robert Small carefully lifted Skye down from her saddle.

A small, plump woman with snapping blue eyes, silver hair, and rosy cheeks appeared in the doorway. "So, you're finally back, Robbie! Is this Mistress Goya del Fuentes?" And without waiting for an answer, she held out her arms to Skye. "You poor dear! Well, you're safe now, and we'll take good care of you and the child. Come inside now!"

Dame Cecily swept Skye and Jean and Marie into the house to a small receiving room where a cheerful fire blazed. "Sit down, all of you. Why Robert made a lass in your condition ride from town I'll never know. A cart would have been slower but safer. No matter, you're here and well. Robert! See what's keeping that shiftless Martha! There should be wine and biscuits ready for four tired travelers!"

"Oh, please Dame Cecily, you must call me Skye. Mistress Goya del Fuentes is such a large mouthful."

"Thank you, child. Now, I am a plainspoken woman, so I am going to say what I have to now and then we will know where we stand with each other." Dame Cecily nodded to Jean and Marie, who were seated on a couch to the right of the fireplace, listening attentively.

"I know I may speak before your servants, as they are also your friends and Robbie has written to me about them."

Skye nodded. Dame Cecily took a deep breath. "My brother has told me something of your history. Poor lamb! How terrible to remember nothing of your life until a year ago. I do not approve of your late husband's business, but I can see you are a lady born. That's plain. And Robert has always spoken highly of Khalid el Bey. That, my dear, is good enough for me. I welcome you to England with all my heart. Our home is yours as long as you wish it. Forever if you like."

Skye felt tears prick her eyelids. "Thank you, Dame Cecily! Thank you with all my heart! Not just for myself, but for my servants too."

"Lord bless me, child, I almost forgot! Robert, I had the old cottage at the end of the garden cleaned and refurbished for you," she said, nodding to the French couple. "I thought you might prefer your privacy."

Jean and Marie were deeply touched. The cottage given them sent Marie into joyful delirium. It, too, was of soft red brick, with a newly thatched roof and small leaded windows. There were two rooms in the cottage. The first was a large chamber with a big stone fireplace, the other a small bedchamber with a fine varnished oak bedstead. The entire cottage was furnished in sturdy carved oak furniture. The stone floors had been scrubbed and swept. There were late hollyhocks and michaelmas daisies growing outside by the door. Dame Cecily, it appeared, had thought of everything. A small booklined room off the library was set aside for Jean to work in. It had an entry into the garden.

Skye was thrilled to see her two servants so well provided for. She could not thank Dame Cecily enough, but the Englishwoman brushed her gratitude aside, her blue eyes twinkling. "No need, child. What are friends for, may I ask?" And she then led Skye back to the main house and upstairs. Skye's apartments took up the southwest corner of the second floor. The sitting room had a large gray stone fireplace with a carved mantel. The two large windows, diamond-shaped and lead-paned, were hung with deep-blue velvet draperies. A deep bay window looked south over a rose garden, now in late bloom. The wide, polished oak floorboards were laid with thick red-and-blue Turkey carpets.

At the far end of the room on either side of the fireplace were arched and paneled doors, both of which led to the bedchamber. Here were windows facing both south and west, which made the room sunny and bright all year long, particularly in the winter. The fireplace here, which backed up to the one in the sitting room, had a pretty tiled border. The draperies here were of rose velvet and matched the bed hangings and bedspread. Here again was a fine Turkey carpet, this one in blues and golds.

Off the bedchamber was a small dressing room. The furniture everywhere was of fine carved oak. There were bowls of fresh flowers in all three rooms. Skye was sure she would be happy here.

Dame Cecily drew forward an apple-cheeked young girl. "This is Daisy, my dear, I've chosen her to look after you."

The girl smiled a friendly, gap-toothed smile, and bobbed Skye a curtsey. "I'm glad to serve you, mum."

Skye smiled back. "Thank you, Daisy. I've been at sea for several weeks now, and more than anything I long for a bath. Could that be arranged?"

"Yes, mum! Let me get your boots off, and while you rest a bit I'll see to setting up the bath."

Dame Cecily smiled approvingly. "I leave you in good hands, Skye. Daisy will show you to the hall in time for dinner."

Less than an hour later Skye luxuriated in a hot tub set before her bedroom fireplace. A pretty curved screen had been drawn about the bathing area. The oak tub was deep, and she sank gratefully into the warmth, feeling the weeks at sea ease away. The air was fragrant with the scent of damask rose soap. Daisy moved quietly around the room, unpacking Skye's trunks, setting out fresh clothes. Skye had been amazed to find in her cabin aboard the *Mermaid* two trunks filled with the latest English fashions. Robbie had laughed, saying, "Algiers is an international port. One can find anything in Algiers."

Daisy came behind the screen and, chatting cheerfully, picked up the soap and began to wash Skye's hair. "Ah now, mum, we'll soon have your crowning glory free of that sticky sea salt. Lord! What a fine color it is!" She scrubbed the dark thick mass, working up a good lather, then rinsed it free and pinned the damp curls on top of Skye's head.

Skye stepped from the tub and Daisy wrapped her in a warm towel. Once dried, she stood before the pier glass examining her figure. Her breasts were certainly fuller than before, and she was beginning to notice a slight rounding of her belly. Khalid's child. What would he look like? Would he have his father's dark hair and golden eyes? Oh, Khalid, I miss you so!

Silently she stepped into her undergarments and let the little maid slip a dark-blue silk gown over her. It was a simple but elegant gown, befitting her station as a wealthy merchant's widow. The only jewelry she wore were the rings given her by Khalid, a sapphire and her gold wedding band. Her hair was brushed dry, carefully plaited, and then wound about her head in a crown effect. Upon it she wore a soft white lawn cap.

The household was small, consisting only of Skye and Robert and Cecily Small, so the evening meal was a simple one. Jean and Marie preferred to remain in their cottage. Skye couldn't blame them, for this was the first time in their married lives that they would actually be alone. How she envied them! She shook herself. Khalid el Bey was dead, and she would have to go on with her life.

Robert Small had created an identity for her that would satisfy curiosities. She would admit to being Irish-born, and the absence of a maiden name and past would be explained in this fashion: She had been brought as a child to a small French Christian convent in Algiers by a sea captain who claimed that her parents, passengers on his ship, had died on board. Since they had paid for their passage in advance, in gold, the sea captain did not know their names. The child, who seemed to be about five, and who called herself Skye, was raised by nuns in the Algiers convent. When the young orphan was sixteen she had been seen by Señor Goya del Fuentes while praying in the church. He had applied to the nuns for her hand, and his suit had been accepted. He had been a wealthy merchant and a respected man. When he had died suddenly, the young widow could not bear to remain in Algiers. Since her late husband owned a house in London, she decided to settle in England. Robert Small, as her late husband's partner, had taken the lady under his protection.

Of course, Dame Cecily knew Skye's real story, but she agreed with her brother that the less spectacular history he had invented was a better one.

Skye's arrival with her two servants and her resettlement at Wren Court was accepted easily by the Smalls' friends and their few relations. The servants, gossiping from house to house, were sympathetic to the beautiful, pregnant widow. Skye was modest and kind, a true lady, even is she was a papist. The memory of Mary Tudor was still too fresh for the people of England to be very tolerant toward Catholicism.

It was almost Christmas before the first frost arrived and that caused the people of Devon to mutter about a hard winter to come. Skye had confided the secret of her memory loss to the local priest. Elderly, kindly Father Paul retaught her the tenets of her religion. Though it evoked no memories, it was strangely comforting. Skye did this because she knew that never to attend church in a Christian land would promote suspicion. It seemed that everyone needed a label, and even a papist label was more respectable than none.

Shortly after Candlemas in February, Marie gave birth to a fine big boy who was baptized Henri. Skye had embroidered some little gowns for the child. She loved sitting in Marie's cottage near the fire, watching while Marie nursed her son. Her own babe was strong and kicked vigorously, to her discomfort and her joy. She had decided to call him James, which was the English equivalent of Khalid el Bey's Spanish name, Diego. As her time drew near she was eager for the baby's birth.

On the fifth of April, Dame Cecily hadn't even time to summon a midwife before Skye's child was born. Marie handled everything, and the birth was a quick and easy one. No sooner had the child slid from between its mother's legs and given its first cry than Skye slipped into unconsciousness.

Handing the squalling infant to Dame Cecily, Marie whispered, "My poor mistress! Ah, well, it's God's will."

When Skye opened her eyes she found herself in a clean nightgown, her long hair freshly brushed and braided. "Give me my son," she whispered to Dame Cecily.

"It's a wee girlie you've birthed, my dear, and never have I seen a prettier child." She placed the sleeping infant in Skye's arms.

Skye looked down at her baby. It was a lovely little creature with a mop of damp dark hair, long dark eyelashes, pink-tinted cheeks, and a red bow of a mouth. The skin was as fair as Skye's own. "A daughter," she said softly, "I didn't expect a daughter."

"What will you name her, my dear?" inquired Dame Cecily gently.

Skye gazed out the windows opposite her bed. In the garden beyond, the spring flowers were all in bloom, and a willow tree drooped its newly sprouted yellow green leaves by a small pond. "I shall call her Willow," she said. "It is fitting that Khalid el Bey's daughter be named after the tree of mourning."

Willow, though she had been born in sorrow, was a child of gladness. Everyone in the house adored the infant, from her mother to the lowliest little maid. All tried to make her smile.

When Willow was five months old, Skye decided it was time to go to London. Robert Small had made only one brief trip away, down the coast of Africa, in the ten months since he had brought Skye to his home. Though it had pleased his sister to have him home, he itched to take the *Mermaid* off on a good long voyage. First, however, he had to go to London and see if Lord de Grenville could obtain letters giving him royal patronage. Skye was prepared to invest in this latest venture, and she, too, desired to go to London.

The *Mermaid* was berthed in Plymouth on the channel side of Devon. Jean would go to London with Skye, but Marie would remain at Wren Court caring for both babies. She had already taken over the nursing of Willow, her large peasant breasts producing more than enough milk for the two children. To Dame Cecily's relief, Skye considered the mild air of Devon more salubrious for her daughter than the climate of London. Dame Cecily could not have been happier. Skye had become the daughter she had never had, and Willow her grandchild. It pained her to part with one, but to part with both would have broken her heart.

Skye was feeling the pain of separation as well. "Oh, I wish you would come with me, Dame Cecily! I have so much to do, and your help would be invaluable. Heaven only knows what condition the house is in, and I shall probably have to refurnish it. Promise me that when it is done, you'll come up to London with Marie and the children."

"Of course I will, my child. Lord bless me. I've not been to Londontown since I was a girl and that's thirty years past! I believe I've a hankering to go again, and I'll come when you've got your house in order."

They rode out from Wren Court on a bright, early autumn morning. Skye had lingered with Willow, loath to leave the baby. Finally Robbie had shouted at her in exasperation, "Dammit, lass! The sooner you get to London, the sooner she can be with you again!" Skye kissed her daughter and, mounting her horse, rode off. The countryside through which they traveled was hilly. They rode by grain fields ready for harvesting, meadows of sheep and Devon cattle, and thriving orchards. Ahead of them the flat granite tableland of Dartmoor thrust up from the rolling hills, and it was there in an inn called *The Rose and Anchor* that they spent the night.

When they had arrived the inn was empty, so Robbie decided they could eat in the taproom. But as the meal was served, a party of riders arrived and trooped noisily into the inn.

"Damn," muttered Robbie irritably, "I wish I'd asked for a private room. They're noblemen, and if they get rowdy we're in for it."

Suddenly a voice boomed across the room and a man detached himself from the crowd. "Robert Small! Is that you, you old sea trout?"

Robbie's eyes lit up, and he quickly stood. "My lord de Grenville! It is good to see you. Join us in a cup of wine."

De Grenville had reached the table. "Your manners, Robbie," he chided. "You've not introduced the lady to me yet."

The sea captain flushed. "Your pardon, Skye. May I present Lord Richard de Grenville. My lord, this is Señora Goya del Fuentes, the widow of my late Algerian business associate. I am escorting her, and her secretary, Jean Morlaix, to her house in London."

Skye slowly extended her hand and de Grenville kissed it. "My lord."

"Madam. A pleasure, I assure you. I find it most reprehensible of Robbie to have such extraordinary luck."

"Luck, my lord?"

"To be escorting quite the loveliest woman I've ever seen to London."

Skye laughed as she blushed. "My lord de Grenville. I fear you'll quite overwhelm me with your flattery. Please, do sit down and join us."

"You're not Spanish," he observed as he seated himself.

"No, I am Irish."

De Grenville poured himself a goblet of wine. "I thought so. Most outrageously beautiful women in the world. Tell me, madam, how do you find England? Is this your first trip here?"

"Yes, it is, and I find England a joy, sir. I have been living at Robbie's home for close to a year now."

"Skye was *enciente* with her husband's child when we first arrived," Robbie explained hastily lest de Grenville misunderstand.

"A son or a daughter, madam?"

"A daughter. Her name is Willow. I have left her at Wren Court with Dame Cecily and her wet nurse. I know not in what condition I will find my husband's house, so until I have time to refurbish it, she is best left in Devon."

Across the room, where de Grenville's party of friends were sprawled about a table, one man, lean, blond and arrogantly handsome, stared boldly at Skye. She was incensed when he caught her eye and then raised an elegant eyebrow in a manner that could have but one meaning. It was as plain a request as though he had spoken aloud, and just as insulting. Angrily she turned away, tossing her head, and listened once more to what de Grenville was saying.

"Very wise, madam. London is not a town for tender creatures."

"So I have heard, my lord," replied Skye. Then, "Tell me, sir, who is the gentleman in your party who stares at me so rudely? The one with the face of an angel."

De Grenville didn't even bother turning around. Her description was enough. "Lord Southwood, madam, the Earl of Lynmouth."

"Robbie, please escort me to my room and arrange to have a tray sent up. The Earl makes me exceedingly uncomfortable. He gazes at me as he would a tray of sweetmeats." She stood, casually brushing her long riding skirt free of crumbs. "My lord de Grenville. I bid you good night." She held out her slim hand and he kissed it. "Madam. I hope we will meet in London. Now, allow me to escort both you and Robbie past your ardent admirer."

But it wasn't to be that easy. As they neared the taproom door, the Earl of Lynmouth moved to block their way.

De Grenville grinned. "Give over, Southwood. The lady is leaving."

"Not before we're introduced, my dear Dickon. You simply cannot hoard all the beauties to yourself."

De Grenville shrugged. "Señora Goya del Fuentes, Lord Geoffrey Southwood. Now, Geoff, let us pass."

"Señora, will you share a goblet of wine with me?"

"No, sir. I will not," snapped Skye. She pushed past him and left the taproom, Robbie in her wake.

De Grenville laughed softly. "Geoff, you've been quite properly bested, I do believe."

Lord Southwood went white about the corners of his mouth. "Who is she, Dickon?"

"The widow of Captain Small's business partner."

"She's not Spanish."

"Her husband was. She's Irish."

"She's magnificent. I intend having her," said Southwood.

"I have heard that your taste runs to women unable to protect themselves, Geoff. Señora Goya del Fuentes is a very wealthy woman. You won't be able to bully her, and she'll not be bowled over by a few baubles or a cheap gown. I wager she'll send you packing."

"How much will you wager, Richard?"

De Grenville let a slow smile spread over his face. Southwood had a magnificent stud stallion that de Grenville coveted. "One year's time, Geoff. At the end of that time you'll turn over your stud, Dragon's Fire, to me."

"Six months, Dickon, at which time you'll turn over to me your magnificently outfitted river barge."

De Grenville winced. His barge was the most elegant on the river, and even the Queen coveted it. Still, he reasoned, the beautiful Señora Goya del Fuentes was no lightskirt and she had obviously detested Southwood on sight. It was unlikely that she would succumb, and besides he wanted that stallion very much.

"Done!" he said decisively. "Your stallion against my barge. The time period to be six months from this day." He held out his hand and Southwood shook it firmly.

"Try not to damage my barge this autumn, Dickon," Southwood said mockingly. "Come spring, I shall want to take my new mistress cruising on the river."

"I won't, Geoff. And you see that my stallion is well cared for and not overbred?"

The two men parted then, each secure in the knowledge that he would soon possess a coveted new toy.

Geoffrey Southwood did not know what intrigued him the most—the lovely widow's beauty, her air of breeding, or her dislike of him. He would enjoy the challenge of seducing and taming her. And he would be the envy of London for owning such a fine mistress. By fair means or foul, Southwood vowed he would have her.

Chapter 14

Skye's house was located on the Strand on the Green in the village of Chiswick outside the city of London. The last building in the row, it was much less pretentious than its neighbors. Farther down the line were the palaces of such great lords as Salisbury and Worcester, and the bishop of Durham.

They had sailed from Plymouth up the coast into the mouth of the Thames. There the *Mermaid* had anchored in the Pool awaiting her chance to dock in London. Skye, Jean Morlaix, and Robert Small had disembarked and ridden ahead. It would be several weeks before the *Mermaid* was assigned a wharf space, and Robert Small trusted his reliable first mate to oversee the ship in his absence.

Skirting the main portion of the city, they soon arrived at Chiswick. It was a small and charming village with an excellent inn, the Swan, on the far side of its green. Here they stopped to refresh themselves with cups of freshly pressed cider, warm newly baked bread covered with pink ham, and a sharp, pale golden cheese. Skye was ravenous and ate eagerly, much to the beaming approval of the fat innkeeper. He poured her another foaming goblet of cider.

"Be you passing through?" he queried.

Skye sent him a blinding smile that quite stunned him. "No," she said, "I own a house here, Master Innkeeper, and I've come to live in it."

"Which 'ouse is that, madam? I thought I knew all the great lords and their families. I grew up here, you see. Ever since there's been an inn in Chiswick, there 'ave been Monypennys in Chiswick. In fact," and here he chuckled, his fat belly heaving with mirth, "no one 'as ever been quite sure which came first, the Swan or the Monypennys! Aha! Ha! Ha!"

Jean and Captain Small looked askance but Skye giggled, thus increasing the innkeeper's approval of her. "I am Señora Goya del Fuentes, Master Monypenny. The house I own is 'Greenwood,' the last one on the Strand. It belonged to my late husband."

"You're Spanish?" his voice was now edged in disapproval.

"My husband was. I am Irish."

"Almost as bad," came the reply.

"*Mon Dieu! Quel cochon!*" muttered Jean.

"Master Monypenny! I will thank you to keep a civil tongue in your head. Señora Goya del Fuentes is a good and gentle lady, and not to be abused while under my protection." Robert Small's hand was on his sword.

The big innkeeper looked down at the little sea captain. "Lord bless me!" he began to chuckle. "She must be a fine lady that the ant would challenge the sparrow! My apologies, ma'am. It's just that the memory of Bloody Mary and her Spanish husband dies hard."

"Bloody Mary?"

"The late Queen. Her that was married to Philip of Spain. Young Queen Bess's half-sister."

"Oh, yes, of course, Master Monypenny. Now I understand," said Skye. She had heard the story of the sad daughter of Catherine of Aragon from Dame Cecily. "Well, I promise you I am nothing like Bloody Mary. My daughter and I have no family left anywhere that we know of, and so we have come to England to make a new life. English hospitality is famous worldwide."

The innkeeper ruffled with pride. "And so it should be, ma'am. So it should be. You'll be quite happy here upon the Strand. Now, if I may involve myself in your business for a moment . . . You say your house is the last one in the row. Tsk! The last tenants left it in shameful condition, and if you'll allow me, ma'am, I'll have rooms for you and your party set aside. The plain fact is that your house is not habitable."

"Robbie! Was the agent not notified to prepare the house for me?"

"He was, Skye."

The innkeeper shook his head dolefully. "That would be Mr. Taylor, wouldn't it? He's a bad 'un, but how were you to know that?"

"Bad? In what way, Master Monypenny?" asked Robert Small.

"He's been renting the house out to youngbloods for their—oh, dalliances, you might say. Charges 'em twice what you asks for the house, pockets the overage, and then collects his commission too."

"And how do you know *that?*"

"He's in the habit of taking a drink here now and then. But he can't hold his liquor. More than two pints and he begins to talk. One night during the late Queen's reign he bragged about how he was cheating the Spaniard who owned the house."

"We had best go and check the house, Robbie." The sea captain nodded. "I should be grateful, Master Monypenny, if you would set aside rooms for us, as well as a private dining room. I shall require a bath upon our return."

"At once, ma'am!"

Remounting their horses, they rode across the green and down Riversedge Street. Skye was impressed by the great houses that lined the waterside. As they neared the end of the street the buildings became less grand, however, the last three being an elegant mansion, a small palace, and finally a charming house of mellowed pink brick. It was set within a private green park. The gates showed rust, and hung loosely open. Robert Small pursed his lips. Pushing open the gates, he led the way into the grounds.

The park was overgrown and unkempt, the woodland filled with brambles, the lawns waist-high in weeds. When they reached the house they found several windows broken and the front door hanging open on broken hinges.

"Master Taylor is going to have a lot to answer for," growled Robbie. "Where the hell is the gatekeeper? He should be guarding the premises. Jean, didn't you pay wages last year for a year's gate-keeping service?"

"*Oui,* Captain, I did, but the monies were forwarded to Master Taylor, the agent."

"It's neither here nor there now," said Skye. "The damage is done. Let us see if the inside has fared as badly."

The three entered the house and gasped with shock as they moved from room to room on the main floor. Then Robert Small ran quickly upstairs inspecting the second and third floors. His face was a thundercloud when he descended again.

"Stripped!" he roared. "There isn't a stick of furniture in the entire house! Nor draperies, rugs, linens, or plate! You've been robbed! The dirty bastard has taken everything!"

"Master Monypenny knew whereof he spoke," observed Skye drily. "I won't be played for a fool, Robbie. Master Taylor must be caught and prosecuted. I imagine, however, that the furnishings are long gone. You were in the house several times, Robbie. Do you recall seeing anything of great value?"

"Just the usual household furnishings."

"Then they're easily replaced. Thank heavens, Marie and the children remained in Devon. Come, Jean, Robbie. Back to the Swan. I am tired and want a bath, and nothing can be done here until tomorrow."

On the following morning Skye rode into the city of London.

She visited the cabinetmaker, the draper, the silversmith, the brass and iron mongers. At each stop she said the same thing. "Deliver my order within the week, and I'll pay you a handsome bonus." Then she paid in full for the work contracted or items chosen.

At the Swan she interviewed applicants for her household staff and with Master Monypenny's aid, employed a Mistress Burnside as her housekeeper, half a dozen housemaids and footmen, a Master Walters for her majordomo, and his wife for her cook. There were four kitchen girls hired, as well as a pot boy. Mistress Burnside had a widowed sister who, with her two plain daughters, would be the household laundresses. The out-of-house staff consisted of a head gardener and head groom, each of whom had two assistants, and a gatekeeper. Skye would soon need a nursery staff to look after Willow, and this would consist of a laundress, a nursemaid, and one assistant. Compared to the great houses on the Strand, hers would be a very modest household.

Skye had inspected her house thoroughly by her second day in London. Below the main level of the house was a large kitchen that opened out into a small vegetable patch and herb garden. There were two fireplaces in the kitchen, both with brick ovens. One would take a whole side of beef. The other, smaller one, was well suited to pots and bread-baking. Off to one side of the kitchen was a cool, stone buttery, and off to the other was a scullery. There was a long servants' hall with a fireplace and quarters for some of the servants.

The housekeeper had a private bedchamber, as did the majordomo and his wife, the cook. The four kitchen maids shared a room, and the laundress and her two daughters shared one. A small alcove set into the chimney wall was padded with a plump pallet and assigned to the little pot boy who was considered too young to be housed with the other male servants. The six housemaids would sleep in attic rooms set aside for them. The six footmen, three grooms, and two undergardeners were housed in the stable loft. The head gardener and his wife would live in a tiny cottage hidden in the little garden and the gatekeeper and his wife in the little gatehouse. Jean and Marie were given an apartment of their own in one wing of the house. Marie would continue in her duties as Skye's chief tiring woman while the nursery staff watched over both Willow and Henri. The nursery staff would, of course, sleep in the nursery.

On the main floor of the house there was a large formal dining hall, a small family dining room, a reception room, and the apartment set aside for Jean and his wife. The second floor consisted of a library, a smaller room for Jean's work, and two big reception rooms that could be opened into one large room for dancing. The third floor of the house held Skye's bedchamber, dayroom, and dressing room, besides two guest chambers and the nursery apartments.

The house was built near the river's edge, but set back enough to allow for a rear garden, the walls of which rose up from the water. Skye had her own private quai. This was a distinct advantage, for it allowed Skye her own barge. She immediately commissioned one built, and, shortly thereafter, a bargeman was added to the staff. Everyone in the house was delighted by this, for river travel was often preferable to land, especially so in times of unrest.

The tradesmen with whom Skye did business were eager for the bonuses promised. Within the week the house was filled with all the things she had ordered. Everything was of the best quality. Skye had warned the tradesmen that she would not accept shoddy goods. She was not aware that many of the goods had been made for others. Merchants had sent her things that other customers would now have to wait several months for.

She hurried from room to room, directing the hanging of draperies, tapestries, and pictures, the placement of furniture. The rooms began to take on life and, finally contented, Skye walked slowly throughout her house. It was well after midnight, and the exhausted servants had long since sought their beds. She entered each room and looked about with satisfaction.

The oak furniture gleamed with a polish that only hand rubbing and pure beeswax could give it. Upon the dark wide floorboards were thick Turkey carpets. The use of carpets was unusual. Many homes, even those of the wealthy, still used rushes mixed with herbs upon the floors. There were colorful tapestries and paintings throughout the house, for Captain Small was clever at ferreting out those noble but impoverished families who were willing to discreetly sell such items. Heavy draperies in velvet and silk hung from the leaded casement windows. Brass sconces adorned the paneled walls. Silver twinkled on the sideboards. The scene was one of elegance and wealth.

As Skye departed each room she snuffed out the beeswax candles carefully. She would not allow fat or tallow in the house, even in the servants quarters, for she disliked the smell. There were porcelain bowls of potpourri in all the rooms. The river was known, after all, to stink occasionally.

She entered her apartment and found Daisy, who had arrived several days ago, dozing by the fire. The girl jumped when she saw her mistress.

"Daisy, you didn't have to wait up. But since you're here, unlace me, and then off to bed with you."

"I don't mind, mistress," said Daisy as she undid Skye's gown and helped her out of her petticoats. She wisked the clothing into the dressing room and soon was back dipping water from the fireplace kettle into an earthenware pitcher. "Are you sure you don't need me further, ma'am?"

"No, Daisy. Go to bed."

The little maid was quickly gone. Skye sat down wearily and carefully rolled off her gossamer stockings. Naked, she walked across her room and had a leisurely wash with her favorite damask rose soap. Sliding into an embroidered pale-blue silk caftan, she extinguished the candles and went to sit in her bedroom window seat, facing the river.

The moon silvered the water. She could see a barge pull into the quai two houses down. Two figures, a man and a woman, climbed out of the boat and went slowly up the steps to the garden. At the top of the stairway they kissed for a long moment. Then the gentleman picked up the lady and they were lost to view. Sighing, she sought her bed, and slept badly. The memory of the romantic scene she had watched burned into her and made her ache. Skye was twenty years old, and for the first time since Khalid's death over a year ago, she deeply wanted a man to love her. She rose, weeping softly, and took a bottle of blackberry brandy from her dayroom sideboard. She then crawled back into the window seat and drank herself to sleep.

Next door, the owner of the small riverside palace was also wakeful. The Earl of Lynmouth paced his bedroom floor excitedly, scarcely able to believe his good fortune. Not only was his new neighbor the beautiful Señora Goya del Fuentes, but he had found a way to victory over de Grenville. He chuckled. He would pay his respects to the lady, but if she had not willingly succumbed by Twelfth Night, then he would blackmail her into submission.

The Earl of Lynmouth entertained lavishly, and his parties were famous. He had recently come up to London to see that his house was properly prepared for Christmas and Twelfth Night. The Queen herself would be attending several seasonal festivities, including his Twelfth Night masque. Geoffrey had been quite astounded to find that the beautiful Mistress Goya del Fuentes was the owner of the little jewel of a house at the end of the Strand, and had watched with interest as the house was refurbished. A connoisseur, he noted her choices with an approving eye as the tradesmen lugged their merchandise into her house.

Now the time had come for him to make his first move to capture the lady. He would woo her gently at first, and then if necessary he would threaten her with exposure. Through a fantastic piece of luck, he had discovered her true history. He owned a one-third share in a ship that traded in the Mideast, and when it had returned recently to London he had gone aboard to see to his interests. Through the bow window of the master's cabin he had seen Robert Small. He asked his Captain Browne, "Do you know who that man is on the next ship?"

"Aye, my lord. That be Captain Robert Small of Bideford in Devon. The *Mermaid* is his ship."

Captain Browne drew in on his pipe, then gently puffed out a curl of blue smoke. "Robbie Small is a lucky devil, my lord. He needn't go off to sea at all, for he's a wealthy man and was born of gentry, too. But the sea's a wanton bitch, and when she gets in your blood it's hard to rid yourself of her."

"Was he born to wealth?" prodded the Earl gently.

"No. The family fortunes were pretty low until he went into partnership with the great Whoremaster of Algiers, Khalid el Bey. How they met I don't know, but they somehow became friends and the bey backed Robbie in several ventures. Finally when he was on his feet, they became equal partners. And so they remained for over ten years."

"What happened then?"

"The bey was killed a year and a half ago, murdered by one of his women. Bless me! He ran the finest cathouses in the East, he did. The most famous of them was called the House of Felicity, and the woman who ran it for him finally did him in. They say she was jealous of his young wife, and thought it was the wife she was stabbing. At any rate, the young widow soon disappeared and it was discovered that she had sold everything her husband owned. The captain-governor of the Casbah fortress went wild with rage. He'd had his eye on the young widow. God help Robbie Small if he ever sets foot in Algiers again, for the Casbah captain knows Small helped the lady Skye leave Algiers."

Geoffrey Southwood felt his heart lurch wildly. "*Skye?*" he asked.

"The bey's wife. Her name was Skye muna el Khalid. She herself is another wild tale. More wine, sir?"

"Tell me!"

And so Captain Browne told him all he had heard about Skye, which was a great deal indeed. And when Geoffrey left the ship, he was elated. His coach clattered back through the noisy city streets and he began to plot.

It was her! There could be no mistake! And he had her, for there was a child. The bey's child? Probably. Robert Small did not act like her lover. She would probably do anything to protect her child, for the child's future would be determined by its family's reputation. As long as she was the respectable young widow, all would be well. She would not want her true story known, for her own sake and for the child's. Yes . . . Geoffrey had her!

Geoffrey Southwood was a wealthy man. Although he seldom discussed it, his paternal grandmother had been a rich merchant's daughter. Over the past few centuries many noble families had married into the monied middle class to increase their finances. The Southwood family understood that money was power. They were not an important family, but their title was an ancient one, earned on the field at the Battle of Hastings.

The first Earl of Lynmouth had been Geoffroi de Sudbois, the third son of a noble Norman family. He had joined Duke William's invasion of England in hopes of winning a place for himself and his descendants, for there was nothing for him in his native France. His oldest brother was his father's undisputed heir and had three sons of his own. The next de Sudbois brother had opted for the religious life, and was already the valued right hand of his prior. The Duke of Normandy's invasion of England was a godsend to Geoffroi de Sudbois, for it offered him a chance to make a place for himself.

His father gave him war-horses and their equipage, along with a small velvet bag of gold. When Geoffroi's oldest brother protested, his father said, "As long as I live, what is mine shall be disposed of as I choose. When I am gone, and it is yours, you may dispose of it your way. Do not be greedy, Gilles. Your brother cannot succeed unless he is properly equipped and mounted. Do you want him to always have nothing? To be constantly coming back here coveting your position, his mere presence a threat to your boys? It will be better for all if he makes a place for himself in England."

The eldest de Sudbois son understood his father's point, and even pressed upon his surprised brother a fat purse of silver marks. This purse proved the means by which he recruited himself a small troop of cavalry. Those who joined him supplied their own horses, mail, and weapons. He paid them one silver mark upon debarkation for England. What booty they could take in battle was theirs to keep, and there was always a chance to win oneself land and even a title.

The young Seigneur de Sudbois and his thirty-five men made an impressive addition to Duke William's invading army. Even more impressive was the soldier that de Sudbois proved himself to be. He managed to fight near his Duke twice, once even preventing a direct attack upon his overlord. Toward the end of one day, he found himself in on the kill of the English King, Harold.

Duke William of Normandy had seen enough of the young lordling to be both amused and impressed. "He's a valuable man," observed the Duke, "and God knows he's worked hard enough to win a bit of this land for himself. I'll give him something down in the south, toward the west. If he can take the land and hold it, it's his."

Geoffroi de Sudbois took and held the little earldom of Lynmouth. He ruthlessly slew the Saxon lord of the holding and all his kin, with the exception of the Saxon's thirteen-year-old daughter, Gwyneth. He raped her upon the hall's long table and, when the girl was proved a virgin, he sent for a priest and wed her instantly. The practical Gwyneth cleaved to her new lord and dutifully sired the next generation. Within a hundred years de Sudbois was anglecized to Southwood, but through the many generations the ruthlessness of the original Norman Geoffroi de Sudbois and the determination of his Saxon wife remained strong traits, even down to the sixteenth-century Geoffrey Southwood.

This Earl of Lynmouth was twenty-eight years old. Six feet tall, he had dark-blond hair, lime-green eyes, and, as Skye had observed, the face of an angel. It was a beautiful face, yet an entirely masculine one. Oval, the forehead was broad, the cheekbones high, the nose long and slim, the mouth sensuous, the chin slightly pointed. His fair skin was tanned, and because his face had no flaws, he kept it smooth-shaven. His wavy hair was cut short. His body was the lean one of a man used to regular exercise.

He had been married twice. At twelve he had wed a neighboring eight-year-old heiress. She died two years later of smallpox, along with her parents. This left him considerably richer, having inherited money, lands, and the barony of Lynton. Sexually active, he had mourned his wife for the shortest time possible and then wed again. The second wife was five years his senior, painfully plain but very wealthy. An orphaned heiress, her guardians had thought themselves stuck with the poor girl until Geoffrey Southwood's father offered for her for his son. Mary Bowen was of an old and noble family. More important, her lands adjoined those of the Earl of Lynmouth's.

On her wedding day, the poor plain bride showed herself enamored of her handsome bridegroom, and grateful to have been rescued from the shame of spinsterhood. On her wedding night, however, her opinion changed. Her shrieks could be heard all over the castle as Geoffrey Southwood battered his way through her maidenhead and impregnated her. During the next six years she delivered a child every ten months. All but the first were daughters, and each was as plain as her mother. In disgust, Geoffrey finally stopped visiting his wife's bed. His seven plain daughters were more than enough for one man to dower.

Mary Bowen Southwood was more than content to remain in Devon. She feared her husband. After the horror of her wedding night she had learned to lay quietly during their mating, occasionally even simulating the response expected of her. When it was first apparent that she was pregnant, he had treated her in a kindly fashion. She was glad to have pleased him, especially when Henry was born. But then had come Mary, Elizabeth, and Catherine. The week after little Phillipa's birth he had been so furious that he slapped her, shouting that she had done it deliberately, that she'd give him a son next time or he would know the reason why. She had learned fear in her subsequent pregnancies. Susan was born next. Geoffrey was in London. Frightened but dutiful, she sent him word. A six months' silence followed. When he finally arrived home he handed down one final ultimatum. "Produce another son, madam, or you'll spend the rest of your life here in Devon with your brood of daughters."

"What of Henry?" she dared to ask.

"Henry goes to the Shrewsburys' household," he said flatly.

When the twins, Gwyneth and Joan, were born, the Countess found herself and all of her daughters moved from Lynmouth Castle to Lynton Court. Geoffrey Southwood had had enough.

From that time on he saw his wife and family once yearly, at Michaelmas, when he arrived to hand over the money needed to run their little household for the following year. He refused to make matches for his daughters, on the premise that they were all like their mother and he would not be responsible for other men's disappointment when the girls produced a string of daughters, as their mother had done.

Mary Southwood was frankly relieved to be rid of her husband, but she worried over her girls. Through personal sacrifice and great frugality she managed to save half of what he gave her each year. Added to a small, secret hoard left her by her late guardians, she slowly built up small dowries for her daughters. She taught them the arts of housewifery. There would be no grand matches, but she would get them all settled. Eventually fate helped her out when Geoffrey Southwood stopped even his yearly visit, delegating that chore to his majordomo.

The "Angel" Earl, as he was known, spent his time following the Court. The young Queen Elizabeth enjoyed his elegant beauty and sharp wit. Even more, she appreciated his astute knowledge of business and overseas trade. Trade was where England's future lay, and the educated Queen needed all the advice about it she could obtain. Elizabeth had already demonstrated herself to be a working monarch, and nothing escaped her sharp eyes or ears. Geoffrey Southwood might have an appetite for the ladies, but he deliberately went out of his way to avoid her maids-of-honor, and his respect for her was much appreciated by the vain young Queen. Best of all, Geoffrey came to Court without the encumbrance of a wife, and was therefore free to play one of Elizabeth's gallants.

The next day dawned bright and blue, as perfect an October day as one could wish for. Skye spent the morning indoors overseeing her household, which was finally beginning to run smoothly, then working with Jean and Robert Small in setting up a new trading company. Later she eagerly snatched up her flower basket and garden shears and escaped to the beckoning outdoors.

The gardener and his assistants had done miracles in a few short weeks. Gone were the waist-high weeds and brambles. Brick walks had been discovered beneath the overgrowth, as well as small reflecting pools and rose bushes. Pruning had brought forth an abundance of late blooms, which Skye now clipped. "Damn!" she swore suddenly, jabbing her thumb on a thorn, then popping it into her mouth to soothe it.

A deep, amused masculine chuckle sent her whirling about. To her anger and embarrassment, the handsome Earl of Lynmouth was sitting on the medium-high wall separating her house from the next. He leaped down gracefully and took her hand. "Just a prick, my pet," he said.

Skye snatched back her hand furiously. "What were you doing on my wall?" she demanded.

"I live on the other side of it," he answered smoothly. "In fact, my pet, you and I own the wall in common. The building next to yours is Lynmouth House. It was built by my grandfather, who also built this charming little house for his mistress, a goldsmith's daughter."

"Oh," said Skye coldly, shocked. "How very interesting, my lord. Now . . . if you will please leave?" she managed.

Geoffrey Southwood smiled ruefully, and Skye noticed that the corners of his strangely green eyes were crinkled with laugh lines. "Now, Mistress Goya del Fuentes," he said. "I realize that we got off on the wrong foot, and I will apologize now for having stared so rudely at you at the Rose and Anchor. Surely, however, you will not be too hard on me? I cannot be the first man who has ever been stunned by your extravagant beauty, now can I?"

Skye flushed. Damn the man! He really was charming. And if they were neighbors, she could hardly continue to snub him. The corners of her mouth turned up in a small smile. "Very well, my lord. I accept your apology."

"And you will join me for a late supper?"

Skye laughed. "You are really incorrigible, Lord Southwood."

"Geoffrey," he corrected.

"You are still incorrigible, Geoffrey," she sighed, "and my name is Skye."

"A most unusual name. How did you come by it?"

"I don't know. My parents both died when I was young, and the nuns who raised me could never tell me." It was said so naturally that he was thrown. Perhaps she wasn't the Whoremaster of Algiers' widow after all. "And was Geoffrey your father's name?" she was asking.

"No. He was Robert. Geoffrey was the first of the Southwoods. He came from Normandy with Duke William almost five hundred years ago."

"How wonderful to know the history of one's family," she said wistfully.

"You haven't yet told me you will dine with me tonight," he said.

Skye bit her lip. "I don't know," she murmured. "I really don't think I should."

"I realize it's a bit unorthodox, asking you to dine late, but I must attend the Queen at Greenwich, and she'll not let me go till late."

"Then perhaps we should dine on another day when you have more time," she replied.

"Have pity on me, fair Skye. I dance constant attendance on

Her Majesty, and it is only rarely that I have any time. My chef is an artist, but cooking for one is little challenge. Unless I provide him with a guest soon I shall lose him. And how can I give my famous Twelfth Night revel without a chef? So you really can't refuse me, can you?"

She had to laugh. He seemed so boyish, and so very handsome in the open-necked cream silk shirt. He was not at all the arrogant nobleman who had accosted her several weeks before. "I should not," she said, "but I will. I would not like to be held responsible by all of London for the defection of your chef."

"I will come for you myself," he replied. Then he caught her hand to his lips and brushed it lightly. "You've made me the happiest of men tonight!" Grasping at a heavy vine growing against the wall, he pulled himself up and quickly disappeared over the top.

Shrugging, Skye picked up her flower basket and returned to the house. If she was to be ready when he came this evening, she had a great deal to do. She stopped, and told herself that this was just a simple dinner, not a romantic liaison.

Robert Small emerged just then from the library. "Well, lass, we're done now. May I treat you to dinner at the *Swan* tavern up the river?"

"Oh, Robbie. I'm having dinner with Lord Southwood. He is, it seems, my neighbor."

"That knave! Christ's toenail, Skye, are you mad?"

"Now, Robbie, he has apologized for his rudeness. I have no friends here in London, and you'll soon be off again. I must start somewhere."

"He has a wife," stated Robert Small flatly.

"I suspected so, but I do not seek a romantic entanglement with Geoffrey."

Robert Small's bushy gray-black eyebrows shot up. "Geoffrey, is it? Well, my lass, so you'll know a bit about the man, attend me. His first wife died when she was a child. His second wife is a woman of no beauty, but much wealth. She's borne him one son and seven daughters, and for her perfidy she and her daughters are exiled to Lynton Court, her childhood home. He sends his steward each Michaelmas to pay the servants there for the year. Cold bastard, I'd say. He's rich, though. At least we don't have to worry about him being after your money."

His dour concern over fortune-hunting men made her laugh. She ruffled his thinning hair. "Dear Robbie, you're a good watchdog, and I thank you. You and Dame Cecily and Willow are my entire family. I promise to be very careful in my relationship with Lord Southwood, but it's only a late supper."

"I'll stay the night, Skye. It's best you have a man in the house."

"Thank you, Robbie. Now, I'd best prepare myself," and giving him a quick kiss on the cheek she ran upstairs to her own apartment. "Daisy!" she called. "Have a footman set up my bath and lay out the peacock-blue velvet gown with the gold thread flowered underskirt."

As the footmen lugged the buckets of steaming water up the back stairs from the kitchen, Skye sat at her dressing table sliding necklaces through her slender fingers. She decided upon a double strand of perfectly matched pale-pink pearls from which hung a teardrop diamond of slightly deeper pink. The necklace had been Khalid's gift. It no longer hurt quite so much to think about Khalid.

The footmen departed and she undressed slowly. Daisy took each garment, and Skye reached for some tortoiseshell hairpins and secured her dark hair. It would not be necessary to wash it tonight, as she had done so yesterday in a mixture of fresh rainwater and essence of roses. Now she walked naked across the room and poured some of the same rose essence into her tub. Daisy averted her brown eyes. She could simply not get used to her mistress's habit of bathing regularly, let alone bathing naked. The young woman liked her mistress, however, and so she bore with her eccentricities.

Skye chuckled. "You can open your eyes now, Daisy. I'm safely in the tub."

"Oh, mum, I don't think I'll ever get used to it."

"Haven't you ever looked at yourself, Daisy? Women have very lovely bodies, but men are never quite so pretty."

"Oh, mum! How you talk! Look at myself indeed! If me mother had ever caught me doing such a thing she'd have beat me black and blue."

Skye smiled to herself and wondered why the English—no, she amended—why the Europeans were so afraid of their bodies. Then she laughed at herself for, though she could not remember it, she too was European. But she couldn't imagine herself bathing only a few times a year, and then in a cotton shift!

She picked up the damask rose soap, built up a rich lather, and washed her face. She lathered the rest of her lithe body, slowly and thoroughly, summoning an almost unbearably sensuous feeling. Good Lord, she thought, as she watched the nipples of her breasts harden, I'm alive again, and I want a man to love. She blushed with the memory of how Geoffrey Southwood had looked at her this afternoon.

Stepping hastily from the tub, she took the big warmed towel from Daisy and began to dry herself. "Bring me a light wool caftan," she said. "It's too early to dress yet. I'll sleep for a bit."

Slipping on the caftan, she added, "Leave the tub till later, I'll rest now, and ring when I want you. Go get your dinner." The little maid curtseyed and left the room.

Skye lay upon her bed, drawing a fur robe over herself. Geoffrey Southwood had a finely turned leg, she thought, and those lime-green eyes had undoubtedly melted many a heart. She was much too vulnerable to be having dinner with him. Oh, why had she accepted the invitation? She was lonely. Perhaps that was why. Khalid had been dead almost two years, and suddenly she was again aware of the fact that she was a woman, a woman who, up until her husband's death, had been well loved. She would have to be very careful lest she present the Earl of Lynmouth with the wrong impression of herself. She drifted into a light sleep and awakened at Daisy's touch.

"The Earl of Lynmouth's footman is below, mum. His lordship will be here in half an hour."

Skye stretched languidly. "Fetch me a basin of rose water, Daisy. Is my gown ready?"

"Yes, mum."

Skye bathed her face, hands, and neck, having shed the caftan. With averted eyes Daisy handed her mistress her silk undergarments, lacing the little boned busk up tightly, smoothing down the several petticoats, the last one threaded through with blue ribbons, as was her silk underblouse. Skye slipped on her new knitted silk stockings which were of the palest blue with a tiny silver thread vine pattern. Her garters were also blue with deep pink rosettes.

Daisy carefully slipped the gold-threaded underskirt over Skye's head, and laced it up. Lastly came the beautiful peacock-blue velvet gown, split to show the embroidered underskirt. The puffed sleeves were slashed to reveal a soft creamy sheer silk underblouse. Skye slipped on her blue satin slippers and stood before the pier glass, a faint smile on her lips. She slid the pearls around her neck, watching with fascination as the pink diamond nestled in the deep valley between her breasts. Yes, it was perfect.

Daisy held up a tray of rings, but Skye selected only a large baroque pearl and placed it on her right hand. She held out her hands and was pleased with the simple effect the single ring created.

Her hands were especially beautiful, slender with long, well-shaped fingers, the nails delicately rounded and buffed to a healthy pink.

She gazed at her image again. *I* am *beautiful,* she thought. Then she laughed softly.

"His lordship is here, mum," said Daisy. "The footman has just come up with word."

"Have the footman tell his lordship I shall be down directly, and escort him into the small receiving room. Have Walter pour him some wine."

Daisy curtseyed. "Yes, mum."

Skye moved slowly to her dressing table and reached for her scent bottle. She daubed the rose fragrance on all the available pulse points, remembering Yasmin as she did. Dear God, she thought, if there is a Paradise, please don't let Yasmin be Khalid's houri. I forgave her for the sake of both our immortal souls, but I couldn't bear it if she was with him when I can't be. The tears sprang to her eyes, and she quickly snatched up a lace-edged handkerchief. Then, fixing a little smile on her lips, she left to join the Earl of Lynmouth.

Geoffrey Southwood had declined both a seat in the receiving room and the wine. With undisguised admiration he now watched as Skye descended the staircase. Reaching the bottom, she swept him an elegant curtsey. "Good evening, my lord Southwood." He admired her lovely breasts which momentarily swelled over her seemingly modest square neckline.

"And a good even' to you, Señora Goya del Fuentes. I hope you don't mind, but I've arranged for the door in our garden wall to be opened. I assume you won't object to a stroll in the gardens."

"No, I don't mind a stroll."

He offered her his arm, and they moved through the house and out into the evening. The air was mild, and the night sky clear. His slim hand covered hers, and as they walked he said quietly, "Are you aware of how beautiful you are? There isn't a woman at Court who compares with you."

"Even the Queen?" she teased.

"Her Majesty is in a class by herself, my pet. No one compares with Elizabeth Tudor."

"Bravo, my lord Earl! The perfect courtier's reply," she mocked mischievously.

"I *am* the perfect courtier, Skye, for only by the Queen's favor can an ambitious man progress."

"You are titled, intelligent, and wealthy," she said. "Why should it matter to you if the Queen favors you?"

The question pleased him, for it showed she had intelligence. Oddly enough, he liked intelligent women. "The Southwoods have never been important in the history of England, Skye. We won our lands with William the Conqueror and our title with Richard, Coeur de Lion, in the Holy Land. That particular Southwood, upon returning to England, advised his family to remain in Devon and not go gadding about. We've taken his advice. Nevertheless, probably thanks to my merchant antecedents, I seem to be an ambitious sort, and Court is the place for ambitious men. The Queen has need of them."

"And what of ambitious women, Geoffrey?"

He smiled as they walked through the wall gate into his garden. "What are your ambitions, my pet? If you seek a titled lover, then I'm your man."

She ignored the remark. "I've just formed a trading company with Robert Small. It would help if I had a royal charter. Help me get it, and I'll give you a two-percent interest in it."

The Earl of Lynmouth was astounded. "By God, sweetheart, you are ambitious!" he laughed. "I'm not sure if I'm shocked or simply amazed."

Skye was as surprised at herself as was Southwood. Where in Heaven's name had *that* idea come from, and where had she gotten the nerve to suggest such a thing? Having ventured it, however, she decided to follow it through. "Well, my lord," she said coolly. "What say you?"

She was serious, thought Southwood, amused. They had reached Lynmouth House by now, and he escorted her up the steps of the marble terrace into a small room with a lovely bow window that overlooked the river and the gardens. A candlelit table had been set up in the bow.

"Let us have some wine," he said, pouring a Burgundy and handing her a goblet. "Now, mistress, what guarantee do you give me that I'll see a return on my investment?"

"Captain Small was my husband's partner in Algiers. Kha—Diego financed him, and our secretary, Jean Morlaix, kept the records. It was up to Robert to handle the rest of it, and he did. He was my husband's partner for ten years. Nothing has changed. The Goya del Fuentes money will finance him. Jean Morlaix remained in my employ after Diego's death. I do not need a royal charter, but it would help enormously. What do you risk, my lord? Neither gold nor prestige. You waste more money gambling. If you would prefer, set a price upon your aid and I will pay you. Then you risk nothing," she finished scornfully.

"Ah vixen," he chuckled, "so you would shame me into it, eh? You're a damned hard bargainer, but I'll see what I can do. After all, a two-percent share in a good trading company is not to be overlooked."

Inwardly she heaved a sigh of relief and, with a casual air, sipped at her wine. His mouth twitched with suppressed amusement, for Geoffrey Southwood could appreciate a jest on himself better than most men. She had outbluffed him, the little devil. What a woman she was, he thought to himself. The thought of her in his bed sent shivers down his spine. For now, however, he would be a gentleman, for to move too quickly with this lady could cost him de Grenville's barge as well as the beauty herself.

The footmen began serving the meal, which began with a silver bowl of cold, raw oysters. Skye happily cracked open the shells and swallowed half a dozen luscious, icy oysters. Southwood ate two to her every one. The next course was bright yellow mussels in white wine with a Dijon mustard sauce, thin slices of Dover sole on a bed of crisp watercress, accompanied by very thin slices of lemons imported from the south of France, and tiny pink shrimp broiled in herb butter. Skye ate sparingly but tasted of everything. The Earl had been quite right—his chef was a master.

The second course cleared away, the third was set on the sideboard. Three ribs of juicy beef with horseradish sauce and a large plump pink ham vied for attention alongside a platter of small quail, roasted golden and stuffed with fruit. Salad of new lettuces, venison slices in red wine, and a rabbit pastry rounded out the third course.

Skye directed a footman to serve her one of the quail, some ham, a slice of rabbit pie, and a dish of salad. The Earl, who sampled everything, looked on approvingly. "I like a woman who enjoys her food," he grinned, his green eyes bright.

"But keeps her figure," she shot back.

"Aye. A pretty woman is far more pleasant to gaze upon, sweetheart."

"Is your wife a pretty woman?"

"Mary? Not really. She's too tiny, like a Spanish dwarf. Her hair is no real color, her eyes a pale brown, her complexion, sallow. Was your husband handsome?"

"Aye," she said softly. "He was very handsome. But more important, he was kind and good."

"How long have you been widowed?"

"Two years now."

"You should think of remarrying, Skye. You're far too lovely to remain alone."

"I know few people here, my lord. And besides, there is no one who could take my lord's place."

"If you don't have friends in England," he ventured, "why did you leave Algiers?"

"The Turkish governor decided I should make him an admirable wife. Since I did not choose to marry him, it became necessary to leave. None of my lord's real friends would have dared to protect me. I was helpless against that powerful beast, but he got nothing of my lord's, neither his widow nor his wealth! I shall build that wealth and make it even greater. My little Willow will be very wealthy."

He smiled slowly at her. "You are an ambitious wench, sweetheart, but damme if I don't approve! The Queen is ambitious too, and though some men may be fearful of such women, I'm not."

The last course was offered then, ripe pears covered with meringue and baked to a faint golden brown, thin sugar wafers, and a clear sweet wine. The Earl apologized for the simplicity of the dessert. As there were only two diners, he had suggested to his chef that he limit the sweets.

When she had spooned up the last of her dessert, Skye sat back in her chair, her sapphire eyes half closed, and smiled. Southwood laughed. "You look like a well-fed cat."

"I am, my lord, and I must have the recipe for the quail stuffing. It was delicious."

"It's yours. But come, sweetheart, up with you! We'll walk in the gardens by the river to settle our meal."

He escorted her outside after first dropping his black velvet cloak about her. The night had turned chilly. The full moon silvered everything, and a faint mist was beginning to rise from the Thames. They walked in silence, watching as a brightly lit barge went by, hearing laughter drift across the water. A steady measured beat of oars and a single lantern announced the approach of the enterprising waterman who offered taxi service to those who wanted to go up- or downriver. They stood watching the moonlit water, and after a while Geoffrey said softly, "I would not offend you, but I would kiss you."

"No one but my husband has ever kissed me," she whispered.

"He's gone, sweetheart," was the hoarse reply. And tipping her pale face firmly toward him, he touched his warm mouth to hers. He kissed her gently, but she could sense the desire that he held firmly in check. The tip of his tongue licked at the edges of her mouth, sending a shiver through her, awakening the long unsatisfied passions. He held her tightly, his masculine scent assaulting her senses. She began to relax within the circle of his arms. He was as big and tall as Khalid had been, and very male.

Then, gently, as suddenly as he had kissed her, he released her and whispered softly, "I will take you home, sweetheart, lest I do something that would lose me your friendship." And without another word he took her arm and walked with her, back through the wall gate, across her gardens, and into her house.

In the moonlit library she gazed openly at him and her musical voice said firmly but softly, "Kiss me just once more, Geoffrey." A quick smile touched his mouth, and then he bent to meet her lips again. This time he allowed his passions a looser rein and the pressure of his mouth forced her lips apart. His tongue ran swiftly along her teeth, pushing through, finding her silken tongue and caressing it with his own.

To Skye's shock, her own passions rose swiftly, fiercely from deep within her. Her tongue fenced skillfully with his, and she quivered at the fire and ice racing through her veins. His big hands caught her face and he kissed her again, this time very tenderly. Then his smooth fingers trailed down her slender neck to drift along the swelling tops of her breasts, and she moaned softly.

"No, sweetheart," he said quietly. "There's no honor in taking a vulnerable woman, and you are very vulnerable right now." And silently he disappeared through the French doors, and she was alone.

Skye stood very still, rigid with shock. She had nearly thrown herself at him, and had he not been the gentleman he was . . . Shivering, she made her way upstairs. Once within the safety of her room, she stood for a bit clutching Geoffrey's cloak about her. It carried the scent of orris root, and she buried her face within the sable collar trying to quiet her pounding heart.

"Are you all right, mum?"

She started. "Daisy? You needn't have waited up for me."

"And who would help you with your gown, I should like to know?" Daisy drew the cloak from Skye. "His lordship's?" Skye nodded. "Ha, ain't he the gallant one!"

"Yes. He is," said Skye, a little regretfully.

Daisy prattled on as she helped her mistress disrobe. "They say he's left a trail of broken hearts from here to Devon. Highborn or low, they all loves the 'Angel Earl.' " She looked slyly at her mistress's flushed cheeks. "They say he's a grand lover, and Lord knows you have no husband to answer to, mum."

"Shame, Daisy!" Skye broke away from her reverie long enough to remember how young her maid was. "You take on London manners and morals too quickly. I think it not wise of you. Beware lest I send you back to Devon!"

"Oh, mum. I meant no harm! But with him so handsome and ye so bonny . . ." she trailed off, her head hanging lower and lower, with such a woebegone expression that Skye almost laughed. She sent Daisy off to her bed, cautioning her to think on her sins.

Grateful to be alone, Skye slowly washed her face and hands and cleaned her teeth. Sliding a simple mauve silk nightgown over her naked form, she climbed into bed. Dear God, how she had responded to the Earl's kisses! And he had known it! She trembled. What kind of a woman was she to respond so fervently? She began to weep softly, ashamed of her wantonness, ashamed of her inability to remain faithful to the memory of her beloved husband. When at last she fell asleep, it was an exhausted and restless sleep.

The next day, as Skye sat hollow-eyed, sipping Turkish coffee in the library with Robert Small, there arrived a messenger in the green-and-white livery of the Earl of Lynmouth. He flourished a bow and presented her with an exquisitely carved rectangular ebony box. The captain raised an inquisitive eyebrow as Skye accepted the box and lifted the lid. On the red velvet lining lay one perfect carved ivory rose, its stem and leaves wrought from green gold. Beneath it was a folded sheet of vellum. It read: "In memory of a perfect evening. Geoffrey." A pink flush rose in her cheeks, but she said merely, "Convey my deepest thanks to Lord Southwood." The footman bowed himself from the library.

"So," remarked the captain, when they were alone again, "the evening went well. I would not have believed it, judging by your woebegone expression, Skye. Perhaps the gift is by way of an apology?"

"You needn't worry, Robbie." She handed him the Earl's note.

Perusing it, he looked back up at her. "Then what is it, lass? Why are you so troubled?"

"Oh, Robbie! He asked if he might kiss me, and—I let him!"

"And you found it distasteful?"

"Nooo," she wailed. "Oh, Robbie! I liked it, that's what's wrong. And worse, I wanted him to make love to me! How could I? What kind of wanton am I?"

"Christ's blessed nightshirt!" roared the little man. He thought a moment, his head in his hands, and then he began. "Listen to me, Skye. I sometimes forget that damned memory of yours still has gaps in it. Khalid has been dead for two years, and it is time you found yourself another man. You're not expected to remain true to his memory forever. There is nothing wrong in what you felt. God Almighty, you're a beautiful young woman, lass, and it's natural you responded to the Earl. He's a handsome devil. Try your wings with him if he attracts you. But remember this—he's a married man. Don't get hurt."

"Oh, Robbie, how could you even suggest such a thing? My lord Khalid—"

"Khalid is *dead,* Skye! He would be the first one to tell you to go on with your life. He wouldn't want you to bury yourself along with him."

"But Robbie, I don't love Lord Southwood."

"Lord, lass, I should hope not. He's married."

"But I still want him to make love to me."

He began to laugh. "What you feel for the Earl is desire, lust, passion. Sometimes those feelings go along with love, but more often not. The churches would like us to feel guilty about such emotions, but don't you do it! Those feelings are human nature. You won't have them with every man you meet, so don't fret." He put a friendly arm about her. "Skye, lass. I know I'm many years older, but if having the protection of marriage and my name would make you feel safe, I'd gladly marry you. I'd ask nothing of you. It would be in name only."

She was stunned. "Why, Robbie, how kind you are. You always have been, since our first meeting. What a good man you are! Thank you, but I must stand on my own two feet. I somehow feel that Khalid would want me to be strong and independent."

"Aye, lass. I think he would, but should you ever change your mind, the offer stands open. Remember that."

She bent and kissed his cheek. "I do love you, Robbie, but not the way a woman loves a man. I could not marry you, even for safety's sake, but never stop being my friend."

"I won't, lass. I won't," he said quietly, thinking, I owe Khalid more than I can ever repay, and watching over you is such a small thing. Lord God, let her find happiness, the fierce man prayed.

Chapter 15

Ever since Elizabeth Tudor had ascended the throne of England, the Earl of Lynmouth had held a masqued ball on Twelfth Night. Not the first year, however, for Queen Mary had died on the morning of November 17, 1558, and Twelfth Night had been only seven weeks later. The Court was still in mourning for her.

This year would be the third time the Earl's fête would be held, and invitations were eagerly sought. Skye received her invitation on the morning of New Year's Day. Geoffrey Southwood came calling and planned to deliver it himself. She had not seen him since that mid-November night, but she had dreamed of his kisses ever since. She hurried from her own apartments, where she had dressed, to the second-floor receiving room. Her burgundy velvet gown was offset by exquisite, delicate ecru lace along the sleeves. The square neckline was low, and bordered by the same lace. A little above it dangled a necklace of small rubies and pearls. Her midnight hair was parted in the center and fell in soft curls, Italian fashion, about her shoulders. It gave her a charmingly youthful appearance.

"My lord Earl! A happy New Year to you," she cried gaily, sweeping into the richly furnished receiving room. Dear Heaven, he was so incredibly handsome, dressed all in black velvet trimmed with sable, wearing a great heavy gold pendant about his neck.

"Mistress Goya del Fuentes, a happy year to you also." His gleaming green eyes swept over her. Christ's bones, she was beautiful! "I have brought you a small gift," he said.

She colored becomingly. "My lord, it is not necessary, and I have nothing for you."

"I will take a kiss, sweetheart, for one of your kisses is worth more than anything else."

"Oh!" Before she could protest he swept her masterfully into his arms, and took possession of her lips. The blood sang, roared, and pounded in her ears and she matched him kiss for kiss until they were both breathless. Her breasts began to swell with longing, the nipples chafing against her silk chemise. His mouth scorched down the side of her neck to her shoulder, then across the tops of her breasts, which threatened to burst the confines of the burgundy gown.

"I want to make love to you," he said softly.

"I know," she answered breathlessly, "but I need more time. I have known no man but my late husband, and I am confused. And afraid."

"I won't force you, sweetheart. Rape holds no charm for me." He led her to the brocade settle and they sat together. He drew a small jeweler's box from his left pocket. "I have been on constant call to Her Majesty," he explained. "We kept Christmas at Hampton Court, but the Queen is now at Whitehall, and I was able to get away for a while. I have bought these because I thought they matched your eyes."

Skye took the proffered box. She opened it without taking her eyes from him. Inside the box were a pair of round sapphire earrings that dangled from two tiny gold beads. She lifted one up to the bright morning sunlight and, like a prism, it caught the light and twinkled a rainbow back at her. The sapphires were among the finest she'd ever seen, and certainly Indian.

"My lord, I cannot. They are far too valuable," she sighed regretfully.

"Geoffrey, sweetheart, and I beg you not to be silly. What harm is there in two friends exchanging gifts on New Year's Day?"

"But I have nothing for you," she protested again.

"Nothing? Have you not given me the hope that someday we might share love between us? And your sweet kisses are far more precious to me than jewels. Come, love, let me fasten the sapphires into your little ears." His hands brushed her curls back, making her shiver, and he carefully set the earrings in their places. "Perfection," he said.

Skye faced the pier glass, turning this way and that to admire the sparkling, richly blue stones. "Damn you," she said softly, "they're beautiful—and I love them!"

He chuckled. "I'm happy to see you exhibit even the tiniest bit of greed, sweet Skye. Now, love, I've something else for you before I go. An invitation to my Twelfth Night masque. Will you come? Perhaps Captain Small will escort you? The Queen will be there. I have not yet broached the subject of a royal charter for your trading company, but I shall do so before the ball, and I will endeavor to present you to Her Majesty that evening."

"Oh, Geoffrey, how lovely! Of course I shall come, and Robbie shall be my escort, though I doubt I can get him into anything overly elegant. Robbie takes no pleasure in lavish dressing."

He nodded, satisfied. "I must get back to Whitehall now, sweetheart." He rose and she moved toward him. He towered over her, making Skye feel very small as she gazed up at him. His long fingers trailed smoothly over her upturned face. "I'm a patient man as long as the prize is worth the wait, my pet."

"I could disappoint you, Geoffrey," she frowned up at him, her face intent.

"I think not, Skye. I think not." He brushed her lips lightly with his. "What would you like for Twelfth Night?"

"My lord! You must not spoil me!"

"Sweetheart, I've not even begun to, but I shall. Until Twelfth Night." She hadn't time to reply before he nodded and, turning, left the room without another word.

Geoffrey Southwood strode down to the river bank and hailed a waterman to take him the short distance back to the palace. "Whitehall," he said, climbing into the little boat and seating himself.

"Aye, me lord," the waterman said as he pushed off into the stream. "I'm going to enjoy de Grenville's barge very much," the Earl said softly to himself. Then he grew somber. It was no longer a game. To his surprise, his heart had become deeply involved. He had not been entirely truthful in letting Skye believe that the Queen had kept him at Hampton Court. There had been several occasions over the past few weeks when he might have returned home. But he had chosen not to because he had wanted time to think.

She had been so very vulnerable that November night, and he could have taken her easily. She was young. She had known a great love. Widowed two years, she was now obviously ready for a man. His bet with de Grenville might have been won then and there. But she had trembled faintly in his arms, and somehow he couldn't dishonor her. Geoffrey was amazed at himself, for he had never been soft, or overly concerned with the feelings of others.

When he had returned to his house that night he had found a plump little maid bringing wood to his bedchamber. His green eyes narrowed speculatively for desire rode him fiercely. He slid an arm about her little waist, and she giggled.

"What's your name, lass?"

"Poll, m'lud."

"How old are you?"

"Thirteen, St. Thomas's Day past, m'lud."

"Are you willing?"

"Aye, sir."

"Are you a virgin?"

"Nay, sir," she said as she shed her blouse, revealing breasts generous for one so young. Her skirts and petticoats rapidly followed, and she was naked.

There were no preliminaries. He loosened his codpiece and, pulling her to the bed, pushed her down and fell on her. He pumped into her methodically until she cried her pleasure. The ache in his manhood was finally soothed. Rolling off her, he lay quietly for a moment and then rose from the bed. Drawing a gold piece from his purse, he gave it to her. "Run along now, Poll." The girl gathered up her garments and, giving him a saucy smile, ran from the bedroom.

He sighed now with the memory. He had been physically appeased, but by no means satisfied. It was Skye he had wanted. There was an innocence about her, though she had been married, widowed, and was a mother. That innocence made him want to love Skye, not betray her.

There was no doubt about it, the Earl of Lynmouth was feeling the pangs of real love for the first time in his life.

Robert Small was not thrilled by the invitation to the masque. "Dammit, Skye, I'm no gallant to be escorting you."

"Now, Robbie, stop grumbling. Geoffrey suggested it himself, though I warned him you'd fuss. The Queen will be there, and he has promised to present us."

His weathered face softened a little. "Well, I'd like to meet Young Bess, I would. What must I wear?"

"Nothing overly ornate. I promise. I have decided to go as 'Night.' Your costume will match mine. I'll have them done, so you need go only for one or two fittings with the tailor."

"Very well, poppet. I can't let you go alone else those elegant Court popinjays overwhelm you."

She kept her word, and on the night of the masque Robert Small found himself dressed quite simply though very elegantly indeed in a black velvet doublet sewn with tiny silver brilliants, and edged in silver lace at the neck and sleeves. The short round black breeches were lined in stiff horsehair to puff them out. He wore black silk stockings and thick-soled black leather shoes with silver rosettes. His short cape was also of black velvet, lined in cloth of silver and trimmed in sable.

Skye presented him with a beautiful golden sword, its handle sprinkled with small sapphires, rubies, and diamonds. To her vast amusement he swaggered before the receiving-room pier glass, a little smile playing across his lips.

"Do you think you might crow?" she teased.

He reddened. "Ah, give over, Skye. But damned if I don't look as good as any dandy."

"You do. I only wish Dame Cecily could see you."

"Thank God she can't! I'd never hear the end of it. She's always trying to rig me out for some party or other, but I've avoided her so far. Now don't you tell on me."

Skye laughed. "All right, Robbie I'll keep this a secret."

He sighed, turned from the mirror, then eyed her critically. "Isn't your neckline a bit low?"

"No, Robbie, it isn't," she said softly, "it's the height of fashion. Now let me have the mirror, if you can tear yourself away." He sniffed in mock offense and she stuck her tongue out at him.

"I'll see the coach is ready, Mistress Peacock," he said, striding grandly from the room.

Skye stood quietly gazing at her image. Her black velvet dress was magnificent, and she knew she should eclipse every woman at the masque. The low, square neckline was unrelieved by any lace at all, but offered a very daring show of white breasts instead. The sleeves, full to just below the elbow, were slashed to show silver lace inserts. The silver lace was repeated at her wrists. The black velvet bell-shaped skirt parted to reveal a black brocade underskirt which had moons, stars, planets, and comets embroidered on it in silver, pearls, and diamonds. Her black silk stockings with their silver lace rosette garters were sewn with tiny diamond brilliants, as were her narrow, pointed, high-heeled black silk shoes.

Her hair, parted in the center, was arranged in a soft chignon at the nape of her neck. This new French fashion would also set her apart from the other women at the masque. They would still be wearing their hair puffed out at each side. Her pearl-and-diamond hair ornaments were shaped like stars and tiny crescent moons.

Her necklace was a magnificently opulent display of blue-white diamonds. There was a matching bracelet. And in her ears were pear-shaped diamonds that fell from baroque pearls. On the fingers of her left hand she wore rings set with a great flashing round diamond, a heart-shaped ruby, and a sapphire. On her right hand was a large, irregularly shaped baroque pearl, and a square-cut emerald.

Her eyes were highlighted with just a touch of blue kohl, but her cheeks were pink with excitement and needed no artifice. Her perfume had been made this past summer from the damask roses at Wren Court, and sent up to London by Dame Cecily at Christmas.

Her mirror told her she was perfection, and for the first time in months Skye felt completely confident despite the fact that tonight, when she arrived at the Earl's house, she would be entering a new and alien world.

"Ready, lass?"

She whirled around and, picking up her silver mask, said brightly, "I'm ready, Robbie." He carefully draped a sable-lined and -trimmed long cape about her shoulders, and descending the stairs together they walked swiftly from the house to the coach. "How silly," remarked Skye, "when I live so nearby to have to take my coach."

"You could hardly walk. That wouldn't make a grand entrance at all, now would it? The beautiful, mysterious, Señora Goya del Fuentes should make a good first impression. I can guarantee that within the next half-hour every noble popinjay at Court will be falling over himself to meet you."

"Oh, Robbie," she laughed, "you sound like a suspicious father."

The coach quickly reached the gates of Lynmouth House and drove up the drive to the brightly lit palace. Arriving at the front door Skye became aware, for the first time, of the grandeur of the building. The dark-red brick palace stood four stories high, towering over the river and its own beautiful, carefully designed gardens. Built early in the reign of Henry VIII, it had all the sprawling, boisterous magnificence of the monarch himself. It was considered a perfect example of Tudor architecture. Footmen in the azure and gold colors of the Southwood family ran to open the carriage door and help the occupants out. Skye took Robbie's arm and entered the big marble foyer where a footman hurried forward to take Skye's cloak. Several women guests were standing nearby and as her gown was revealed, they gasped. The corners of her mouth twitched, but she feigned indifference. Slipping her hand through Robbie's arm again, they began to ascend the wide staircase.

"Well done, lass," he murmured softly, and she winked mischievously at him. They gained the landing and stood in the wide arch to the ballroom, waiting until the majordomo asked, "Names, please?"

"Sir Robert Small, and Señora Goya del Fuentes."

Skye's dark feathery eyebrows shot up. *Sir* Robert, indeed. Once again, Robbie had managed to surprise her.

"Sir Robert Small, and Señora Goya del Fuentes," called out the majordomo, and suddenly the room became quiet and they faced a sea of upturned faces. Slowly, the two black-clad figures descended the three wide steps. Geoffrey Southwood, resplendent in white and gold, came forward to take Skye's hands and kiss them. She felt a delicious tingle race through her.

"Damme, madam, you outshine every woman here! Good evening, Sir Robert, I see you decided to use your title tonight."

"I would do honor to your revels, m'lord. I thank you for including me."

"May I steal Skye from you, sir?"

"But of course, m'lord. I see de Grenville across the room, and I've been wanting to talk to him." Robbie bowed and walked away from them, his carriage erect and proud.

"The dancing won't begin until the Queen arrives," he said. "Walk with me now, and I'll show you some of my house."

"But your guests—"

"—are far too busy eating, drinking, and gossiping to notice my absence. Besides, if another man stares at you, I'm apt to find myself involved in a duel. Come, madam. I want you to myself." And allowing her no further protest, he led her from the ballroom and through a small door. "The picture gallery," he announced, "complete with a full complement of Southwood portraits."

"I would have expected them to hang at your seat in Devon," she remarked.

"They do when I'm there. These family paintings have traveled between London and Devon as often as I have. An eccentricity of mine." For a moment they walked in silence, and then they stopped. He said simply, "Skye." And there was such longing in his voice that she thrilled.

Looking shyly up at him, she wondered at the intense passion in his lime-green eyes. Her palms flattened against his broad chest as though she would hold him off. "Say nothing, my darling," he commanded her, and brushed her lips with his.

"Geoffrey!" she whispered frantically.

His mouth moved gently over her face, down the side of her neck, across the tops of her breasts. He buried his face in the deep scented valley and felt her heart jumping erratically beneath his mouth. "Let me love you, Skye. Dear God, how I ache for wanting you, sweetheart." They stood together like that, the black figure and the gold-and-white one, not moving.

There was a discreet scratching at the door, and Southwood instantly stepped back. "Enter!"

The door swung open, "My lord, the Queen's barge has been sighted but a few minutes from here," announced the footman.

"Very good." The footman discreetly withdrew. "I must go to welcome Her Majesty. I'll take you back to Robbie, my darling, and we'll talk again later."

With Robbie on one side of her and Richard de Grenville on the other, Skye joined the other guests in the garden near the dock, awaiting the arrival of the Queen.

"Damme, if you're not a succulent sight," said de Grenville.

"Thank you, m'lord."

"Getting mighty close with old Geoff, aren't you?" remarked de Grenville. "From the way he behaved at the Rose and Anchor I'd have thought you'd have not spoken to him again."

"Geoffrey apologized very prettily for his behavior, m'lord de Grenville."

"You know, of course, that he's married," de Grenville pressed.

"My lord, what exactly is it you seek to tell me?" Skye asked firmly.

De Grenville was discomfited. It would hardly be gentlemanly or sporting to tell her of the wager he and Southwood had entered into. "I simply do not wish you to be hurt, my dear, and Geoff is known to be a bit of a rake," he said innocently.

"You're most kind, m'lord," she said coolly.

Trying to regain the lost ground, he changed the subject. "Ah, Young Bess herself! Look, my dear Skye, the Queen comes."

They stood looking out over the garden, across the colorful sea of guests. The Queen's barge had docked and now the Earl of Lynmouth was handing his royal guest out. For a brief moment Elizabeth stood viewing her subjects. Then a small cheer rippled across the garden. The young Queen was just twenty-seven, and even from a distance Skye could see that she was lovely. Tall for a woman and with an angular slenderness, she, like Skye, had chosen to wear her hair differently than current fashion dictated. Parted in the center, it fell in long, red-gold waves down her back. It was dressed with many strings of pearls. The Queen had chosen to represent "Springtime" and was gowned in apple-green brocade, heavily encrusted with gold embroidery and diamonds. Her beautiful long aristocratic fingers sparkled with rings. Her almond-shaped eyes glittered like the finest jet and her smile was merry.

Lord Southwood led his honored guest through the garden, through the lines of bowing and curtseying courtiers, and into the ballroom. The ballroom, like the gallery across the hall, extended the length of the house. The Queen seated herself on a small throne set upon a raised dais, and one by one the guests approached her to present themselves. Southwood stood near her throne.

Escorted by both Robbie and de Grenville, Skye was brought before the Queen.

"De Grenville, you rogue! 'Tis good to see you," smiled Elizabeth. "I was not aware you were up from Devon."

"Just today, Majesty," said de Grenville, kissing her hand. "Would I miss Southwood's fête? And a chance to gaze upon England's fairest?"

Elizabeth dimpled prettily. "And who would you present to me, Dickon?"

"First, Majesty, an old friend and Devon neighbor, Sir Robert Small, captain of the *Mermaid*."

Robert Small knelt reverently and kissed the Queen's hand. "Madam," he began, but his eyes filled with tears and he could not go on.

"Why, sir, what honor you do me," said Elizabeth kindly.

"All England thanks God for Your Majesty," said Robert Small, somewhat recovered.

"All England should thank God for stout seamen like yourself, Sir Robert," replied the Queen. "You are our future." Elizabeth's gray-black eyes then flitted over Skye.

"Mistress Goya del Fuentes, Majesty," said Geoffrey, from the Queen's left.

Skye's curtsey was graceful.

"The lady from Algiers?"

"Yes, Majesty," answered Skye, her eyes modestly lowered.

"I understand your late husband was a merchant prince there."

"Yes, Majesty." Skye looked up, gazing directly at the Queen.

"You and Sir Robert are business partners? A bit unusual for a woman, is it not?"

"As unusual as it is for a woman to be Queen in her own right, Majesty. But I have never believed that being a woman meant one lacked intelligence. Certainly Your Majesty has disproven that notion." The deep-blue eyes held the grayish black ones.

Elizabeth Tudor's eyes narrowed a moment as she studied Skye. Then she laughed. "You desire a charter of me," she said. "We will talk on it soon." Turning to Southwood, she said girlishly, "My feet itch, m'lord. Let us begin dancing."

Dismissed, Skye swept the Queen another curtsey, and moved away swiftly on the arms of her two gallants, her black skirts billowing.

"By God," said de Grenville admiringly, "the Queen likes you. She likes damn few women, Skye. What's this about a charter?"

"Robbie and I have formed our own trading company, m'lord, and Lord Southwood is aiding us in obtaining a royal charter."

Damn the man! thought de Grenville. So that's how he got to her. I must think hard on this or I may yet lose my barge. He was about to ask her to dance when Lord Southwood, having opened the ball with the Queen, approached them and claimed her. Eyes sparkling, Skye gave him her hand, and they moved off into the figure leaving Robert and de Grenville by the door.

"He seems quite taken with her, Robbie," de Grenville murmured pensively.

"Aye," replied the captain, "and I'm afraid she with him."

"Lord and Lady Burke," intoned the majordomo.

"Who are they, Dickon?" asked Robbie.

"Southwood's neighbors on the other side. He's some Irish chieftain's heir. I suppose Geoffrey felt bound to ask them."

The Earl slid an arm tightly about her as they danced the intricate figure. "If one more of those fops leers at you," he muttered between gritted teeth, "I shall resort to my sword."

Her laughter bubbled up soft, warm, and rich. "La, Geoffrey," she teased, "surely you're not jealous."

"Yes, I'm jealous, and we'll discuss it later, sweetheart, rest assured." Skye laughed, delighted.

She was having the most wonderful time of her life. The handsome Earl was outrageously attentive, and there wasn't a man here who hadn't complimented her. She danced every dance, ate supper surrounded by half a dozen gentlemen besides de Grenville and Robbie, and drank just enough sweet wine to add to her gaiety. At midnight everyone unmasked to delighted shouts, though most had long ago identified their friends beneath the ornate masks.

Across the ballroom, Niall Burke stared in rigid shock at the beautiful woman in the magnificent diamonds and black velvet who stood directly across the room from him, laughing up at the Earl of Lynmouth. It couldn't be! It simply could not be! Skye was dead! They had all explained that she was dead, told him and told him until he'd had no choice but to accept it.

"By God," he heard the man next to him saying. "Southwood was always a lucky devil. If Señora Goya del Fuentes isn't already his mistress then she soon will be, judging by the looks passing between them."

"She's lived in the East," another man chimed in, "and I imagine she knows some of the things those harem girls know. God, I wonder . . ."

"Don't be a young fool, Hugh! Southwood has marked her for himself as plainly as if he'd put a brand on her forehead. If he catches you sniffing around her he'll skewer you without a second thought."

The two men moved away, leaving Niall Burke to his whirling thoughts. How could two women look so alike? Somehow he must meet this Señora Goya del Fuentes, but who did he know who could introduce them?

"Will you dance with me, Niall?"

"What? Constanzita, love—what is it?"

Constanza laughed, shaking her dark gold curls. "How can anyone daydream in the midst of all this revelry?" she asked.

"I'm sorry, my dear. I was admiring the lady across the room in the black velvet costume. She looks quite familiar."

"Señora Goya del Fuentes? Perhaps you do know her. Though her husband was a Spaniard, she is Irish."

He thought he might be sick, but he gripped his emotions. "How do you know that, Constanza?"

"She owns Greenwood, the house on the other side of this one, the last one in the row. Our bargeman and hers are brothers. The maids and the bargemen gossip, and I hear things from my tiring woman. They say the Earl is mad for her."

"A lady does not listen to servants' gossip," he cut her off curtly. "I wish to go home now."

She was hurt, and protested, "But it's just after midnight. Even the Queen is still here. It would be rude to leave before the Queen herself leaves."

"I am not well, Constanza," he said sharply, "and I wish to leave."

Instantly contrite, she reached up to feel his forehead. "You do feel warm, my love. We will make our apologies to Lord Southwood, but say that I am ill. He will understand that better."

They moved across the room and approached the Earl of Lynmouth, who was gazing down at Skye, his white velvet-clad arm around her midnight velvet shoulders. They made an extraordinarily handsome couple. Southwood smiled as they approached.

"My lord Burke, I hope you and your lovely lady are enjoying yourselves." Geoffrey smiled graciously. "Allow me to present our new neighbor, Señora Goya del Fuentes. Skye, sweetheart, Lord and Lady Burke own the house on the other side of me."

"Also built by your grandfather for a *belle amie?*" she teased him.

The Earl laughed. He was so intent on Skye that he did not notice Niall Burke's stunned look. *Her voice!* It was her voice! Her name and her voice.

"Lord and Lady Burke. I am delighted to meet you," she looked straight at Niall without a flicker of recognition. Her voice reflected only politeness. Niall Burke thought he was surely going mad. Mastering his fear and anguish, he said, "You'll forgive us, my lord, if we leave early. Constanza complains of one of her violent headaches."

"I am sorry," replied the Earl, immediately sympathetic.

"Have you tried infusing witchhazel bark in warm water, then soaking a soft linen cloth in it and putting it on your forehead, Lady Burke?"

"Why thank you, Señora Goya del Fuentes, I have not heard of that but I shall try it," murmured Constanza. Feeling Niall's grip on her arm becoming insistent, she curtseyed and turned away.

"What a strange man," said Skye, watching the Burkes' retreating backs. "He stared so intently at me."

Geoffrey laughed. "I wonder why. Could it be because you're the most beautiful woman here?" He lowered his voice. "Sweetheart, you know what I want to say to you."

"Yes," she replied softly, her cheeks growing hot.

"If I come to you tonight, my darling . . ."

"I know I'm behaving like a damned coy maid," she answered him, "but no man had ever loved me but my dearest lord. I don't know if I could let you, Geoffrey. I want you, but I'm afraid. Can you understand?"

"When the Queen leaves," he said quietly, "go home and wait for me. We will talk, Skye. I love you, and what is between us must be resolved. You feel that, too, don't you?"

She nodded at him, her eyes huge and deepest blue. He smiled reassuringly at her, and the icy fear she had felt deep inside her dissolved in a quick, warm glow. He loved her! He had said so plainly!

Her soaring thoughts were interrupted as de Grenville arrived. "The Queen would speak with you, Mistress Skye. Allow me to escort you," he offered.

"We shall both escort you, my love," said the Earl firmly.

As they reached Elizabeth, the Queen ordered her page to bring a stool for Skye. Then she waved the two gallants away without a word, her beautiful hands gesturing imperiously. "You're popular with the gentlemen, mistress," Elizabeth commented as the two men moved away.

Skye laughed. "My lord de Grenville is an old friend of my business partner, Sir Robert Small. Like Robbie, he feels he must protect me."

"And that rogue, Southwood?"

"The Earl does not feel . . . protective toward me," Skye twinkled and Elizabeth laughed, the deep gray eyes bright.

"An understatement, mistress!" she chuckled. "A woman of wit, I see. I like that! Tell me of yourself now. How did you come to be Sir Robert Small's partner?"

"Of myself there is little to tell, Majesty. I am Irish, or so I have been told. I was left in a convent in Algiers at a very young age and I know nothing about my background. Several years ago I was wed to a wealthy Spanish merchant of that city. Robbie was his partner. When my lord died two years ago I was forced to flee Algiers because a Turkish governor had plans to force me into his harem. Robbie rescued me and my husband's French secretary, Jean Marlaix, and his wife Marie. She and I were both with child when we fled. My daughter was born here in England, for which I thank God."

"So you arrived here a poor widow, and Sir Robert Small took you in?"

"Poor? Oh, no, madam! I had, by Moslem law, one month to mourn my husband. During that time I secretly arranged for the sale of all my husband's goods and properties and I had the monies transferred to England. Oh, no, madam! My daughter and I are hardly penniless."

"'Pon my soul, mistress, you are a cool one. I like that. Indeed I do. So you have gone into business with Sir Robert Small, have you? Good! I like an intelligent woman, one who uses her brain as well as her body. Are you at all educated? You must be."

"Yes, Majesty. I speak and read English, French, Italian, Spanish, and Latin. I can write and am competent with figures."

"Very well, mistress. I am impressed with what I see and hear. Cecil will arrange an appointment with you and Sir Robert. We will all talk. I think perhaps a royal charter will be forthcoming."

Skye rose and curtseyed deeply. "Majesty, I am most grateful."

Elizabeth stood. Instantly the Earl of Lynmouth appeared by her side.

"Southwood, I am weary. It has been a busy holiday season. Escort me to my barge."

The Queen and her escort moved between the bowing and curtseying guests, a path to the door opening before them. Robert and de Grenville took possession of Skye once more.

"Will you stay, Skye lass?"

"No, Robbie, I am tired. I have already bid Geoffrey good night. Please escort me to my coach. But you remain if you like."

"I'll go. I'm longing for a good pint and a warm wench. The atmosphere here is too rarefied to suit me. De Grenville, will you join me?"

"Aye," came the smiling reply.

"Take my coach," offered Skye.

"Ah, lass, bless your generosity."

They left her safe inside her house, and drove off. Skye handed her cloak to Walters, her majordomo. "Lock up," she said, "Captain Small will not be back tonight."

"Very well, madam."

Skye hurried up the stairs to her apartment, where Daisy awaited her.

"Oh, mum, did you see her? Did you see Young Bess? We watched her barge from the top of the house!"

"Yes, Daisy, I met the Queen. We spoke twice this evening, and I shall see her again."

Daisy's eyes were round with excitement. "Is she pretty, close up?"

"Yes, Daisy, she is very pretty, with lovely fair skin and red-gold hair and bright gray eyes."

"Oh, mum, when I tell me mother back in Devon that I saw the Queen's barge, and that my mistress even spoke to her! She'll be so proud!"

Skye smiled. "Tomorrow I shall tell you what the Queen wore tonight, but for now help me get ready for bed."

Obediently Daisy went to work, unlacing her mistress's gown, helping her disrobe. The beautiful velvet gown was brushed carefully and hung back in the wardrobe. Silken undergarments were gathered up to be given to the laundress. Skye slipped into a pale-pink silk gown with a deep V neckline secured by tiny pearl buttons. The long full sleeves floated, the skirt clung.

Daisy brought a silver basin of warmed rose water, and Skye washed her face and hands and cleaned her teeth. "Shall I brush your hair, mum?"

"Nay, Daisy, I'll do it. It's late. Go to bed."

Daisy curtseyed. "Good night then, mum."

"Good night, Daisy."

The door closed behind the little maid, and Skye sat down at her dressing table. Slowly she removed the diamond and pearl ornaments and drew the gold and tortoiseshell pins from her hair. It tumbled down, a night-dark cloud. Picking up her brush, she vigorously brushed the tangles out, all the while wondering if Geoffrey would come . . . and if she really wanted him to. What would happen if he did come?

She laughed. What would happen, indeed! She would become his mistress, of course. She frowned. Was that what she wanted? To become some nobleman's mistress? Oh, damn! She was burning for a man's caress, the hardness of a man's body on hers. Might she not have a discreet affair and let it go at that? Surely he would understand her desire for privacy. If he did not, then she would stop the affair.

The sound of something scraping against her window startled her. She ran to the window and looked out, then quickly jumped back. Pebbles were being thrown at the window! She laughed and flung the casements wide. Below stood the Earl of Lynmouth, still in his white and gold costume, grinning impudently up at her. "I'm coming up," he whispered, loudly enough for her to hear. "Leave the windows open, Skye."

"But how," she began, and gasped as he reached out and grasped at a thick vine growing up the bricked side of the house. He swung himself up and began climbing. She watched, holding her breath, until he was safely on the sill.

"Good evening, sweetheart," he drawled lazily, vaulting lightly into the room. In one fluid motion he drew the casements shut behind him and pulled her into his arms. "Skye!" His voice was husky with emotion. His hands reached up to tangle themselves in her hair. Her deep blue eyes grew wide and her breath caught in her throat. She could not speak. "Sweet, sweet Skye," he whispered, and then his mouth took full and complete possession of hers. Geoffrey kissed her passionately, deeply, the kiss vibrating through her. Thrill after thrill rippled through her as his lips gently persuaded hers to open, allowing his silken tongue to rove unchecked, to meet and subdue hers. "Skye, sweet, sweet Skye," he murmured against the softness of her neck, her final defenses weakening. She shivered deliciously.

His fingers undid the little pearl buttons at the deep V of her gown. One arm held tightly about her slender waist. His other hand sought one firm and perfect breast, cupping it, fondling it, his eager mouth seeking the tightly closed flower of her nipple. The warm mouth closed over its quivering prisoner, his tongue expertly encircling it again and again until she thought she could stand no more and whimpered a small protest. In response he lifted his swooning treasure up and carried her to the bed. There he resumed delightful loveplay concentrating this time on her other breast.

Her body was now helpless to the passion he was igniting in her, yet her mind rebelled at the thought of seduction. Desperate, she tried to stop him, finally finding her voice.

"Geoffrey, no! Oh, please no!" For a moment he didn't hear her and she cried out softly again, this time twining her slender fingers in his hair and pulling. "Geoffrey! Oh, Geoffrey, please no!"

Slowly, reluctantly, he raised his head from the warm bounty of her breasts. His lime-green eyes were glazed and heavy with passion. "Tell me, Skye," he said quietly, "tell me."

She gazed at him helplessly, all the logical reasons for stopping now whirling out of her reach. Their eyes locked, and he said quietly, "You're shy of this for you've always been a virtuous woman. I know that. I cannot wish away my wife. If I could I would do so. I love you, and I sense beneath the respectable widow a naughty little sensualist who hungers for me as much as I hunger for her." She flushed. "What is so wrong in our pleasuring each other?" She sighed, still trying to find words. He was so damnably persuasive. Then Geoffrey Southwood reached out and, taking her hand, drew it to his codpiece. Beneath her fingers she felt the hard throb of him.

"Oh, Geoffrey!"

"I won't beg, Skye." He had the weapon to force her, but somehow he couldn't bring himself to use it. He wanted to win her fairly for the victory would be so much sweeter. I do love her! he thought exultantly. Oh, my love, let me have the precious gift of you! And as if she had heard his silent plea, she sobbed, "Oh, Geoffrey, yes! Yes! Yes! Yes!"

He pulled her from the bed and gently drew her gown away. To his surprised delight, she reached out and, with trembling fingers, undid his ruffled shirt. Together they drew his breeches and hose off, and then fell back upon the bed. He wanted to take her then and there, but getting a mighty hold on himself, he held back. She was not to be used quickly. Her surrender would be so much better for the waiting.

She lay shyly, half afraid and confused, almost as though she were a maid once more. The Earl moved downward upon the bed and grasping her right foot began kissing it—the top, each toe, the arch, and the heel. His lips moved oh so slowly to her ankle, and up her leg to the shapely calf, her dimpled knee, her long silken thigh. Moving downward again, he performed his tender ministrations on her left foot and leg.

Returning to her lips, he nibbled at them briefly, leaving her gasping before finding again the sensual warmth of her breasts. Once more he sucked eagerly on the ripe fruit, tempting them to tiny aching peaks, making them tingle with anticipation. Her beautiful body was an unexplored land and he didn't want to miss a single inch of it.

How firm her waist was. He nuzzled the curves of it, feeling the warm smoothness against his cheek. His hands held her firmly about the hips as his lips slipped across the silken flesh of her belly. His tongue probed teasingly into her little navel, then slid lower, seeking the very core of her. Gently he parted the lips of her vulva. It was already half open, the coral-red flower of womanhood wet and pouting with desire. Bending his head he kissed it, tasting the sweet-salt taste of her. She gasped her shock, her fingers twined tightly in his dark-blond hair, and her body arced to meet his mouth.

Smiling his pleasure, he lifted his head up and said quietly, "Not yet, sweetheart. It's much too soon yet."

"Please," she pleaded. Her excitement was so great that she thought she would die if it weren't satisfied.

"Not yet, Skye," he repeated. "I will teach you to enjoy the anticipation, to prolong the pleasures." He turned her over gently and she felt him licking her back, her shoulders, her buttocks, her legs. Slowly, rhythmically, his knowing tongue stroked her smooth skin, increasing her fever. Her arms lay above her head and she clawed at the sheets, digging fiercely into the mattress. Then, suddenly, he laid his naked body on top of her and rubbed his great organ between the cheeks of her bottom.

Now she fought him, catching him unawares, and throwing him off her, rolling onto her back, hissing angrily, "Bastard! You're no angel but a devil! No more!"

Laughing, he pinned her down and kissed her until she couldn't breathe. Then he raised her legs and, drawing them over his shoulders, buried his face between them. His tongue found her honey, and he used her furiously until she came, his mouth forcing her climax.

"Damn you! Damn you!" she cried, weeping in frustration for she still was not satisfied.

"Look at me, my hot little bitch!"

She squeezed her eyes tightly closed. "No!"

"Look at me, Skye!"

At the cruel sharp note in his voice she opened her sapphire eyes and looked into his green ones. "I've fallen in love with you, bitch, and I'll not take you like a whore." He rubbed his big blue-veined organ against her belly. "This is what you want, isn't it?"

"Yes!"

"You'll have it in good time, Skye. In fact . . . I'll give it to you now." He spread her wide. "All of it, sweetheart!" He drove deeply, enjoying her gasp, the incredulous look on her face.

He was huge and he filled her to overflowing, pushing upward to touch at her very womb as he moved his great shaft skillfully, drawing it nearly all the way out, then thrusting home again. For a moment Skye thought she would be torn asunder, but her body stretched to receive him, almost devouring him in her desperate hunger. She clawed at his back and he caught her arms and pinioned them above her head. She bit into his shoulder, drawing blood, then licked furiously at the wound. He slapped her very lightly, cursing softly at her sharp little teeth.

The pleasure and the pain mingled about and within her. She had known great love, but never had she known such passion. It consumed her, leaving room for nothing else. Onward he drove her, and she reached peak after peak, believing each time that it was not possible to go any further, yet cresting higher and higher. Behind her closed eyelids the world exploded into a rainbow of shattered glass. She felt the contractions of an orgasm so great that she believed death was about to overtake her. Over and over and over again her body shuddered with the force of her passion.

He had joined her in ecstasy, climax for climax, then slowly he regained his senses and managed to roll off her body. For a moment he could but stare at her. She was white and barely breathing. Sitting up, he tenderly gathered her into his arms. She was cold and he strove to warm her. No woman had ever driven him as far as she had done. No woman had ever satisfied him as much as she, and no woman had ever given of herself as fully as she.

Yes, he loved her. And de Grenville could keep his damned barge. He had no intention of jeopardizing his love over an insane bet. Why had he made the damned bet? If Dickon dared breathe a word of their foolishness, he'd call him out.

She stirred in his arms, and slowly her beautiful blue eyes fluttered open again. She searched his face fearfully for a sign of reassurance. He gently smoothed her tangled dark hair from her forehead and said simply, "Don't ever leave me, Skye."

"I won't, Geoffrey."

For Geoffrey Southwood this was the first love he had felt since his pretty, young mother had died in another futile attempt at childbearing, when Geoffrey was still quite young. His father's only son, Geoffrey had been born just ten months after his parents' wedding day. His mother next produced a daughter, Geoffrey's only full sister, Catherine, who was married now and living in Cornwall. His stepmother had birthed his two half-sisters, one of whom was now wed to a Worcestershire baron, the other to a wealthy Devon squire. She had died, along with a stillborn son. His father had not married again.

His father had been proud of Geoffrey, but had forbidden what he considered soft treatment for his son. At seven, Geoffrey had left his own home to grow up in the household of the Earl of Shrewsbury, as his own son was now doing. He lived with half a dozen other young nobles, learning manners, morals, politics, and the business of being a great lord, but there was no room for love in that life. It was three years before he saw his home again and then he was allowed but a single month's visit. Only his youngest half-sister, Elizabeth, was still at home, the two older girls already having been settled in other noble households to learn the business of becoming successful wives and mothers. Though Beth had admired the elegant and polished ten-year-old boy, young Geoffrey was far too puffed up by his own importance to pay the little girl much attention.

The following year when he returned for his month, Beth was gone. The next year he was twelve, and married the little heiress whose life had meant so little to Geoffrey and whose untimely death left him wealthy in his own right. Both his mother and stepmother had died. He scarcely knew his sisters, his father had flatly discouraged affection, and his mousy, unimaginative wife was not to his taste and never had been. This mysterious and beautiful woman who lay by his side had given him more than any other person. It was perhaps not so surprising, then, that he was falling in love with her with an innocence extraordinary in a worldly man.

He wrapped an arm about her and she nestled close, her thoughts beginning to reassemble. Her beloved Khalid had given her much joy, but she admitted to herself that she had never known such passion as this. It was frightening, yet it was magnificent. Their bodies seemed to have been created expressly for one another.

That Geoffrey had wanted more than a one-night affair with her had been obvious from the first. He said he loved her, and she was beginning to believe it. Too, Skye was not foolish. She knew she was a stranger in a country foreign to all she had known in Algiers. And when Robbie left, as he soon would, she would be without a man's protection. Her business had to be run here, not from Devon. If she intended staying in London then she must have a protector.

She should marry again, but after Khalid el Bey, who would suit her? She was too exotic and, she believed, too well-born, to wed with a mere London merchant. On the other hand, she was not sufficiently high born for a lord. Since Geoffrey was married, there seemed only one course open to her. Though she shrank from it, she knew she must take it. To cap the argument, there was also Willow to think of.

It would not be so awful. Geoffrey was handsome, and in love with her. He would treat her well, and since she need not rely on him for financial support she would retain a great measure of independence. This would set her above other men's mistresses. And as his acknowledged mistress she would be safe from other men, for no man in his right mind would dare approach the Earl of Lynmouth's woman!

Geoffrey's breathing had become quite regular. How handsome he was in sleep, very much the Angel Earl of his nickname once sleep took the cynical and faintly arrogant look from his face. There was an almost vulnerable look, though he was indeed a strong personality. She let her eyes wander from his face to his wide shoulders and broad chest, down to his narrow waist and slim hips. His legs were long, shapely, and covered with a fine pale golden down. His feet were slender, high-arched, the nails neatly pared. Her eyes wandered upward again to his sex, limp now and settled cozily in its nest of soft blond hair. It looked so sweet and harmless now, yet a short while ago it had been a great, blue-veined beast driving her to pleasures she hadn't known existed. She wanted to reach out and touch him.

"I trust it all meets with your approval, sweetheart."

She started and color flooded her face. She gasped.

He chuckled, then opened his lime-colored eyes and, reaching up, pulled her down into his arms. "So, witch, you were taking inventory of me. I ask, does it meet with your approval?" Kissing her ear, he ran his tongue around it, then thrust in and tickled her.

She squirmed, shivering deliciously. "Stop it, Geoffrey! Yes! Yes! Your assets certainly do meet with my approval."

He cupped a breast in his hand, rubbing the nipple. "The Queen will be resting for the next few days, so I am free. I want to take you away somewhere and spend all my time making love to you."

"Yes!" she replied, slightly surprised at herself.

He chuckled again. "How flattering you are, and how honest. I approve, sweetheart. I know of an inn about half a day's ride up the river. It's small and elegant, and the food is excellent. I am well known to the landlord."

"Do you take all your mistresses there?" she said more sharply than she would havé wished.

"I have never taken any woman there," he said softly, understanding her. "It is my own special place when I wish to escape the trials of being who I am. I thought we would go there and see if, after spending several days with me, you would like to become my mistress. That way, if you decide against it, our liaison will remain our secret. Though it would please me to shout our love to the world, I would not embarrass you publicly."

"Geoffrey. I am so sorry I spoke in haste. And I thank you for being so considerate."

"Sweetheart. I have had several mistresses in my day, but you've been a wife. It's hard for you, I know, to reconcile yourself to this position." He took her face in one hand and kissed her tenderly. "God, you've got the sweetest mouth!"

She felt herself growing languid again and she leaned back. Sighing happily, her deep blue eyes warm, she said, "Damn you, Geoffrey. What is it you do to me that one kiss renders me weak—and wanton besides."

"What do you do to me, Skye, that renders me insatiable?"

Quickly they were in each other's arms again, their mouths and tongues and hands devouring each other. Bodies entwined, they kissed until their mouths were bruised and both were breathless. Already aroused, his manhood beat against her thigh. Reaching down, she caressed him with teasing fingers, reaching out to cup the soft pouch beneath his shaft, running a sure finger firmly beneath it, hearing his gasp of surprised pleasure.

There was no excruciating waiting this time. She parted her thighs easily and he slid into her warmth. Confident now, she tightened her vaginal muscles about him as Yasmin had taught her. "Jesus!" he cried out softly as the wave of pleasure overpowered him. He drew back to thrust deeper yet, and again she tightened around him. "Stop, witch!" he begged. "It's the most delightful torture I've endured, but stop before I die. I want to pleasure you, too!"

Her arms were tight about him and as she loosened her grip on him he began to murmur softly to her, "Little witch, I knew that beneath the ladylike demeanor there was a passionate wanton. Open yourself to me, my darling. God, how warm and sweet you are! How your little honey oven burns for me—pleasures me—loves me!" He moved rhythmically with long, smooth strokes, each thrust seeming to go deeper than the one before. She could feel herself opening wide to receive him, taking him all, wanting even more. Oh, God, she wanted more! Sobbing, she felt her climax bearing down on her like a great wind, slamming into her with such force that she fainted, hearing as she slid away into the dark warmth his cry of pleasure.

Her first awareness was the kisses he was covering her face with. Dear God, she thought, that he can rouse me to such heights! She opened her eyes and smiled tremulously at him, her eyes brilliant with tears. He smiled back and ran a slim finger tenderly down her nose. "You've bewitched me, my blue-eyed love. Tomorrow afternoon we shall ride upriver to the Ducks and Drake. For several days we shall do nothing other than make love in a beautiful room that overlooks the river, and eat and drink sweet wine. I shall bind you to me so you'll never want to leave me, sweetheart. Never!" His mouth closed over hers again, kissing her deeply. Then he loosed her and rose from the bed. He drew on his clothing quickly and smiled down at her. "We had best keep our liaison a secret for now, sweetheart." His green eyes glittered. "Though you've probably not made up your mind about me yet, I've made up my mind about you. I mean to have you, sweetheart!" He bent again and placed a firm, light kiss on her forehead. "Sleep well, my darling. I've no doubt I've fair worn you out." He walked across the room, lifted a tapestry hanging on the wall, and pressed a panel. A door swung open.

Skye gasped. "Where," she demanded, "does that passage lead?"

"To my house," he replied, a hint of laughter in his voice. "Remember—my grandfather built this house for his mistress."

"Then there was no need to climb up to my window?"

"No, sweetheart, but I did think it was most romantic, didn't you?"

She began to laugh. "Geoffrey, I'm not so sure you're not a madman!"

He grinned. Then, blowing her a kiss, he disappeared through the passage and the door swung shut behind him.

"What manner of man have I involved myself with?" she said softly aloud. A damned interesting one, the voice in her head answered, and she laughed into the darkness.

Chapter 16

The following morning, Skye sent Daisy to find Robert Small. The little captain had rolled in, a good hour past dawn, much the worse for wear. When he finally made an appearance, rumpled and red-eyed, Skye winced. "Oh, Robbie, how many pints did you drink?"

He gave her a weak grin. "It wasn't the pints so much as the wenches. They were twins, and just sixteen. Ah, youth!"

"Did your friend de Grenville survive?"

"Barely. Thank God we had your carriage. I left him in the care of his majordomo. For a Devon sailor, though, he has a mighty weak stomach."

Skye bit back the laughter bubbling in her throat. It would have been unkind. "I'm going away for a few days," she said quietly. "Though this is a secret, I will be upriver at an inn called the Ducks and Drake. Should there be an emergency you'll know where to find me."

"You'll not be alone." It was a statement.

"No, I'll not be alone, Robbie."

Robbie sighed. "Skye, lass, I'll not have you hurt. Southwood is such a cold bastard."

"Not with me, Robbie. Besides, though this will sound terrible, I do not love him. I doubt I shall ever love anyone again. Khalid is too strong in my memory. But I do like Lord Southwood. And Robbie, you know that I must have a powerful protector. Come spring, you'll be off again, and be gone for months. I am a woman alone. I have no family but my daughter. My whole life began with Khalid. I have no past. With the Queen's charter, our business should flourish and with the Earl's protection I will be free to run it, and free from the bothersome advances of other men."

"But the price, Skye."

"Being Southwood's acknowledged mistress?" she laughed.

"What else is there for me? Marriage? With whom? And you know that I need wealth to give me the power and respectability that will secure Willow's future. I loved Khalid and I was proud of him, but what future would my daughter have if it were known here that her father was the great Whoremaster of Algiers? No, Robbie, the price is not greater than the rewards. The Earl of Lynmouth has never had an acknowledged mistress of my stature, and I don't expect him to replace me soon. When Willow is grown she will be an heiress with a powerful 'uncle.' I shall be able to make a good match for her."

Robbie shrugged. "You've thought it all out, I see, as usual. There's no arguing with a logical woman. Should I wish you happiness, then?"

"He loves me, Robbie. It's not just that he's said it. He means it. A woman knows when she's being lied to, Robbie, and I hope I'm not easy to fool."

"Ah, lass. I only want you happy."

"I know, Robbie. Don't fret. I'm not unhappy."

He patted her hand awkwardly, and she bent and kissed his ruddy cheek. "Oh, Robbie, what would I do without you? You're my best friend!"

In the early afternoon Robbie stood in the doorway and watched sadly as she rode off down the drive of Greenwood, keeping her red horse to a slow trot. Earlier he had gone down to the Thames and arranged for a waterman to take her little trunk upriver to the Ducks and Drakes. He sighed. He wished he were happier about the liaison.

Skye had been radiant when she departed. She wasn't worried and enjoyed herself very much. Dressed quite elegantly in a black velvet riding habit, ecru lace at the sleeves and a froth of lace bubbling up at the neckline as well, she cut a superb figure. Her cloak was made up of alternating bands of sable fur and black velvet with heavy carved gold frog closings. The attached hood was edged in the same dark sable, and made a perfect contrast to her creamy complexion. Her black boots were of the finest Spanish leather, her cream-colored scented gloves of French kid. Her big red gelding adored her with a singular devotion.

As Skye had explained to Robbie, she and the Earl would meet a mile or so from the Strand, on the river road. They were less likely to be seen together at that point. The afternoon was cold and clear, and Skye fought the urge to set her horse acantering. Since noon was the dinner hour, few people were out. She had ridden for some minutes when she heard the steady beat of hooves behind her and turned to see a tall man riding a large black stallion.

"Señora Goya del Fuentes, I bid you a good day."

"Sir?"

"Niall, Lord Burke. We met last night at the Earl of Lynmouth's gala."

Her gaze swept over the tall dark man with the silvery eyes. He was really quite attractive, she thought, but he looked disapproving of her, and Skye found herself growing annoyed.

"Oh, yes, of course. How is your wife's headache, my lord?"

"Gone, thank you." He moved his horse next to hers. "Do you generally ride unescorted, madam? A dangerous practice, I would say."

"I am meeting someone just a short ways away, my lord. I scarcely thought a groom necessary," she dismissed his question. How dared he criticize her! But Lord Burke was not easily dismissed.

"I understand you were raised in Algiers." The silvery eyes looked at her searchingly.

"Yes, my lord, I was."

"Your parents were Irish?"

"So I was told, my lord."

"Didn't you know them?" He was incredulous.

"I do not remember them, my lord. I was brought by a sea captain to the convent of St. Mary and placed in the care of the nuns there."

"Your name is unusual," he noted, after a moment.

"It was what I called myself when I arrived there, though the nuns added Mary to it, thinking Skye not quite Christian." Now why had she embroidered her tale? What did it matter if her name was Skye? Damn the man! Why didn't he go about his business? She was almost sure that Geoffrey was around the next bend in the road. She flashed Burke a sweet smile. "I must go now, sir. My friend will be waiting." And before he could protest she put spurs to her horse and was gone.

He could not make a display by following her, so he was forced to continue at a sedate trot. As he rounded the curve in the road, he saw her moving away accompanied by a man on a big chestnut stallion. It was likely Lord Southwood, thought Niall bitterly, remembering the gossip he had overheard last night.

Now Niall was more confused than ever. She looked and spoke like Skye O'Malley. Even her name was the same. It had to be his

Skye and yet . . . He shook his head. She gave no sign of recognizing him.

Then it struck him that perhaps she had survived after all, but had been despoiled by her captors, incarcerated in a harem, and was ashamed to face him. Maybe she was putting on an act for his benefit? Ah then, said his saner self, how pray tell did she escape captivity? And there was a child, too. And Captain Sir Robert Small, a most reputable man, not only supported her story, but appeared to be her protector.

Then another thought struck him. A sea captain had left her in Algiers. Had it been Dubhdara himself? Was it possible she was one of the old man's bastards? God knows he'd had enough of them. The old satyr had never denied his urges. But if Dubhdara had done that, the question was, *why?*

Sighing, Niall turned his horse back toward the Strand. He had been on his way home when he saw her riding out from her house, and he followed her in order to speak with her. He was being foolish. It was just a coincidence of names and looks. He had a wife who loved him and his Skye was dead. He had to believe that. Otherwise he might well go mad.

The Earl of Lynmouth and Skye rode happily together. Geoffrey Southwood was wildly in love for the only time in his life, and he was now to have three lovely days alone with his beloved.

"You're beautiful," he growled, and she laughed happily, throwing back her head so that her hood fell off, exposing her face and the pure white pillar of her neck. He wanted to stop, pull her from her horse, and cover that smooth creamy throat with his kisses. "How is it," he continued, "that you are as fair in sunlight as in moonlight? Do you know you've bewitched me, Señora Goya del Fuentes?"

She colored becomingly, her lashes making charcoal smudges against her pink cheeks. "My lord, you make me feel shy of you."

"Why, Skye! Didn't anyone ever pay you outrageous compliments?"

"My husband." It was stated simply.

"Sweetheart, sweetheart. I *am* sorry! Would you rather we went back?"

"No, Geoffrey. I don't want to go back."

He breathed a sigh of relief and cursed himself for a fool. This was only her first adventure, and she was hesitant. Reaching out, he took her hand and silently they rode on together. All about them the English January day was magnificent—the sky a cloudless bright blue, the sun a sharp piercing yellow, the air cold, crisp, and invigorating. Their own warm breath and the horses' heaving breaths made tiny clouds. The Thames River valley rolled gently, on and on. The lovers seemed entirely alone in the world, like Adam and Eve.

Skye rode quietly with her thoughts. She liked this man, though she doubted she would ever love him or any other man again. Love was both a passion and a pain. She didn't think she could bear another loss like the loss of Khalid. If she simply enjoyed Geoffrey's company and his lovemaking, she would be safe from hurt.

As the January sun began to sink away they came to a charming small inn set upon the river bank. It was separated from the road by a low stone wall that opened into a brick courtyard. Upon either side of the entry hung an oval sign depicting a drake surrounded by several ducks. The building was whitewashed and half-timbered, with a thatched roof and lead-paned bow windows that had window boxes filled with holly and ivy. From the great brick center chimney rose a curl of gray-blue smoke. As they clattered up to the inn door an ostler ran out from the stable to take their horses. Geoffrey's hands lingered on Skye's waist as he lifted her from her horse, and she felt her skin tingling against her silk undergarments. Taking her hand firmly in his, he led her into the inn.

"My lord Southwood!" A tall, moon-faced man came forward. "Welcome, my lord, my lady. We received your message this morning, my lord, and your room is ready. There will be no other guests for the duration of your stay."

"My thanks, Master Parker. I think we will have dinner as soon as it can be made ready. It's been a cold ride."

"Very good, my lord! Rose! Where is that lass? Rose!"

"Here, Dad!"

"Escort my lord Southwood and his lady to their room, girl."

Rose, a very buxom young lady whose ample bosom threatened to overflow its blouse, bobbed a curtsey, and smiled saucily at the Earl. "This way, m'lord, madam," she said, leading them not upstairs but down a short sunlit hallway and into a small wing off the main inn building. The door swung open to reveal a charming white room with a bowed window, large fireplace, and big carved oak bed with heavy green and white linen hangings. Dark beams timbered the walls and ceiling. On one side of the fireplace was a round polished table holding a brown glazed earthenware bowl filled with pine boughs. There were two matching chairs. At the foot of the bed was a blanket chest. There was a seat built into the window, with plump cushions of the same homespun green and white linen as the bed hangings.

Rose touched a brand to the perfectly laid fire and it blazed up instantly. "Your trunks are on either side of the bed, m'lord," she said. "Can I bring you anything?"

Geoffrey looked to Skye. "Sweetheart?"

The little maid almost sighed her envy of the beautiful lady. "A bath," pleaded Skye. "I can smell nothing but horses."

He smiled down on her, then turned to Rose. "Will you see to it, love?" His big hand cupped the girl's face, and he looked down into her bovine brown eyes.

Rose nearly fainted. "A-aye, m'lord. A b-bath. At once!"

He dropped his hand and she spun about and fled. He laughed softly, and Skye chided him, "Oh, Geoffrey, what a wicked man you are."

He grinned at her. "I suppose I am," he admitted. Then "I'll bathe with you. I stink of horses too." Reaching out, he pulled her into his arms, pushed her hood off, and loosened her hair so that it tumbled down her back in a shining black mass. One strong arm pressed her tightly against him. The other hand caressed her silken hair. She could feel herself growing weak with his touch, and fought to control her emotions. His green eyes mocked her efforts, and for a moment she became angry and struggled to escape him. He released her instantly.

"I'll never force you, Skye," he said aloud. The thought lay between them: because I don't have to.

There was a scratching at the door and then a sturdy boy lugged in a small round oak tub. Several other boys carried in buckets of water. Rose ordered the tub placed before the fire, and set a carved screen about it. When the tub was filled and the male servants gone, she asked, "Shall I stay and help you, madam?"

"Thank you, Rose. I should appreciate it." Her blue eyes twinkled wickedly. "Sorry, Geoffrey, but the tub is much too small for us both, as you can see. You will have to bathe after me." It was a small but delicious revenge, and she was hard pressed not to laugh. She slipped behind the modesty of the screen and slowly removed each garment.

Sitting on the bed, he watched through narrowed eyes as first her velvet riding habit and then her perfumed, silken undergarments were handed over the screen to the solicitous Rose. Soon he heard the water splashing gently as she lowered herself into the tub.

"Will you need help, madam?"

"No, Rose. I can wash myself."

"I'll take your riding habit and cloak to be brushed, ma'am, and your underclothing to be washed. Then I'll come back."

"Don't bother, I will care for my lady," said the Earl as he escorted the servant girl to the door and firmly thrust her out. To sweeten the rebuff he slipped a gold piece down her front and, patting her backside, sent her on her way. The door was shut, the bolt slammed home. "And now, madam!" He strode across the room and yanked the carved screen aside. She sat covered by suds, her dark hair loosely pinned on top of her head. She looked up at him mockingly.

"My lord?"

He stripped off his clothes, letting them lie where they fell, and strode purposefully toward the tub.

"No!" she shrieked, "you'll flood the room!"

He grinned wickedly. "Then get out and let me bathe."

"I am not through!"

"But I am ready!"

"Oh, damn you, Southwood! Hand me a towel."

He held it just out of her reach so that she was forced to stand in order to get it. The suds sluiced down her lush form, and Geoffrey Southwood drew in his breath sharply. The beast in him stirred. Clinging to an end of the towel as she grabbed it he pulled her over and kissed her. Her small full breasts, wet and warm, pushed demandingly at his chest.

"Skye, oh sweet Skye!" His voice was rough with longing. Then suddenly he felt the ground give way beneath him and he landed rudely in the warm, scented tub. She was laughing uproariously, the red mouth wide and luscious.

"There, Master Lecher! Cool your heels, and wash the stink of the road from your handsome body! Geoffrey! Geoffrey! How accustomed you must be to getting your way with women! Shame, my lord! Fie! We barely arrive and you ogle the maidservant. Then you kiss me, ogle the wench again, and pat her backside! Yes! I saw it! Then attempt to climb into *my* tub for another kiss and a cuddle. No, my lord! If you would have me as your own then I will demand fidelity. Are you capable of fidelity, Geoffrey Southwood?"

For the briefest instant he was angry. Angry with this nameless female, the Whoremaster of Algiers' woman. How dare she impose conditions on him? But as he gazed at her he felt the anger dissolve. She was right. She wasn't some common trull to love or ignore as the spirit moved him.

"*Touché,* sweetheart," he admitted ruefully.

"I'll teach you manners yet, Southwood," she said mischievously.

"Scrub my back," he shot back and, laughing, she complied.

She had decided in the early hours of the dawn that if she was to become his mistress it must be on her terms. She would not be one of many. She must be his only love. She would give to him affection and respect, but in return he must give her the same. And as she would be loyal and faithful to him, so must he be to her. She had, just now, won their first battle.

They ate in their room by the fireplace. It was a simple but very tasty meal of boiled lobsters, artichokes in oil and vinegar, newly baked bread with sweet butter, whole apples baked in pastry with colored sugar sprinkled over them accompanied by clotted cream, sharp cheese, and a pitcher of white wine.

Afterward they lay back against the plump goose-down pillows on the lavender-scented bed and, holding hands, fell asleep. Skye woke to watch the firelight dancing against the wall. Instinctively she knew he was awake too. Turning, she lay her head against his heart.

"What a wench you are," he said softly, and stroked her hair. "I've fallen in love with you, Skye. You know that, don't you? I've never loved before, sweetheart, but as God as my witness I do love you."

They made love tenderly, lingeringly, then slept, awakened, and made love twice more. As Geoffrey had promised her, the next three days were spent in an orgy of lovemaking, eating, and drinking. And even if they had wished to change the program they would not have been able to do so, for they awoke that first morning to find a January snowstorm swirling about them.

As gleeful as children, they piled wood upon the fire and then snuggled naked beneath the down coverlets just before Rose arrived with a breakfast of hard-cooked eggs, thick slices of country ham, bread, cheese, and nut-brown ale. It snowed all that day and they never stirred from their bed except to feed either the fire or themselves. Skye could not believe how often and easily he aroused her, fulfilled her, loved her. Each time she thought surely it could not happen again, and yet it did.

On the second day the snow stopped and the sun shone again. They dressed and played outdoors in the snow like youngsters, much to the amusement of Master Parker and his wife. But Rose was outraged. It was unthinkable for the gentry to behave in such a fashion! Especially such a handsome, romantic gentleman as the Earl.

Skye's cheeks were red with the cold and she shrieked with mock terror as the Earl pelted her with snowballs. She got back at him by teasing him into position beneath the roof and then sending a well-aimed snowball into the piled-up snow on the edge. It tumbled down over him like an avalanche, leaving him sputtering his surprise.

That night they sat before the fire, Skye in her simple white caftan and Geoffrey in a green velvet robe. They roasted chestnuts in the coals of their fire, picking the sweet, hot meats from the shells, burning their fingers in the process. He found a lute in the common room of the inn and brought it back to their little room. To her surprise he played and sang quite well. He sang her several naughty ditties that left her weak with laughter, and when he saw that she was helpless he put the lute down and pounced on her. Giggling, she fought him off, tickling him mercilessly until he too was helpless with mirth.

They lay panting upon the bed, and then suddenly he was kissing her frantically. "Skye! Skye! Dammit, woman, love me a little!"

"But Geoffrey," she protested, "I do!"

"No, sweetheart, you love what I do to your passions but you feel nothing for me. You're so fair, so charming, so intelligent! I thought it was enough, but it *isn't* enough. I want you to care as I care."

"Oh, Geoffrey!" There was genuine regret in her voice. "I don't know if I shall ever love again. It hurts so damned much to love. I like you, and I had thought we would be friends. It's more than most men have with their mistresses."

"You're not just any woman, my love! I want more of you, Skye, than most men have of their mistresses."

"You have no right!" she shouted at him. "You do not take me, I give myself freely! Because I want to, and only because I do want to." She was kneeling on the bed, her hair swirling about her sleek, beautiful shoulders. "I will be no man's toy! Understand that, my lord Earl."

Her sapphire eyes flashed blue fire, her creamy skin was rosy with emotion. At that moment she was the most beautiful thing he'd ever seen. Still, he was furious at her. He was Geoffrey Reginald Michael Arthur Henry Southwood, the seventh Earl of Lynmouth, and she was only a nameless woman without a past. He was the "Angel Earl," the man for whom all women pined. She was the first to have the gift of his true love. And he would have hers!

His voice was dangerously low and tinged with scorn. "I'll not beg you, Skye. But if you cannot learn to love again and yet you still give your body, then you're no better than a common whore."

She went white with shock, her eyes huge. Lashing out, she hit a blow to his cheek which left the red imprint of her fingers. Instantly he struck back, matching her blow. Then flinging himself on her, he pinned her beneath him.

"Your husband is dead! Can't you understand?"

Struggling wildly, she screamed at him. "Don't speak of him! Don't you dare to speak of him! He was kind and wise and good, and I loved him! Do you hear? I loved him! I loved him as I shall never love anyone else!"

"Instead," he raged at her, "you'll make a mockery of his love by behaving like a whore! You'll lock your heart away while satisfying the lusts of your body. Very well, sweetheart, if you wish to be a whore I'll show you how!"

His hands went to the neck of her caftan and with several quick motions he tore the silk garment from her easily. He squeezed her breasts, his knee jammed brutally between her thighs.

"No! Geoffrey!"

His lime-green eyes glittered in the firelight, and he bent to capture her mouth. She turned her head aside quickly and he lost his balance. He fell into the pillows. She scrambled from beneath him, her feet finding the floor. She fled across the room. But reaching the door, she realized the hopelessness of her situation. She was stark naked, and could hardly escape.

She faced him as he lazily stalked her across the room. "Geoffrey, please." She held out her hands in supplication. His eyes were pitiless as his body pressed hard into hers. She felt the wall behind her.

"Whores," he said tonelessly, "are often taken in alleys, standing up, their backs to the wall." Forcing her thighs open, he ordered, "Put your arms about me, whore! Wrap your legs about my waist and see how the other members of your sisterhood behave!"

She fought him wildly now, trying to twist her body away from him, struggling, clawing at his eyes. He slapped her and she burst into tears, tears of shame, tears of fright. "Please," she whimpered, "*please* not like this."

Her tears stopped him and he suddenly stepped away. She crumbled toward the floor and he caught her and carried her to the bed, cradling her against his chest as he sat down. "Damn you, Skye! Damn you for the heartless, blue-eyed bitch you are. I only want you to love me."

"It hurts to love," she sobbed, "I don't want to be hurt again."

"Sweetheart, living hurts, and loving is part of living, as is death." His anger had disappeared in the face of her obvious pain. "Skye, my darling, love me as I love you."

She began to cry harder. She wept for the woman she could not remember, for Khalid el Bey, that tender and noble man. She was so very tired.

"Love me, my darling," he whispered tenderly. "Let your heart soften again. Oh Skye, I would set you above all women, even my wife. Love me, sweetheart!"

She had built a wall about her heart and now she felt that wall being breached, piece by piece.

"You're no wanton, to lie with me simply for pleasure. You do feel, though you won't admit it. Don't you, my darling?"

She looked up at him, her eyes streaming. "Yes," she whispered, so low that he had to bend to hear her.

"You will not betray the love you felt for your husband if you love me, Skye. That you can—and must—love again is a tribute to the love you shared with your husband. Now share your love with me, my darling."

There was a long silence. At last he heard her say softly, "Yes, Geoffrey."

With infinite care he lay her upon their bed and gently kissed the tears on her cheeks, moving down her throat, her chest, her exquisite breasts. He worshiped at the shrine of their perfection, nursing on each nipple. Protectively she enfolded him in her embrace, cradling him, and, exhausted, they fell asleep.

In the gray-white light of the January dawn she awoke to find that he had thrust gently into her. The hardness within her seemed natural and good. "I do love you," she said quietly, and slowly he began the primitive rhythm that would culminate in searing passion for them both. She moved with him, savoring the sweetness of him, and suddenly she knew that all the barriers had crumbled away. She loved this tender and arrogant lord who sought to possess her so completely. She loved him. He would never know, of course, for men never did, that though she loved him there would always be a secret part of her that belonged to her alone. But she loved him, of that she was sure.

Their rhythm quickened and then the blazing white light of

the dawn blended with the pulsing golden light in her mind as he brought her twice to perfect fulfillment. She cried his name and felt his strong arms about her, heard his voice soothing her, his lips kissing away the salty tears she hadn't even been aware of shedding.

"You are mine, and I am yours," she said finally, easily.

"Aye, sweetheart," he answered. "We belong together, and we will be together. In the spring I shall beg leave from the Queen and take you down into Devon to my home."

"But your wife—"

"Mary and her daughters do not live at Lynmouth," he said. "It is you who shall be its mistress."

That afternoon they left their secret sanctuary at the Ducks and Drake and rode back to London. The day was cold and windy and overcast, and threatened snow again, but they were happy.

"I want you to move into my house," he said as they rode. "The apartment next to mine is for the Countess of Lynmouth, and we will redo it for you."

"I don't know, Geoffrey. I have my own home, and I plan to bring my daughter up from Devon soon. I haven't seen her in several months. She should be in her own house, not in yours."

"Then keep Greenwood, darling, but let me redo those rooms for you. You can travel easily between the two houses using the underground passage beneath the garden. You can be with your little girl during the day, and with me in the evenings."

"Very well, Geoffrey, as long as I may keep my own home. But until the rooms are redone I will remain at Greenwood. Will you dine with me this evening?"

"I will, sweetheart, but first I must return to Court and pay my respects to Her Majesty."

Soon they turned their horses into Greenwood's driveway.

"Welcome home, ma'am," called the gatekeeper.

Skye threw him a smile and waved. Approaching the house, Skye was pleased to see a groom hurry from her stables. As they reined in their horses the Earl dismounted and lifted her down from her horse. His arms remained wrapped around her and, flushing prettily, she looked up at him.

"Do you love me, Skye?" he demanded softly.

"I love you, Geoffrey," she answered, her bright blue eyes never wavering from his.

"And will you be my lady fair, sweetheart?"

"Yes! Oh, yes!"

He bent and kissed her lingeringly, lovingly. "I'll send word when I can come this evening," he said. Mounting his stallion again, he cantered off down the drive.

She entered the house dreamily.

"So you're back, and looking as dewy-eyed as any foolish maid."

"Good day to you, Robbie." She smiled sweetly at him. "Come have a glass of wine with me."

"Wine, is it?" he grumbled, following her upstairs to the little salon.

"Yes, wine! Wine to celebrate the fact that I'm in love! Oh, Robbie, I'm in love again! I never thought I would be able to love after I lost Khalid, but I love Geoffrey!"

Lord have mercy, thought the sea captain as Skye, humming a tuneless ditty, poured out generous portions of ruby-red wine for the two of them. Robbie sat slumped in a chair, his gaze on the floor. *How can I tell her what de Grenville told me while in his cups last night?* he thought. *How can I tell her that Southwood seeks to make her his mistress in order to satisfy a bet? Now the bastard's gone and captured her heart. Damn! I'd rather be in the middle of a South Atlantic hurricane!* He raised his eyes slowly.

She raised her goblet high. "To my Lord Southwood! Long life!" she toasted.

Robbie raised his goblet lifelessly. "Aye," he answered tonelessly. *Christ! She's so happy! I haven't seen her happy since Khalid died. Ah, hell! It's too late for me to save her from him. Let her find out on her own. Let her be happy for now.* He gulped down his wine and sat back against the velvet cushions.

"I've news too," he said. "We're to see the Queen and Cecil the day after Candlemas. We'd best have that first voyage mapped out by then."

She was suddenly all business. "Have you decided where? And what?"

"Jewels and spices. In case of shipwreck," he crossed himself, "at least we can save half the cargo. We'll go down and around the Horn into the Indian Ocean, across to the Spice Islands, for a cargo of pepper, clove, nutmeg, mace, and ginger. Then on to Burma for rubies, for the best rubies come down to Rangoon from Mogok in the central part of the country. In India we'll take on cardamom, diamonds from the Golconda, and pearls. In Ceylon there's cinnamon and sapphires to be had."

"Be sure," said Skye, "to buy only the Kashmir blue sapphires. Khalid always believed their color was the best."

"I know. It's going to be a long voyage, lass. I may not be back for a year or even two, depending on conditions."

She smiled at him affectionately. "You look forward to it, Robbie, don't deny it. You've been landlocked for almost two years now and your feet itch to walk a deck. It's all right, my dear, I understand, and it's time for you to go. I am so grateful to you for your friendship, but I am myself again at last, and I must build my own life."

"I know, lass, but I don't want you hurt, or taken advantage of by anyone. That damned trick memory of yours worries me. In many ways you're still an innocent."

"I have Geoffrey now, Robbie."

"Rely only on yourself, Skye! Love Southwood if you must, but put your trust in no man!"

"Robbie! How cynical you are!"

"Not cynical. Truthful."

There was a scratching at the door, and Skye called out, "Enter."

A footman brought in a piece of paper on a small silver tray. Skye took the folded parchment and opened it. "Damn!" she said.

"What is it?"

"Geoffrey has been called away." She turned to the footman. "How was this delivered?"

"One of the Earl's grooms, mistress."

"You may go."

The servant turned and left.

"What does he say, Skye?"

"Very little," she said, frowning. "Just that there's a problem in Devon."

"You could probably use a good night's sleep," remarked Robbie wryly, and she laughed at his irreverence.

"Considering your reputation as a swordsman, this is surely a case of the pot calling the saucepan black," she teased.

He guffawed heartily.

The days sped by. She heard nothing from Geoffrey. And then came the day of her appointment with Cecil and the Queen. She dressed elegantly but soberly. William Cecil, Lord Burghley, Her Majesty's chief advisor, was not a man to be swayed by a show of bosom. Her gown was dark-blue velvet, its severity relieved by a small white lace ruff at the neck. The sleeves were slashed and edged with gold, her white silk underblouse showing through the openings. She wore a gold chain interspersed at intervals with small flat plaques of carved white coral roses. Her shining hair was parted in the center and drawn into an elegant chignon at the nape of her neck.

The river was frozen solid, so they went to Greenwich in Skye's coach. Cecil awaited them in a book-lined room. He wasted no time but came directly to the point. "If we grant you a royal charter, what does Her Majesty gain?"

"A quarter share in the cargo, an accurate map of the area—for we're carrying two cartographers on each vessel—and of course we're available to do any errands Her Majesty may require along our route," replied Robert Small.

"How many ships?"

"Eight."

"That will be the number going. How many will you bring back?"

"Six at the minimum."

"You overestimate, I think, Captain Small," snapped Cecil.

"No, my lord. I don't. Barring a typhoon, I will actually return with all eight. But a serious storm could lose me one or two."

"What of pirates, or mutiny?"

"My lord, every captain in my fleet has been with me for several years, as have all my ships' crews. These men are used to working together under both good and bad conditions. They are a loyal and disciplined lot, unlike most crews. They'll bring their ships through Hell if necessary, but they'll bring them home to England."

Cecil smiled thinly. "Your confidence is commendable, sir. I shall look forward to being amazed." He turned to Skye. "And where, madam, do you come into this?"

"I finance it," said Skye quietly.

"You must have great confidence in Captain Small," said Cecil drily.

"I do, sir. He was my husband's partner for some years, and never failed him once."

"And your husband was . . . ?"

"Don Diego Indio Goya del Fuentes, a Spanish merchant of Algiers."

"The Spanish ambassador claims never to have heard of him, madam."

"I would hardly think the Spanish ambassador to the English Court would be well acquainted with the residents of Algiers, my lord," said Skye coolly.

"Perhaps not, madam. I merely mention it in passing. It is my duty to protect my Queen."

"If you feel, my lord Cecil, that this venture is a danger to your Queen, or would bring some discredit upon her, then I shall withdraw my request for a charter, and you must rule against us with Her Majesty. However, to do so casts doubt upon not only my honor, but on Sir Robert's as well. I am but newly come from Algiers, but Captain Small has always been a loyal and good servant of England."

"Madam, you misunderstand me. I merely said that King Phillip's man knew not of your late husband's family."

"Why should he? My husband's family came to Algiers several generations back. The original Goya del Fuentes was, I believe, a younger son. There is still a branch of the family in Spain—near Granada or Seville. I can never remember which."

Cecil sighed, exasperated, and Robbie hid a smile. Skye was doing a fine job of confusing the chancellor. It relieved him to see her fast thinking. Now he need not fear leaving her when he went back to sea.

"Really, my lord," Skye allowed a slightly annoyed tone to creep into her voice, "what it is that bothers you I cannot imagine. I ask for nothing other than Her Majesty's sponsorship. In return I offer her a quarter share of the profits, the latest mapping of the area, and my ships will be bringing to the peoples of the East word of our Queen's greatness. This hardly seems to me a suspicious undertaking."

"Dammit, madam, you deliberately twist my words!" roared Cecil.

"Do I indeed, sir? Pray then, enlighten me as to exactly what it is you *do* mean."

A burst of tinkling laughter interrupted them, and from a shadowy recess in the room the Queen quickly appeared.

"Do not mind Cecil, Mistress Goya del Fuentes. He is overcautious of our welfare, and we are appreciative of his efforts. Although we might do without any other of our servants, we could not do without him. Come, my friend, you need not know the lady's pedigree in order to do business with her. Our treasury is not so full that we cannot use the profits from this voyage, and it costs us nothing more than our goodwill. Captain Small's record speaks for itself."

"Very well, my lady Queen. I will see the charter is granted if you so desire."

"I do, my lord Cecil. Work out the pertinent details with Captain Small. Mistress Goya del Fuentes will come and have a glass of wine with us." The Queen strode from the room and Skye, after curtseying to Cecil, followed her.

As the door closed upon the women the chancellor remarked, "She's a beautiful woman, Sir Robert, and she has a brain. Her Majesty approves of intelligent women."

"She is the daughter I never had," replied Robbie.

"Indeed," murmured Cecil. "Then are you aware that she spent several days and nights in mid-January with Lord Southwood at the Thameside inn called the Ducks and Drake?"

"I am," said Robbie, his anger beginning to rise. "You seem to be keeping a rather close watch on an unimportant and harmless young woman, my lord."

"A woman of Irish descent who was wed to a Spaniard . . . both traditional enemies of England," Cecil observed drily.

"And is Lord Southwood also under suspicion?" snapped the captain.

"Only to the extent that a valuable servant of the Queen might be subverted."

Robert Small was on his feet. "By God, sir! I'll hear no further slander against Skye! She has suffered greatly, and yet remains a sweet and good lady. There is not a devious or disloyal tendency in her, I assure you."

"Sit down, sit down, Captain Small. Our own investigations have borne out your words. I would, however, like your personal thoughts about her relationship with Lord Southwood. You need divulge no confidence, of course, but the Earl is a valuable man to the Queen."

"He claims to be in love with her," answered Robbie, "and God help her, for she's in love with him."

"Curious," said Cecil. "It is not the Earl's custom to take women seriously. Then perhaps he really is in love with her?"

Far away, at that very moment, the gentleman in question was raging violently at his pale and cowering wife. Geoffrey Southwood had rarely felt such overpowering fury. "Bitch! Bitch!" he shouted at her. "You've killed my only legitimate son! Christ's body, how could you be so stupid? You knew there was smallpox about, and yet you wrote to the Countess of Shrewsbury and asked to have Henry sent home for Twelfth Night. Without my permission. As God is my witness, Mary, I could kill you!"

"Then why don't you, Geoffrey?" she baited him. "You hate me, and our daughters! Why not kill us all?"

Her hysterical outburst calmed him somewhat. He eyed her coldly. "I am going to divorce you, Mary. I should have done so years ago."

"You have no grounds to do such a thing."

"I have all the grounds I need, Mary. You produce nothing but daughters. The one son you bore me you wantonly killed. You refused to hostess my friends, yet you hoard the household monies I send you to dower your daughters despite the fact I have forbidden them to wed. I have grounds, Mary, but if needs be I'll produce half a dozen men who'll claim intimate knowledge of you."

She went white with shock. "You truly are a bastard, Geoffrey," she whispered, horrified.

He hit her a blow that sent her to her knees.

"A bastard!" she repeated. He turned and left. They were the last words she ever spoke to her husband. By nightfall Mary Southwood lay ill of smallpox herself, as did every one of her daughters. She died several days later. Mary, Elizabeth, Catherine, and Phillipa joined her. Only the three youngest girls, Susan and twins Gwyneth and Joan, survived. The Earl was saved because he had had a light case of smallpox as a child.

The Countess and her daughters were buried with a bare minimum of ceremony, the bell in Lynmouth Church dutifully tolling their passing as the carts carried their coffins to the family cemetery. Geoffrey told his three daughters of their mother's and sisters' deaths. They were so young, only four and five, that he was not sure they really understood him. Looking at them closely for the first time, he decided that they were really somewhat comely. Leaving detailed instructions as to their convalescence, he departed Devon for Court.

He had been in Devon for over two months, and spring had come to England. The Court had left Greenwich and was now at Nonesuch. The Earl of Lynmouth was welcomed back warmly, particularly by the ladies, for news of his loss had preceded him. Anxious to see Skye, he fretted until he could get to London. He could not go until the Queen gave her permission. He waited for the right moment to beg that permission.

In London Robbie prepared to take his leave of Skye. The *Mermaid* and her fellow ships waited now, fully provisioned, in the Pool. He had put off his departure until the last possible moment, for Skye was quite easily upset of late, the least little thing sending her into tears. He had sent to Devon for his sister, Marie, and the two children. The sight of Willow, now almost two, had cheered her somewhat.

He knew what distressed her. It was Southwood's apparent desertion. Since the Earl had returned with her from their tryst in January there had been no word from him other than the cryptic message that he was needed in Devon. Robert Small told himself once more that the man was a bastard, plain and simple. Seeing Skye grow so pale and listless, he silently cursed the Earl and bemoaned the fact that there was nothing he could do to cheer her.

Finally Robert Small could delay no longer. On the night before he sailed Skye arranged a small dinner party for him at her house. De Grenville was their guest, dining with Skye, Robbie, Dame Cecily, Jean, and Marie. De Grenville intended to sail with Robbie as far as the Channel. The meal was delicious, but Skye only picked at the food. Her merriment was forced. At least, she thought sourly, Southwood had done her one good turn by arranging an introduction to the Queen, thereby helping them obtain a royal charter. As to love . . . it was all either passion or pain.

De Grenville was soon in his cups, and he leered at Skye in a friendly fashion. "For a learned and modest woman you cost me dearly, Mistress Skye. Now that the Earl of Lynmouth is back at Court I suppose he'll be taking my barge."

He was back! And he'd never even sent her word! "Why should he take your barge, Dickon?" she asked absently.

Robert Small suddenly came to life. "That's no story for Skye's ears, Dickon!" he protested, kicking his friend beneath the table.

But de Grenville paid him no heed. His hostess's rich wine had fuzzed his wits. "Why shouldn't she know, Robbie? When I turn my barge over to Geoff it will be all over Court. Don't know why I bet him anyway, but I did want that stallion."

Skye felt a premonition of disaster run through her. "What bet is this, Dickon?"

"Enough, de Grenville!" cried Robert Small desperately, glancing toward his sister and Marie.

"No, Robbie," snapped Skye. "I believe I should hear what Dickon has to say. Pray, sir, enlighten me as to what you and my lord Earl wagered."

"I bet my barge against his prize stud stallion that he couldn't make you his mistress within a six-month period. Looked like such a sure thing. You certainly cut him dead at the inn in Dartmour. Didn't think he was your type at all. But then, my father always said women were a fickle lot and not to be trusted."

Cecily and Marie both gasped. The Gallic Jean shrugged philosophically. But Robbie, who knew her best of all, held his breath in anticipation of the explosion that immediately followed.

"The bastard!" she raged. "The damned bastard! I could kill

him! I *will* kill him! No, I won't—I shall do to him what Marie did to Captain Jamil!" Bursting into tears, she picked up her skirts and fled the room.

Marie and Cecily rose to follow her, but Robbie stayed them with a gesture and went after her himself. He saw her running across the terrace, down into the garden. His short legs pumping hard, he ran after her calling, "Skye, lass! Wait for me, Skye!" She stopped, but her back remained toward him. As he reached her he could see her shoulders shaking. He walked around her and gathered her into his arms. She wept wildly. "Oh, lass, I am so sorry. But don't waste your tears on him. He's not worth it, Skye. He's not worth any grief."

"I l-l-love him, Robbie," she sobbed, "I l-l-love the bastard!"

He sighed. He was going to have to hurt her further, but there was no help for it. Best she know the worst from him than have some ass like de Grenville tell her. He drew her over to a carved stone bench and they sat down.

"I want you to hear this from me, Skye. Southwood's only son and his wife and four of his daughters are dead of the smallpox. That's what sent him down into Devon in January. De Grenville tells me the rumors at Court are that the Queen has already picked out an heiress for him, and Geoffrey Southwood would never say no to a wealthy match. And now that he no longer has a son, it is imperative that he remarry. The sooner the better, I would say, for with a new wife he'll have little time for you, lass."

She raised her face to him and he thought, as he had thought a hundred times or more, that she was the most beautiful woman he had ever known. Tonight when he left her he would visit a sweet young whore of his acquaintance, but on the long nights at sea it would be Skye he thought of, not little Sally. It would be Skye's face that he would easily recall to mind, the young prostitute's fading from memory within an hour of their parting.

"You understand what I'm saying to you, Skye?" He looked anxiously into her wet sapphire eyes. "You understand that in all likelihood it's finished with Southwood."

She sighed. "I am carrying his child, Robbie. In six months' time, more or less, I shall present the seventh Earl of Lynmouth with a child, and I pray God it's a son! And I also pray that his rich, new wife does precisely what his last rich wife did—deliver girls!"

"Marry me, Skye."

"You are prejudiced, Robbie," she smiled wanly. "Take me back inside and I'll bid de Grenville goodnight. What time do you sail tomorrow?"

"We catch the midday tide. I'll come in the morning to bid you farewell."

They walked back through the garden and into the house. De Grenville had fallen asleep in his chair.

"*Il est un cochon,*" muttered Marie.

"No," said Skye.

"He hurt you, *mignon.*"

Skye shrugged. "Better I heard it from him than from a stranger, Marie. Alas, our good wine does not agree with him."

Suddenly the small dining-room door was flung open and Skye's bargeman stumbled into the room beside her majordomo, Walters, who gasped, "Madam, the Queen comes!"

"What!?"

The bargeman spoke up. "The Queen, mistress! She's almost here! She sent a messenger ahead of her on the river."

"My God, I'm not dressed properly to receive her! Quick, Marie!" And she raced upstairs to her own apartment, calling to Daisy as she ran. "Fetch the burgundy-colored silk with the gold-and-cream-stripped underskirt. The rubies! My gold ribbons! Marie, go back downstairs and have Walters clear the dining room. I'll want ham, cheeses, fruits, thin sugar wafers, and wines. Have them set on the sideboards in the banquet room. Wake de Grenville and have Robbie sober him!"

Marie turned and ran from the room while the maids fluttered about Skye. She quickly changed her clothes. "Hawise, watch the window! Sing out the second you see the Queen's barge!"

A few minutes later, as Skye smoothed the wrinkles from the elegant silk gown, Hawise called, "The Queen's barge is rounding the bend, ma'am!" Skye flew from the room and down the stairs. Catching Robbie and de Grenville by the hands, the trio sped across the terrace, down another garden, and reached the barge, landing moments before the Queen's boat bumped it. The two men stepped forward to aid Elizabeth as she disembarked, while Skye swept the monarch a magnificent curtsey, her wine-colored skirts billowing gracefully, her dark head lowered in perfect submission.

The young Queen eyed her hostess approvingly. "Rise, Mistress Goya del Fuentes. 'Pon my soul, you make the most elegant and graceful curtsey I've ever seen!"

Standing, Skye thanked the Queen with a smile and Elizabeth

said, "We hope you'll forgive us this unorthodox visit, but it was brought to our attention that Sir Robert sails tomorrow. We could not allow him to leave on such a lengthy voyage without giving him our good wishes."

Robbie flushed with obvious pleasure. "Majesty, I am overwhelmed by your kindness."

"Madam," said Skye, "will you take refreshment?"

"Thank you, mistress. Sir Robert, de Grenville, you may escort me. Southwood, take Mistress Goya del Fuentes and Mistress Knollys."

The Queen moved off, leaving Skye stricken. Here was Geoffrey stepping up from the Queen's barge, handing out a ravishing lovely red-headed girl.

"Skye, may I present the Queen's cousin Lettice, this is Mistress Goya del Fuentes."

Lettice Knollys smiled in a friendly fashion, her pale skin glowing and youthful. "We're of an age," she said. "May I call you Skye, and you call me Lettice?"

"But of course," Skye answered. God in Heaven, was this girl the rich match the Queen proposed for Geoffrey?

"It's good to see you, Skye," the Earl of Lynmouth murmured softly as he escorted both women up the garden to the house. Behind them the other half-dozen barges that had escorted the Queen were unloading their passengers.

"What a charming house you have," remarked Lettice. "I have always wanted a small house on the Strand. You do not come to Court, do you?"

"There is no need. And besides, I am not of the nobility. If the Queen invited me, however, I would, of course, obey."

They had reached the house now, and as they entered, Southwood said quietly, "Lettice, I must speak with Skye. Keep the Queen occupied for me." Before Skye had time to protest he had whisked her into the library and shut the door firmly.

"I cannot leave my guests! The Queen will notice!" she protested.

"Madam, I have been parted from you for three months now. Have you no warmer welcome for me?"

"Sir, you presume a great deal! I do, however offer you my deepest sympathy on the loss of your wife and children."

"You knew? How?"

"De Grenville told me earlier this evening." She turned and walked a little ways from him. "I understand I am also to wish you felicitations on an upcoming marriage. Is it Mistress Knollys? And will you honeymoon on your barge?"

"I don't own a barge."

"Why, sir," she said scathingly, "did you not win de Grenville's barge? I understood the wager was his barge against your stallion. He is quite distressed by the loss of the animal."

"Damn de Grenville for a fool!" swore the Earl. "Sweetheart, listen to me! The bet was made when you snubbed me, on the first day we ever met. I had no intention of collecting on it. It had nothing to do with our falling in love later on. I intended to tell Dickon so, but I forgot it when I was summoned to Devon. That worthless bitch I married had brought my son, Henry, home when there was smallpox in the village. He came home only to die! That she and four of her girls perished as well is only God's judgment. Then it was touch and go with the three youngest. I stayed on until they were well. I am not entirely heartless, Skye. They're but four and five."

"You might have written me!"

"Frankly it did not occur to me. I am not a man of words, Skye. The pox swept through my estates like wildfire, and I was kept damned busy. My bailiff died, among others, and until I could replace him I did his work."

"You've been back at Court for a while, my lord! You might have sent me a message. A posy of flowers. Something! But you were too busy finding an heiress to replace your dead wife! I hate you, Geoffrey! I will never forgive you! You used me like a common trollop! You lied to me!" Angrily she turned away so he might not see the tears springing into her eyes. "I was warned that you were the biggest bastard in London, but God help me I would not believe it!"

"You're right," he admitted. "I have spent the time since my return to Court arranging my next marriage." Her shoulders shook, and his ears caught a muffled sob. "The lady I wish to make the next Countess of Lynmouth is one of the most beautiful women in London. She is wealthy, so I need not fear that she seeks my money. Her manners are flawless and she is an excellent hostess, able to deal graciously with those of high and low estate. She is the perfect mate for me."

His voice was filled with such love and admiration that each word he spoke was like a great knife thrust into her heart.

"There was only one problem that might have prevented the match," he continued, "so it was necessary that I convince the

Queen that, despite this impediment, I would have no other woman to wife."

"I-I-I am not interested, my lord Earl." Turning, she tried to push past him, but he held her fast. Her face was pressed against the velvet of his doublet. "I *must* return to my guests," she pleaded.

He ignored her. "The lady in question is not English. She claims to be an Irish orphan who wed a Spanish merchant and was then widowed. So I have represented her to the Queen. I know, however, that the story is not true. She was a captive slave of unknown background who was fortunate enough to catch the eye of the great Whoremaster of Algiers. He took her under his protection, and when he was murdered she fled Algiers with his wealth. But I love her, and I want her for my wife. I have convinced the Queen of the wisdom of my choice. She has given me her permission for us to wed."

Skye pulled away from the Earl, and when she looked up at him her eyes were blazing blue fire.

"I do not know how you have obtained your information. Though your facts are correct you know nothing at all! Yes, I was brought as a captive to Khalid el Bey—that was his name, my lord Earl. I had no memory of who I was or where I had come from, but he didn't care. He might have made me a whore in one of his houses, or he might have made me his concubine. He did neither. I was indeed under his protection. *But,* my lord Earl, I was also *his wife!* Are you so narrow-minded that you believe a marriage doesn't exist unless it is celebrated by a Christian priest? The chief mullah of Algiers wed me to my lord Khalid! I was well and truly married!"

She was pacing back and forth now, her burgundy silk skirts swishing angrily. Her hair had come loose, and as she turned to face him again it swung fiercely with her. "My daughter, sir, bears her father's Christian surname, for he was a Spaniard by birth, driven from that cursed land by the cruelty of the Inquisition. I expect, my lord, that even you can understand that! You will find in the baptismal registry of St. Mary's Church in Bideford the name of Mary Willow Goya del Fuentes!

"I could not wed with you, my lord! It would be grossly unfair to mingle my unknown blood and tainted body with such as yours. I fully understand the great honor you do me, but *no!*" And pushing past him, she fled the room.

Geoffrey Southwood stood stunned and disbelieving as Robert Small entered the room and closed the door behind him.

"What the hell did you do to her?" growled the little captain.

"I asked her to marry me."

"Why?"

"Because I love her!" shouted the Earl. "I told her I knew the truth of her past, and it mattered not. I even have the Queen's permission."

"Laddie, laddie, you're a fool. Did she tell you that she has no memory prior to her life in Algiers?"

"Yes."

"Listen to me, my lord. I am old enough to be your father, and I'll speak to you as one. Her husband was my best friend in all this world. He was born the second son of an old and noble family, but fate decreed that he live a life far different than that for which he believed himself intended. Whatever his profession, he was a true gentleman in every sense.

"You love Skye. So did he, with all his heart. She was his joy, his pride, and he wanted nothing more than to spend his life with her and the children they wanted to have. He had just learned, before he was murdered, that he was to be a father, and his happiness came close to making me weep." Robbie breathed deeply and turned to sit. Southwood sat across from him. "I invented Skye's background in order to protect her and the child. Now, Geoffrey lad, I will help you to bring Skye around, for the stubborn wench loves you and has sighed and wept enough over you these last few months. I don't suppose she told you she's with child?"

"Oh my God!" the Earl whispered.

"No?" said Robbie drily. "Well, she is angry with you. Well, we must be firm then. I have just the way to settle this, but you must go along with me in all I say. Agreed?" Southwood slowly nodded. "Come along then, lad, and I'll show you how to neatly trap a vixen."

They came back out to the large salon where Skye and the Queen were holding court together, surrounded by a laughing group of courtiers. They worked their way forward carefully until they were next to the young Queen. Elizabeth was looking especially lovely, her glorious red-gold hair a mass of long, loose ringlets, her smoky eyes sparkling. Her gown was of apple-green silk embroidered heavily with gold, small pearls, and topaz.

"Is the guest of honor finally among us?" said the Queen, laughing. "Pray, sir, where have you and my lord Southwood been?"

"Settling the details of the match that's so dear to your kind Majesty's heart. As Mistress Goya del Fuentes' *parentis in absentia,* it was my duty. Now, madam, with your gracious permission I shall delay my departure by one day in order to give the bride away. Can your Majesty persuade the archbishop to waive the banns and wed the happy couple tomorrow?"

Stunned, Skye began to speak, but the Queen clapped her hands with delight. "Sir Robert, it's an excellent idea! Yes! Yes! The wedding shall be tomorrow at Greenwich. You shall give the bride away, and I shall hostess the wedding party!"

"Majesty, we are honored," said the Earl, placing a firm arm about Skye. "Are we not, sweetheart?"

"Aye, my lord," said Skye loudly and sweetly. Then, while everyone chattered excitedly about them, she hissed, "I'd sooner have the pox than marry you!"

"Come, everyone," cried the Queen. "If Mistress Goya del Fuentes is to be ready to wed at one o'clock tomorrow then we must leave her now. Away to Greenwich!" She turned to Skye. "My dear, you're a delightful hostess. We have enjoyed ourselves so much. You shall be a credit to the Southwood family, I know. Lynmouth will escort me home. Hie yourself to bed and rest. I should imagine you'll get little sleep tomorrow night if your betrothed's reputation is fairly earned." Chuckling, the Queen departed for her barge.

Skye rounded on Robbie furiously. "I'll not marry him, do you hear? I'll not marry him!"

"Indeed you will, Skye lass," said Robert Small with infuriating calm. "Be sensible, my dear. He knows the truth of your past, and yet he loves you and wants to marry you. Think, Skye! You'll be the Countess of Lynmouth. And think of the child you're carrying. Refuse Lynmouth and no one will believe the baby is his, for what woman in her right mind would not marry her child's father? Then the question will be asked whose child is it. And since you have not socialized with anyone it will be assumed that you coupled with a groom or a footman. The child is lowborn, people will say. Then what will happen to Willow?" With every word he uttered she felt more and more trapped. "I'll go happily off to sea now, knowing you're safe, loved, and cared for, Skye," he finished.

"Damn you, Robbie! If Khalid knew what you'd done—"

"He'd fully approve, Skye, and you know it," snapped the gruff little man. "Come along now. The Queen is right, and you need your sleep tonight. Tell Daisy what gown you'd wear tomorrow so the maids may freshen it."

"I will choose nothing!" she said stubbornly.

"Then I will, my dear. Come along now, lass." He took her hand and walked her upstairs to her apartment. "Daisy, girl, to me," he called, and the buxom maid appeared.

"Sir?"

"Your mistress is to be wed at one tomorrow to the Earl of Lynmouth. What in her wardrobe is suitable for a wedding gown?"

Daisy's brown eyes grew round with awe and delight. "Oh, sir! Oh, ma'am! How wonderful!"

Skye turned away sulkily and stamped into her bedchamber, where she threw herself on the bed. Daisy looked questioningly at Robert Small.

"Don't fret, girl," the captain reassured her. "Your mistress is simply in a mood. Let's have a look at her wardrobe."

Daisy led the way to Skye's dressing room. Robert Small's mouth fell open. "Sweet Jesus!" he exclaimed, "I've never seen so many fine feathers in my entire life."

Daisy giggled. "These are only the ones suitable for a wedding, sir. The simpler things are hung in another room."

Robert Small shook his head, then began to study the gowns. White was ruled out, for Skye was a widow. And somehow a bright color seemed inappropriate. Then his eye was caught by a rich, heavy, candlelight-colored satin. "Let's see that one."

Daisy drew the gown forth and held it out for his inspection. The simple bodice was cut low and embroidered in seed pearls. The puffed sleeves, which ended just below the elbow, were slashed and the openings filled in with a fine cream-colored lace. Below the elbow the sleeves hugged the arm in alternating bands of satin and lace. The wrists were ruffled by a wide band of lace. The underskirt was embroidered with delicate seed pearls and tiny diamond flowers. The dress had a small, starched, heart-shaped lace collar edged in tiny diamonds that rose up behind the neck. The underskirt was a graceful bell shape.

"Aye, Daisy, my girl! This will more than do! See it's pressed and ready by ten in the morning. Your mistress is being married in the Queen's own chapel at Greenwich, and the Queen is giving the bridal feast afterward. They'll also be spending the night there."

"Oh . . . sweet Mary, sir! Will I be allowed to go? My mistress will be needing me, I'm sure."

"Aye, girl, you'll go."

The little maid nearly swooned in her ecstasy. "Lord, sir! Wait till me old mother hears that I'm maid to the Countess of Lynmouth! She'll be so proud! Oh, sir! You don't think Mistress Skye will want someone else, do you? I'm nothing but a simple Devon girl."

"Your mistress will want you, Daisy, never fear. See to the dress now, and have a scented bath ready for your lady at dawn. Wash her hair, too."

"Yes, sir." Gathering up the beautiful gown, Daisy left Robert alone. He walked back to the bedroom.

"Are you finished sulking, lass?" he asked.

"I never sulk!" she snapped, sitting up. "I simply dislike having my life settled for me by other people. Do I have no choice in this?!"

"No, lass, not this time. You're angry with Southwood, and so you seek to spite him by making his son a bastard. Yes, I do believe it's a boy you carry. But the Earl has suffered enough, being caught in a loveless marriage, having his heir die. Without even knowing that his potent seed has already taken root in your fertile womb, he offers you marriage. It's hardly an insult, my dear."

"And what of my wealth? Is it to be poured into the Lynmouth coffers along with that of his first two wives? No! No! I won't be left helpless and dependent like poor Mary!"

Robert Small smiled a slow smile. "So that's what's bothering you, lass."

"Part of it," she admitted.

"Don't fret, Skye lass, I'm not about to leave you helpless. The Earl directed me to have a marriage contract drawn up tonight, which he'll sign in the morning. You'll have to give him a good dowry, Skye, but the bulk of your wealth will remain in your hands. This house will remain in your hands, and I've made you my heiress, providing that if anything happens to me you'll care for Cecily. That way you'll have plenty for Willow."

"Robbie! Oh, Robbie!" she began to weep softly.

Embarrassed, he clumsily put his arms about her. "Give over, lass," he muttered gruffly. "For pity's sake don't cry all over me. I like it better when you scream. Who else could I leave Wren Court to, Skye? You're the daughter I never had, lass, and you're as dear to me as if you were my own."

"Thank you, Robbie. You're the best friend I've ever had." She wiped her eyes and Robbie tried to muffle a sniff.

"Now listen to me, Skye. We're giving Southwood twenty-five thousand gold crowns for dowry, and of course you come with your clothing, plate, and jewelry. All the rest of your wealth, the money Khalid left, the shares in our partnership, this house, and

Wren Court remain exclusively yours. He can't take them, so you are free and independent."

"Will he sign such a contract, Robbie?"

"He'll sign, lass. The Queen would have his head if he refused, for Young Bess is very much her own woman, like you." He patted her shoulder. "It's very late, Skye, well past midnight. Rest now, my dear. I will see you in the morning."

"Which gown did you choose, Robbie?"

"The creamy satin with the pearl and diamond embroidery," he answered, smiling.

"It's the one I'd choose, were I interested in this marriage."

He chuckled. "Sleep well, Mistress Goya del Fuentes. Tomorrow night you'll be Lady Southwood, Countess of Lynmouth. Not bad for such an ugly wench." He ducked the pillow she threw at him as he strode from the room, laughing merrily.

Chapter 17

Skye's wedding morning was a rainy spring day. She stretched in a leisurely fashion, dimly aware of activity about her, then suddenly sat straight up in bed. She was being married in a few hours, and there was so much to be done! A steaming tub was already waiting before the fireplace.

"Good morning, m'lady," chorused Daisy and the two undermaids, bobbing curtseys.

"Not 'my lady' yet, Daisy," said Skye sharply. The two maidservants giggled, then gasped, their faces reddening as Skye rose from her bed, drew off her gown, and walked naked across the room. Daisy, who was used to her mistress's eccentricities with regard to nudity in the bath, smirked smugly at the red-faced underlings and helped Skye up the two steps and into the big tub.

Skye sunk gratefully into the bath. The sweet-smelling oily water caressed her skin and lapped about her shoulders. Daisy drew a screen about the tub, leaving her mistress to a few moments of privacy, while she guided the undermaids in the laying out of the bride's clothing.

So, thought Skye, *today is my wedding day. How different it is from the joyous day that I wed you, Khalid. Oh, my dearest lord, how I loved you. But you are gone, Khalid, and this strange English lord has caught at my heart. I may be wealthy, dear Khalid, but the honest truth is that the widow of an Al-*

gerian "merchant" is scarcely on a social footing with a belted Earl. Yet, he would make me his Countess. It's not simply to get me in his bed, for I have already been there. He claims to love me, yet he left me without a word for weeks. Dare I trust him? Or will he break my heart? Oh, God, I wish I could know. I want to be loved, but even more I want to be safe again.

"Mistress," scolded Daisy, "you've not yet begun to wash." Daisy took up the soft cloth herself and began to scrub her mistress. Skye continued to muse silently as Daisy moved on to wash her mistress's hair. Daisy's chatter caused Skye to lose her train of thought and she exploded. Relenting at the hurt look on Daisy's face, Skye confided, "I've wakened with a terrible headache, Daisy, and I don't want it later on at Greenwich."

Daisy became concerned. "Ah, m'lady, I'll have an herbal draught made up at once. Hawise," she turned to one of the serving maids, "ask Dame Cecily to please make up an herbal tea for m'lady's headache."

Skye left her tub wrapped in a large warmed bathsheet and, seated by the fire, endured Daisy's further ministrations. Her hair was rubbed free of excess water, brushed and brushed and brushed again until it was dry, then rubbed with a piece of silk until it shone with deep blue-gold lights. Meanwhile, the second of the undermaids knelt paring her mistress's toenails.

"What I really need is something to eat," declared Skye. "Bring me bread, meat, and wine. I'm starving. See to it, Daisy. Jane, either the Earl will like my feet or he won't." She stood up and the bathsheet dropped. Daisy wrapped her mistress in a loose pink silk robe, then hurried off to see to the food. Picking up her pedicure equipment, Jane departed as well. Skye sighed with open relief. It was so lovely to be alone. But the sound of chuckling spun her around.

"Geoffrey!"

"Good morrow, wife." He stood before the tapestry that hid the secret passage door.

"Not quite yet, my lord," she answered sharply. "How long have you been standing there?"

"Long enough to be reminded what a magnificent creature you are, madam," he drawled lazily, his green eyes sweeping boldly over her.

A flush stained her entire body, and she shook her cloud of hair. Did he really love her, or was it only lust to possess her? She determined to try and find out now. He could cry off when she had finished, but that was better than being owned by a man who had no real feelings for her. Walking deliberately to the door, she locked it and then said firmly, "Sit down, my lord. Will you take some wine?" He nodded, and she poured him a small goblet from her sideboard supply.

"Well, madam," he demanded after accepting the goblet and leaning back. "What is it?"

She drew a deep breath. "How brave you are to wed with me, my lord, but are you sure you really want to take to wife the widow of one of the most notorious men in the history of Algiers? I remind you that I recall nothing whatever prior to my life with Khalid el Bey. He made me what I am. God only knows what tainted blood flows in my veins. My mother might have been mad and my father a murderer. Think carefully, my lord. Is this the sort of woman you would take to wife?"

"Why, Skye," he drawled, "are you trying to discourage me?" She shook her head. He continued. "Did Khalid el Bey teach you to read and write?"

"No," she answered. "I already knew."

"What else did you know, my love?"

"Different languages, mathematics," she said slowly. "The knowledge was just there . . . though I don't remember acquiring it."

"You've hardly a peasant's look," he observed, "and you've been damnably well educated for a man, astoundingly for a woman. From the moment we first met I knew that we should be more to each other than simply friends.

"I wanted to know more about you and I inquired of a sea captain of my acquaintance, one who knew Robert Small and of his association with Khalid el Bey. The captain left Algiers several days after you and Small did. The story of your flight from the Turk was on every tongue in the city, particularly because your loss was said to have rendered the unfortunate man impotent."

Skye choked back her laughter with the confirmation of her revenge on Jamil. But she didn't know whether to be angry at Geoffrey Southwood for this invasion of her privacy, or flattered that he had been so deeply interested in her. She was, above all, pleased to know that Geoffrey wanted her even though he knew of her past.

"You've signed the marriage contract?" she asked him coolly.

"Aye. Your dowry is most generous, my love. With your permission I shall put it in trust for our first son. I don't need it," he countered. It was her move.

One winged dark eyebrow raised slightly. "You read the contract, didn't you? My wealth remains mine."

"Of course, my dear. I will dower any children we have. I know you'll want to provide for Willow. But if you had not a pennypiece, Skye, I'd have gladly dowered your daughter."

"Yet, it was said that you refused to dower your own."

"They were Mary's brats," he replied bitterly. "Little brown wrens like their mother, obviously capable of bearing only daughters. The three who survived the pox, however, seem to have something of me in them. They'll be good company for Willow, and since I can see from the mutinous expression in your eyes that you'll give me trouble unless I dower my daughters, I promise to do so."

"I shall be a good mother to your children, Geoffrey."

"I know that, Skye." He rose and moved toward her, the longing in his eyes almost too painful to behold, but she held him at arm's length.

"Not yet, Geoffrey. Please, not yet."

"You have not forgiven me then." It was a statement.

"I can understand your not writing to me from Devon. It must have been terrible for you there. Yet when you returned you sent no word, and I had to learn from de Grenville of your misfortunes. And he said the Queen was arranging a match for you with an heiress. What was I to think?"

"You might have trusted me, Skye."

"How could you expect my trust after I learned of the infamous wager that you made with Dickon?"

"Damn, Skye. I never meant to collect from him! Surely you see that the wager happened before you and I truly met."

"Your reputation preceded you, my lord, Geoffrey Southwood, the Angel Earl, the great cocksman, and breaker of hearts."

"Enough, dammit. Woman, you argue with too much logic. I love you, Skye. I will always love you. In a few short hours we are to be wed. Let us forget what is past and begin afresh. We are well matched, madam." He held out his hand to her then. Slowly, after a long, agonized wait, she took it.

"One question," he said, "and I shall never ask this question again. Did you love him?"

"Yes," she replied gravely. "I loved him. I awoke from some unremembered horror to find safety with him. He gave me a name, an identity, a reason for living. He was my husband, he was my lover, he was my best friend. I will never forget him." She continued after a silence. "I find it strange to say this, but though Khalid el Bey will always hold a claim on a part of my heart, I love you also, Geoffrey. Why else would I have been so angry and so hurt?"

The lime-green eyes regarded her now with hope as well as longing. "Then I am forgiven, Skye?"

The smile she offered was tremulous. "Perhaps, my lord," she said mischievously.

"Madam, you try my patience," he growled, but his lips twitched at the corners and his eyes were bright with both relief and mirth.

"You had best cultivate patience, my lord, for I will be no meek wife, Geoffrey. I will be an equal partner with you in this marriage. Equal in all things."

She was more trusting now, and immediately he took advantage. Pulling her toward him, he wrapped both his arms about her, then bent to find her lips. A delicious tremor shot through her and she sighed deeply. "Madam," he said, kissing the corners of her mouth, her eyelids, the tip of her nose, "it's a cool, wet day, and were we not to be wed in just a few hours I should take you to bed right now."

"Do you require several hours, my lord?" Her face was a study in innocence.

"Vixen!" he murmured huskily, burying his face in the scented tangle of her hair. She felt his kisses burning into the satiny skin of her neck. With a low moan she threw her head back and his lips devoured her throat, setting her pulse to racing.

"Beware, madam. Tonight I shall seek revenge for your sharp tongue. But today when you enter the Queen's chapel, you will look chaste, not newly tumbled." He loosed her slowly and she swayed unsteadily. He laughed softly and, turning, departed through the secret door behind the tapestry.

Skye stood trembling. Dear God, how he could arouse her. And he knew it. She became aware of pounding at the door. "Mistress Skye! Mistress Skye! Are you all right?" She flew to the door and opened it to find Daisy, Hawise, and Jane standing there with anxious faces.

"I wanted to be alone," she conjured as best she could.

They gave her funny looks, then continued into the room bearing a breakfast, which was placed on a small table. Two footmen followed and removed the tub. Jane folded the screen and put it away while Daisy and Hawise drew the breakfast table and a chair up near the fire.

"Cook says you are to eat everything. Knowing how you've picked at your food lately, and you'll not eat much later," said Daisy. "Also, it will be hours before the bridal feast."

Skye sat down and, lifting the cover on the largest dish, found two perfectly poached eggs in a light cream sauce of sherry and dill. A small platter held several thin slices of pink ham, and wrapped inside a napkin set in a basket were several slices of steaming hot bread. Two crocks held butter and honey, and there was a carafe of deep red wine. She was suddenly ravenous.

"Tell Cook she is to be commended on the menu, Hawise. I shall eat it all! Daisy, my jewel case, please. I must pick out my jewelry while eating. Jane, find the gown I had made up for Dame Cecily and bring it to her. Then fetch Willow and her nurse."

The two undermaids hurried off and Daisy brought Skye's huge jewel box. Skye pursed her red lips, considering. Simple pearls were too dull, diamonds too harsh. What was needed was some color! Her fingers sifted impatiently through the many necklaces until she located what she sought. She smiled, quite satisfied with the turquoise necklace. Each polished oval turquoise was surrounded by alternating translucent pearls and fiery diamonds. There were matching earbobs, and two hair ornaments shaped like butterflies. "These," she said, handing them to Daisy. "Now for rings . . . a turquoise for luck, a pink pearl for constancy, and a sapphire to match my bonnie blue eyes."

Daisy giggled. Setting aside the chosen pieces, she removed the large case. "I've a message for you from Captain Small, m'lady. He says though the river's calm, it would be best to go to Greenwich in the carriage. The rain is quite heavy."

"Very well, Daisy. Ah, here's my little love," cried Skye happily as her bedchamber door opened to admit Willow and her nurse.

"Mama! Mama!" the child cried, running into Skye's open arms. "Smell good! Willow likes," she said, burying her little face in her mother's neck.

Skye swept the baby up and cuddled her in her lap. "Today, my poppet," she said, "I have a fine present for you. I shall bring you home a papa. Would you like that, Willow?"

"No!" said the baby stoutly. "No new papa! Want Uncle Robbie!"

Skye chuckled. "So it's Uncle Robbie who has captured your heart, my darling. You've good taste. But you'll soon love your new papa too and he'll love you."

Willow pouted, her little rosebud mouth set in disapproval.

The thick dark lashes that fringed her golden eyes—eyes like her father's—swept down to brush her pink cheeks, then swept upward in such a flirtatious adult manner that Skye caught her breath with surprise.

"Will my new papa bring Willow presents?" she asked slyly.

"Indeed he will, greedy one," replied her mother, amused.

"What?" The question was an imperious demand.

"I don't know, my pet. Perhaps a new gown, or a necklace, or a wee basket of sweetmeats."

"Maybe I'll like my new papa," said Willow thoughtfully. "Do you like him, Mama?"

Skye laughed. "Yes, poppet, I like him very much. Now give Mama a kiss and run off to play with Maudie. If you are very good I'll bring you something from Greenwich Palace."

Willow kissed her mother and then trotted happily off with her nurse. Skye finished up the last of her meal as the mantel clock struck half past eleven.

"Oh, Lord! You must leave here by noon if you're to reach Greenwich on time," exclaimed Daisy. "You, Jane, Hawise! Bring the mistress's clothes." She handed Skye a pair of cream-colored stockings so finely knitted they seemed spun of cobwebs. Skye slid them on carefully. Beaming, Daisy handed her the garters with silver lace rosettes, each flower center a tiny freshwater pearl. Skye's undergarments were pure silk. A small-boned corset made her small waist even tinier. Her farthingale was a modified one, for Skye had no wish to look like a merchant ship under sail. Before putting it on, she sat quietly while Daisy did her hair.

It was brushed once again, then parted in the center and drawn back over her ears. Daisy fashioned the thick, silken mass into an elegant and graceful chignon that centered on the nape of Skye's neck. The butterfly ornaments were secured, one in the front, one on the right side of her head. As a finishing touch Daisy carefully set two perfect pink rosebuds into the chignon.

Skye sat and stared at her image. A flawless-faced woman stared back at her. *Is that me?* she thought. And for the first time in many months she began to wonder who she really was. Who had she been before Khalid el Bey had found her? Suddenly she desperately wanted her own identity back.

"Madam," Daisy's voice interrupted her thoughts. "We *must* hurry!"

Skye nodded and stood. On went the farthingale, and then it was time for the gown. Chattering excitedly, Jane and Hawise fastened it up. Skye smoothed the skirt and stepped in front of her pier glass. A slow smile lit her features. She was well satisfied. She looked every inch the Countess of Lynmouth. Geoffrey would have every reason to be proud of her.

"Oh, my lady," breathed Daisy reverently, "you're beautiful!"

"Thank you, Daisy. Now my cloak, lest the rain spoil my gown."

A deep-blue velvet cape was draped about her shoulders, and Skye left her apartments to descend the staircase. Robbie and Dame Cecily awaited her and she swept them both a low curtsey. "How magnificent you both look!" Truly she'd never seen either of them looking better.

Dame Cecily's gown was of elegant black silk with an underskirt of cloth of silver. She had a white lace ruff at her neck and lace ruffles at her wrists. On her silver hair she wore a peaked cap of stiff black silk edged in silver lace. Upon her ample bosom rested a silver chain with a heart-shaped pendant cut from turquoise. Dame Cecily's light-blue eyes twinkled with pleasure. "My dear Skye, how can I thank you for this beautiful gown? And an ermine cloak! I was despairing over what to wear to Greenwich, and on such short notice too!"

Skye was pleased by the older woman's evident delight. "I had the ensemble made for your birthday next month," she confessed. "Now I must find you another gift."

"Dear child! This is more than enough, and what matter that you've presented it to me a wee bit early? This is the perfect occasion to wear such a fine gown."

"Nevertheless you'll have a gift on your birthday too," vowed Skye.

"Is there no compliment for me then, lass?" complained the little captain.

"Why Robbie, you know you're the prettiest of us all," teased Skye.

"Hummph!" said Robbie, but a small smile played about his mouth, and he preened without knowing he did so. Skye hadn't seen him so magnificently attired since the night she had first met him. Like his sister, he was garbed in black, but where she wore silk he wore velvet, the doublet heavily embroidered with gold thread, aquamarines, pearls, and rubies. The sword at his side had a gold-filigreed hilt with a large ruby knob. "Let us go, lass," said Robbie as he heard the coach draw up before the house. When the front door was opened the wind blew their capes wildly about them and rain thrust its way into the house, wetting the marble floor. Without a word the tallest of the footmen swept Skye up and carried her out through the tempest to the safety of her carriage. A flustered Dame Cecily and blushing Daisy were also deposited carefully. Robert Small climbed in under his own steam.

The trip to Greenwich was a relatively easy one, for the roads had been emptied by the ferocity of the storm. The rain drove against the brightly painted coach, pouring down the windows in sheets. It was impossible to see out. Skye felt a surge of pity for her coachman, high up on the box, muffled against the weather but still prey to it. Even worse off were the footmen who clung behind the vehicle, the rain pouring down over them.

Inside the coach, Skye clung to Robert Small's hand. She had not been frightened when she married Khalid el Bey, but now she was a little afraid. Added to her trepidation was the realization that she would soon have to tell Geoffrey of the child. She could well imagine his joy, but then what if it was not a son? Would he one day attempt to banish her, as he had poor Mary Bowen? She felt her spine stiffen. She would never allow him to treat her in such a fashion. And if he ever tried, she would appeal to the Queen.

The coach slowed to a clattering halt at Greenwich, and the ladies were carried into the palace by the Queen's own guards. Greenwich Palace, much beloved of Henry VIII, was built along the river for a seemingly endless distance and stood three stories tall. A palace official escorted them to a small room next to the chapel where they might freshen themselves and repair any damage to their clothing. Daisy helped Skye and Dame Cecily off with their cloaks. The hood of Skye's cloak had protected her head, so there was little to do.

Dame Cecily drew a small lace-edged square from a hidden pocket in her gown and pressed it upon Skye. "For luck, my dear, and I wish you great happiness," she said tearfully, kissing the younger woman. Then Dame Cecily disappeared into the chapel, Daisy following behind.

Suddenly everything was moving too quickly. Robbie was there, leading her through the door, into the chapel, and up the aisle. The room was packed. Skye didn't know most of them, although she spied de Grenville, Lettice Knollys, the Queen, and Lord Dudley, who was rumored to be her lover. Even Lord and Lady Burke were there.

Geoffrey stood waiting before the altar, resplendent in hunter-green velvet. Matthew Parker, the archbishop of Canterbury, waited behind Geoffrey.

Slowly she and her beloved Robbie moved up the aisle. Skye felt as if her legs were encased in glue. Ahead of her, Geoffrey Southwood radiated approval of her attire. His eyes smiled encouragingly. They stopped, and Robbie firmly placed Skye's hand into Geoffrey's large paw. Geoffrey's warmth transmitted itself to her. He gently squeezed her hand and she drew a deep breath of relief. It was going to be all right.

The archbishop droned through the service, and, as they knelt, their heads close together, Geoffrey whispered softly to her, "Courage, my love." She felt a stab of love for him race through her. The unease she had felt at the sight of the hot, crowded candlelit chapel was slowly being dispelled by his love. Matthew Parker pronounced them man and wife and, turning them about, presented the newly wedded couple to the assembled congregation. They smiled happily into the sea of faces that all smiled back at them . . . all but one. Why was Lord Burke's face so dark with anger? He was such a strange man, and why was he here at all? She turned away and curtseyed low to Queen Elizabeth, who was magnificently attired in purest white silk sewn with gold thread, diamonds, and palest blue aquamarine. Her Majesty spoke graciously.

"Rise my lady Southwood, Countess of Lynmouth. We are pleased to have you at Court, and welcome you right heartily."

"Majesty, how can I thank you for your kindness? It is all so much."

"You may show your gratitude, my dear Skye, by being a good and faithful wife to your lord, and by cleaving to him only," replied the young Queen primly.

"I shall, Majesty," replied Skye, fervently kissing the hand Elizabeth extended.

"That will be a terrible blow to all the eager gallants," murmured Lord Dudley softly to Lettice Knollys. She swallowed back her laughter with much effort.

"And now," cried the Queen gaily, "let us away to the bridal feast! Let the Earl and Countess of Lynmouth lead the way to the Great Hall!"

Skye sent Geoffrey a startled look. Taking her arm, he reassured her, "I know the way, my love." Accompanied by capering musicians who played on reedy pipes, lutes, and drums, the couple led the Queen and her court into the Great Hall of Greenwich Palace.

Outside, the rain beat fiercely against the tall ornate windows, but inside, the great hearths burned cheerfully with enormous oak logs. The head table accommodated the bridal couple, the Queen, Lord Dudley, and Captain Sir Robert Small and his sister, who had acted as the orphaned bride's parents. The rest of the Court knew their places, many from habit, and found them now either along the length of the T-shaped head table or at smaller tables set up along the walls.

The servants placed an enormous salt cellar upon the main table. Two standing winged silver griffons and two standing gold lions together held up a carved coral seashell filled with salt. The goblets were pale-pink blown Venetian glass, the Queen's crest carved upon an oval piece of garnet and affixed to each. Golden plates were placed before those at the head table. The other guests seated above the salt had to be satisfied with silver, and those below the salt with simple crockery.

A parade of liveried servants began the circulation of an enormous feast. The first course consisted of the usual bowls of icy cold raw oysters, mussels and scallops broiled with herbs and butter, tiny prawns in white wine, thinly sliced salmon on a bed of young watercress, whole sea trout, and great loaves of both brown and white bread. The next course offered sides of beef, whole roast red roe deer, legs of lamb. A whole great boar with wicked curved tusks rested upon a huge silver platter which had to be carried in by four footmen. There were small, sweet roast suckling pigs with apples in their mouths, gingered capons, big pink hams, swans stuffed with fruit, geese, roast pheasants and peacocks served with their full colorful plumage, larded ducks, steaming pies made with lark, pigeon, dove, sparrow, and rabbit. There were bowls of new lettuce, scallions, radishes, and artichokes. The servants kept everyone's goblets full to the brim with a deep red heady Burgundy.

Skye ate little, disliking huge feasts where the menus were far too heavy. A few oysters, a capon wing, a thin slice of suckling pig, and some lettuce satisfied her. She noted thankfully that Geoffrey was as abstemious as she, choosing oysters, a small slice each of the beef and the goose, an artichoke, and some bread and butter.

The last course of sweets and subtleties arrived with a profusion of colorful molded jellies, fruit pies, plum cakes, early strawberries with bowls of clotted cream, early cherries from France, oranges from Spain, and wheels of Cheshire cheese. There was, of course, an enormous sugar-iced wedding cake. To Skye's great relief, the cake did not have the usual marzipan bride and groom figures with their overly endowed sexual organs and breasts. Instead, the cake top was decorated by a small bouquet of tiny white roses and blue forget-me-nots, all tied with silver ribbons. Somehow Skye knew this was the Queen's touch, and she leaned across Lord Dudley and thanked her.

The Queen smiled quietly. "He loves you very much, Skye. I have not seen such true love and devotion in all my life. How I wish I might have such a love to help me sustain my great burdens."

"Why surely you can, madam!" said Skye. "There are any number of gentlemen willing to lay their hearts at your feet."

The Queen smiled again, sadly this time. How innocent the new Countess of Lynmouth was! How sheltered she must have been before coming to England. "There are many men willing to lay their hearts at my feet, Skye, but none really loves me. They seek my crown, or a part of it. They do not want Elizabeth. A queen who rules in her own right has no true love. She is wed to her country. That is the harshest to serve of all lords."

"Oh, madam!" Skye's eyes filled with tears.

The young Queen gently brushed a tear from the bride's cheek. "Why, my lady Southwood, what a soft heart you have. But weep not for me. I knew my fate a long time ago. I accepted it, and I wanted it." Then thoughtfully she said, "I think, my kind-hearted little Countess, that I shall call upon you to serve as one of my ladies. An honest, open heart is a rare thing at Court."

Skye shortly found out how right the Queen was. After the tiny cordial glasses of spiced hippocras wine and thin sugar wafers that officially ended a banquet were served, the dancing began at the other end of the hall. The bride danced first with her new husband, then with Lord Dudley. After that she was prey to all the gentlemen. Several were forward enough to suggest assignations while staring boldly down her dress. Skye was shocked. The morals of the Islamic world she remembered had been quite strict. Here at Greenwich they appeared to be lax indeed.

She soon found herself partnered by the scowling Lord Burke. Did the man never smile? "My felicitations, madam. You have done quite well for yourself." His tone was most insulting, and she found herself once again infuriated by the man. She fixed him with a level gaze and asked, "Why, my lord, are you so hostile to me? Have I done you some injury of which I am not aware? Pray speak, sir, that I may correct whatever fault it is that offends you."

Wordlessly he drew her from the dance floor and led her to the table where refreshments were being served. His silver eyes probed her face, never looking away. Suddenly he asked, "Have you ever heard of the O'Malleys of Innisfana Island, madam?"

She thought a moment, then replied, "I am sorry, Lord Burke, but I have not. Is it important to you?"

"No," he said roughly. "It is of no account, madam." But he appeared almost distraught. *Why?* she asked herself.

Dame Cecily bustled up just then. "It's time you got ready for bed, my dear. Here are Mistress Lettice and some of the Queen's ladies to help you."

"Lady Southwood." Lord Burke bowed curtly over her hand. Then he turned and walked away.

Skye and her female companions left the hall discreetly. "Her Majesty," confided Lettice Knollys, "has given you an apartment in a quiet part of the palace. You'll be quite private. How I envy you this night! Southwood is said to be a magnificent lover!"

"Lettice!" scolded another of the Queen's ladies, "if Her Majesty should hear such loose talk, you'll be sent down to the country."

The Queen's red-haired cousin tossed her beautiful head. "The Queen would sell her soul to be the bride this night if Lord Dudley were the groom."

"Lettice!" cried several scandalized voices, "you speak treason!" but Lettice Knollys simply laughed. "Ah, here we are, Skye," she announced as she paused before a door.

The guards flung open the door, and the chattering women entered into a prettily furnished bedchamber where Daisy awaited her mistress along with two palace maids.

The large oak bedstead held up ornately twisted bedposts which were hung with pink velvet hangings. To the left of the bed, casement windows looked out toward the rain-swept river. To the right of the bed was a large stone fireplace, now blazing with enough warmth to have removed all dampness from the room and rendered it cozy.

Daisy and her two assistants set to work immediately disrobing the bride. Wearing only a single petticoat and her underblouse, Skye bathed in rosewater from a silver basin. Then her hair was taken down and brushed until it gleamed. The blue-gold lights were the envy of most of the women in the room. Now Daisy brought forth the nightgown, the two undermaids removed the last of the bride's clothing, and the nightgown slid down and over her. The Queen's ladies gasped in shock and envy, for the nightgown clung to Skye as if it had been painted on her. It was made of pure white silk, the bodice forming a deep V, the sleeves wide like butterfly wings, the skirt a mass of tiny pleats.

"God's blood!" Lettice Knollys voiced all their thoughts. "That gown will not be long on you, my dear Skye."

"But will he leave it in one piece?" murmured one woman. The rest of the ladies giggled.

Skye blushed and then laughed nervously. "It is said to be a copy of one worn by the Pope's mistress."

"Hurry," called one of the women, "I can hear them coming." They helped her into bed, plumping the fat lace-edged pillows behind her back and smoothing the down-filled satin coverlet. She felt very foolish, the center of all this attention in what should have been a private moment. She remembered how she and Khalid el Bey had slipped away from their guests on their wedding night to ride down the moonlit beach to the Pearl Kiosk. But she was not in Algeria, she was in England. It was not Khalid el Bey she eagerly awaited, but Geoffrey Southwood.

The door burst open, admitting a laughing crowd of men and women. Geoffrey Southwood was pushed forward. He was barechested, "We've half undressed him, madam," said Lord Dudley with a drunken grin. His arm was around the Queen in a proprietary manner, and Elizabeth was flushed and looking very pretty.

"I shall finish the job myself," said Lord Southwood firmly. "For the Countess and myself, I bid you all a good night."

"Come, everyone," the Queen called, throwing the newlyweds a sympathetic look. "I have not yet tired of dancing."

The courtiers and servants all filed out and the Earl shut the door behind them and threw the bolt hard. Wordlessly he stripped off the rest of his clothing and blew out the candles. The firelight played on his lean frame and golden hair. He turned and held out a hand to her. "Come to me, Skye."

She rose from the bed and walked toward him. A slow smile lit his face. He took in the full effect of her gown and the grin grew. The tiny skirt pleats undulated to show her long legs, and when she stood before him he quietly hooked his hands on either side of the neckline and tore the gown away. Laughing, she flung her arms about him. He could feel his passion flame and, taking her face in his hands, he pressed a kiss upon her half-opened lips.

"I love you, Skye," he murmured huskily.

"And I love you, my lord," she answered, her deep blue eyes shining.

His hands slid slowly from her perfect shoulders down her

smooth, long, fair back, until he could cup and gently squeeze each sweetly rounded buttock. "I have missed you so," he sighed, softly bending his head to capture a taut nipple in his warm mouth. Teasingly his tongue encircled it again and again until he felt her quiver. Sliding to his knees, his mouth moved with maddening slowness downward until at last his probing tongue slipped between the pouting lips of her woman's center. She whimpered, "Please!"

He raised his head and gazed at her. "Please what, Skye?"

"Please!" she repeated, and pulling away from him, fled to the bed and flung herself upon it. Laughing softly, he joined her, pinioning her beneath him. "Do you want me, my wanton little wife?" he teased. "No, Skye, don't turn your head away from me. I want to see your lovely face when I take you. Ah, sweetheart, there's nothing wrong in wanting this. Tell me, love! Tell me!"

"Yes! Yes! Yes!" she half sobbed, and he filled her full, his own excitement mounting as her beautiful eyes told him all the things she was even now too shy to say aloud. He was incredibly gentle, and this very gentleness roused her wildly. Her passion again acted as a spur to his own desire until it exploded within her as hers exploded.

They lay exhausted and then he pulled her into his arms, caressing her soft hair, her trembling body. "Ah, love," he murmured low, "now we have officially sealed the bargain we made today before the archbishop. I love you, Skye, and I shall always make you happy. I swear it!"

She turned in his arms so that she faced him, and said quietly, "Your child already grows in my womb."

"Thank you, my darling," he answered. Puzzled by his lack of surprise, she realized that he must have guessed her secret.

"Geoffrey—you *knew*? Is that why you asked me to marry you?" He could see the hurt mounting in her eyes. "I am no bitch to be bred!" she cried furiously.

"I did not know until after I had asked you," he said quickly.

"Robbie told you," she accused. "Damn him for a meddling old woman!"

"Aye, he told me. I was close to either strangling you, or beating you black and blue. You are the most stubborn, wayward witch I've ever met, Skye Southwood! The child you carry is *both* yours and mine, and I want it! You've no right to deny it me simply because your pride fears I might love our child more than I love you! I will love the babe, but I shall never love anyone or anything as I love you, Skye. Whatever I had to do to get you to marry me I would do again!"

She was stunned by the intensity of his voice, and unable to find the words of reply. She heard him begin to chuckle softly, and the chuckle grew until the chamber was filled by the sound of his laughter. "So!" he crowed. "I've finally rendered you speechless, you overproud, overtalkative Irish wench! Mayhap now you will finally admit to my mastery over you. Surely no one has ever rendered you speechless before now."

The angry reply died on her lips at the sight of his bright lime-green eyes, which were tender and full with love.

"I have a terrible temper," she said in a small voice.

"Aye," he agreed gravely, "you do."

"I do not like injustice of any kind."

"Nor do I, my love. Nevertheless, it is not a perfect world we live in, as you well know. And there are no perfect humans living in it, as you also know."

"I will not be chattel, Geoffrey. I have guided my own destiny too long."

"Were you so independent with Khalid el Bey, my darling? I cannot imagine the wife of a Moorish gentleman being given such great freedom."

What a strange conversation to be having on my wedding night, she thought. *Here I am lying naked in my second husband's arms calmly discussing my previous lord!* "Khalid," she said slowly, "respected my intelligence. It was he, along with his secretary, who taught me how to run his business and handle his investments. He used to jest that if anything happened to him I should surprise everyone by being able to take care of his interests."

Geoffrey Southwood mused on his wife's words. He had, since meeting Skye, thoroughly investigated the reputation of Khalid el Bey. It had not been easy, for the distance between Algiers and England was great, but his curiosity had been piqued by this man of notorious repute who had taken in and then lost his heart to a nameless lost waif. What he had learned had surprised Geoffrey. Despite his rather unsavory business, Khalid el Bey was considered a gentleman. He was noted for his honesty, his charitable nature, and his charm.

It was this last that gave Geoffrey Southwood the most difficulty. It had never mattered to him whether his woman of the moment had had other men; but Skye was different—and she was his wife. Was she already comparing her two husbands? It fretted him, and unwittingly he crushed her to him.

"Geoffrey!"

His mouth savaged hers, blazing a burning trail down her neck and across her breasts. "Do you compare me to Khalid el Bey, Skye?" he asked fiercely.

She understood instantly. He had never really been secure in a woman's love. Her heart went out to him. "Oh Geoffrey," she said softly, wrapping her arms around him. "There is *no* comparison. Khalid was Khalid and you are you. I loved him for what he was as I love you for what you are." She raised his head and kissed his mouth sweetly. "I love you, my lord Southwood, but sometimes you play the fool."

And he did feel very foolish.

"Is this how you would spend our wedding night, my lord?" she asked teasingly. "Now that we have discussed my first husband, shall we speak of the many ladies who have graced your bed, sir?"

"Madam," he growled, trying to gather the remaining shreds of his dignity, and then he heard her muffled giggles. "Oh, witch," he laughed, "would anyone believe such a conversation between two lovers who are newly married?" Then he covered her face with kisses, and she sighed happily, which only made him laugh again.

"I shall not be able to hide my condition much longer, Geoffrey," she said thoughtfully, "and the Queen has asked that I join her ladies."

"When is the babe due, my love?"

"In early autumn, after the harvest."

"Do you feel all right?" he asked anxiously.

"Sometimes in the evenings I feel queasy," she admitted. "It's the smell of roasting meat that does it to me, though tonight, thank God, I was not so distressed."

"I want you in Devon as soon as possible," he said. "We will hide your condition a month and then you must go."

"It would be better if I went in two or three," she said. "To admit my pregnancy in less than two months' time would be to bring the Queen's anger down upon us. She is a very moral lady, Geoffrey. Besides, it will be safer for me to travel later than now. We can avoid following the Court for a month or so, for Her Majesty will not deny us a honeymoon. Then, when we do return to the Queen's service, I shall feign sickness. Everyone will be praising your virility long before we make our joyful announcement. Then, if you wish to escort me to Devon, it will be permitted and we will offend no one."

"I begin to see," said the Earl of Lynmouth, "why Khalid el Bey trusted your judgment. To find such a clever mind lodged in such a beautiful body is astounding."

"I trust you mean to flatter me, my lord," she said drily.

"Yes, witch. I mean to flatter you!" And tumbling her back amid the plump feather pillows of their bed, he kissed and tickled her until her happy laughter could be heard as far away as the ballroom.

Chapter 18

Niall Burke slouched deep in a large chair in the study of his London house, staring out as the gray dawn rose over the dark and rainy river. A fire crackled merrily in the large fireplace, but the big Irishman scowled blackly, ignoring its warmth. He clutched in his clenched fist a large goblet from which the odor of spiced red wine rose. Around the house the sou'wester that had dampened Lord Southwood's wedding was roaring itself out.

A blast rattled the windows, and Burke glowered again. The wedding of Mistress Goya del Fuentes and the Earl of Lynmouth had been hell for Niall. He and Constanza stood with the rest of the Court watching as the most beautiful bride he'd ever seen was married to a very handsome groom. It had been torture. For, in his mind, he saw again the candlelit chapel of the O'Malley tower house, and a hollow-eyed, frightened young bride whose face was whiter than her gown. He remembered how he had flung open the chapel doors only a moment too late, how she had fainted upon seeing him, how he had outrageously demanded the *droit du seigneur.* Most of all, he remembered how sweetly she had yielded.

"Skye!" he whispered softly, saying her name aloud for the first time in many months. "Oh, Skye, how I love you!" He was so painfully confused, and the new Countess of Lynmouth was responsible. She was *his* Skye's identical twin. He ached with longing for her, yet he was ashamed. Upstairs slept his sweet and faithful young wife, alone in their bed while he sulked downstairs, lusting in his heart for another woman, a dead woman, and another man's wife.

Damn the Countess of Lynmouth, he thought bitterly, reaching for the decanter. What he should be thinking of was an heir, not a dead woman. He had been married to Constanza for almost two years now, and there had been no sign of a child. Had he not scattered his share of bastards about, he might be worried about himself, but obviously the fault lay with Constanza. He had wanted to return home to Ireland with both a wife and a child. The MacWilliam was growing old, and the reassurance of another heir would cheer the elderly man greatly.

They had lingered on Mallorca for several months after their marriage, then begun a leisurely wedding journey through Mediterranean Spain, to Provence in France, and up to Paris. They had stayed the winter in Paris—a happy, gay time in which he had fully initiated her into the sensual world of lovemaking and she had proved an eager pupil. Sometimes he wondered if perhaps she wasn't too eager. Had he not been certain of her virginity when they had first made love, he would have had his doubts about Constanza's character, for her enthusiasm was, he thought, unseemly. Then he cursed himself for a fool. How many men mounted cringing, cold women who lay like stone beneath them "doing their duty" while they said the rosaries to themselves, hating what was being done to them? Constanza enjoyed their lovemaking. He ought to be glad.

He would go to her now. He would slip into her bedchamber and she would be warm and fragrant with sleep. He would kiss her awake, then take her slowly, savoring her passion. She would whimper with pleasure and claw at his back. He made to rise but a wave of dizziness overcame him and he fell back. The room seemed overwarm. He sipped again at his wine, and suddenly he was so tired. His eyes closed, the heavy goblet fell from his grasp to the rug, and a small snore issued from his open mouth. Niall Burke slept a deep drunken sleep.

A few minutes later the library door opened softly and very slowly. Constanza Burke and Ana looked into the room. A look of annoyance crossed young Lady Burke's face and her pansy-purple eyes narrowed in anger. "He is drunk again," she snapped. "He has been drinking all night. In the name of all that is holy, Ana, what manner of man is he?"

"He is unhappy, *niña*. Perhaps it is the lack of a child that makes him so."

"Can he sire one on me in this condition?" she snapped. Then her voice softened. "Ana, fetch my cloak."

"*Niña!* No, no! Not again!"

"Ana, I burn! I must or I shall die."

"I will soothe it, *niña*."

"It is not enough, Ana! I must have a man! I must! If you won't fetch my cloak I shall go without it and my white nightgown will be a beacon to the entire household."

With a sob Ana went for the dark, enveloping cape. Constanza walked across the room and stood looking down at her husband. Why had he drunk himself into a stupor? This had begun only recently. When they first came to London all had been well, but in the last few months he had changed, quite suddenly, and for no apparent reason. Now he often drank himself into a stupor. Perhaps if he hadn't changed, she herself wouldn't have changed. But Constanza knew this wasn't so.

It had all begun so insidiously. One night, in an excess of passion, he had taken her four times. But when finally he lay contented and happy, she lay awake and yearning. It was not that he had not satisfied her. He had. Each time had been better than the last. But suddenly it was not enough. And it never was enough anymore. She had grown edgy with her constant longings.

Then, one day, their head groom had been helping her to mount her mare and his hand slid up her leg farther than it should have. She said nothing and the hand moved higher yet until it was stroking the soft, wet place between her thighs, bringing her to a swift, delightful climax. The hand was slowly withdrawn and, without a word spoken between them, Constanza rode out from the stables with the head groom, his face impassive, riding at her side.

When they returned an hour later he lifted her down from her horse and carried her into the darkened stable loft. Constanza had been driven half mad by the friction of her saddle and the motion of her horse against her already inflamed body. She offered no objections when the head groom pushed her skirts up to her waist. He stared down at her for a moment.

"So it's true, then," he whispered wonderingly.

"What?"

"Ladies pluck their cunny hair," he answered. Then he dropped on top of her. What Harry lacked in skill he made up for with vigor, pumping against her until he had fulfilled her twice.

Afterward she felt guilty and ashamed, but as her needs far outweighed her guilt the interludes with Harry became a regular part of her life. At Court she was ogled by several young bucks, but instinct told her to be wary.

Sometime later, she had lost a little of that wariness and agreed to an assignation with Lord Basingstoke, an older gentleman who seemed pleased to believe he had seduced a bride. But even having two lovers was not enough for Constanza any longer. Her lust was a sickness she could not rid herself of, and soon she did not even wonder at herself anymore. She was careful, however, that no one knew her terrible secret. She was not a wicked woman, and she loved her husband. But she would not, could not, stop.

Constanza did not hear Ana return. She looked up only when the heavy velvet cloak was dropped over her shoulders.

"M'lord?" asked Ana.

"Leave him," she answered quietly. "He is sleeping soundly, and in any case I will not be long."

"*Niña,* please. I beg of you."

"Ana! I cannot help myself." And so saying, Constanza Burke swept from the library and out of her house through a little-used side door. In the half-light of the early morning she made her way to the stables and the room in the loft where Harry slept. With a proprietary air she opened the door and, looking in, saw a naked Harry sleeping with an equally naked Polly, one of the kitchen maids. For a few moments she watched them, fascinated, then Polly opened her eyes and stared at her mistress, horrified. Constanza smiled and put a warning finger to her lips. Shrugging off the cloak, she stripped her white silk nightgown from her lush body and climbed into bed on the other side of Harry.

Polly lay stiff and frozen next to the groom. Suddenly her mistress's face was over hers, looking down at the frightened girl.

"Suck him," came the soft command. "Together we can drive him mad. What a bull he'll be then."

Polly scrambled to obey her mistress, no longer afraid. And while she eagerly did her part Constanza's little tongue darted into and around Harry's ear. The sleeping man stirred. Polly worked feverishly while Constanza blew softly into the groom's ear. Harry groaned as his loins were filled with a fierce burning, and he opened his eyes, amazed by the sight that greeted him. His mighty shaft grew until Polly could hold it no longer and fell back. The groom was quickly atop her, ramming fiercely. Constanza watched, her slim fingers playing with herself until suddenly she felt Harry's eyes upon her and looked up to meet his lascivious grin.

He had not spent himself yet, though Polly lay gasping her pleasure beneath him. Rolling off the girl, he pulled Constanza beneath him and teasingly moved himself against her engorged and throbbing sex. Constanza whimpered and strained her body upward. But he denied her. Instead, and with a refinement that shattered her, he rubbed himself over her entire body until she was begging him to take her. With a wink at Polly, Harry jammed himself forcefully into Constanza and moved swiftly back and forth until he finally wrung from her a series of cries.

Afterward, as the three of them lay side by side, Polly ventured shyly, "My friend Claro would never believe this—and her a popular madam with her own place. But if you wasn't the mistress, I'd introduce you to Claro. She could sure use a girl like you."

Harry laughed at the outrageous idea, but later, when she had returned to her own bed, Constanza thought the idea over. Perhaps it was the answer to her problem. When the yearning overcame her she could sneak off to the whore's house and indulge herself. She would be masked, but that would add a certain piquancy to her performance. Suddenly the horror of what she was thinking swept over her and she scrambled from her bed to kneel at her prie-dieu.

"Holy Mother," she fervently prayed, "let me not do this terrible thing. Wipe my mind clean of such thoughts. I beg thee!"

Then her eyes strayed to the exquisite leather-bound book that lay on the table by her bed. It had been a gift from her lover, Lord Basingstoke, and had been brought to England by a Portuguese sea captain who had obtained it in India. Constanza rose from her knees and, sitting back on the bed, opened the book. Inside were pages and pages with beautiful and colorful illustrations of men, women, and animals performing a wide range of sexual acts, from the most pristine to the most perverted. Mesmerized, she slowly turned the pages. Her breathing had quickened and, despite her recent activity, she felt her need growing again.

Ringing for her maid, she ordered her bath and asked that her riding clothes be laid out. By the time she approached the stables the fires of her desires were growing again. She stood quietly while Harry saw to the saddling of their mounts, but the impatient tapping of her riding crop against her boot told him that her passions were riding high once more. He sighed. Her fires seemed unquenchable, though God knew he tried. There had never been a woman he couldn't satisfy but, by Heaven, the mistress was a rare one.

They rode sedately from the house along the river road to a secluded thicket where they tethered the horses. He took her on the mossy ground, his excitement heightened by the foul words she whispered breathily in his ear. As always, he was amazed by the capacity for pure lust in this madonna-faced woman. Later, as they rode on, she said in her soft, slightly accented voice, "I want to meet Polly's friend, Claro."

"Woman, you're mad!" he exclaimed. "I'm amazed that your

husband hasn't found out about you cuckolding him with me *and* Lord Basingstoke. Are you looking to get caught?"

"Let me worry about Niall. I want to meet the whore. If you won't arrange it with Polly then I must do so."

"If having a hundred cocks up your hot little cunt will help you, Connie, then I'll speak to Poll. 'Tis a sickness with you, I know that. There was a girl in my village in Hereford like you. She just couldn't get enough."

"What happened to her, Harry?"

"She died of the pox," he answered matter-of-factly. "What would you expect?"

Several days later, with Niall Burke off hunting with friends for a week in Hampshire, Constanza Burke and Harry rode into London. She fully expected to be led into a dank slum, so she was pleasantly surprised to find herself before a small well-kept house on the London Bridge itself.

The house was whitewashed and half-timbered, and each of the three stories extended out over the other, making it look a bit like a cake. One side of the house faced the street—the bridge actually was a street—while another side looked down onto the river traffic. This was a source of continuing delight to the bargemen, who enjoyed ogling and joking with the scantily clad women who sat fanning themselves in their windows on hot summer afternoons.

"I'll wait for you," Harry said, helping her dismount. She drew her hood up and knocked at the door. A little maidservant opened it almost immediately and Constanza quickly entered and followed the girl down a short hallway to a pleasant sunny room with a bay window overlooking the river.

An attractive blonde with sky-blue eyes awaited her, and when the servant girl had left, the woman spoke in a husky voice. "Good afternoon, my lady. I am Claro. Polly said you wished to see me. Now you do, so how may I serve you?"

Constanza felt suddenly shy and, turning away, mumbled, "I have made a mistake in coming here."

Claro laughed breathily. "No, my dear. Poll has told me *all* about you. You have an itch that needs constant scratching, and you would join me on occasion. Please don't be embarrassed. I should be delighted to have you with me. You'll stay masked whenever here, and no one will ever know your real identity. Is it a bargain, my dear?"

"You don't even know fully what I look like," said Constanza. "How can you be sure I'll be a success?"

"My dear," was the devastating reply, "as long as you will give the gentlemen a good jogging, it matters not if you're as ugly as sin itself. Remember that no one will ever see your face. I've half a dozen pretty lasses for those who like beauty with their play."

"What about the money?" asked Constanza.

"We'll split your earnings fifty-fifty," came the reply.

"*No!* I want none of it! Oh, God! Why did I come here?"

Claro laughed, then put a friendly arm about Constanza. "Don't be frightened, lovey. Being a whore takes getting used to, but you'll do beautifully." She sat Constanza down, gave her a small glass of a restorative cordial, then sat opposite her. "D'you think I was born a lightskirt then? My father was a nobleman with lands, but I ran off with my cousin and when he'd filled my belly, he left me. I couldn't go home. What else could I do?"

"You had a baby?" Constanza's purple eyes were wide with surprise.

"No," laughed Claro, "I wasn't so innocent that I didn't know how to get rid of the brat."

Constanza felt sick, and swallowed hard. Oblivious, Claro continued. "Your using a mask will certainly be enticing, but I wish you also had a specialty that would set you apart. A mask is not enough."

Constanza stared at her hostess, her fear suddenly gone. Claro was, she realized with surprise, simply a business woman. The cordial was beginning to work, and now Constanza had a wicked idea. "I have a book," she said.

"A book?"

"A book from the East, full of beautiful pictures of men and women, and some with animals. What if I offered each man who comes to me the opportunity to chose a page and duplicate that page?"

Claro's baby-blue eyes widened. "God's toenail! You've a quick mind for this, my dear. It's perfect! Now, when will you come to us?"

"Tonight," answered Constanza. "My lord is away for several days, and the truth is that I burn."

"Do not bother returning home now, my dear. Send your groom back for your book while you rest here," purred Claro. She rang a small silver bell and said to the little servant girl, "Take Madam to the Rose Room."

Wordlessly Constanza followed the maid out the door. As the door closed on the two, Claro spun about, hugging herself with glee. "Oh, Dom!" she said softly to the air above her. "Oh, my darling brother, at last I have a means of vengeance on Niall Burke for you! That milk-faced girl is his wife. His wife! And I'll make the fine Lord Burke's wife the most infamous whore in London! That, added to the death of your late bitch wife Skye, should destroy him for good!" And Claire O'Flaherty laughed wildly.

So it began. Soon gentlemen of the Court were circulating stories of the "Book Lady" who occasionally entertained at the house of the nobility's favorite whore, Claro. The Book Lady performed the most unspeakable and delicious acts of perversions. The Book Lady's lust was inexhaustible. That she was a lady was evident, but who she was was a favorite guessing game of the men who frequented Claro's house, and Elizabeth Tudor's Court.

And Constanza Burke, living her secret life, had never been happier. She had her husband, and Lord Basingstoke, and Harry the groom, and a host of noble lovers. Who would ever suspect that the innocent-looking Lady Burke of Elizabeth's Court was the wicked Book Lady?

Luck rode with her, for Niall Burke was lost in his personal world of sad memories and was hardly aware of his wife any longer. Had the Countess of Lynmouth not looked so much like his Skye, he would have gone on with his life. But now, seeing her frequently, his wounds bled again and again. What a fine joke fate had played on him, and he laughed bitterly and drank deeply of his wine.

One evening his wife's personal servant, Ana, entered his library and curtseyed before him. "My lord, I must speak with you." Ana was in a most difficult position. She could not allow her beloved child to go on as she was, yet to expose her sins to her husband would be worse. Ana believed that if she could force Lord Burke from his depression, perhaps he would again become a loving husband. Constanza would then cease her wicked adventures before it was too late.

"Well, Ana, what is it?"

"My lord, my *niña* is not happy, and it is because you are not happy." His black look made her falter, but summoning her courage, she continued. "You've been neglecting Constanza, my lord, and you know that I speak the truth. Why can it not be as it once was between you? Surely you don't love her any less."

He sighed. The old woman was a busybody, but she spoke honestly and he knew it. "We Irish are subject to black moods, Ana, and Constanza must get used to that. She's a good little lass."

"Why do you not go home to Ireland, my lord?"

"I will not return until I can return with my wife *and* my son."

"There is little chance of that if you see my mistress so infrequently," snapped Ana tartly.

"Peace, woman!" shouted Niall Burke. "For the moment the mood is upon me, and I must bear it until it passes. Your mistress has had two years to produce an heir, and I've seen no sign of a son or daughter. She has not complained to me of neglect, and seems well enough entertained these days. Christ, she's in the house less than I am!"

"And don't you wonder where she goes?"

Niall Burke's silver eyes narrowed. "What are you saying, woman?" he asked ominously.

A wave of fear rushed on Ana, almost suffocating her. "Nothing, my lord, nothing!" she gasped and quickly backed out of the room. Oh God! She had almost given it away. Leaning against the wall, she wept silently, the hot, salty tears stinging her eyes and swelling them. Ana was not young anymore. Going through this awful fear again was surely a curse.

She remembered back eighteen years ago to when she and Constanza's beautiful mother had been carried off by Moorish pirates. When they had finally been returned, she had sworn an oath that her mistress's virtue was untouched. Under the circumstances, she hoped God would forgive her the lie. The lady Maria had already been pregnant with her husband's child when they were abducted, and to have told the truth would have left open to question the validity of the child's heritage. In the end, the Conde questioned it anyway. Still, to protect the girl she had raised, Ana had lied. Since all the others who had been caught in the raid had disappeared into the slave markets of the East, no one questioned her story.

But Ana would always remember it vividly. The pirates had struck after sunset, using the darkness to creep up upon the Conde's summer villa located in a remote part of the island. The entire village had been lined up for inspection. The children, the young girls, the youths, women of childbearing age, and healthy, strong-looking men were herded onto the pirate vessel. The remaining unfortunates were quickly slaughtered. At the villa the procedure was similar but the young Condesa and her duenna were treated gently, and locked aboard the ship in a small cabin furnished with only a Turkish couch, a low table, and some floor pillows. The ship had been underway for several hours before anyone bothered with them. Then the door burst open and the ship's captain swaggered in. The three men at his back leaped forward and tore the clothes off the shrieking young Condesa. Ana attempted to shield her mistress from the lustful stares of the four men, but the captain dealt her a fierce blow that sent her reeling to the floor. Stunned, she could only watch in horror as the handsome Moor scrutinized her naked mistress. He walked about her slowly, squeezed a buttock, hefted a pear-shaped breast as if testing its weight, felt the soft texture of the silvery blond hair. He made a comment to his three companions in their guttural language and they laughed. The Moorish captain bent and dragged Ana up by her hair. "Is your mistress a virgin?" he asked her in flawless Spanish.

"No," gasped Ana. "She is the wife of a wealthy and powerful lord, the royal governor of these islands. He will pay a fortune for her safe return."

The men laughed uproariously. The Moorish captain said, "Some fat pasha will pay a hell of a lot more to have your mistress in his harem than her stiff-necked husband will pay for her return. And since she's no virgin we may enjoy her first."

The two women's eyes widened and Ana screamed, "No! I beg of you, captain, take me—but leave my mistress untouched!"

"Why, wench," laughed the Moor, "did you think we wouldn't have you too? Hey, Ali, this one's eager for a little loving! Do your duty well by her!"

What had followed was a nightmare Ana could never quite forget. That she was raped several times was of no importance, to Ana's mind, for she was a peasant and such things, though distasteful, happened to peasants with great regularity. Her position on the floor, however, gave her a clear view of the lady Maria, who had been thrown on the couch above.

At first the Condesa had struggled and screamed as the handsome Moorish captain rammed himself in and out of her. But her cries soon became cries of passion rather than shame as the captain, inflamed by her blond beauty, prolonged his performance. At last he could no longer contain himself, and poured himself into her. His place was quickly taken by one of his men, and then another, and finally the last.

Ana listened with horror as Maria exhorted each man to greater efforts, begging for more when one was spent and another took his place. The captain and his three officers quickly left Ana in peace so that they might spend the night in a long debauch with the young Condesa. Ana could not believe either her eyes or her ears. What had happened to her child to turn her from a sweet girl to this . . . this terrible woman?

When at last the four men stumbled wearily from the little cabin, Ana crept over to where Maria lay. The Condesa's body was wet with sweat and semen, the hollows beneath her purple eyes dark with exhaustion. She beamed her sweet smile at Ana. "Ah, sweet body of Christ, my dear Ana, I have not been so well fucked since we left Castile."

"*Niña,* you are mad! You were a virgin on your wedding night! I myself saw the blood on your sheets."

Maria laughed her tinkling laughter. "Chicken's blood," she said. "The Conde would not have known a virgin if he'd had one. On our wedding night he was hot to possess me, and I pretended to be shyly reluctant. It took him two hours to get my nightgown off." She laughed again. "And when I finally let him take me I shrieked and struggled. When I pretended to shove him away, I broke the small bladder of chicken's blood I had secreted for the occasion, then I pretended to faint. There, however, I overdid it. The Conde, alas, is not a particularly vigorous lover, and since our wedding night he handles me with such delicacy that it is like being fucked with a feather. I have been wild with desire for months now, but I dare not take a lover. There are no secrets on Mallorca."

"My dearest," begged Ana, "what is it you tell me? That you were not pure when you married the Conde? It is not so! I, myself, watched over you! When could you have had time to deceive me? When? You studied, made your devotion regularly, gardened, and rode. All decent pursuits!"

"Ana, Ana, what an innocent you are," said Maria. "My guardians left us alone in that jewel of a house. Though our bills were paid they never appeared from one year to the next. I was easy prey for those who liked to deflower innocents."

"Who, *niña?* Who?"

"Our good priest for one, my Ana. I was six when he first took me on his lap and slipped his hand up my gown to touch my sex. I was eleven when he finally took my virginity in the confessional. You sleep soundly, my old duenna. After that I chose my own lovers from among the gardeners, the grooms, my tutor, and the gypsies who camped on our lands several times every year. It was their old queen who gave me the chicken's blood in the bladder. I need loving, Ana. I must have it! I almost lost my mind these past months, but God, what lovers the Moors are!"

Poor Ana was overcome. She had raised this girl from birth, and believed she knew her well. How could something so pure and fresh-looking be so filled with evil? Dear Holy Mother, how could she not have seen it? Then her great love for Maria overcame her abhorrence.

"*Niña,*" she said quietly, "we are in grave danger. These Moors mean to sell you into a harem. You would not like being confined, or sharing one man with a hundred other women. If you tried to deceive your master you would first be terribly tortured and then killed."

"Do not fear, Ana," came the confident reply. "The Moors will not sell me. They will ransom us back to my lord husband."

"*Niña,* how can you be sure?"

"I am with child, Ana. I will bear the Conde a child next year. They cannot sell a pregnant woman. I should make some lovely houri with a big belly! I have told Captain Hamid this, and have agreed to service him and his crew for the term of our stay with him.

"Maria!"

The young Condesa laughed. "Do not scold me, dear duenna. I'll wear them out before they wear me out. Besides, soon I shall be too fat with my baby. And once the child is born all I will have again will be my husband." She sighed bleakly.

The beautiful Condesa calmly accepted the role of ship's whore and was available at any hour of the day or night. Ana could only watch helplessly, and pray that their ransom would be paid quickly. When it was, and they were returned to Palma, Ana watched with amazement as her mistress, now pale and demure as befitted a young Spanish matron of noble blood, fell fainting into her anxious husband's arms. Soon, under the stern eyes of the Archbishop of Mallorca and the Conde, Ana swore on the holy relics kept in the Palma cathedral that her mistress had remained untouched by the Moors during the period of her captivity. This extraordinary restraint was due to their respect for her impending motherhood.

But the Conde was suspicious. Even when Constanza was born six months later, a fat full-term baby, he still doubted. Ana never knew why, for Maria had never given the Conde any reason to doubt her. Ana liked to believe that Maria had died of a broken heart, brought on by the Conde's distrust. In reality she died of the complications of childbirth. The greatest of these complications was a massive dose of venereal disease. The doctor, used to his fine and elegant lady patients, never even identified the pox as the true cause of Maria's death. And the Conde believed she had died of shame at having been held captive by infidels.

It came to Ana now that her Maria had been an evil creature who had passed on her devil's seed to the innocent Constanza. Now Constanza was tainted too, and there was nothing Ana could do about it. Sooner or later Lord Burke would find out the double life his wife was leading, and when that happened . . . Ana shuddered and an icy sense of disaster surrounded her.

Ana's complaints had roused Niall from his black mood. He saw that he could not rest until he knew the truth about the new Countess of Lynmouth. There was only one man who could tell him.

The fierce storm that had torn through England had delayed the sailing of Robert Small's fleet. Despite careful precautions, several ships had been damaged and it would take some weeks to repair them. The Devon captain was therefore still in London, and Lord Burke sought him out, finding him at the King's Head Inn. The two men exchanged pleasantries and then Niall seated himself opposite the captain and said straightforwardly, "I need your help in unraveling a mystery, sir."

Robert Small sipped his ale and regarded the Irishman quietly. He replied, "If it's in my power, m'lord."

"Several years ago," began Niall, "I fell in love with a young girl. She was already betrothed, and my father did not think her highborn enough for me. She was wed to another man and bore her husband two sons before being widowed. My own marriage had been a farce, and was annulled by the Church. My father then agreed to a marriage between the lady and myself. Not only had she proven herself a good breeder, but she was wealthy by then. We were formally betrothed, but before we could wed, it was important to my lady's family interests that she make a sea voyage. I joined her on that voyage."

Robert Small felt an eerie sense of premonition creep over him.

"We had almost reached our destination when we were attacked by pirates. In the last moments of the battle one of those devils kidnaped my lady."

Robert Small felt a trickle of nervous sweat roll down his back. His stomach, full with a rich dinner and stout English ale, began to roll. Dear Christ, what was Lord Burke after? "What is it you want of me, my lord?" he asked abruptly.

"The truth, Captain. You brought to England a woman known as Señora Goya del Fuentes, the widow of your dead partner, allegedly raised in a convent in Algiers. I might have accepted that story except that the lady is the identical twin of my lost betrothed. Identical! Yet when I questioned her she seemed honestly to have no knowledge of Ireland or the O'Malley family." He paused. "At the bedding of the Earl and Countess of Lynmouth, Lady Southwood's gown slipped and I saw a tiny mole at the crest of her right breast. The possibility of two women who look so alike and bear the same name, I must reluctantly accept. But that two unrelated, coincidentally identical women should have the same mole I do not think possible. I believe the Countess of Lynmouth is the lost Skye O'Malley, and I think you know the truth of this matter. Why will she not acknowledge me or her past?"

"Because, my lord, she has no memory of anything prior to Algiers," said Robert Small calmly. "The only thing she was ever able to tell us was her name. Later on, she realized she was able to speak, read, and write in several languages. She had a strong sense of values, acquired somehow, but who she was and where she came from is all unknown, though I, of course, recognized her accent as Irish.

"The doctors explained that she suffered a shock, something so painful that her mind chose to blot everything out rather than face the terrible event—whatever that was."

"My God," Niall Burke was white-faced. "Tell me, Captain, was she truly married to a Spanish merchant, or is her child the result of rape?"

Robert Small hid a smile. North Africa was hardly a safe world, especially for women, but it wasn't much different here. Why did all Christian Europeans think of Moslems as sex-crazed fiends? "Willow is the result of a great love," he said. "Skye was indeed wed to my Algerian business partner. His name was Khalid el Bey, and it was he who rescued Skye. He adored her and she him. When he was murdered it almost destroyed her, and I brought her to England to escape the advances of the Turkish governor who was behind Khalid's death. She met Lord Southwood, and they fell in love.

"Now, my lord Burke, I have told you all I know, and I would appreciate it if you would return the favor. Who is she? Where is her home? You say she bore her first husband children? Are they living?"

"Her name is Skye O'Malley. Her first husband, may his soul burn for all eternity, was Dom O'Flaherty. He gave her two sons, both living. Her father was Dubhdara O'Malley." Here Robert Small whistled softly through his teeth, for what seaman had not heard of the great Irish pirate-merchant, Dubhdara O'Malley? "On his death," finished Niall, "she was made the O'Malley of Innisfana, pending the majority and aptitude of one of her half-brothers."

"How have they fared without her?" asked Robert Small.

"Her uncle, the Bishop of Connaught, has taken charge—much to my father's annoyance," smiled Niall. "When Skye disappeared the MacWilliam, my father, thought to avail himself of the O'Malley interests. But the O'Malleys have always been independent, for all they do owe us fealty."

The two men sat in companionable silence for a few moments, then Robert Small sighed, "Well, my lord Burke, what do you intend to do with this knowledge? I must warn you that Skye should have no shocks now. She is with child."

"But she's just wed . . . !" Then Niall Burke flushed and finished weakly, "Oh."

Robbie chuckled softly. "She's a beautiful woman."

"What am I to do now, sir? I can hardly tell the Countess that she is my lost betrothed wife."

"Why not tell Southwood about her background, my lord? Leaving out, of course, your personal involvement with her," suggested Robert Small. "Geoffrey should know. Then write to the Countess's uncle and explain the situation. It is only decent that her family know she is alive. Geoffrey Southwood loves Skye dearly, and after their child is born I am sure he'll want her to know of her past. Perhaps knowledge of it will bring her memory back."

Niall Burke was thoughtful, then said, "Be there, Robert. Help me tell him. I'm in a difficult position."

"I understand." Robert Small debated with himself for a moment, then asked, "Tell me, my lord Burke, do you love her still?"

"Yes," said Niall Burke without hesitation, "I still love her. I have never stopped loving her, though God knows I have tried. The memory of her has haunted my every hour, waking and sleeping."

"And your wife?"

"Constanza is my wife, Robert. I may have done her a great disservice by marrying her, but until death parts us she is my wife, as Skye is Lord Southwood's."

"I am relieved to know that you are a sensible man, my lord. You see, Skye is the child that neither my sister nor I ever had. We love her dearly, and would not see her hurt. She remembers nothing before she awoke in Khalid's house, and she obviously does not remember you. I will arrange for us to see the Earl immediately, for the repairs to my fleet will be completed soon and I must sail when they are. This storm has delayed me long enough."

Robert Small was as good as his word. Within the hour he sent a note to the Earl of Lynmouth that read, "Imperative I see you alone, without Skye's knowledge, immediately. Meet me aboard my ship tonight at ten."

Geoffrey Southwood, raising an elegant blond eyebrow at the cryptic message, made an excuse to his bride and rode off, promising a swift return. Arriving at the docks, he was escorted aboard the *Mermaid* to the captain's cabin, where he was surprised to find the Irishman, Burke, waiting with Robert Small.

Geoffrey flung his cloak to the little cabin boy and, nodding to both men, sprawled his long frame into a chair. "Well, Robbie, what's so important that you would take me from my bride on my honeymoon?"

"Have some wine, my lord," said Robbie. "You know Lord Burke?"

"We've met. The Burgundy, Robbie."

Robert Small poured wine for himself and his guests, and when the cabin boy had served the goblets, Robbie instructed him, "Stand watch outside, my lad. We're not to be disturbed unless the ship is sinking. Do you ken?"

The boy grinned. "Aye, sir!" he said, and closed the door behind him.

Robert Small sat back and drew a long deep breath. "Geoffrey, I've news that should make you happy, but it is of a *very* delicate nature. For several months Lord Burke has been quite confused by Skye's name and appearance. When you were bedded at Greenwich several nights ago he saw a mole on Skye's . . . um, Skye's . . . Skye's person!" he gasped, as Southwood's green eyes darkened.

"The tiny star?" Geoffrey asked softly.

"The very same," answered Niall.

"You've big eyes, Irishman," said the Earl, his voice soft with warning.

Niall bit back a hot-tempered reply. Damn the arrogant, possessive English bastard! Robert quickly resumed. "When Lord Burke saw the mark on Skye he was able to make a positive identification, although he was still quite confused as to why Skye did not acknowledge knowing him. He has mentioned names and places to her and is convinced that she has no knowledge of them. So he came to me this afternoon."

"And?" Geoffrey Southwood's voice was icy.

"She is Skye O'Malley," said Niall Burke. "The O'Malley of Innisfana, herself, and vassal to my father, who is the MacWilliam. Skye O'Malley disappeared several years ago off the North African coast and was presumed dead. Robert Small has explained her loss of memory to me. I felt, my lord, that you should know her true identity, but the captain and I were fearful of disclosing these facts to Skye herself."

Geoffrey Southwood's eyes narrowed just slightly at Niall Burke's familiar use of his wife's name. "Tell me of my wife's family," he said pointedly.

"Both her parents are dead, her father just a year before she was lost. She has a stepmother and uncle of whom she is quite fond, five older sisters, a younger brother, four younger half-brothers, *and two sons* by her first marriage. He's dead, my lord," Niall finished quickly, seeing the Earl go white about the lips.

"Did she love him?"

"Certainly not! He was a bastard who delighted in mistreating her. He was dead before she left Ireland, proving that there is a God in Heaven."

Geoffrey Southwood's eyes narrowed further and glittered dangerously at the impassioned tone in Lord Burke's voice." And what, my lord, was your connection with *my wife*?"

"We grew up together," said Niall. The lie slipped coolly off his tongue. "Her father was the O'Malley of Innisfana, her mother, Margaret McLeod, of the isle of Skye. When Dubhdara O'Malley died he made Skye his heiress until one of her brothers was old enough and showed an aptitude for the family seafaring business. Skye had always been her father's favorite, and had her father not finally sired some sons it probably would all have gone to her anyway. After the O'Malley died she swore her fealty to my father, as had all the O'Malley chiefs before her."

"And what was she doing on a ship off the North African coast?" demanded the Earl.

"The O'Malleys have been great sea rovers for centuries. Her trading fleet had made inquiries of the Algerian government with regard to beginning trade. When the Dey of Algiers learned that the O'Malley chief was a woman he insisted on meeting her before he would continue their negotiations. Representing my father, I accompanied her on that voyage. A severe storm tore the Dey's protective pendant from our mast, and when the storm ended we fought a sea battle with Barbary pirates. They didn't know that we were under the Dey's protection. We had almost succeeded in driving them off when one pirate swung across the gap between the ships and carried off the O'Malley. Before we could retrieve her a fog bank separated the ships. I had been severely injured, and was taken to the island of Mallorca. The rest of the O'Malley fleet sought for Skye, with the Dey's aid, but no trace of her was found."

"And that," explained Robert Small, "was because she wasn't channeled through a regular slave market, but disposed of in a private sale."

"Her family should be notified, Southwood. With your permission I should like to write to her uncle, who is the Bishop of Connaught. Captain Small and I thought that perhaps, after your child is born, you would tell her."

"Lord Burke is a gentleman, Geoffrey," said Robbie apologetically, "but since he was all for rushing to your house and telling Skye of her past, I found it necessary to explain her delicate condition to him."

"I congratulate you on your good fortune," said Niall feelingly. "I understand you lost your only son recently."

"Thank you," said Geoffrey, softening a little.

Robert Small heaved a sigh of relief. They weren't going to kill each other. "Well, gentlemen, we all have Skye's interests at heart," he said. "We've agreed then that Lord Burke will inform the O'Malleys of this happy turn of events, but that Skye will not be told until after the birth of her child."

The two young men nodded their assent, and Robbie raised his goblet. "To Skye and her happiness!" he declared.

Geoffrey Southwood smiled for the first time since entering the cabin, his green eyes meeting Niall's silver ones. "That's an easy toast," he said, and Niall Burke smiled back, raising his own goblet.

Suddenly, from outside the cabin there arose a small uproar. The piping voice of the little cabin boy was heard protesting in concert with a deep masculine voice. Southwood cocked his head. "Sounds like de Grenville," he said. The words had hardly left his mouth when the door burst open to admit that gentleman. The little cabin boy was close to tears and clung valiantly to the nobleman's doublet.

"I *told* him he couldn't come in, Captain! I told him!"

"That's all right, lad," said Robert Small in a kindly tone. "I can see you've done your best, but in this instance you've been outgunned. Go back and guard my door again. You did well."

The boy wiped tears away with his sleeve. Saying "Aye, s-sir," he took up his post again.

Robert Small turned coolly to de Grenville. "Well, Dickon, what is so important that you forced your way in here?"

De Grenville shook his flowing lace cuffs free of imaginary

wrinkles. "A once-in-a-lifetime opportunity for you, Robbie! Hello, Southwood . . . Burke. Mayhap you gentlemen will join us." He turned again to the captain. "Robbie, fate smiled on you when it delayed your sailing. I've been sent word that the 'Book Lady' is to perform at Claro's tonight, and I've obtained time in her bed for both of us!"

"The 'Book Lady'?" the Earl interrupted.

"Ah, Geoff, you've been so busy in the wooing of your new wife that you've missed this delicious phenomenon. She's just appeared at Claro's in the last few months. They say she's a bored noblewoman, but she's always masked so who's to know for certain? Her manners are flawless, and she speaks like a noblewoman, so the gossip may be right."

"Perhaps she's just a good actress," suggested the Earl.

"I think she's well bred. Her bone structure and skin texture are fine," replied de Grenville.

"Why do they call her the 'Book Lady'?" asked Niall Burke.

"Ahhh," breathed de Grenville again, "there's the fascinating part. Let's face it, gentlemen, a whore's a whore, but the Book Lady is an *artist*. She's got a naughty book from the Far East, filled with the most gorgeous illustrations of people fucking. If you desire, you pick a page and she'll duplicate it with you. They say she's expert in all she does, and she certainly loves her work. There's been talk of her and Claro having a contest to see who can fuck the most men in a twenty-four-hour period. By God, Robbie! We've a good time ahead of us tonight! Southwood! Burke! Will you join us?"

"No, Dickon, not I. What man married to my Skye would seek other entertainment?"

A hot pain pierced Niall.

"What excuse did you use to Skye when you came here?" asked Robert Small.

"That I'd a surprise for her," answered the Earl, "and I do." He drew forth from his doublet a large sapphire teardrop on a delicate gold chain. "D'you think she'll like it?"

"A Ceylon blue! God, what a beauty!" ejaculated de Grenville.

"Aye, Skye will like it," said Robert Small. "It matches her eyes."

"That's just what I thought," remarked the Earl, grinning, and again Niall winced.

Geoffrey Southwood stood and picked up his cloak. "Thank you, Robbie, and you, too, my lord Burke. Robbie, be sure you come to say good-bye to Skye before you sail."

"I will," promised the captain. Then he and the other two walked to the gangplank with the Earl.

At its foot waited a sailor holding Southwood's chestnut stallion. After mounting, Southwood waved to Robert and rode off in the direction of the Strand. Lord de Grenville turned to his two companions. "Well, gentlemen, are you for Claro's with me?"

Robert Small nodded. "I could use an entertaining memory to warm me on the long and lonely nights of this voyage. Aye, Dickon, I'm with you. And you, Lord Burke? Claro has some of the loveliest pox-free girls in London."

Niall considered a moment. "Aye, I'll join you. I don't think, however, that I'm up to your Book Lady. I'll happily settle for a pretty lass who fucks well."

De Grenville signaled his coach and the three men climbed in and were off. "Claro will fix you up right enough," prophesied de Grenville.

And Claire O'Flaherty, seeing the three men coming through her front door, panicked until she realized that, although she'd been a guest in the MacWilliam's castle, she'd never met Niall Burke. As the daughter of a minor and impoverished vassal, Claire had not been considered important enough to merit the heir's attention. So he would not know her. But Constanza must be warned.

Claire ran lightly up the stairs to the beautiful room that showcased her star attraction. Constanza, having just arrived, was alone. She was rouging her nipples when Claire burst in.

"Your husband's here," announced Claire, "but I don't believe he's come for you. He's not angry or upset at all. He's with friends."

"Who?"

"Lord de Grenville and Sir Robert Small."

Constanza checked a small book open on her bedside table. "De Grenville and one guest are scheduled with me for the entire night," she said. "Rose took the appointment. De Grenville said something to Rose about his friend going off on a long sea voyage."

"Then it must be Sir Robert," said Claire, giddy with relief. "But if Rose got it wrong then I'll send her up here and you get out fast. I'll make your excuses. Unless, of course, you'd like your husband to know?" She glanced slyly at Constanza.

"And spoil my fun?" laughed Constanza nervously. "Never!"

Claire slipped from the room and, with much show, descended the staircase. Her blond hair was piled high. Her sky-blue eyes sparked with malice. Her skin was very white except for the cheeks, which had been reddened with pomade. Her nipples were rouged. She wore a deep-blue gown so entirely transparent that her body was plainly visible. She was adorned with ropes of pearls.

"Lord de Grenville," her feline, husky voice purred. "Welcome! Welcome to you and your guests. I recognize you, Sir Robert, but the other gentleman is a stranger."

"Niall, Lord Burke, Claro. He's looking for a bouncing lass and some good bedsport."

"I shall see to him myself," smiled Claro broadly. The thought of bedding the man who had loved Skye O'Malley was simply too tempting.

"By God!" muttered de Grenville enviously. "I've been trying for months to pry those plump white thighs apart, and she'd have none of me. You merely walk through the door and she's at your feet!"

Niall eyed Claro dispassionately. Yes, she would do quite nicely. In his depression over Skye he had been disinclined to seek his wife's bed for several weeks, and yet he needed a woman to vent his frustration upon. This one would do quite nicely. With her big, pillowy, white breasts and avid, wet red mouth, she was totally unlike his dainty, gentle little Constanza. He smiled boldly at her, a smile that did not reach his cold silvery eyes, Claire noticed.

She could feel the suppressed violence in Niall as he slipped a hard arm about her, and she shivered with delight. Maybe this time, for the first time since that last wonderful time with Dom, she would feel something.

She smiled coyly up at him. "Come on, lovey," she said in that husky voice. Taking him by the hand, she led him up the stairs to her room. The door had barely closed behind them when he was pulling her into his arms and kissing her with a brutality that left her breathless. She heard the sheer gown rip, and felt the cool air on her skin. He picked her up, tossed her on the bed, pulled his own clothes off, and flung himself on her. He plunged into her without ceremony and she gasped with the pain he was inflicting on her in his desperate rutting. He was even bigger than Dom had been. Thrusting her hips to meet him, she felt her climax building. Yes, it was the first time since Dom that she had felt any satisfaction from a coupling. And, to her great surprise, he delayed his own pleasure until she had had hers. No man had ever done that for Claire.

The release was a purely physical one for Niall. The woman beneath him was a coarse creature, but she served her purpose and he had to admit she moved well. He had thought to take her once and leave, but now he decided to spend the night, as she apparently expected him to do. Why not? "You're a good tumble." He grinned and laughed when she shot back, "So are you, Niall Burke!" He hoped de Grenville and Robert Small were having as good a time as he was.

They were. The room in which Claro showcased her most famous whore was not used by anyone else. It had been decorated at great expense. In an age when glass was a rare and almost prohibitively expensive thing, the Book Lady's room had a great mirror built into its ceiling and two large standing mirrors in gilt frames on either side of the bed. The bed was enormous, with ruby velvet hangings, large fat pillows, and a red fox coverlet. Before the great fireplace was an Oriental type of couch, set low to the ground and covered with pillows. Next to the bed was a walnut bookstand upon which rested the famous book. Over the fireplace were hung dainty silver chains with gold wristlets, and next to the fireplace stood a tall white vase with a supply of hazel switches. Heavy red velvet brocade drapes shielded the windows. The floor was covered by a thick blue and red carpet from Turkey.

The three occupants of the room were all naked, poring over the book of love. The woman sat between them on the large bed, each man absently fondling a firm golden breast. "Impossible!" muttered Robert Small, studying the picture. "Not at all, Captain," came back the breathy answer. "It simply takes a bit of time and some patience. Would you like to try it?"

Robert Small looked at the petite golden-skinned creature and was rather shocked by what he saw. The woman was lust incarnate. Constanza pressed herself against him and, reaching down, fondled his sex. "Such a great weapon for such a little man," she murmured. "Can you wield your sword well, Captain?"

"Aye," he growled as he kissed her open mouth. "Come on, de Grenville, let's teach this hot little minx a good lesson!"

De Grenville's eyes glittered as he pressed against Constanza from behind. "Damme, Robbie, it's going to be a good evening! Geoff will be sorry he didn't join us!"

At that moment the Earl of Lynmouth, having reached his home, entered his bedchamber and found his wife lying on the bed, asleep. His valet entered silently behind him and closed the door. Geoffrey Southwood looked tenderly at the picture she made. She was wearing a demure white silk nightgown. The deeply scooped neckline offered him a generous view of her pretty breasts. Smiling, he drew off his clothes. Geoffrey bathed in the warm water set out by his valet, then waved away the white silk nightshirt offered him.

Placing the sapphire on the bedside table, he said pointedly, "Good night, Will." The valet chuckled as he left the room. Marriage had not paled Lord Southwood's appetite!

For a few moments Geoffrey watched Skye in sleep. She was so outrageously lovely that his breath caught in his throat. What he had learned tonight was astounding in one sense, yet not truly surprising. It had always been obvious that Skye was a lady as well as an educated woman. Now that he knew her to be the mother of two sons as well as the adorable Willow, Geoffrey was greatly encouraged. Surely the child she now carried beneath her heart was his son and heir, and not another daughter.

Suddenly he became aware of his great need for her and, gently rolling her over on her back, he kissed her mouth. She murmured and stretched. Pulling her gown down over her shoulders, he bared her to the waist. Then, with a shrug, he pulled the gown off entirely. The sight of her slim body, the belly just beginning to round, roused him painfully, the desire slamming into him sharply. He buried his face in the valley between her breasts and murmured her name.

Her arms were quickly about him. "Geoffrey, my love. I fell asleep waiting for you."

"I've been watching you sleep and, God help me, even in sleep you rouse me, my love." His mouth was closing over hers, his tongue exploring the roof of her mouth, then flicking downward to tease at her sensitive breasts. She caught at one of his hands and pulled it downward to the sweet core of her. She rubbed against him and he felt the wetness of her.

"You see, my darling, what a shameless creature I am. I desire you too!" Then catching his tumescence in her hand, she guided him to her and sighed with pleasure when he thrust deep.

"Witch," he muttered, "wives are not supposed to enjoy their husband's attentions so much."

"I shall say my prayers then," she teased, wriggling provocatively beneath him.

"You must say them to Venus, the goddess of love," he growled. He redoubled his efforts and soon she was crying out. Satisfied that he had mastered her, he took his own release. Niall Burke might play the old family friend all he wished, but Geoffrey Southwood knew a man in love when he saw one. Skye, however, was his alone, and he would never let her go.

Recovered, she leaned over him and demanded, "Where is my surprise?"

Muttering about greedy women, he reached over to the bedside table and dangled the gift before her.

Skye gasped. "Oh, Geoffrey, it's magnificent!" She sat cross-legged before him and slipped it over her neck. It dangled provocatively between her small impudent breasts as he had known it would. "And you went out especially tonight to get it for me. Thank you, my darling!"

And looking at her sitting there, the delight of a child on her face, he vowed again that no one would ever take her from him. She might be the head of a large Irish family, but they had managed these last few years and they'd have to continue to manage without her. She was his wife! His!

"Geoffrey, you look so fierce. Have I displeased you somehow?"

"Nay, sweet," he reassured her smilingly. "I was just thinking how very much I love you."

She crept into his arms and put her dark head against his shoulder. "And I love you, my darling. Oh, Geoffrey, I am such a terrible woman! I cannot help but think how lucky we are that Mary died."

"D'you think I would have let you go? Never! From the moment I first saw you in Dartmoor I meant you to be mine. I will never let you go, Skye! You belong to me!" And then his mouth was taking fierce, harsh possession of hers, and she was meeting his passion with her own, matching him kiss for kiss, caress for caress, until they were again joined in the blazing union so familiar by now, yet never the same. It left them both weak and breathing hard.

Afterward he gently scolded her. "We cannot go on like this, my angel. We must be careful of the baby."

"I know," she answered softly, "but Heaven help me, Geoffrey. I love you so, and I love it when you make love to me."

He smiled in the dimness of the room and, pulling her close, sighed, "Go to sleep, my naughty little wife. Too soon we must return to Court to serve the Queen. Then you'll have to curb your appetite, for the Queen allows her servants very little time to themselves."

She nestled next to him. "I'll find time, Southwood. Never fear!"

Chapter 19

"Hurry, milady," scolded Daisy. "You know how the Queen dislikes it when her ladies are late to vespers."

"None of the Queen's other ladies are about to give birth," grumbled Skye. "Let any of the others become pregnant and they're sent home to the country immediately. But not I! Oh no! The Queen must have her 'dearest Skye' near her. I wonder if she will allow me the time to birth my son?"

"Remember, milady," cautioned Daisy, "that you're not supposed to give birth for another two months. Keep it in your mind, ma'am."

Skye laughed ruefully. "Thank God it's not really that long! If I don't have this child soon I think I shall burst." She smoothed her gown over her protruding belly. "There! I am finally presentable. Give me my pomander, girl." Catching it up, Skye hurried from her apartment and through the maze of palace corridors to the chapel. She could hear the sweet, fluting voices of the choirboys singing: "Therefore we before Him bending, this great sacrament revere." Avoiding Geoffrey's little frown, she slipped into the pew beside him.

"I couldn't wake up," she whispered.

He took her hand and squeezed it. "You should be down in Devon," he whispered back, and she nodded.

The service was brief. The Court then trooped gaily off to the dancing, which would be followed by supper. Elizabeth's sharp dark eyes scrutinized her favorite lady as they all moved through the halls, and she thought, *So Southwood tasted of forbidden fruit before his last wife died. I wonder what they would have done if she hadn't died?* Then the memory of Robert Dudley's dead wife, Amy, assailed her. Elizabeth tried to push it away. But this time, as had happened before, she could not banish the thoughts. Amy Dudley haunted Elizabeth Tudor. The Queen was a person of strong and certain morals, and she knew that she had coveted another woman's husband. Now that other woman was dead, dead under distinctly mysterious circumstances, and the Queen wondered what the truth of the matter really was. It was not the first time she had wondered.

She did not believe, as many others did, that Robert Dudley had had his wife murdered by a hired killer. Elizabeth knew Dudley too well. His lust to be King of England was great and consuming. All he had had to do was wait, just a little time, until Amy died a natural death. She had been mortally ill. No purpose would have been served by killing her and, thus, casting suspicion upon himself. No, Robert had not ordered Amy's death.

But there were two other possibilities. One was that her dear Cecil or someone else who did not want to see Dudley become her husband and their King had arranged Amy's death, well aware of the furor a suspicious death would cause. The other possibility was that poor little Amy, in revenge against Elizabeth for stealing her husband's love or else in despair over her doctor's grim verdict, had thrown herself down the staircase, knowing that this unhallowed death would destroy Robert and Elizabeth's chances of marriage.

Could someone love a man as deeply as Amy Dudley had loved Robert, and one day come to hate him with equal passion? Elizabeth wondered whether this could be. Oh! If only Amy had died a natural death! Sometimes Elizabeth felt actually responsible. It wasn't fair! Angrily, she managed to put the subject from her mind and looked again at the Countess of Lynmouth.

I really should let Skye go home to Devon, she mused, *but there are so few women who amuse me. Perhaps in a week or so,* she considered.

The Queen also noted how radiant the Countess of Lynmouth was. Her gown was of mulberry-colored silk, cut low to reveal her very full breasts. There was an attempt at modesty in the soft creamy lace tucked into the bodice. The same lace overflowed the sleeves. Skye's dark hair was styled severely, drawn into a chignon at the nape of her slender neck, and tucked into a net of very thin gold wires. The long double rope of pearls she wore about her throat were a source of envy to every woman in the room, including Elizabeth.

Skye did not join in the dancing, remaining instead on her footstool by the Queen's chair. She watched the others dance, and was content. The Queen loved dancing and scarcely sat at all during the entire evening. When he was not partnering Her Majesty, Lord Dudley stood by her throne. At one point his hand dropped to Skye's bare shoulder. She froze. Dudley laughed softly.

"I've heard Southwood brag of the fineness of your skin." His long, elegant fingers moved slowly downward to the swell of her breasts. He stroked her lightly, casually. "He does not lie," drawled Dudley insolently. Slowly, he drew his hand away.

"You play a dangerous game, my lord," said Skye in a low, furious voice. Skye studied the Queen's favorite without bothering to conceal her scorn. He was a handsome enough man, if one were drawn to his type, she considered. He was tall and elegantly slender, and always dressed himself with foppish care. His long, aristocratic face and slender hands enhanced his . . . well, elegance. She had to admit it. He was not an easy man to overlook, even among the well-dressed courtiers. But Dudley did have one flaw, as though nature, having designed him so well, could not bear to endow a mere mortal with everything. His dark red hair, his mustache, and his very short, carefully clipped beard were all very sparse.

His dark eyes were slightly hooded and he never managed to look one directly in the eye. By contrast, however, his words were brutally straightforward.

"I enjoy the game I play, my dear, and I shall win it," he said sharply. His eyes now held a mocking expression. "You'd like to slap my face, wouldn't you, Lady Southwood? But you can hardly slap your King, can you?"

"You're not the King yet, Lord Dudley!" Skye was shocked by the man's boldness.

"But I will be, my dear, never fear. Bess must wed and produce heirs for England. The council would far prefer a good, solid Englishman to some mincing foreigner. Would you like to be the King's mistress, m'dear?"

"You're insufferable," Skye raged, struggling to her feet. "And, my lord, you are insulting!" Finally standing and balancing herself, she walked slowly away with as much dignity as she could muster. Finding an empty chair in the card room, she sat down and joined the game. She was very angry, and played with a fierce concentration.

She had never liked Robert Dudley, finding him overly ambitious, and arrogant to boot. Given free access to the Queen's apartments, he came and went at will, particularly when the women were likely to be in states of undress. His eye was bold, and when the young, love-besotted Queen was not looking, his hands were even bolder. Skye was shocked that he would so lewdly approach a woman in her condition. She prayed that Elizabeth would not choose him for a husband. She smiled. The young Queen was sharper and a great deal wiser than those around her gave her credit for. If only love would not cloud her judgment.

The pile of gold coins before her grew higher, and then de Grenville was leaning over her asking, "May I escort you in to supper, Skye?" Her anger cooled, Skye gave him a bright smile and stuffed her winnings into the little silk pouch that hung from her waist. She excused herself from the card table, to the relief of the other players.

"Aye, Dickon, I am famished!" she said. "Where is Southwood?"

"With the Queen. I've news of Robbie."

"Oh, Dickon, tell me! Is he all right?"

"A small merchant fleet that's just put in to London hailed him on the Indian Ocean side of Cape Horn. His entire fleet was intact—and so was Robbie. I've letters for you which I'll bring around tomorrow."

They had reached the dining room. Courtiers in full, colorful finery were milling about, chatting and helping themselves from the vast buffet. "I shall eat nothing but Colchester oysters," announced Skye, piling her plate high.

"The outrageous vagaries of breeding women," teased de Grenville.

"I don't know how on earth you would know about that, Dickon," Skye teased in return. "The moment your wife shows sign of being with child, you banish the poor woman to Devon."

"For her own good, Skye. And of course, the child's health as well," he responded piously.

"Nonsense! It's so you can wench in the best brothels in London without suffering a guilty conscience." Skye laughed, speared an oyster, and swallowed it whole.

De Grenville reddened. "You're too forward for a woman," he muttered, "and far too beautiful for a lady about to give birth."

"And if I weren't pregnant would you be trying to make love to me, Dickon?"

"For God's sake, Skye!" protested de Grenville.

"Just asking, Dickon. You see, I love Geoffrey. I would like to have you for a friend, as would my husband. It would distress me to have to be constantly fending you off. Beauty does not necessarily mean a loose moral character. Did you know that?"

"Any man attempting to toy with Geoffrey Southwood's wife would be suicidal," muttered de Grenville. "For my health's sake, Skye, I think of you as I do my own dear sisters."

Skye patted his arm in a kindly fashion. "I am very relieved to hear that, Dickon," she twinkled up at him.

"Whore!" The outraged shout accompanied by a sharp crack brought instant silence to the room. Skye and de Grenville turned, startled, in the direction of the uproar. Everyone was staring toward a corner of the room where Lionel, Lord Basingstoke, stood towering over a beautiful golden-haired woman who cowered on her knees, clutching her bruised cheek. The nobleman was in a high rage, his face as red as his velvet doublet. The veins on his neck bulged and his pale eyes glittered with fury. Raising his hand he struck the woman again and repeated, "Whore!"

Several gentlemen dashed forward and restrained the apoplectic man. "My God!" someone hissed. "That's Lady Burke, the Irishman's wife." The woman was weeping softly. *Lord,* thought Skye, *she's absolutely beautiful.* Then, almost before she realized what she was doing, Skye pushed through the crowd to the sobbing woman. Leaning down, Skye put a tender arm about her and helped her up. "There, my dear. By tomorrow there will be something else to gossip about, and this will be entirely forgotten," Skye said gently. Constanza threw her a grateful look.

"Christ's blood, Lady Southwood!" cried Lord Basingstoke, "Don't touch her! She is foulness beyond measure! No decent woman should even speak her name."

"Fie, my lord!" Skye's voice rang out. "You abuse a lady, and you dare do it in the Queen's presence!"

"That she dares to show herself to the Queen is an outrage in itself!" shouted Basingstoke. "The most evil of whores in the presence of the most innocent and virtuous of women!"

"You make a great deal of noise, my lord," said Skye wearily. "I've yet to hear what causes your outrage."

"And I should be interested too, sir." Niall Burke pushed his way forward. Pulling one of his gloves from his doublet, he struck Lord Basingstoke across the cheek. "You are challenged, my lord. Where? And when?"

"No, Irishman. She's not worth it. I'll not have your death on my conscience, nor will I be killed for such as she! God Almighty, man! Can you really be so blind? Constanza has been my mistress for months. Yes, she's been cuckolding you, but far worse, she's been cuckolding me also. And not with just one man, but with *any man* who had the gold to buy her!" Basingstoke wrenched Constanza from Skye's protective grasp. Holding her hand high, he declared in his booming voice, "Gentlemen! I give you the Book Lady! Madame Claro's most famous attraction! The busiest cunt in Londontown!"

A collective gasp rose from the assembled court, the women shocked yet titillated, the gentlemen pressing forward for a closer view. Constanza's violet eyes widened in horror at the knowing, leering looks. Trembling uncontrollably, she fainted.

"My lord Basingstoke!" A path opened instantly through the jostling crowd, and the Queen moved regally forward. "My lord Basingstoke," she repeated. "These are appalling charges. Where is your proof?"

"I have proof, ma'am, but I should not like to present it publicly."

"Sir! You saw fit to begin this affair publicly, so that is how we will air it. Speak or else tender your apologies to Lord Burke without delay."

"Madam, as you will." Basingstoke sighed, and then began. "Several months ago I made Lady Burke my mistress. After a time I gave her as a token of my affection and admiration a rare book of . . . of pictures. Pictures of . . . ah . . . lovemaking." A snicker ran through the crowd but was silenced by the Queen's quick frown. Basingstoke continued, "I soon began to hear stories of a new attraction at Madame Claro's, a woman they called the Book Lady, and several weeks ago I heard of a contest to be held at Claro's. It was to be a battle between Claro herself and the Book Lady, a contest . . . forgive me, Majesty, for my bluntness, over who could fuck the most men within a day-and-night period. The wagering was great, and as there was to be no charge for entry to Claro's that day I went with friends to observe the fun. My God, ma'am! The men were coming and going out of the women's rooms so quickly it would make your head spin! A tally was called as each man left. Observers were permitted, for a gold piece, to stand at the doors of each bedchamber. I decided to watch. Imagine my shock in discovering that the infamous Book Lady was my own mistress!"

"And just how did you discover it, Lord Basingstoke?" demanded the Queen. She had no choice but to hear the whole story.

"Constanza has an unusual identifying mark. Also, my book was open on a bookstand next to the bed. I have been promised that there are no two in existence."

Elizabeth Tudor pursed her lips thoughtfully. This was the worst scandal to occur at her Court since she had become Queen. "I want the men who have visited the Book Lady to step forward," she said. "Come, gentlemen! I'll wager you weren't so shy with the whores at Claro's!" And Elizabeth's eyes widened at the number of men who finally stepped forward. "Bless my soul, sirs, I thought you were kept well busy chasing my maids of honor," she remarked sourly to the large group of shamefaced courtiers. Choosing ten, she dismissed the rest. "Have you all seen the lady's birthmark?" They nodded solemnly. "Very well then, gentlemen. Each of you is to step up to Lord Burke, and whisper to him the description of that mark."

Niall Burke stood rocklike, his face an icy and impenetrable mask as, one by one, the ten embarrassed men moved up, whispered, and then slipped away, disappearing into the crowd as quickly as they could.

"You also, Basingstoke," commanded the Queen. When Constanza's accuser had finally stepped back Elizabeth asked, "Very well, Lord Burke, do these men speak the truth?"

"Aye, madam, they do, to my everlasting shame."

Constanza had revived and, cradled in Skye's arms, moaned as if in terrible pain. Niall sent her a bitter yet pitying look.

"Do you wish to withdraw your challenge, Lord Burke?" asked the Queen in a softer tone than she had used during the awful interrogation.

"No, madam. Lord Basingstoke, for all his fine outrage, is nevertheless responsible for being the first to debauch my wife and bring dishonor upon my name. I will not withdraw my challenge."

"Very well, sir, we will settle this matter here and now. Lord Dudley, will you see to it? The ballroom will do. See to the seconds."

"I will act as Lord Burke's second," Geoffrey Southwood stepped forward.

Skye gave a little cry of distress and the Queen reached over and patted her. "No danger, my dearest Skye, I promise. Sirs, this *will not* be a fight to the death. Do you both understand what I say? Honor must be served, but that is all!"

Lord Dudley chose a reluctant second for Basingstoke from among the men who had admitted to visiting the Book Lady. "Birds of a feather," he quipped, receiving contemptuous looks in return for his humor. The others knew that he had been a visitor to the lady involved, but had not dared admit it before the Queen.

The paneled ballroom was quickly cleared of chairs and tables, and the musicians in the gallery above were dismissed. Skye helped Constanza Burke to her feet and led her to stand by the Queen. Elizabeth would not even look at the distraught woman, but said quietly, without moving, "From tonight, my lady Burke, you are banned from this Court." Constanza bowed her head.

The combatants stood at either end of the room. Having shed their elegant and ornate doublets, they stood in shirts open at the neck. With an air of great self-importance, Dudley bustled back and forth between the two groups. Whip-thin rapiers, made of the finest Toledo steel, were brought forth, tested, and chosen by the seconds.

"What a pity you can't kill the pompous bastard, Niall," Geoffrey Southwood murmured.

"God's will be done," said Niall Burke in a low voice as he very loosely attached to his sword the protective tip ordered by the Queen.

"A-men," answered the Earl piously, pretending to inspect the tip.

"More lights!" commanded the Queen, and fresh tapers were brought.

"The gentlemen and their seconds forward, please," commanded Dudley. "Now, sirrahs, this is a combat to satisfy honor. Honor will be satisfied when one of the combatants is totally disarmed and helpless. Is that understood?" The participants nodded. "Seconds to neutral corners, please. Gentlemen, *en garde!*"

So began an exquisite ballet of courtly battle technique. The combatants were fairly evenly matched. Basingstoke was not quite as tall as Niall, but he was heavier. They circled each other slowly, engaged in a brief flurry, separated quickly. Each was guaging the other, testing for strengths, seeking weaknesses.

The courtiers leaned avidly forward, fascinated, silently egging the combatants onward. The young Queen stood quietly, only the faint quivering of her long, elegant hands betraying her nervousness. She was frankly disgusted by the beauteous Lady Burke's disgraceful behavior, but at the same time thrilled by the sight of two stalwart men brought to battle by that very behavior. If only men would fight over her like that, thought Elizabeth.

Constanza Burke watched with a sense of growing desperation. What would Niall do to her? Probably kill her. God knew she deserved it. Why did she have this awful sickness? What drove her to these terrible acts of perversion? She wept softly.

Skye, Countess of Lynmouth, watched the battle nervously. Thank God the Queen had ordered the protective tips. If Geoffrey had to fight he wouldn't be injured. Why had he volunteered to second Lord Burke? She hadn't been aware of any friendship between them. Still, he was their neighbor on the Strand. And she felt a deep pity for both the Irishman and his unfortunate wife. Khalid had told her about women like Constanza Burke, women who could not get enough loving. Skye knew that Lady Burke was not wicked, but sick. She suddenly felt tired. When this was over she would beg the Queen's leave to go home for her lying-in.

Niall Burke circled his opponent, parrying a vicious thrust. Leaping forward, he executed a quick riposte. His eye checked the protective tip on his sword. It was loose, and would soon be off. He pressed his attack hard, the anger burning coldly and deeply within him.

Lionel Basingstoke, valiantly defending himself, knew he had made a terrible mistake in allowing his pride and his temper to overrule his sense. He had seen the loose tip on his opponent's sword and he fully realized Lord Burke's intent. He was going to die. And over a worthless tramp. Why had he not simply given her the beating she deserved and left her to pursue her lusts? His body grew wet with fear and anger.

The two men battled back and forth until, older and heavier, Basingstoke began to tire. In a moment of rashness he again allowed his temper the upper hand and, yanking the protective tip from his sword, snarled at Niall, "All right, you damned Irish cuckold, let's end this now!"

Niall's silver eyes narrowed speculatively, and then he grinned, savagely, wolfishly. The idiot Englishman had made the first move, and now he could kill him without any qualms. Flicking the tip off his own blade, he replied, "I hope you've a legitimate heir, you stinking English pig, for if you've not your line ends now!" And he lunged forward, slipping easily beneath his opponent's guard to bury his blade in Basingstoke's chest.

A look of complete surprise crossed the Englishman's face and then he fell forward. As he fell, his own blade flew upward, opening a small but very bloody flesh wound on the Irishman's chest. It blossomed scarlet on Lord Burke's white silk shirtfront.

An unearthly shriek shattered the utter silence. The Court turned, expecting to see Constanza Burke's hysteria. But it was the Countess of Lynmouth who stood rigid, her eyes staring inward at some nameless terror. She screamed once again, then cried, "I've killed him!" She wept piteously. "Oh, sweet Christ, I've killed him!" A spasm of pain crossed her face and suddenly her gaze returned to the scene before her. Clutching at her belly, she fainted, sliding slowly to the floor in a crumpled heap.

In the uproar and confusion that followed, both Geoffrey Southwood and Niall Burke leaped forward to catch her, but the Earl was first to his wife's side, shooting Burke a venomous look. Cradling Skye in his arms, he pushed past the babbling courtiers and carried her through the palace and down to the river bank where his barge was docked.

"The Countess is going into labor," he told his bargemen. "Row for home and row as you've never rowed before! A gold rose noble to each of you for getting us there safely."

The cool air revived Skye as they pulled away from the river bank. Her eyes opened. "Geoffrey?"

"I am here, my darling. How do you feel?"

"The baby's coming."

"I know. You clutched at your belly and then you fainted. Damned provident, this duel. People will believe it brought on the premature birth of our son." He glanced anxiously at her.

"I remember, Geoffrey. I remember everything!" she breathed.

He sighed. "I know, Skye," he answered her quietly. "I saw the look on your face before you fainted. What brought it all back, my darling? Burke's injury?"

"Yes! The pirates shot at the jollyboat and wounded Niall. His shirt was so bloody I thought he'd been killed. When he was wounded again now it all came back to me. He is all right, isn't he?" The Earl nodded. She fell silent, a pensive look on her face.

"I love you, Skye."

The heart-shaped face tipped up, and the sapphire-blue eyes looked unwaveringly into his. "And I love you, Geoffrey, my darling. I do!"

He held her close. Of course she loved him. She was in pain now, in labor with his child, a child conceived in a moment of love, conceived when Niall Burke had been wiped out of her memory. But when the child was birthed, and she had time to think clearly, would she love him then?

Skye lay quietly in his arms, her mind whirling. O'Malley! She was Skye O'Malley! *The O'Malley of Innisfana!* She had two sons, Ewan and Murrough! Oh God! Who had looked after her boys all this time? Anne! Surely Anne would have looked after them, and Michael, and her half-brothers too. Lord! Who had cared for the O'Malley shipping interests? She would ask Geoffrey, for surely he knew. It seemed he knew her identity. *And* she would be interested in knowing how long he had known it!

She felt the pain beginning deep within her, so deep that her toes tensed. She let it sweep upward. Breathing deeply into it took the edge off of it. Skye wasn't even aware that she was clutching her husband tightly, but Geoffrey relished the fierce grip that almost rendered his elegant hand pulp.

"My sons?" she said. "What has happened to my sons?"

"They're safe with your stepmother."

"And the family?"

"Your uncle took care of them, and the O'Malley interests. He's now Bishop of Connaught."

"How long have you known my identity?"

"A few months. Lord Burke went to Robbie just after our wedding. At the bedding ceremony he noticed that very fetching little star on your breast. I was curious that, having been like a brother to you all your life, he would know of such a mark."

"I am curious too," said Skye, and though he knew she lied, he loved her all the more for loving him enough to try and protect him. "I am more curious," she continued, "that he was not suspicious of my identity prior to seeing my birthmark. Surely I have not changed so greatly."

"Señora Goya del Fuentes didn't react to his hints. And though she looked like Skye O'Malley, her credentials were impeccable. He has since told me he thought you were one of your father's by-blows."

Another wave of pain swept over Skye, but she giggled despite it, and Geoffrey was forced to laugh too. "It would have been just like Da to leave a bastard daughter in a convent in Algiers. How did he account for the name being the same?" The pain receded.

"He couldn't, and that almost drove him mad. There was simply no explanation."

"Yes," she said thoughtfully. "I imagine it would have driven him mad. Niall was always an impatient man."

"He's in love with you, Skye."

"I know, Geoffrey."

"And you?" He knew he shouldn't ask her, not now, but he couldn't stop himself.

"Geoffrey, my dearest husband, I am yours and I want to be. When I have finished this business of birthing our son I shall tell you all about Niall Burke, and Skye O'Malley. And when I have finished my tale I shall still be yours because I choose to be."

It was what he wanted to hear, or was it? Still, he had to be content with it for now. They both fell silent, listening to the slap-slap of the oars against the water as their barge knifed through the river down to Lynmouth House. The pains were coming more frequently now, and with the knowledge that this was her fourth child, the Earl despaired of reaching home in time. Suddenly Skye groaned, and cried out sharply.

"My love, what is it?" He felt so damned helpless.

"The child is being born, Geoffrey! I can wait no longer. You must help me birth it!"

"My God, Skye! In the barge?"

She managed a chuckle. "Tell your son!"

"What do I do?" He was sweating, but this was his child, and he'd manage.

"First, draw the drapes and bring in the lantern," suggested Skye, and when he had accomplished these two simple tasks she said, "Help push my gown up." That done, she inched her silken undergarments off, and he stared at the swollen, blue-veined belly that would soon be emptied of their child. Suddenly a flood of water spewed forth from her body, wetting the seat cushions. She arched as another pain began to push the child from her body.

"Geoffrey!" she gasped through gritted teeth. "I can feel the head. Look! Look!"

Fearfully he forced his eyes downward. "My God!" he whispered, awestruck, as the child began to emerge from her body. "What do I do, Skye?"

"Turn the child slowly as he comes forth, Geoffrey. Be very careful not to drop him for he'll be slippery with the birthing blood. Ahhhh, Jesus! Mary!" Another pain racked her.

Quickly he rolled up the sleeves of his silk shirt, his bejeweled doublet having been left behind at Greenwich. Skye groaned again, and her convulsion pushed the child's shoulders forth. Leaning forward, Geoffrey wiped the beads of perspiration from her forehead with his handkerchief. "You are magnificent, madam, and I love you," he said admiringly. Then he gently turned the child, and saw the baby's tight little face, wiping the blood from it with the same handkerchief that had wiped its mother's face. The baby's eyes opened, looked dispassionately at its father, a disturbing, strangely familiar look, and then slipped forth fully born into the Earl's waiting hands with a howl of pure outrage. One swift look told the Earl what he wanted to know. "*A son!*" he exulted. "You've given me a son, Skye!"

"Of course I have," she said weakly. "Did I not promise you one?"

"The cord? We've nothing to cut it with."

"It'll wait," she said, and then fainted.

The Earl's bargemen, hearing the newly born infant's cry, and his lordship's shout, grinned at each other and put their backs into their work. Shortly afterward they reached their dock at Lynmouth House and, to their surprise, found Daisy, Dame Cecily, and the midwife waiting for them.

"Lord Burke rode in with Daisy but a few minutes ago to tell us you were coming," said Dame Cecily. "Is Skye all right? Is she in labor?"

"The child is born!" exulted Geoffrey, when he heard their voices. "I have a son!"

Entering the barge, the midwife finished the job by cutting the cord and wiping the newborn free of birthing blood. She wrapped him in a clean swaddling cloth, and handed him up to Daisy. Skye had regained consciousness, and she groaned as another, weaker pain cut through her.

"You've not yet borne the afterbirth, my lady. Let me help you." The midwife pressed down hard on Skye's belly, and with one quick pain the afterbirth slipped out onto a linen towel spread by the efficient midwife. Quickly the woman cleansed her patient free of all evidence of her recent travail, then signaled to the litterbearers. The Earl carefully lifted his wife from the barge, and tenderly placed her on pillows in the litter. Skye held out her arms. "Give me my son."

Geoffrey took the baby from Daisy, and placed him in his mother's arms. Alert, but quiet now, the child returned his mother's scrutiny. His small round head was covered with soft, damp blond curls, his eyes were a deep sapphire blue, and his features were his father's. Skye smiled happily. "Oh, Geoffrey, I have indeed given you a son! He's you in miniature. I'll wager his eyes turn green within the year."

Mother and child were escorted to the house and tucked carefully into bed. The midwife handed Skye a goblet of wine into which she'd mixed herbs. "This will help you sleep, madam, and will also help rebuild the blood you've lost." Skye obediently drank it down and Geoffrey, sitting down next to the bed, took his wife's hand. Her beautiful blue eyes were heavy with weariness, but the warmth of his strong grasp communicated to her all the love that he felt for her. She sighed, contented. Geoffrey Southwood smiled tenderly at her. "Go to sleep, my love," he said, and when her eyelids finally closed he left her sleeping under the watchful eyes of Daisy, their slumbering son in his cradle by his mother's bed.

The Earl of Lynmouth walked next door to his own apartment. Wordlessly he stripped his bloodstained clothing off and climbed into the steaming tub his body servant had prepared. He scrubbed himself down and then, climbing out, dried himself off. His valet then wrapped him in a long, warm gown and, murmuring congratulations, left his master alone.

Geoffrey Southwood poured himself a goblet of pale golden wine and sat before the blazing fire. The child was safely born. He had a healthy, lusty son, an heir. But did he still have a loving wife? She had refused to discuss Niall Burke with him, which led Geoffrey to believe that she had once loved him. Now that her memory had returned, would she love Burke again? "When I am finished with this business of birthing our son I will tell you of Niall Burke," she had said. "I am yours because I choose to be," she had also said. Damn her proud and independent Irish spirit! Then he chuckled ruefully. It was this very independence that made her different from other women, that made her Skye.

Draining his goblet, Geoffrey climbed into his chilly, empty bed, then lay tossing restlessly. He dozed, then awoke with a start. This was the first night since their marriage that he'd been without her, for even in these last weeks of her pregnancy he'd slept with her, in her bedchamber, snoring contentedly against her warmth. *I must be getting old,* he thought with a touch of humor. These sheets were cold and musty with lack of use, and there were lumps in his fine mattress.

"God's blood!" he said, suddenly leaping up. "I will not sleep here a minute longer!" And padding barefoot across the cold floor to the door that connected his room with hers, he stomped in. Poor Daisy was horrified, having never seen her master in his nightshirt.

Skye, sitting propped up with pillows behind her, the child at her breast, bit her lip with suppressed mirth. "My lord, have you come to see our wee Robin?" The baby made a murmur of distinct annoyance as his mother's voice disturbed his concentration.

"I'm cold," announced the Earl pettishly.

Skye's eyes twinkled. "I have never seen the sense," she said, "in a man sleeping apart from his wife simply because she has just borne a child." With her free hand she flung the bedcovers back in invitation. "Climb in, Geoffrey. I am cold too without you."

Scandalized, Daisy pursed her lips together, but the Earl and Countess of Lynmouth simply giggled like two naughty children, and snuggled close. Then Geoffrey turned his attention to the tiny golden-haired infant who rooted noisily at his mother's breast, his tiny fingers kneading her.

"He's working hard enough at it," observed the Earl.

"My milk won't be in for a day or two. All he's getting now is a watery liquid," said Skye.

"Is that natural?" He was instantly concerned. "Should we have a wet nurse for him?"

She laughed. "With all the children you had, you should know more, my love. My present condition is quite natural. I shall get a wet nurse for Robin in about a month, but during the time it takes me to recover from this birth I shall have the pleasure of giving my child suck."

"So you already decided upon his name, have you? All by yourself?"

"I have," she replied, unconcerned. "He is Robert Geoffrey James Henry Southwood. Robert for my dearest Robbie, Geoffrey for you, James for my uncle Seamus, and Henry in honor of both the late king, and Robin's dead half-brother. His godparents will be the Queen and Lord Dudley. He will be vain enough to believe I have named the child for him in order to please the Queen. He should therefore prove an excellent godfather to Robin in an effort to impress the Queen."

Geoffrey Southwood chuckled admiringly. "By God you're a wickedly clever minx, my dear. The Queen and Lord Dudley! I don't believe anyone has yet given them a godchild, not both of them together. What a stroke of genius! I most assuredly approve." Warmed by her ripe body, he was beginning to feel expansive.

Noting it, Skye smiled. "Daisy, put Robin back to bed. Then you may watch over him the rest of the night please."

"Aye, madam." Daisy took the child. Her flush went unnoticed as her mistress drew the bed draperies, thus making a private little world for herself and the Earl.

Geoffrey Southwood's eyes were bright with love and admiration. "I was so damned lonely for you," he said.

"And I for you. If you'd not come into my bed I should have called for you."

"Would you?" He was as pleased as a child, his green eyes lighting up.

"Aye, I would. Now go to sleep, my darling. 'Twas a brave thing you did delivering Robin. Thank you, my love." She nestled next to him and, sighing happily, he put a protective arm about her. Within a few minutes he was sleeping soundly, his slow regular breathing a comforting sound.

Now it was Skye who lay awake. How strange it was that this elegant, assured man to whom she was married could suffer such terrible pangs of insecurity. How hard it must have been for him these last few weeks—knowing the truth of her identity, unable to tell her yet fearful she would learn of it. Fearful because of Niall Burke.

For the first time since her memory had returned those few

short, yet somehow long hours ago, she thought of him. There were touches of silver at his temples that had not been there four years ago. In the morning Geoffrey would want to know about Niall and what was she to tell him? Should she lie? She knew Niall still loved her. Now she understood those searching looks he had given her, the intense questioning. If she chose to lie she knew she could ask Niall for his help. He'd not like it, but he'd help if she asked him to.

She moved restlessly, and Geoffrey's protective arm slipped loose. He sighed and turned on his other side, away from her. She couldn't lie to Geoffrey. She couldn't! The truth might be softened, but an outright lie could bring disaster. She had no wish to hurt Geoffrey. She loved him. But did she not also love Niall? Hadn't her memory fled because he was the most important being in her life? Her mind had gone blank rather than accept Niall's death.

Four years ago. Four long years. And in that time so much had happened. Khalid el Bey, her beloved second husband. Could she love him any less because her memory of Niall had returned? No. He would always have a place in her secret heart. And their daughter, Willow, with Khalid's black lashes and golden lion eyes was the living proof of that love.

And Geoffrey. She loved him also as he loved her. Their love had grown into something wonderful. Could she walk away from him now?

And Niall. What of him? Long ago, and far away in what almost seemed another life, they had shared one ecstatic night of blinding passion. They had tried to build a life together based on that night, but fate continued to separate them. He had a wife now, a wife who obviously needed him desperately. As she had a husband.

But she loved him still. Yet she loved Geoffrey. It was madness! How could a woman love two men at the same time? "Damn!" she swore softly to herself.

"Tell me," Geoffrey's calm voice commanded.

Skye gave up all thought of lying and answered simply, "I was betrothed to him after my first husband died. I thought you were asleep."

"How can I sleep with you tossing so, my darling? Did you love him?"

"Yes."

"Do you love him now that your memory has returned?"

"I love you," she said.

He smiled in the darkness. "But do you love him?" Geoffrey persisted.

"No!" she said quickly.

He frowned slightly at the too-quick denial. Was she lying to protect his feelings or to hide something from him? "Did he ever know you?"

"Geoffrey!" Damn!

"Did he?"

Oh Lord, help her not to rouse his suspicions. "No," she said with what she hoped was just the right tinge of righteous annoyance. "He never knew me." She felt him relax, and said a quick prayer of thanks. Now, the tension gone, she was suddenly exhausted. "I am tired," she yawned.

Once more he enfolded her in his protective clasp. "Go to sleep, my dearest wife," he said. "Go to sleep."

In the house to the right of them, however, the master and mistress were far from sleep. In the uproar that had followed the duel the Queen had instructed the Burkes be brought to her. "My lord," she addressed herself to Niall, her dark eyes very large and angry. "I have already told your wife that she is no longer welcome at this Court. As for you—you deliberately disobeyed my orders and killed Lord Basingstoke. For that I could have you beheaded. Do you realize that?" In her dancing costume of pale green watered silk, ecru lace at the neck and sleeves, Elizabeth ought to have appeared young and mild. But this was Elizabeth at the angriest Niall had ever seen her, and the frivolous dancing gown was obscured by her flaming red-gold hair and snapping dark eyes. In this rage, Elizabeth flamed as hotly as her father, the infamous Henry the Eighth.

She continued. "We understand that you were sorely provoked, Lord Burke. Nonetheless you are also banished from Court, *and* from England for the period of one year. Your wife, however, is never to set foot in my realm again. We give you one month in which to prepare for your departure."

"The woman called Claro?" Niall asked in an unwavering voice. "I beg Your Majesty's permission to deal personally with her."

"We do not wish to hear of it, my lord," said the Queen slowly and with particular meaning, "lest we be forced to review our clemency to you."

"That is understood, madam."

"Farewell, then, my lord Burke," said Elizabeth, extending him her hand. He kissed it. Elizabeth pointedly ignored the subdued Constanza, as she had ignored her throughout the interview.

Niall Burke slowly released the beautiful, bejeweled hand. "You are ever gracious, Majesty." Grasping his wife's arm, he led her through a side door, down a maze of corridors, and out into the courtyard to their carriage. He pushed her up into the coach, and shouted to the liveried servant on the box, "Home!" Then he climbed in and sat opposite her. The vehicle lurched forward. Niall Burke sat back in his seat and looked at his wife. "Amazing," he said after a long while. "Simply amazing! Despite the fact that you are obviously the biggest whore in Christendom, you look like an angel."

Her violet eyes wide, she cowered from his brutal appraisal.

"What's this, Constanzita? Shyness? Why shy with me when you are as familiar with every man in London?"

"What are you going to do with me?" she asked him, finding her voice and unable to bear the strain any longer.

"What the hell can I do with you?" he countered. "You are my wife, may God have mercy on me. I must surely be cursed. My first wife was a religious fanatic who couldn't bear any man's touch and my second turns out to be a notorious whore who encourages every man's touch! The one woman in the world I ever truly wanted loses her memory and marries another!"

Constanza Burke relaxed just a little. For a moment she was free of his searing contempt. "What do you mean the *only woman* you ever really wanted?"

He looked coldly at her. "The Countess of Lynmouth is Skye O'Malley. She did not die, as your father assured me she must have done, but she did lose her memory." He gave her a brief explanation of what had happened.

"Is that why you've been so unhappy and preoccupied these last few months?"

"That is why," he said, "and how fortuitous for you, my dear. It made it so much easier for you to play the whore."

She wondered if his own sorrow might make him receptive to her anguish. "Please try and understand. I cannot help this terrible need, Niall. I truly can't."

"I know it, Constanza, and that is why I must do what I must do. We are banished from England and we must go home to Ireland. I cannot have you running about the countryside bringing further shame upon my name. You'll be confined to your apartments in my father's castle. You'll never leave them, my dear, and you'll have a warder of my choosing who will never leave your side except when I bed you. And I'll do that often, my dear, for since I am forced to remain shackled to you to prevent my name from becoming a joke,

I must therefore breed my legitimate heirs on your well-used body."

"Especially since you can't breed them on the fine Lady Southwood!" she snapped back. Realizing her folly too late, she was unable to escape the blow he aimed at her. The sound of it echoed inside the carriage, and her head swam with the force of it. She felt his hand cruelly locking itself into her hair, and her neck snapped back as he yanked her about to face him. His silver eyes were narrowed. His harsh voice ripped into her like shards of ragged glass.

"Listen well, my dear, to what I have to say. I could take you home now and beat you to death. I could strangle you and dump you in the Thames, and no one would care, not even me. Nothing would be said for your actions have merited death.

"But you are my wife. And though I am forced to confine you, as the only way of assuring your faithfulness, I will get my sons on you, and you will live in luxury. *But never,*" and he yanked her hair harshly, "*never* do I want to hear *her* name on your lips! Do you understand me, Constanza?"

"Y-yes!"

"Yes, what?"

"Yes, my lord."

"Very good, my dear. I am pleased." Letting her go, he pushed her back into her seat. Lowering the coach window, he called to his driver to stop. "My horse is tied to the back of the coach," he told Constanza. "I am returning to the palace for the Countess's tiring woman, and then I am riding to Lynmouth House to warn them that the Countess is in labor with her child. I will see you at home later."

She nodded dumbly, but he was already gone. A moment later two footmen climbed into the coach, and sat opposite her. "Master says we're to guard you as you've not been yourself," said the older one dourly. She ignored them, looking after Niall as he galloped off.

Despite the lateness of the hour and the empty streets, the trip to the Strand seemed to take forever. The footmen had been eating onions, and the already fetid air in the closed coach was unbearable quite quickly. Constanza was becoming paler by the moment, her mind bursting with all Niall had said.

In Ireland she would be incarcerated—for the rest of her life. She was to be a brood mare. The thought repelled and excited her at the same time. Shifting nervously in her seat, she boldly eyed the younger of the two footmen whose eyes were glued to her full breasts. The boy flushed guiltily, turning even redder as Constanza's pointed little tongue swiftly licked around her pink lips. The familiar longing now began. Imprisoned! Watched over constantly! She would go mad! Somehow Ana would have to help her to escape Niall. But right now, Constanza had to satisfy her hunger. Who knew when she would get another chance?

"Stop the coach!" she commanded imperiously. "You!" Her accusing finger pointed at the older of the two footmen. "You stink of onions! Ride up top. I am close to fainting."

Accustomed to obeying orders, the man called to the driver to stop and scrambled up the coach's side to join the driver. As the vehicle began to move again Constanza wordlessly fell to her knees before the remaining footman, fumbled with his livery and, bending her head, took his organ into her mouth. The boy could only gasp with surprise as his mistress's insistent lips and tongue drove him. When he thought his delight could be no greater, she rose and, lifting her skirts, impaled herself on him. The footman swiftly tore her bodice open and pushed his face into her breasts. He kissed, sucked, and bit on them, prodding her to frenzy as she jogged up and down on him. She spent twice, then, when she was weak and languid, the footman became emboldened. Lifting her up, he turned her over and shoved her face down on the opposite seat. Her skirts pushed above her waist, her little white bottom glowed pale and he entered her from behind. His beefy hands fumbled beneath her, squeezing her breasts rhythmically with each stroke of his rod as he murmured the foulest of obscenities in her ear. A moment before his climax he reached one hand beneath her to tweak at the little button of her sensuality, and they shuddered their satisfaction in unison.

He had barely drained when she bucked him away from her, straightened her skirts, and sat calmly down to lace her bodice. "Fix your livery!" she hissed. "And remember that one word will cost you your position." She was calmer now than she had been all evening, and now she was able to think.

When they reached the house, she sought Ana. "He knows all," Constanza announced without preamble. "That fool Basingstoke provoked a duel. Niall killed him, but we've been banished from both Court and England."

"Santa Maria protect us! Ah, *niña,* I warned you! My lord will surely kill you now!"

"I'd rather he did. But he is taking us to Ireland and I am to be forever imprisoned in my apartment there while I breed his heirs!"

"Get down on your knees, *niña,* and thank the Holy Mother! The lord is merciful."

"No! No, duenna! I will not be locked up! You must help me escape!"

"*Niña, niña!* Be reasonable! My lord is willing to forgive you. Where could you go?"

"Perhaps Harry will help me."

"No, *niña!* You have been fortunate. Be a good wife now."

They argued for close to an hour, Ana urging restraint, Constanza becoming more frantic. Then suddenly the door was flung open, and Lord Burke strode in. "Good! You are both here. Ana, I am pensioning you off and sending you back to Mallorca."

"No!" cried both women in unison. Ana flung herself at Lord Burke's feet. "Please, my lord, no! Constanza is my baby! I cannot leave her! Do not make me, I beg you!"

Niall Burke lifted up the weeping woman. "Ana, it is precisely because of your love for Constanza that I must send you away. You knew of her perfidy, and yet you protected her. You would do so again. Had you come to me immediately, this scandal might have been avoided."

"Please, my lord—"

"Ana, no more." His voice was stern but kindly. "It is because of your love for my wife and the care you have given her that I pension you rather than send you onto the streets. Bid your mistress farewell now. You'll leave in the morning and carry with you my instructions to my agent in Mallorca."

Helplessly, Ana hugged Constanza to her, the tears running down her worn old face. "*Niña,* do as I have bid you, for the sake of the love I bore both you, and your poor mother."

"Do not leave me, duenna! Do not leave me!" Constanza wept. "Niall! Please, I beg you!"

Lord Burke separated the two women. "Neither of you can be trusted," he said wearily, and firmly escorted Ana from the room, stopping to lock the door behind him before he walked Ana to her room.

"My lord," she pleaded once more.

"Adios, Ana. God go with you."

"Be kind to her, my lord."

"I have let her live to bear my sons, Ana, yet I am not sure I am wise in doing so."

As Ana departed the next morning she remembered the sadness in his voice. From an upper floor of the house Constanza waved to her, calling, "Adios, Ana mia. Vaya con Dios!"

Ana was taken by coach to the London docks, and escorted aboard a Mallorca-bound vessel. On her person she carried two letters. One was to the governor, Constanza's father. It explained that the climate of England had proved detrimental to Ana's health and, as Ireland was no warmer, Lord Burke was pensioning off his wife's loyal retainer. She would be given a cottage on Constanza's dowry lands, and an annual stipend. The second letter directed Lord Burke's Mallorcan agent to make the proper arrangements for Ana.

The vessel on which Ana traveled was fortunate. As there were few ships in the London Pool, it sailed within two days. Ana's thoughts, however, remained behind in England, with her mistress.

Chapter 20

A LINE OF BRIGHTLY DECORATED CARRIAGES EXTENDED DOWN the Strand from the entry of Lynmouth House. Gaily caparisoned horses, their elegant riders bandying the latest gossip, rode past the carriages and up the driveway of the beautiful riverside mansion. Lady Southwood, two weeks past childbirth, was receiving. Everyone sought to congratulate the Queen's favorite lady on the birth of the Lynmouth heir.

The truth had been broadcast about the lovely Countess of Lynmouth. She had not been raised in a French convent. She was in fact an Irish heiress who had suffered from a complete loss of memory since being kidnaped by pirates! She had been betrothed to the Irish Lord Burke at the time of her disappearance. The same Lord Burke whose wife provoked the terrible duel that killed poor Basingstoke. It was all too delightfully scandalous.

Scandal bred scandal. Some cousins of Geoffrey Southwood's, the ones who stood to inherit his title and estates if he died without male issue, then petitioned the Archbishop of Canterbury to declare the Earl's current marriage null and void and his new son, Robert, a bastard. Their justification was Skye's previous contact with Lord Burke! The uproar that followed was monumental, with Geoffrey Southwood calling his cousin out and badly wounding him in a duel. It was still not certain whether the foolish man would live.

Lord Burke, a gentleman even if he was Irish, had saved the situation by bringing forth a document signed by the Pope and attested to as genuine by the Spanish ambassador. The document had dissolved Lord Burke's betrothal contract with Skye O'Malley, who was presumed deceased. Constanza's father had been a careful man! The Archbishop of Canterbury subsequently declared that no impediment had existed at the time of the marriage between Lord and Lady Southwood. Therefore, their son, Robert, was legal issue. The archbishop had baptized the boy himself, with the Queen and Lord Dudley acting as the child's godparents.

But there was even more! Lord Burke had invaded the house of the prostitute, Claro, stripped her naked, and whipped her through the streets of London to the edge of the city. He left her there to brave a mob of lustful men and outraged goodwives. Returning to his own home, Burke discovered his wife, her jewels, and his head groom gone. The Queen had lifted his banishment until he could find Constanza. She seemed to have disappeared off the face of the earth. The Court agreed that the past half-month had been simply exhausting!

The Countess of Lynmouth received her guests in state, propped up in her bedchamber with its gold-embroidered rose velvet hangings. She wore a heavy cream-colored quilted satin bedgown, embroidered with pearls and turquoise in a floral design. Her beautiful dark curls were held back by a matching pearl-and-turquoise ribbon. Her pink cheeks and sparkling blue eyes attested to her good health and quick recovery. Southwood finally had a lucky marriage. The lady was a good breeder who'd probably give him a son every year or two.

Plump goosedown pillows, their lace-edged white linen covers smelling faintly of lavender, propped the Countess up. A pink coverlet that matched the rose velvet hangings was spread over the bed. Next to the canopied bed a carved and gilded walnut cradle displayed the lace-capped heir who slept, oblivious, through the admiring exclamations.

The room was a treasure trove of gifts, all tastefully displayed in honor of their donors. Chief among the gifts was a set of twelve silver cups set with sapphires, the baby's birthstone. They were from his godmother. Lord Dudley had presented his godson with a leather case containing twelve silver spoons. The child's crest was on the front, his birthdate on the back.

Everyone who came brought gifts. Young Robin had a dozen silver rattles of various designs and at least that number in teething rings. There were several christening cups, many lengths of excellent cloth, and a number of well-filled purses. There were gifts for Skye too. Frivolous bits of lace and ribbons, little jewelry, and nosegays of late-September flowers. Through it all, Geoffrey Southwood stood by his wife's side watching over her with loving pride. She had been most loving since Robin's birth, and that more than anything else she could have done, reassured Geoffrey.

But Skye did not feel sure of herself. Niall Burke had not yet come to see her, and how could she know what was really in her heart until he did? Why did he not come? And when he finally did, at last, she was totally unprepared.

Autumn had been late in coming, and even now at October's end the trees were just at their golden peak. Geoffrey had been gone ten days, down into Devon to oversee the arrangements for his wife and son's arrival there. The Queen had finally, though reluctantly, agreed to let Skye go at least until the spring.

Skye sat, this bright October day, beneath an apple tree in her riverside garden. Her yellow skirts were spread about her like a flower. Willow, now two and a half, played nearby under the watchful eye of her nurse. The baby slumbered on a blanket beside his mother in the warm afternoon sun. Skye was relaxed and content when Daisy came to announce, "My lord Burke has called to pay his respects, milady. He is waiting in your little library."

Skye rose slowly with far more calm than she felt. "Take Robin to his nurse, Daisy," she instructed, then walked quietly across the lawn and into the house. She stopped for a moment to check her hair in a mirror, carefully tucking an errant lock into the golden net that confined her dark curls. Her hand was trembling, which didn't surprise her, for her heart was racing wildly. Taking a deep breath, she grasped the door handle firmly, straightened her shoulders, and walked purposefully into the library.

"My lord, it is good to see you again." Her musical voice did not waver, and she produced just the right note of cordiality.

Niall turned. The silvery eyes were still bold and clear and bright, but now there were tiny wrinkles around them. His fair skin was clear and he stood as tall and straight as ever. But there was a maturity, an alluring quiet strength about him now, growth marked by time and molded by suffering. His dark hair was accented by a bit of gray near the temples. Gone was the rash young man she remembered and in that young man's place stood a mature and, yes, a most attractive, self-assured man.

"You've become even more beautiful—if that is possible. Motherhood becomes you, Skye."

"Thank you, my lord." She moved to the table. "Will you take wine?" How formal she sounded! Was he laughing at her?

"Are you uncomfortable with me, Skye?"

"It is . . . awkward, Niall. Until six weeks ago I remembered nothing beyond four years ago—in Algiers."

"Sit down with me, Skye. Sit down and tell me what happened. I almost lost my mind when I lost you."

She sat across from him in a brown velvet chair and calmly began. "I was transferred from the ship that took me to another that same day. That part is hazy. They did not harm me, for the Moslems believe the mad to have been touched by God's hand. Believing you dead, I had temporarily lost my mind. When I became aware again I was in the house of Khalid el Bey. He cared for me. He loved me. Eventually we were married." She told her story simply, finishing with, "I was pregnant with Khalid's child when I fled Algiers. Willow is his daughter. The rest you know." Her eyes never left Niall's during the recitation.

"Did you love the infidel?"

Skye felt a cold anger surge through her. How dare he speak to her that way? "Khalid el Bey was a great gentleman," she said, slowly and deliberately. "I loved him deeply. He was kind and good, and beloved of all who knew him. How dare you refer to him that way?"

"Skye, forgive me. My own troubles have colored my feelings toward all women lately. Thank God for Khalid el Bey. Had he not rescued you, God only knows what would have happened to you."

"Why have you come, Niall?"

"I am returning home to Ireland, Skye. I thought I might carry some messages for you, and tell your family when you will return."

"I do not know when I'll return," she said. "I am told that Uncle Seamus has taken excellent care of the business. My life is here now. All I want are my sons. I would like them sent here to me."

"But you're the O'Malley of Innisfana, Skye."

"I am also the Countess of Lynmouth, Niall. But tell me, have you found your poor wife?"

"I found her. She is not well. She'll be better off in Ireland."

He was so bitter, she realized. Fate had not dealt kindly with him. "I am sorry, Niall," she said. "So very sorry."

"I neither need nor want your pity, Skye," he snapped. The words he did not say hung between them: *I want your love!* He rushed on. "Constanza nursed me back to health. They all said you were dead, that a lady couldn't possibly have lived through such an experience. At first I wouldn't listen, but even the Dey of Algiers couldn't find you. Finally I had to listen. I was lonely, and Constanza was pretty and . . . so innocent. I had to marry for the MacWilliam's sake, for the Burke name. I had forgotten the difference between just a lady and a certain Irish lady." He sighed so sadly that she came close to weeping.

"Whatever your fate, Niall, mine would not have changed. I should still be married to Geoffrey now."

"Would you?" His tone challenged her.

For the first time since she had entered the room Skye looked straight at Niall. Her sapphire-blue eyes with their hint of green snapped, "Yes, I would. Had my memory remained whole I would have moved Heaven and Hell to return to you, Niall Burke, but the thought that you were dead all but destroyed me. In my heart and mind I must have believed myself responsible for your death and I could not face what I thought I'd done. My mind went blank. Now my memory has returned and I thank God for it, for it allows me to be reunited with my sons and my family. But understand this, Niall. I cannot change what has happened during the last four years, and I am not sure I would want to change it. How many women have known the love I have known?"

"Love?" he shouted at her. "More likely you mean lovemaking! That's all you damn women think about! I would have thought Dom O'Flaherty had cured you of lust!"

"And if he had," she shouted back, "would you have been so hot to bed me? No! You wouldn't have wanted me." Then her heart went out to him. "Niall, oh my poor dear, how badly you've been hurt! Once my lord Khalid told me of women like your Constanza. It's a sickness with her, Niall. She cannot help what she does."

But he was infuriated by her pity. "And what is your excuse, madam. That lusty boy who howls in your nursery was no seven-month babe."

"What a cold, self-righteous bastard you've become," she said softly.

He snarled and, catching her by surprise, yanked her roughly toward him. She found she could not move and his big hands tangled in her hair as his mouth crushed down on hers. With brutal deliberateness he kissed her slowly over and over until she could not avoid responding. His mouth seared hers. He kissed her purple-shadowed eyelids, her temples, and again her mouth.

Thrill after thrill slammed through Skye. Oh dear God! His mouth forced back the memories she had so long denied. The girl she had been cried out soundlessly to him. Then, as suddenly as he had grasped her, he thrust her from him. "Yes," he spat. "You are all alike, you women! Ready to lift your tail for any man who rouses you!"

She slapped him as hard as she could. "No wonder your wife seeks other men," she said, and rejoiced to see his face crumble. He had hurt her and she wanted to hurt him. He turned on his heel and slammed from the room.

Alone, her hand tingling, she wept. What had happened to him in the past four years to change him so? Was it not she who had suffered the most? She could understand his bitterness over Constanza, but why did he direct his hostility toward her? The afternoon shadows lengthened, a servant came to light the fire, and still she sat with the tears running unchecked down her face.

The library door opened once again, but she did not look up. Strong arms wrapped about her, pulling her against the comfort of a familiar velvet-clad chest. "I'll kill the arrogant bastard for hurting you," Geoffrey's cool voice surprised her.

"He hates me," she sobbed. "He truly hates me. And for what? What have I done to him?"

"Do you hate him?"

"No!" she sobbed.

"Then he's a fool to scorn your love," came the reply.

"I don't love him, Geoffrey. Not now. But he was once my dear friend and now he hates me. I did him no hurt, and that is what I cannot bear." She wept as he held her tenderly, stroking her dark hair. Finally she managed to calm herself. "When did you get back?" she sniffed.

"A little while ago. Daisy told me Lord Burke had called on you, slammed angrily from the house shortly thereafter, and that you'd not come out of the library since then."

"Is all well in Devon?"

"All is well, and in readiness to receive us. My girls eagerly await you as well as their stepsister and half-brother."

"Let us go tomorrow!"

"All right," he agreed, "we'll go tomorrow."

"Geoffrey?"

"What, my darling?"

"I love you!"

A happy grin split his handsome face. He walked to the library door and turned the key in the lock. She saw the grin fade into a look of passion. "Oh, yes!" she breathed in answer to the unasked question. "Yes! Yes! Yes!" And holding out her hand to him, she drew him close. For a long, long moment he held her face in his hands, looking down into it. Then his mouth touched her gently, searchingly, and her lips parted eagerly beneath his, sending shivers of hot and cold up her spine. His kisses deepened and she became aware that his hands were loosening her laces, drawing her skirts off. Her own fingers were pulling at the bone buttons on his doublet, and when they had undressed each other, they slipped to the floor before the warm fire. His elegant fingers stroked her long back, her rounded buttocks. She grew bold, pushing him onto his back, her small tongue lapping eagerly at his nipples. "Damn you, Skye," he growled through gritted teeth. "Ahhhh, God, sweetheart!" Her tongue followed the thin golden line of hair downward from his belly. She breathed deeply of his warm male scent, like a kitten licking lovingly at a kindly hand. She loved his great manroot with her tongue. He shuddered with pleasure. For several months now he had been denied the delights of her body. Strangely, he had remained faithful. Once having loved her, no other woman could satisfy him.

To fall upon her would have been so easy. He ached to bury himself deep within her, but Geoffrey Southwood was that rare man who gained his greatest pleasure by giving pleasure. Skillfully he turned her onto her back and slowly rained burning kisses over the long pure pillar of her throat. "I have longed for weeks to love you again," he murmured, placing his lips against the jumping pulse at the base of her throat. His mouth moved to the tiny star mole at the swell of her breast. "Sweet, ah my darling, how sweet you are."

They were lost in each other. Hands and lips loved and loved and loved again until the line between reality and fantasy wavered and finally disappeared altogether. They caressed, they tasted, they hungered until finally they were joined in one undying blaze of love that left them physically shaken, but strangely stronger. The gold-orange firelight played over their entwined bodies like a jealous third lover. Exhausted, they slept where they lay, waking an hour later to cuddle, to speak in hushed whispers of little things. They were man and wife, they were lovers, and yet they sometimes felt momentarily shy of each other.

"The harvest was good on the estates," he said.

"Did you visit Wren Court?" she asked.

"They eagerly awaited Dame Cecily."

"She's as anxious to get home as we are. Oh, Geoffrey! Thank you for loving me, *really* loving me!"

"I love you as you love me, my darling. 'Tis love returned."

"'Twill always be returned, my dearest husband."

What Niall Burke would not have given to hear those words. He had left Lynmouth House in a high rage. The meeting had not gone at all as he had planned. He had dared to hope that she would fling herself into his arms and beg to be taken home to Ireland. He had believed she would be ashamed of what had transpired in Algiers. Instead, she had behaved totally unlike the sweet Skye of his memory. His memory was faulty: Niall had conveniently forgotten the woman who had led her men into battle with Barbary pirates.

Moving through his house, he unlocked the door to his wife's bedchamber and walked into the room. "Good evening, Mrs. Tubbs, and how is your patient tonight?"

A tall, stocky woman rose from her chair by the bed and came forward. "She was able to take some soup this evening, my lord."

"Good. Go and get your own meal now. I will sit with Lady Burke until you return."

"Thank you, my lord." The big woman bobbed a curtsey and was gone.

Niall Burke sat down by the bed and stared at the sleeping woman who was his wife. Her beautiful pale golden skin had grown sallow, her glorious dark golden hair—braided now in two plaits—had become a lusterless brown, and lank. But a few months ago she had been the loveliest girl alive, and now—He sighed. Poor Constanza. He could never forgive her for what she had done, but they might begin again, and if he could get her with child perhaps she would become once more the sweet girl he had fallen in love with back on Mallorca.

Her pansy-purple eyes opened. "Niall?"

"I am here, Constanzita."

"Take me home, Niall."

"When you are strong enough to travel, my dear, we will go home to Ireland."

Constanza shuddered. Ireland. That wet, gray land. The MacWilliam's stronghold would be cold and gray too. She longed for warmth, for the sun, for Mallorca. "If you take me to Ireland I shall die. I want to go home to Mallorca."

"We will see what the doctor says, Constanzita," he said. "Go to sleep now."

Her eyes closed wearily, and he was struck by how frail she was. It amazed him that she had managed to withstand the rigors of the London underworld where he'd found her. She had fled with his head stableman. Knowing her nature quite well, Harry had set her up in two rooms and pimped for her. He sold her jewelry, then began to live riotously on the proceeds, setting himself up in quarters in a nearby tavern. Lavish spending soon emptied Harry's pockets, but his taste for high life abated not one whit. He beat his mistress cruelly, accusing her of not working hard enough. She could earn twice as much if she'd cut down on the amount of time she spent with her customers and if she took only four hours to sleep a night.

Polly the kitchen maid, hearing of Harry's whereabouts from her married sister who lived in the same slum, crept above stairs to find her master. Niall had taken Polly up on his horse ahead of him and, breathless with excitement, she had directed him to where Constanza lived.

Niall was hard put not to become sick when he found his wife, half-delirious with fever, on the floor in a tiny room. She lay on a filthy pallet, the stink of the unemptied chamber pot permeating the room. Even little Polly, raised in the same degree of poverty, gasped with shock.

"'Er 'ull be no good to ye," cackled the old crone who owned the house, "unless o' course ye likes to swive 'em when they 'alf dead."

"Close your trap, old hag," snapped Polly. "We're taking the lady out of here."

"Lady, is it? Lady?" screeched the old woman. "She owes me for rent, that one."

"Where is the man who was with her?" asked Niall.

"'Andsome 'Arry? 'E ain't been around since she got ill. Got 'imself a newer, younger doxy."

"How much rent is owed?"

The old woman eyed Lord Burke craftily. "A shilling," she said.

The Irishman reached for his purse, but Polly intervened. "You wouldn't get a shilling for this room in two years' time, old hag," she declared, outraged. "Give her no more than two silver pennies, my lord."

Instead Niall Burke pulled a half-crown from his purse and handed it to the woman, whose eyes bugged with greed and shock. "This woman was never here, and neither were we," he said quietly.

The landlady snatched the coin, bit it, and stuffed it into her apron pocket. "I ain't never seen any o' yese," she declared, quickly disappearing from the room.

Niall and Polly got Constanza to her feet. "You'll ride with her, lass, and I'll lead the horse," he said, thankful for the rainy dark night that would cover their return to the Strand. Niall Burke had long ago tired of feeding the gossip mills of Court. When they finally reached the Burke house the servants had all retired excepting one sleepy stable boy who took the horse off to its stall. Lord Burke carried his unconscious wife up to her rooms, where he and Polly stripped the filthy garments off her thin body. Niall then filled the small oak tub with warm water he and Polly lugged up from the kitchens themselves. They washed her, including her matted, lice-ridden hair. Constanza, half conscious, protested weakly. They hauled her from the tub, toweled her off, put a clean gown on her, and plaited her dried hair into two braids. She was finally tucked into bed.

Back down in the kitchens of the house, Lord Burke emptied the little tub and sat down at the table. Polly rummaged about in the larder and found half a roasted capon. She put it on a wooden trencher with some bread and placed it before her master. She then poured him a goblet of brown October ale, and stood back. But Niall motioned her into the bench opposite him. Tearing off part of the capon breast, he shoved the meat toward her. "Eat up, lass! You've worked hard this night. And pour yourself some ale too."

Shyly, Polly obeyed him, somewhat astounded. "Thank you, my lord."

"That was a kind thing you did, lass. I might never have found my wife without your help. She's a very sick woman, Polly. Sick in spirit and body."

"I never thought a lady would act that way, begging your pardon, my lord."

He smiled. A curiously innocent little sparrow was Polly. He could have shocked her with tales of great Court ladies all over Europe who whored for one reason or another. "Polly, you seem a bright lass. I'm going to offer you a chance to better yourself, but it will not be easy. I need someone to look after my lady. She can never again be left alone. If I am not with her then someone else must be. She is ill now, but when she gets well she'll try and cozen you, but you mustn't let her. Do you think you can do it?"

"Aye, my lord. But there's one thing you should know. Harry was sometimes my lover too and once when my lady caught us, she . . . she . . ." Polly's face was beet red. "She joined us," the servant finished with a rush. "I know I can care for her, but I wanted you to know that."

Niall choked on his ale. Constanza had certainly been inventive. "Part of caring for Lady Burke will be telling those who ask that she is not strong in mind, Polly."

"I understand, sir."

So he had hired Mrs. Tubbs to keep watch by night, and young Polly cared for Constanza during the day. The first doctor engaged was told only that Lady Burke had been abducted and the experience had unhinged her mind. He cupped and bled her, which only weakened her further. Niall sent the physician on his way and brought in a second doctor, this one recommended by Lord Southwood.

The man turned out to be a knowledgeable Moor. He examined Constanza thoroughly, stopping to make notes, clucking sympathetically. At last he went with Lord Burke to a private room. "My lord, your wife is a very sick woman, emotionally and physically. She will need a special diet, rest, sunshine, and medication." He paused a moment as if weighing something. Then he asked, "Do you have the pox, my lord?"

"God, no!"

"Your wife does." It was said flatly. "One of the worst cases I've ever seen."

"I'm not surprised," Niall said quietly. "You see, Doctor, my wife is indeed ill. She is a woman for whom one lover is simply not enough. Do you understand what I am saying?"

"I do, my lord, and I am sorry. I have heard of such cases. I can treat her symptoms, but unless you can prevent her folly, she will kill herself. Frankly, I am not sure it is not already too late."

Niall sought his study. He lit no candles but sat quietly by the dancing fire. *Well, Father,* he thought, *I shall not be bringing this wife home to Ireland yet.*

Dr. Hamid returned the next day.

"Good evening, Doctor," Niall greeted him.

"My lord."

"Come see me after you have examined Constanza."

"Very well, my lord."

Niall sighed. He remained in thought for some time and then became aware that he was not alone.

"My lord?"

"Oh, Doctor. Come into my study and sit down, man. How is Constanza?"

"A bit stronger, but not as well as I hoped for, my lord."

"Could she travel?"

"Ireland? It would kill her."

"No, Doctor Hamid. Mallorca. She had expressed a desire to go home. If it is possible, I would grant her wish."

"The sun would be very good for her, my lord, but she is not yet strong enough for the trip."

"In a few weeks?"

"It is possible. Yes! In fact, if she knows she is going it will improve her attitude greatly."

"Then I shall tell her. In the meantime I will go home to Ireland to see my father. I have been gone over four years."

Niall Burke was on his way home within three days, riding across the verdant stretch of England that brought him to its westernmost port, where he quickly found a ship bound for Ireland.

The first sight of his beloved homeland, the softly undulating green hills, the dramatic, cloud-tossed skies peculiar to Ireland alone, combined with his lengthy absence brought tears to Niall's eyes. But once the ship had docked and he was on a horse once more, sentiment gave way to sheer eagerness to reach the MacWilliam's stronghold. He was stunned to find his family expecting him, and wondered how in the world they'd known of his coming. As he approached his home, he saw a figure riding out to meet him, and his heart caught when he recognized his father. The old man had grown thinner and was even frail, Niall noted as his father came closer. But he had not lost any of his fabled authority or proud bearing.

"So you let the O'Malley escape again, and she's already spawned a son for her new lord," was his father's greeting. It was as if Niall had never been away.

"I have a wife now," he reminded his father, more than a little defensive.

"Another barren field upon which your seed lays fallow. Where is she?"

"I left her in London. She is ill."

"Humph! I might have guessed as much."

"Father, I cannot stay. I came because I wanted to see you. Our climate is killing Constanza and because Ireland is no better I am taking her home to Mallorca."

"Better you bring her here to Ireland to die. Then we can rewed you to a strong Irish girl who'll give me grandsons. Foreign wenches transplant badly in Irish soil."

"She will probably die anyway, Father. She misses the sun, and I would have her last days be happy."

"In that case I'll see which maidens of good family are available for marriage. Or perhaps a young widow with sons . . ." the older man mused.

"Make me no matches, Father!"

"I want my grandchildren about me before I die!"

And so it went between them for the few days of Niall's visit. On the day of his departure Seamus O'Malley, the Bishop of Connaught, arrived with his two great-nephews, Ewan and Murrough O'Flaherty, requesting that Niall escort them to their mother in England. Though the children would slow him down, Niall agreed. He was pleasantly surprised when Seamus O'Malley offered an O'Malley vessel to take them directly to Devon.

"Is my niece happy?" asked the bishop.

"She claims to be," said Niall sourly, "but then, women are apt to be fickle."

Seamus O'Malley hid a smile. "You must learn to accept God's will, my son," he murmured piously.

Niall Burke bit back the urge to tell the good bishop to go to Hell. "I shall endeavor to pray for patience," he said with obvious insincerity, and Seamus O'Malley chuckled.

"Can you leave tomorrow, Niall? Skye writes that she is anxious to see these imps of hers. Poor Skye . . ." He trailed off. There were no words to express what the bishop thought about his niece's tragedy.

After a moment Niall said, "I can leave tomorrow, though I devoutly pray that this trip aboard an O'Malley vessel will not be as eventful as the last one was."

Ewan and Murrough O'Flaherty proved easy to chaperone. Six and seven, the boys were anxious to see their mother, yet frightened of encountering a woman they barely remembered. This trip was their first away from Ireland, and despite their anxieties they were very excited.

Niall Burke bid the MacWilliam an affectionate farewell. "If you need me, the governor of Mallorca will know where I am," he said, "and I promise you I'll come home this time."

"Good! I'll not die, my lad, until I see the next generation."

Niall shot his father a parting grin, then rode off with his two young charges. The few days' voyage proved uneventful, a time of clear skies and good winds. On the last day they sailed past the Isle of Lundy, across the tidal bar, and up the Torridge River to Bideford. The little O'Flahertys were wide-eyed, having never been in a town before. Openmouthed, they gazed at the activity about them in the bustling port town. Niall, unable to resist indulging them a little, took them to a delightful riverside inn for cakes and watered wine. He was able to rent two horses, and as it was not quite the noon hour, there was plenty of time to reach Lynmouth Castle. Before they rode off, the innkeeper's young wife supplied the little party with bread, cheese, and crisp apples. "Boys get hungry," she said with a cheerful smile. Niall smiled back and mischievously dropped a coin into her bodice. "Buy some blue ribbons to match your eyes," he answered.

Ewan and Murrough were silent now, more nervous as each clop of the horses hooves brought them closer to their mother. Niall's thoughts centered on Skye, also. They had parted so bitterly, and it had been his fault entirely. That Constanza's behavior should have driven him to suspect Skye of immorality! What a fool he'd made of himself! Of course she loved Southwood. It was tragic, for Niall, that her memories of him had only returned *after* she had fallen in love and married. But then, as she had pointed out, had she not been wed, he was. Why had he taken his frustrations out on her? They stopped by a clear stream to rest the horses and eat the simple luncheon that the innkeeper's wife had pressed on them.

"'Tis not like Ireland," observed Ewan.

"Everything is so neat," Murrough said. "I want to go home."

"Now, lads, give it a chance. Your mother is so anxious to see you."

"What of the *Englishman* she's married?" asked Ewan. His scorn was barely concealed. Niall's amusement was great.

"Lord Southwood is a fine gentleman, boys. You'll like him."

"We're not staying here," continued Ewan. "My brother and I are O'Flahertys of Ballyhennessey, and I've my own lands to care for in Ireland. We'll only visit with our mother."

"Your mother only recently regained her memory. When she did, her first concern was for you both. You are not to disgrace her in front of the English and let the English say we're uncouth barbarians."

"To Hell with the English!" snapped the boy.

"A sentiment I'm inclined to agree with, Ewan O'Flaherty, but nevertheless you will behave yourself and not disgrace the Irish," replied Niall, cuffing the boy playfully. "Now mount up, lads. If we're to reach your mother before dark we must ride hard for Lynmouth."

They had their first view of Lynmouth Castle just before sunset. Situated on a bay between two headland points, the castle faced the Isle of Lundy. The oldest part of the castle was a Saxon round-tower onto which the next several generations had built. The result was a small but totally charming mixture of Saxon, Norman, Gothic, and Tudor architecture. Below the dark-gray tower the house was pale gray stone, covered in spots with deep-green ivy. Just then the red late-afternoon sun colored its slate-turreted towers and warmed its fields. Slowly the horses clopped across the well-worn oak drawbridge into the castle courtyard. A stable boy hurried out to take their mounts and a servant led them inside the castle.

"I am Lord Burke. I have brought the Countess's two sons from Ireland," said Niall.

"This way, my lord. The young masters have been expected though we knew not when you would arrive."

The footmen led them to the family hall. As they entered the room, two things struck Niall. The room was beautiful, windowed on both sides and facing the sea. And Skye seemed so absolutely right at home in this room, standing by a window, simply gowned in mulberry velvet. Her magnificent blue eyes widened with surprise at the sight of him and the two children. "I've brought you your lads, Skye," he said quietly. "Good evening, Southwood. I hope I may rely on your hospitality tonight."

The Earl nodded and moved to place his arm tightly about his wife's shoulders.

"These are my sons?!" Her look was incredulous. "Geoffrey! They were still babies when I saw them last!" Tears were rolling down her cheeks. "Ewan! Murrough! Come to Mama." Her arms opened wide and were filled instantly by the two young boys, who clung to her, unashamed, sobbing their own happiness and relief. "Oh my darlings," she wept, "I did not realize until this moment how very very much I'd missed you both." She hugged them again. "Let go of me, little monkeys, and let me look at you." She untangled them from her neck and set them back. "Well, you're nothing like your father, either of you—and I thank God for it. You're pure O'Malley with your black hair and deep-blue eyes. Ewan . . . you are seven now, and Murrough is six?"

"Yes, Mama," they chorused.

"Then," she said wistfully, "you will soon be sent to a good family as pages. But first we will get to know each other again. I would present you to your stepfather, the Earl of Lynmouth."

The boys both turned and, under Niall's threatening gaze, made a leg to Lord Southwood. Having seen Niall's stern look, Geoffrey chuckled inwardly with suppressed amusement. So the two little savages resented him? Well, that was only natural. He bowed back to the two children. "Ewan and Murrough O'Flaherty, I am most pleased to have you as my stepsons, and welcome you to my home."

"And they must meet the other children, Geoffrey," said Skye. "You have three stepsisters, boys. Susan is six, the twins, Gwyneth and Joan, are five. And you have a half-sister, my daughter Willow. She is three and a half. Your new baby half-brother is called Robbie. Come my darlings, and I'll take you to the nursery to greet them." She had said nothing at all to Niall, nothing.

"I had forgotten that she hates as fiercely as she loves," said Niall softly.

"You hurt her badly the last time you met," replied Geoffrey.

"I know. God only knows I never meant to, but suddenly we were quarreling."

"It was kind of you to bring Skye's boys from Ireland. Did you settle your wife there safely?"

"Constanza is still in London. I went to see my father. I shall leave for London tomorrow. My wife is very ill and I am taking her home to Mallorca."

Geoffrey nodded. "Let me have a servant show you to your room," he said politely.

A few minutes later Niall stood alone in his room. Like the lovely family hall he had just left, this room faced the sea. The sunset was staining the waters below him a dark wine red, and in the early-evening autumn haze he could see the Isle of Lundy, that mysterious pirate haunt. Skye would be happy here, thought Niall, within the sight and smell of the sea.

Dinner that night was simple, and a restrained, almost uncomfortable affair. The children were not there, having eaten earlier in the nursery. Ewan and Murrough were more comfortable now. Their stepsisters were in total awe of them, and they had instantly fallen under the spell of their half-sister, Willow. Their infant half-brother had been dismissed as uninteresting.

The Southwoods and Lord Burke sat at the high board. Below them were only a few retainers, for the Earl was not holding state. The meal was simple, the conversation spare. Finally only Niall and Geoffrey and Skye remained sitting, the others having either left the hall or gathered about the fireplace. Niall knew he could not leave in the morning unless he first spoke with Skye. She had managed to avoid speaking directly to him all evening while making it appear as if nothing was wrong. Niall realized he must take the direct route.

"Skye," he said quietly, looking directly into her eyes, "I would tender my apologies for our last meeting."

Her lips turned up in a little smile. "You were under a great strain, my lord," she replied pleasantly. The smile did not reach to her blue eyes, which were devoid of all expression. "Now I hope you will excuse me, my lord. It has been an exciting day, and I am weary." She didn't pause to wait for an answer. Bending to Geoffrey, her eyes warm now, she said, "Do not be long, my darling."

He caught her hand and, turning it, kissed the palm lingeringly. "I won't, my love." Her hand caressed his face.

Niall felt himself painfully the intruder in witnessing this short intimate moment. Skye paused at the door to the hall and, turning, said, "God speed, Niall." Then she was gone.

"She really has forgiven you, Niall. But you hurt her and she is proud."

"She was always proud," he said. "Proud and defiant of the entire world. I think that's why her father loved her best, and left the O'Malleys in her charge." Niall rubbed his forehead wearily. "Ah, that is history now, history of another time, another place. And, I'm thinking of another woman. Well, I'm off to bed, Southwood. I plan to make an early start. If I don't see you in the morning, I thank you now for your hospitality."

Geoffrey Southwood watched his guest depart, and felt sorry for him. Then, shaking himself, he went to prepare for bed. When he joined his wife, Skye was brushing her lovely dark hair. "You were hard on him, my love."

"I will not be vulnerable to Niall Burke ever again," she said grimly. Then, switching moods, she wound her arms about him and he laughed softly.

"Witch, are you flirting with me?"

"Yes! Kiss me, Geoffrey!"

He pretended to consider her demand. "I must think on this, madam," he said, moving away from her.

"Beast!" she hissed, launching herself at his back.

He turned in time to catch and crush her against his chest. Pinioned, she was helpless. "And now, madam," he said softly as he nibbled her lips.

"Love me, Geoffrey! Please love me!"

"With pleasure, my darling," and his mouth closed over hers.

She gave herself to him unreservedly, once again surprising him by the intensity of her passion. Her lips were petal-soft beneath his, parting to allow his tongue entry. Never freeing her lips, he lifted her up and carried her to their bed. He laid her gently amid the pillows, then drew off his silken nightshirt. Her sapphire eyes devoured him, his lime-green eyes responded in kind. She quickly drew her own sheer nightgown off, flinging it to the floor, and then held out her arms to him. He sat on the edge of the bed and took her face in his strong hands, looking deep into her magnificent eyes.

"No, Skye, don't make love to me in order to wipe out memories of Niall Burke. I am not afraid of those memories, and neither should you be. You cared deeply for the man once, and I know that those feelings can never be erased completely, nor should they be. I know he hurt you, but he was in pain himself. Forgive him, my darling, for his sake but for mine as well, so that when we love I know it is because of the feelings you have for me, not the deep resentment you still harbor for Niall Burke."

The tears spilled from her eyes and ran down her face. "Damn you, Southwood, I don't deserve you! Hell, yes! I'll forgive the bastard, for he's to be pitied. I came to terms with the portion fate allotted me, but Niall did not, and hated me while railing at fate. As if I were responsible for what happened to us! And yes, I hated him for inflicting such hurt on me. He made me feel guilty for being happy with you when he had such misery with Constanza. Understand one thing though, I have never made love with you in order to wipe out memories of Niall Burke!"

She looked adorably indignant, and he chuckled, "I am relieved to hear that, madam." He reached out and slowly fondled an impudent little breast, a lazy smile turning up the corners of his mouth and lighting his eyes. An elegant finger teased a pink nipple to rapt attention, then trailed leisurely between her breasts and downward to the place between her legs. The heel of his palm pressed firmly, then rubbed. Her breathing was more pronounced now, and her eyes glittered through half-lowered lids. "Oh, sweetheart," he murmured, "you were perfectly fashioned for loving," and his head dipped down to taste the soft flesh of her breasts. As often as he had done this, it still wrung a passionate cry from her throat that set his heart to beating wildly. He moaned.

His hands moved downward, imprisoning her slender waist for a moment, then slid lower to cup her buttocks. His own long body moved over hers, and Skye reached out to cup and fondle his manroot. Her soft hands played with him skillfully, teasingly rubbing the wet opening of the sensitive organ. "You could rouse a marble statue, witch!"

"Love me, Geoffrey," she whispered urgently, and spread her legs to receive him.

Slowly, with sweetly practiced skill, he entered her while watching her beautiful eyes mirror what she felt. He drew back and her eyes cried distress. He plunged deep and the pleasure that leaped into that blue gaze added to his own joy. When she finally begged him for sweet release, and her dark feathery lashes lay quivering against her pale cheeks, he felt her spasms break one after another like breakers crashing on the beach. Assured of her happiness, Geoffrey Southwood found his own heaven, reveling in the lovely body that moved so skillfully beneath his, reveling in the sharp nails that dug into his back, in her cry of surrender as his aching manhood burst and flooded her with his burning tribute. She was his, his alone.

Chapter 21

The Earl and Countess of Lynmouth left Devon briefly after the New Year in order to host the Earl's famous Twelfth Night gala in London. Invitations were at a premium again this year, and London's best dressmakers and tailors were overbooked, overworked and overwrought in everyone's mad scramble for the perfect costume. The Countess of Lynmouth's well-filled purse assured her prior knowledge of all of her guests' themes. In order that she not offend any by a similar garb, a discreet bribe here and there had been necessary.

To her amusement, several of the women were copying her idea of the year before, when she had come gowned in black velvet as "Night." Some of them had been clever enough to reverse that role, so there would be at least half a dozen "Days" and four "Afternoons" as well. There were to be the requisite number of "Springs," "Summers," "Winters," and "Autumns." The Queen was coming garbed as "The Sun," which was the worst-kept secret in all of London. The three ladies who had had the same idea had been taken by fits of hysteria when they had to change their gowns. "The Moon" and "Harvest" were also popular themes, but no one except Skye had thought of coming as a jewel. She was to be costumed as "Ruby." As Daisy and her mother had made the dress in Devon, this was the best-kept secret in all of London. Geoffrey would be dressed as "Emerald" in dark green.

The night of the masque Skye stood before her pier glass more than pleased with what she saw. The deep-red gown was magnificent but not gaudy. The underskirt was silk sewn all over in a swirling ornate design with tiny rubies and gold thread that glittered with every movement of light. The overskirt was heavy velvet, the slashings in the velvet sleeves showing the matching silk of the underskirt and repeating the design of tiny rubies. The neckline was daringly low, causing the Earl to comment, "I do not know if I approve of your generosity in showing to the Court the sweet treasures that are mine alone to enjoy." Skye had laughed and replied, "But think of the envy it will cause, my lord." He had laughed, "What a naughty vixen you are," and suddenly placed about her neck a beautiful necklace of large rubies. "My Twelfth Night's gift to you, sweetheart." As she gasped, he bent and fastened matching drop earrings into her ears.

"Oh, Geoffrey!" Her hand touched the necklace reverently. "They are extraordinary." Turning, she kissed him sweetly. The heady perfume of her body assailed him, and he felt a stab of desire.

"For mercy's sake, my love, thank me later! At this moment I am seriously considering the disarrangement of both your gown and your hair."

She giggled happily, flushed with pleasure and excitement. "Oh, I love you!"

He forced his passion away and muttered, "I'd truly rather be home with you in Devon than here now, preparing to allow half of London to eat and drink me out of house and home as well as ogle my wife's breasts."

Skye laughed, delighted, then sat and allowed Daisy to put the finishing touches to her hair. The ladies of the English Court were currently frizzing their hair, but Skye would have none of that. Her own glorious tresses had been coaxed into a chignon at the nape of her neck. The chignon was decorated with red silk flowers. Her hair was parted in the center and two small curls, lately named love-locks, dangled on either side of her face.

Skye stood up, satisfied, and pirouetted before her husband. "Well, milord?"

"There is nothing I can say that you don't already know, my pet." She smiled. He asked, "What of me, madam? Am I not worthy of notice?"

Mischievously she eyed him as boldly as any gallant would eye a lady of his fancy, and the Earl's mouth twitched with amusement at her mimickry. She circled him slowly, looking him up and down critically, and then said, "You've got the best-turned leg of any man at Court, my lord, and the emerald-green velvet compliments those superb eyes of yours. The ladies will be hard put tonight to remember you're mine—but they had better!"

He bowed elegantly, acknowledging the compliment. Laughing, arm in arm, they descended the stairs to the great ballroom of Lynmouth House.

The first carriages were beginning to arrive, and Skye and Geoffrey stood regally at the top of the main staircase greeting their guests. The ballroom filled quickly. Even the Queen arrived early, escorted by the handsome Lord Dudley, among others.

"We intend staying late, my dear Skye," announced Elizabeth. "You and Southwood give the best party of the year!"

"It was to avoid disappointing Your Majesty that we returned to London—temporarily," said Geoffrey. "Skye is not quite over your godson's birth."

"This 'twill not tax you too badly, my dear?" questioned Elizabeth anxiously.

"No, madam. The sight alone of your dear face strengthens me," replied Skye.

The Queen's eyes twinkled. "What a perfect courtier you are, my dear Skye. Certainly a fit mate for Southwood!"

The Earl bowed at the compliment and offered his hand to Elizabeth as the first dance began. Lord Dudley partnered Skye. She did not really like the Queen's favorite, a fact of which he was quite well aware. Unfortunately, her very aloofness excited Robert Dudley. He was a man who loved danger, and the thought of seducing this beautiful woman beneath the very noses of both Elizabeth and the lady's husband was deliciously tempting.

Robert Dudley's view of himself was such that it simply didn't occur to him that he, the most popular man at Court, could be sincerely rebuffed. He blandly assumed that Skye was being coy, though there was nothing of the coy maiden in Skye's personality. If he had known her well, Dudley would have realized this. As he partnered her his eyes feasted on the pearly luminescence of her skin, then plunged deep into her décolletage. What sweet round little apples she hid beneath her bodice. The perusal was all done quickly, for though Elizabeth had thus far denied him total possession of her royal body, she was a very jealous woman.

Skye ignored the greedy eyes that made her feel almost unclean. What she was unable to ignore were Dudley's outright suggestive comments. "Why do you dislike me, my beauty? You would be wise to cultivate my favor."

"I do not dislike you, my lord," said Skye, looking at him evenly. But Dudley's smirk of triumph faded when she continued, "But neither do I like you."

"Then why the hell did you make me your son's godfather?"

"You were my husband's choice," lied Skye. She was thinking, though I may antagonize you, my lord Boorishness, you'll not take it out on my Geoffrey. "You see, my lord Dudley, I always obey my husband as a good wife should," she finished demurely.

"God, how your very virtue inflames me," muttered Dudley.

"I do not seek to inflame you, sir."

"But nevertheless you do, madam." He shot a quick glance toward Elizabeth, but she was well occupied. Catching Skye off guard, he led her from the dance figure and guided her into a private alcove within the ballroom. Before she had recovered her shock, Robert Dudley's arms wrapped quickly about her. Skye was outraged, and she struggled fiercely against him. "Sir! Loose me at once, my lord!" she demanded.

His low laughter was almost a growl. "No, my pretty Skye, I shall not. Enough of this coyness now, madam. I long to taste your ripe lips, and," he lowered his head to kiss the tops of her heaving breasts, "these far sweeter fruits."

She tried to free her arms. Revolted, she pulled away from him, but he tightened an arm about her while his other hand grasped and held her head in a firm grip. Desperately she tried to turn away from the lips descending on hers, but she couldn't, and Dudley's mouth ravaged hers wetly, trying to force passion where there was none. She dared not scream, for the enamored Queen would believe her the aggressor. Robert Dudley, of course, knew this. His tongue pushed past her teeth, thrusting deeply with obvious meaning. Confident, his hands were boldly lifting her skirts now, and knowing she had but one chance before he coolly raped her, she swiftly lifted her knee to find his vulnerable groin. She was rewarded by instant release, and a look of acute pain on Lord Dudley's surprised face.

Without a word Skye fled the alcove, her cheeks burning. She was fortunate that Dudley's chosen rendezvous place had been secluded. Neither their entrance nor her embarrassed flight was observed. Snatching a goblet of iced wine from a passing footman, she forced herself to sip slowly while the beating of her heart dropped back to normal. She stopped before a mirror, set her wine down, and smoothed her hair and her gown with shaking hands.

The filthy, arrogant bastard! How dare Dudley attack her? She had done everything to discourage him, but he could not be put off. She couldn't appeal to the Queen, for Elizabeth was in love with him and would brook no criticism of her precious Robin. *I don't ever want to return to Court,* Skye thought desperately. *We can probably beg off in the spring, and perhaps by next autumn we shall have been replaced in the Queen's affections by others. Then we can remain in Devon and raise our children in peace.* She grew calmer with thoughts of Devon and, picking up her wine, discreetly joined her guests.

In the alcove she had so hastily vacated, Robert, Lord Dudley, was still doubled over, retching. Waves of pain continued to wash over him for a few minutes, but gradually he began to feel better. The little bitch, he thought, half-angry, half-intrigued. He rubbed his injured member ruefully, still unable to quite believe she had refused him. Women simply did not refuse Robert. She would regret this. One day he would have her. *And,* he vowed, she would beg him for his favors. Straightening his garments, he left the alcove.

Skye managed to avoid Dudley the rest of the evening, but Geoffrey, ever sensitive to her moods, saw that something was wrong. Discreetly he led her aside. "What is it, my love."

"Dudley just tried to rape me," she said angrily.

"What?"

"Lower your voice, Geoffrey!" She placed a warning hand on his arm to restrain him. "He has pressed his unwanted attentions on me before, but you know as well as I do that the Queen would not believe it if I told her. He counts on that."

"He didn't—"

"No. I jammed my knee into his groin. I'll be surprised if he can dance again this evening."

Geoffrey winced automatically, but could find in his heart no sympathy for Dudley. "How would you like to leave for Devon immediately after the masque, my darling?" he asked.

"Oh, yes!" Her face lit with joy.

"We'll pause just long enough to change into something warm and easy. We'll be off with the dawn. I know of a marvelous inn along the road where we may spend tomorrow night." He kissed the tip of her nose.

"Like the Ducks and Drake?"

"Better!" He smiled down at her. "Would you mind if we continued to stay down in Devon, forsaking the Court and London?"

"No! It would please me greatly to remain in Devon. I am afraid I am a country mouse at heart, my lord. I hope the news does not disappoint you."

He enfolded her in a warm and loving embrace. "I find, my darling wife, that I have no wish to share you with anybody—except perhaps our children."

"Only perhaps?" she teased.

"Skye, if the shocking truth be known, I don't wish to share you with anyone, including the children! Now, let us go back to our guests before we're missed."

At the midnight supper de Grenville and the recently wed Lettice Knollys found the tiny crowns in their pieces of Twelfth Night cake and were crowned Lord of Misrule and his queen. For the rest of the evening de Grenville kept the party lively ordering naughty forfeits from the guests. Even poor Lettice could not escape her consort of the evening. Dickon ordered her first to be blindfolded, and then to kiss the six gentlemen whom he chose.

"One of them is your husband, Walter, my dear, and you must tell us which."

Poor Lettice was in a terrible quandary, for Walter was not the most inspired of lovers. Blindfolded, her ears became sharper and she could hear amid the giggles a great deal of scuffling. Pursing her pretty cherry lips, she received her six kisses—one a peck, two hearty busses, two that were wet and sloppy, and one very passionate kiss that sent a hot thrill racing through her.

"Well, Lettice?" demanded de Grenville of the blindfolded woman.

Lettice pretended to consider the dilemma. She was quite sure that none of them had been Walter, but she was desirous of knowing the identity of the man whose kiss had thrilled her so. "The last gentleman was Walter," she announced firmly. "I am quite sure."

A great burst of raucous laughter greeted this statement, and when the blindfold was snatched off Lettice found herself facing Lord Dudley. "Ohhhh," she cried, blushing in pretty confusion, "but I was so very sure! He kisses me just the way Walter does."

"None of them was Walter, my dear," chortled de Grenville.

"Really, Dickon!" Lettice stamped her foot in apparent outrage, and there was more good-natured laughter. Robert Dudley smiled to himself as he put an arm about the Queen. Lettice Knollys was an outright minx. When he'd kissed her she'd thrust her sharp little tongue into his mouth with a delightfully practiced skill. He eyed her from beneath carefully lowered eyelids, and saw to his amazement that she was eying him, just as intently and just as discreetly. Well, well, thought Dudley, a possible playmate on those nights when Bess drives me to distraction and then sends me on my way unfulfilled.

The evening progressed, growing merrier and merrier. Finally the Queen and her intimates departed and were followed shortly thereafter by the other exhausted, exhilarated, and drunken guests. The last of them waved out the door, the Earl and Countess of Lynmouth joined hands and ran up the staircase to their apartments where their body servants awaited them.

"I've your night things all ready, m'lady," smiled Daisy.

"No," said Skye, "my lord and I are but stopping to change. We are off for Devon! Have the girls pack my nightgown and toilet articles now, and get me the deep-blue wool traveling dress and the matching velvet cloak with the sable lining and trim."

"But m'lady," protested Daisy, "we've not packed to leave."

"You and the others may leave tomorrow or the day after. My lord and I prefer to travel quickly."

"Yes, m'lady."

In his bedchamber Geoffrey was issuing similar orders. "The large traveling coach," he instructed his majordomo. "My lady will want to nap along the way. Send a rider ahead to the Queen's Head Inn to say that we will be stopping there in late afternoon. I will want their best bedroom, a private dining room, and accommodations for the coach and the staff."

"At once, m'lord!"

Within the hour a great traveling coach, the crest of the Southwood family emblazoned upon its side, lumbered down the Strand. A coachman and a footman sat upon the box. A groom rode behind the coach leading two horses. He was followed by six men at arms. *This* coach would not fall prey to highway thieves. Another six preceded the vehicle. It was four o'clock on a cold January morning, and sharp little blue stars dotted the clear dark skies above them.

Inside the coach the two occupants sat snuggled beneath an elegant red fox rug, hot bricks wrapped in flannel at their feet. Geoffrey Southwood's arm was about his wife. His other hand fondled her breasts, his mouth lazily explored her lips, her throat, his teeth nibbled on her little earlobe. "Do you remember what we were doing just a year ago tonight," he murmured.

She giggled happily. "Something very similar, if memory serves, my darling. But not in a jouncing coach."

"I don't believe we've ever made love in a coach," he observed thoughtfully.

"Geoffrey!" Her voice was husky with shock.

He chuckled. "I cannot help it, pet, you're the most damnably tempting piece, and I want to bury myself deep in you."

She felt herself go weak with desire. He had the most wicked ability to rouse her with no more than a word. She tingled with hunger for him, and wondered if that was wrong. In a burst of outraged virtue she exclaimed, "My lord, this is not right."

"Indeed it isn't, my darling. I have made love in a coach, and it is wretchedly uncomfortable as well as awkward. We shall wait until we reach the Queen's Head Inn. But then I promise, madam, to show you no mercy." He ceased his teasing of her already aroused person, and Skye tingled with delicious anticipation of their stop at the Queen's Head Inn.

The coach rumbled through the early-morning countryside. Winter was in strong evidence upon the quiet land, brown with fallow fields, and dotted by frozen puddles. The bare trees stood black against the lavender-and-gold dawn sky. Here and there smoke rose from a chimney. Once a barking dog dashed from a farmyard to run alongside the coach for a short while, snapping at its wheels, but it soon fell behind. Inside the rolling vehicle the Earl and Countess of Lynmouth slept fitfully, the motion of their carriage jerking them back to semi-consciousness every now and then.

The horses were changed after several hours, giving the Earl's party time to relieve themselves and break their fast. The innkeeper, mightily impressed by the crested coach, its occupants, and the liveried entourage, offered Lord Southwood and his sleepy wife a private parlor. Almost immediately thereafter two servants arrived, their trays laden with clear hot soup, ham, spiced apples in honey, cheese, bread still steaming from the oven, and sweet butter. The innkeeper himself brought in two pitchers, a frosted one filled with brown October ale, the other with sweet apple cider.

The smells wafting from the trays wakened Skye fully, and under her husband's tolerant and amused gaze she fell to the food with gusto. The soup took the chill from her bones, and put color back into her cheeks. She smacked her lips over a piece of hot buttered bread with thin salty slices of ham, and enjoyed it so much that she ate another, the second with an added embellishment of cheese.

Sighing contentment, she sat back, and Geoffrey chuckled. "Sometimes I find it hard to believe you're old enough to be my wife."

"I was hungry," she said simply.

"I'm having the innkeeper pack us a basket, for, if you remember, our next stop offers no such amenities as this. It's only a place to change the horses. Is there anything you fancy?"

"Hard-cooked eggs and winter pears," she answered promptly, and when he looked at her strangely she laughed and said ruefully, "No, Geoffrey, I am not breeding again . . . yet." She nuzzled his cheek, saying, "I love you so much, my lord husband. I want a houseful of your sons."

What Niall Burke would have given to hear those words. On the island of Mallorca he felt as out of place as a chicken in a fox's den. By good fortune, Doctor Hamid had a cousin on the island who was also a doctor. Though Spain had been swept clean of the Moslem Moors, here on its Mediterranean islands located halfway between Europe and North Africa, the tolerance was greater, due in part to centuries of intermingling and intermarriage.

Ana, overjoyed to see her mistress, was brought back from retirement and, along with Polly, took over Constanza's care. Niall knew that his wife would not dare misbehave here on Mallorca as she had in England. There was no reason to separate Constanza and Ana. He bought a small house in the hills above the city. The house afforded them the greatest privacy and had little room for entertaining.

Upon seeing his child, the conde turned furiously on Niall. "What have you done to her?"

Niall sighed, and led his father-in-law from the bedroom out onto the patio. "That she is ill is of her own making, Francisco. I tell you this not to hurt you but so you may understand her. Do not withdraw your love. There is a very strong chance that Constanza will not recover. I brought her home because she may die, and despite her perfidy I want her happy."

"What has she done?"

"Constanza is a woman for whom the love of one man is simply not enough."

At first the Conde was uncomprehending. But as his son-in-law's words began to penetrate he grew red, then white with anger. "Just *what* is it you are saying to me, my lord?" he demanded.

"Constanza is a whore."

"You lie!"

"To what purpose, Francisco? Ana will verify all I say. I sent Ana home because she could not control Constanza. Without meaning to, Ana aided her. Constanza caused such a scandal at the English Court that she was exiled from England permanently. I thought of taking her home to Ireland, but she is badly diseased, cannot bear children now, and will probably die soon. I might have obtained an annulment of this marriage, Francisco. That would have embarrassed you. You are, after all, still King Phillip's governor on these islands."

"I am not surprised that the licentious English Court corrupted my child. Look at its bastard Queen, the daughter of the great whore-witch! England is as damned as its Court."

"As an Irishman, Francisco, I'd like to agree with you. But I can't. Elizabeth of England is young, but I sense greatness in her. She will lead her country well. Her Court is elegant and intelligent, witty and bright. And not particularly licentious, Francisco. Oh, there are some who play at lewd games, but when you think of carnality, the French Court is far ahead of any other in Europe."

The older man's stern face crumbled. Whom could he blame? "Then what am I to think, Niall? Is the fault mine? Where did I fail Constanza?"

"You didn't, Francisco. It will take you time, as it did me, to understand that the fault is not in you. The fault is in Constanza, deep within her, eating outward like a maggot inside a perfect fruit. To the eye the fruit is beautiful, the skin firm, the color exquisite. Inside, however, is rot, and decay. Constanza herself is probably not to blame."

Suddenly the Conde was weeping. "Ah, Blessed Mother, my poor child! My poor child!"

"Francisco, Constanza is dying and there are no other children. Have you ever thought of marrying again? I do not understand why you never did. Now, if you wish your line to continue, you must do it. You are not an old man, and there is time for you to sire sons."

A surprised glance met Niall's. "It is strange that you mention that," he said. "After Constanza's mother died I was left alone by the matchmakers. I suspect that was meant to give me time to grieve. But shortly thereafter I withdrew from society entirely, appearing only when it was necessary to my duties. After you married Constanza and left this island I became lonely, and I began to socialize again. I have recently received an offer of marriage with the orphaned granddaughter of an old friend of mine who lives here on Mallorca. I hesitate because the girl is only fourteen."

"Could you be happy with her, Francisco? Is the match a good one?"

"Yes, I should be happy with Luisa. She is pretty, she is pious, and she has indicated she could be happy with me."

"Then for God's sake, man, marry her and get yourself some heirs!"

It took Constanza Burke two years to die, and in that time her new stepmother bore the Conde two sons and became pregnant with a third. Neither woman could abide the other. Luisa much resented her stepdaughter because Luisa's children might have to share the Conde's wealth someday with Constanza. She refused to believe that Lady Burke was dying.

Constanza believed that Luisa embodied criticism of her, particularly when her first half-brother arrived not even ten months after her father's wedding day. The second was born eleven months later, and when he was but three months old Luisa announced that she was pregnant again. "Her fertility is a reproach to me," Constanza wailed to Niall. "She delights in being the perfect Spanish wife in order to show the island that I am not! She is what neither my mother nor I could be—a mother of sons. God, how I hate her!"

Though Luisa was a perfect wife for the Conde, she was far too smug and stuffy for so young a lady. She was not the beauty her stepdaughter was, but she was quite pretty, with creamy gardenia skin that she zealously protected from the sun, smooth, blue-black hair that she wore neatly netted at the nape of her neck, and dark brown eyes that would have been beautiful if there had ever been any emotion to liven them.

Niall did his best to protect his wife from her stepmother. Whether Luisa was deliberately cruel or simply thoughtless, Niall could never be sure. Things finally reached a head one afternoon when Luisa said something—Niall never found out what it was—and Constanza stumbled from her bed shrieking, "Get out of my house, you damned fecund cow!" Then she collapsed. Ana ran to her mistress while Polly hustled the young Condesa from the room.

"Take your hands off me, girl," snapped Luisa, attempting to break Polly's hold on her arm.

"On your way, mistress, or I'll put a curse on your unborn brat!" Polly squinted her eyes and twisted her mouth to give her threat serious meaning.

"Oh!" Luisa crossed herself and, wrenching free, fled out the door to her carriage.

Constanza was unconscious for several hours. Dr. Memhet was called, and shook his head. "She will not last the night, my lord. Your vigil is almost over." The priest was called, and gave the dying woman extreme unction. He was a young priest, and the dying woman's confession left him white and shaken. Never before had he heard such evil from a woman's lips. He fell wearily to his knees, hoping his prayers might help a little.

The Conde arrived, wisely leaving his wife at home, and then they all sat and waited for death to claim its victim. Ana wept softly while telling her beads. Polly wiped her mistress's forehead free of icy perspiration. And Niall sat pensively by his wife's bedside wondering, not for the first time, if it might have all been different if he had taken Constanza directly home to Ireland instead of exposing her to London.

The clock on the mantel ticked off the long minutes, its little bell clanging the passing hours in a bright, cheerful fashion that marked a direct contrast to the somber vigil. Then in that darkest and loneliest time of the night, between the hours of three and four, Constanza opened her violet eyes and gazed about her. Her glance lingered lovingly on the three people she cared for the most, her husband, her father, and Ana. They moved to her side instantly.

With great effort Constanza reached out a pale hand to touch her old duenna's wet cheek. Ana's plump shoulders shook, but she swallowed the grief that threatened to explode in her throat. Next Constanza looked to the Conde and smiled sweetly. Francisco Cuidadela felt suddenly old and lonely. With Constanza went his last link with her mother, the love of his life. He felt that a part of him was dying too.

Lastly Constanza turned her head toward Niall. "I am so sorry about all of it, Niall," she said. "Remember that I truly loved you."

"I know, Constanzita," he said soothingly. "It was the illness, not deliberate."

She looked vastly relieved then, as if he'd lifted a weight from her. "Then I am forgiven?"

"You are forgiven, Constanzita." He bent down and lightly kissed her mouth. She sighed deeply and was gone. For a moment he stared down at her, remembering the lithe and lovely girl with the exquisite golden body and hair who had offered him her innocence in a flower field. *What had happened?* Gently he kissed her eyelids one final time and, turning, left the room.

Behind her he could hear Ana, finally free to vent her grief, wailing pathetically. He stood in the anteroom of his wife's apartment for a moment, not quite sure what to do next. Then, quickly, he came to a decision. "I am going to sign over Constanza's Mallorcan holdings to you, Francisco, all except a small house and vineyard, which I think Ana deserves. She should also be paid a pension of twelve gold pieces yearly. We will have the lawyers arrange that.

Polly wants to return to England. I want her to have a dowery of ten gold pieces, her passage, and that little string of seed pearls that was Constanza's. I want the London town house for myself. But the rest is yours."

"Please, Niall, my daughter is not yet cold, and you callously speak of dividing her possessions as the soldiers spoke at the foot of Christ's cross."

"Francisco, I have been living in Hell for two years now. I will do my final duty by Constanza and see to her burial, but I want to go home. Now. You will mourn in your fashion for a full year, but you have a wife and two sons by your side. I have no wife, no sons, and no time for Spanish conventions. I will see to the details of all arrangements today, for I intend sailing home as soon as I can."

Niall Burke was true to his word. Constanza's body was moved to the governor's palace where it lay in state for two days. She had been dressed in her wedding gown, and the bier was banked by white gardenias with their shiny green leaves. Pure wax tapers had been placed at both her head and her feet. On the morning of the third day the funeral mass was sung in the Palma cathedral, where they had been wed. Constanza was buried with a minimum of fanfare on a hillside overlooking the sea, and that same afternoon a ship sailed from Las Palmas to London. Lord Burke and a mistress Polly Flanders were on it. On Mallorca, except for the few who had known them, it was as if Constanza Maria Alcudia Cuidadela and Niall, Lord Burke, had never existed.

Several weeks later, after an uneventful voyage, Niall saw Polly safely placed with a good family as a ladies' maid, her precious dowry with a reputable banker. He longed to go south to Devon to see Skye, but after a drinking bout with some old friends at Court he knew he would probably not be welcome. The Southwoods, he learned, had not returned to Court but preferred the country. Only once a year did they come to London, after the New Year, in order to give their famous Twelfth Night masque. The beautiful Countess had presented her husband with a second son, John Michael, Lord Lynton. They were divinely happy, a most perfect couple.

Niall Burke left London for the west coast of England and sailed home to Ireland. Delighted to have his son back, but anxious for his happiness, the MacWilliam paraded before Niall every suitable available woman between the ages of twelve and twenty-five. He was thoroughly rebuffed.

"You've got to take a wife," the old man argued. "If you won't think of yourself, think of me. I need another heir!"

"Then you marry again! Twice I've wed because it was my duty and both marriages were disastrous. The next time I marry it will be for love and for no other reason!" shouted Niall.

"You're talking like a child!" the MacWilliam yelled back. "Love indeed! Christ bear me witness, I've spawned me a fool for a son! No wonder Skye O'Malley married her fine English lord!"

"Go to Hell, old man!" snarled the heir to the Burke fortunes. And he slammed from the hall and spent himself riding his great red stallion at breakneck speed across the hills. Later he rested the foam-flecked animal on a cliff above the sea, and stood staring west across the blue waters. He knew the old man was right, damn him. But right or wrong, he'd not wed again except for love. Niall sighed. It was Skye he loved. He would always love her. He did not believe he could take another wife to his heart and his bed, not while Skye lived. Once he had tried to fool himself, and the result had been the destruction of an innocent girl. Poor Constanza, asking his forgiveness on her deathbed. "It was I who should have asked your forgiveness, my poor Constanza," he said aloud. Then, mounting the stallion, he rode off to get gloriously drunk and dream futile dreams of a woman with hair like a dark night cloud and eyes the blue of the seas off the Kerry coast.

Skye was living a waking nightmare. After a sunny, warm March had come a cold, wet April. The disease had begun in the village of Lynmouth, the dreaded white throat sickness. It struck at children in particular, attacking one child, skipping its brother. Before she could isolate the children in the castle, Murrough O'Flaherty and Joan Southwood were ill.

Skye put the two children in the same room, the better to tend them. Having had the sickness as a child, she was not afraid of nursing the little ones, but she would allow none of the others near them. Geoffrey and the rest of the children were isolated in another part of the castle. Daisy volunteered to help her mistress. "I ain't never caught the white throat," she said, "though I've nursed its victims aplenty with my ma. She never caught it neither."

"They have a natural immunity," said Skye to her husband.

"What's that?"

"The Moorish doctors believe that some people have a special defense against certain diseases while others survive a disease and never get it again even though exposed. They call this an immunity. Obviously Daisy and her mother are immune, though they have never had white throat."

"And you are immune just because you did have white throat!" he said triumphantly.

"Yes," she answered. "That is why Daisy and I will nurse Murrough and Joan."

"What will you need?"

"Plenty of water, clean clothes, and oil of camphor."

"I'll see to it, my love."

"How many have we lost in the village?"

"Nine, so far."

"Jesu assoil their poor souls," she said.

It was a long and frightening procedure, but fortunately neither child was stricken severely. They were weak and feverish and cranky. The dreaded dirty white patches appeared first on their tonsils, and then spread to the rest of the throat, but though they coughed constantly, that was the worst of it. Nevertheless Skye and Daisy were totally exhausted, and neither spared herself in the care of the children. The crisis was surmounted after a period of twenty hours during which the two women spent all their time placing and replacing hot camphor cloths on their little patients' throats and chests. Finally the fever broke, the coughing eased, the white patches began to fade. The two women watched over the children for another day and night before they would admit they had beaten the disease.

At last Skye and Daisy allowed two of the other servants into the sickroom to take over. The children needed rest and light food to rebuild their strength while their two devoted nurses needed sleep before they dropped of exhaustion. Daisy sought her own room and fell, fully clothed, across her bed. Skye stumbled into her chamber to find a steaming tub awaiting her.

"I can't," she said. "I must sleep."

Geoffrey Southwood led his wife to a chair and sat her down. "You'll sleep better for being clean, my darling," and he gently undressed her, drawing off her gown and petticoats, slipping off her shoes and rolling down her silk stockings. Placing her in the tub, he smiled at her sigh of bliss and gently washed her. He dried her off, slid a nightgown over her, and carried her to their bed and tucked her in. Bending, he dropped a kiss on her forehead. "Sleep well, my dearest," she heard him say before blackness reached up to claim her.

Skye slept for almost two days, and awoke to find her world in shambles. Daisy had awakened first, and was standing over her mistress's bed. One look at Daisy's open country face caused Skye's heart to accelerate.

"What is it?"

"The young master, little Lord John! White throat! The Earl is nursing him."

Skye tumbled from the bed, reaching for her velvet dressing gown, struggling into it as she ran. "Where are they?"

"The floor above the nursery, m'lady."

Skye's first instinct was to rail at Geoffrey. How dare he keep Johnny's illness from her? Why had he not awakened her? Then she realized he had tried to spare her for a few brief hours so she might regain some strength. She sped down the corridors of the castle, climbing the stairs to the wing above the nursery floor, and pushed into the room.

"No!" she cried.

Geoffrey sat stunned, tears running down his face, the limp body of baby John in his lap. He looked up, his eyes mirroring such acute pain that she could not tell if her grief was for him or for the son they had just lost.

"I did everything you did," he wept helplessly. "He couldn't breathe, Skye! He couldn't seem to catch his breath, and I couldn't help him. His eyes, Skye! His blue eyes . . . so like yours . . . pleading for help, and I couldn't! I couldn't do anything."

She fell to her knees to gaze upon the body of her youngest child. He had looked so like her, with his fair skin, sapphire eyes, and dark hair. He had been Geoffrey's favorite, not Robin his heir, but Johnny, her elfin child, everyone's favorite, who was more of Ireland than of England. A muffled sound in the doorway caught her attention, and she raised her head to see Daisy, a fist stuffed in her tear-streaked face. Johnny had been her favorite too.

Feeling very old, she pulled herself up and, taking the limp body from Geoffrey's lap, gave the child to Daisy. "See to it, lass. I must comfort my lord."

Daisy fled from the room, holding the little boy close to her chest. Her weeping was quite loud now. Skye put an arm about her husband. "Come, my love. Come with me," she begged him. He rose to his feet and, stumbling along by her side, allowed himself to be led downstairs to their apartments. "Hot wine!" she ordered her husband's body servant, and when it was brought she added herbs to it and helped him drink. Mistress and servant undressed their lord and got him into a silk nightshirt. Skye nervously noted that Geoffrey was warmer than he ought to be. Tucking him into bed, she asked, "Do you feel all right, my darling?"

"Tired. So very tired," he muttered. Then, "Too hot," and he threw back the coverlet.

Skye put her hand on his forehead. It was burning. His fever was spiraling quickly. "Get me a bucket of cold water and some clean cloths," she ordered Will, the manservant. The Earl coughed, a sharp, barking sound, and fear gripped Skye. "No!" she whispered. "Dear Holy Mother, *please,* please no!"

Will returned with water drawn from the deepest well on the lands. It was so icy that it burned Skye's hands when she dipped a cloth into it. The Earl winced when the cloth touched his skin. "I must get your fever down, my love," she apologized, but he did not hear her, for he was lost in delirium. In the hours that followed they kept him well wrapped in bedclothes while his forehead was bathed constantly. Both the sheets and the Earl's nightshirt were changed three times, the used linen all burned to prevent the spread of infection.

Then suddenly Daisy appeared. "I've brought you a tray. It's in the anteroom."

Hollow-eyed, Skye looked up at her servant and then glanced away distractedly. "I couldn't eat."

"My lady, it will not do my lord any good if you fall ill, too. The children need you also, for they are badly frightened by their little brother's death. Now the Earl is ill, and that will be hard on the little ones."

I am frightened too! Skye wanted to shout. But she nodded wearily, glad for Daisy's firmness, and went into the anteroom. The tray had been lovingly prepared with a silver dish of small scallops broiled in sweet butter and herbs, ham, a little bowl of new lettuce and young scallions, a bread pudding, an iced cake, and a carafe of wine. Skye ate mechanically, not tasting any of it, simply chewing and swallowing until the dishes were empty. Rising quickly, she went back into the sickroom to find that the Earl's fever had broken. He was shivering violently and Daisy was piling more coverlets on his bed.

"Hot bricks," commanded Skye, and Will rushed to obey.

Geoffrey began to cough violently and gasp for air. Skye forced his mouth open and peered in. The Earl's throat was covered with dirty white patches, and a grayish membrane was forming that constricted his breathing.

"Keep his jaws open," said Daisy to her mistress. And with one quick motion, the girl reached down and hooked the membrane out of Geoffrey's throat. She threw it in the fire. The Earl was now able to breathe. "If we can keep that scum from cutting off his air then we can save him, m'lady. If it hardens he will die," she said straightforwardly.

"No!" Skye shook her head grimly. "I will not lose him!"

Together they began the tedious process of laying on hot camphor cloths. Several more times Daisy pulled an ugly mucous membrane from her master's throat, easing his breathing. The hours crept by until one full day had passed and it was night again. The fever came again and went again. He was having more difficulty breathing as the membranes formed much more quickly now and were becoming more difficult to get out. His color was pasty and his chest labored harder with each harsh breath. Skye could feel panic beginning to creep upward from deep within herself. They could not seem to conquer the disease, only to slow it down.

Suddenly Geoffrey Southwood opened his lime-green eyes. "Skye!" His voice was hoarse, and he coughed that terrible barking cough.

"I am here, my darling." She bent anxiously over him.

His marvelous eyes roamed slowly and lovingly over her face as if committing it to memory. "Take care of the children, Skye."

"Geoffrey, my love, you must not say things like that!" Her voice was edged in hysteria.

He smiled a gentle smile at her and, reaching up, touched her cheek with his elegant hand, as though bestowing a benediction. "What a joy you've been to me, my darling," he whispered, and then he gave a deep sigh and died.

The room was silent. Neither Daisy nor the manservant dared to move.

"Geoffrey! Please don't frighten me so," Skye begged. "You're going to get well, my love! You will! And we'll go to Ireland this summer as we planned, to see my family and so that Ewan may formally pledge his fealty to the MacWilliam." She went on talking to him of family things and plans they had made.

Finally Daisy gently put an arm about Skye. "He is dead, my lady." She began to sob. "The Earl is dead, and you must face it now. The children must be told and the funerals for wee Johnny and his father must be planned."

To Daisy's immediate relief, Skye burst into wild sobbing and flung herself across her husband's body. "Not gone!" she wailed. "No! No! No! Not dead! Not dead!"

Her cries could be heard throughout Lynmouth Castle, and the cry was quickly taken up by others. Daisy and Will pulled Skye from her husband's form. She fought them like a madwoman, but finally their combined strengths prevailed and they were able to get her to her own bed. She collapsed there, sobbing.

"Get the children," Daisy whispered to the manservant, and when he had brought them, Daisy brutally roused her mistress from her grief. "My lady! The children are all here with you now. They need you, my lady! They need you now."

Skye raised her ravaged, tear-swollen face to stare at the frightened group of youngsters clustered together in the bedroom doorway. Geoffrey's three daughters from his second marriage—Susan, nine, with her father's haunting green eyes, and the eight-year-old twins, Gwyn and Joan—these three were now orphaned. Her own three—Ewan, ten, Murrough, nine, and Willow, six and a half—looked confused and tried to hide their fright. And Robin, three, *their* son, was now the Earl of Lynmouth. *Go away and leave me to my grief!* she wanted to shout at them. But then she heard Geoffrey say again, "Take care of the children, Skye."

Gathering herself, she stood up and smoothed her rumpled gown. "Your father is dead, my children," she said quietly. Then she lifted little Robin to a table, where he sat, wide-eyed, staring at her. "Robin, you are now the Earl of Lynmouth. To you, my lord Earl, I pledge my fealty." And she curtseyed to him.

Then the other children were standing before Robin, and pledging their fealty. Robin was confused. "Where is Papa?" he lisped.

"Gone to Heaven, my son," said Skye softly.

"Like Johnny?" His little brow was furrowed.

"Yes, Robin, like Johnny."

"Can't we go too, Mama?"

Susan sobbed, but was quelled by a fierce look from her stepmother.

"No, Robin, we can't go yet. One may only go when God calls, and God has not called us yet." Skye could feel strength flowing back into her limbs. Geoffrey had been right. The children needed her. She lifted her son from the table and gathered the other children about her. "We must all be brave, my dears," she told them, and kissed each in turn. "Now go back to your rooms, and pray for your father and for Johnny."

The children dutifully filed out. "Fetch the priest," she said to Daisy. "Will," she turned to the manservant, "I want you to ride to London with a message for Her Majesty. Wait in the anteroom while I write it."

The note informed the Queen of Geoffrey's death, and requested royal confirmation of Robin's inheritance. Will left immediately. The priest was told to schedule the funerals for the following day. The sixteen-month-old John, Lord Lynton, would be buried in the same grave as his father. Then Skye called for a bottle of cherry brandy and drank herself to sleep, an act she had cause to regret when the morning dawned clear and far too sunny for her throbbing head. It was tragically ironic. The April weather had turned mild overnight and there were no new cases of white throat in the castle or in the village. Having taken the Earl, the epidemic seemed to have satisfied its lust for lives.

Chapter 22

Robert Dudley, the foppish Earl of Leicester, hummed a merry tune as he traveled the road down to Devon. About him, his escort echoed this mood. The Earl was on a mission for Her Majesty, which lent great importance to this trip. Added to this was the fact that it was June and England was enjoying beautiful, sunny weather. Roses of every possible hue peeped from dooryard gardens and tumbled extravagantly over rock walls. In the green meadows fat young lambs gamboled amid the sweet clover. Every millpond had at least one family of swans, elegant snow-white parents with their gray cygnets, sailing as proudly across the barely ruffled waters as treasure-laden Spanish galleons.

Lord Dudley was in an excellent mood. Unwittingly, the Queen had given him something he wanted very much. Bess could not possibly have known when she sent him off to see to the welfare of their godson, the little Earl of Lynmouth, that the child's mother concerned him far more than Robin did.

Geoffrey Southwood's death had been a terrible shock to the Queen and the entire Court, for the Angel Earl had been very well liked. True, he and his lovely Irish wife had not been to Court for two years, but they always came up to London to give their Twelfth Night masque, always the best party of the year. Only a few short months ago they had astounded everyone once more by the marvelous originality of their costumes, coming to their last masque as "The New World." The beauteous young Countess had been gowned in cloth of gold trimmed lavishly in rich dark beaver and set off by Colombian emeralds, while Lord Southwood had been equally resplendent in his cloth-of-silver suit trimmed in fox, and sewn all over with Mexican turquoise.

So much for earthly glories, thought Robert Dudley wryly. Southwood, so lively and virile in January, was quite dead and buried on this glorious June day. Now perhaps his wife would be more amenable. And if she was not, there were means through which he could persuade her to be more cooperative. So pleased with himself was the Earl of Leicester as he came in sight of Lynmouth Castle in early evening that he burst into a currently popular and very bawdy song, much to the grinning delight of his soldiers.

Watching his approach from the open ramparts of the castle, the widowed Countess of Lynmouth was filled with trepidation. It had taken the Queen several weeks to answer Skye's letter announcing Geoffrey's death. When she did, Elizabeth had confirmed little Robin's inheritance. But she had also appointed Robert Dudley the child's guardian. Skye had protested, pointing out as diplomatically as possible that Geoffrey's will had made her the sole guardian of all their children. But the Queen was adamant. Skye had full control over the others, but the little Earl of Lynmouth was to be under royal protection from that time on.

Skye was most unhappy. She did not trust Dudley. To be sure, his behavior had been most circumspect since the incident of the Twelfth Night masque two years before. But she knew he would not give up easily. And in her widowed state she was unprotected and easy prey. He would not hesitate to use the young ones to force her hand, and so Skye had quickly done what she could to protect herself and the children.

Ewan and Murrough O'Flaherty had been sent home to Ireland, along with the twins, Gwyneth and Joan Southwood. Over a year previously, Skye and Geoffrey had betrothed these children to each. The twins had expressed the desire to remain together, and the boys were quite fond of them. The four would all be safe in Anne O'Malley's care and would marry in a few more years. The twins' nine-year-old sister, Susan Southwood, was sent to the household of Lord Trevenyan in Cornwall to learn the housewifely arts from his wife. She would be wed to the Trevenyan heir, an excellent match for both young people.

Only Willow and Robin remained with their mother. Skye had plans for the little Earl, but she would need the Queen's permission to carry them out. She had therefore waited to approach Elizabeth until she knew Lord Dudley was away from Court. Willow could easily be removed from Lynmouth. In case of danger the Smalls at Wren Court would protect her. If Skye had to fight Robert Dudley, it would be on her terms, not his: the children would not become weapons in his hands.

Below her, she could hear the thudding of the horses' hooves as they passed over the wooden drawbridge, then clattered into the castle courtyard. Gathering her cloak about her, she left the ramparts and hurried to her own apartment to await word from her majordomo that Lord Dudley had arrived. When the announcement came she calmly smoothed her skirts and descended to the Great Hall to greet her unwelcome guest.

As she entered the room Robert Dudley felt a momentary stab of compassion. She had grown thinner and looked tired. Yet despite the changes, she was still the most beautiful woman he had ever seen. Her black silk mourning gown was enormously becoming and the jet-edged cap framed her heart-shaped face in an outrageously flattering way. Widowhood became her, thought Robert Dudley.

"Welcome to Lynmouth, my lord." Her voice held no warmth.

"Am I truly welcome, my dear Skye?" he inquired playfully, kissing her hand.

"The Queen's majesty is always welcome in this house, my lord Dudley, and you represent the Queen. I trust your men have been suitably cared for by my people?"

"Thank you, madam, yes."

"You will wish to see the Earl," she said. "At the moment, however, his lordship is asleep. I shall send him to you in the morning when he awakens. I apologize for our being unable to entertain you, Lord Dudley, but this house is in deepest mourning. You will excuse me now, sir."

Dudley felt a surge of quick anger. He was being dismissed like a servant. "No, madam, I will not excuse you," he snapped.

"My lord!" Skye looked outraged. "I would pray for my husband! You have no right to deny me the solace of prayer."

"Would not a flesh-and-blood man be a better solace, sweet Skye?"

Her beautiful blue eyes widened. "*You? After Southwood?* Oh, Dudley!" she laughed harshly. "If you seek to amuse me, sir, you have certainly succeeded, and I thank you. I have not laughed once since my Geoffrey died."

He flushed a dull red color. "You try my patience, madam!"

"And you try mine," she snapped. "How dare you come into

my house and suggest what you suggest? It was bad enough that you attacked my virtue when Geoffrey was alive, but to continue to assault me in my grief is despicable!"

"Madam, I will have you." There it was. Blunt and open.

"Never."

"Let me remind you that I am your son's governor."

"But not mine!"

"I can have the boy removed from here at any time. And unless you cooperate, I shall."

"I shall appeal to the Queen!"

"On what grounds, sweet Skye? I have only to tell Bess that you are suffering from acute melancholia brought on by Southwood's death. That I think your moods are bad for the children. Better yet, the children shall remain here at Lynmouth, but I shall remove you to London! What will you tell the Queen, and which one of us will she believe?"

"No!" She was helpless until the Queen replied to her last letter and she was free of Dudley. She dare not take the chance of being separated from Robin and Willow. Dudley smiled, knowing that she had assessed the situation intelligently and knew she had no choice.

"You will have supper with me, and afterward I will have you," he crowed triumphantly.

"I pray that you excuse me from supper. What you force me to is distasteful, and I find I have no appetite. I will come to you, for I will not take you into the bed I shared with my husband. Give me a few hours to compose myself."

He nodded. "Very well, sweet Skye. I will excuse you from supper. I shall eat in my rooms, and you will come to me at ten o'clock tonight. Is it agreed?"

"Yes, my lord." She turned from him and quickly left the room. If it had not been for the children she would have thrown herself from the castle heights. No! She would have plunged a dagger into his chest, and thrown his body into the sea! Why should she suffer because of that revolting man?

Daisy waited for her in Skye's bedroom. "From the look on your face I'd say Lord Dudley's not changed his tune." Skye had taken her tiring woman into her confidence because she believed she might need Daisy's aid.

Skye explained wearily, "He has threatened to send me from the children unless I yield myself. I must, of course, especially since I don't believe he knows yet that the five older children are gone.

When he learns of that all hell is apt to break loose around us, Daisy."

"Unless, of course, you please him. He'll be more amenable if he thinks he's won you over," observed Daisy.

"If the Queen agrees to my suggestion for Robin's future, then the fine Lord Dudley will have nothing to blackmail me with at all."

"But in the meantime you've got to warm his bed, and he'll not be happy if you are aloof with him."

"How can I receive him warmly, Daisy? I despise the man! How could I take a ridiculous popinjay like that for a lover after my darling Geoffrey?"

"Alas, madam, it's not a matter of what you want. The Earl would want you to protect little Robin's inheritance," said the ever-practical Daisy. "Lord Dudley has the power now. Men always do."

"Not always," said Skye softly. For the first time in several years she was experiencing her youth again, in her memory. Safe in Geoffrey's love, she had almost forgotten that she was the O'Malley of Innisfana. Now she was trapped, for Robin was an English peer, and she could not steal his ancient heritage in order to return to her own. But there might be a way out of this, if only the Queen agreed to her plan. For tonight, however, there was no escaping Lord Dudley. She shuddered.

"I've had the girls draw your bath, my lady," said Daisy quietly. "There'll be breast of capon, salad, and fresh strawberries with cream for your supper after your bath."

Skye nodded absently. Undressing automatically, she stepped into her tub. The warm water was fragrant with her favorite scent, roses. Daisy carefully pinned up her hair, and Skye sank deep into the water. She did not think Dudley meant to flaunt her before the world. Elizabeth Tudor could not be used that way. Too, it had been less than two years since Dudley had finally received his earldom. Therefore, he would plan to leave Skye in Devon, taking his pleasure of her on occasional trips down to see to the "welfare" of his godson, the Queen's ward. He would have to be very careful lest he rouse the suspicions of the Queen regarding his true motives.

Taking the soap from a small porcelain dish, she chuckled to herself, realizing that her daily bathing was a habit picked up in Algiers. Many of the English Court ladies were just as shy of soap and water as their kitchen help. She rose from the tub, and Daisy wrapped a warmed towel about her. Stepping from the tub, Skye sat down on a bench by her fire. Two little undermaids carefully rubbed the beads of moisture from Skye's shoulders and then, kneeling, dried her feet. Skye stood up, dropping her towel, her slender arms raised above her head. Daisy, armed with a thick lamb's wool puff, liberally dusted her mistress with rose powder, muttering all the while, "Indecent is what it is! In her middle twenties, five babes, and she still has the figure of a young girl!"

Skye laughed. Though Daisy was younger than she was by a good five years, she was, in the manner of a beloved servant, maternal in her feelings toward her mistress. Still smiling, Skye took up the crystal flacon of attar of roses and daubed the scent on herself, suddenly remembering Yasmin and the women in the House of Felicity. *I seem to have gone backward instead of forward,* she thought wryly.

Daisy held out the gown, and Skye slipped into it. Of coral silk, it had wide flowing sleeves, a very low, scooped neckline, and a full skirt that fell in graceful folds. There was no waistline. The gown fastened beneath the breasts, molding them. How Geoffrey would have loved this gown, she thought, blinking back tears. She had had it made in London last winter, and had not had a chance to wear it before he died. For a moment she considered tearing it off rather than wear it before Robert Dudley. But she realized that nearly everything she touched would hold memories of Geoffrey.

"You may all leave me now," Skye said. "Good night, girls." The door closed behind the three, and she glanced toward the mantel clock. An hour to go. She nibbled on a bit of supper, surprised to find that she had an appetite. The strawberries tasted particularly good, and it came to her that she hadn't really tasted food since Geoffrey had died. She had eaten because she had to, but she might have been eating dried leaves.

She paced the room nervously, wishing that her monthly courses were upon her so she might have refused Dudley. Oh, good God! Why had she not told him that? It would have mattered very little. He would simply have waited until she could receive him. Better to get it over with now.

She thought for a moment on the man who awaited her, seeking to find something about him that would make her ordeal less terrible. She could not deny that he was handsome. Tall and well formed, his complexion fair, his hair and elegant mustache a reddish-ginger color, his eyes velvet brown. But his eyes were too close together, hinting of a slyness she had seen exhibited more than once. And although his manners were perfect, there was a marked arrogance about the man. Far worse was his ambition which, like his love of himself, was monumental. She could not like him and that was all there was to it.

It lacked five minutes to the hour when Skye wrapped a dark velvet cloak about her shoulders and left her apartment. The castle was quiet, everyone but the watch being asleep. Lord Dudley had been placed in the east wing of the castle, far from Skye's rooms in the southwest sector. She walked swiftly, praying she would encounter no one who might witness her shame. Pausing a moment outside Lord Dudley's bedchamber, she drew a deep breath and then, before she could allow herself to flee, reached out and opened the door.

He turned from the fireplace and grinned toothily at her. Outside on the castle heights the watch was just calling the hour. "How prompt you are, my dear. May I attribute it to your eagerness to be with me?" He chuckled. Walking toward her, he reached out and took her cloak and let it slide to the floor. "By God, madam!" he swore softly. "You choose your gowns with care!" Pulling her into his arms, he kissed her hard. She struggled instinctively, but he pinioned her tightly against his chest, saying fiercely, "No, madam! There'll be none of that! You may play the grieving widow publicly, but don't tell me that you're not really hot for a man between your legs. Geoffrey Southwood was a man who loved a woman well, and you've not had any loving in several months. Unless, of course," and he leered unpleasantly at her, "there's a willing stable boy about."

"You're a bastard, Dudley," she spat at him.

"No stable boy?" he mused. "Then you'll give yourself willingly to me, sweet Skye." Drawing her to a wall mirror, he stood her before it and, positioning himself behind her, carefully drew the coral silk down over her shoulders. His fingers caressed the smooth skin, and then suddenly his lips were burning into the bare flesh. "Southwood always bragged about your skin," he murmured, intoxicated by the softness of her.

Skye felt her flesh crawl under this first assault, and his references to Geoffrey almost made her swoon. "Please, my lord," she said low so he might not hear the tremor in her voice, "If you have any feeling for me at all, do not speak of Geoffrey to me."

Lord Dudley glanced up at her curiously. Shrugging, he drew her gown down a little more, exposing her breasts. His left arm held her tightly against him while his right snaked forward to cup her right breast. "Exquisite," he said with the appreciation of an experienced connoisseur. "Just a handful, but more would be wasted."

Skye closed her eyes, forcing back tears as the gown slipped lower, and his hand followed it, sliding over her belly. Then the gown was lying on the floor and she was completely naked. Dudley's breathing quickened and became harsh. He pushed her forward over his arm, and his free hand roamed her bottom. But when he attempted to insert his finger within her she squirmed away from him crying, "No!"

Dudley chuckled, pleased, and undid his deep-brown dressing gown. "We'll eventually do that too, my sweet Skye, but first things first." He was now as naked as she was and she looked to his sex with fear. He did not fail to notice. He was not overly thick, but he did have the longest manroot she had ever seen.

"I want you to sit on the edge of the bed," he commanded, and when she did he continued, "now lie back, my sweet Skye. Yes, that's it." He slid his hands beneath her buttocks and drew her down toward him. He spread her legs wide.

She knew then what he intended, which did not lessen the shock when he knelt before her and put his head between her legs. He fastened his mouth to her. She shuddered, which he misinterpreted as the beginnings of her passion. To her anguish, Skye was remembering when Geoffrey had first loved her thusly, his mouth and tongue using her gently with feathery, tenderly passionate touches. Dudley, however, feasted greedily on the succulent pink flesh, his tongue thrusting and stabbing at her provocatively. He demanded a response. Skye bit her lips until they bled. He was rousing her, and she could not help but respond.

The sweet flow from her body told him so. With a grunt of satisfaction he rose and, lifting her slightly, took her there on the edge of the bed. Bending down, he imprisoned her between his two strong arms. He murmured into her ear. "I am now inside you, my sweet Skye. How ready you are to receive me, lovey! Your little honey oven burns my lance with the fiery flow of the passion you would like to deny me, but can't." He moved within her fiercely and she cried out in passion, hating herself for her weakness.

Triumph was written all over the face that loomed above her. "I want to get further inside you, lovey. Clasp your legs about me," he ordered. Afraid to disobey him, she complied. With a groan of pure pleasure he drove so deeply that she would have sworn he touched her very womb. To her great surprise, he was concentrating on her response rather than his own. And though she hated him, her body treacherously yielded itself.

With a chuckle of satisfaction Robert Dudley suddenly withdrew from her. "I have learned to control my body, sweet Skye. I am not quite ready yet to yield to passion. Why—we have scarce begun, my pet! You're much too delicious an armful to devour so quickly. I am now in the mood to play with you for a while."

He eyed her lasciviously. "What a pretty little girl Papa has. Is she a good little girl?" He looked to her questioningly, and when she looked back at him blankly, he said, "You must play along, my sweet Skye. You must call me Papa. Didn't you and Southwood ever play such games?"

She shook her head, and he chuckled again. He sat up and pulled her onto his lap. "Such games can be fun, my pet. Come now, and tell Papa if you're his good little girl."

"I . . . yes."

"Come, Skye, don't be shy with me. Are You Papa's good little girl?"

"Yes—Papa."

"Ah ha!" He pounced upon her answer, grinning toothily. "Now here's a small lie, sweetness. No one can ever be good all the time, now can they?"

"No—Papa."

"Then you have lied to me, my sweet naughtiness."

"Yes, Papa." God, but the man was a fool!

"Then I must punish you, my wicked little girl."

"No! Dudley, this is ridiculous!"

"Ah, wouldn't be defiant with your papa? I shall definitely have to punish you!" And quickly Lord Dudley turned Skye over his knee and, raising his hand, began to spank her. She shrieked and tried to wriggle free but, laughing delightedly at her reaction, he paddled her harder until her bottom tingled.

She had only been spanked once before in her entire life. It had happened when her father had sent her home to learn how to be a lady instead of a sailor. She had spent the week annoying her older sister Peigi, and Peigi had finally spanked her. Skye had retaliated quickly by filling her sister's bed full of wriggling, live crabs. No one since had ever spanked her.

"By God! By God!" she heard him pant as she tried to escape him. "That saucy backside of yours begs for spanking. How your little cheeks blush rosy for me, my pet." Now he was lifting her up and quickly pushing her face down upon the bed.

"No! Damn you, Dudley, no!" she sobbed, knowing full well what he intended. But he was already on her, holding her down by the neck while he pushed carefully into her in the Greek fashion.

"Bastard! Boy lover!" she snarled at him, but he only laughed.

"Your little rose is tightly closed to me now, but in time 'twill stretch to receive me as eagerly as your sweet cunny does."

For a few moments he used her thusly, and the terrible memories of her first husband and his abuses came racing back to assail her. Then he withdrew from her and, turning her over, thrust into her in proper man-woman fashion.

This time Dudley was ready to allow his own passion full control. After he had satisfied her once, he took his own release. Skye did not think it possible to hate a human being as much as she now hated him. Even once sated, he could not leave her be. Pulling her onto her side and into the curve of his arm, he stroked her perfect, small breasts, the shapely curve of her hip, the soft round of her bottom.

"Damme, sweetheart, you were fashioned for loving. That silken skin of yours would rouse a eunuch. Still, I would prefer a bit more fire from you."

"Oh, no, my lord! You can force me to your bed with threats against me and my children and you can order me to perform whatever perversions please you, but you can never force my emotions. Do you suddenly find the possession of my person not enough for you?" She could not disguise the triumph in her voice, and she hoped it rankled him.

Lord Dudley was far too sophisticated the courtier to be easily angered by her barbs. Her very inaccessibility had intrigued him in the first place, and her distaste still did. He could force her body to yield itself, but he wanted to hear her cry of surrender echoing in his ears. At the moment, however, all he heard was defiance. He pulled her beneath him again, excited by that defiance.

"Whoreson!" she hissed.

"Bitch!" His mouth savaged hers as she raked her nails down his back, and bit at his lip. "Owwww!" Dudley pulled away from her but laughed when he saw the look of battle in her eye. "Little Irish barbarian," he murmured in her ear. "I fully intend taming you, and I will!"

"You'll grow old trying, my lord!"

"Why sweet Skye, you give me hope," he shot back, deliberately twisting her words as he jammed his knee between her soft thighs, forcing them open. Now Skye tried to claw at his eyes, and Robert Dudley caught her hands and, pulling them above her head, successfully immobilized her while he once again assaulted her. Then, sated for the moment, he turned on his side and fell asleep, one leg thrown carelessly over her body, imprisoning her.

She lay rigid with fury. He was not going to leave her alone. Her coldness intrigued him, yet if she could pretend passion, he would be equally intrigued. Dear God, if only the Queen would answer her letter favorably so she could get out of this!

The Earl of Leicester stayed two days and three nights at Lynmouth, and there was only one thing upon which he and his hostess agreed during that time. That agreement centered about little Lord Southwood. "He's Geoffrey's son, and no doubt about it!" said Dudley admiringly. "By God, if he were mine I'd burst my buttons. You've bred a fine son, madam. Are your Irish sons as fine? I have not yet had the opportunity to greet them."

"They are in Ireland," she answered.

"I was given to understand that they were here with you."

"Only part time," she said sweetly. "Ewan is, after all, the O'Flaherty of Ballyhennessey. It is necessary that he and his younger brother remain on his estates part of the year. They have taken their betrothed wives with them, and are at present in the safe custody of my uncle, the Bishop of Connaught, and my stepmother, Lady Anne O'Malley."

"Their betrothed wives?"

"Gwyneth and Joan Southwood. Geoffrey and I betrothed our children over a year ago. They all adore each other. Is it not fortunate?" Her beautiful face radiated innocence.

"Southwood had another daughter. Where is she?" Robert Dudley's voice was very carefully controlled.

"Susan? Susan is with Lord and Lady Trevenyan's household down in Cornwall. She was matched with their heir a long time ago. I do believe Lady Trevenyan and Susan's mother were cousins."

"So only your daughter and son are here? You're clever, my sweet Skye. Far cleverer, frankly, than I had anticipated. Still I do hold the trump card with Robin, don't I?" He smiled. "I must return to Court today lest my dear Bess grow suspicious, but I will return as soon as I can. When I do I will look forward to more pleasant hours in your bed."

She made a face at him, and he laughed as he raised her hand to his mouth, and kissed her fingertips. Soon Dudley took his leave, slowly kissing her hand again. Smiling for the benefit of her servants, she said in an undertone, "You're a pig, my lord."

Dudley laughed again, and rode off as he had come. Singing.

Free of him at last, Skye fled her castle and walked the cliffs above the sea. The bright day and the brisk clean wind helped to lift some of her melancholy, but she still felt dirtied. She had almost forgotten that men like Dudley existed. Dom O'Flaherty had been like Dudley, though lacking his refinements. But Dom had been dead for many years and in the love and tenderness and warmth of men like Khalid and Geoffrey she had almost forgotten that there were men whose sexual satisfaction was gained only by the pain and shame they inflicted.

The next day, however, Skye had a happy surprise. Robert Small had returned from his long voyage. Stopping at Wren Court only long enough to assure Dame Cecily of his safety, he came directly to Lynmouth. From her favorite retreat high upon the open battlements, she recognized his dearly familiar form upon his little bay gelding. Gathering up her skirts, Skye flew from the top of the castle down the winding flights of stairs out into the courtyard and onto the drawbridge.

"Robbie! Oh, Robbie! You're safe! And you're home!" She was laughing with joy, sobbing with relief, and overwhelmingly glad to see her small protector. Everything was always all right when Robbie was home to look after her.

The gelding stopped, and the little man slipped from its back to gather the beautiful woman into his arms. They hugged each other in full view of the entire castle, and then Robert Small kissed her soundly on both cheeks. "How is it possible that you've grown prettier, my lass?"

"Oh, Robbie, your tongue is so smooth that I sometimes think you're Irish."

He chuckled, and slipped his arm through hers. "I find that I have an Irish thirst right now. Will you take me into your fine house, and offer me a bit of wine to clear the Devon dust from my throat?"

She laughed. It was a clear and happy sound, one she had not made since she had lost Geoffrey and their younger son. Leading Robbie to the Great Hall, she sat him down and brought him the wine herself. He took a deep draught and then said quietly, "I was sorry to learn about Geoffrey, and the child."

"Who told you? De Grenville?"

"Yes. He met me in Bideford. Damn, Skye, sorry is . . . hardly a good enough way to—"

"Say nothing, Robbie. We're friends. I know what is in your heart."

"The Queen's confirmed your son as heir?"

Skye looked hard at her old friend. "Yes, but she's overridden Geoffrey's will and made Robert Dudley my son's guardian."

The sea captain frowned, beginning to understand that trouble was in the air. "From your tone, Skye, I think I am home just in time. Must I again rescue the poor widow?"

"I think this time I must rescue myself, Robbie." She stood and began to pace while she explained. "Geoffrey and I left Court after Robin was born, and retired here to Devon. My uncle sent my Irish sons to us, and we were a happy family—my sons, his daughters, and our two boys. Then Geoffrey died, and Johnny. The Queen was quick to recognize Robin as Geoffrey's legitimate successor, but she sent the Earl of Leicester as his guardian. It is my supreme misfortune that Robert Dudley covets me."

"Why, the damned lecher," cried Robbie. "Is not Bess enough woman for him?"

"The Queen has most certainly not yielded her person, Robbie. She wants him, I believe, but dares not compromise herself. Still, she dotes on him and spoils him fearfully. She will hear not a word against him. How can I dare tell her that he has forced me, and will continue to do so as long as he can use my son to control me?"

"The bastard!" said Robert Small fiercely. "You mean that he's already—?"

"Aye, Robbie. *He's already.*" Then she said grimly, "But I may yet outsmart Lord Dudley. Geoffrey and I had spoken of betrothing Robin to de Grenville's littlest daughter, Alison. If I can gain the Queen's permission to this match, then I shall ask that de Grenville be made Robin's governor. I have written to Her Majesty about this, but it will be weeks before she replies."

"Then go up to London and obtain her permission during a personal audience."

"What?"

"Go up to London, lass! I will go with you. I must anyway in order to report the success of our mission to the Queen. It is our trading company that made the voyage, and what would be more natural than that we both report to Elizabeth?"

"Successful? We were successful! How successful? Lord bless me, Robbie, it should have been my first thought!"

He laughed. "Nay, love, you've had other troubles. But now I'll make those troubles disappear! Not a ship lost, Skye! Not one! D'you know the odds against that? Five men though, in a bad storm in the Indian Ocean. Other than that, we might have been sailing in a millpond. I've never encountered such good weather. The holds of all the ships are crammed to overflowing with spices. I've a fortune in rare jewels. And, as an extra bonus, m'dear, when we stopped to take on water at a small African port I obtained us a fine cargo of ivory! If you hadn't been a rich woman before, Skye, you are now! And the Queen's coffers will not suffer by this, either."

Her blue eyes sparkled with delight. "Can you be ready to leave tomorrow, Robbie?"

"Aye, lass, I can. Give me a good hot dinner and an unbroken night's rest, and I'll be ready."

Suddenly the door to the room burst open and Willow ran in, followed by a small blond boy. "Uncle Robbie! Uncle Robbie!" She launched herself straight at him.

Robert Small caught her up, his weathered face split in a wide grin. "Willow, lass! Can it truly be you? Why, you're half grown!" He kissed her soundly on both cheeks, then put her down.

Willow flushed with pleasure, then smoothed her gown. "I am now seven," she said importantly.

"Are you indeed? How proud your father would have been of you. You have the look of him." His air of being impressed was just what the child wanted. "Now tell me, lass, who is this wee lad?"

Willow drew the boy out, and said gravely, "May I present my brother, Robin, sir. He is the Earl of Lynmouth."

Robert Small made an elegant leg to the child. "M'lord, I am honored to make your acquaintance. I knew your late father, may God assoil him, and I respected him greatly."

The boy looked up shyly, and the little captain was struck dumb. The boy was his father's image. Seeing Geoffrey Southwood looking at him through this small boy's eyes was very disconcerting. "May I call you Uncle Robbie too?" came the shy question.

"Indeed you may, laddie!" Robert Small lifted the delighted boy up onto his shoulders. "Willow! You and Robin come with me and I'll show you the presents I've in my saddlebags for you."

Skye smiled, glad to see her children happy again. It had been so solemn at Lynmouth for so long. She walked from the Great Hall out into the castle gardens that ran along the cliff tops. At the garden's end she passed through the gates into the Southwood family cemetery, and made her way to Geoffrey's tomb. She had plucked a single white rose on her way through the gardens, and now she lay it on Geoffrey's grave.

"Robbie is back, Geoffrey," she said, "and the voyage was a wonderful success. I'm putting your percentage into Robin's coffers, my darling, and I shall go up to London myself to speak to the Queen. I must rid myself of Dudley! 'Tis not just his lust that frightens me, but his greed. The man is too ambitious, Geoffrey. Oh, my darling, I need you so very much! Why did you have to leave me?"

Then she sighed deeply. This simply had to stop. She had gotten in the habit of coming to Geoffrey's grave every day, and speaking to him as if he were actually there. It gave her a strange comfort. Immediately following his death she had believed she felt his presence near her. But that feeling was gone now.

"It's because you really are gone from me now, isn't it, my love?" she whispered sadly.

A gentle sea wind teased at her hair. She felt the unbidden tears suddenly slipping down her cheeks, and for the first time since his death she cried without forcing herself to stop. There was no one to see or hear her, and she did not need to be brave for the children's sake.

It was there that Robert Small found her. Wordlessly he gathered her into his arms and offered his silent sympathy. He said nothing, for there was nothing he could say. But his very presence, familiar and loving, gave her comfort. As her sobs finally lessened he sought for and found a reasonably clean silken square in his doublet and offered it to her. She wiped her eyes and blew her nose. "Better?" he asked.

"Thank you. I cried when he died, but only for a moment, for the children were all there, and they were frightened, and my wailing would have only made it worse for them. There hasn't been much time for mourning since then."

"Until today."

She nodded. "I suddenly realized that he is actually gone. I am really alone again, Robbie."

"You'll remarry one day, Skye."

"Not this time, Robbie. I've buried two men whom I loved greatly, and I'll not go through that again."

"Then you will have to take a powerful lover, m'dear. You've already seen that a beautiful widow is the prey of blooded rakes."

"Never! I intend to rid myself of Lord Dudley and then return to Devon to live until Robin is of age. He and Willow are my chief concerns. And Robbie—should anything happen to me, I have arranged that you and Dame Cecily be my daughter's guardians. I knew that would be all right with you."

"What is it you're planning, Skye? I can almost see the little wheels turning in your pretty head."

She smiled softly. "Nothing, yet, Robbie. First I must go to London. Time enough afterward to decide my fate."

The following morning, Skye and Robbie departed from Lynmouth and headed northeast to London. A messenger had ridden on ahead of them to see that Lynmouth House was ready to receive its mistress, and to take word to the Queen that Sir Robert Small had returned to England and sought an immediate audience with Elizabeth, in company with the Countess of Lynmouth. They reached London safely several days later. Upon entering her house, Skye found to her fury that the Earl of Leicester waited for her.

"Your impetuousness in following me to London delights me, my sweet Skye," he teased, kissing her hand.

She snatched her hand from his grasp. Skye had a headache from riding in a closed coach on a warm day, the dust from the road having necessitated the closing of the windows. She glared stonily at Dudley while, below, her Robert Small was hard put not to howl his laughter at the look of surprise on Dudley's face when she said to him, "Go to Hell, m'lord!" Pushing past him, she stamped up the stairs to seek the comfort of her own apartment.

Foolishly he followed along next to her. "I hadn't expected the pleasure of your company for several more weeks, my sweet Skye," he murmured in what he believed was a seductive voice. "I must dance attendance on Bess at Whitehall until well past midnight, but afterward my sweet Skye . . ." he breathed.

Skye stopped in midstep and whirled about. "There will be *no* afterward, my lord Dudley! My head aches! My monthly courses are upon me! I have spent three days being bumped to bits in a coach and three nights avoiding drunks and bedbugs in noisy inns. I am tired. I intend going to bed. *Alone*! Now get the hell out of my house!" And she continued on her way upstairs. The next sound was the mighty slamming of her chamber door.

Openmouthed, the Earl of Leicester could only stare after the Countess of Lynmouth. Below him, Robert Small chuckled softly, then drawled, "She's a bit testy from the trip, my lord. But then, having once had a wife yourself, you'll understand that."

Dudley stared at the little captain for a moment then slowly descended the stairs and said menacingly, "Don't try to interfere, Captain. I have already laid my claim to the lady."

Robbie felt cold anger begin burning within him. "The decision is with the lady, my lord. Remember that, lest I should have to remind you of it."

Dudley moved toward the door, then turned. "Bess and Cecil will see you tomorrow morning at ten o'clock. Think not to undermine me with the Queen. You cannot." Then, after a brief bow, Dudley left.

Arrogant bastard, thought Robbie savagely. Skye was right. She would best be rid of him, and quickly. He was no fit guardian for Robin, and he'd drive her to something rash if he continued to harass her. She'd not take it much longer.

The following morning as they were ushered into William Cecil's closet Robbie thought he detected the light of battle in Skye's bearing. The black of mourning became her, adding to her warrior's appearance. They greeted Cecil, and then Robbie sketched out the success of his voyage to the Queen's chief advisor. Cecil nodded, listening, then said, "Your report is most encouraging, Sir Robert. Both Her Majesty and I agree that England's future prosperity lies in trade. Your success indicates the wisdom of that belief."

"Will it be possible to see the Queen, sir?" asked Robbie. "I have a small token to present to her, and I know that my lady Southwood would speak privately with her regarding the future of her son, the little Earl."

"The match with de Grenville's daughter? I have advised Her Majesty to permit the betrothal, Lady Southwood. It is a good one and in the best interests of both families."

"Thank you, my lord. But there is one other thing I must speak with Her Majesty about."

"My dear," said Cecil in a kindly fashion. "If you would accept a bit of advice from an old man who knows the Queen well—*don't.* Elizabeth Tudor, like her father before her, is blind in both eyes when it comes to those she loves."

"I must try, sir," persisted Skye.

William Cecil smiled ruefully. The Countess of Lynmouth was a strong and stubborn woman. But then, so was the Queen. Seeing these two lock horns should prove interesting if not actually explosive. "I will call Her Majesty now," he said, resigned.

Elizabeth Tudor entered the room a few moments later. She was expecting the French ambassador that morning, and was dressed in a magnificent cloth-of-gold gown adorned with ropes of pearls. She was, if possible, growing more regal with every passing day. "My dear Skye," she held out her hands in greeting, "how good it is to see you again." She turned. "Sir Robert! Cecil tells me your voyage was successful. We are very pleased!"

"It was quite profitable, madam, and I have brought you a small token of my crews' affections for their beloved Queen." He lifted a beautiful cedarwood casket and held it out to her. "Every piece there is a part share belonging to every man. Each man gave voluntarily and with love, a piece of the fruits of his labor."

The Queen accepted the small chest and placed it on the table. She opened it slowly and her eyes widened appreciatively at the riches within. There were Indian Ocean pearls in every shade of white, cream, pink, gold, and black. She fingered flashing Burmese rubies, sparkling Ceylon sapphires so like dear Skye's marvelous eyes, cold and fiery Golconda diamonds. There were also several silk bags filled with precious spices—fat nutmegs, long smooth sticks of cinnamon, pods of vanilla beans, tiny, sharp cloves, and round black peppercorns.

The Queen beamed at the captain delightedly. "Robert Small, your men could not have given me a lovelier gift. You'll thank them for me, and tell them this: the Queen says that as long as England has such brave sons, she will be invincible. Now, gentlemen, you will leave us so that dear Skye and I may visit. I want to learn all about my wee godson's progress."

The two men bowed from the room. There was a long silence after they had gone. The Queen spoke first. "Cecil has persuaded me that the match you propose between little Robin and Alison de Grenville is a suitable one. We have therefore given our permission, dear Skye."

"Your Majesty is most kind. But I would beg a further boon."

Elizabeth inclined her head.

"Since Your Majesty has approved this match, would you not also relieve Lord Dudley of his guardianship of my son, and appoint Dickon de Grenville in his place? Under the circumstances 'twould be more natural, and certainly more convenient for de Grenville than for my lord Dudley."

"Dudley remains my choice," said Elizabeth firmly.

The tone of the Queen's voice irritated Skye. Why was she interfering this way? "May I remind Your Majesty," she said sharply, "that my late husband made me sole guardian over our children, an arrangement Your Majesty chose to overrule though I could never see the sense of it."

"Only in the case of my godson, madam," retorted the Queen. "The child needs a man's influence in his life. I have provided him with the best man in England for that influence."

"Robin has de Grenville and Robbie as well as his half-brothers for male influence, Majesty," argued Skye.

"Dudley is proud to have the care of little Robin Southwood. He has told me so himself, *my dear Skye,*" the Queen argued back.

"I do not wish Robin to be under the influence of anyone from Court, madam. Not now. He is far too young. *I* am his mother, and that decision is my right."

"No, my lady Southwood," the Queen replied icily. "Robin's fate is my decision as his Queen! Lord Dudley will remain his governor."

Skye finally lost her fine Irish temper. "Dammit, madam! Don't you really know why Dudley wants charge of my son?"

"Yes, my dear Skye, I do," said Elizabeth Tudor.

Shocked, the Countess of Lynmouth looked deeply into the Queen's jet-black eyes. What she saw there made her shiver. "My God," she said softly. "*You do know*! Oh, madam, how could you? How could you give me to that man? My husband and I were always your loyal servants. Is this how you reward our loyalty?"

The Queen looked angrily at Skye. "Madam, you try my patience, but because I value you I shall explain. Repeat what I tell you, however, and I shall deny it while you languish in the Tower. I shall never marry, my dear Skye, for if I did I should be neither a Queen nor a woman in my own right. I have seen how men can overrule women. As long as England has only a Queen to rule her, that shall not happen to me.

"My half-sister, Mary, never fully recovered from what my father did to her, and to her unfortunate mother, Catherine of Aragon. Their lives were ruined by my father. Poor Mary! He had cosseted and spoiled her from birth, then suddenly one day all that love was withdrawn and she was torn from her own mother, whom she never saw again, and declared a bastard.

"My own mother, I am told, was under constant pressure to produce a son. When she failed her life was wantonly taken. As for me, I never knew where I stood with my father. One day I was his darling, the next day I was sent down to Hatfield in disgrace. I learned, my dear Skye. I learned.

"Jane Seymour was, I think, fortunate to die. For all his fine mourning he did not care, for he had what he wanted—a son! Of my other three stepmothers Anne of Cleves was wise enough to give Henry Tudor what he wanted the most—a quick divorce. Poor Cat Howard, my mother's cousin, lost her head as my mother did. I can still hear that tragic girl's frantic cries when she realized they had come to take her to the Tower. She tried to reach my father, and they dragged her screaming from his chapel door." The Queen shuddered with the memory.

"Catherine Parr was fortunate enough to outlive my father and marry the man she loved. I went to live with her and her new husband after my father's death, you know. The Lord High Admiral of England, Sir Thomas Seymour, was my stepfather. He was the handsomest man I've ever seen, and the greatest rogue who ever lived. While my stepmother grew bigger and sicker with his child, he planned my seduction. He did not think Catherine would survive the birthing and he sought power to thwart his older brother, Edward, who was my little brother's guardian. He might have succeeded with me, for I was so innocent, but Kate realized his intent when she caught him kissing me in a very unfatherly fashion. I was sent from her house in disgrace, and when she died some weeks later of a childbed fever, Tom Seymour tried to marry me. He shortly thereafter lost his head. There were those who sought to implicate me in his perfidy, but I escaped them! I quickly learned that women who seek power in a man's world—and make no mistake about it, my dear Skye, this is a man's world—women like that have no friends among either sex. I am a woman who has power. I do not intend to hand it over to a man, not after all I have learned, and all I have suffered.

"After my sister Mary became Queen she became more and more suspicious of me. Strangely it was a man who was responsible for saving me: my brother-in-law, King Philip of Spain. Nevertheless I was sent to the Tower, and there I renewed my brief acquaintance with Robert Dudley. I love him, but I can never be his wife, and I most certainly will not be his mistress. He is not wise enough to understand this so I flirt with him, and I give him the things he wants, in order to keep his hopes alive and his interest in me from straying. I cannot lose him. I cannot.

"At the moment Robert Dudley wants you and I am pleased to give you to him for you are no threat to me. You despise him. And always will, I suspect. Yet you will give yourself to him because I am your Queen, and I command it."

"You can do this to me?" Skye repeated softly. "I who have been your friend? Your loyal servant? My God, madam, you are your father's daughter! The English lion has spawned as vicious a cub as he himself was!"

Elizabeth winced. "Careful, my dear," she warned.

"You are indeed the Queen of England," said Skye ominously, "but then, I am Irish. While Geoffrey Southwood lived I forgot it . . . but no more!"

Elizabeth Tudor laughed. "What a firebrand you are, my dear Skye. But we both know you are quite helpless before my royal office."

A quick retort sprang to her lips, but she forced it back. "Have I Your Majesty's permission to retire?" she said evenly.

The Queen held out her beautiful hand, and Skye kissed it briefly. "You have my leave to retire, Lady Southwood. Go home to Devon, and plan my godson's betrothal to Alison de Grenville. It will help to keep you busy, and out of trouble."

Skye backed out of the Queen's closet to rejoin Robbie and William Cecil. Her color was high, and her temper matched her flaming cheeks. She curtseyed to the chancellor and, with a furious look toward Robbie, swept from the room.

"It seems it is time for me to leave, my lord," observed Robbie drily.

The two men shook hands and parted, Cecil to return to his paperwork, Small to escort the Countess of Lynmouth, when he finally managed to catch up with her, back to Devon.

Skye was in a rage and refused to linger in London another hour. So the Queen thought to hand her over to Robert Dudley while she played her "perhaps I will, perhaps I won't" game. The bitch! Skye had no intention of meekly waiting for the fine Lord Dudley to use her as a plaything. For Robin's sake she would appear to submit. But *somehow* she intended being revenged on Elizabeth Tudor.

Skye looked across at Robbie, who sat pensively smoking his pipe. "I want you and Dame Cecily to take the children for a few weeks," she said. "I must go home to Ireland. It is a trip I have delayed far too long."

"What did the Queen say to you, Skye?"

"She said I must play the whore for her precious Earl of Leicester. She means not to marry, Robbie, but she'll not admit it publicly. She fears a man's dominance over her more than anything else. She wants Dudley, but she'll not take him to husband. She has decided that I am no threat to their love, as so many others might be, because I dislike the man. Therefore, as long as I satisfy his lusts Elizabeth Tudor stands in no danger of losing her gallant. God! Geoffrey must be spinning in his grave to see me used thusly! And by the Queen!"

"It's monstrous!" Robert Small was deeply shocked. "What will you do?"

"What can I do, Robbie? I must submit for my son's sake, and both the Queen and Dudley have counted on this. As long as I keep her secret and yield to Dudley, my son's inheritance is safe."

"And this is your final word on the matter? No, Skye, I don't believe it. You've some plan that you're not telling me about."

"Robbie . . . are you loyal to the Crown?"

"Of course! I'm an Englishman."

"And I am an Irishwoman, Robbie. We Irish have never been overfond of the English monarch impressed upon us. While Southwood lived, his loyalties were mine. And they might even have remained my loyalties had Elizabeth Tudor respected me as I once respected her. But she is just like all English rulers! She uses everyone around her to her own ends, overlooking kindness and friendship. She is a brilliant woman. I have no doubt she will govern England well. But after what she has done to me, she is my bitterest enemy!

"Two of my children, nevertheless, are English, and I will not confuse them by tampering with their loyalties. Robin is the Earl of Lynmouth, a peer of this realm. The title is old. Geoffrey was proud of it and rightly so. Robin owes his allegiance to his Queen and, perhaps because he will be an attractive man as his father was, Elizabeth will treat him well.

"Willow was born here in England, and she is your heiress. I cannot endanger you and Dame Cecily, and I know that my dearest Khalid would not thank me for placing his only child in a dangerous situation. So for all your sakes, whatever I do it will be done in secret."

"Did Geoffrey ever adopt Willow legally?" asked the captain as their coach jounced along.

"No. He meant to, but we simply never got to it. Why?"

"Because I do want to adopt her, Skye. She's legally my heiress, but 'twould please me greatly if she also bore my name. And, I suspect it would be safer for Willow to be a Small. I've known you since you were an innocent slip of a girl blindly in love with Khalid, and I recognize the light of battle when I see it in your eye." He sighed. "You're going to make war on the Crown, aren't you?"

She smiled a rueful little smile. "I honestly don't know what I'm going to do yet, Robbie. But as a loyal subject of the Queen, it would be better if you didn't know my plans."

"Humph!" sniffed the little man. "I'll remind you that I'm your friend before I'm anything else, your fine ladyship!" Then he grew serious. "Be careful, Skye. Bess Tudor is the lion's cub, and can be very dangerous."

"So I have found, Robbie, and I'll be wary. I think, however, that I have discovered a way to get at her without her ever knowing it's me. Let me go to Ireland first, and then we shall see."

"When will you go?" he asked her.

"In a few days. I must first send a message to my uncle, for I prefer to travel in an O'Malley ship."

And some four days later the Bishop of Connaught sat in his study reading his niece's letter for the second time. The O'Malley of Innisfana was finally coming home, though this was to be a secret visit. She wanted her flagship, the *Seagull,* to meet her off the Isle of Lundy on Midsummer's Eve and she wanted her uncle aboard. Seamus O'Malley was well pleased. It was high time his niece remembered who she was. And on Midsummer's Eve, it was he who reached over the ship's rail to pull her up the final few feet to the deck.

Her smile erased the years. She leaned over the railing and called down to the little sailboat that had ferried her from the mainland. "Ten days, Robbie, unless it's stormy."

"God speed, lass!" was the sure reply, and the little boat turned and headed back toward the English coast.

Skye walked directly to the main cabin in the stern. She flung her cloak on a chair, poured herself some wine, and stood looking at the two men who were waiting for her to speak. "Well, Uncle," she smiled teasingly, "have I changed so much? MacGuire, you've gotten fat, but it's good to see you again."

"Mistress Skye, we thought surely you were dead," and then his voice broke.

She reached out a hand to comfort him. "But I'm not dead, MacGuire. I am quite alive, and I have come home now."

The old seaman blinked rapidly and Skye turned to her uncle. "Well, m'lord Bishop, I've never heard you so quiet in my entire life. I owe you a debt, Uncle, for your care of the O'Malley fortunes. I can never repay that debt, for it's too large, but I do thank you with all my heart."

Seamus O'Malley found his voice at last. "I would not have believed it had I not seen it with my own eyes. I thought once that you'd reached the peak of your beauty, but I was wrong. You're lovelier now than ever before, if that's possible. And there's something else about you, something I cannot put my finger on." He shook his head. "No wonder Niall Burke refuses to marry again."

She paled slightly at the mention of his name, but not enough that her uncle noticed. "Is he widowed then?" she managed to sound casual.

"The Spanish girl died before he even brought her home to Ireland. They're not strong, those girls from warm climates." He paused and looked at her craftily. "But for fate intervening, you and Niall would be long wed. The match could be remade now that you're both free."

"No! I didn't come home to be mated, Uncle. I am the Countess of Lynmouth, and I shall remain the Countess of Lynmouth until my son is grown, and takes a wife. I am here because I would wage war on Elizabeth Tudor, and to do so I'll need my fleet."

"*What?!*" both men chorused.

"The Queen of England has insulted me unforgivably, Uncle. But my battle with her must remain a secret one. I cannot endanger my young son, the Earl of Lynmouth, or my little daughter."

"What in Hell are you going to do, Skye?" demanded Seamus O'Malley.

"Elizabeth Tudor believes that trade is the key to making England great. She is right, Uncle, it is. I have seen how trade has made the East wealthy. My own English vessels—mine and my partner's—have already begun increasing the Queen's wealth, but now in order to punish her I will harry the trading vessels coming into England of which the Queen now receives a percentage. I cannot refuse to trade for England, for that would endanger Robin's inheritance. But if my ships and others like them are pirated, then trade benefits the English Crown nothing. I shall not be harmed. For who would suspect the innocent widowed Countess of Lynmouth of pirating?

"Mind you, I want no killing. I value all who are in my employ, officer and common seaman, English and Irish alike. Those of my Irish ships that pirate my English ships will proceed to Algiers to dispose of the cargoes. I will profit, but Elizabeth Tudor most certainly will not."

"Why this war on England, Niece?"

"Not England, Uncle, Elizabeth Tudor herself. I have no quarrel with the English."

"Very well, then. Why the war on Elizabeth Tudor?"

"Because to hold the man she loves, but will not bed or marry, she would use me as her whore. She easily forgets that my beloved Geoffrey was her most loyal and devoted servant. As am I—or was. She is ruthless in the pursuit of her own desires, but I will not be used thusly by anyone, even the Queen of England!"

"Think carefully, Niece," the bishop was greatly troubled. "If you are ever connected with this scheme the Queen will not be merciful. She can't afford to have her perfidy made public. How will you protect your children?"

"I am arranging my little Robin's betrothal with Alison de Grenville, a daughter of Sir Richard de Grenville, who is safely in the Queen's favor. It's an excellent match for the girl and Dickon is a good friend. He'll look after Robin's interests if anything should happen to me.

"Robert Small, the dearest friend I have in this world, is legally adopting my daughter, Willow. He was her father's best friend, and is childless. We are business partners, and before he sailed on his last trading voyage three years ago he made Willow his heiress. He has a fine house near Bideford. He and his sister adore Willow, and she adores them. It was Captain Small who brought me out to meet you tonight."

"You've thought carefully of your English children, Niece, but what of Ewan and Murrough O'Flaherty? Could not English vengeance fall on them?"

"The O'Flaherty holdings are too small, too unimportant, and too isolated for the English to bother with, Uncle. Besides, my Irish sons are doubly related to my English son by their betrothals to Robin's half-sisters, Geoffrey Southwood's daughters. If Robin stands in the Queen's favor, then his half-brothers will, too."

Seamus O'Malley nodded, satisfied that all precautions had been taken. "We'll need a base of operations in England that can't be traced to you or the O'Malley family," he said.

"MacGuire!" said Skye. "Set a course for the Lord of Lundy Isle's castle. It's the only safe landing on the whole of the island. Adam de Marisco is the master there. He's the last of his line and, I am told, as much a cutthroat as anyone. But de Marisco makes his living giving sanctuary and selling supplies to privateers and smugglers. We'll find a haven on Lundy for our ships."

"You've thought this all out, haven't you, Niece? Dubhdara would be damned proud of you—but then, he always was. Do you intend to sail with your ships?"

"Nay, Uncle. MacGuire will head up these expeditions, and I trust him to chose responsible young captains who'll not be recognized by others. Neither you nor I, Uncle, must be involved because we are easily recognized. The ships must sail without any identifying marks or flags. I have already thought out a means of communication during the piracy, a system that will totally confuse our victims. But we'll discuss that later."

"I'll go change the ship's course," said MacGuire. "If you'd like to get out of those skirts, you'll find all your old things in that chest across the room. I stored them away myself," he muttered shyly.

"Why, MacGuire, you're getting positively kindly in your old age," teased Skye.

The weathered captain eyed her boldly. "They'll probably be a bit tight in the britches, and across the front," he noted. "You've grown a bit, I'm noticing." He went out, chuckling over having had the last word.

Chuckling too, Skye opened the small sea chest. There, lovingly stored amid small bags of lavender, were her sea clothes. She lifted a silk shirt, and shook it out. Her double-legged skirt, her long, soft, woolen hose, her thigh-length doeskin doublet with its staghorn and silver buttons, her Cordoba leather boots, and her wide belt with its silver and topaz buckle were all there.

Seamus O'Malley saw the quick tears shining in his niece's beautiful eyes. "I'll be on deck getting some air, Skye. Perhaps you'd like to take some time to change."

As she heard the door close behind him she began to undo the fastenings on her gown. Off it came, and her petticoats, and silk stockings, and the small, ribboned corset. The trappings of Her Ladyship, the Countess of Lynmouth, lay in a heap on the cabin floor. In the mirror she watched, fascinated, as the O'Malley of Innisfana was reborn before her eyes. MacGuire had only been half right, and she solved the problem by leaving the top button of her shirt open.

In the bottom of the trunk she found her small jeweled dagger and—good Lord!—her sword of fine Toledo steel with the gold-and-silver-filigreed handle. She buckled it on, sure that Adam de Marisco wouldn't be impressed simply by a well-turned leg.

A knock sounded on her door, and her uncle reappeared. "We're about to land, Skye."

"Send MacGuire ashore to contact Lord de Marisco, and set up a meeting between us. I will wait aboard until he is ready to see me."

"I take it," said Seamus O'Malley, "that de Marisco is not expecting a woman."

"He's expecting the O'Malley of Innisfana, Uncle," said Skye with a smile. "It's not my fault if he doesn't know that the O'Malley is a female."

The bishop laughed. "Let us go topside, Niece. There'll be no real dark this night, as it's Midsummer's Eve. We'll get a good look at the island. I imagine its inhabitants will be celebrating the holiday with pagan fervor."

They left the cabin together, and after Seamus O'Malley had given MacGuire his instructions, the two O'Malleys stood at the ship's rail. Lundy got its name from the old Norse word, lunde, which was the word for puffin, a bird. The island loomed above the ship, great granite cliffs towering darkly into the lavender half-dusk. The place had a barbaric beauty about it. The island was covered in pasturage upon which herds of sheep grazed. It also served as a breeding ground for sea birds. At one end of the island was a lighthouse. At the other stood the ramshackle ruins of de Marisco Castle, with the only landing place on the island.

MacGuire's boat bumped the quay. Securing his craft, he quickly walked the length of the stone pier. At the end of the pier a ship's supply shop had been set up alongside an inn. The inn was not crowded yet. MacGuire sat down at a table. A very buxom serving wench in a soiled blouse leered over him. "Wot's your pleasure, Cap'n?"

"I want to see de Marisco."

"Everyone does, dearie, but he don't see just anyone."

"He'll see me. I'm expected. From the O'Malley of Innisfana's ship."

"I'll go ask," said the girl, walking off.

O'Malley looked about him. The walls of the inn were the original stone walls of the castle, and they were damp with green mold. The rushes on the floor had seen better days, and were matted down and mixed with old bones for which several scrawny dogs now snarlingly vied. The few tables were none too clean, and both the fireplace and the tallow torches smoked.

The wench returned. "He says you're to follow me."

MacGuire got to his feet and hurried after the girl. Anything was better than this hellhole. The serving wench led him up a flight of open stone steps, stopping at the top to knock on the massive oak door. "In there, Cap'n." MacGuire pushed through into the room, and his jaw dropped in surprise.

The room was positively opulent, the most splendid the Irishman had ever seen. The walls were hung with velvet and silk tapestries, the stone floors covered by magnificent, thick sheepskins. A huge fireplace burned with sweet-scented applewood even on this Midsummer's Eve. On the long oak table were two large golden, twisted candelabra burning beeswax tapers.

In a great thronelike chair at the table's head sprawled a giant.

Though he was seated, MacGuire could see that he must stand at least six foot six inches tall. His hair was as black as night, as was his full, well-barbered beard. His eyes were a sensuous smoky blue. He sported a gold earring in his left ear. His doublet was of fine, soft leather, his white silk shirt was open, revealing a thick mat of hair growing upward from his navel. His hose were a dark-green wool, and his huge brown leather boots rose well over his knees. In his lap sat two pretty young girls, both naked from the waist up, who were feeding dainties from silver platters to the lord of Lundy.

"Sit down, man!" came the booming command. "Glynis!" Adam de Marisco dumped one of the girls from his lap "Serve my guest."

The girl good-naturedly picked herself up off the floor, rubbing her prettily rounded posterior as she did so, and poured a goblet of wine for MacGuire. MacGuire swallowed hard at the close proximity of the girl's big breasts. The nipples were as large as Spanish grapes.

"She's yours for the night," chuckled de Marisco, and Glynis cheerfully plumped herself into the Irishman's lap. MacGuire grinned, delighted. "I like your style of hospitality, by God I do, m'lord! If the O'Malley doesn't sail tonight, I will gladly accept your gift." He raised the goblet to his host. "Your health, sir!"

De Marisco nodded. "I'll see your master as soon as he comes ashore. This will be a busy night, with many celebrations. Would the O'Malley and his men like to join us?"

MacGuire hid a smile. "I'll go immediately, and take the O'Malley your invitation." MacGuire stood, dumping poor Glynis.

De Marisco was bored tonight. As the Irishman left the room, he wondered if the O'Malley's visit would herald any excitement. He doubted it. But several minutes later his smoky eyes widened with surprise as the captain returned with the O'Malley. "Christ's sacred bones!" he swore. "*A woman!?* What the hell kind of a joke is this, MacGuire?"

"My lord, this is the O'Malley of Innisfana."

"I don't do business with women," came the flat reply.

"Afraid, my lord?" drawled Skye softly.

With a roar of outrage the giant stood, dumping the one remaining girl from his lap. She scrambled up and cowered with Glynis while Adam de Marisco stomped over to Skye and towered over her in his most intimidating manner. MacGuire began getting a sick feeling in the pit of his stomach. Though he was a brave man, he was old, and he hadn't a chance against this giant.

De Marisco stared fiercely down. The woman, instead of trembling like the other two females, stared boldly up at him. He began to cool down a little, and realized that he liked what he saw. He began to chuckle. She was a brave one, and beautiful as well.

"I own," she began abruptly, "close to two dozen ships of various sizes. One of my fleets has just finished a successful three-year voyage to the East Indies. I'm a rich woman. I have a quarrel with someone in a high place. To avenge myself against this person I'll need assurance that Lundy Isle is open to my ships. You'll be paid well."

De Marisco was instantly intrigued. "How high a place?" he asked.

"Elizabeth Tudor," came the cool reply.

"The Queen?" He whistled. "Are you serious, woman, or merely mad?" He peered down at the woman who faced him. "By God, you *are* serious!" He began to chuckle, and the chuckle grew into a great roar of mirth that shook the entire room.

Skye stood her ground, unblinking. "Well, de Marisco, do we do business or do we not?"

"How much?" A crafty look narrowed his eyes.

"Name your own price—within reason," she answered.

"We'll discuss this alone, O'Malley," said de Marisco. "MacGuire, why don't you take Glynis and her sister downstairs."

"M'lady?" The Irishman looked to Skye.

"Go along, MacGuire. I'd spend a full year feeling guilty if I denied you such choice company. Tell the men that they may come ashore for the celebrations. Alternate the watch so they may all have a bit of fun." MacGuire hesitated, and Skye laughed. "Oh, Lord, man, you're such an old woman! De Marisco, give my man your word you'll not harm me, or we'll never get down to business."

"You've got it. Good God, Captain, do I look like a ravager of helpless women?"

MacGuire reluctantly withdrew, and de Marisco motioned Skye to the chair the Irishman had recently vacated. Pouring her some wine, he shoved the ornate silver goblet at her. She sipped at the ruby liquid, smiling appreciatively at the excellent vintage. De Marisco eyed her closely again, and then reopened the discussion. "So I may name my own price—within reason, eh?"

"That is correct."

"I don't need money, madam. There's precious little to spend it on here, and I've more than enough at any rate. So what's within reason, eh?" He drank a bit of wine. "What's your name? I can't believe your intimates call you just O'Malley."

She gave him her best smile, and he felt his heart lurch. "My name is Skye."

"For the island?"

"My mother came from there."

"You look Irish, but your speech is of England and of Ireland. Why?"

"You are certainly nosy, de Marisco. I offered you a straight business proposition, not the story of my life."

The smoky blue eyes narrowed. "I like to know with whom I'm doing business, Skye O'Malley."

Her eyes flashed. He continued. "You tell me that you wish to wage war on the Queen of England. Before I risk my small standing, I'd like to know why I should join your personal war."

She considered a moment, then nodded. "My late husband was the Earl of Lynmouth. You can see the lights of my castle from your own windows. When Geoffrey died several months ago, from the white throat, he left me sole guardian to our combined families, my own children, his children, and our son, who is Geoffrey's heir. But Queen Elizabeth overruled his will in the case of Geoffrey's heir, and sent her favorite, Robert Dudley, to be our son's governor. The Earl forced his attentions upon me, and when I complained to the Queen she told me quite frankly that she wanted me to accept those attentions. She expects me to act as her whore in order to keep her favorite happy. Both my late husband and I were loyal servants to the Queen while we were at Court. I don't deserve this shabby treatment, but I can't endanger my son by doing anything openly against Elizabeth."

De Marisco sucked in his breath sharply. He was an ethical man in his own way, for all his business "ventures" were considered unorthodox. "Well, she's Harry Tudor's brat for sure, and as ruthless as both her father and that witch who spawned her, Anne Boleyn. All right, Skye O'Malley, Countess of Lynmouth, tell me what you plan and then we'll see if I'll help you."

"My English fleet brings great riches to England, and the Queen accepts a fat share of it. Her coffers fill daily with the profits of all ships doing business from England. If my Irish ships rob selected vessels, including my own so that no suspicion falls on me, then I hurt the Queen in an area where she can least afford it. But the pain will not be made public. That is why I need the island of Lundy, de Marisco. It is only eleven miles off the Devon coast, and I can be here and back within a single day if necessary.

"My privateers can be safe here on Lundy, and no one will be the wiser. You wouldn't try to tell me that all the goods going through this island are legal trade, now would you?"

Adam de Marisco laughed pleasantly. "It seems, Skye O'Malley, that you need me a hell of a lot more than I need you. Nevertheless I'm not adverse to a bit of piracy, so I'll make you a proposition. You can have my aid, and sanctuary on Lundy for your ships in exchange for one percent of the goods you take, and—" he paused a moment, then finished quickly, "and if you'll spend this night in my bed."

She went white. Recovering quickly, she said, "Two percent of the goods taken, and not a penny more."

"One percent, and this night," he repeated, a mischievous smile flickering across his handsome face.

"Why?!" she burst out.

"Because you are beautiful and a lady, and I know of no other way for someone like me to possess something so fabulously rare as someone like you." She seemed genuinely troubled, and he continued, "Come, Skye O'Malley, if you really desire vengeance on your enemy then no price is too high. It's only one night, sweetheart."

Skye was torn. She knew her plan was flawless, but it could succeed only if she had the use of Lundy. She thought of Elizabeth Tudor calmly admitting to using her. She thought of Robert Dudley and his perverted, degrading possession of her—a possession which had in all likelihood only just begun.

Now Adam de Marisco wished to possess her also, but he at least offered a fair return. She sighed, ruefully recalling Robbie's warning that unless she married again she would be prey to men. She looked at the huge man, and realized that he was not unattractive. If she were lucky, he was also not as debauched as Dudley. "Until midnight," she bargained.

He shook his head. "The whole night, and no weeping or lying limp like a dead thing."

"Dammit, man, I'm no whore to perform for you!"

"Precisely, Skye O'Malley. You're a beautiful and, I suspect, a passionate woman. I want no holding back of those passions because of mistaken virtue. I should be far more shocked by a lack of fire in you than an abundance of it."

She blushed furiously, and his laughter rumbled about the room like distant thunder. "Is it agreed, then?" He held out his hand. She hesitated, then grasped the great paw with her own elegant hand. She wasn't protecting any maidenhead, and so much was at stake. "It's agreed," she answered him.

"I should like to hear you say my Christian name, Skye O'Malley."

"Very well, Adam, I agree."

"I'm not a bad fellow," he said. "I won't hurt you."

That innocent reassurance comforted her. "I'll have to direct my people first. I'll need an hour or two, and I'd prefer it if our liaison tonight were kept secret."

"Of course," he assured her. "I have no need to brag."

"And then there's my uncle, the Bishop of Connaught. He travels with me."

Adam de Marisco had the good grace to look abashed, and a small giggle escaped Skye. He grinned at her. "That's a nice sound, Skye O'Malley, you should laugh more often. Well, now, and how do we rid ourselves of the bishop?"

"He has a partiality to good French Burgundy. You wouldn't happen to have any on this rock of yours?"

"I'll send a small cask out to the ship at once," promised the lord of the isle.

Skye returned to the *Seagull* along with the wine. Bonfires were already springing up on the hillsides of Lundy in celebration of the summer solstice, and her crew headed ashore to join in the festivities. Skye went directly to her cabin and put on her dress. It was a pale wisteria-colored silk with a simple scooped neckline, and long tight sleeves—most unfashionable, and she'd worn no farthingale beneath it, but what could Adam de Marisco know of current fashions? It was soft and feminine, and when she loosened her hair and brushed it about her shoulders she knew she created a pleasing picture. Strangely, Skye wanted him to be pleased.

Stopping by her uncle's cabin, she found Seamus O'Malley already enjoying the wine. "The lord de Marisco has been most hospitable, Uncle. We have almost reached an agreement, and I am going ashore to have supper with the gentleman. Will you join us?" She knew he would refuse.

"Nay, Niece, I am quite comfortable here with my book on the Life of Saint Paul, and the excellent Burgundy sent by our host. It is really quite superior."

She bent and kissed his dark head. "Good night then, Uncle. Sleep well."

"You also, Skye."

She went ashore again, this time wrapped in the anonymity of a dark cloak. She arrived at Adam de Marisco's chambers to find the table laid with a cold supper. Adam took her cloak, his hand lingering a moment on her shoulders. When she tensed he said quietly, "I've never raped a woman, little girl. Let us go easily, and you'll not regret your decision, I promise you."

"I'm not so little, de Marisco," she retorted. "I'm tall for a woman, and taller than many men."

He turned her about and lifted her so that she was at eye level with him. "My name is Adam, little girl, and though you are tall for a woman, I top you by a good foot." Setting her back down, he asked, "Are you hungry?"

"No."

"Then we'll eat later." And before she realized what it was he intended, he had her gown unlaced and was pulling it off her. She gasped, clutching at her chemise, but he paid her no mind. Loosening her grip on the fragile silk, he stripped her naked. Lifting her into his arms, he carried her from the room into an adjoining bedchamber. One arm cradled her while the other hand pulled back the bedcovers. He gently tucked her into the biggest bed Skye had ever seen.

She lay quietly watching as he pulled his own garments off. Clothed, Adam de Marisco was impressive. Naked, he was magnificent. Perfectly proportioned, he had thighs like tree trunks, shapely, well-muscled arms, a lean torso, and a great broad chest covered in a thick mat of dark hair. His arms and legs were also liberally furred. He was, in fact, the hairiest man she'd ever seen. He watched her reaction to his nudity, a faintly amused smile upon his sensual lips. Quickly he climbed into bed with her.

Skye braced herself for his assault, and when nothing happened she turned slightly to look at him. He was gazing at her, and she blushed, caught in his careful scrutiny. He reached out and drew her close. The arm that held her was strong, the body against which she was pressed was warm and clean-smelling. She was held quietly this way for several silent minutes. Then Adam de Marisco kissed her and, to her immense surprise, the kiss was a firmly tender one. His mouth was fragrant.

"Lovemaking," he said calmly, "is a great art, Skye O'Malley. I spent four years of my life at the French Court, for my late mother was a Frenchwoman. I have made a rather outrageous bargain with you and you've accepted my terms, for you are a rather outrageous woman. We are two healthy, attractive people, and I cannot enjoy making love to you if you are fearful of me. So, little girl, we will just lie here in each other's arms until you are comfortable."

The silence was deafening. For the first time in her life Skye was at a complete loss. "De Marisco . . . Adam . . . I don't know you. I've never made love to a man I didn't know. To a stranger."

"And how many men have you *known,* Skye O'Malley?"

"I've had three husbands," she said in a small voice. There was no need to explain about Niall Burke.

"You've outlived them all?"

"Aye."

"No lovers?"

"None, except Dudley, of course. But then that's not my wish."

"Did you love any of them, little girl?"

"The last two, both very, very much. Losing them was so painful that with both deaths I thought I would die. But of course I didn't."

"Do you have children?"

"Two sons by my first husband, a daughter by my second, and one living son by Geoffrey. And, of course, I am stepmother to Geoffrey's three daughters. My younger son by Geoffrey died in the same epidemic that killed his father."

Her soft voice caught and Adam pulled her back into his arms. "You've learned that love can cause pain as well as pleasure, haven't you? Let me comfort you, little girl. Let me comfort you."

His mouth was closing over hers again, and Skye felt no resistance in herself at all. His lips were warm and experienced, and she felt a delicious thrill run through her as she realized that he was wooing her, really seeking her favor. He covered her face with little kisses, then took her lips again, this time parting them masterfully, touching only the very tip of her tongue with his. The effect was devastating, and she shivered violently.

One hand traced gently over her jawline, her slim throat, a rounded shoulder, moving downward to cup a small breast already firm with desire. The warm mouth followed the fingers, kissing, tasting, biting playfully. She was turned, her long hair pushed aside, the back of her neck tenderly saluted, the long line of her back lovingly traced in fire. She gasped, then blushed pink as her buttocks were first kissed, then gently nipped.

His kisses branded each long leg at the rounded calves and slim ankles. He sucked on her toes, and Skye came close to fainting, so sensuous was that sensation. She was turned again to lie once more on her back while his lips began an upward sweep of loving. He inhaled the marvelous woman smell of her that was mixed with the scent of wild roses. His tongue reveled in the pure silk of her inner thighs, the moist coral flesh of her womanhood.

"Let me comfort you, little girl," she heard him say again, and her own voice answered, sobbed, "Yes!"

He was unbelievably gentle, raising her just slightly, and slowly, so slowly filling her full of himself until she thought surely she would burst, so big was he. His great body covered her slim one as snow covers the land. She was pressed deeper and deeper down into the mattress as he drove deeper and deeper into her willing flesh. He became more vigorous and she reveled in his passion.

This was not Robert Dudley seeking to crush her spirit by degrading her body. This big man sought to give pleasure, a pleasure she had believed possible only with true love.

She could feel her climax rising fast, and she cried out, wanting him to know. "Oh, Adam! It is good!" Then she was lost in a storm of passion as great as any storm she had experienced at sea, and she heard him cry out triumphantly.

He rolled away and they lay side by side, panting, and then she said quietly, "Adam de Marisco, I hope you'll comfort me again before this night is done!"

And he laughed, a wonderful warm rumble of mirth. "Fear not, Skye O'Malley! You'll be well comforted!" And then he was kissing her again, *and it was good*!

Chapter 23

IT HAD BEEN AN UNUSUALLY LOVELY SUMMER. IN AUTUMN, SKYE looked back on the last several months with deep satisfaction. Half a dozen treasure ships had been taken, robbing Elizabeth Tudor's coffers of much-needed revenue. Only two had been her own ships. The others had been funded by wealthy courtiers, including Dudley, and Skye felt no guilt over robbing them. The monies from the ships other than her own found its way into church boxes . . . paid delinquent taxes for poor but hardworking farmers . . . and the sick, the old, and the hungry were astonished when they began receiving gifts of medicine, firewood, food, clothing, and small bags of coins.

With winter coming, however, the parade of ships would be slowing down. The sudden increase in piracy off the Devon coast had only just begun to attract royal attention. Now Skye would have her privateers lie low, and if the royal curiosity had been piqued it would be forced to remain unsatisfied. She chuckled. It had all been so unbelievably easy. Suspecting nothing, the trading ships had been like fat white ducks that had waddled by mistake into a fox's den.

Every attack had gone smoothly. Amazingly, there had been no loss of life in this venture, for each vessel taken was captured by not one, but two ships. Outnumbered, outmanned, and outgunned, the trading vessels did not care to fight. Their cargoes were transferred quickly and quietly by silent, well-trained seamen who, responding to whistles and hand signals, gave no hint of their nationality. The privateers disappeared with their booty as quickly as they appeared. The whole affair was eerily well done.

The small royal commission sent to investigate returned to London at a loss. No one had even the slightest idea of who was behind this genteel pillage. The pirates had to be English. How else did they know when ships were due, and the courses the ships would take? Since the piracy stopped as suddenly as it had begun, the royal commission concluded that the incidents had been isolated and coincidental. The Queen was so informed.

Skye had decided that she might avoid giving the Twelfth Night gala because she was in mourning. Accordingly, she sent Elizabeth Tudor her regrets, and went off to Lundy to confer with Adam de Marisco over the spring pirating schedule and the signals that would be used between the two castles.

The giant lord of Lundy had become her good friend and, after that Midsummer's Eve, her occasional lover. She had awakened to find herself clasped in his arms, his smoky eyes studying her intently. She returned the stare, then added a blazing smile that made him sigh with relief.

"Then you're not angry with me?" he said.

"No, of course not. Why should I be?"

He grinned ruefully. "Little girl, you're not just some wench. In a half-drunken moment I demanded a rather outrageous price for my aid. You're a great lady, Skye O'Malley, and you held to the bargain we made better than many men would hold to a bargain. Now, however, I have a problem. My instinct is to imprison you in this tower and make love to you for at least a month without stopping. But I can't do that, can I?"

"No, Adam de Marisco, you can't," she said, "but I thank you for the compliment."

"I'd marry you!"

"Oh, Adam, what a lovely man you are, but I'll not marry

again. Besides, aren't you wary of a woman who's buried three husbands?" Her lovely eyes twinkled mischievously, but he looked so crestfallen, this great bear of a man, that she soothed him. "I'll be back, Adam, I promise you."

And in fact, she had come back, several times throughout the summer. In between their incredible sessions of lovemaking they had talked and become real friends. This was a whole new experience for Skye. Apart from the obnoxious Robert Dudley, her lovers had been men to whom she was married, excepting that one long-ago night with Niall. She was not a promiscuous woman, but the plain truth of the matter was that she needed to make love with someone she liked, especially now, for the Earl of Leicester had been to Lynmouth twice more to make demands upon her.

Robert Dudley delighted in degrading her, or "taming" her, as he called it. He derived intense pleasure from forcing her to total submission, but though he could force the body, her soul eluded him. This kept Dudley returning. After these nightmares of lust Skye invariably fled to Adam de Marisco. His honest adoration and vigorous sexual worship of her were like a clean sea wind after the passing of a garbage scow. Adam did not raise her to the exquisite soul-rending heights that Geoffrey had, but he gave her pleasure and was delighted that she cared enough to give him pleasure in return.

It had been a melancholy Christmas and New Year. Skye had kept to the Southwood family customs, decorating the Great Hall with pine and holly, burning a Yule log, offering the wassail bowl to the carolers and mummers, but it had not been the same without Geoffrey. Skye's sons and twin stepdaughters remained in Ireland and she hadn't seen them since the previous summer when she had made her secret visit home. Susan Southwood preferred to remain in Cornwall with the Trevenyans. Only Robin and Willow were at Lynmouth. Dame Cecily had contracted a bad chill and remained at Wren Court. Skye insisted that Robbie remain too, so that his sister would not be alone.

Several days into the New Year, Skye decided to go to Lundy. Sending to Wren Court for news, she learned that Dame Cecily was up and about again. They would be delighted to have the children and would return with them to Lynmouth in time for Twelfth Night, which they would all spend together. Skye intended asking Adam de Marisco to come back with her and join them in the celebration. His presence might soften the pain of the memories that continued to assail her.

Dressed in her doeskin doublet, boots, woolen hose, and a heavy wool cloak, she sailed the eleven miles to Lundy alone. Skye now kept a small boat moored at the foot of the cliffs on which Lynmouth Castle was located. In the first sleepless nights following Geoffrey's death, she had wandered aimlessly about the castle and, during those nocturnal wanderings, had found a passage that wound down and down and down to emerge into a small, well-hidden cave just above sea level. She had emerged from the cave into the bright moonlit night to find herself on a comfortable-sized ledge, the sea lapping just a few inches below her feet. The moon was full and the tide high, which meant that the sea would never rise higher than this. The cave wouldn't flood except possibly in an extremely severe storm. Looking closely along the rim of the ledge, she had finally found the flight of stone steps she sought, and the round, barnacle-encrusted heavy iron ring. Obviously some long-dead Southwood had had an interest in the sea.

She had come back later with Robbie, and they had thoroughly explored the cave, finding iron torchholders, rusted, but still serviceable, at intervals along the walls. Daisy's fifteen-year-old brother, Wat, had been assigned to clean out the cave, to keep torches always burning, and to see that Skye's boat was always in readiness.

She had never fully tested her knowledge of seamanship since her memory had returned, for there had been no need or desire. The first time she had again sailed in a small boat had been with Robbie on that inaugural trip to meet her own Irish ships, and once she sailed with MacGuire to St. Bride's for a reunion with her favorite sister, Eibhlin. Eibhlin had grown plump but was as tart as ever. Returning to Innisfana, Skye had taken the tiller from MacGuire and discovered that her sailing skill was entirely intact.

Home again at Lynmouth, she had taken to sailing out occasionally into the Bristol Channel. The first time she was caught in a sudden summer's afternoon squall she had felt not fear, but pure exhilaration sparking her. After that, all doubts about her skill disappeared.

Skye hesitated before sailing to Lundy on that cold January afternoon. The day was far too beautiful, a real weathermaker if her sailor's instincts were correct. Still, it had been a depressing two weeks at Lynmouth Castle, and she longed to laugh and be frivolous.

"Little girl!" Adam greeted her, delighted. "You must be fey, my beautiful Irish witch! I've been thinking about you for days." He enveloped her in a bear hug that left her breathless. Picking her up in his arms, he carried her upstairs to his lair.

Laughing, she protested, "Adam! What will people think?" But she was glad. She felt safe and warm and happy in this man's arms.

They undressed each other quickly and made delicious passionate love until, sated, they lay back amid the tumbled feather pillows, warm beneath an enormous fur coverlet. He reached for her hand, found it and held it tenderly in his grasp. "I wish to Heaven that you could love me, Skye O'Malley," he said quietly.

"I do, Adam," she protested. "You're one of my best friends." But she knew it wasn't what he wanted to hear and she felt suddenly sad, realizing that she could not go on using this gentle giant to ease her own sorrows when he felt so much more deeply for her than she did for him. "Adam de Marisco, I never meant to hurt you, but it seems to me that I have. I beg your forgiveness."

"No, little girl. I started this. I have been well punished for my arrogance. However, I am going to send you home now. I can no longer just spend time with you in bed and not have all of you."

She understood and, rising quickly, dressed. "I came today to ask you if you'd come to Lynmouth for Twelfth Night."

He looked up from buttoning his shirt. "I'll come. They say lovers can't be friends, but we are."

Outside the sky was darkening fast. A single clear star hung overhead, and in the west the last of the sunset was a cold lemon-yellow smudge on a stale-gray horizon.

"Snow coming," he noted.

"I thought so too. Come with me now."

"No, but I'll come later tonight, for 'twill start to storm by early morning." He helped her down into the boat. "The wind's from the west, little girl. You'll be home quickly." Untying the boat, he threw the rope to Skye.

"I'll have the cave entrance well lit, Adam. Until later!" She blew him a kiss and he pushed her craft away from the stone quay. The breeze caught quickly at her sails and she was off.

The fresh winds sent the little sailboat skidding swiftly across the tops of the waves and though it was dark when she reached her mooring, this was still, she was sure, the fastest passage she'd ever made from Lundy. She secured the boat tightly. Taking a torch from inside the cave, she lit the ledge beacons so Adam might find his way safely. Then she began climbing up into the castle. She thought she could hear sounds of revelry, which was indeed confusing. Arriving at the level of her apartment, she moved along the hidden interior passage until she reached the door that would admit her to her rooms. Flipping the hidden lock, she stepped into her antechamber, pulled the door shut behind her, and drew the tapestry back into place. She could now hear definite sounds of merrymaking below in the Hall. Puzzled, she moved toward the door that led into the public hall, but the door opened suddenly and Daisy flew in, slamming it behind her.

"Oh! Mistress Skye! Thank God you're back!"

"What is going on down there?" demanded Skye.

"Right after you left, milady, Lord Dudley and a group of his friends arrived. He was furious to learn you weren't here, and then he just took over, ordering a feast, sending into the village for some girls."

"What!?"

"Maids," he said. "They had to be maids," Daisy explained tearfully.

"Oh my God," said Skye. "Are the girls all right, Daisy? I'll send them home immediately. They're probably frightened to death. The Earls of Lynmouth haven't allowed that sort of abuse in years. Trust Dudley, the fiend, to revive such an appalling custom!"

"It's too late, milady. The girls have already been ruined," said Daisy.

"Are they all right, though?" asked Skye.

"All except little Anne Evans. She bled quite heavily."

"Christ's bones! Anne Evans is but twelve! Damn! Damn! Dudley will pay for this! I'll raise such hell with the Queen now that she'll be forced to punish him this time!" Skye slammed into her bedroom. "I shall have to pay a bounty to the families involved. Were any of the girls walking out yet?"

"Four, milady."

"And something to the young men to marry them immediately. Damn!" She whirled on Daisy. "Don't stand there gawking, girl! Get me a dress! I can hardly go below like this, can I? The lilac velvet should do. No farthingale, just three petticoats, I'm not at Court." She tore off her sailing clothes. *Dudley*! her mind raged. The slimy snake that Elizabeth Tudor had dropped into her private garden. It was bad enough that he had power over Robin and that he could use her as his occasional whore, but to come into her home uninvited! And with his cronies, too! To rape innocent village girls entrusted to her care!

Thick-fingered, Daisy struggled with her mistress's gown. Stumbling, she almost spilled the contents of a jewel case at Skye's feet. "Easy, my girl," soothed Skye, plucking an amethyst necklace from the box and clasping it around her neck.

"They're fearfully drunk," whispered Daisy, terrified. "Maybe you shouldn't go downstairs, my lady. Lord Dudley is the worst of all. It was he who hurt little Anne Evans."

Skye put a gentle hand on Daisy's cheek. "Listen to me, my girl," she said. "I know it would be easier to bolt my door and go to bed. Dudley would not know I'd returned, and God knows I dread facing him. But I am the Countess of Lynmouth. Lord Dudley has, in my absence, abused my hospitality and injured my charges. It is my duty to set things right. I should betray the trust Geoffrey left me were I to do otherwise, Daisy. D'you understand?"

Daisy bowed her head, ashamed, then said, "I'll warn the guard you're back. If there's any trouble, they'll come."

"Good girl!" Skye hurried from the room and downstairs. The noise from her uninvited guests grew louder with every step she took, but even so, the sight that met her eyes when she entered the Hall brought her close to fainting. Dudley and his friends sprawled around the high board in shirt-sleeves and hose. At either end of the table were the remains of what had obviously been a very generous feast. Most of the unfortunate village girls were naked or almost so, and imprisoned in the laps of their drunken captors. But what brought Skye close to hysterics was the sight of poor little Anne Evans, naked, on all fours in the center of the long table. One of the big castle mastiffs had been brought to a state of sexual excitement, and was just now being positioned in such a way that the child would soon be ravished by the dog.

"Sweet Jesus." Skye heard a voice behind her exclaim, and she turned to find the captain of the castle guard and his men all ranged at her back.

"Get the girls and that beast," she said. "Take the maids to the housekeeper. Have her attend to their injuries and put them to bed."

"And the dog, milady?"

"It's not his fault. Send him to the kennels, Harry."

The men-at-arms and their captain jogged into the hall and, taking the half-drunken courtiers by surprise, began removing the weeping, frightened girls. The mastiff was yanked off the table and Anne Evans, her eyes blank, was borne from the room.

Robert Dudley lurched to his feet shouting, "How dare you! I'm here in the Queen's name as governor to the lord of this castle. How dare you?!"

"I dare, Dudley! *My* men obey only me. I wonder what Bess Tudor would think of this performance, my lord? Rape! The perversion of innocents! D'you think I'll be silent this time? I'll shout this outrage to the skies! How dare you come into my house and abuse my people? Shelter and food I gladly offer you, but nothing more. You are not lord here, Dudley!"

Robert Dudley's eyes narrowed. There she stood, so damned proud, the Irish bitch. Why couldn't he break her the way he'd done with so many others? Including his late milksop wife, Amy. He remembered the last time he'd seen Amy alive. She'd told him she had a canker in her breast, and would die soon. When? he'd asked, not at all affected by the hurt in her eyes. A year, maybe two, she answered him, weeping. That's not soon enough, he had told her brutally. I could be King were it not for you. I don't care how you do it, but be dead soon! Your life is over, anyway.

Dudley hadn't known whether she actually had the courage to kill herself, but she had. And she'd done it in such a way as to cause an appalling scandal. She had done it deliberately, using her last chance to destroy his dreams of being King. Elizabeth, once hot to wed him, had backed off. And he'd never quite regained with her that high favor, despite the fact that he was her obvious favorite. Yes, his wife had planned her death brilliantly. Who would have predicted such a thing of the weak Amy.

To his infinite frustration, he could not bring Bess Tudor to heel, but he damn well would bring this haughty Irish beauty to her knees. She was going to learn tonight who the master was. Gulping some of her excellent Burgundy, he lurched to his feet.

"Where the hell were you?" he demanded. "And where is my ward?"

Furiously she strode into the hall and up to the board, her scornful glance taking in his rumpled appearance, ignoring the leers of the other men. "Your ward is visiting with his sister at Wren Court. He'll be back tomorrow."

"And where were you?" he pressed.

"Go to Hell, Dudley! I'm not your business."

There was drunken laughter at this, and the Earl of Leicester flushed a dull red. She stood there defying him, and he felt his anger double. "Bitch!" he snarled, leaping at her. His fingers dug into her soft upper arm and she felt bruises begin to form.

"Where were you?" He shook her.

Skye attempted to pull free. "Dudley! You're drunk! Disgustingly drunk!"

"She's a fractious filly, Leicester," came a mocking voice. "You can't seem to control *any* of your woman, can you?"

"I am not his woman!" shouted Skye. "I am Geoffrey Southwood's widow, and I ask that you all remember that!"

"You're my whore, madam, because if you are not, then I'll remove your son from your custody! Remember that well!"

"Never, Dudley! Never! Never! Never!"

Angrily Dudley pushed her until she sprawled backward upon the same spot where little Anne Evans had so lately been abused. "That's it, Dudley," sounded the same mocking voice. "Show the wench who's master here. We'll all help you! Right, men?"

She was being dragged onto the table, her skirts brutally lifted, her arms and legs yanked apart. Nightmare faces with bulging, bloodshot eyes, laughing mouths, tongues that licked quickly at dry lips, loomed over her. She was almost suffocated by the sour smell of wine. At least a dozen men leered at her, men who a year ago had eagerly sought the honor of an invitation to the Southwood's Twelfth Night masque, who had once paid her elegant compliments. Now these same men leaned over her like a pack of savage dogs.

She began to scream, screaming ceaselessly though she doubted anyone could hear her. Dudley's body flattened hers, and she felt him seek entry into her body. Skye struggled wildly, twisting this way and that. One foot wrenched free and she kicked out viciously, the sole of her foot finding a target. She managed to slip from underneath Dudley, but he was less drunk now and mounted her again. Before she could twist aside he thrust himself into her. Skye screamed.

Then suddenly a huge roar of outrage echoed in the Hall. The painful grip on her arms and legs was loosened. Dudley was lifted off her in the middle of his rutting and thrown clear across the room, causing the others to scatter. Adam de Marisco helped her up. "Do you want me to kill the bastard, little girl?"

"Yes!" she sobbed, then, "Oh, God, no! It's Dudley, the Queen's pet, Adam. You must not! Just put them out! All of them! Now!"

The castle's men-at-arms had returned and, under de Marisco's direction, put the Earl of Leicester and his cronies out into the cold night. Then the lord of Lundy returned to the Hall where he wrapped a cloak about the shivering woman and held a cup of wine to her lips. "Drink it, little girl, it will warm you."

She gulped from the goblet gratefully. Finished, she said, "Thank God you came, Adam. Oh God, I wish I could kill him!"

"Who will come the next time, Skye O'Malley?"

"What?"

"I said who will come the next time? You were lucky tonight. Who will rescue you the next time? You need a husband, my dear. You're far too beautiful to be alone, and you simply cannot protect yourself. Now listen to me—if you can't protect yourself, how can you protect your children?"

"I've kept them safe so far!" she retorted hotly.

"By sending them away from you, Skye. Alone and unprotected is no way for a woman to live."

"Then marry me, Adam!"

He shook his head. "No, little girl, it would never do for the widowed Countess of Lynmouth to wed a simple island lord. I know now I've neither the great name nor the power you need."

"But you love me."

"Oh, Skye O'Malley, I do love you, but I've my pride, too. You'll never love me, and I'm old-fashioned enough to want a woman who will truly love me. Think, little girl. There must be someone who has the name and the power, and with whom you might live in peace, possibly even in love."

She shook her head. But he refused to give up and when Robbie and Dame Cecily arrived the following day, they immediately agreed with Adam de Marisco, and added their voices to his. Robbie was horrified that Robert Dudley would make so free with Lynmouth Castle.

"I'm writing your uncle," he said. "He's bound to come up with a good match for you."

"No!" she was becoming agitated, and paced the Hall frantically. "I cannot go through the pain of loving and losing someone again, Robbie. I cannot!"

The giant Adam de Marisco looked on in amazement as Captain Sir Robert Small, just a shade over five feet tall, shouted at his beloved friend in a voice that would have split stone. "At what cost, Skye? The Queen bides her time. It amuses her to please Dudley, knowing you're no threat to her. But what if Elizabeth decides to wed you to Dudley? Or bestow you and your fortune upon some other man she wishes to honor? She can do it, Skye. And if she does, there'll be no premarriage agreement as there was with Southwood. You'll lose everything you have and find yourself dependent upon your husband for pin money." He could see the effect his words were having on her. She looked totally panicked, and he felt sorry for her. But she had to see the danger she was in. "Have your uncle make you a match. You don't have to marry just anyone. There'll be several men to chose from, and the choice is yours. It won't be like when your father forced Dom on you.

"In the spring I must begin another voyage, lass. I would feel happier knowing I leave you safely wed. Besides protection, you need a husband to take your mind from schemes such as last summer's piracy."

"You knew?"

"It had your fine touch, lass. And when Jean rendered me the year-end accounts, I showed no losses even for our two ships that were pirated."

"I would hardly rob you, my business partner," she said indignantly.

He chuckled. "What did you do with the rest of the cargoes?"

"They were sold and the money was dispersed among the poor and the churches."

"It was a good jest on Bess Tudor, Skye, but no more. You were lucky not to be caught. Next time, you could be. I want you to promise me you will not go pirating again."

"No, Robbie, I've not finished with the Queen yet. Besides, I've Adam to protect me."

Adam de Marisco shifted uncomfortably. "You'll have your new husband to protect you, little girl," he said as Robbie and Dame Cecily nodded mutual approval.

Skye threw up her hands in mock exasperation. She understood how right they were. "Very well then, you can write to my wily uncle, and I'll send my own note with yours."

Their two letters were enough to rouse Seamus O'Malley, the Bishop of Connaught, from an attack of winter doldrums. With the holidays over and Lent just ahead, he had been feeling depressed. Robert Small's letter instantly ended his dark mood. Mounted upon a fine bay gelding, he hurried off to see the MacWilliam.

The overlord of Middle Connaught was delighted to hear that Skye O'Malley was again in need of a husband. Here was the answer to all his problems. This was the one woman Niall would marry happily, and he would finally see some grandsons!

"On the same terms as before?" he asked the bishop.

Seamus O'Malley looked pained. "My lord," he said, "my niece is a very wealthy woman now in her own right. She is the widow of a belted Earl."

"An Englishman!" was the scornful reply.

"But a titled one," rejoined the bishop smoothly.

"She may be too old now to breed safely," mused the MacWilliam slyly. "She's at least five and twenty."

"And at the peak of her fertility!" came back the quick reply.

The two men argued for some time. The minutes strung themselves into hours. Finally an agreement was reached and the bishop said, "I want a proxy marriage now, as soon as possible."

"Why?" demanded the MacWilliam suspiciously.

"Because Skye is not overly enthusiastic about marrying. I'm afraid if we wait until after Easter she may change her mind. There's no time to prepare a big wedding now, so if we don't wed them by proxy now, we'll have to wait until after Lent. D'you really want them to wait?"

"Jesus, no!" swore the MacWilliam. "There's been enough waiting already between those two! Have your priests draw up the contracts as quickly as possible so they can be taken to England and signed."

"They don't have to go to England to be signed," said Seamus O'Malley. "My niece has given me permission to act for her." And then he thought, *God forgive me, for Skye will have murder in her heart when she learns what I've done.* Skye had indeed given him permission to act for her, and although she hadn't spelled it out he knew that his aid was required only in the matter of seeking prospective bridegrooms. Skye would make the agreement all by herself. Still, he reasoned, he was the eldest O'Malley, and there wasn't a court that wouldn't uphold his right to make a final decision.

Three weeks later the walls of Lynmouth Castle echoed with the outraged shrieks of its chatelaine. The servants, who had never seen the beautiful Countess in such a fine tearing Irish temper, wondered whether they should flee. Daisy, in the very eye of the storm, sent a groom at top speed to Wren Court to fetch Robert Small. The little captain arrived and hurried up the stairs of the castle in the direction of the screams and breaking crockery.

Skye stood in the center of her antechamber, broken crystal and china about her. Her dark hair was loose and swirling and she wore only petticoats and a low-cut white blouse. At the sight of Robbie, she burst into tears and threw herself into his arms. He held her and made soothing sounds until she finally quieted. Still holding her, he asked, "What is it, Skye lass? I can't help you unless I know what is happening."

"It's all your fault, Robbie! All yours! You all had at me! All of you! You and Adam and Dame Cecily all insisting I must marry to protect myself. Now look what you've done!"

He thrust her from him. "What did we do?" he demanded.

"What did you do?" she cried, her voice beginning to rise again. "Let me tell you what you've done! That wicked devil who calls himself my uncle, that saintly man of the Church that you asked to help me seek a new husband, that bastard has already wed me by proxy. I'll have it annulled! I'll not be wed against my will!"

Robbie didn't know whether to laugh or cry. He was astounded by Seamus O'Malley's actions and wondered why the man had acted in such haste. While Skye continued to pace and swear, Daisy caught his eye and held out a parchment to him. He took it and began to read, admiring as he did so, the cool way in which the elder O'Malley had taken complete advantage of his unsuspecting niece.

"I am glad," wrote the bishop, "that you have come to your senses and decided to marry again. To this end I have matched you with Niall, Lord Burke. Your wedding was celebrated by proxy on February third of this year with myself standing in to represent you. You may expect Lord Burke to arrive in England shortly. I do not have to tell you that the MacWilliam is very pleased with this match, as am I." The letter went on for several more sentences, ending with the bishop's hope that the union would be fruitful. The marriage contracts were enclosed, and Robbie was pleased to see that Seamus O'Malley had seen that his niece's wealth remained in her hands. Her uncle had done an excellent job.

Drawing a deep breath, Robbie said, "I cannot see why you're so upset, Skye lass. You were to wed with Burke several years ago and you weren't distressed by the idea then."

"I was but a girl, Robbie, and I believed I loved him. When I regained my memory Niall was horrible to me. What happened to separate us was not my fault, yet he blamed me. He accused me of all sorts of terrible things. He is spoiled, and I hate him. I told my uncle several months ago that I'd not wed with Lord Burke."

"If not Lord Burke, Skye, then who?"

"I don't know, Robbie, but *anyone* would be better!"

"The marriage is valid, lass. There isn't a court anywhere that would invalidate either the contracts or the proxy ceremony and there are no grounds for annulment. Whether you like it or not, you're now Lady Burke."

"Go to Hell!"

Robbie began to chuckle. "By God, I never thought to see you bested, but that sly old ecclesiastical fox has done it and done it well."

Skye's blue eyes began to narrow and grow smoky with anger. But Robbie was so tickled by the situation that he failed to note her growing rage. He prattled on. "At least he's chosen you a *real* man. Lord Burke is similar in character to both Khalid and Lord Southwood. No, indeed, you can't complain, Skye lass." And his mouth fell open with shock as the crystal decanter shattered just above his head, spattering diamond shards of glass and ruby-red droplets of wine down the wall.

"This match has been made by my uncle, Lord Burke, and the MacWilliam with the sole purpose of breeding another generation. Well, without my cooperation they can't get the new generation, can they?" she said softly, ominously. Then she continued, "Geoffrey has not been dead a year. I cannot possibly be a proper wife to Lord Burke while I am still in deep mourning. And then, of course, there is my semi-mourning for another year. As you are certainly aware, Robbie, propriety must be strictly observed."

Robbie began to look worried. "You can't mean you're going to deny him his rights?"

She laughed, a harsh sound. "His rights? What rights?"

Robbie felt a sinking sensation. "He's your husband," he said weakly.

"*I* didn't pick him. It was all your idea, and de Marisco's and my uncle's and the MacWilliam's. All I asked was the right to chose, for I am the one involved. I am entirely capable of planning my own destiny. Instead, I have been married off without even the courtesy of a single discussion. Well, Robbie, if I must live with the consequences, then so must you all—including Niall Burke."

Robbie's sinking feeling deepened. What had they done? Not just to her, but to Niall Burke as well? He did not regret his advice. Marriage had been the only solution. But the Bishop of Connaught had acted high-handedly. Robbie suddenly realized that he knew her better even than her own family did. Well, why not? When Skye had left them she was still a girl, her character just beginning to form. They still thought of her as a young girl. Those two sly old men hadn't stopped to realize that a cleric and a provincial nobleman could scarcely conceive of the kind of life Skye had led in the last several years. What could they know of men like Khalid el Bey? He sighed. God, how much simpler it would have been if Khalid had lived. Skye would have had a dozen of his children and grown pleasingly plump on Turkish pastries. Then he chuckled at himself for being a fool. She simply wasn't that kind of woman.

"You cannot hold Lord Burke responsible for this situation.

Though I am sure the idea of finally being wed to you has him ecstatic."

"He of all people should have known better than to wed with me without my personal consent."

"Perhaps your uncle convinced him that he had it."

In actuality Niall Burke had been astounded when, arriving home from a hunting trip, he had found Seamus O'Malley and his father sitting together getting companionably drunk.

"Behold! The bridegroom cometh," chuckled the bishop.

Niall Burke felt his anger rise. "I warned you," he snarled at his father, "I warned you to make no matches for me!"

The old man snickered. "You are being married February third, my son."

"The hell I am!" was the outraged reply.

"My niece will be so disappointed," the bishop cackled, and the MacWilliam joined in his laughter, the two old men doubling up like fools.

Niall wondered if the smoky peat whiskey they were drinking had been tainted. His bewilderment caused the two to laugh harder, tears running from their rheumy eyes and down the worn old faces. Finally the bishop wheezed, "My niece, Skye, has given me her permission to arrange another marriage for her, now that Lord Southwood is dead. Your father and I have decided that since you were once intended to wed, you should do so now."

"And Skye is coming to Ireland to wed me?" Niall was incredulous.

"No. We're celebrating the marriage by proxy on February third. You are to go to England, for she'll not come to Ireland and rob her little son, the Earl, of his rightful inheritance."

"What's the hurry?" Niall was suspicious, knowing these two old schemers for what they were.

"Lent, my lad. You know we cannot celebrate a marriage in that solemn season. D'you truly want to wait till after Easter to wed and bed Skye? After all these years?"

"Very well then," said Niall. "I agree."

"He agrees!" wheezed the MacWilliam with helpless mirth.

"Praise be to God!" cackled the bishop, gasping for air. Niall Burke thought them both drunk, or mad, or possibly both.

The contracts were signed the following day, and all Niall could think about from that point on was that Skye would soon be his. How sweetly modest she still was, even after all this time. What an adorable creature to have her uncle arrange the match instead of making the contracts herself. After all, she was hardly a maiden and not likely to be shy of him. His mind was so full of memories of Skye that the woman he had known so unhappily in England faded and the girl he had known so long ago took her place.

Consequently he was unprepared for the cold woman who greeted him at Lynmouth Castle. It was but a few weeks after their marriage, when the winter weather had cleared. He had left the MacWilliam's stronghold to travel across Ireland and take an O'Malley ship from the east coast town of Cobh to Bideford. In Bideford he repeated what he had done several years prior, and hired a horse for the ride to Lynmouth. He came alone, unheralded, without an escort. Riding across the lowered drawbridge into the courtyard, he said to the servant who ran out to greet him, "Tell the Countess that her husband has arrived." The servant's mouth dropped open, then he turned and ran.

Niall Burke calmly stripped off his riding gloves and strode into the castle. As he entered the hall, Skye came toward him. She was dressed totally in black. She was cool and elegant and very formal. "You should have told us you were coming, my lord. Have my servants seen to your retainers?"

"I have none. I came as soon as the weather cleared. There was no time to send word ahead."

"We'll have rooms readied for you, my lord." He looked puzzled and she explained, "My husband is not dead a full year, my lord. I am still in mourning."

"I am your husband, Skye."

She smiled frostily. "My late husband," she amended in a tone meant to convey how crassly he was behaving.

"Then why did you marry now, Skye?"

"My uncle had my permission to seek possible *candidates* for a marriage for me and nothing more. Instead he arranged this proxy marriage. I did not even know of the wedding until two days ago."

"You didn't want to marry me?"

"It is of little importance to me whom I wed, though I should have preferred having a choice. You see, Lord Burke, it was necessary that I take a husband." She told him about Dudley and her need to protect both herself and her children.

Her words stunned him, and as their import sunk in he was torn between anger, pity, and laughter. In his eagerness to regain her, he had accepted a simple explanation for a situation that he ought to have known was not simple. From her icy demeanor, he decided that the MacWilliam would have a long wait for a grandchild. Oh, he could shout and bluster about his marital rights, but he suspected that would gain him only scorn. He decided that he would play the gentleman and wait. A rueful smile touched the corners of his mouth, for it seemed he was forever waiting for Skye O'Malley.

"You do need a permanent man in your life," he said, "and who better than me? We loved one another once. Perhaps we will again."

"Or perhaps not," she said. "Love, it has been my experience, brings more bitterness than sweetness. I have lost two men I loved to death. I have the memory of bitter words between us, and although I forgave you because Geoffrey asked me to, I cannot forget those words."

"I regretted them the moment they escaped my lips."

"You were ever impulsive, Niall. Impulsive and heedless of the havoc your actions wrought. You are now my lawful husband but unless I can learn to love you again this marriage will be in name only. I have never given myself to a man I disliked."

"You liked Dudley?"

"I despise Robert Dudley as I did Dom. They took, yes, but I *never gave*! Do you understand me?"

"And I do not make a habit of forcing unwilling women, my dear *wife*. I have no intention of doing so now. Do you understand me?"

"Then we should get on quite well, Niall Burke. You will keep to your place, and I to mine."

He bowed mockingly to her. "It shall be just as you say, madam. Has the Queen been notified yet of this match?"

"The messenger left for Hampton Court the same day I received word from my uncle."

"Then Elizabeth should know by now that a man stands by your side at Lynmouth."

And Elizabeth did know. The Queen had been angry at first. "How dare she?" stormed Elizabeth. "She has not my permission!"

"Aye, she does, madam," put in Cecil, Lord Burghley.

"She does?"

"Indeed," the chancellor said smoothly. "You signed the papers several months ago when the Bishop of Connaught applied for permission for his niece to wed again. I believe that Lord Burke was at one time betrothed to the Countess of Lynmouth. It is an excellent match, madam. Skye O'Malley is head of the O'Malleys of Innisfana, a wealthy seagoing family. She will not, I suspect, leave England until her son can manage his own estates—which will not be for a long time. Her family will never dare to rebel against the Crown for fear of reprisals against her. We have therefore neutralized a potentially powerful enemy. The same can be said of the Burkes. Niall Burke is the only heir to the MacWilliam of Mid-Connaught. He and his people dare not act against England as long as his heir is in England, and he will be as long as his bride cannot leave. That is why I advised you to sign the papers allowing the Countess to wed again."

Elizabeth pursed her lips. Leicester would be very disappointed. Still, he had had his fun, and she didn't want him becoming overly involved with Skye. Why, he might have eventually desired marriage with the lovely Countess. And surely dear Skye could not have remained forever impervious to darling Robert's charms. What woman could? No, it was better that dear Skye had married again.

"I think it would be wise, under the circumstances, to transfer the guardianship of little Lord Southwood to his stepfather," remarked William Cecil.

"Yes," said the Queen thoughtfully. "But Rob will be upset. The child is a rich prize. Find him another such prize quickly so we may sever the connection immediately." She turned to one of her secretaries. "Send our felicitations to Lord and Lady Burke along with the transfer of guardianship of the young Earl of Lynmouth. Also, a purse of a hundred gold marks and a pair of silver candelabra. Say we will be happy to receive them at Court anytime."

Lord Burghley was pleased. She might be her father's cub, but she was his student. He, Cecil, had guided and taught her well, and at that moment he was proud of her. "I think Lord Dudley would be pleased with the guardianship of the Dacre heiress. She was the posthumous only child of Lord John Dacre. Her mother died in childbirth."

Elizabeth Tudor nodded. Yes, Rob would be pleased with such a rich prize, and the royal influence would be needed more in the north where border families like the Dacres swung back and forth in their allegiance. There was no question of the young Southwood's loyalty.

The royal messages were dispatched along with the royal gifts. Skye cared nothing for the purse of gold marks or the silver candelabra. But her delight in the transferral of Robin's guardianship to Lord Burke was boundless. Niall watched her sardonically as she exulted in her victory.

"It seems," he remarked pleasantly, "that I have managed to be of some use to you."

"You must feel quite fulfilled," she answered sarcastically.

"I am more fulfilled than you are, my dear. How you exist with cold iced water in your veins instead of warm red blood is beyond me."

"Yes, I've heard about your barmaid," she answered with a nonchalance she did not feel.

"Have you?" he drawled and the corners of his mouth twitched in a way that infuriated her.

"They call her the 'Devon Rose' I am told. Is that because she is overblown, or because she smells?" Skye's face was a study in innocence.

Niall Burke burst out laughing. "Dammit, woman, your tongue is knife-sharp! You're a hell of a lot more interesting than the maid I knew ten years ago, Skye."

"Yet you feel it is necessary to take and flaunt a mistress, sir."

"Madam, I am a man, and whether we discuss it or not, you do deny me of my marital rights. I am willing to be patient, but I am not willing to be celibate."

"I have been in mourning."

"For a man dead a year. We have been wed two and a half months."

"Dead a year today," she said, her voice trembling. "Would it were you instead of Geoffrey." And she ran from the room so he could not see her weeping.

Niall swore softly. He had liked Geoffrey Southwood, but he was fast becoming sick of his ghost. He had thought that she would thaw and accept their marriage sooner or later. Instead she had grown colder and more distant with each passing day. They could not leave Lynmouth until little Robin was six or seven and could be sent to page in another household. In the meantime, he must live in Geoffrey Southwood's house, fathering Geoffrey Southwood's son, but not husbanding Geoffrey Southwood's widow who was now *his* wife.

The children had accepted him easily enough. Willow had said flatly, "You're my third father, y'know. The first died before I was born, and the second just last year. I hope you'll stay longer."

"I shall do my best," he had told her gravely.

Robin had been delighted to have another man in the family again. "What shall I call you?" he asked.

"What would you like to call me, Robin?"

"I—I don't think I could call you 'Papa.' It's what I called my father." The boy's voice was tremorous.

"I understand. Why don't you call me Niall? That's my name, and I've no objections if your mother doesn't."

For the children it had been a settled matter, but for the adults it was simply not that easy. Niall had taken over the management of the Lynmouth estates, and Skye had had no objections to that. She seemed always preoccupied. After their argument of the afternoon Niall vowed he would charm her that evening at dinner, but she did not appear at table.

"Where is your mistress?" he asked Daisy, who was eating with the other upperservants down the board. Daisy rose from her seat and came to stand beside him. She curtseyed, then said, "I believe she may have taken the boat out, my lord."

"Her boat?"

"Aye, my lord. The boat is moored below the cliffs. My little brother, Wat, cares for my lady's boat. He'll be happy to show you the way, sir."

Niall finished his meal, thoughtful, and then waved the boy over to him. "Did Lady Burke take her boat out, Wat?"

Wat shuffled his feet, but nodded.

"Do you know where she went?"

"Don't know, sir." But Wat suspected that his lady had gone to Lundy. He knew her moods by now.

"Do you think she'll be back tonight, lad?"

"Maybe, maybe not, my lord. Sometimes she stays all night, but sometimes she comes back, late. Her and the sea is friends."

Niall smiled. "Thank you, Wat. I'd like you to show me the boat mooring now."

"Aye, my lord," was the obedient reply, and Niall hid another smile. The boy was obviously loyal to Skye. She engendered fierce loyalties. Niall could see that young Wat resented what he considered an intrusion into his mistress's private life. So, as he followed the boy, Niall spoke quietly to the lad.

"Did you know that I've known your mistress since she was a slip of a girl? I know how good she is with boats. But I worry. You see, Wat, I love her."

The boy said nothing, but Niall noted that the stiff set of his shoulders eased somewhat. He trotted silently along ahead of the tall Irishman until they finally reached the cave. Lord Burke's eyebrows rose in surprise, and his lips pursed softly. It was a good-sized space and well lit to boot. He saw the wide-mouthed entrance and walked out onto the ledge, noting the steps to the water, the iron ring. Niall turned to the boy. "You can go back, Wat. I'll stay here a bit."The boy seemed in a quandary, but then shrugged and headed back up the stairs. It wasn't his business to tell the gentry what to do.

The April evening was warm and pleasant. Niall sat out on the ledge, the cave wall at his back, watching the sunset. The sea was calm and dark and above him he heard the mewling cries of a nest of gull babies settling in for the night. The sky now began to darken, the first pale stars twinkling tentatively as if they weren't quite sure it was time for them to be there. Niall Burke sat quietly on the hard stones of the ledge. Soon the sky was black, the stars no longer pale but diamond-bright. A faint wind sprang up, and the air grew damp. Still, he waited. He was deeply curious. Where had she gone? Would she be back tonight? Here was a whole new aspect of Skye's life that he hadn't known of. It was growing cold and he wished he had thought to bring his cloak. Soon, then, as if he had voiced the thought aloud, he heard Wat saying:

"I've brought you a cape, m'lord, and Daisy said you were to have a flask of wine."

Niall stood stiffly, and taking the fur-lined garment, wrapped it tightly about his chilled body. "Thank you, lad," he said as he uncorked the flask. He drank deeply and was grateful for the warmth that hit his innards like molten rock, then spread upward. Wat nodded and lit the ledge beacons. "The mistress be late tonight. Could be she not be back till late," he ventured.

"I'll wait," said Niall.

Wat disappeared back into the cave, and Niall could hear his steps as he mounted the stairs. It was quiet again, only the gentle slap of the sea against the rock of the ledge to cut the silence. The star formations overhead moved slowly across the heavens, and new ones took their place. Niall dozed, waking suddenly to find the sky gray with the early dawn, and Skye's small boat sailing toward him. Slowly he rose, shaking his lean frame loose, and walked down the steps to take the rope she tossed casually to him. Fastening it to the ring, he reached down and pulled her up. She moved past him, and he smelled the scent of tobacco on her sea clothes. Jealousy surged up in him and he had a difficult time controlling his voice.

"Where the hell were you?" he demanded.

Her blue eyes narrowed. "At sea," she replied shortly.

"I waited all night!"

"Did you? I'm touched, but you wasted time you might have spent rutting with your Devon Rose in a warm bed."

She was mounting the stairs and he leaped after her.

"You weren't at sea all this time," he said flatly.

"No?" She looked over her shoulder, a mocking expression on her beautiful face.

"Not unless you've taken up smoking tobacco, Skye."

"What?"

"Your clothes reek of it!"

She stopped and sniffed at her doublet. "You're absolutely right, Niall," she said, and continued on her way without another word.

Astounded, he stood rooted to the stairs for a few moments. The bitch had a lover! It was the only possible explanation. What was it about him that sent his wives seeking other men? Nothing! he decided, slamming his fist into his palm. He remembered women who had lain panting with passion beneath him. He would not allow memories of Constanza's treachery to obliterate good sense.

Suddenly, he heard the door click shut above him and he returned to the present. The little bitch! To hold him off in the guise of mourning for Geoffrey Southwood when all the while she was sailing off to join a lover! How they must have laughed at him, she and her lover. His rage grew. Who was the man?

He mounted the stairs purposefully. There would be no more waiting. Her little game was over. And after he had settled the score with her he intended sinking her damned boat so she could not run off again. This might be Lynmouth Castle, and she might be the Countess of Lynmouth, but she was also Lady Burke, a fact he was about to bring home to her.

Time had taught Niall Burke the value of subtlety. Reaching the door that led into his own apartment, he entered and called to his body servant. Mick came running. "A bath!" ordered his master, and the deep oak tub was filled with hot water. Niall spent a good half-hour washing, including his short-cropped dark, wavy hair. Climbing out, he toweled himself vigorously while standing before the fire. His body was still long and lean, and had matured well. He was warm and the blood raced in his veins as he thought of Skye. Mick held out his dressing gown and he wrapped it tightly about him. Then he went through the door that connected their bedchambers.

Skye, too, was freshly bathed, as the tub before the fireplace bore evidence. She sat naked at her dressing table brushing her long black hair while Daisy turned back the bed. Startled by his entry, she reached for the lacy shawl that lay on the edge of the table. He snatched it away. Suddenly wary, she sprang up.

"Daisy! Get out!" His voice barked the command.

"Daisy! Stay!" she countermanded desperately.

Frantically Daisy looked back and forth between the two, caught in a terrible quandary. Niall took a menacing step toward the servant woman and, with a shriek, Daisy fled, slamming the door behind her. Niall calmly threw the bolt, then leapt across the room in two strides to close and bolt the connecting door that separated their two apartments. In doing so he successfully captured Skye, who had been trying to escape through that door.

He towered above her, his handsome, craggy face dark with rage. His eyes blazed a chill, silver fire, colder than anything she had seen in those eyes before. Real fear began moving upward from her belly, and she fought to hide it from him.

Niall pinioned his wife against the door, his arms making prison bars on either side of her. Neither of them spoke for the space of several heartbeats, and he did not fail to notice the frightened pulse leaping at the base of her slender throat. At long last, Skye managed to whisper hoarsely:

"You have no right."

"More than your lover!" he snapped, his eyes fastened on her perfect small breasts, their rosy peaks rigid with fear.

Bewildered, caught off guard, she nearly stammered. "My—lover? I have no lover!"

"You stay out all night and come home with your clothes reeking of tobacco smoke and tell me you have no lover? What then, madam, is your explanation? And think not to tell me this is not my business. You're my *wife*."

Christ's bones! she swore silently. She couldn't tell him, for he'd never understand. How could she say, you hurt me, and I sailed off to Lundy because I have a friend there? How could she tell him that she and Adam de Marisco had spent the whole night just talking, that the reason her clothes smelled of tobacco was that Adam had recently taken up a pipe? How could she explain the lord of Lundy to a husband? Niall would never know that Adam had indeed once been her lover, for de Marisco was no more eager to tangle with Lord Burke than Skye was for him to know.

She looked up at him and was frightened by what she saw in those silver eyes. "I have no lover, Niall," she repeated.

"Then you've taken up tobacco, my dear?"

"Yes!" she answered him desperately.

In answer he caught her chin in one hand, and kissed her deeply, his tongue plunging swiftly into her mouth. When he released her lips he smiled cruelly. "You're a liar, Skye! Your mouth and breath are sweet with no hint of tobacco. What else have you lied to me about? For over two months you've denied me with this pretense of mourning. And I, great fool that I am, believed you and respected your grief, and all the while you were sneaking off to fuck with your lover!"

Angrily he yanked her away from the door. Sweeping her up in his arms, he strode across the room to the big bed. "Well now, madam, you'll fuck with me!" and he dumped her down onto the feather mattress.

While he undid his robe she scrambled up, only to be shoved back onto the bed. "Oh, no, my dear! What you give to *him,* you'll give to me too!"

"Whoreson!" she snarled at him as his body crushed her flat, but he only laughed. Infuriated, she struggled against him like a madwoman.

His mouth came down hurtfully on hers, and she clenched her teeth tightly together. His hands tangled in her dark hair, holding her head still. She closed her eyes to blot him out, but she couldn't close out his voice, which crooned in her ear. "Are you going to be my wife willingly, Skye, or is it going to be rape? Maybe that sort of thing excites you, eh, my darling? I'd rather you'd let me love you and that you would try to love me back."

"Love you?" Her scorn was thick. "You sicken me! And to think that I once preferred you to Dom O'Flaherty!"

He wanted to hit her. What had happened to them? All desire left him. Rape was not his style. To her surprise, he rolled off her. But when she tried to rise he held her back. "No, madam! From now on you'll sleep with me. But I'll not give you further excuse to hate me by taking my rights by force. You'll have to ask me for loving, my darling. And you will, Skye. You will."

Relief made her brave. "Never!" she spat.

He laughed, and pulled her into his arms so he might caress her breasts. "Those two pretty apples of yours have grown plumper," he observed.

"I thought you just said you wouldn't make love to me unless I asked," she said, trying to squirm away from him.

"I said I wouldn't take my 'rights,' Skye. I never said I didn't intend to enjoy your delicious little person."

"Oh!" she gasped, outraged. "That's not fair!"

"You'd rather I'd rape you?" he asked in mock surprise.

"I didn't say that!"

"Then just what is it you want of me, my darling?"

She opened her mouth to speak, then shut it. Let him tease and play his stupid games. She would never yield, nor would she give him the satisfaction of protest. Niall, allowing his hands the freedom of her body, roaming the marvelous skin, noted the grim line of her mouth. He smiled to himself. She would never know how close to rape she had come.

His hands and his mouth wreaked a wonderful torture upon her, and Skye bit her lips and pressed her nails into her balled palms until the pain eased some of the unholy pleasure he forced on her. When he believed he had driven her far enough, he stopped abruptly and, rolling over, went to sleep. She lay next to him, her whole body trembling, and silently hated him as much as she had ever loved him.

Skye quickly discovered that Niall intended being master in everything, not simply in their bedchamber. As soon as she was able to escape him, later that same day, she fled down the winding interior staircase of the castle to the boat cave. She stood horrified at the place where her vessel should be moored. The boat was gone! "Wat!" she shouted. "Where are you, boy?"

"Don't bother calling for Wat, my darling." Niall had followed her. "He's been given a place on a fishing boat, and will no longer be serving here."

She whirled and her voice shook with anger. "Wat was *my* servant! How dared you reassign him? And I suspect you know where my boat is."

"I do."

"Where?" she shouted at him.

"Precisely where you left it, Skye."

Puzzled, she turned to look again at the empty mooring.

"Look closer," he instructed.

She moved down the steps further, and as the sun played on the calm sea, her eyes caught a glimpse of something in the water and comprehension dawned. Slowly she backed up the stairs to the ledge, rage permeating every fiber of her being. She turned to face him, and Niall Burke saw anger as he'd never seen it before.

"Whoreson!" she hissed. "Bastard! You sank my boat! How dare you! How dare you!" And her fist lashed out to hit him a blow that caught him off guard and actually staggered him.

He grabbed at her, successfully holding her arms, and looked down into her face. The hatred he saw there was as fierce as her blow had been. Silently he cursed his father and Seamus O'Malley for ever believing that he and Skye could be reunited. "Aye!" he said through clenched teeth. "I sank your damned boat! I'll not have you running off to your lover again and possibly passing off his bastards as my sons."

Outraged, she let out a piercing shriek. "Do you consider me so without honor then, Niall Burke? And I repeat, *I have no lover*!" Then she wrenched out of his grasp and ran back up the stairs.

Skye was very worried. It was time for the spring parade of ships to be arriving from the Indies. Word had come from Bideford that very morning that half a dozen ships, the largest grouping ever, would be here within the next few days. She had to get word to de Marisco and her fleet, which was waiting now on Lundy for her instructions. If she could not go to them, then they must come to her.

When evening fell Skye climbed up the west tower of the castle. In the tiny topmost room that faced Lundy, she lit two small signal lights in stone dishes and placed them in the window. One was set up high, the other low. Across the clear calm of the sea a boy at the top of de Marisco's keep looked hard, rubbed his eyes, and looked again. Then he hurried to find his master. Adam de Marisco looked across the eleven miles of water with his spyglass. One high, one low. The meaning was "Come at once. I need you." They had set up that signal after last winter's unfortunate episode with Lord Dudley. But why would she need him now? What of her husband? Still, Skye wasn't a woman to take things overhard. If the signal was there, then she must need him.

Several hours later, for the winds had been light and he had been forced to tack back and forth in order to reach Lynmouth Castle, he sailed into the cave and up to the mooring. Skye's boat was gone, but she stood awaiting him.

"Adam! Thank God you've come! I was afraid you wouldn't see the signal tonight." She made his craft fast, and he climbed out.

"Where is your boat, little girl?"

"My husband sank it, Adam. He believes I use it to go to a lover. My sea clothes picked up the scent of your damned tobacco last trip over, and he smelled it on me."

De Marisco whistled softly. "How did you explain it?" he asked.

"I didn't."

"Dammit, Skye! You must drive the man mad. Well, perhaps you'll calm down when you are with child."

She laughed harshly. "There'll be no children, Adam, for the marriage is in name only. I angered him so that he's sworn never to take me unless I ask—and I never shall! But that's not why I called you here. I received word this morning that six ships are due into Bideford within the next few days—three English, two French, and a Dutchman sailing in convoy."

"You've got the route they'll take?"

"Yes, Adam!" her voice was excited. "I'd like to take them all! D'you think MacGuire and his men can do it?"

Adam de Marisco stroked his chin reflectively and his smoky blue eyes sparkled. "Where would you do it?"

"Off Cape Clear. There are plenty of places to hide there."

"By God, you're a bold wench! Yes! Yes, I do believe MacGuire and his men can pull it off!"

"Good! Then tell him those are my instructions," Skye chuckled. "Lord Dudley owns a half-share in one of those ships. He'll be ruined."

"The Queen will make it up to him," observed Adam.

"Indeed she will, but it will be hard for her to do so, for her own coffers are none too full right now and she will be further strapped by the loss of her share from these goods."

"Where do you want the goods sent, Skye?"

"I think we should hold these cargoes till midsummer. The flow of ships is greater then and the furor will have died down. It wouldn't be safe to dispose of the cargo now."

"If you've no further instructions, little girl, I'll be on my way. I don't think Lord Burke would be too pleased to find me here."

"To Hell with him! Oh, Adam! Get me another boat. I shall go mad penned up here."

"I don't know, Skye. I'm not sure you're wise to defy him. Wait a bit, little girl, until your anger is cooled. I'll return here in a fortnight. If it's stormy then I'll come the first clear night after that."

She pouted slightly then said, "Oh, all right, Adam, but why do I get the feeling you're in sympathy with *him*?"

He grinned up at her from his boat. "Because I am, little girl. I cannot imagine being wed to you and not loving your tempting little self. I wonder whether the man's a saint or a fool."

She laughed and threw him his rope. "I'm not sure what he is either, de Marisco."

"Don't you think that it's time you found out?" came the reply, and then the lord of Lundy's little boat slipped out into the sea, its bow pointed for home, scuttling away like a crab on the morning sand.

She stood perplexed, then shrugged. Men! They were always trying to tell a woman what to do and they invariably stuck together. Still, Adam's words haunted her. What *was* Niall Burke all about? She realized she didn't know. Looking back, she saw the spoiled child-woman she had been at fifteen, the "Black" O'Malley's darling. And she remembered how she had felt when she had first met Niall Burke, a sudden realization that she had met *the* man whom she would love the rest of her life. What an innocent thing she'd been! For she had loved two men since, learning that it was possible to love more than one man.

But had she ever really loved Niall Burke or had she been sexually aroused? Hating poor Dom so violently had helped turn her toward Niall. What had the Skye O'Malley of ten years ago known of life, of the world, of a man and a woman?

It had been a shock to find herself summarily wed to him without her own consent. Still—and she frowned to remember, instead of accepting the positive aspects of the situation—she had reverted to the child she had once been instead of acting like the woman she had become. Was it then so surprising that he treated her like a child?

After all, he understood her need for freedom, which was a good start. He was attractive, with no disgusting habits such as swilling his food or breaking wind in public. He liked the children, and they liked him. When she thought of the type of man she might have been married to, Niall Burke shone by comparison.

Still, he had sunk her boat, and he accused her of taking a lover. She sighed, having failed to convince herself that Niall was either a devil or an angel.

She returned to the Great Hall to find Niall romping noisily with Robin and Willow. She sat at the board quietly watching them, a soft smile on her lips. He was so good with her children. She thought guiltily that she had given Khalid and Geoffrey children, and was Niall not entitled to children also?

"Hungry, madam?" He sat down next to her. "Be off, you little wild beasts!" he called to the children. "Kiss your mother, and then find your beds."

Skye enfolded the children in her arms, gently nuzzling Robin's soft golden hair, kissing the top of Willow's dark head. "Good night, Mama," said her little son. "Good night, Robin. God give you happy dreams." "Good night, Mama," smiled Willow. "I like our new father, don't you?" she said enthusiastically.

Niall's lips twitched and his silvery eyes locked for a moment onto her sapphire ones. Skye flushed as his deep voice drawled lazily, "Well, Mama? Do you like me?"

"Don't be silly, Niall!" she muttered. "God give you sweet dreams, Willow. Now run along."

The children ran to hug Niall, and then hurried out. "Where were you?" he asked quietly.

A sharp reply sprang to her lips, but she swallowed it back. "I was below in the boat cave," she said.

"And the signal lights from the west tower window?"

So he had seen them! "Oh, I must tell Daisy to extinguish them," she said, as if to herself. Then she turned and uttered a small white lie. "The lights are a prearranged signal to my ships on Lundy Isle. MacGuire is there."

Comprehension dawned on Niall. MacGuire smoked a pipe! "Is that where you were the other night? On Lundy?"

"Yes."

"Why the devil didn't you tell me?" Good Lord! She'd been with MacGuire, and he'd acted the jealous fool! A lover!

"I didn't like your manner of asking," she answered loftily, knowing where his thoughts had led him, but unwilling to correct his mistaken impressions.

"Dammit, Skye. I'm always the fool where you're concerned. Forgive me, my darling."

With this apology she felt a rush of warmth toward him. She hadn't actually lied to him when she told him that MacGuire was on Lundy. It was he who had assumed that she had spent her time with MacGuire. Her time with Adam de Marisco had been just as innocent, but that would be far too hard to explain. She wasn't sure Niall would believe that she was simply friends with the lusty young giant. Better to leave things as they were.

"I forgive you, my lord," she said sweetly. Standing and looking at him demurely, she said, "Shall we to bed, husband?" Then she walked slowly from the Hall.

He lingered for a few minutes, sitting on a bench before the fire, drinking a small goblet of white wine. She was an enigma. And he only now realized that she hadn't told him why she was signaling her people on Lundy, or even what they were doing on the island. Well, he thought, I must learn to trust her. In time she'll tell me. As for now, it would appear that I'm melting the ice.

When he reached his own bedchamber he found Mick waiting with his bath. Swiftly he washed, toweling himself vigorously dry, wrapping a robe about him. Then he entered Skye's room. Two undermaids were removing Skye's tub from the room.

"That will be all, Daisy." She wore only a shawl.

The door closed after the tub and three servants. Niall stood, momentarily hesitant, unsure of what he should do. He feared to leap at her lest he had misread her signals.

Turning from the fire, she allowed the shawl to slide to the floor. She smiled as his silvery eyes warmed and grew wide with appreciation. Slowly she walked toward him, stopping before him to loosen the tie that held his dressing gown. One hand lay flat on his chest, the other slid beneath the fabric of his gown to move tantalizingly over his chest, teasing at his flat nipples, twining in the soft dark hair of his chest. Niall felt his breath catch in his throat. Her hand moved upward to caress his shoulder, and around to his back where her nails raked delicately downward, producing a shudder from him.

Her blue eyes held his captive, her mouth curved seductively in a little smile. Then her hands were opening his gown wide, pushing it off him, and she was pressing her own nude body against his. Her lips nibbled at his ear, her hands caressed his hard buttocks, and then he heard her murmur, "Love me, my lord husband!"

"Skye . . ." his voice was husky, he wasn't sure he could move, and the ache in his groin was fierce.

"Come!" She took his hand and led him to her bed, gently pushing him back onto the fur coverlet. He felt like a child, not quite willing to believe the lovely gift being offered him, afraid to enjoy it lest it disappear. Amazed, he allowed her to caress and kiss him, and then she mounted him, kneeling to capture his manhood and imprison it between her breasts. He almost sobbed his pleasure when she took him firmly in one hand and rubbed the tip of his penis around the hard nipples of her breasts. Then, while he was recovering, she raised her body and plunged downward, burying him deep within her. He lay momentarily imprisoned between her silken thighs, and then, as if he'd received a signal, he grasped her buttocks and, with a swift move, turned her over so she lay beneath him.

"It's better the stallion mount the mare than the mare the stallion," he said, and then he was kissing her passionately. Her mind began to whirl. Once, so long ago that it seemed more a dream than a part of her life, he had taken her innocence. And now, just when she thought she would never do it, she had given herself to him again. It was as glorious as she remembered, and she could not understand why she had denied him for so long.

"I love you, Skye," he said when the storm was over and he held her close. "Perhaps someday I will regain your love again, but I thank you for now."

"I will not deny you again, Niall. As for the other, we must begin anew, you and I. What was between us so long ago is unimportant compared with what may be between us now. You must accept in your heart that I have deeply loved two other men. You readily accept the fruits of these unions. Why not the fact of them? I have accepted that when you believed me dead you turned to poor Constanza. Now these others who invaded our lives for such a short but sweet time are gone, you and I are left alone together. We will go on from here and, God willing, I will love you again."

It was enough. More, in fact, than he had dared hope for.

Holding her firmly, he fell asleep, content. For a while longer Skye lay awake in his gentle clasp. She had made her peace with him, and she was glad.

The other castle inhabitants soon realized that their Countess and her new husband had made their peace. It was going to be a beautiful summer. When the Queen sent a summons requesting the Burkes' presence at Court, Niall sent back a charmingly worded message begging Her Majesty to allow them the summer to honeymoon in private. The Queen, in love with love, returned her royal consent.

May arrived, its festive first day a perfect, warm, breezeless one. The fruit trees were heavy with blossoms and the lilacs full and sweet. A maypole was set up on the village green and, to everybody's delight, a troupe of morris dancers arrived with their musicians. Everyone from the castle and the village saw the afternoon performance. A raised dais was set up on the edge of the green and little Robert, the four-and-a-half-year-old Earl of Lynmouth, presided over the festivities under the guidance of his mother and stepfather. In attendance were Dame Cecily and Willow Small. Robbie had indeed formally adopted Willow besides making her his heiress. Robert Small had left on a long sea voyage and his sister had been feeling sad and alone.

The twelve dancers were dressed in greens, reds, yellows, blues, and purples, their costumes covered with gaily tinkling brass bells and silk ribbons of white, silver, and gold. There were five musicians, two with reed pipes, two with tabors, and one with a bagpipe. The dancers split into groups of three and began to caper about in rhythm with the music. It was wonderful entertainment, and the eyes of the child Earl and his sister were huge with delight.

Skye's two children were happier now than they had been since the tragic deaths of Geoffrey Southwood and baby John. The sporadic visits of Robin's erstwhile guardian, Lord Dudley, had frightened them both. Although not old enough to understand what was happening between their mother and the arrogant nobleman, they had sensed that something was very wrong, and were frightened for both Skye and themselves. Now, however, everything was very happy, with Skye and Niall occasionally giggling like naughty children and spending a great deal of time in their bedchamber. Neither Willow nor Robin understood why their parents needed sleep so much.

The six-ship convoy that Skye had been expecting arrived on schedule, and was neatly pirated off Cape Clear by the O'Malley ships. The convoy's arrival in Bideford with their holds picked clean was the talk of the countryside. Skye was hard put not to shout her triumph. She had known of the successful venture before word arrived from Bideford. A green beacon shining its light from de Marisco's keep on Lundy had told her. Satisfied with her first success of the spring, Skye melted back into her husband's arms and temporarily forgot the world.

Chapter 24

Elizabeth Tudor was fresh from the hunt. Damp tendrils of russet hair curled about the sides of her face and clung to the nape of her neck. Her black velvet riding habit was wet and stuck to her shoulder blades in dark patches. Her eyes were sharp and her cheeks flushed as she listened to Cecil's report.

"The convoy," he said, "was attacked off Cape Clear. Three of the ships were English, two French, and one Dutch. They were stripped completely. Both the French and Spanish ambassadors have registered strong complaints with me."

"Why?" demanded Elizabeth. "Has it been proven that these pirates are English?"

"No, madam, it has not. They fly no flags whatsoever and their men are commanded by a series of hand and whistle signals. However, one of the French captains said that the lines of the marauding vessels are English and the three English captains agree."

"God's foot!" swore the Queen. "That Englishmen could attack the French and the Spanish-Dutch I fully comprehend. But that they could pirate their own countrymen is despicable. Tell me, Cecil, are these the same pirates who robbed us last summer?"

"It would appear so, Majesty."

"I want them caught," said the Queen flatly.

"Of course, my dear lady," said the chancellor, smiling. "I have taken the liberty of formulating a modest plan, which I now present for your approval. King Philip of Spain, your late sister's husband, has married the French Princess, Isabelle de Valois. He now presses the suit of his Hapsburg nephew, Charles, as a possible bridegroom for you. To this end, a Spanish treasure ship is coming from the New World, and will be offered to you in the name of the Archduke Charles.

"We will use this ship as bait. The supposed merchant vessels that accompany your treasure ship will actually be our own warships in disguise. Thinking to snatch an easy prize, these bold privateers will find themselves caught in our net. The Spanish have already agreed to this plan and will send one of their ships along with ours to meet the treasure ship and explain the plan to its captain."

"How will the pirates know about the treasure ship, Cecil?"

"Word will be spread about on the London waterfront, in Plymouth, and in Bideford. That should be enough."

"Do it then!" commanded the Queen. "I want these pirates stopped." And then she departed the chancellor's closet, leaving her chief advisor alone.

Cecil sat down heavily, his nimble mind mulling over a thought he had decided not to voice to his mistress quite yet. The lines of the ships might be English, but Cecil doubted that their crews were. The attack off Cape Clear had given him the idea, for Cape Clear was in Ireland. He would wager his personal fortune that the pirates were Irish. This line of thought had led him to another. He suspected that they were disposing of their stolen cargoes through Lundy Island, which was notorious for that kind of business. And Lundy was but eleven miles by water from Lynmouth Castle. The mistress of that castle was the Irish-born heiress of a great seafaring family. To boot, the lady had a grievance against the Queen.

Cecil might never have suspected the woman except for the memory of her face when she left the Queen many months ago. A beautiful face, an angry face, a proud face—as proud as Elizabeth Tudor herself. Cecil sighed. The one thing he'd never been able to teach the Queen was not to use the people about her so ruthlessly. In that respect she was like her father, Henry Tudor.

He could not prove it yet, but he suspected that the lovely Countess of Lynmouth was cleverly revenging herself on the Queen by attacking one of her most important revenue sources. Cecil smiled to himself. The lady was a very worthy opponent, but the whole business ought not to have happened in the first place. Had the Queen remembered the loyal service of both the late Earl and his wife instead of sacrificing everything to her love for Dudley, none of this would have happened. Cecil did not like Robert Dudley. The man was a bad influence on Elizabeth, her one terrible weakness. She had come frighteningly close to marrying him, and Cecil still shivered at the memory, recalling the painful scene he had had with Elizabeth right after Amy Dudley's death.

Elizabeth Tudor had been denied many things in her life, but she had salved her pride by reminding herself that one day . . . one day she would be Queen of England. And when she was, no one would ever deny her anything again. But insignificant little Amy Rosart had caused a scandal and her death had cost Elizabeth the only man she wanted. For that, a grateful Cecil prayed daily for Amy's soul.

Unfortunately, the Queen would not let Dudley go. Keeping his foolish hopes alive by indulging him outrageously was the means through which she held on to him. The lovely Skye Southwood had been part of that indulgence, and now the Queen was paying for her unnecessary cruelty.

Privately Cecil sympathized. What Elizabeth had done to her had been outrageous. Nevertheless, he could not allow the lady to rebel against royal authority, even discreetly. It could set a dangerous precedent if it ever became public knowledge. Cecil intended keeping the affair a private one.

Several weeks later Skye paid a regular visit to Bideford to inspect her warehouses and learned of the Queen's treasure ship. Hurrying back to Lynmouth, she set the signal lights ablaze in the west tower, and then fidgeted several hours waiting for de Marisco. Niall was off visiting the furthermost part of the estates and was not expected back that night. Matt, Wat's younger brother, had taken over the care of Skye's new boat and the responsibility of the cave. He ran upstairs to tell his mistress that the lord of Lundy awaited below.

Skye hurried down the interior staircase to greet Adam, a small pang of remembrance touching her as he swept her up and kissed her soundly on both cheeks. "Little girl! You obviously took my advice, for you're blooming!"

"I did indeed, Adam, and thank you. Now please put me down. I'm dizzy with the height."

He regretfully complied. "Why the signal, Skye?"

"News! Marvelous news, de Marisco! In an effort to impress the Queen and turn her thoughts favorably toward the Archduke Charles, Spanish Philip has sent our Bess a treasure ship from the New World. It's filled with Inca gold, Mexican silver, and emeralds from the Amazon mines. I'm going to take that ship! I'm going to pluck it from the sea and pick it clean!"

"No, Skye, you're not. Something is wrong here. I sense it. Where did you learn of this ship?"

"The entire town of Bideford buzzes with the news, Adam."

At that, he looked even more concerned. "As does Plymouth m'dear. My men brought me word of this ship over a week ago. It is obvious that someone wishes to attract our attention. I suspect a trap."

"But if we took their ship anyway, and escaped with Bess's gold in spite of their trap—?" mused Skye.

"It is too dangerous!" protested de Marisco. "To begin with we have no idea if this ship actually carries treasure or not. They say it travels in convoy with four other merchant vessels. That in itself rouses my suspicions. Why is such a valuable ship unguarded, traveling only with merchant ships?"

"Perhaps so as not to arouse suspicion."

"Then why broadcast the fact of its coming? No, Skye, this stinks. This is a trap. Don't risk yourself, your men, or your ships."

"But if the vessel is genuine, Adam. All that gold! To be able to take all that gold from the Queen!"

"Little girl, don't let desires for vengeance overrule common sense. The Tudors are merciless when dealing with their adversaries. You've been lucky so far. Ignore this. That's the wise thing to do."

"Let us investigate the rumor further, Adam. If we cannot prove the truth of it then I will let it go. But if the treasure proves to be a real treasure ship, then I *must* take it!"

Adam de Marisco shook his head. "Even if you're not caught, there's no safe way for us to dispose of such a prize."

She flashed a quick smile. "We can dispose of it through Algiers after we melt all the gold and silver down and have it formed into new bars. I will want to take some of the emeralds for myself, for a necklace and earrings. It will give me great pleasure to wear them beneath the Queen's nose, secretly knowing where they came from."

"How will you find out more about the ship?"

"De Grenville is stopping here in a day or two, on his way home to Cornwall. He'll know. When he has gone I'll signal you to come."

"Does Lord Burke know of your activities?"

"No," she answered him in a low voice.

"The Burkes, the O'Malleys, the O'Flahertys, the Southwoods, the Smalls. There are five families involved in your schemes, little girl. Bring ruin on yourself, and you'll bring ruin on them *all*. Think carefully before you tilt with the Tudors one more time. Right now there is nothing to involve you with any of our past piracies, but one more venture is all that's needed to bring destruction to you and all those others. Let it go, Skye. Forget the Queen. Please!"

Diamond-bright tears glittered in the sapphire eyes. "*Forget?*" her voice trembled. "Oh, de Marisco, do you have any idea what it is like to be a woman? To be forced to give yourself against your will? How do you imagine I felt when Dudley pushed himself into me? Every time he touched me I felt fouled beyond belief, but I bore it because I had *no other choice*. A woman rarely does.

"Elizabeth Tudor did that to me, Adam. Another woman did that! She handed me over to Dudley without a thought for me or for my dead Geoffrey or for our loyal service to her. I was a *thing* to be used by the Queen and her favorite. No, Adam, I cannot forget!"

"All right, Skye," he sighed, for how could he argue? "But this will be the last time. I don't relish seeing your pretty head on the block—or mine either!"

"Just this last time, de Marisco."

Adam de Marisco returned to Lundy, deeply troubled. What had begun as a lark was deadly serious now, and he was afraid. Skye's lust for vengeance was overriding all good sense, and he was worried. Why hadn't he seen this coming and put a stop to it before she became obsessed?

Two days later de Grenville arrived at Lynmouth from London. He was full of amusing gossip and chatter about the Court. Skye possessed herself of great patience, not wanting to give herself away. At last, with Dickon and Niall relaxed and well in their cups she asked casually, "What is this I hear of a treasure ship for the Queen from King Philip? Bideford is full of rumors."

"Aye," smiled de Grenville drunkenly, "he hopes to push the suit of his nephew, Charles, by showing Bess how nice it is to have rich relatives."

"Then the ship is real, Dickon?"

"Oh, yes."

"Isn't the Queen afraid that she may lose her ship to the pirates who have been raiding off the coastal waters here and near Ireland?"

"That's why I'm here," de Grenville chuckled craftily. "Gonna take four warships out to meet the *Santa Maria Madre de Cristos* and escort her into Bideford."

Skye giggled. "No pirates would attack a merchant vessel surrounded by four warships. Even *I* know that." She reached for the pitcher and, leaning across him, sloshed more wine into his goblet. Her movement offered him a fine view of her breasts, and she noted with amusement that his breathing quickened. Niall appeared to have fallen asleep, his dark head lying upon his crossed arms.

"My ships gonna be dis—disguised, Skye. Gonna look like plain old trading vessels, as helpless as the real one. Just five little ships all ready to be plucked." He hiccoughed, then swilled more wine, spilling some of it on his doublet.

Sudden comprehension shot through Skye. "Are you telling me, Dickon, that the *Santa Maria Madre de Cristos* has sailed alone across the Atlantic without escort?"

He nodded. "King Philip felt it was safer that way. No one would believe that one lone, unprotected ship carried such treasure. After the ship put to sea, William Cecil thought to catch the pirates by sending my ships out disguised. Pirates attack little helpless convoy. Only this isn't helpless. Good ol' Cecil. Always the crafty one."

"Why Dickon, how clever! Thank heavens the Queen is acting at last to rid us of these pirates. Robbie and I lost two ships to them last summer," she said indignantly. "Where will you meet the treasure ship?"

"Three days out off Cape Clear."

"Then they sailed the Southern Star route," she gently probed.

"Um," he nodded.

"When will you meet the Spanish, Dickon?"

"A week from today," he muttered, then slipped forward to fall asleep on the table near the snoring Lord Burke.

Skye smiled, satisfied, and signaled to Daisy, who had remained quietly in her place below the salt during the evening. "You lit the tower beacons?" Skye whispered.

"Just before dusk, m'lady. Lord de Marisco is already waiting below," Daisy whispered back.

"Have these two carried to bed, Daisy, and have my bath ready,

I'll not be long." She hurried from the Hall and using an entry door at the end of the room, hurried down the interior staircase to the cave. "Adam!" she called as she reached the bottom, and he stepped from the shadows.

"Well, little girl, what news?"

"The ship is real! It's the *Santa Maria Madre de Cristos,* and for the next week it travels alone and unescorted!" she burst out.

"What! What of its escort?"

"There are none! In a week's time de Grenville and four of the Queen's warships disguised as merchant ships will join the Spaniard three days off of Cape Clear. Until then the *Santa Maria* is unprotected!"

"What's her course?" de Marisco asked tensely.

"Southern Star."

"It's too good!" he began to pace. "De Grenville simply told you all that?" Adam was incredulous, his smoky blue eyes darkening.

"I got him drunk," she explained. "Dickon never could hold his wine. He always says what he shouldn't when he's drunk." She was remembering that long-ago evening when a drunken de Grenville had told her of the bet he'd made with Geoffrey.

"Are you sure he was drunk?"

"Very sure, Adam." She chuckled. When he looked at her strangely she said, "An old debt Dickon owed me has been settled by tonight's information."

"Where is he now?"

"Dickon? I gave orders to have the footmen carry both him and Niall to bed."

"Your husband was drunk?"

"Yes. It was strange," she mused. "I've never seen Niall unable to hold his wine. I hope he's not sickening. More likely, he's tired. He's been out riding the estate for two days."

"Do we go, Skye?" he asked.

"We go Adam. I've a feeling. Call it a hard Irish hunch, but if MacGuire and his men leave Lundy at once they can intercept the Spanish ship and be safely home before de Grenville and his men rendezvous with her."

"And its cargo? Where do we store that impossible cargo, little girl?"

"Not Lundy, Adam. If the Queen's men suspect us they'll be all over your island, and losing you your head would be a poor way of repaying your friendship. Not here or Innisfana, either."

"Where, then?"

"Inishturk Island! The location of my sister's convent, St. Bride's. There are caves there that I discovered years ago when I—uh . . . spent some time visiting Eibhlin. MacGuire knows the caves, and the English will never think of looking there. In time we'll smelt the gold and silver down. They can be easily disposed of in Algiers once they're formed into bars."

"This is the last time, little girl," he said quietly but firmly.

"I know, Adam."

"I'll miss you, Skye O'Malley."

"We needn't stop being friends, Adam, simply because we'll no longer be doing business."

"Little girl, for such a smart woman you are sometimes a bit of a fool. It hurts me to see you and I know I can never have you. So when this business is done, I'll not see you again. Lundy will be closed to you, Skye O'Malley."

"Oh, Adam," she said softly, looking up sadly into his face, "I never meant to hurt you."

"I know that, little girl. It was always friendship for you, but for me it was more. You're like a star, my darling: bright and beautiful and unobtainable. I am only a simple island chieftain, Skye O'Malley, not a star-catcher, but oh how I wanted to say to Hell with common sense and keep you for myself."

Her face was wet and her blue eyes overflowed hot tears. He gently traced a tear down her cheek.

"Don't ever stop being my friend, Adam," she whispered.

"Never, little girl!" he answered, and then his arms closed about her and his mouth came down on hers. He kissed her gently, yet passionately, and then quickly stepped back. "I never did get to kiss the bride. Farewell, little girl! I'll get word to you when the operation is completed."

Then he was gone, out onto the ledge, down the steps. Through the haze of tears she saw his boat draw away, heading out into the channel, bound for Lundy. Strong arms turned her then and she wept softly against the familiar velvet-covered chest.

"I don't suppose you'd care to explain to me why you're meeting in this cave with that giant of a man?" asked Niall quietly. Skye cried harder and he continued, "I hope I'm not going to have to challenge him to a duel to protect my honor."

"N-n-no!" she sobbed.

"Who is he, Skye?"

"A-A-dam de Marisco, the lord of L-Lundy Island."

"Go on, love."

She managed to bring her sobs under control and, sniffing noisily, sought for her handkerchief. He handed her his and she wiped her eyes and blew her nose.

"Should I be jealous?" he asked. She began to wonder how long he'd been standing in the shadows on the stairs. Blushing, she peeped up at him from beneath the thick fringe of black lashes.

"You weren't exactly fighting off his advances," Niall noted humorously. "But every time I leap to conclusions about you I find myself standing hip-deep in the wrong. So if there *is* a reasonable explanation for your meeting secretly in a cave at night with an attractive man who seems to enjoy kissing you, I would enjoy hearing it."

Skye sneezed, then sneezed twice again. Niall shook his head and, picking her up, started up the stairs. "You'll tell me after you're tucked warmly in bed," he said. He carried her into her bedchamber. "I believe your mistress has caught a chill," he told Daisy.

"I've a hot tub ready, my lord," she replied. "I'll take care of her."

"No, Daisy. I will. You're dismissed for the night, lass."

Skye's servant hesitated, then shrugged and obeyed. She would never, she decided, understand the gentry. She sometimes wondered if they understood themselves.

Skye kicked her shoes off and stood quietly as her husband unlaced her. "I thought you were drunk," she said.

He smiled. "I thought you might. You were doing such a fine job of picking de Grenville's brain that I didn't think you needed me." He got the gown unfastened, and drew it off her. Then he undid her petticoat and underblouse, and pulled them off too. Kneeling, he took her garters off and unrolled her stockings. When she was naked he picked her up and deposited her in the hot tub. She sighed deeply and closed her eyes. "I know," he said, "that cave can be damnably damp and cold." She murmured agreement and came close to purring when he began soaping her back.

Niall's mouth turned up again in a small smile. Less than half an hour ago he had stood in the shadows, on the cave stairs, and watched a strange man make love to his wife. A month ago he might have acted rashly. Now, however, he knew better. She loved him. He knew it, even if she wasn't willing to admit it yet. He rinsed her back off with the sponge and moved on to the more interesting portions of her anatomy.

He felt his desire mounting but pushed his hunger down. First he wanted to hear her explanation. Lifting her from the tub, he wrapped her in a large towel and placed her on the settle by the fireplace. He took a smaller towel and rubbed her dry. Ignoring the pale-blue silken gown Daisy had laid out, he tucked Skye between the down feather bed and fox coverlet.

He undressed and washed himself lightly, then dried off and climbed into bed beside her. Turning to look at her, he said quietly, "Now, madam."

"Adam de Marisco is my friend," she said.

"Adam de Marisco is in love with you," he returned bluntly.

"But I was never in love with him," she said. "It was he who insisted I marry again, and he has fussed at me ever since to make peace with you. I believe he sees your side of things better even than mine," she frowned.

"I'm relieved to know that the lord of Lundy is on my side," murmured Niall wryly, "but that still does not tell me why the two of you were meeting in secret."

She sighed. "It began long before we were wed, Niall. After Geoffrey's death, when Lord Dudley forced himself upon me, I complained to the Queen. In effect Elizabeth gave me to Dudley as a toy, for his pleasure. I will never forgive her for that, for all she is Queen of England. In fact, her authority ought to mean a greater sense of responsibility. I wanted revenge on her and I still do. The privateers who have been harrying this coast since last summer are mine, my O'Malley ships and crews. Adam de Marisco allowed us sanctuary on Lundy, and helped us to dispose of the cargoes."

"His price for this aid?" Niall managed.

"A percentage of the profits, Niall," she said sharply, then continued. "In a few days we will take the *Santa Maria Madre de Cristos,* King Philip's treasure ship meant for Elizabeth. She will never see so much as one gold piece!"

Niall was so stunned that for several minutes he could not speak at all. Various emotions rose and ebbed within him like a tide. Amazement and admiration at her daring. Anger that she should endanger them all in her quest for revenge. Sorrow that he had not been there to protect her from Dudley. He didn't know whether to kiss her or kill her.

"You can't beat me," she said, anticipating him. "I am with child."

"Good God, woman!" he burst out, and she began to cry. Then Niall started to laugh. "You're the most impossible female God ever created, Skye. You wage war on England, and still retain all you possess. Did it never occur to you that you might be caught?"

"No!"

"Indeed, and why not?" He was fascinated.

"There is nothing to connect me, de Marisco, or the O'Malleys with any acts of piracy."

"You're sure?"

"Aye. My ships fly no flags. My people do not speak, they communicate with whistles and hand signals. The cargoes have been carefully disposed of, and I even pirated two of my own ships last summer to keep suspicion away from me."

"But Cecil has obviously sent de Grenville to capture the pirates. You can't take this bait."

"My fleet sails tonight from Lundy. By the time Dickon and his people meet the *Santa Maria* its cargo will have been long since removed and stored safely in caves on Inishturk. This is my last venture against the Queen, Niall. I swear it."

"And de Marisco kissing you? I trust that was a last venture as well?"

"He was saying good-bye," she said softly.

He pulled her into his arms and brushed her lips with his. "When is the child due?"

"Our baby will be born early next winter."

"There will be no more *adventures,* Skye," he said sternly. "I want your promise."

"I must think on it," she said mischievously.

"Madam, your word!" he thundered.

"Very well, my lord," she lisped meekly, and he looked at her suspiciously. Skye giggled. "I'm having a necklace and a pair of earrings made from the emeralds taken from the treasure ship. I shall so enjoy flaunting them under the Queen's nose."

Niall laughed again. "Impossible!" he said, and kissed her again.

Less than a week later, on Midsummer's Eve, Skye and Niall stood in the west tower of Lynmouth Castle and watched the celebration bonfires spring up on Lundy. Three, lined up straight in a neat row, told her what she wanted to know. The *Santa Maria Madre de Cristos* had been successfully taken and its cargo was already hidden. A deep satisfaction swept over her. Turning to her husband, she said, and meant, the words he had so eagerly worked to hear.

"I love you, Niall." With a glad cry he swept her into his arms and kissed her passionately.

The Devon summer was sweeter that year than any summer they remembered. But in London, Elizabeth Tudor fumed with impotent rage. King Philip's treasure ship had been boldly pirated from under de Grenville's very nose. The King was both outraged at the incident and frankly scornful of Elizabeth's ability to keep order in her own land. This piqued Elizabeth more than the loss of the treasure. She had borrowed heavily from the goldsmiths to finance her household, anticipating the wealth of the treasure ship. Now she was heavily in debt and several of her creditors had already shown they were not intimidated by her royal office.

"Is there no evidence to connect Lady Burke with the piracy, Cecil? Surely there is *something* we can use?" William Cecil had finally confided his suspicions to Elizabeth.

"Madam, there is *nothing*. All the O'Malley ships are where they should be, and there is no evidence of the treasure ship's cargo anywhere. We searched both Innisfana and Lundy."

"I want her arrested, Cecil."

"On what charges, madam?"

Elizabeth whirled to face him and he saw the angry red patches on her white cheeks. "I am the *Queen,* Cecil! I do not need formal charges! Lady Burke has offended me, and I want her in the Tower!"

"Madam!" Cecil was shocked. "This is not like you."

"Dammit, Cecil, we know she is guilty!"

"We *suspect,* my lady Elizabeth." He had not spoken to her so familiarly, so gently, since she had become Queen. "We only suspect, and since the *Santa Maria Madre de Cristos* was taken, no other ships have been pirated despite the fact that this is the busiest season for shipping."

The Queen remained adamant. "I want her in the Tower," she said. "Perhaps, if we frighten her, we can force her to confess. I need that gold, Cecil! My creditors press me."

Cecil sighed. If Lady Burke had hated Elizabeth before, she would hate her far more very soon. The Irish were so damned emotional! Offending both the O'Malleys and the Burkes could rouse all of Connaught, starting a conflagration that might spread through Ireland. We don't need a war in Ireland now, Cecil thought wearily. "What of Lord Burke?" he asked.

"He is to remain in Devon," said Elizabeth. "He is forbidden to come to London or to go to Ireland. Let him look after that she-wolf's whelps."

"The Countess has many admirers, madam. They will not be happy to see her imprisoned unjustly, and the talk could be detrimental to Your Majesty."

"Then do it secretly, Cecil. Send de Grenville. Since he lost me my ship, let him see if he can redeem himself by delivering the

Countess safely and secretly to the Tower. Tell the governor there is to be no official record of the lady. If no one knows she is in London, and her husband is confined to Devon, then there will be no Court gossip."

"I do not approve of this, madam," Cecil tried one more time.

"But you will obey me nevertheless, my lord," returned Elizabeth.

He nodded. "You are my Queen, and you've always learned from your mistakes. I expect you will in this instance, too." He couldn't resist making his opinion clear.

The Queen's head shot up. Cecil's face was impassive, but was there a hint of a twinkle in his eyes?

The late Devon summer offered promise of a bountiful harvest. Along the roadside late wild roses and Michaelmas daisies fought a territorial war. The haying had long since been done, and the grain lay stacked in the fields. The apple trees were heavy with fruit, some early varieties ready for picking, the later ones not quite ripe. The apple presses would soon be busy turning out Devon's famous cider.

Into this peaceful setting rode Richard de Grenville, a troupe of the Queen's own at his back. Dickon was troubled, even horrified, and under orders he did not understand. He had been incredulous when Cecil gave him those orders.

"I know that you like wine, my lord," said Cecil, "and you've been known to be loose-lipped when in your cups." Here de Grenville flushed guiltily. "It would be most unwise to babble this news, for the Queen wishes total secrecy." De Grenville had nodded.

Richard de Grenville and his men clattered over the drawbridge and into the courtyard of Lynmouth Castle. He dismounted and made his way into the castle, where he was informed that Lord and Lady Burke were in the small family hall. Arriving there, Dickon stood for a moment, unobserved, looking at Skye and her family. Then his heart contracted. Skye moved, and he could see that she was with child. She sat with Lord Burke. His arm was loosely about her expanded waist, his big hand gently caressing the living mound of her belly. She lay her head back against his shoulder and smiled up at him, a smile of such incredible sweetness that de Grenville thought he would weep. Well, he couldn't stand there forever. He cleared his throat and stepped noisily into the room.

"Dickon!" she cried. "It's good to see you!"

Robin and Willow ran to greet him.

"Madam," Dickon said coldly, without preamble. "I arrest you in the name of the Queen."

The glad greeting died away. Slowly Niall Burke got to his feet. Though his voice was calm, he could not mask his anger. "If this is a jest, de Grenville, it's a poor one. My wife can stand no shocks at present."

"It is no jest, my lord."

"The charges, sir?"

"I have not been given a list of charges, my lord. My orders are to escort Lady Burke to London as quickly as possible."

"And when you arrive in London . . . ?"

"The Tower, my lord," said de Grenville softly.

Skye cried out, and the children clustered about her knees, frightened.

"I will not allow you to remove my wife in her condition. She carries the MacWilliam's heir."

"Unless you are prepared to battle the Queen's guards, my lord, I intend taking her today."

Niall wore no weapon, but he towered over de Grenville. "Over my dead body, Englishman!"

De Grenville drew his sword and Skye shrieked, "My lords! No!" She got awkwardly to her feet. "Dickon, for pity's sake, what is this all about?"

"God bear me witness, Skye, I do not know. My orders are to bring you quickly and secretly to London where you are to be lodged in the Tower. Lord Burke, you are forbidden to leave Lynmouth. That is all I was told to say, and it's truly all I know."

"You can't transport a woman who is six months gone with child all the way to London."

"I have orders, my lord."

"I can use the traveling coach," said Skye quietly, and the two men turned to stare at her. "If we go slowly and carefully there should be no danger to my child. I know not why the Queen does this, but if I must go to London to straighten this out then I will. You will give me time to prepare, Dickon? My servants and I will be ready in the morning."

"You can only take one servant, Skye."

"Very well," she said. Then, "Niall, I am tired. Will you escort me? You understand, Dickon, that I prefer to dine alone tonight in my rooms with my husband and children."

De Grenville mumbled his assent as Niall escorted his wife from the room. In their apartment Skye sent the children off with

Daisy and turned to Niall. "They know nothing," she said positively. "If they did, Dickon would know the charges."

"But they're suspicious," he said. "Suspicious enough to arrest you."

"They can prove nothing!" argued Skye firmly. "They will try to frighten me, but they will not succeed. If they had any evidence at all they would be tearing Lynmouth and Lundy apart. They have nothing. The Tudor bitch seeks to outbluff me, but I'm a better opponent than she's used to dealing with."

"She can keep you imprisoned as long as she chooses, Skye."

"I know. You must not disobey her, Niall. You must stay at Lynmouth and watch over Robin and Willow. You must watch over Lynmouth."

"But how can I help you if I remain here?"

"Adam de Marisco!" she said quietly. "Set two lights in the topmost window of the west tower, one high and one low. Have you got that? He'll come. You can get word to Ireland through Adam."

He put his arms about her and buried his face in her beautiful black hair and soft neck. "Skye . . ." There was such anguish in his voice.

"Do as I ask, Niall. I will not endanger Robin's inheritance, nor give the Queen an opportunity to steal Southwood's son from me. Oh, how she would enjoy that, barren stock that she is!"

Helplessly he held her, knowing he had no real part in this war. She had begun it without him, and now it seemed she would end it without him. All he could give her was his love to carry with her into imprisonment.

Supper was a subdued affair. Skye told the children, "You must not be frightened for me. I will come home again. Obey Niall as you would me, for I expect good reports of you." She then tucked them into bed, kissing each one tenderly. Next she supervised Daisy and the maids with the packing. "Be sure you don't forget the feather bed," she reminded them. "It's cold by the Thames in winter. And Daisy, see that several casks of Burgundy and malmsey are packed into the baggage wagon. I prefer my own wines." Finally she lay next to Niall, curled spoon fashion against him, and he felt her trembling, heard her soft weeping. He said nothing, only held her close.

When morning came she dressed warmly, pulling her long knitted wool stockings on, following with first a silk and then two lightly spun wool petticoats. Her gown was of heavy dark-blue silk with pearl buttons, long sleeves, and a high neck. Her hooded cloak was lined in silk and edged in fur. Her short boots were fur-lined. Daisy arranged her thick dark hair in a low chignon.

Skye bid her children good-bye in the privacy of her rooms as she did not want them frightened by the soldiers who would escort her to her coach.

"Why is the Queen arresting you, Mama?" asked Willow again.

"I don't know, my chick," she replied. "It is just a misunderstanding. You must not be afraid for me."

"W-w-will they c-cut off your head," quavered Robin, close to tears.

"Gracious, no, my darling! Where on earth did you ever get such a grim idea?"

"Willow said that's what happens to people who go to the Tower," he answered.

"The Queen was in the Tower once when she was just a Princess. And so was Lord Dudley, and so were any number of people I could name, Robin. None of them had their heads removed."

"But Willow said . . ." insisted Robin in defense of his adored older sister.

"Willow is an ignorant little girl who has obviously not been paying attention to her lessons and who badly needs a switching," said Skye, hugging her son fiercely. She realized that Willow was badly frightened by her dramatic departure and, opening her other arm, said, "Oh, chick, come here and let me hug you too. But don't cry, for there is nothing to weep about." Willow flung herself into her mother's arms, pressing as close to her as Skye's pregnancy would allow, and then it was Skye who came close to weeping. The two heads, one so dark like her own, one so fair like Geoffrey's, came together and she kissed them both, then gently disengaged them and stepped away.

"I must go now, my loves. Obey Niall, and make me proud."

"Good-bye, Mama," Willow's eyes swam with unshed tears, but she gamely held them back.

"G-good-bye, Mama," Robin stood straight.

"Good-bye, my lord Earl," she replied, and then hurried from the room before the children saw her own tears.

Niall was waiting for her in their private family hall. Seeing the look on her face, he quickly caught her to him and kissed the hot tears that slid down her cheeks. "It's my condition," she muttered.

"I know," he soothed, "it must be, for you'd never give the Queen a victory over you. I know that."

"No," she sniffed, fumbling for her handkerchief. "I certainly wouldn't!"

He laughed. "That's my girl!"

She wiped her eyes. "I must not keep Dickon waiting." She stuffed the handkerchief away in an inner pocket of her cloak.

"You're the most incredibly brave woman I know, Skye. Don't fear, my love. I'll let nothing happen to you. I have friends, and so do you. If the Queen thinks to harm you, she'll not succeed. The secret of your arrest will not remain a secret long."

"I'm not afraid, Niall," she replied. Her eyes were clear now and she was calm. He felt a surge of pride sweep over him. *God help Elizabeth Tudor,* thought Niall, *for she's never tangled with a wildcat like my Skye.*

In the courtyard the horses stamped in the crisp air, their hot breath visible. Daisy, who had insisted on going into captivity with her mistress, was already seated in the coach. Carefully Niall helped his wife into the vehicle. Clambering up after her, he tucked a fur robe about her legs. Her blue eyes regarded him calmly and she said softly, "Perhaps you'd have done better to marry a meek miss than a wild widow."

He chuckled, answering just as softly. "I had me two meek misses, madam. I far prefer the widow. I always did." Then he kissed her, a sweetly gentle kiss that set her heart fluttering wildly.

"Oh God, I shall miss you, Niall Burke!"

"There's time to flee, my love. You've but to claim you're in early labor, and then it's off to Lundy through the cave with that English buffoon, de Grenville, none the wiser."

"No!" she said sharply. "I mean to beat Bess Tudor, and keep it all!"

"You're a stubborn woman, Skye O'Malley, but I believe you'll win."

"Oh, I will, Niall! I will!"

He took her small hand in his, and kissed it slowly, first the back, and then the palm. "Farewell, madam, I'll look after all here."

She felt a catch in her throat as he stepped out of the coach and shut the door firmly behind him. She watched him stride over to Dickon and speak with him, his face grim.

"I want you to travel carefully, de Grenville. I am holding you personally responsible for the safety of my wife and unborn child. Do you understand that? If anything happens to either of them I will personally slay your wife and family and burn your bloody house."

"I'll be careful, my lord," said de Grenville. "I'd not take Skye at all in her current condition were I not under direct orders from the Queen."

"I understand," said Niall quietly. "Will you keep me informed of any news? And if she may have visitors, go to see her so she won't be lonely."

De Grenville nodded. Mounting his horse, he led the procession of soldiers, coach, and baggage wagon from the courtyard of Lynmouth Castle across the drawbridge and out onto the road. To his vast surprise, the road was crowded with people for over two miles. Tenant farmers, villagers, merchants and fishermen, gamekeepers and castle servants, young and old stood cheek by jowl lining both sides of the road, all quietly supporting their mistress. Here and there, de Grenville heard a voice call out: "God keep your ladyship, and bring you safely home to us!"

What the hell is Bess Tudor about? de Grenville wondered. *What has Skye done that no one knows about, yet has offended the Queen so terribly?*

The trip, which should have taken but a few days, took well over a week. The coach moved at a sedate pace, stopping frequently so the lovely Countess might stretch her legs or refresh herself. They started late in the day and stopped early. When de Grenville suggested they might move a little faster, Skye took to her bed, thus delaying them an additional day. Thereafter, de Grenville gritted his teeth and kept his peace.

When they finally arrived in London, de Grenville transferred Skye to a closed water barge so her coach with the Lynmouth arms emblazoned on the doors would not be recognized. The coach and its servants were returned immediately to Devon.

Parted from the familiarity of her coach and servants, Skye felt some of her courage ebb away, though from the serene look on her face no one would have known it. She had learned long ago that to show fear only encouraged one's enemies. Carefully de Grenville handed her and Daisy down into the waiting barge, then joined them.

"I always wanted to take you out on the river in my barge," he said in a lighthearted attempt at conversation.

"I am sure, Dickon," she answered, "that cruising on your barge would be far preferable than the cruise I am about to take on this one."

"Skye, damme, what is going on between you and the Queen?!"

"I really have no idea at all, Dickon," she replied sweetly, and turned her face away from him to gaze out on the river.

He sighed deeply, but made no further attempt.

Skye breathed slowly, concentrating hard on the simple act of drawing air into her lungs and expelling it. Each beat of the oars brought her closer to imprisonment and God only knew what else. But, she swore silently to herself, she would admit nothing! She would beat the Queen at this cat-and-mouse game if it was her last act on this earth.

A soft rain began to fall. The twilight was a mauve-gray about them. It was quiet on the river, and there seemed to be no other boats upon the water. Then Skye's heartbeat accelerated. For ahead of them the Tower of London loomed tall, dark, and menacing in the early evening. The barge turned shoreward, and the child in her womb kicked as the craft bumped the stone quay. She placed a protective hand over her belly thinking as she did so, *Fear not, my child, I will protect you.* Yes, said a nagging voice in her head, but who will protect *you*? She shivered.

De Grenville leaped from the boat to help Skye out. She stood for a minute savoring her last moments of freedom, then turned to mount the stairs to the Tower. The steps were smooth with age, and slick with the rain, and to her annoyance she slipped once, but de Grenville caught her beneath the elbow and steadied her.

She stopped to regain her balance, then pulled away from him. "I am not afraid, my lord."

"It was only the steps, Skye, I know," he answered, all the while thinking how brave the lady really was.

The Tower governor met her at the entry, looking extremely distressed as he noted her condition. To be sure, she wouldn't be the first woman to give birth here, but how he hated imprisoning pregnant women! Anything could happen under these conditions. The governor greeted his prisoner as warmly as was appropriate.

"Please take supper with my wife and me, Lady Burke. It will give your servant time to ready your rooms. I'll send my own people up with your baggage, and see that the fires are laid."

"Thank you, Sir John," answered Skye. Turning, she said, "Farewell, Dickon. Please tell Her Majesty that if I had really wanted to come to London, I should have done so long before this. I wish a list of the charges against me, and if there are none then tell the Queen she holds me illegally." She turned again. "Sir John, your arm please. I am so ungainly these days."

Richard de Grenville left the Tower and made his way to Whitehall where the Queen was currently in residence. He went directly to Cecil, Lord Burghley's apartment and asked to see him immediately. The secretary, by now inured to the usual request for haste, was surprised when Cecil told him to send in Sir Richard at once. When the door had shut behind Dickon, Cecil motioned him to a chair and asked, "What took you so long, sir? Was there difficulty at Lynmouth?"

"No, my lord, none at all, although Lord Burke is very angry and Lady Burke is confused about why the Queen would arrest her. There is one complication, and that was what delayed us." Cecil looked inquiringly at him and de Grenville explained, "Lady Burke will be delivered of a child within a few months. It was necessary, therefore, to travel slowly."

"Damn!" swore Cecil. "I warned the Queen, and now—" He stopped himself.

"My lord," Dickon plunged in, "why has the Countess been arrested? What has she done?"

"Done? Why she has done nothing that we know of, Sir Richard. She is merely under suspicion."

"Oh." He desperately wanted to ask under suspicion of what, but he dared not.

"You may go now, Sir Richard. You'll remember, of course, not to discuss this mission with anyone."

"Yes, my lord." He turned to go, hesitated, then turned back and asked, "May I visit Skye occasionally, my lord? She's apt to be lonely."

"No, Sir Richard, you may not. Her presence in London is to remain strictly a secret. If anyone saw you there, you could not possibly explain your visits to the Tower." When de Grenville looked crestfallen, Cecil added in a more kindly tone, "Perhaps you may see her before Christmas, Sir Richard, and carry her greetings home to her family."

Alone, Cecil sat back, satisfied that he had effectively isolated Lady Burke. They would leave her alone for a few weeks to stew over why she was there. If she was really guilty, she would be quite thoroughly frightened by the time they got around to her interrogation. He smiled.

Some days later, however, Cecil was not smiling with regard to the matter of Lady Burke. Standing before him was an irritatingly implacable Irish nun who identified herself as Sister Eibhlin née O'Malley, of St. Bride's Convent, Inishturk Island.

"I have come," she said in a soft but firm voice, "to attend my sister in her travail."

At first Cecil pretended ignorance. "Madam," he answered coldly, "I have no idea to what you refer."

Eibhlin flashed him a hauntingly familiar mocking smile. "My lord, let us not waste time. Your signature was on my sister's arrest warrant. I have spent the last several days traveling here at breakneck speed from the west coast of Ireland. I mean to be with Skye, and unless you give me leave to join her, I shall find some means of getting to the Queen and making this whole affair public. The O'Malleys have held their peace thus far, for Lord Burke assures us this is but a misunderstanding."

"Why?" demanded Cecil, now becoming irritated, "why should I allow you to be with your sister, madam? I will not allow her husband. Why her sister?"

"My brother-in-law is a fine fellow to be sure, sir, but I am a midwife by profession. Skye needs me."

"She has her woman with her."

"Daisy? An excellent lass for doing hair or caring for my sister's clothing and jewels—but as a midwife? I fear not. The mere sight of blood sets the poor girl to swooning and there is much blood connected with a birthing. Did you know that? Perhaps though, you would prefer that my sister suffer."

"Good God, woman!" snapped Cecil. "We wish no harm to Lady Burke. We would have sent someone to help her when her time came."

"I can well imagine," rejoined Eibhlin scornfully. "Some ancient crone with dirty fingernails who would undoubtedly infect both Skye and the babe. What do you know, my lord Cecil, of midwifery?"

The Queen's closest advisor felt his temper rising higher. The woman was insufferable. "Madam," he thundered, "getting into the Tower is easy. It is the getting out that will be hard."

Again she smiled that mocking smile, and this time he recognized it. It was the Countess of Lynmouth's smile. *Strange,* thought Cecil, *the nun doesn't look like Lady Burke at all but for the mouth. I would never believe them even related but for that smile . . . and that annoyingly superior attitude.* "I am not afraid, my lord." She answered him, and he acknowledged that she wasn't. Ah, these over-proud Irish, he again thought. "Go then, madam. My secretary will issue the necessary papers," he said.

"I trust I shall be free to come and go, my lord. There will be necessities I must get when my sister's time comes."

"No, madam," said Cecil. "It would be too simple for Lady Burke to escape the Tower in a nun's robes. Whatever you need you must either take in with you or have the servants fetch from the markets. You may enter the Tower, but once you leave it you will not be allowed back inside. Those are the conditions."

"Very well," answered Eibhlin. "I will abide by your conditions." She bowed faintly to him and, turning said regally, "Farewell, my lord. My thanks."

Several hours later, clutching the precious parchment in her slender hands, Eibhlin O'Malley entered the Tower of London and was escorted to her sister's apartment high in one of the several towers. As she mounted the stairs, Eibhlin was pleased to see that the soldier who escorted her was respectful, and that the building seemed clean, relatively draft-free, and had no noxious odors.

Skye was sleeping when she arrived, but Daisy practically fell on her neck with undisguised relief.

"Oh, Sister, thank God you're here!"

Eibhlin's generous mouth twitched with amusement. "Now, Daisy, is it as bad as all that?"

"Sister, I have never even helped birth a kitten. I was so afraid I'd be alone with my lady when her time came. Lord Burke would surely kill me if I'd let anything happen to either Mistress Skye or the child."

"Well, you need worry no longer, Daisy. I'm here, and I intend to stay!"

When Skye awoke, Eibhlin was well settled into the Tower suite. "How on earth did you get here?" she exclaimed, hugging her older sister.

"About ten days ago a giant of an Englishman arrived at St. Bride's and told me you needed me. I was hurried across Ireland on the back of a bony horse, put on a tossing ship, and set down at Lynmouth. Niall told me the rest, and sent me up to London to be with you."

"And Cecil let you in here? I am surprised. I've seen no one but Daisy and the guards since the morning after my arrival. I think I am supposed to be made afraid through continual isolation."

"But being a sensible woman, sister, you are not afraid, I suspect."

Skye smiled. "No, Eibhlin, I'm not."

"Then you've gained no more sense with the passing years, little sister, than you had at ten," replied the nun tartly, and Skye laughed.

"Oh, Eibhlin, it's so good to have you with me!"

Later the two sisters bundled together in the large bed that took up almost the entire bedroom. It was hung with Skye's own garnet-colored velvet hangings. The sheets, feather bed, goosedown pillows, and fur coverlets were her own. A fire blazed in the corner fireplace, warming the cold early December night and scenting the room with the fragrance of applewood. Because it was at the top of one of the towers, Skye's bedchamber was totally private. It was the one place where she was free of being overheard. Now she and her sister spoke softly, but freely.

"Have they presented you with a list of formal charges?" asked Eibhlin.

"No, which confirms my suspicions that they suspect me of piracy but have no proof. I have not even been questioned." She chuckled warmly. "No, they have no proof, Eibhlin. They will have to let me go eventually, and I'll have made Bess Tudor doubly a fool!"

Eibhlin looked thoughtful. "Be careful, sister, that it's not you who rides for a fall. Elizabeth is England's acknowledged Queen, and if she chooses she can keep you here until you rot."

"If she tries," said Skye, her voice becoming hard, "the Burkes and the O'Malleys will rouse all of Connaught against her. And if Connaught rebels, all of Ireland will follow. There are enough hot-heads in Ireland waiting just for an excuse."

"My God, Skye, you're bitter! Why? Why this unremitting hatred for the English Queen?"

Slowly, leaving out no detail, Skye told her sister of the Queen's decision regarding Robin's guardianship and of Lord Dudley's continuing rape and abuse of her. Niall had not explained these things to Eibhlin.

"And I thought I was the rebel," said Eibhlin. "By God, Skye, you're a cool one. So the Queen knew of Lord Dudley's conduct and allowed it. Then she's gotten what she deserved! Now, however, our problem is to free you."

"She can do nothing without proof!" maintained Skye stubbornly.

"She needs no proof to keep you here," repeated Eibhlin. "What we must do now is convince her to her satisfaction that you are not guilty."

"How?"

"I don't know yet. I must pray on it."

Skye laughed. "It will take a powerful prayer, Eibhlin. Go to sleep. My conscience is as clear as an innocent babe's." And so saying, she tied the ribbons of her lace-edged lawn night cap firmly beneath her chin and, lying back, quickly fell asleep.

Eibhlin, however, lay awake thinking. Skye was right. The Queen had presented no formal charges of piracy against the Countess of Lynmouth, which meant that she indeed had no proof. But until she was convinced that Skye had had no part in the piracy, she would hold her prisoner, though she dared not act openly against her. It was a standoff.

The following morning as Skye was finishing her daily exercise period on the battlements, a captain of the guards stepped up to her. "Good morning, my lady. I am to escort you to Lord Cecil."

"Very well," said Skye, her heart quickening. So at last they were going to question her. She was looking forward to the challenge of pitting her wits against Cecil's. She followed the guardsman through a maze of corridors until, finally, he ushered her into a paneled room with a small oriel window that overlooked the Thames. Seated at a long table were Cecil, Dudley, and two other men. She believed one was the Earl of Shrewsbury, the other Lord Cavendish. Seeing no chair for her, she said icily, "You surely do not expect a woman in my condition to stand, my lords?"

"Please remember that you are a prisoner here, madam," said Lord Dudley meanly.

"And," continued Skye, "unless *that* man is removed I shall leave this minute, Lord Burghley."

"Please bring a chair for Lady Burke," ordered Cecil. "Dudley, be silent."

"I hope," remarked Skye boldly as she settled herself with much display, "that you'll be good enough to explain the meaning of my imprisonment. I have been kept in total ignorance for weeks now, and I am beginning to find this situation quite intolerable."

A grim smile touched the corners of Cecil's mouth. "We were desirous of speaking with you in regard to the recent piracies occurring in Devon."

Skye raised an elegantly winged eyebrow. "If you wished to speak to me, sir, why did you not simply do so? Was it necessary to imprison me? I am well aware of the piracy. I lost two ships last year myself. I regret to say that the Queen's commission could not find the perpetrators. A fine penny it cost me!"

"You do not seem to have suffered overmuch financially," remarked Cecil.

"I am a very rich woman, as you are well aware, my lord Burghley. Nevertheless I dislike losing money. My ships must be properly maintained, my captains and their men paid. They, in turn, feed the economy. It is a satisfactory circle which is broken when the spectre of piracy arises."

"Clever, madam, but not clever enough to fool us," snarled Dudley.

Skye turned her cool gaze on Robert Dudley. "You have grown paunchy with too much good living, my lord, but your brain is just as soft as ever." The Earl of Leicester grew beet-red, and though his mouth opened and shut several times, no words issued forth.

Shrewsbury and Cavendish snickered, and Cecil himself was hard pressed not to laugh. His turn, however, was coming.

"If, my lords, you have formal charges to place against me, then do so! If not then release me, for you hold me illegally." She then spoke directly to Cecil. "Lord Burghley, you insult me greatly by asking me to come before this panel. I will not appear before you again without formal charges, nor will I at any time come before any group of which Lord Dudley is a part. And you need not ask me why because you know why." She stood, turned, and walked to the door.

"Stop her!" shouted Dudley to the guardsmen.

Skye whirled, surprisingly graceful despite her girth. Her deep-blue eyes blazed with contempt. She placed her hands protectively over her belly and said fiercely, "I carry within me the heir to the MacWilliam. Lay rough hands upon me and harm that child, and even my pleas will not be able to stop the flame that will ignite all Ireland! If the Queen wishes war with my people, we will be happy to oblige her!" Then she turned again and left the room, unopposed.

"Why didn't you stop the little Irish bitch?" demanded Dudley of Cecil. "Who cares if her cub strangles on its own cord?"

"My lord," said Cecil evenly, "you sit on this panel because the Queen requested it and I am, in all things, the Queen's loyal servant. You were not my choice, however, and I shall ask Her Majesty to reconsider her request. I agree with Lady Burke. You are offensive. Gentlemen, you are dismissed until the same hour tomorrow when we shall again attempt to question the Countess of Lynmouth."

It was not to be, however, for Skye had felt the first pangs of labor as she made her exit. Slowly, gritting her teeth against the pain, she followed the guardsman back through a maze of corridors, almost fainting as she climbed the stairs all the way back up to her tower, forcing her legs to climb again and again, though they were leaden and she could hardly lift them. Nearing the top, she groaned and sat down heavily.

Startled, the young captain of the guard turned. "My lady!" he cried. He leaped back down the steps. Supporting her with his strong arm, he helped her up the last few steps to her apartment, shouting for aid as he went. The door was flung open and both Eibhlin and Daisy hurried out to take Skye from the captain.

"D'you need anything?" he asked worriedly.

Eibhlin smiled reassuringly at the young man. "No, thank you, Captain. We have everything we need. I would, however, inform the Tower governor that Lady Burke has gone into premature labor." She lowered her voice to a whisper easily audible to both Skye and Daisy. "I hope we don't lose them both. All this nonsense of arresting my poor sister, and what are the charges, Captain? There *are* none! Well, thank you for your aid. You're a good Christian lad, and I'll pray for you." Then she shut the door firmly between them and the guard.

"Oh, Eibhlin!" Skye was laughing between contractions. "You're the most unholy nun I've ever met! You terrified that poor, nice young guardsman. Now he'll run all the way to Sir John, and tell him I'm at death's door."

"Good! We'll make them all feel guilty," crowed Eibhlin as she and Daisy helped Skye undress. "What did Cecil want?"

"Me to confess to piracy. It's as I thought. They have no proof." She winced as a wave of pain rolled over her. Suddenly her waters broke, flooding into a puddle at her feet. "Eibhlin! I think this child is going to be born right now!"

"Daisy! Quick, lass, drag the table in front of the fireplace."

Daisy struggled with the long oak table, grunting as she fought to push it across the room.

"Eibhlin! Help her! I can stand alone."

Together the two women swung the oak board around before the blazing stone fireplace. Then Daisy ran upstairs to Skye's bedchamber and came back down with the goose-down pillows, a pad, and a sheet that she and Eibhlin placed on the table. They then helped Skye up onto the table, and she half sat with her legs spread, the pillows propping her shoulders as she labored. Eibhlin washed her slender, strangely elegant hands in the basin that Daisy provided. Some weeks before, the nun had instructed Daisy concerning her birthing-room duties and now Daisy performed without fault.

The nun-midwife leaned down to examine her patient. "Holy Mary! The child is half-born," she exclaimed. Reaching out, she carefully turned the slippery infant.

"I—told—you," gasped Skye as a final contraction racked her.

And then the child, fully born, began to squall loudly. "Is—he—all right? All his fingers—and toes?"

Eibhlin swiftly wiped the baby off and gazed down at the tiny face. "*She's* fine, Skye! All her fingers and toes!"

"She? Oh, damn!" Then Skye laughed weakly. "Willow will love having a little sister, and I am happy to have another daughter, but the MacWilliam is going to be very disappointed."

"You'll have others," remarked Eibhlin drily.

Skye sent Eibhlin an amused look, thinking how good it was to have her matter-of-fact big sister with her. How long, she wondered, would the Queen allow Eibhlin to stay now that the child was born? A thunderous knocking began on the door.

"Quick, Daisy, tell whoever it is that they can't come in," directed Eibhlin.

Daisy ran to the door and opened it a crack. "You can't come in," she said to Sir John, the Tower governor. "My lady is having her baby."

"I've brought my wife to help you," said Sir John, and before Daisy could prevent it Lady Alyce pushed into the room and hurried over to where Skye lay. Seeing the newly born infant on its mother's stomach, Lady Alyce's eyes twinkled conspiratorially. Bending down, she whispered, "Groan loudly, my dear." Understanding filled Skye's eyes and she groaned long and piteously. "Oh dear," cried Lady Alyce, running back to her husband, who waited patiently at the door. "It will be hours, John. You'd best go along. I will come back when I've news. Close the door, girl."

Daisy gladly complied, breathing a sigh of relief as she did so. The Tower governor's wife laughed softly and smiled down at Skye. "There, my dear, that should give you peace for a little while longer. Besides, it never does to let men know that having babies can sometimes be easy."

"Thank you, madam. I've never had a baby so quickly. Each one comes faster than the previous one."

"How many have you had, my dear?"

"This child is my sixth, but it's my second daughter."

"Oh, a little girl! I had a little girl once. . . . She would have been fourteen this past Whitsun. She died of the white throat, eight years ago. Her name was Linaet."

"I lost my late husband and our youngest son the same way," said Skye.

The two women fell silent, then Lady Alyce asked, "What will you call this babe, Lady Burke?"

"Deirdre."

"Skye!" cried Eibhlin. "Deirdre's fate was a tragic one."

"She was held prisoner by her King. My innocent child is being held prisoner by her Queen. She was born in captivity, in a most infamous place, Eibhlin. The name is fitting. And as I have not the comfort of a priest, you must baptize my daughter, dear sister."

Lady Alyce looked troubled. "Why are you here, my dear?" she asked.

Daisy took Deirdre from Skye and began cleaning and dressing her. Eibhlin cleaned her sister free of all traces of the birth. Skye explained to the kindly older woman. "No one has told me why I am here, madam. No charges have been leveled against me. I hoped . . ." she hesitated, "that your husband might know."

"Alas, my dear, no! Oh, I wish I could help," she cried. "It seems so unfair."

"Do not trouble yourself, Lady Alyce. We Irish are used to being misunderstood and mistreated," said Skye sweetly.

"Well, at least I can stay here for a few hours," said the Tower Governor's wife. "If they think the child is being born, they'll leave you be. Later, having been witness to such a hard birth, I will of course advise my husband that your sister must stay a month or two if you and your poor weak infant are to survive."

Skye smiled. "You're a true friend, ma'am. But do nothing to endanger yourself or Sir John with the Queen. The Tudors, I have found, can be most unkind even to their friends. I have learned this first hand."

"What does the Queen know of the Tower except whatever my husband tells her?" replied the good lady. And she plumped herself down in a comfortable chair before the fire. "I understand, Lady Burke, that you've the best malmsey in England. I am mighty partial to malmsey."

The following morning Lady Alyce informed her husband that the poor, imprisoned Lady Burke had managed, though the dear Lord only knew how, to give birth to a wee girl child. "Both she and the little lass are very weak, and will need constant nursing for the next few months if they are to survive," said Lady Alyce firmly. Her husband recognized her mood. She would brook no interference.

"My dear," he said mildly, "it is all right with me if Lady Burke's sister remains with her, but the final decision is not mine to make."

"You have some influence, John. Use it! I don't understand

what the Queen is about imprisoning poor Lady Burke, *and* without charges."

"Hush, my dear! I can see that our distinguished guest has made a conquest of you, but we must trust that the Queen and Lord Burghley know what they are doing. I will send word now to the Queen."

Elizabeth had been having one of her infrequent and painful menstrual flows when word was brought to her of Lady Deirdre Burke's birth. "God's nightshirt," she swore irritably, "she has done it deliberately!"

"Done what, madam?" said Cecil.

"Had her child in the Tower! The tone of Sir John's missive is quite sympathetic to Lady Burke, and I am not sure I like it! Why should he sound faintly disapproving of me, and tenderly concerned for that . . . Irish rebel?"

"New mothers and their infants always have a tendency to evoke sympathy from those around them," Cecil soothed.

Elizabeth turned around, her lovely, long, red-gold hair swinging with her. Her face was white and pinched with pain. "You'll not be able to question her for several weeks now! Damn! I wanted her exposed for the pirate bitch she is! D'you know that she threw Dudley out of her castle into the middle of a snowstorm last winter?"

Ho! thought Cecil, *so that's the reason behind this vendetta. Precious Lord Robert has been offended. Little did I think when I sought to get at the truth of the Devon pirates, that I should give Dudley an opportunity for revenge. I must think on this.* He smiled at the Queen in a kindly fashion. "Come, my dear, back into bed with you. You're not well, and this matter will wait. You're perfectly right. We'll not be able to pursue the matter until Lady Burke has recovered from the birth of her daughter. Sir John's wife, Lady Alyce, was present at the birth and says it was a hard one. I imagine it will take Lady Burke several weeks to recover."

Elizabeth climbed back into her bed, and drew the velvet coverlet up about her. "Oh, Cecil!" she wailed. "Sometimes I think it would have been better if I'd been born a simple maid. The mantle of royalty weighs so heavily upon me, and I am but a frail creature!"

"Nay, madam, you but look frail. But when you sprang forth from your mother's womb, of Henry Tudor's strong seed, you had the heart of a lion. You need have no fear of your ability."

Elizabeth sighed, "Oh, Cecil, you are my strength. I will rest now." She closed her eyes. "I will leave you to handle Lady Burke as you see fit."

William Cecil smiled his wintry smile. "I will not fail you, madam."

"You never have, old friend," said the Queen softly as she fell asleep.

Chapter 25

ADAM DE MARISCO COULD NOT BELIEVE HIS INCREDIBLE luck. For several months now, ever since he'd been summoned to Lynmouth to learn of Skye's fate, he had felt helpless, useless, weak. Now he had the means to free her, and it was God's own good fortune that had brought it to him. The idea of how to utilize this chance, however, was de Marisco's own, and having the idea had instantly restored Adam's self-confidence. Now he greeted Lord Burke, welcoming him warmly to Lundy. The big Irishman had grown haggard with worry and lack of sleep.

De Marisco pushed a dram of peat whiskey into Niall's hand. "Drink up, man. I know now how to bring her home safe."

"How?" Lord Burke gulped the smoky amber liquid down, reveling in the burning sensation that spread upward from his belly and into his veins.

"There's a well-hidden cove down by my lighthouse, and in that cove right now is a ship—a ship of dead men. The tidal currents around the end of the island are erratic and they drove the vessel ashore. It was found two days ago, floating half-beached in that cove. I've already given orders that no one is to go near the ship, and I've already placed in its holds my share of the booty from the *Santa Maria Madre de Cristos.* The men who carried the cargo to the holds for me are a family of mutes. I've always seen to their welfare and, as they are grateful, they will never give me away. They wouldn't even if they could talk.

"This ship is of English design, yet the bodies aboard her appear to be Arab or Moorish. I will wager they are Barbary pirates. What killed them I know not, but if we can take the ship in tow and bring it up to London, I believe we can convince Cecil that these unfortunate dead men are part of whoever was responsible for the recent piracies. Especially considering what they'll find in the hold. That should free Skye!"

Niall Burke's face began to relax itself as he digested de Marisco's idea. "It's possible!" He thought a moment. "Did you find a log on board?"

"Yes, but it's all in a funny kind of scrawl that bears no resemblance to any writing I've ever seen."

A slow smile lit Niall's face, crinkling the corners of his silvery eyes. "It's probably Arabic, and you're probably right, de Marisco! They're Barbary pirates! We do have one problem, though. We can't destroy the log. It would be very suspicious if no log were aboard. But if Cecil finds someone who reads Arabic the log might prove that this is not a pirate ship. We must have that log read."

"Who the hell do you know who reads Arabic?" demanded de Marisco. He was beginning to lose confidence.

"Skye does," answered Niall, laughing.

"Damme! Is there nothing that woman can't do?"

"I am reassured to learn that you don't know the answer to that, de Marisco," said Niall, suddenly serious.

Adam de Marisco topped Niall Burke by at least two inches. He drew himself up now and, looking down on Skye's husband, said, "Little man, I believe it's time we cleared the air. Yes! I loved her, and possibly I always will. I was not, however, the husband for her. I knew that, and as proud as I would have been to be her husband . . ." His words faded, and for a moment there was total understanding between them, and then Adam de Marisco finished, "She loves you, and you are a fool if you'd believe I'd ever come between you. Now, little man, can we get on with the business of retrieving Skye from Elizabeth Tudor?"

"Dammit, de Marisco, you make me feel like a green boy with his first love. But anytime you think I'm not big enough to take you on, give me a try. Little man, indeed! Give me your hand, you damned Englishman! I'm forced to admit that I like you."

If only Skye could have seen them standing there grinning at each other, both in love with her and now both united in friendship in an effort to aid her! The two men clasped hands and two pairs of eyes, one silvery gray, the other smoky blue, met in a gaze of understanding.

"We'll need one other man to help, and Robert Small can do it. He'd never forgive me if we excluded him. He can read some Arabic. Maybe he can decipher enough of the log before we present it to Cecil. At least we'll know if the book contradicts our story. He's just back home. His sister sent me word today and I sent back a message asking him to come to Lynmouth. Can you have that ship taken in tow to Lynmouth Bay? It's best no one else know what we're planning."

"I'll give orders at once. My mute brothers can do the job nicely," answered de Marisco.

"What of the bodies?"

"They stink like the very devil," observed Adam, "but I'm leaving them aboard to give credence to our tale. Otherwise Cecil will say we made the whole thing up."

"How will we explain the time lapse? It's been months since the *Santa Maria Madre de Cristos* was taken. Where the hell has this ship been in the meantime?"

"Why she's been a-pirating, Niall Burke! The wily infidels have been off across the sea pirating the waters of New Spain. She must have taken the *Santa Maria* on her way out last spring. We all know how the Moors hate the Spaniards, and cannot resist the opportunity to strike out at them." He chuckled richly. "It's a damn good story if I do say so myself!"

"Aye," agreed Niall admiringly. "I'm thinking you're wasted on your island, de Marisco. Court is obviously the place for you!"

"Christ, no! I'd die penned up in that putrid city playing the gallant to that vain bitch, Bessie Tudor! Wasting my time, and my money on useless clothes, cards, and highborn, high-priced doxies. Give me Lundy, barren rock that it is, and the sea, and I'm a happy man."

"You don't mention sons to follow you, de Marisco. Why?"

Adam de Marisco smiled wryly. "Because they'll be none, Niall Burke," he replied. "Fate has a grim sense of humor. When I was fourteen I was taken with a fever that rendered my seed barren. I've the appetite of a damned satyr where women are concerned, yet I've never fathered a child. I went to an old witchwoman in Devon several years ago in hopes of learning why. When she questioned me and learned of the fever I had had as a boy, she told me she couldn't help, that the life had been burned out of my seed. She said she had heard of such cases before. With not so much as a daughter to my credit thus far, I had to believe her.

"That's another reason helping Skye is important to me. Her little son, Robin, and I are the last living descendants of the first Southwood." He chuckled at Niall's incredulous look. "Aye, Irishman! The de Mariscos are the bastard branch of the family.

"The first Geoffroi de Sudbois brought over from Normandy his mistress, Mathilde de Marisco. Actually as the story has come down, he intended to wed with the lady when he made his fortune with Duke William. Like him, she was a second child, so her portion was very small. After my noble ancestor had taken Lynmouth he found it more practical to wed with the old lord's daughter, and so the fair Gwyneth became the mother of the legitimate line.

"Mathilde, however, was a bold and ambitious wench. She far preferred coming to England as Geoffroi's mistress to remaining in Normandy as a poor relation in her brother's house or entering some insignificant nunnery. She lived for several years in the west tower of Lynmouth Castle making poor Gwyneth's life a hell. But then one day her eldest son was caught attempting to smother one of the legitimate Southwoods in his cradle, and the fair Gwyneth put her dainty Saxon foot down. Mathilde and her offspring had to go. Lundy belonged to Lynmouth then, and so Geoffroi deeded the island to Mathilde de Marisco, her sons, and their descendants forever.

"Down through the generations the de Mariscos have wed with Southwood bastards, Southwood younger daughters, or their French cousins. In fact my grandmother and the late Geoffrey Southwood's grandfather were brother and sister. Since I am the last of my line, the last of the bastards of Lundy, young Robin is the last of the Southwoods. I have enough family feeling to want to protect both him and his mother. They are dear to me."

"Does Skye know this?"

"Nay. We never discussed it," said Adam de Marisco.

Niall Burke didn't have the courage to ask why. Whatever had happened between Skye and Adam had happened before he had wed her and it was not his business. Adam de Marisco was definitely an honorable man. He looked long and hard at the lord of Lundy, and Adam returned his look. "You're quite a man, cousin," said Niall Burke. "Now, let's rescue that wench of mine before she gets into further mischief."

Several hours later Niall found himself and his host aboard a ship towing the Moorish vessel toward the Devon coast. Robert Small awaited them at Lynmouth. The little man was furious.

"I leave you to care for Skye, and come home from a short and profitable voyage to find her in the Tower of London! Is this how you watch over her? And you, Adam de Marisco! You're no better, going along with her foolishness! You are the ones who should be in London, not my Skye! I understand from my sister that she was with child. She must have delivered it months ago! Is the Tower the place for a new mother, and my niece or nephew? Do you even know whether the babe is male or female?"

"Dammit, Robbie, be silent!" roared Niall. "Sit down and listen to me! Skye is perfectly safe. There is no evidence against her. I was forbidden London, or even Ireland. I was told to remain at Lynmouth, and Skye begged me to comply for Robin's sake. She doesn't wish to cost him his inheritance. My child was safely delivered last December 12th, but I know not its gender, for even de Grenville was not allowed to see Skye, though he says Cecil had promised him he might.

"There has been no way to help Skye safely until recently. Now I will risk the Queen's displeasure and go to London, for de Marisco has solved the dilemma. For pity's sake, Adam, tell him before he strangles us both."

Slowly, carefully, Adam de Marisco outlined his plan.

"It's possible," Robert Small nodded thoughtfully. "Have you the log?"

Adam de Marisco brought the flat book to Robbie, and he opened it. "Yes," he said immediately. "It's Arabic." He was silent for a few minutes as he perused the log. Then he said slowly. "The ship is the *Gazelle* . . . out of Algiers . . . and she has been a-pirating." His spirits rose. "They picked up some men in a longboat several weeks ago, and shortly after that their crew began sickening and dying. The men in the longboat perished almost immediately. This last entry was made ten days ago. It says simply: 'Allah have mercy.' " Robbie looked up. "The poor devils." He pushed the pages back, reading swiftly here and there, and suddenly his weathered face split into a smile. "Here's a piece of luck! An entry made early last spring says, 'Took a cursed Spaniard today,' and their heading that day was in the Atlantic off the coast of Ireland! They were on their way out then. The rest of the book has many entries of piracy against the 'infidel,' but they were primarily Spaniard-hunters, which is greatly to our good. If Cecil is suspicious enough, and can find someone who reads Arabic, this should confirm your story. I'll go through the rest of the log more carefully tomorrow to be sure there's nothing that could harm Skye. In the meantime, send the *Gazelle* off to London tonight. We'll have to wait until she arrives before we do. Otherwise we lose the element of surprise."

It was difficult to wait, but they did. Adam de Marisco returned to Lundy where he paced his entire island at least two dozen times during the next few weeks.

Robert Small rode home to Wren Court, where he spent his time handling the business of the trading company that belonged to him and Skye. French Jean, Skye's secretary, took the brunt of Robbie's bad temper and, but for his loyalty to his mistress, would have packed up Marie and the children and returned to Brittany.

Niall worried that their plan might fail. What would they do in that case? But he kept his fears from the children. The separation from his mother had matured Robin Southwood. Without Skye to shield and protect her little son, with his stepfather's strong and kind influence, the young Earl of Lynmouth was made very aware of his position and rose to the challenge.

Willow, her mother's daughter for all she looked like Khalid el Bey, tried hard to replace Skye, sitting between Robin and Niall at the high board and presiding over the household staff. At first the servants tolerated her with benign amusement. Soon, to their horror, they discovered a far sterner taskmistress than their own Countess was. Their complaints to Niall fell upon deaf ears. Unless Willow was in the wrong he supported her fully, and the young girl blossomed under her stepfather's wise support.

Several weeks slipped by, and then finally Robert Small received word that the *Gazelle* and her escort ship, *Mermaid,* were at anchor in the London Pool. He rode hard for Lynmouth. That night in the west tower of the castle a green signal light beamed across the eleven miles of water separating Lynmouth and Lundy. At dawn the following day, three caped riders clattered across the castle drawbridge and down the lane to the London road.

It was rainy that late March day, and the empty roads were muddy. The fog was thick in some places, thin in others, and a gray mist hung like ribbons above the newly planted brown fields. There was no wind at all, and the millponds were still and as smooth as glass. The trees waited expectantly, their buds eager for the April sun. Here and there on the hillsides clumps of yellow and white daffodils and narcissus proved that winter had gone, even if the air was chill and damp.

The three men road silently, their heads down, their shoulders hunched against the steady rain. At midday they stopped at a roadside tavern to wolf down bread, cheese, and bitter brown ale. They were on the road again within the hour, and traveled in the steadily worsening rain until several hours after dark. Finally they broke their journey at a small inn that seemed clean but undistinguished, and therefore unlikely to attract anyone who might recognize Lord Burke.

Niall was pleased to find that the stable was dry, the stalls filled with fresh, clean straw, the stableman knowledgeable. He tsk-tsked disapprovingly as Lord Burke led in the three tired horses. "I hopes your business justifies riding these beauties in this weather," he scolded, and Niall hid a smile.

"And when," he answered, "have the Irish ever been known to abuse good horseflesh? Have them ready to go at dawn, man!" He flipped the openmouthed stableman a silver coin and strode away, grinning to himself. The animals would be well cared for after their long day.

Robbie and de Marisco were waiting for him in the taproom. The men revived a bit with hot mulled wine. "The horses will be ready to go at dawn. What's for dinner?"

"Meat pies," said Robbie.

"Filling," answered Niall, and de Marisco grunted his agreement.

They ate with very little conversation, shoving pieces of the hot, flaky pies into their mouths, washing it down with the mulled wine, finishing off the meal with a wedge of cheddar and some crisp apples. The innkeeper then showed them to a dormitory-style room beneath the eaves, where the three men fell asleep instantly upon husk mattresses.

The innkeeper woke them shortly before dawn. "Today ain't no better than yesterday, gentlemen. I got a hot breakfast waiting for you in the taproom."

They splashed cold water into their eyes, pulled on their boots, and found the taproom. They discovered their appetites again as the innkeeper's pretty, buxom daughter ladled hot oat porridge into the wooden trenchers, covering it with stewed apples. She cut them chunks of steaming wheat bread and smeared it liberally with butter and honey, plunking it all down before them. The girl drew them tankards of brown ale. As she placed the foaming mugs upon the table Adam de Marisco slid a bold arm about her waist.

"And where were you when we rode in cold and hungry last night, my pigeon?" he leered at her.

"Safe in me maiden's bed, and away from the likes of you, my fine lord," retorted the girl pertly, slapping his hands away.

Niall and Robbie chuckled, but Adam persisted. "You'd send me out into the cold rain with that long cold ride ahead of me, without so much as a kiss to warm me?" His hand slid beneath her skirts.

"It would appear to me you're already too warm, my lord!" responded the girl. "I think you needs cooling off." And she calmly dumped the tankard of ale over de Marisco's head and spun away from his pinching fingers.

Lord Burke and Robert Small howled and Adam, bested, joined good-naturedly in their laughter. The innkeeper hurried over with a towel, relieved to see that his daughter's impertinence would not bring awful retribution down upon him. "Your pardon, my lord, but Joan is a headstrong girl. As my youngest, she has been spoiled terrible. Get into the kitchen, girl!"

"Don't send her away. She's the prettiest thing we've seen in days, and she's a good girl to keep herself for her future husband," responded Niall. Then he turned to the girl. "But sweetheart, no more ale over de Marisco. You'll give him a helluva chill, and I haven't time to nurse him."

"He's just to keep his roving hands to himself, me lord," returned Joan, tossing her chestnut curls boldly.

"He will," promised Niall, and Adam nodded gravely.

They finished their meal in peace. Soon, ready to go, their cloaks drawn tightly about them, their hats pulled down over their eyes, they paid the reckoning and headed for the door. Joan was sweeping the floor near the doorway and, unable to resist, de Marisco pulled the startled girl into his arms and captured her cherry-red mouth in a passionate kiss. He kissed her slowly, lingeringly, expertly parting her lips to fence with her tongue until her initial resistance became eager compliance.

Satisfied, Adam let her go gently, steadying the swaying girl as he dropped a gold coin down her bodice. "Don't settle for any less than *that,* my pigeon. You'll be a long time married," he told the starry-eyed young girl. Then he was gone.

The day was as unpleasantly cold as the previous one had been, and when they finally stopped for the night they were chilled to the bone, exhausted, and still forty miles from London. The inn was noisy and crowded. The food and the service were poor.

"I'm for going on tonight," said Niall. "We can rent fresh horses here, and exchange them for ours another time. I'd rather spend a few more wet hours on the road and then sleep in a clean bed, free of the fear of being robbed."

His two companions nodded and Robbie noted, "You're apt to be recognized here, Niall. We're too close to London to suit me." So after supper they rode on through the rainy, windswept night, finally arriving at Greenwood at two o'clock in the morning. Niall had thought it best not to stay at Lynmouth House, for fear of drawing notice. The startled gatekeeper let them in, recognizing Robbie.

Niall cautioned the old man that he was not to speak to anyone of their arrival. If asked, he was to deny that they had been there. The lady Skye's life depended upon it. The gatekeeper looked to Robbie for confirmation. He nodded solemnly.

The sleepy house servants were confused, but as easily reassured by Robert Small. The maidservants scurried about preparing three bedchambers and laying fires. Three tall oak tubs were set up by the fire in the kitchen and the three men soaked the chill from their bones. The motherly housekeeper prepared a hot mulled wine punch and served sliced ham on warm bread. Clean, dry, wrapped in dressing gowns that had belonged to the late Lord Southwood, the three sat at the table eating, drinking, and talking.

When their beds were ready they went quickly to their bedrooms.

Niall was grateful that the sheets had been warmed, but as he lay there, strangely wakeful, he knew it was a different warmth he needed. His body ached for a woman. No, not a woman. Skye. Since she had left the previous autumn he had remained totally faithful. Caught up in the business of running her estates, caring for her children, and trying to free her, he hadn't had time to serve his own needs.

In the morning he and Robbie and de Marisco would force the issue with Cecil and the Queen. Niall wanted his wife and child back! The child! Was it the boy that his father and he had wanted for so long? He'd know in a few hours. Niall sighed deeply and suddenly he was asleep.

The sun was up when he awoke and immediately yanked the bellpull. Shortly a little maid appeared with hot water for washing. "Are Sir Robert and Lord de Marisco awake yet?" he asked.

"Just, m'lord," she bobbed a curtsey. "Your bells rang within minutes of each other."

"Have the clothes I brought in my saddlebags been freshened?"

"Aye, m'lord. I'll bring them right up."

He washed and then dressed carefully. His clothes, selected shrewdly for this occasion, were rich, but subdued. His shirt was the purest white silk, his doublet of deep-blue velvet, embroidered discreetly in silver. His hose were striped silver and blue. And he wore a heavy silver chain with a silver and sapphire pendant. Smooth-shaven, his jaw showed a strong determination that William Cecil would find hard to miss.

Niall broke his fast in his room with fresh bread, cheese, and ale. He then joined de Marisco and Robbie. Walking to the bottom of the garden, they hailed a waterman for the trip down the river to

Greenwich Palace, where the Queen was currently in residence. Niall kept his cloak wrapped well about him, obscuring his features. The rain had stopped, but the day remained gray and threatening.

They arrived at Greenwich and, disembarking, hurried into the palace. Luck was with them: Cecil had not yet arrived in his closet, and on duty was only one young secretary who failed to recognize any of the three. When the chancellor arrived in his long, furred black velvet robe, he was immediately surrounded by the three men and borne off to his private rooms.

Unafraid, Lord Burghley settled himself comfortably at his desk and said to the anxious secretary, "I am not to be disturbed, Master Morgan." The secretary bowed out, and Cecil turned to his three visitors. He eyed them dispassionately, then spoke. "My lord Burke, I distinctly remember forbidding you London."

"I've come to bring my wife and child home, m'lord. You have had Lady Burke here almost six months and I've not yet been informed of the charges against her."

"She is under suspicion, my lord."

"For six months? And of what?"

"Piracy," was the cool reply.

"What! You're mad, man!"

"Niall, Niall!" Robbie spoke. "Cecil, my friend, be reasonable. Lady Burke is a beautiful woman who, I've no doubt, has stolen many hearts. But ships? I think not. Proof?"

Cecil frowned and Robbie almost shouted with glee. They still had no proof! "I will be frank with you, Cecil. I thought piracy was your suspicion, because of the O'Malley ships. Poor Niall refuses to see the logic of it."

"And you do?" said Cecil.

"Indeed I do. The O'Malley of Innisfana has access to ships and a knowledge of shipping lanes and schedules. Add to that her isolated coastal castle, and you have all the ingredients for piracy—except, of course, one important one."

"What is missing, Sir Robert?" Cecil was fascinated.

"Motive, my lord," said Robbie. "Where is Lady Burke's motive? She is already one of the wealthiest women in England, possibly the wealthiest, and she is not greedy for more riches. Everyone knows her to be generous and charitable. She is not a seeker of thrills. So why would she risk her son's inheritance and her own position, by breaking the Queen's law? Above all things, my dear Cecil, Skye is a good mother.

"No . . . there are no grounds for your suspicions, nor justification for holding her. None besides Bess Tudor's jealous spite, and you know it, Cecil."

Cecil looked both annoyed and uncomfortable. "The piracies ceased with Lady Burke's arrest," he said.

Niall's look was as black as a storm cloud, but Robert Small put a steadying hand on him. "The piracies stopped over a year ago, more than six months before you arrested Lady Burke."

"The *Santa Maria Madre de Cristos* was taken off Ireland late last spring!"

"But not by Lady Burke," replied Robbie, "for she was but newly married and on her honeymoon. The Spaniard was taken by Barbary pirates, and we have the proof. Cecil, this giant who's accompanied Lord Burke and me is Adam de Marisco, the lord of Lundy Island." Cecil began to look interested. "Well over a month ago de Marisco found a ghost ship floating off his island. Naturally he claimed it for salvage."

"Oh, naturally," murmured Cecil.

Robbie ignored the sarcasm and continued with his story. "When de Marisco opened the hold of the ship and saw the treasure within, he realized the implications at once. He went immediately to Lord Burke, and Niall sent for me. The ship's log is in Arabic, of which I have some small knowledge. There is an entry made early last summer that coincides with the date of the piracy of the *Santa Maria*. The entry reads: 'Took a cursed Spaniard today.' This was obviously the ship that captured the *Santa Maria*'s cargo. It was on its way to the New World to go a-pirating, which it did. There are entries disclosing a transfer of cargo between the Moor's ship, which is called the *Gazelle*, and another Barbary ship.

"The bulk of King Philip's goods were being sold in the markets of Algiers before word even reached London that the treasure was gone. We found only some of King Philip's treasure cargo aboard the *Gazelle*, as well as cargo from other ships. These were among the stores. I am sure the manifest that the Spanish ambassador gave you lists these items." He pulled a velvet bag from his doublet and, opening it, poured a stream of unset green emeralds upon Cecil's desk.

The chancellor gaped openmouthed at the flashing blue-green fire that lay blazing before him. For a moment the silence was thick, then Cecil found his voice. "Where is the crew of this ship, my lord de Marisco? You can hardly expect me to believe this fairy tale of an empty ship floating conveniently off your island."

"The crew of the *Gazelle* are still aboard her—in various stages of decomposition, my lord," replied Adam. "I would have buried the poor bastards, but Robbie said you'd not believe us unless you saw them, and I can see that he was right." He shook his huge head, disappointed in human nature.

"Where is this ship?" William Cecil croaked.

De Marisco smiled broadly, a wicked smile, his teeth blinding white against his wind-bronzed skin and black beard. Cecil had not noted until now that the giant wore a gold earring. His black hair was shaggy, and his smoky blue eyes mocked in a way that made the Queen's chancellor lower his gaze.

"The *Gazelle* lies under tow by Robbie's *Mermaid* in the Pool, m'lord. You are free to remove the cargo and to inspect the bodies before we sink her. The log didn't disclose what killed her crew, and anyhow, she'll be considered a bad-luck ship now. She's best off at the bottom of the sea with her men."

Cecil was incredulous. "D'you mean there's a ship of dead men in the Pool? Christ's bones! They might be carrying the plague! Are you mad?"

"They didn't die of plague," stated Robbie calmly. "More likely a passing sickness brought aboard by some shipwreck victims they rescued."

"But a ship of rotting bodies? Here in London?"

"You were ready to disbelieve me without the bodies, Cecil. I've brought the log along too. You may be able to find someone here in London who can speak Arabic, and read it, and thus corroborate our story."

Cecil looked sourly at the three men, determined to find someone who could read Arabic. Still, he knew that if Robert Small seemed this confident he must be sure of his story. But Cecil was suspicious. There was something just too convenient about the tale.

"We'll take you to the Pool ourselves, Cecil," said Lord Burke, "and then perhaps you'll give me back my wife and my child. By the way, I'd be interested in knowing whether I have a son or a daughter."

"A daughter," said Cecil absently. "I'll have to inform the Queen about this interesting turn of events. Very well, we'll go aboard the *Gazelle* to inspect her. Where are you staying?"

"*A daughter!*" Niall exulted, feeling no disappointment at all. "I have a daughter!"

"We're at Greenwood," said Robbie, "Skye's small residence next to Lynmouth House. We felt it was a bit more discreet."

Cecil nodded, glad they had considered that.

"I want to see my wife and my daughter," said Niall.

"In time, my lord. In the Queen's good time."

"For God's sake, Cecil, have you no pity in you?"

"My lord! You are forbidden London, and yet you came. You're in no position to ask me for anything. Await my word on this matter at Greenwood and be thankful that I haven't ordered your arrest. And please avoid being seen. Master Morgan!"

The secretary nearly fell through the door.

"Master Morgan, show these gentlemen out through my private entrance."

They were dismissed, and Cecil was once more in control of the situation. Robbie could see that Niall wanted to argue. He looked to de Marisco, and Adam clamped a firm hand on Lord Burke's shoulder. "Come on, man," said Adam gently. Niall sighed, an angry, frustrated sigh, but he nodded and followed Robbie out of Cecil's closet.

In the tower, Skye had awakened with a sense of hopeless futility. She relieved herself in the chamberpot, and then, picking up Deirdre, changed her wet napkin. Climbing back into bed with her daughter, Skye put her to her breast. They would question her again today as they had been questioning her nearly every day for the last month and she would fight them again today as she had been fighting them for the last month. She would ask for a list of the charges against her, demand her immediate release, and say nothing more. Dudley had been removed from the council, but the Earl of Shrewsbury frightened her with his cold eyes and exaggeratedly polite ways.

Deirdre suckled noisily, smacking her little lips with pleasure, and Skye smiled down at the baby. Gently she rubbed the little head with its silky dark curls. Yesterday they had threatened to take the baby away from her. She had stared at them in stony silence, refusing even to acknowledge the threat, but she knew she would have to send Deirdre down to Devon with Eibhlin very soon. Dearest Eibhlin! She had imprisoned herself with Skye, never once leaving the Tower for fear of not being allowed back inside. Recently even Daisy had ceased her trips to the city markets when Lady Alyce had sent a warning that if she left, she'd not be allowed to return.

Now Dudley, though removed from the council, was sniffing about the Tower like a wolf after a staked goat, and Skye was genuinely frightened. She was the Queen's prisoner, and helpless if Elizabeth's favorite chose to assault her. The baby hiccoughed, Skye patted her back. I will not be beaten, she thought. I won't!

At Greenwood Niall Burke paced helplessly. Outside the rain

drizzled softly, pale gray dripping into the darker gray river. Along the river banks the yellow willows had begun to send forth their pale green leaves, but the rain showed no signs of letting up. The graceful trees reminded Niall of his stepdaughter.

Before he had left Lynmouth she had come to him and said, "You will bring my mama home, Niall? Promise me!" And he had looked down into her little face—heart-shaped like Skye's, but with features he didn't recognize—and he had promised.

Downriver in the Pool, Lord Burghley leaned weakly over the *Gazelle*'s rail, vomiting the entire contents of his belly into the roiling dark waters of the Thames. Next to him, and just as sick, was the Spanish ambassador's second secretary, a Christian Moor who could read Arabic well enough to stumble through the passages pointed out to him by Robbie. He had corroborated the story told Cecil by Niall, de Marisco, and Small.

The sight that had greeted the men had been hideous, a vision neither would ever be able to forget. Bodies. Rotting bodies, scraps of cloth and flesh still clinging to the skeletons. And the smell! The terrible, terrible smell that even their clove-studded pomander orange balls couldn't wipe out. Cecil couldn't even remember later how he was transferred over to the *Mermaid,* but he was there after a little while and a cup of strong red wine was pressed upon him. He gagged, still smelling the rot. His whole body was cold and clammy with perspiration. He mastered his stomach, and took a sip of the wine, but the smell of death was still in his nostrils and he retched, tasting the sour bile of his now-empty stomach mixed with the strong wine.

A sympathetic Captain Sir Robert Small handed him a basin into which Cecil spat. "Try another sip, my lord. It'll stay down, eventually." Cecil swallowed again, and although his stomach rolled rebelliously the wine remained where it was. Warmth began to seep back into his body.

"Well," said Robbie, "You've seen the evidence with your own eyes, my lord, and the Spaniard's confirmed the log entry. Will you now release Lady Burke?"

"Aye," said Cecil weakly. "It would appear that we have made . . . an unfortunate mistake."

"When?" Robbie's voice was sharp.

"In a few days, Sir Robert. I must tell the Queen and then, of course, Her Majesty must sign the release for Lady Burke."

"You'll let Lord Burke see his wife and child?"

The wine was strengthening Cecil. "No," he said firmly. "Lord

Burke was forbidden to leave Devon. The Queen is not to know he's here now, for it would anger her to learn that he disobeyed her. I will tell her that I have sent for him to come up to London and escort his family home, knowing Her Majesty would want it so. That way, when we release Lady Burke, her husband's appearance will not offend the Queen."

At Greenwich, Elizabeth Tudor had dismissed her maids of honor, and lay contented in Robert Dudley's arms, luxuriating before a crackling fire. Her dressing gown was open to her navel, and she purred with pleasure as he stroked her small breasts.

"Bess, for God's sake let me!" he pleaded, as he had pleaded so many times before. He didn't know why he allowed her to do this to him. She used him to satisfy her curiosity about sexual matters, but she never actually gave anything of herself.

"No, Rob," she chided demurely. "I must remain a maid until I wed." She felt his ill-concealed lust, and wondered, as she had wondered so many times before, why this selfish, shallow, ambitious man attracted her so.

I wed, she had said. Not *we wed,* he reflected bitterly. Was what the gleefully malicious gossips said true? Were his chances of being England's King over with? Angrily he bent and kissed her. It was a brutal kiss, a cruel kiss of such intense love-hate that Elizabeth shivered with delight. "I want you, Bess," he muttered furiously, "and I mean to have you!" He yanked her beneath him and, straddling her, pushed her skirts up, exposing her long, slender legs with their black silk stockings, gold lace garters, and milk-white thighs.

"Rob! Rob!" she protested as he fumbled with his own clothing, "what you're doing is treason! Stop at once! Would you rape your Queen?" But her black eyes were dancing with excitement. This was the furthest they had ever gone in their charade.

"Aye, Bessie, I'd rape you! You've played your teasing game with me once too often. You can hang me afterward, but by God, I'll have you now!" He had managed to release his swollen organ from its bindings. *She'll not hang me,* he was thinking. *One good spending, and she'll belong to me forever! I should have done this three years ago!*

Beneath him the Queen struggled physically and mentally. As he rubbed his hardened manroot against her throbbing clitoris she wondered if she dared let him do this thing to her. Maybe just this once, so she could truly know what it was all about. *No*! No man must ever have dominion over her! Look what had happened to her mother, to Anne of Cleves, to poor Cat Howard! Subjected to her father by love, lust, and ambition, they had all paid a terrible price. If she let him do this to her even once and there was a child, she would be forced to marry him! Never! No!

Suddenly there was a knock on the door. "Majesty, it's Lord Burghley. He says it is urgent."

"Tell him to go away!" hissed Dudley.

"We will receive him!" the Queen cried out, and the Earl of Leicester swore violently. "Bitch! Oh, God, Bess, you're a bitch!" He struggled off her, pulling his clothes together. "Straighten your gown, for pity's sake, Bess! If being Queen is more important to you than being a woman, then you'd best look like a Queen."

The door opened, and the maid of honor announced, "Lord Burghley, Your Majesty." The maid of honor was red-haired Lettice Knollys. She cast Dudley an amused glance, and he knew that she knew. She'd probably been listening at the door. Another bitch!

"Madam," Cecil bowed. "I regret disturbing your leisure, but I have received important information in the matter of Lady Burke."

"She has confessed?" Elizabeth looked eager.

"No, madam. It would appear that she is not guilty at all. The evidence presented me is irrefutable. Sir Robert Small and Adam de Marisco, the lord of Lundy Isle, came up from Devon to present it."

"And what is this evidence?"

Her chancellor told the story simply but thoroughly. "Their story would appear to be a logical explanation of the pirating of King Philip's treasure ship, especially since much of the treasure was on this ship. Since no evidence can be found against Lady Burke, and believing that you will want to release her now, I have sent for Lord Burke."

"You take a great deal upon yourself, Cecil," said Dudley arrogantly.

"D'you now speak for the Queen, Leicester?" Burghley snapped. His hatred of Robert had not lessened over the years. Now he fully intended seeing that Lady Burke was released. Damn the vain fool and his role in all this! Had Dudley not forced himself upon the beautiful Countess of Lynmouth and had Elizabeth not condoned his outrageous behavior, Lady Burke would never have needed to revenge herself on the Queen. William Cecil did not for one moment believe the tale of the *Gazelle,* but he would swear with his dying breath that he did, for it was the best way out of an impossible situation. Which portions of the *Gazelle* story were true and which were not interested him not at all. Cecil gazed expectantly at the Queen.

"You think I should release her, don't you, Cecil?"

"Yes, Majesty, I do. It is only just, and you have always been Justice's champion."

"D'you think she is guilty?"

"No, madam. I did once, but no longer. How can I, in the face of such overwhelming evidence? Sir Robert said he could understand my suspicions, given the circumstances and the O'Malley history, but Lord Burke could not see my point at all." William Cecil shrugged. "These Irish are such volatile children."

"Very well, Cecil. Write the order for Lady Burke's release in the custody of her husband. She is not to be freed until he arrives to claim her. You may tell her today, though."

"Madam, once again your generous nature has served you well. I am proud of you." The Queen bridled with pleasure.

"I am feeling gay again," she said. "Will you send my maids to me as you leave, my lord? And Rob, you must go as well, for I long for the company of my own sex now." She smiled archly at him.

The chancellor bowed himself politely out of the Queen's presence, but the Earl of Leicester pushed angrily past him and out into the antechamber, bumping into Lettice Knollys as he went. He swore a particularly vile oath, and Lettice laughed softly.

"Bitch!" he snarled. "Don't you dare to laugh at me!"

"Oh, Robert," she said low. "Why don't you let me give you what my cousin won't."

He gaped at her. She wasn't a bad-looking wench with her amber cat's eyes and red-gold hair. She had nice big tits too, he noted. But he wasn't sure he'd understood her. "What the hell do you mean?"

"Bess won't lie with you, Robert, but I will," she answered frankly.

"What of your husband?"

"Walter?" Lettice laughed again. "What about him?"

A slow smile lit Dudley's features. He was beginning to feel expansive again. He backed Lettice skillfully into an alcove and slipped a hand into her bodice. The warm, full breast that overflowed into his palm grew taut with unconcealed desire. "Jesus, sweetheart," he muttered, well pleased, "you're a fine piece of goods, and all set to diddle, I'll wager."

"I'm already wet for you, Rob," she admitted, "but it must keep. Come to my apartment tonight. I am not on duty to the Queen after eleven." She casually removed his hand, and moved away.

Robert Dudley watched her go, feeling very satisfied. If Bess wouldn't, there was always someone else who would. Discreetly, of course, for there was still a chance he might be King.

Late that afternoon Skye started with surprise when Lord Burghley was ushered into her rooms. The chancellor, himself a grandfather, was enchanted by the sight before him. Lady Burke, her hair loose about her shoulders, sat upon the floor playing with her little daughter. The baby lay on her back, kicking her little feet and legs, cooing softly. "Good afternoon, madam," said William Cecil. "I bring good news."

Skye scrambled to her feet. "Daisy, take the baby." The maidservant picked Deirdre up and hurried from the room. Skye smoothed her skirts. Pouring two goblets of wine, she offered one to Cecil. "Sit down, my lord," she motioned him to a seat, "and tell me your good news."

"You're free, madam."

Her beautiful eyes grew wide with surprise, then dark with suspicion. "Just like that, my lord? 'You're free.' " She could feel her temper rising. They had snatched her from her husband and family, endangered her unborn child, imprisoned her without charges, and now they calmly said, "You're free." Skye fixed her gaze steadily on Cecil. "I am free to go home?"

"In a few days. The release is now being drawn up, and the Queen will sign it tomorrow. Your husband will be allowed into London to escort you home to Devon."

"Perhaps *now* you will be so kind as to tell me why I have spent the best part of six months here?" asked Skye.

A wry smile touched William Cecil's lips, and his eyes twinkled for a brief moment. "Skye O'Malley," he said quietly, "we both know the truth of why you are here, though you'd not admit to it and I have not the evidence I need to prove it. Over the last two years you have cost Elizabeth Tudor considerable revenues with your piracies. When we set out to trap you with the *Santa Maria Madre de Cristos* I thought we would be in time to catch you with the booty. I was wrong. You are well organized and a frighteningly intelligent and bold woman.

"Your husband, Sir Robert Small, and the lord of Lundy Isle have gone to enormous lengths to present me with evidence supporting your innocence. I am accepting their story and freeing you, but hear me well, my lady of Innisfana. You have seen that a royal whim can imprison you without explanation. Should there be further trouble in Devon we shall know where to find you. The next time, nothing will free you. I think the Queen has paid dearly for her appalling error in judgment. I do not like Dudley either, m'dear."

Not a muscle in Skye's face moved during his speech, nor did her eyes betray her. Cecil was impressed. She was truly a worthy and an impressive adversary. "Well, madam, what have you to say to me?" he demanded.

"That I am glad to be going home, Master Cecil," Skye answered calmly. "That I will be happy to see my husband. And that," she added mischievously, "if you can find no proof of my alleged crimes, then I must be judged the innocent that I am."

Cecil drained his goblet. "I suppose you must," he answered thoughtfully. He rose and moved to the door. "It was a good revenge, madam, well organized, well thought out, and well executed. I salute you."

Skye flashed him an impudent smile, silently acknowledging the praise. But she said, "La, sir! I know not what you mean."

The door closed behind Cecil and, for a brief moment, Skye stood still, listening to his footsteps retreating down the stairs. Elation began to build. She had won! She had beaten Elizabeth Tudor! She had beaten the Queen of England! Then as suddenly she began to cry, the tension of the last few months releasing itself in the tears that poured down her face.

The door from the bedchamber opened and Eibhlin and Daisy both hurried in. "Skye!" Eibhlin flew to her sister's side. "Skye, my love, what is it? What did Cecil want? Are you all right? Oh, damn these English anyhow!"

Daisy was shocked by Eibhlin's cursing. Her servant's disapproving face moved Skye from tears to laughter. "We're free," she laughed. "We're going home! I've beaten the Queen!"

"Is it a trick?" asked Eibhlin.

"No. There is no evidence against me, and Robbie and de Marisco have somehow managed to convince Cecil that I am not guilty."

"I'd be interested in knowing just how," said Eibhlin.

"So would I, my sister," returned Skye, now calmer and more thoughtful.

They did not have long to wait. The following day Sir John brought Skye the signed order for her release. "You are to go tonight, Lady Burke. Lord Burghley does not wish you to be seen leaving the Tower. You'll go by river barge to Greenwood under cover of darkness. Your husband is waiting there for you. You are ordered to quit London by tomorrow night."

"Thank you, Sir John, and my thanks to you and to Lady Alyce for making my sojourn with you as pleasant as it could be."

The Tower governor smiled good-naturedly. "I am not often thanked for my hospitality," he said humorously. Then he took her hand and raised it to his lips. "God speed, Lady Burke."

In the dark of a rainy evening three muffled figures made their way from the Tower through the river gate, and into a waiting barge. A guard on the walls thought he heard a baby's cry. Skye and Eibhlin breathed deeply of the saturated air which carried a scent of the sea and then, laughing softly at themselves, smiled at one another. The barge cut smoothly through the black waters. Peeping through the curtains every now and then to ascertain their position, they spied quick glimpses of the city of London. Soon the elegant palaces and houses of the Strand were visible, and Skye felt her heart quicken as the barge swept by them all and swung around the bend to make for Greenwood's landing. Lynmouth House stood dark next door, and only a few lights shone at Greenwood.

The barge bumped the landing, and the guardsman accompanying them leaped out to secure the craft. Then he helped the passengers to the dock, starting with Eibhlin, to whom Daisy handed the baby. Then Skye and lastly the faithful serving woman stepped out. Their few bags were placed on the dock. "The rest of yer things will be brought tomorrow, my lady," said the guardsman. Then he jumped back down into the barge, loosed its rope, and the boat swung back out into the current and headed downriver.

For a moment they stood in the windy night, looking around. "Why is no one here to meet us?" whispered Daisy fearfully.

"I have no idea," replied Skye, "but there are lights in the house." She moved determinedly up the steps from the boat quay, toward the house. Eibhlin, with Deirdre cradled in her arms, followed her sister. Daisy struggled behind with their bags. The long glass doors of the library glowed with reflected firelight as she put her hand on the door handles and pushed them open.

Niall Burke turned, startled, as the wet night wind rushed into the room. Finding his voice, he gasped, "Skye!"

"Aye, my lord. I'm home, and a poor welcome it is with no one to meet us at the quay."

"We didn't know you were coming! Adam! Robbie! Skye is home!"

The inner library door crashed open, and de Marisco and Robert Small rushed into the room. The lord of Lundy stopped just short of kissing her, his smoky blue eyes meeting her sapphire gaze, saying all the things he dared not say aloud. "I don't know how you did it, Adam, but thank you," she said softly. Adam de Marisco nodded mutely, and Skye turned quickly to Robert Small. "My dear Robbie, thank you also. I am certainly blessed in my friends."

The little captain wiped the tears from his eyes. "No more mischief now, lass. The next time we may not be so lucky."

"So Cecil tells me," she said drily. "Eibhlin, give me Deirdre." Gently taking the sleeping infant, Skye walked across the room to where Niall stood. "My lord, may I present you with your daughter, Deirdre. She was born December 12th, and is now almost five months old."

Wonderingly Niall lifted the blanket and gazed for the first time upon his sleeping daughter. "Christ," he said softly, "she's so little! And she's so beautiful."

"Little?" snapped Eibhlin. "She's most certainly not little! She was little when she was born. She's a fine big girl now, and growing every day." She snatched the baby back from Skye. "I trust there's a cradle in this house, sister?"

"Daisy will show you, Eibhlin."

Eibhlin looked to the two men. "Come along, you two great buffoons," she snapped. "He's not going to kiss her until we've gone," and she herded the three others from the room.

Niall Burke stood looking down at his wife. "Oh, my love," he said softly, his voice trembling. "I have missed you as I never thought it possible to miss you again. It's now three times you've been taken from me, Skye."

"But never again, Niall. Only God can part us now. I promise you!"

"That's a promise I intend for you to keep, my love," he said, and then he was kissing her, and the pent-up ardor exploded in a wave of fire that, had it had substance, would have ignited the house and all of London. Their lips explored the familiar territory so long denied. She clung to him. His fingers tenderly caressed her upturned face, gently brushing away the tears that were slipping slowly down her cheeks.

"I will never again let you go away from me," he said again. "I will give you your head in many things, but not in all matters, Skye. You are too headstrong for your own good. This affair might have ended tragically, but for a bit of luck and Adam de Marisco's clever thinking. He loves you greatly, my darling. It's almost too painful to behold. And Robbie. You're the daughter he never had, Skye, and you've hurt him terribly. Had we lost you, I don't think he'd have survived you by very long."

"It's over, Niall. I swear it!"

He smiled a slow smile at her. "I want you," he said quietly.

"I want you," she answered.

He held out his hand to her and she took it, delighting as his warm fingers closed around hers in the lovely and familiar sensation. Together they walked from the library, and upstairs to Skye's old bedroom overlooking the river. Wordlessly they removed their clothing. As she undressed, the memories crowded in about Skye. Walking to the window, she stared out and saw that the night had begun to clear. Storm-tossed clouds chased the quarter moon across the sky and here and there stars were suddenly visible.

How long ago had she stood in this very spot letting Geoffrey into her room? A lifetime ago, surely, and now that was over and done with. She smiled with the memory of her "Angel Earl" hanging on a vine, and then put the memory from her.

She turned back to Niall. He stood watching her struggle with her memories, understanding what she must be going through. Proudly she walked over to him and, standing on tiptoe, wrapped her arms around his neck and kissed him. "It is our time now, my lord husband. Our time, now and always!" With a glad cry he swept her up and carried her to their bed.

In the morning the sun shone warm and bright for the first time in days. Spring had finally had its way in England. Skye awoke content and relaxed for the first time in months, blushing rosy with happiness at the memory of the previous night. Mischievously she straddled the sleeping Niall, lying on his stomach, and began to brush her soft breasts against his back. Shortly her labors were rewarded by a murmuring, and then he said sleepily, "That's nice, Rose lass, don't stop."

"*Rose*? Oh, you knave!" she shrieked, outraged. Grabbing a handful of his dark hair, she yanked with all her strength.

"Ow!" he roared, his body shaking with laughter. Turning over, he imprisoned her on top of him, and she felt his manhood, hard and seeking. They were face to face, and his silver eyes glittered. He raised her carefully and then lowered her, slowly impaling her inch by sweet inch onto his lance. Her eyes were wide with surprise, and fast clouding with desire.

His hands reached up to play with the perfect round fruits of her breasts, and he lifted his head to nurse on a dark nipple, eyes widening in surprise at the milk that suddenly filled his mouth. Fascinated, he continued suckling, and more excited than she had ever been, Skye found her hips moving in the age-old rhythm of pleasure. She was shocked by herself, and by him, for neither of them could stop. Unable to control herself any longer, Skye pulled away from him and, arching her body, threw back her head, and took her release. Her pleasure increased when she felt him taking his as well.

She collapsed atop him, and he gently laid her on her side. When his breathing had quieted he said tentatively, "Dear God, Skye, I apologize."

"For what, my love?"

"For stealing my daughter's breakfast," he answered, shamefaced.

She laughed softly. "Don't worry, Niall. I have two."

"Two?"

Skye giggled, openly amused now. "Two breasts, my dearest fool! One is more than enough for Deirdre's breakfast, and I'd best fetch her, for Cecil told me yesterday that we must leave London today without fail."

"Don't go, my love," he pleaded. "It's been so long."

"You had Rose to keep you company."

"No, love. From the day we reconciled our differences and became truly wed there has been no one else." Sapphire eyes locked into silver ones knew he spoke the truth.

"Thank you, Niall," she said. "Thank you for that."

There was a sharp rap on the door and Eibhlin's tart voice called, "Your daughter needs to be fed, and we must be on the road soon. If you've not been well reunited by now, then nothing will help you!"

Laughing, Skye slipped a gown about herself, and opening the door took Deirdre from her sister. "Have Daisy arrange my bath, Eibhlin, if you please," she said. "If I'm going to spend the next several days traveling, I am going to start out clean."

Eibhlin smiled back. "You're radiant, little sister," she said, and was gone.

Skye walked back to the bed and lay Deirdre upon it. Fascinated, Niall leaned over and gazed down at his daughter, who puckered up her little face and began to howl. "Good God, what have I done?" He drew back, terrified.

Skye snatched the baby up and put her to the breast. Deirdre's small hands kneaded her, and though she watched her anxious father with suspicious blue eyes, she suckled noisily without interruption. "It occurs to me that she has never seen a man up close," said Skye. "She was frightened. In a few days she'll be very used to you, my love." Satisfied, Niall watched with pleasure as his wife fed their child. Afterward they spent a few minutes playing with Deirdre. After tasting her father's fingers, the baby consented to hold on to them while her father pulled her back and forth. It was a game she particularly enjoyed, and she began to look at Niall with less suspicion.

When the maids arrived with Skye's tub, Deirdre was sent off with her aunt to be prepared for the long journey home. Niall retreated to the room next door, dressed in his traveling clothes, and then checked the coach while Skye finished dressing.

The Lynmouth traveling coach had been secreted in Greenwood's stables so that nobody would know the Burkes were staying there. The coachman and footmen had spent a happy few days in the company of Greenwood's friendly maids. Now, under their master's watchful eye, the coach was drawn from the stables and the six matched grays were harnessed to it. The luggage was packed in, and the water. Wine bottles were filled and secured. An open woven wicker basket was carefully fitted into an iron rack attached just three inches above the seat in the center. Lined in silk with a small down mattress, it would shortly hold Lady Deirdre Burke. Daisy would sit on one side of the basket and Deirdre's doting aunt would sit on the other. Beneath the seat a kitchen maid stored two baskets packed with bread, cheese, hard-cooked eggs, ham, and fruit.

In the small family dining room of Greenwood, Robbie, Adam, Eibhlin, Skye, and Niall enjoyed a quick breakfast of ham and egg pudding, bread, and fruit. They had a hard day's riding ahead of them. They were all eager to be on the road, away from the nightmare that London had become.

Daisy and the baby were already settled inside the coach when Eibhlin climbed in.

"Should we draw the curtains?" asked Daisy.

"Please don't," answered the nun. "All I've seen of London is a darkened river and the Tower. I've never been here before, and I don't ever expect to come back. I would like to take a memory of this city back to Ireland with me."

Niall helped his wife mount her horse. Sitting on the animal gave Skye a feeling of freedom that made her giddy. Mindful of the need for secrecy, she drew her hood about her face, noting that the coat of arms had been carefully removed from the coach doors.

The coach and the four horses with their riders moved through the streets, London's morning sounds surrounding them.

"Milk! Who'll buy my good, fresh milk?"

"Violets! Sweet violets!"

"Herring! Fresh-caught herring, ha-penny a pound!"

"Pots! Bring out your pots to mend!"

The solemn little party, well disguised, rode stolidly onward until they gained the high road. When they had traveled several miles outside the city, Skye threw back her hood with an exuberant gesture, and let her long, dark hair billow behind her. Her blue eyes sparkled, and her cheeks were pink with excitement and with the joy of riding. At the top of a hill she stopped and gazed back at the city.

"How did you convince Cecil to free me?" she asked her three rescuers.

"You mean Niall didn't tell you?" demanded Robbie.

"I imagine he'd other things on his mind," murmured de Marisco.

"Well, how did you do it?" she repeated, and they told her.

"You mean you sacrificed your share of the *Santa Maria Madre de Cristos* for me, Adam? Your share was what you 'found' on board the *Gazelle*?" she asked when they had finished. "I'll make it up to you! I swear it!"

"You're free, Skye, and that's all any of us cared about," he protested, embarrassed.

"I included your emeralds, the ones you took for yourself. They were added to the *Gazelle*'s treasure," said Niall calmly.

"You took *my* emeralds?"

They all waited for the explosion. But Skye began to laugh. "By God," she said, "I've beaten Elizabeth Tudor well and true, and in a manner I never expected to."

"What do you mean, Skye?" asked Robert Small.

"Why, Robbie, the Queen has gained nothing except some gold, and a few cold stones, but I have the true treasure. I have the three of you. Niall, my beloved husband, and my friend Adam, and my dearest Robbie. Until Bess Tudor has a husband and loyal friends like mine, she has nothing of value at all. I pity her."

They stared wonderingly at her, realizing that Skye really did pity the Queen whom she had bested. The three men felt a burning sting behind their eyes, and each blinked rapidly, unashamed.

Skye gazed at each of them long and lovingly, and her smile was as bright as the morning. "Gentlemen! I'm for home!" she cried. And wheeling her horse about, Skye O'Malley galloped off in the late-April sunshine, and down the road to Devon.

AUTHOR'S NOTE

In 1979, with three books published or about to be published, two of them fictionalized histories of real women, I decided to write a novel based on Grace O'Malley, the renowned pirate queen of Connaught. However, the more I researched, the more I discovered that Grace—while heroic in nature—was actually considered rude, crude, and generally lacking in the more genteel characteristics of a historical romance heroine. Of course the histories of that time were written mostly by churchmen, or by men educated by the church. A strong, independent woman like Grace would hardly be approved of. Still there just wasn't quite enough to Grace for me to write an entire novel about her. She left Ireland only once, when she had a sea battle with Barbary pirates in the Bay of Biscay, off of Portugal.

At first I was disappointed because the particular era in which Grace lived was extremely rich with exciting history. But I wasn't ready to give up on it, so Grace's fictional "cousin," Skye O'Malley, came into being. Skye was not a woman to hang about, merely trolling off the coast of Ireland for prizes. She traveled far and wide, including to exotic north Africa, and later came into contact with England's queen, the great Elizabeth Tudor, through Skye's third husband, Geoffrey Southwood, the earl of Lynmouth, who was known as the "angel earl" because he was so handsome.

Due to her steely nature and magnificent cunning, Elizabeth I is frankly one of my favorite historical characters. I love writing about her. A child when her mother was beheaded, Elizabeth was sent away from her father in both disgrace and disfavor, while a host of enemies conspired against her. Nevertheless, the savvy and determined young woman survived to become England's queen and, in my story, to meet Skye O'Malley.

In my imaginings, Elizabeth and Skye become worthy opponents. At first admiring and respectful of each other, these two friends transform into impassioned enemies. The two strong and fascinating women have many a battle in this novel: though they shared some basic characteristics, they were fundamentally very different. Skye's passions were for her family, who were all very close and loving, and her power came from the wealth she built through her shipping empire—which in turn allowed her to spar with England's queen. Elizabeth's power, however, came from her sovereignty. I remain utterly intrigued by the court of Elizabeth, especially by Lord Burghley, who was so very clever and masterful at leading his royal mistress away from her destructive emotions, and by Robert Dudley, who was in my opinion a proper villain with kingly ambitions of his own.

Like most historians, I have put my own particular spin on the time period. The places and the people in this book are based upon my own thorough research, and my hope was to breathe life into this fascinating era. So thank you for your time, dear reader. I do hope you enjoyed Skye O'Malley's story, and the glimpse into a time when pirates roamed the seas, magnificent and formidable royalty ruled the land, and passions (I am quite sure) ran high as some of the most powerful personalities in history collided.

Bertrice Small

ABOUT THE AUTHOR

Bertrice Small is a *New York Times* bestselling author and the recipient of numerous awards, including the 2006 Career Achievement Award for Historical Romance from *Romantic Times Book Reviews*. In keeping with her profession, she lives in the oldest English-speaking town in the state of New York, founded in 1640. Her light-filled studio includes the paintings of her favorite cover artist, Elaine Duillo, and a large library. Because she believes in happy endings, Bertrice Small has been married to the same man, her hero, George, for forty-four years. They have a son, Thomas; a daughter-in-law, Megan; and four wonderful grandchildren. Longtime readers will be happy to know that Nicki the cockatiel flourishes, along with his fellow housemates: Pookie, the long-haired greige-and-white cat; Finnegan, the long-haired bad black kitty; and Sylvester, the black-and-white tuxedo who is the self-appointed bed cat.